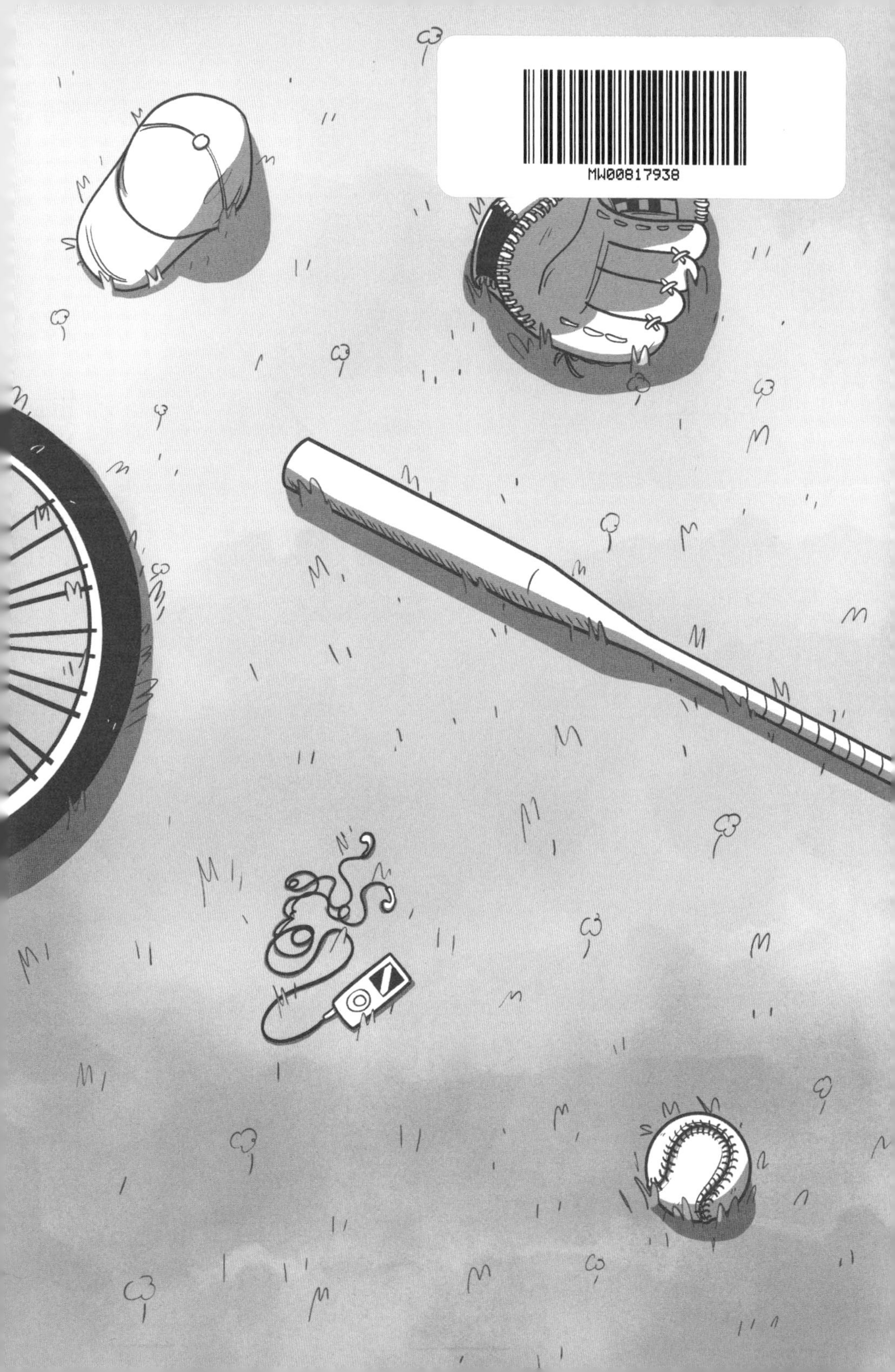

GRAND SLAM ROMANCE

GRAND SLAM
ROMANCE!
BOOK 1

OLLIE HICKS   EMMA OOSTERHOUS

ABRAMS COMICARTS SURELY ★ NEW YORK

SURELY publishes LGBTQIA+ stories by LGBTQIA+ creators, with a focus on new stories, new voices, and untold histories, in works that span fiction and nonfiction, including memoir, horror, comedy, and fantasy. Surely aims to publish books for teens and adults that lend context and perspective to our current struggles and victories, and to support those creators underrepresented in the current publishing world. We are bold, brave, loud, unexpected, daring, unique.

SURELY Curator: Mariko Tamaki
Editor: Charlotte Greenbaum
Editorial Assistant: Lauren White-Jackson
Designer: Andrea Miller
Managing Editor: Marie Oishi
Production Manager: Alison Gervais
Flatter: Wren Rios

Library of Congress Control Number 2022945346

ISBN 978-1-4197-5801-0

Text and illustrations © 2023 Ollie Hicks and Emma Oosterhous

Printed and bound in China
10 9 8 7 6 5 4 3 2 1

Abrams ComicArts books are available at special discounts when purchased in quantity for premiums and promotions as well as fundraising or educational use. Special editions can also be created to specification. For details, contact specialsales@abramsbooks.com or the address below.

ABRAMS The Art of Books
195 Broadway, New York, NY 10007
abramsbooks.com

For Emma. Here is as much of my love for you as could be contained in book form. From those first whirlwind weeks to a love that sustained me through the worst years of my life. If my silly jokes make you laugh, then it's all worth it.
—OLLIE

This book is for Ollie, of course.
For when only half of me had left Europe.
—EMMA

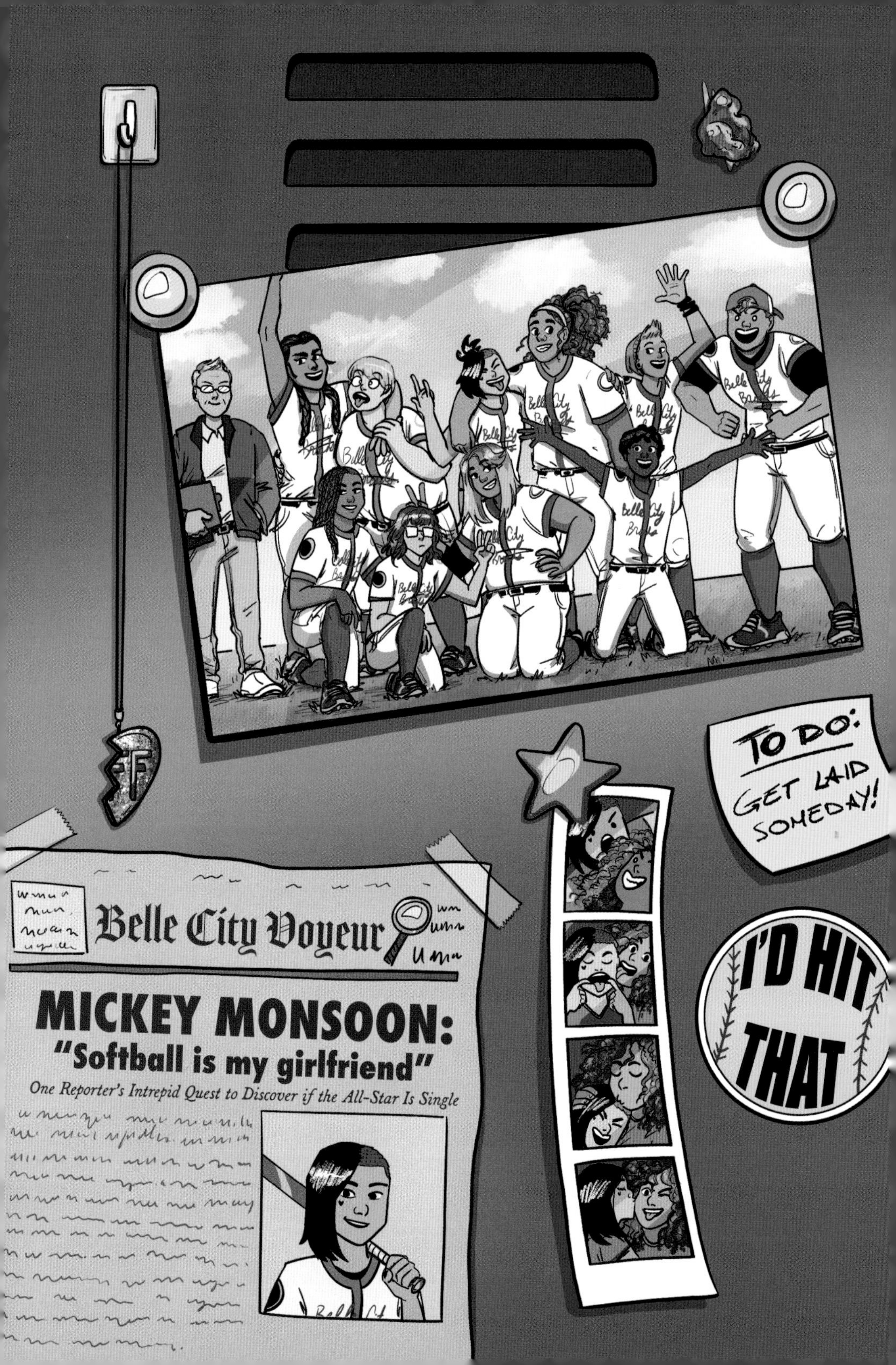

Belle City Braves
TO DO:
GET LAID SOMEDAY!
Belle City Voyeur
MICKEY MONSOON:
"Softball is my girlfriend"
One Reporter's Intrepid Quest to Discover if the All-Star Is Single
I'D HIT THAT

BCB Media Guide

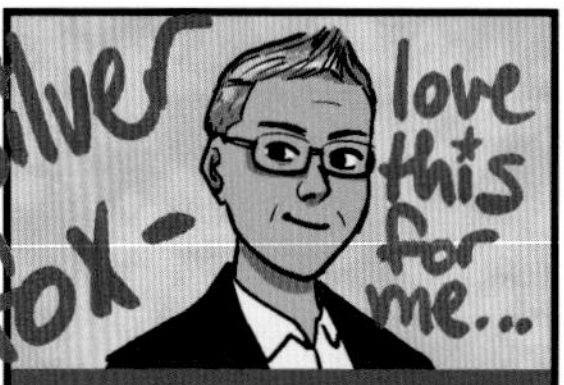
silver fox -
love this for me...

Coach Meredith

Ask anyone in Belle City who their favorite team is, and they'll say the Belle City Broads (BCBs). Formed in 1942 to raise the spirits of the local city folk, they were suspended from their first game for brawling with hecklers. Their motto? "Stupid bitches live forever." Since then, they have become true hometown heroes, winning the Statewide Softball Tournament multiple times, most recently in 2013. Currently sponsored by legendary dive bar Meredith's and coached by none other than Meredith herself, this team is tantalizingly close to reclaiming their former glory. The team is captained by Flo Diaz (voted Most Kissable Lips three years running) and their MVP is Mickey Monsoon, who debuted for the team five years ago at the age of 17.

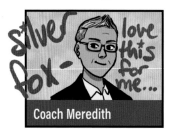

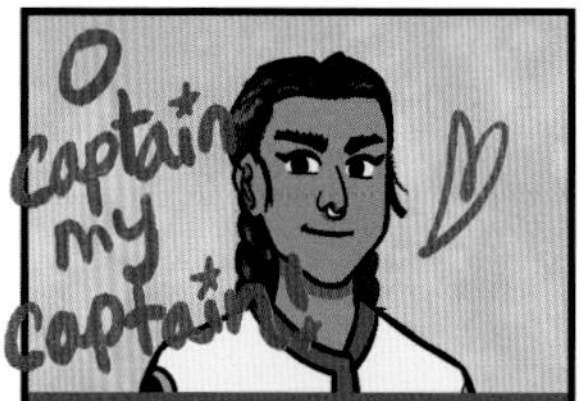
O captain my captain!

#21 Flo Diaz 1B

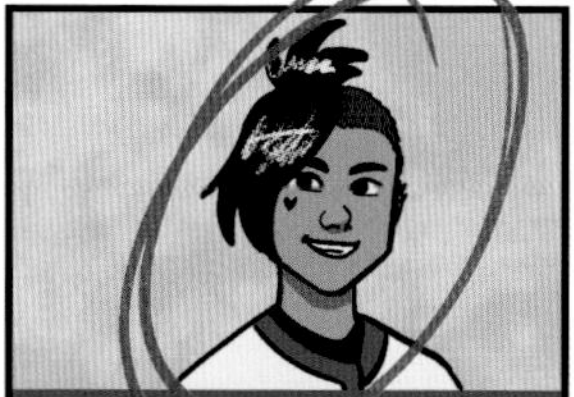

#69 Mickey Monsoon P

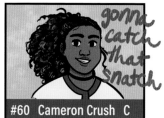

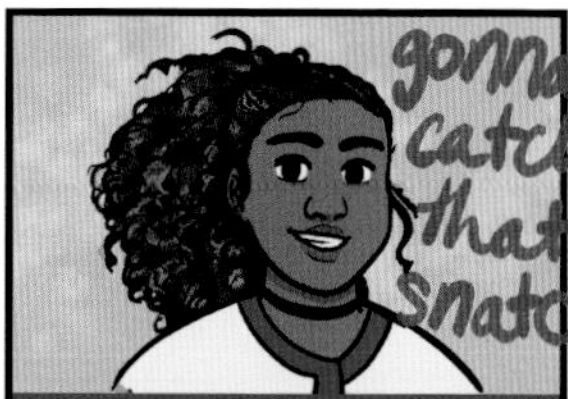
gonna catch that snatch

#60 Cameron Crush C

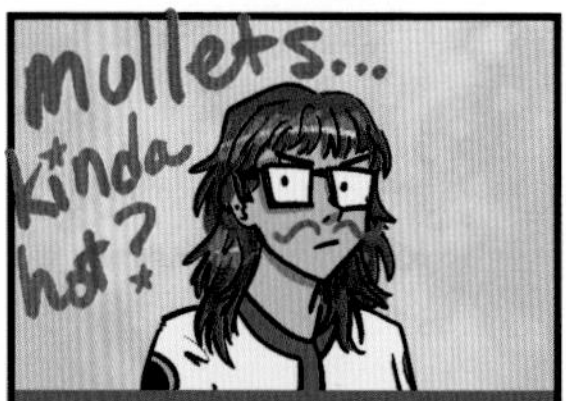
mullets... kinda hot?

#87 Lex Royale 2B

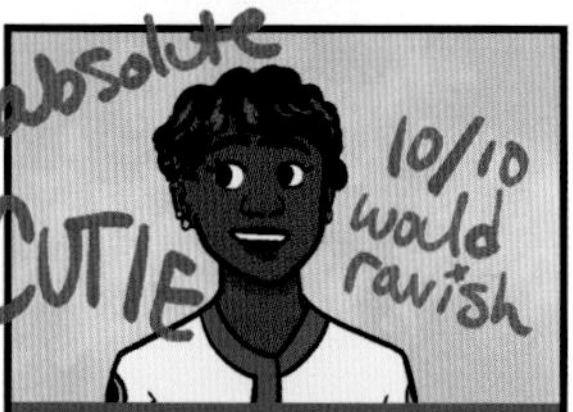
absolute CUTIE
10/10 would ravish

#57 Dusty Hart 3B

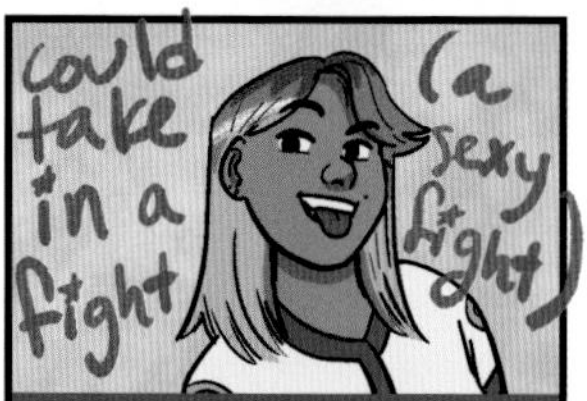
could take in a fight
(a sexy fight)

#17 Gabby Santos SS

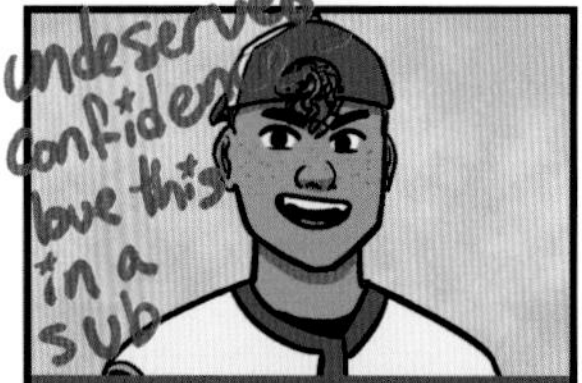
undeserved confiden
love this in a sub

#41 AJ Battle LF

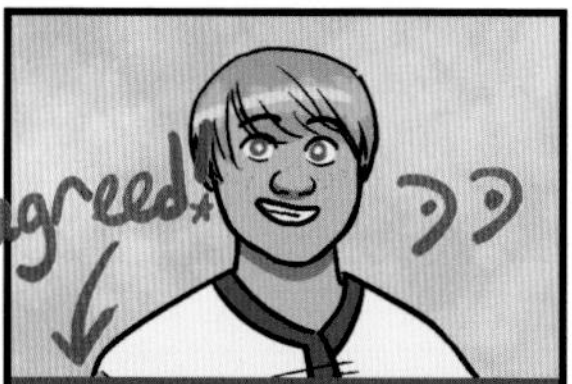
agreed

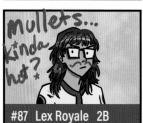

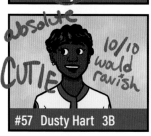

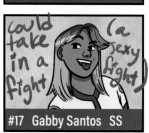

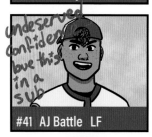

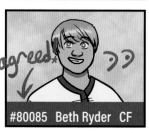

#80085 Beth Ryder CF

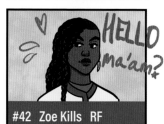

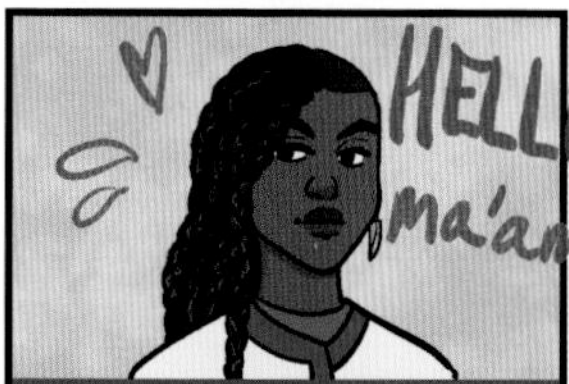
HELLO ma'am?

#42 Zoe Kills RF

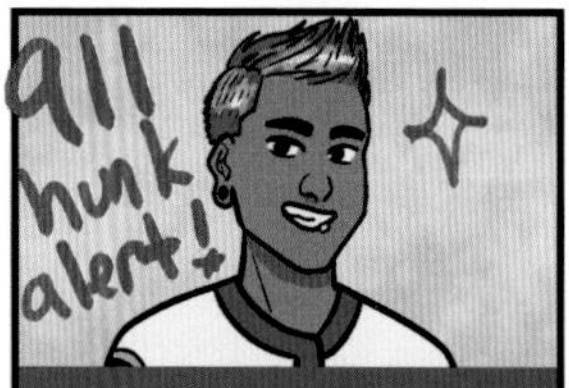
all hunk alert!

#420 Ash Bustamante EP

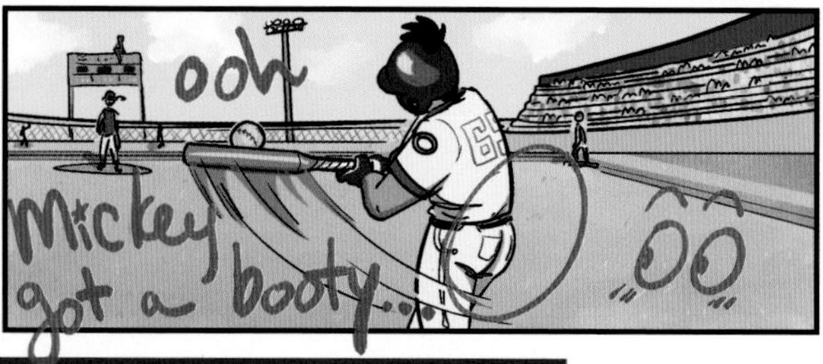
ooh
Mickey got a booty...

- Belle City Broads -

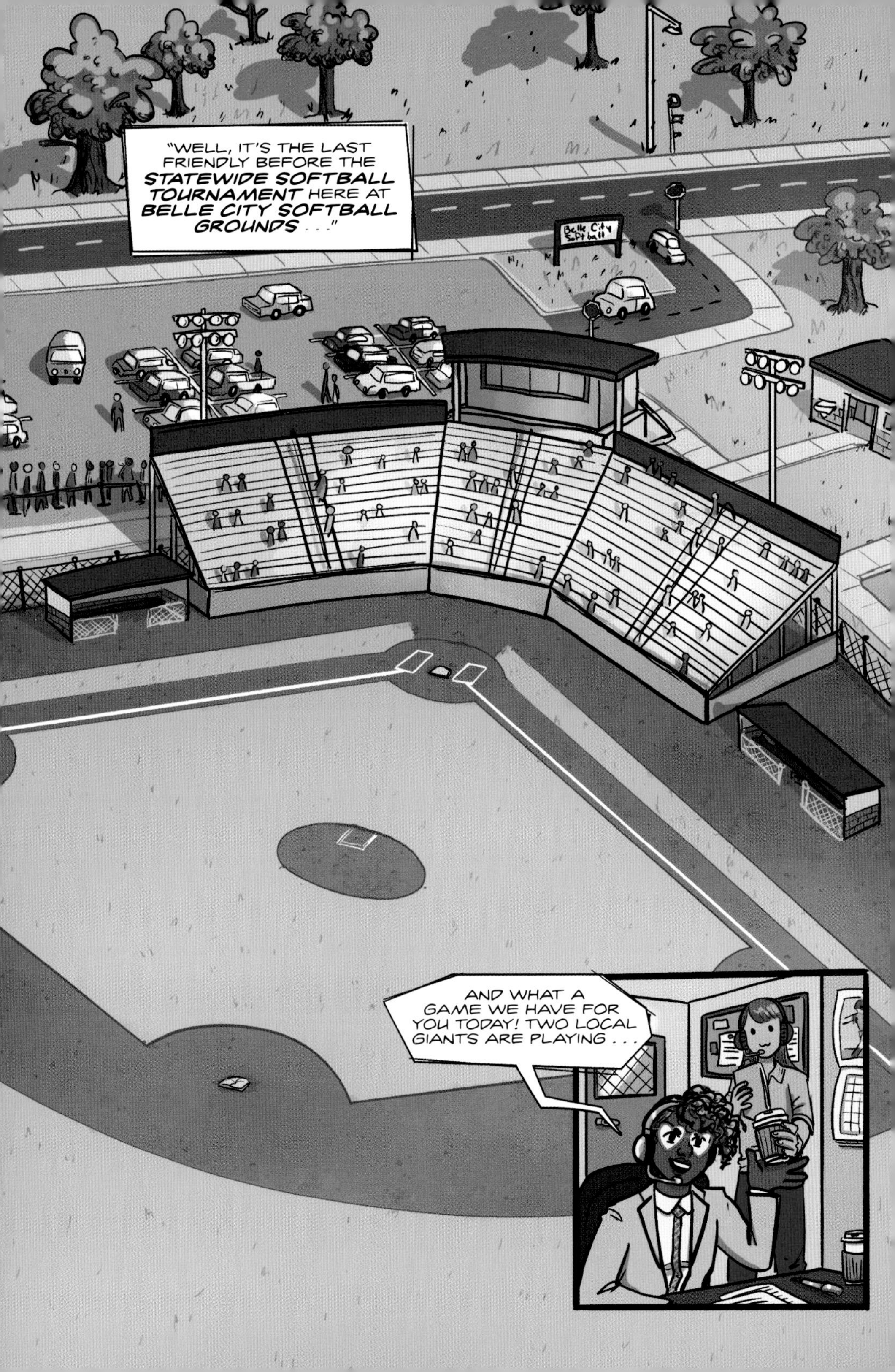
"WELL, IT'S THE LAST FRIENDLY BEFORE THE STATEWIDE SOFTBALL TOURNAMENT HERE AT BELLE CITY SOFTBALL GROUNDS . . ."
Belle City Softball
AND WHAT A GAME WE HAVE FOR YOU TODAY! TWO LOCAL GIANTS ARE PLAYING . . .

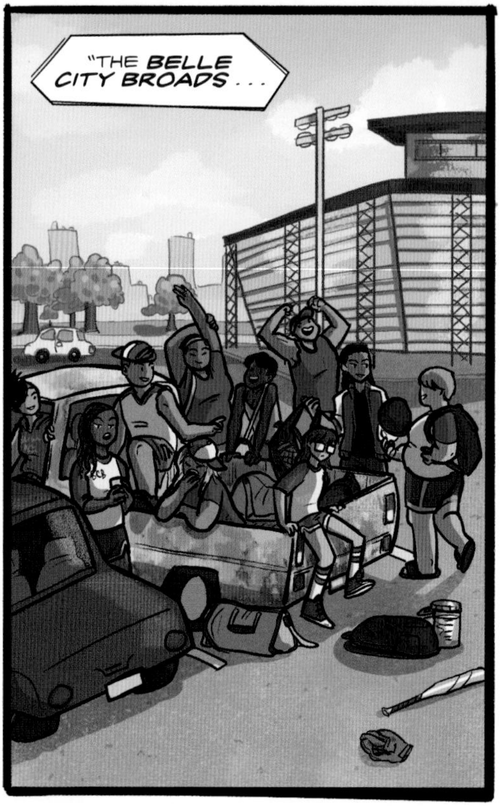
"THE **BELLE CITY BROADS** . . .
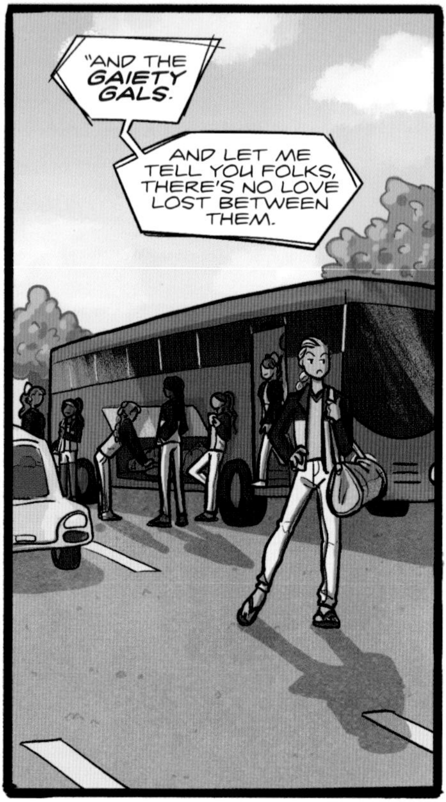
"AND THE **GAIETY GALS**.
AND LET ME TELL YOU FOLKS, THERE'S NO LOVE LOST BETWEEN THEM.
BCB
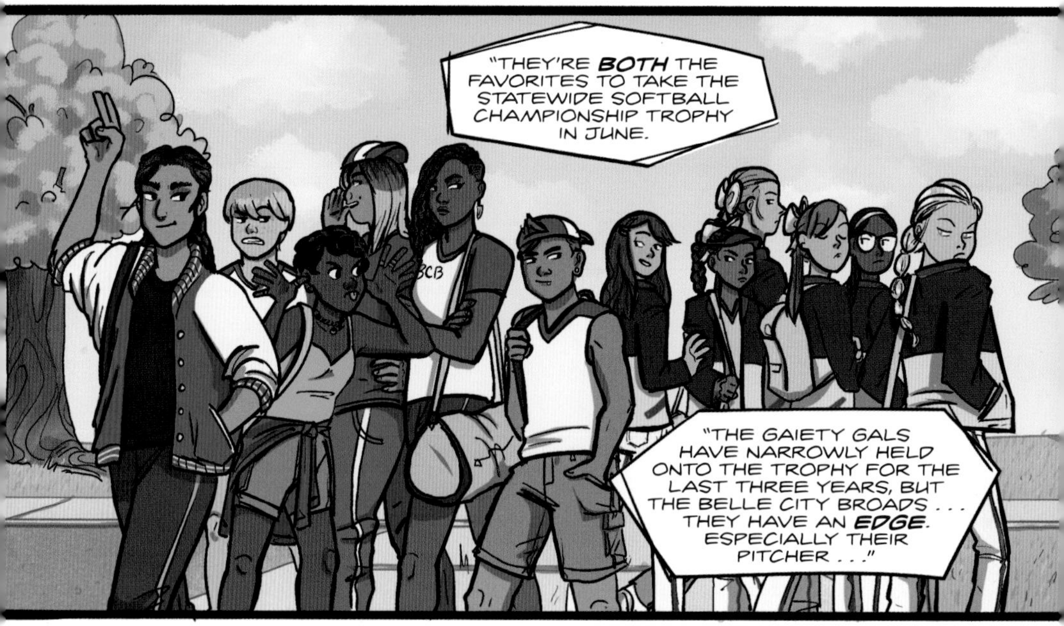
"THEY'RE **BOTH** THE FAVORITES TO TAKE THE STATEWIDE SOFTBALL CHAMPIONSHIP TROPHY IN JUNE.
BCB
"THE GAIETY GALS HAVE NARROWLY HELD ONTO THE TROPHY FOR THE LAST THREE YEARS, BUT THE BELLE CITY BROADS . . . THEY HAVE AN **EDGE**. ESPECIALLY THEIR PITCHER . . ."

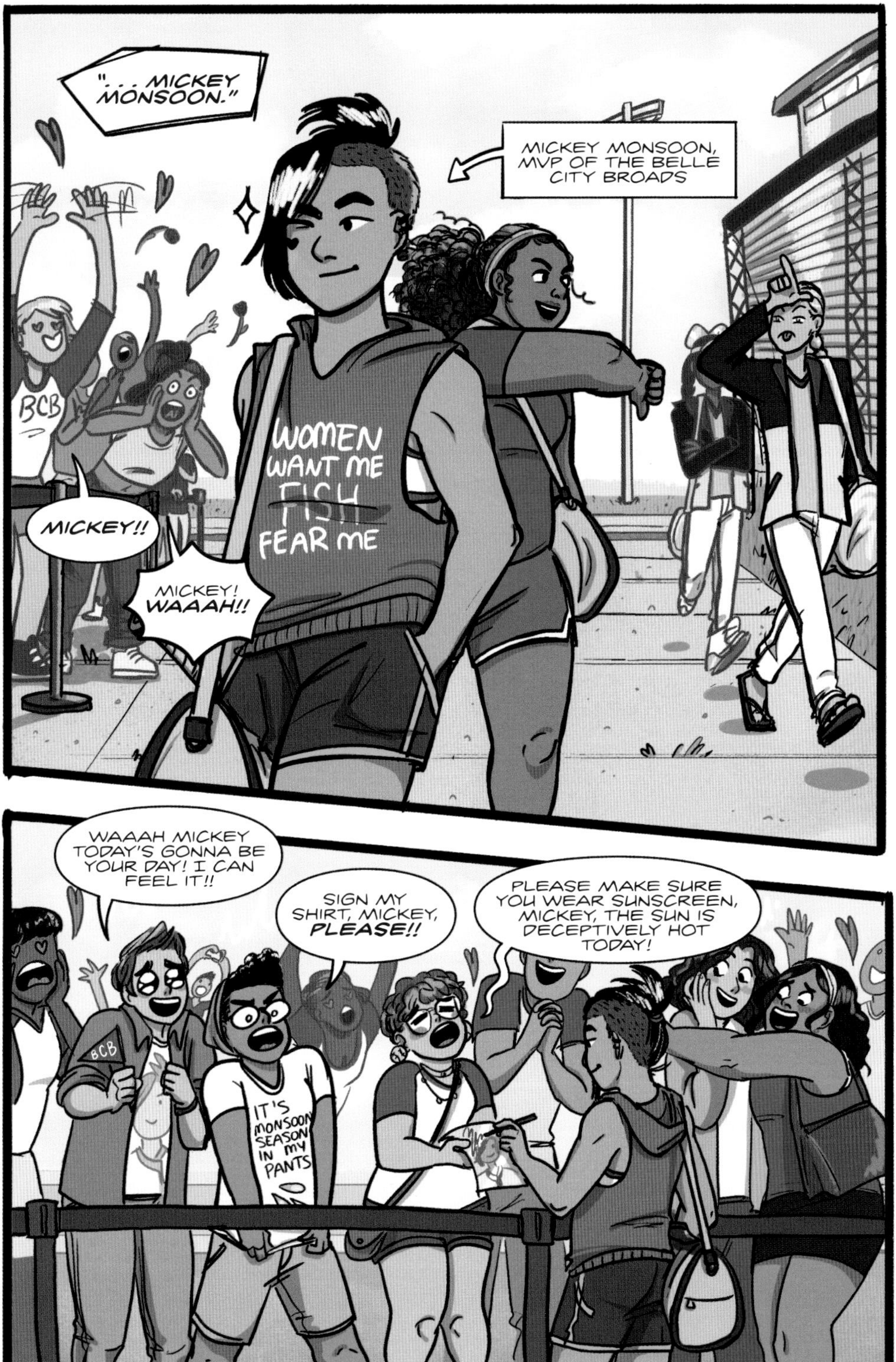
". . . MICKEY MONSOON."
MICKEY MONSOON, MVP OF THE BELLE CITY BROADS
WOMEN WANT ME FISH FEAR ME
MICKEY!!
MICKEY! WAAAH!!
WAAAH MICKEY TODAY'S GONNA BE YOUR DAY! I CAN FEEL IT!!
SIGN MY SHIRT, MICKEY, PLEASE!!
PLEASE MAKE SURE YOU WEAR SUNSCREEN, MICKEY, THE SUN IS DECEPTIVELY HOT TODAY!
BCB
IT'S MONSOON SEASON IN MY PANTS

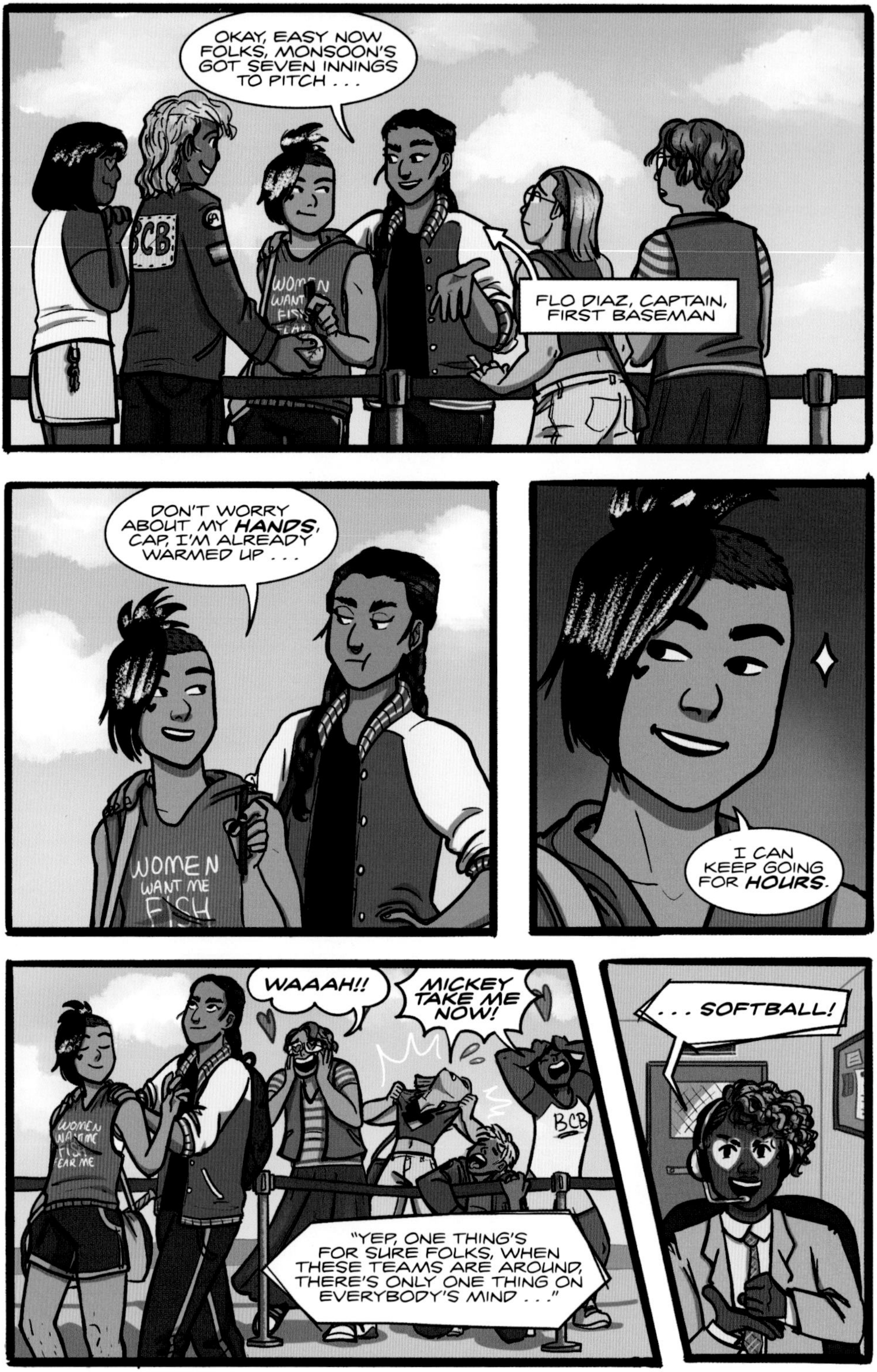
OKAY, EASY NOW FOLKS, MONSOON'S GOT SEVEN INNINGS TO PITCH . . .
BCB
FLO DIAZ, CAPTAIN, FIRST BASEMAN
DON'T WORRY ABOUT MY **HANDS**, CAP, I'M ALREADY WARMED UP . . .
I CAN KEEP GOING FOR **HOURS**.
WAAAH!!
MICKEY TAKE ME NOW!
WOMEN WANT ME FISH FEAR ME
BCB
"YEP, ONE THING'S FOR SURE FOLKS, WHEN THESE TEAMS ARE AROUND, THERE'S ONLY ONE THING ON EVERYBODY'S MIND . . ."
. . . SOFTBALL!

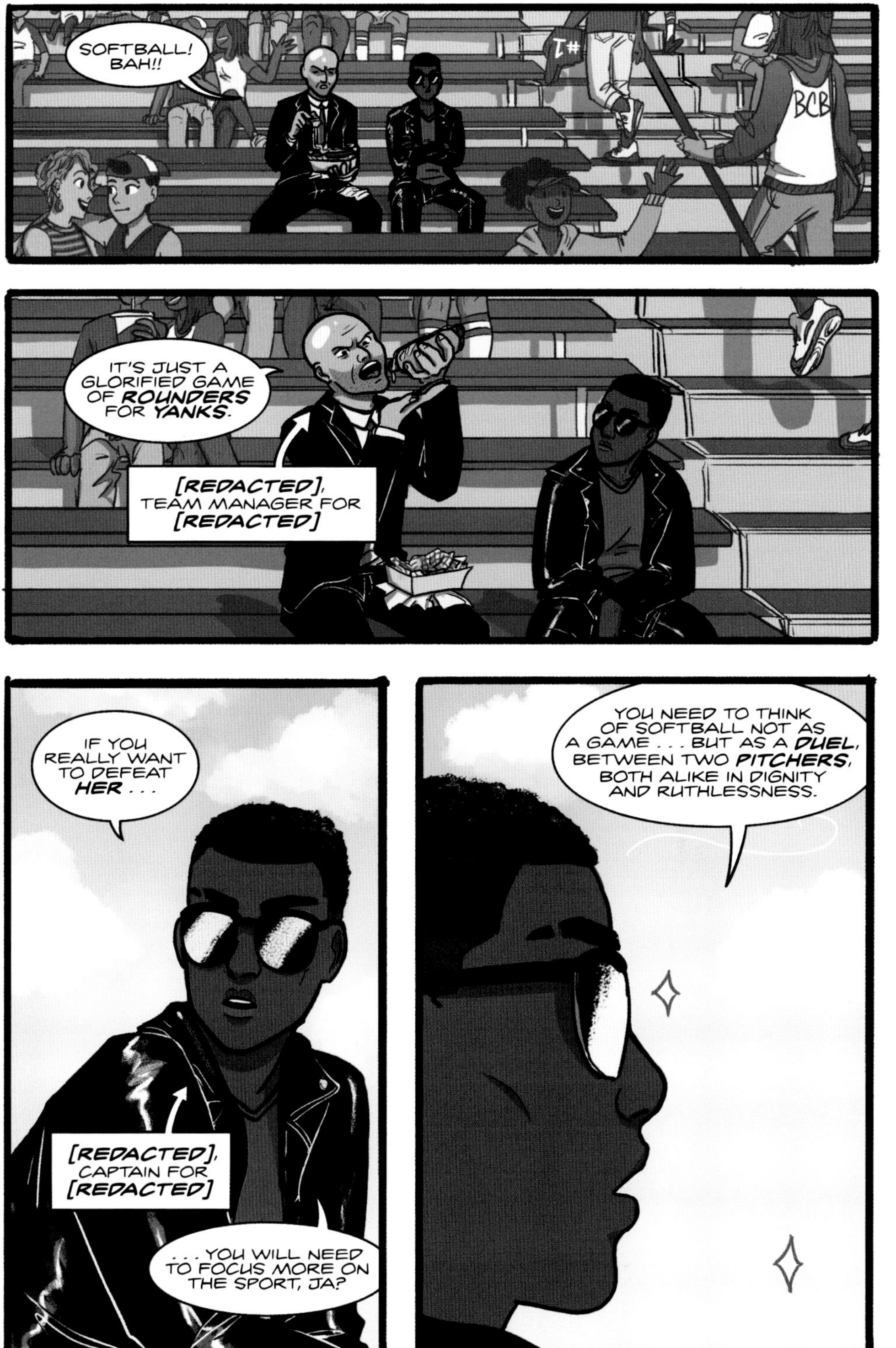
SOFTBALL! BAH!!
BCB
IT'S JUST A GLORIFIED GAME OF **ROUNDERS** FOR **YANKS**.
[REDACTED], TEAM MANAGER FOR **[REDACTED]**
IF YOU REALLY WANT TO DEFEAT **HER** . . .
[REDACTED], CAPTAIN FOR **[REDACTED]**
. . . YOU WILL NEED TO FOCUS MORE ON THE SPORT, JA?
YOU NEED TO THINK OF SOFTBALL NOT AS A GAME . . . BUT AS A **DUEL**, BETWEEN TWO **PITCHERS**, BOTH ALIKE IN DIGNITY AND RUTHLESSNESS.

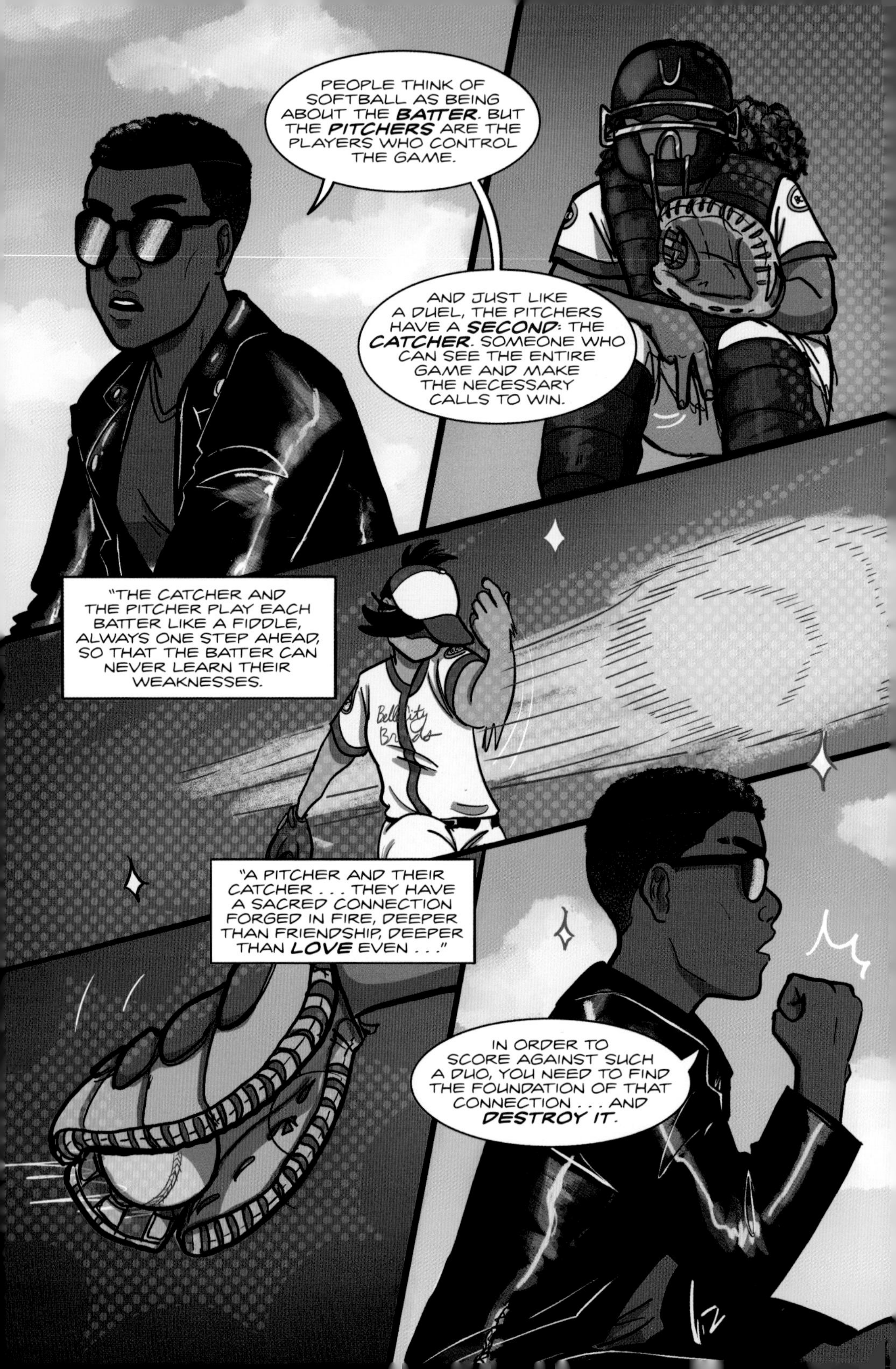
PEOPLE THINK OF SOFTBALL AS BEING ABOUT THE **BATTER**. BUT THE **PITCHERS** ARE THE PLAYERS WHO CONTROL THE GAME.
AND JUST LIKE A DUEL, THE PITCHERS HAVE A **SECOND**: THE **CATCHER**. SOMEONE WHO CAN SEE THE ENTIRE GAME AND MAKE THE NECESSARY CALLS TO WIN.
"THE CATCHER AND THE PITCHER PLAY EACH BATTER LIKE A FIDDLE, ALWAYS ONE STEP AHEAD, SO THAT THE BATTER CAN NEVER LEARN THEIR WEAKNESSES.
Bell City Birds
"A PITCHER AND THEIR CATCHER . . . THEY HAVE A SACRED CONNECTION FORGED IN FIRE, DEEPER THAN FRIENDSHIP, DEEPER THAN **LOVE** EVEN . . ."
IN ORDER TO SCORE AGAINST SUCH A DUO, YOU NEED TO FIND THE FOUNDATION OF THAT CONNECTION . . . AND **DESTROY IT**.

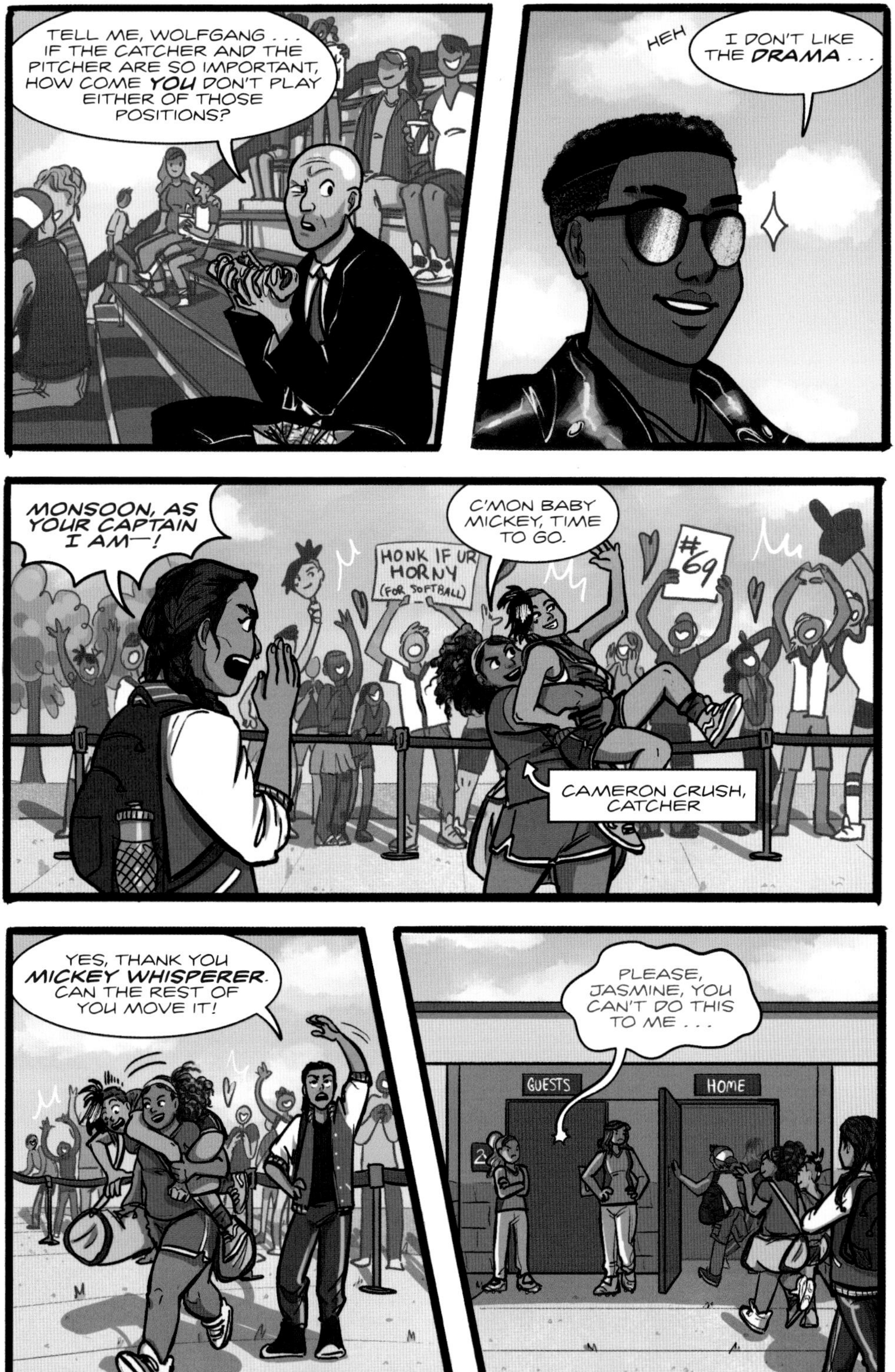

TELL ME, WOLFGANG . . . IF THE CATCHER AND THE PITCHER ARE SO IMPORTANT, HOW COME **YOU** DON'T PLAY EITHER OF THOSE POSITIONS?
HEH
I DON'T LIKE THE **DRAMA** . . .
MONSOON, AS YOUR CAPTAIN I AM—!
HONK IF UR HORNY (FOR SOFTBALL)
C'MON BABY MICKEY, TIME TO GO.
#69
CAMERON CRUSH, CATCHER
YES, THANK YOU **MICKEY WHISPERER**. CAN THE REST OF YOU MOVE IT!
PLEASE, JASMINE, YOU CAN'T DO THIS TO ME . . .
GUESTS
HOME

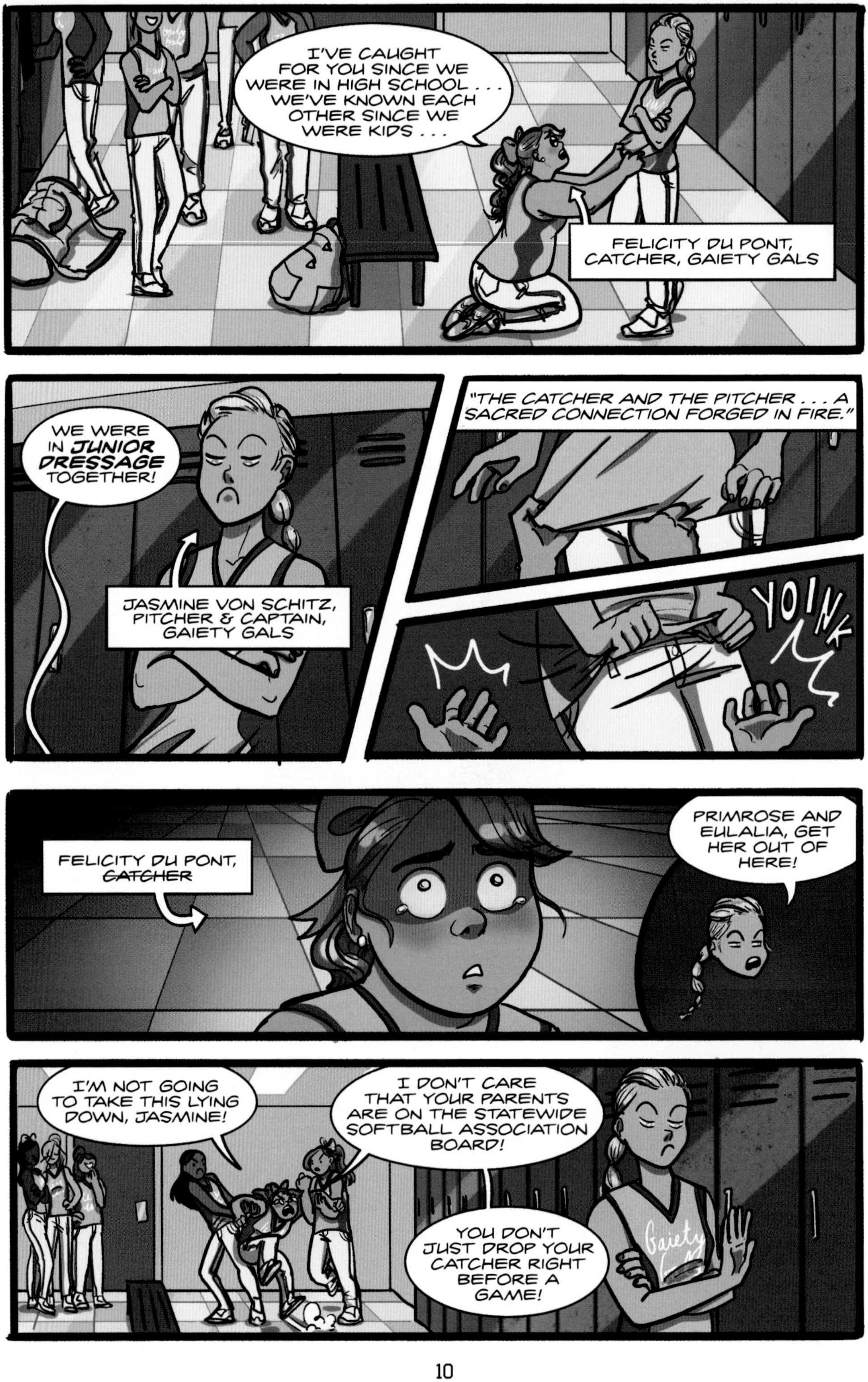
I'VE CAUGHT FOR YOU SINCE WE WERE IN HIGH SCHOOL . . . WE'VE KNOWN EACH OTHER SINCE WE WERE KIDS . . .
FELICITY DU PONT, CATCHER, GAIETY GALS
WE WERE IN **JUNIOR DRESSAGE** TOGETHER!
JASMINE VON SCHITZ, PITCHER & CAPTAIN, GAIETY GALS
"THE CATCHER AND THE PITCHER . . . A SACRED CONNECTION FORGED IN FIRE."
YOINK
FELICITY DU PONT, ~~CATCHER~~
PRIMROSE AND EULALIA, GET HER OUT OF HERE!
I'M NOT GOING TO TAKE THIS LYING DOWN, JASMINE!
I DON'T CARE THAT YOUR PARENTS ARE ON THE STATEWIDE SOFTBALL ASSOCIATION BOARD!
YOU DON'T JUST DROP YOUR CATCHER RIGHT BEFORE A GAME!

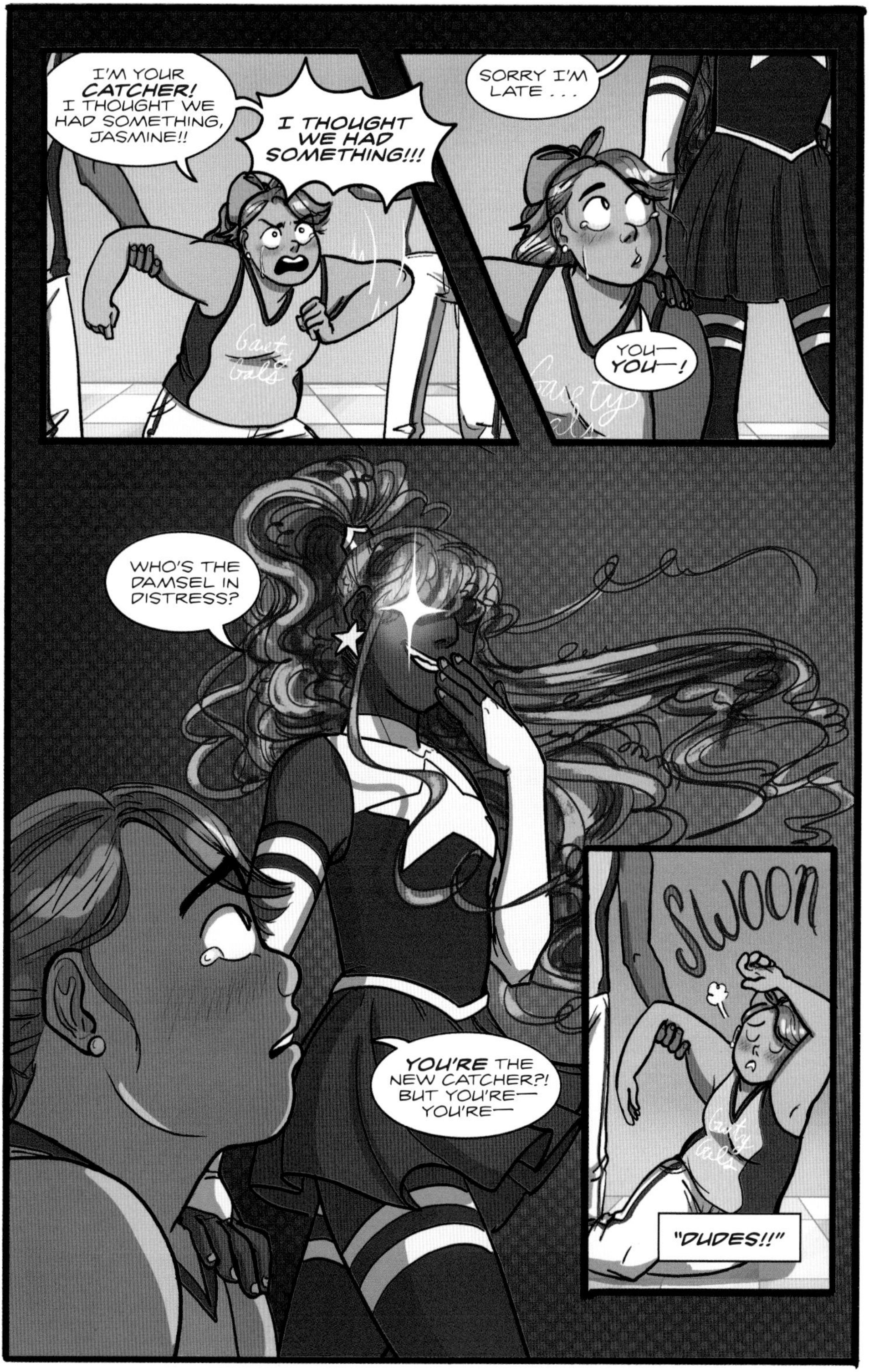
I'M YOUR CATCHER! I THOUGHT WE HAD SOMETHING, JASMINE!!
I THOUGHT WE HAD SOMETHING!!!
SORRY I'M LATE . . .
YOU— YOU—!
WHO'S THE DAMSEL IN DISTRESS?
YOU'RE THE NEW CATCHER?! BUT YOU'RE— YOU'RE—
SWOON
"DUDES!!"

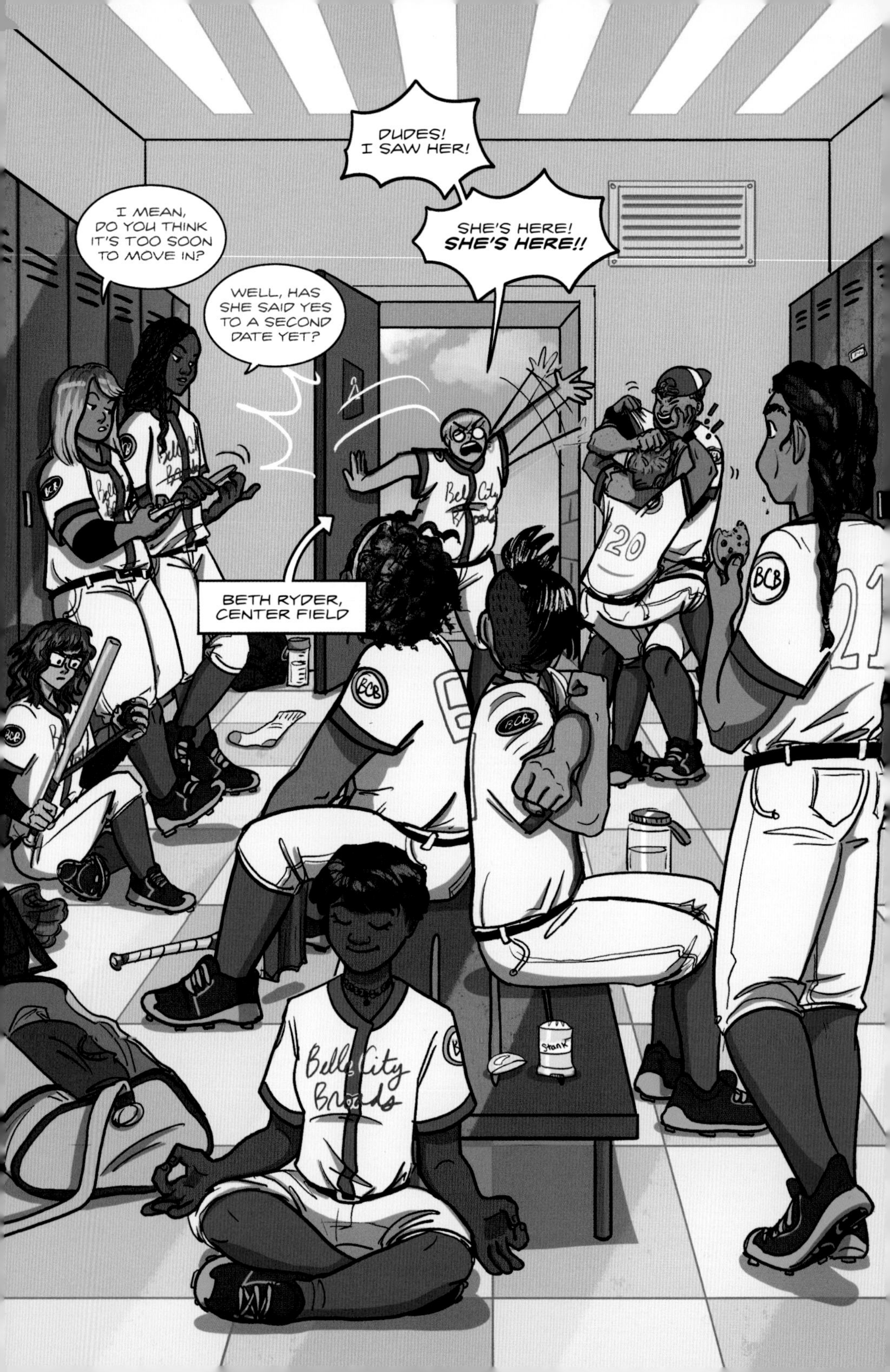
I MEAN, DO YOU THINK IT'S TOO SOON TO MOVE IN?
WELL, HAS SHE SAID YES TO A SECOND DATE YET?
DUDES! I SAW HER!
SHE'S HERE! ***SHE'S HERE!!***
BETH RYDER, CENTER FIELD

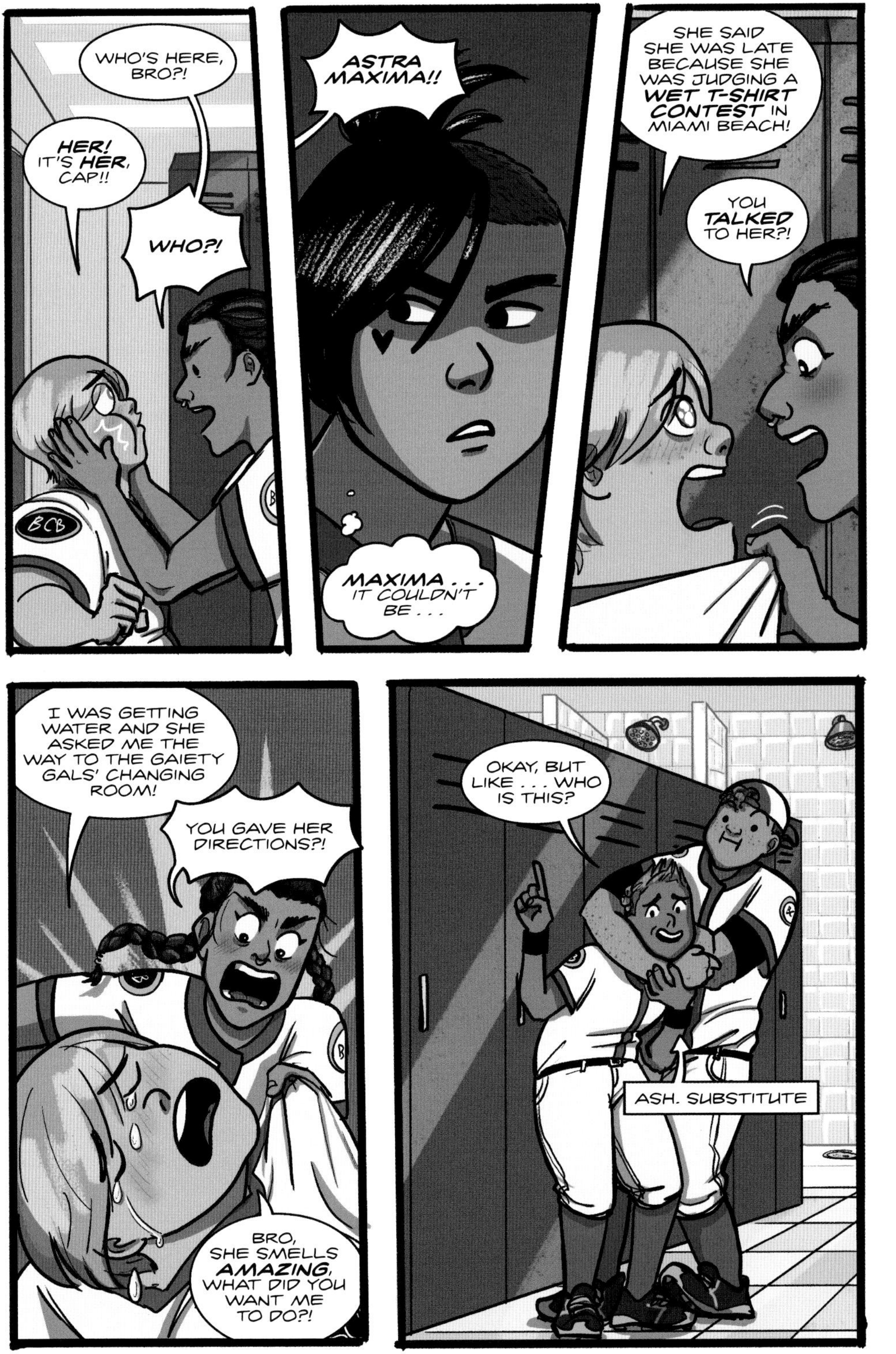

WHO'S HERE, BRO?!
HER! IT'S HER, CAP!!
WHO?!
ASTRA MAXIMA!!
MAXIMA . . . IT COULDN'T BE . . .
SHE SAID SHE WAS LATE BECAUSE SHE WAS JUDGING A WET T-SHIRT CONTEST IN MIAMI BEACH!
YOU TALKED TO HER?!
I WAS GETTING WATER AND SHE ASKED ME THE WAY TO THE GAIETY GALS' CHANGING ROOM!
YOU GAVE HER DIRECTIONS?!
BRO, SHE SMELLS AMAZING, WHAT DID YOU WANT ME TO DO?!
OKAY, BUT LIKE . . . WHO IS THIS?
ASH. SUBSTITUTE

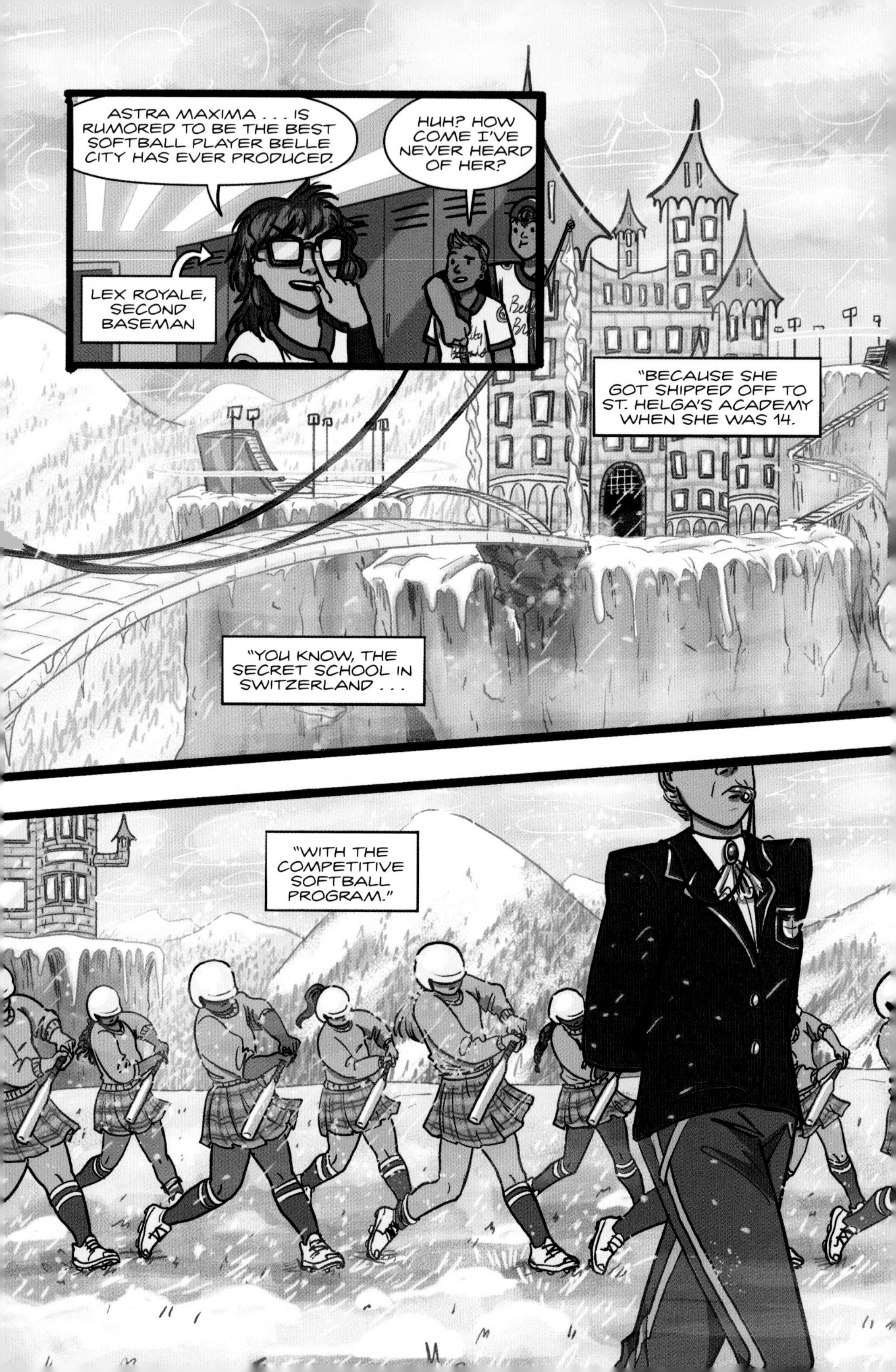
ASTRA MAXIMA . . . IS RUMORED TO BE THE BEST SOFTBALL PLAYER BELLE CITY HAS EVER PRODUCED.
HUH? HOW COME I'VE NEVER HEARD OF HER?
LEX ROYALE, SECOND BASEMAN
"BECAUSE SHE GOT SHIPPED OFF TO ST. HELGA'S ACADEMY WHEN SHE WAS 14.
"YOU KNOW, THE SECRET SCHOOL IN SWITZERLAND . . .
"WITH THE COMPETITIVE SOFTBALL PROGRAM."

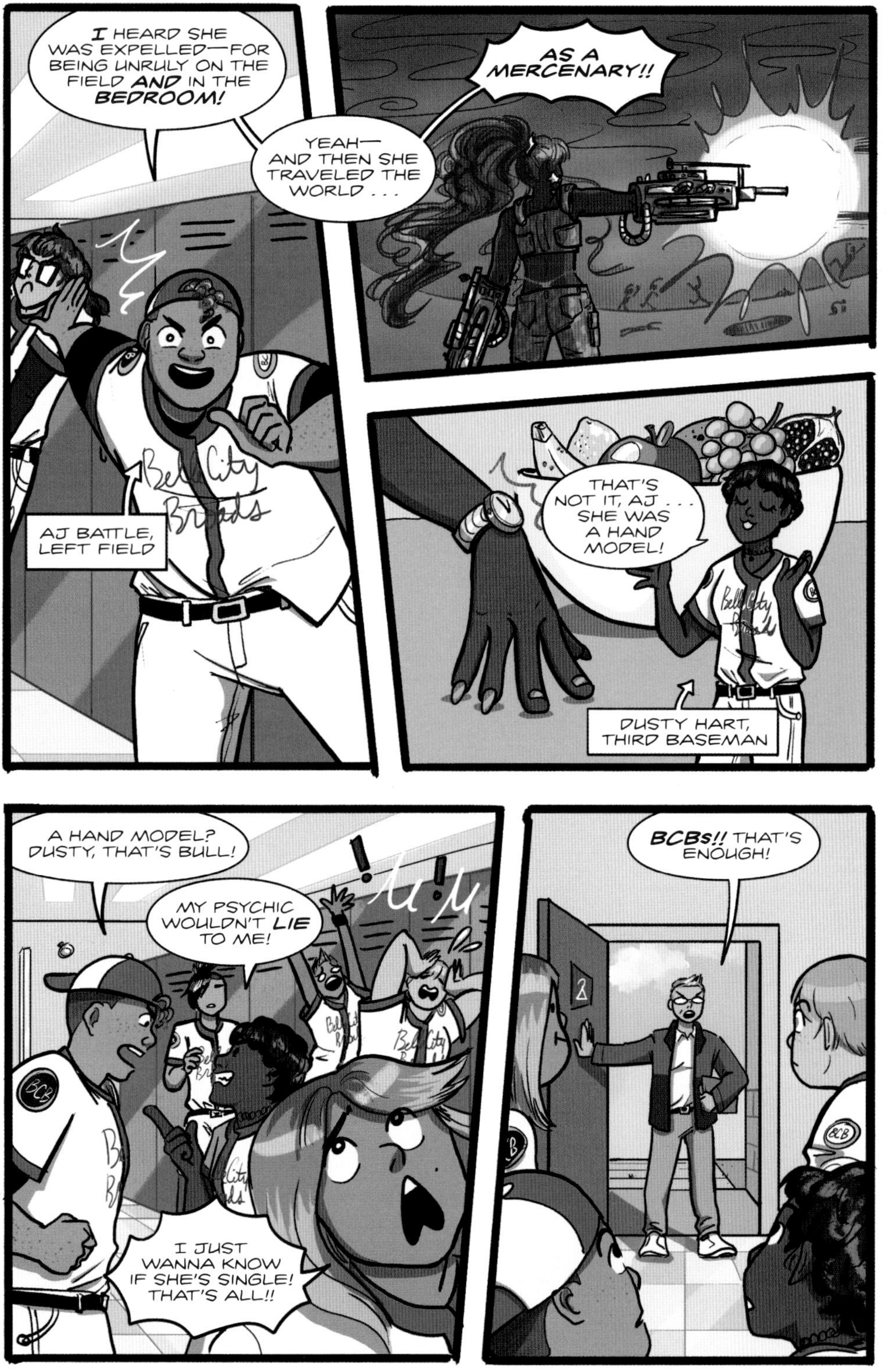
I HEARD SHE WAS EXPELLED—FOR BEING UNRULY ON THE FIELD AND IN THE BEDROOM!
YEAH—AND THEN SHE TRAVELED THE WORLD . . .
AJ BATTLE, LEFT FIELD
AS A MERCENARY!!
THAT'S NOT IT, AJ . . . SHE WAS A HAND MODEL!
DUSTY HART, THIRD BASEMAN
A HAND MODEL? DUSTY, THAT'S BULL!
MY PSYCHIC WOULDN'T LIE TO ME!
I JUST WANNA KNOW IF SHE'S SINGLE! THAT'S ALL!!
BCBs!! THAT'S ENOUGH!

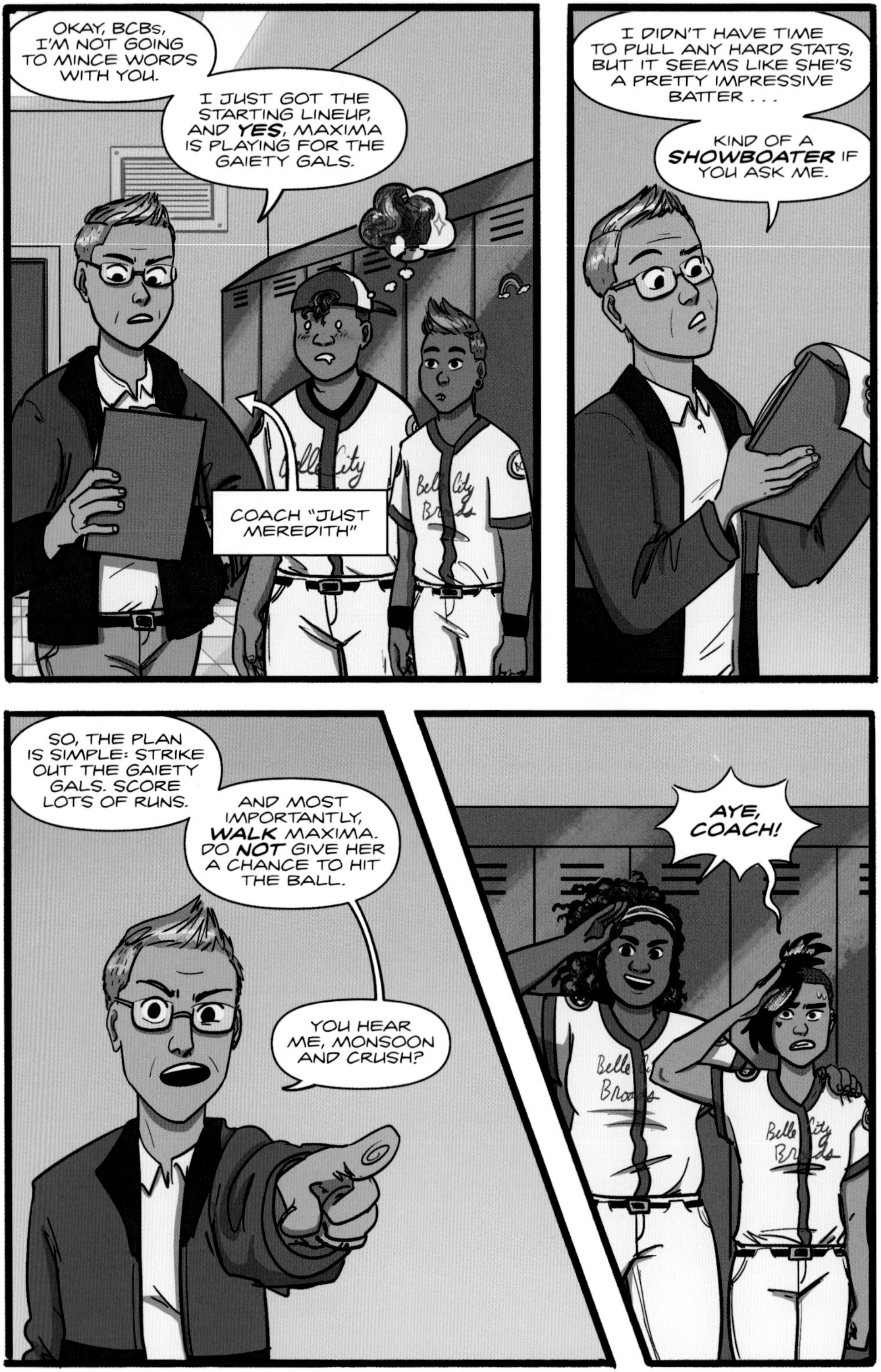

OKAY, BCBs, I'M NOT GOING TO MINCE WORDS WITH YOU.
I JUST GOT THE STARTING LINEUP, AND **YES**, MAXIMA IS PLAYING FOR THE GAIETY GALS.
COACH "JUST MEREDITH"
Belle City
Belle City Broads
I DIDN'T HAVE TIME TO PULL ANY HARD STATS, BUT IT SEEMS LIKE SHE'S A PRETTY IMPRESSIVE BATTER . . .
KIND OF A **SHOWBOATER** IF YOU ASK ME.
SO, THE PLAN IS SIMPLE: STRIKE OUT THE GAIETY GALS. SCORE LOTS OF RUNS.
AND MOST IMPORTANTLY, **WALK** MAXIMA. DO **NOT** GIVE HER A CHANCE TO HIT THE BALL.
YOU HEAR ME, MONSOON AND CRUSH?
AYE, COACH!
Belle City Broads

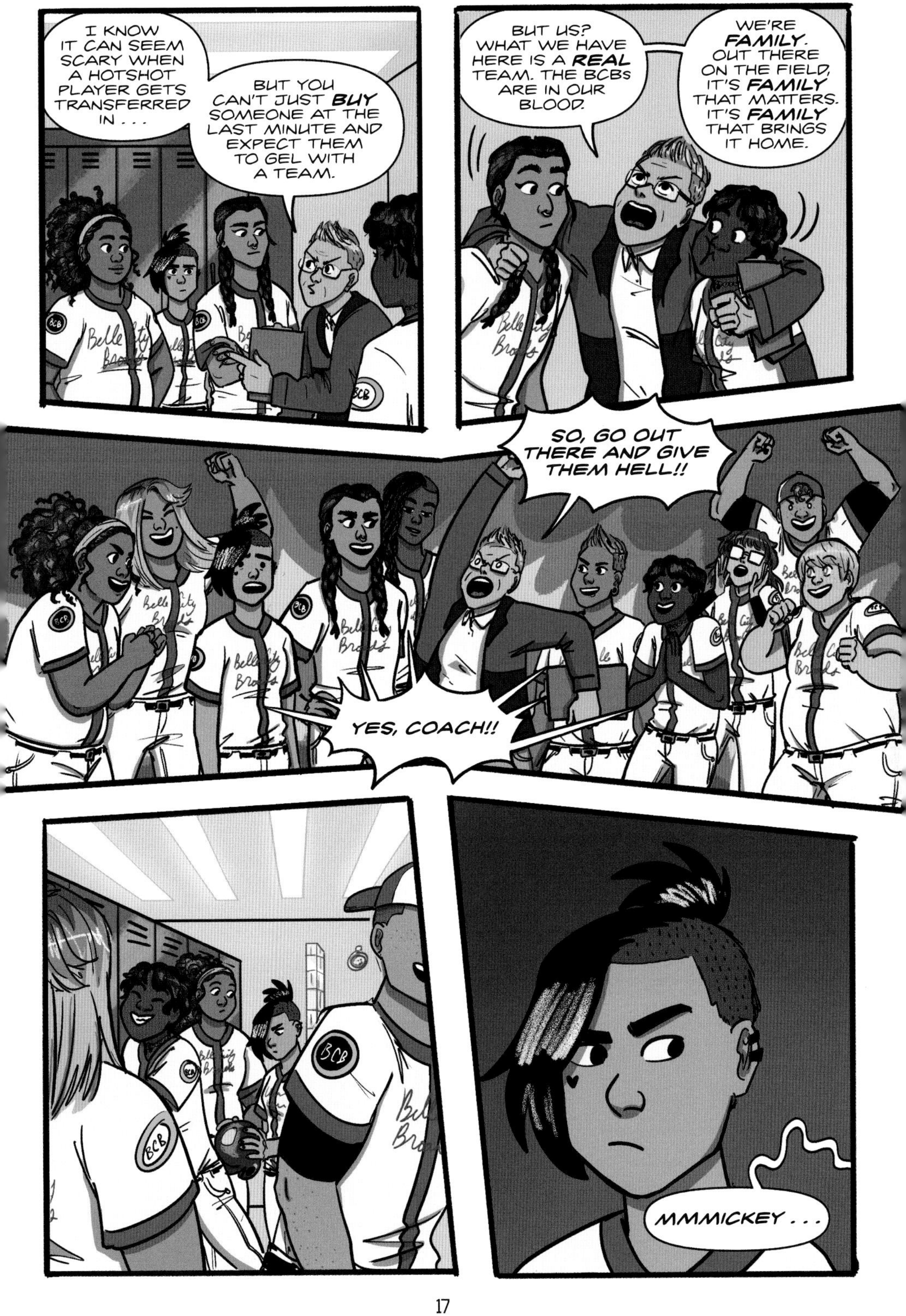
I KNOW IT CAN SEEM SCARY WHEN A HOTSHOT PLAYER GETS TRANSFERRED IN . . .
BUT YOU CAN'T JUST **BUY** SOMEONE AT THE LAST MINUTE AND EXPECT THEM TO GEL WITH A TEAM.
BUT US? WHAT WE HAVE HERE IS A **REAL** TEAM. THE BCBs ARE IN OUR BLOOD.
WE'RE ***FAMILY***. OUT THERE ON THE FIELD, IT'S ***FAMILY*** THAT MATTERS. IT'S ***FAMILY*** THAT BRINGS IT HOME.
SO, GO OUT THERE AND GIVE THEM HELL!!
YES, COACH!!
MMMICKEY . . .

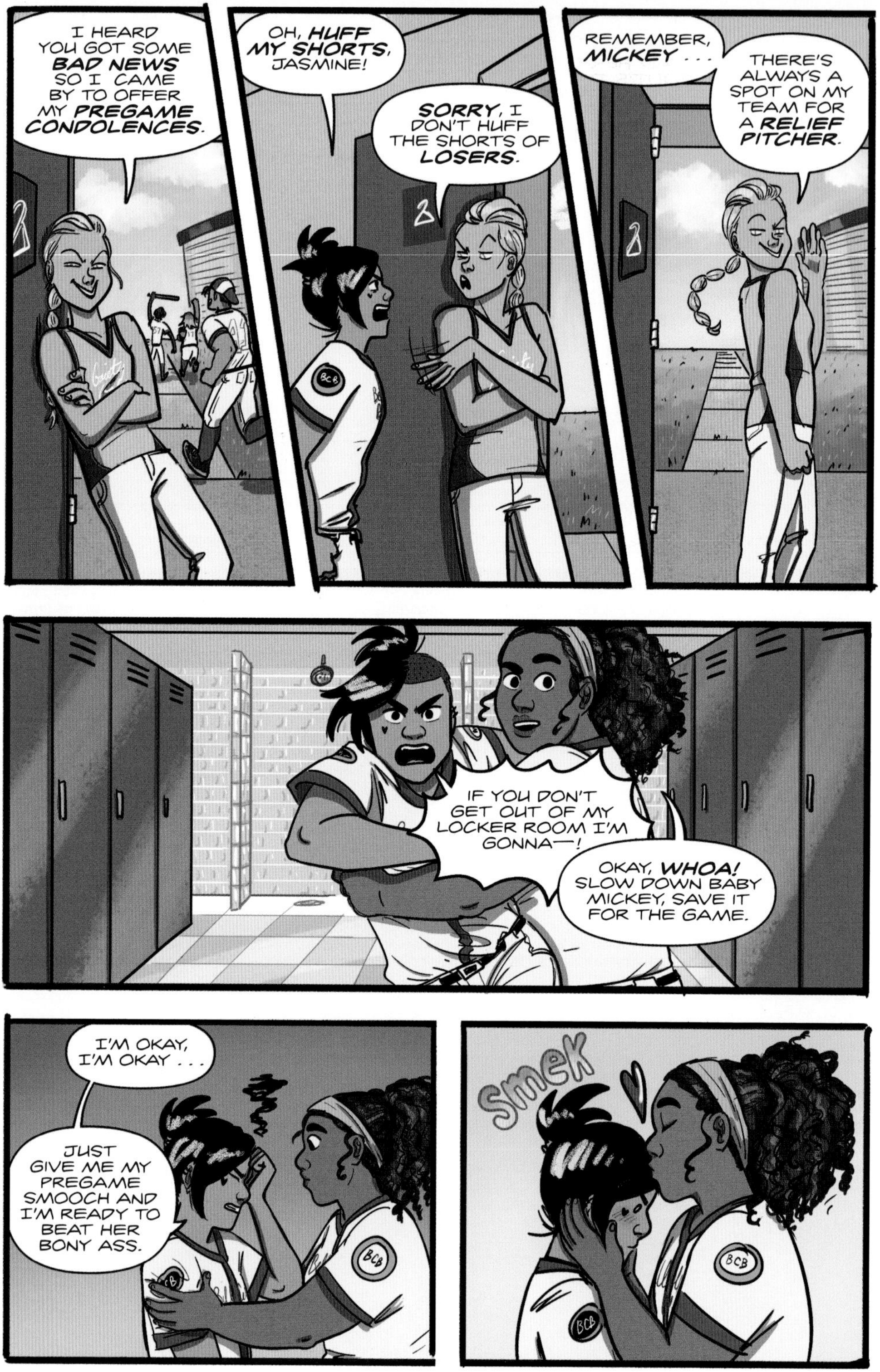

I HEARD YOU GOT SOME **BAD NEWS** SO I CAME BY TO OFFER MY **PREGAME CONDOLENCES**.
OH, **HUFF MY SHORTS**, JASMINE!
SORRY, I DON'T HUFF THE SHORTS OF **LOSERS**.
REMEMBER, **MICKEY** . . .
THERE'S ALWAYS A SPOT ON MY TEAM FOR A **RELIEF PITCHER**.
IF YOU DON'T GET OUT OF MY LOCKER ROOM I'M GONNA—!
OKAY, **WHOA!** SLOW DOWN BABY MICKEY, SAVE IT FOR THE GAME.
I'M OKAY, I'M OKAY . . .
JUST GIVE ME MY PREGAME SMOOCH AND I'M READY TO BEAT HER BONY ASS.
SMEK

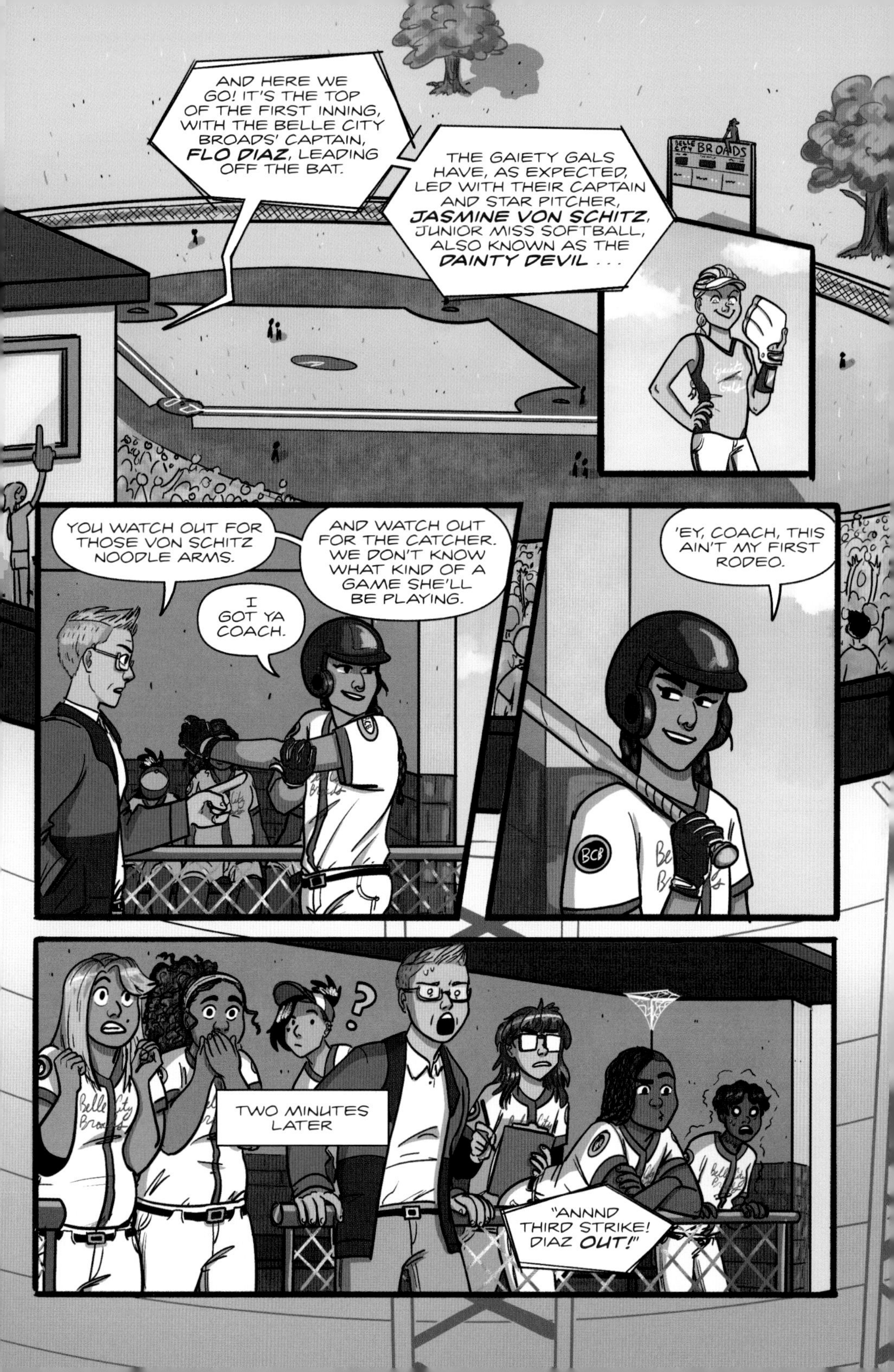
AND HERE WE GO! IT'S THE TOP OF THE FIRST INNING, WITH THE BELLE CITY BROADS' CAPTAIN, **FLO DIAZ**, LEADING OFF THE BAT.
THE GAIETY GALS HAVE, AS EXPECTED, LED WITH THEIR CAPTAIN AND STAR PITCHER, **JASMINE VON SCHITZ**, JUNIOR MISS SOFTBALL, ALSO KNOWN AS THE **DAINTY DEVIL** . . .
BELLE CITY BROADS
YOU WATCH OUT FOR THOSE VON SCHITZ NOODLE ARMS.
AND WATCH OUT FOR THE CATCHER. WE DON'T KNOW WHAT KIND OF A GAME SHE'LL BE PLAYING.
I GOT YA COACH.
'EY, COACH, THIS AIN'T MY FIRST RODEO.
?
TWO MINUTES LATER
"ANNND THIRD STRIKE! DIAZ **OUT**!"

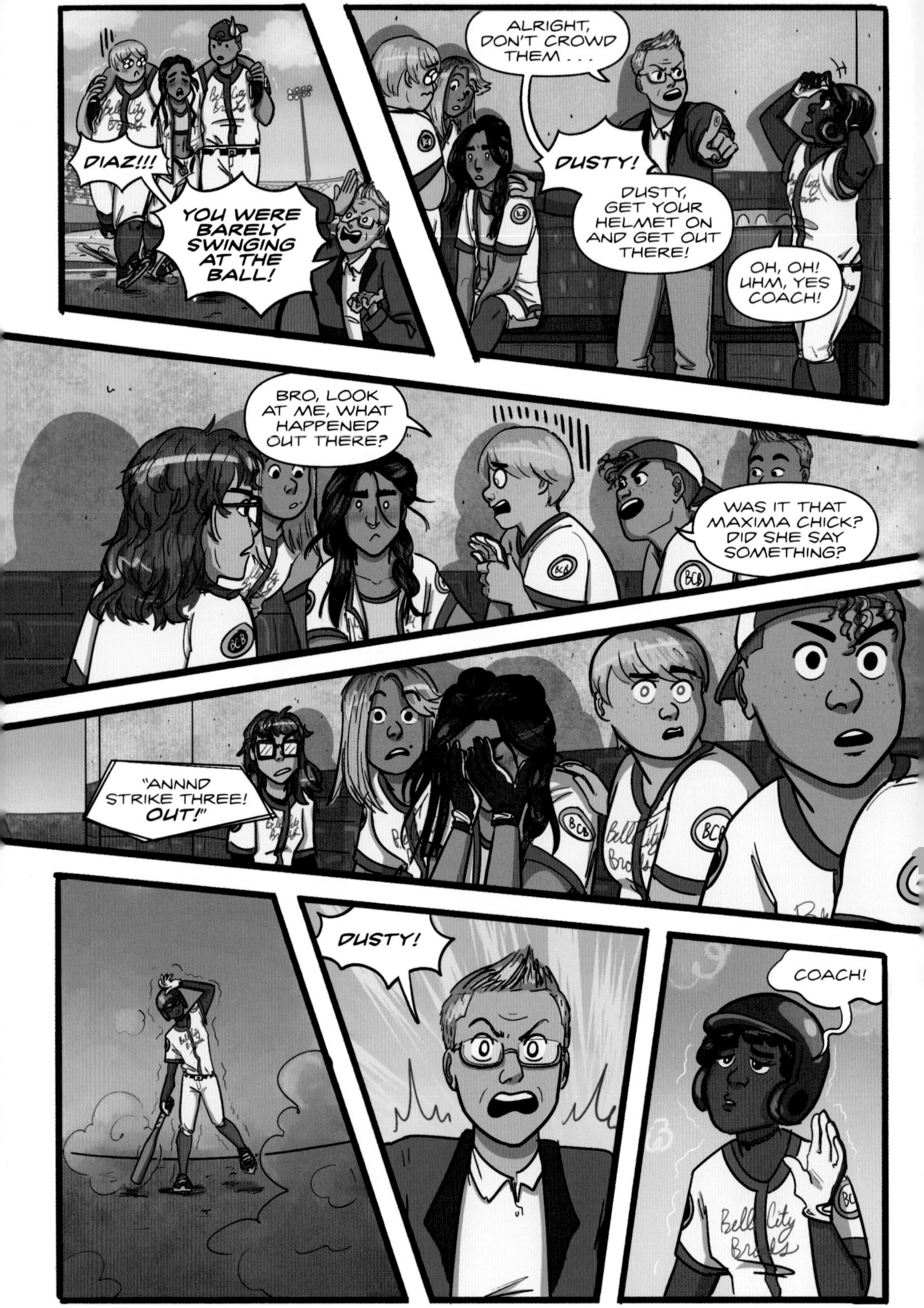
DIAZ!!!
YOU WERE BARELY SWINGING AT THE BALL!
ALRIGHT, DON'T CROWD THEM . . .
DUSTY!
DUSTY, GET YOUR HELMET ON AND GET OUT THERE!
OH, OH! UHM, YES COACH!
BRO, LOOK AT ME, WHAT HAPPENED OUT THERE?
WAS IT THAT MAXIMA CHICK? DID SHE SAY SOMETHING?
"ANNND STRIKE THREE! OUT!"
DUSTY!
COACH!

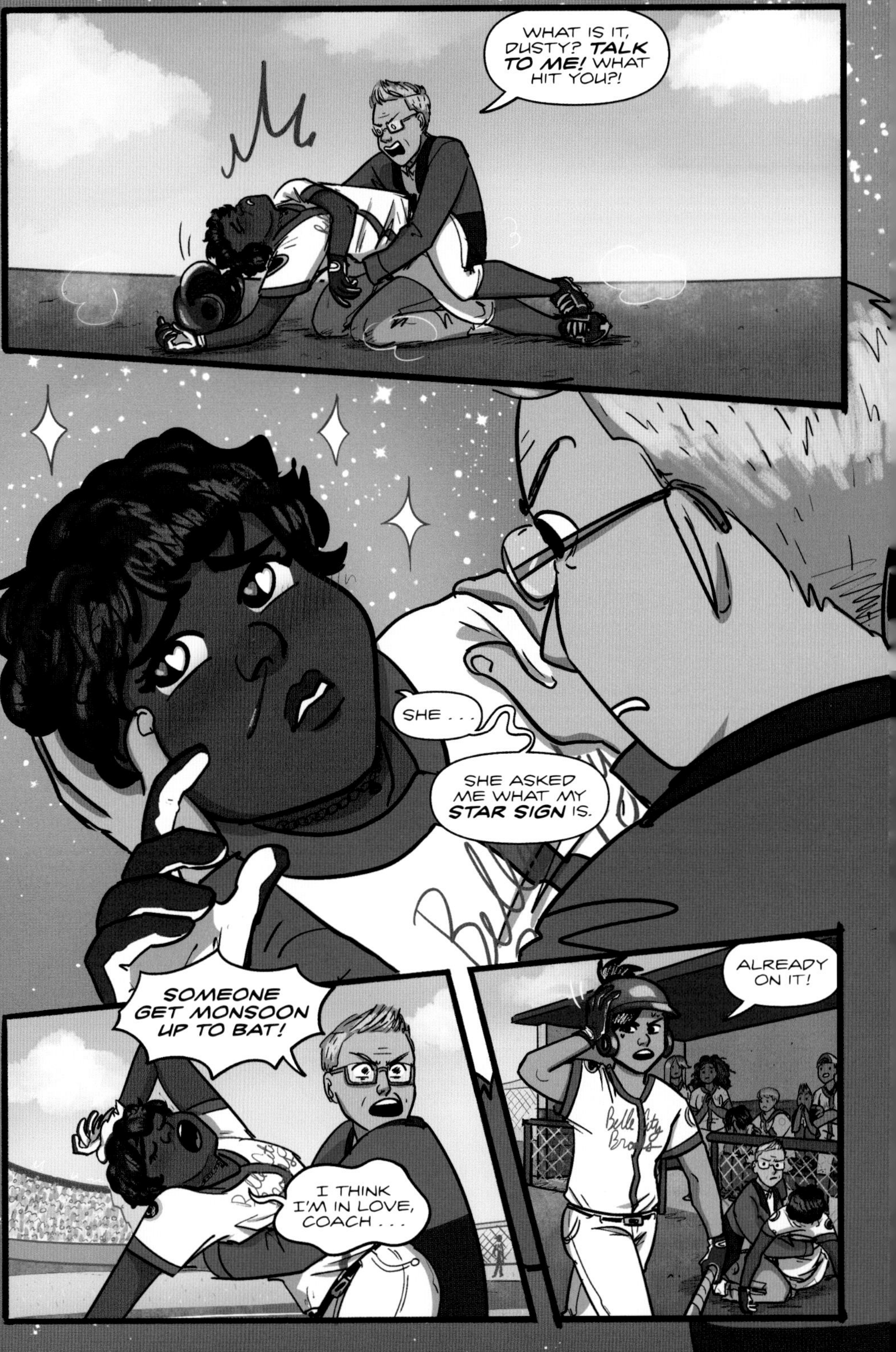
WHAT IS IT, DUSTY? **TALK TO ME!** WHAT HIT YOU?!
SHE . . .
SHE ASKED ME WHAT MY **STAR SIGN** IS.
SOMEONE GET MONSOON UP TO BAT!
I THINK I'M IN LOVE, COACH . . .
ALREADY ON IT!

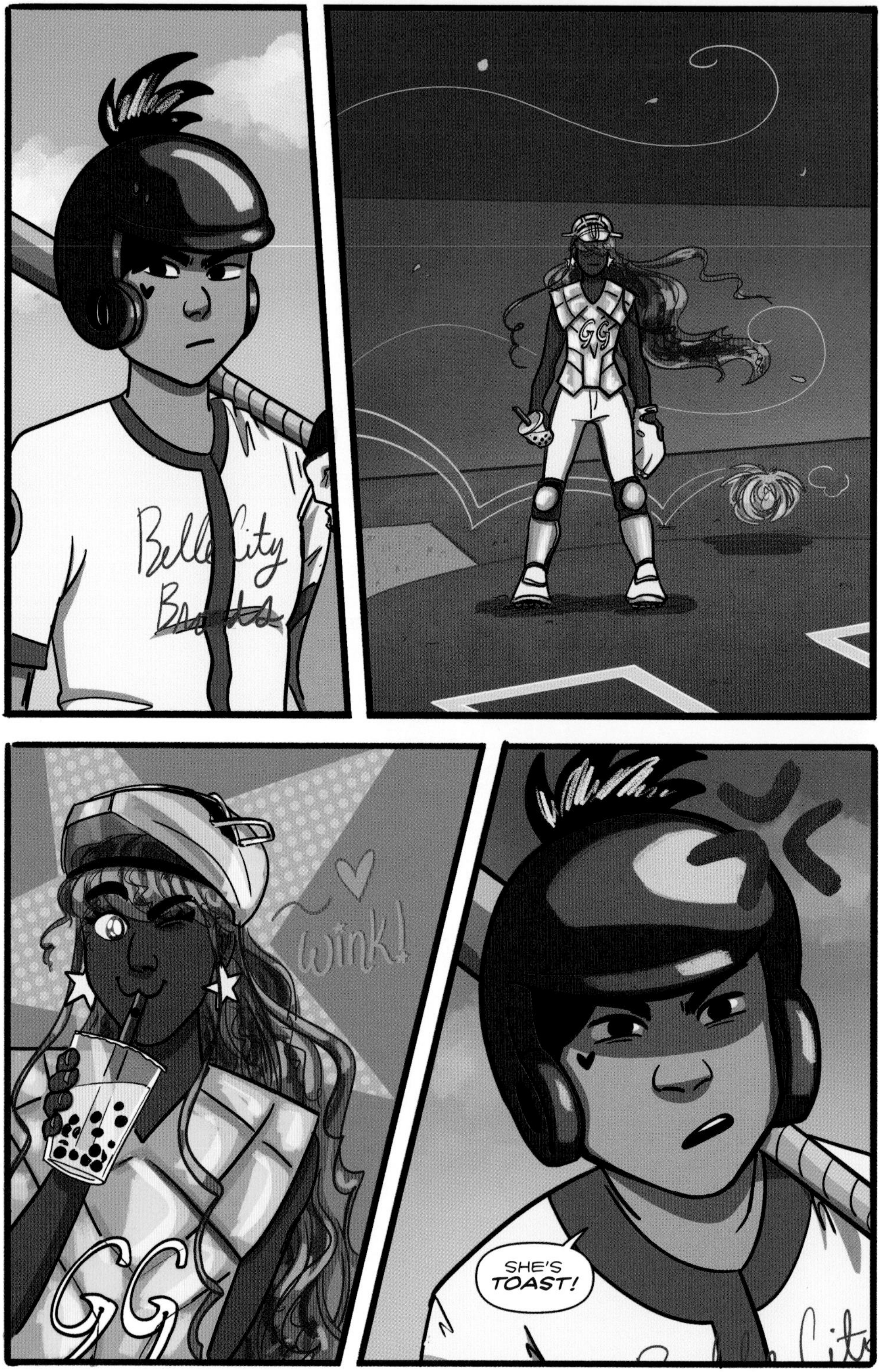
wink!
SHE'S TOAST!

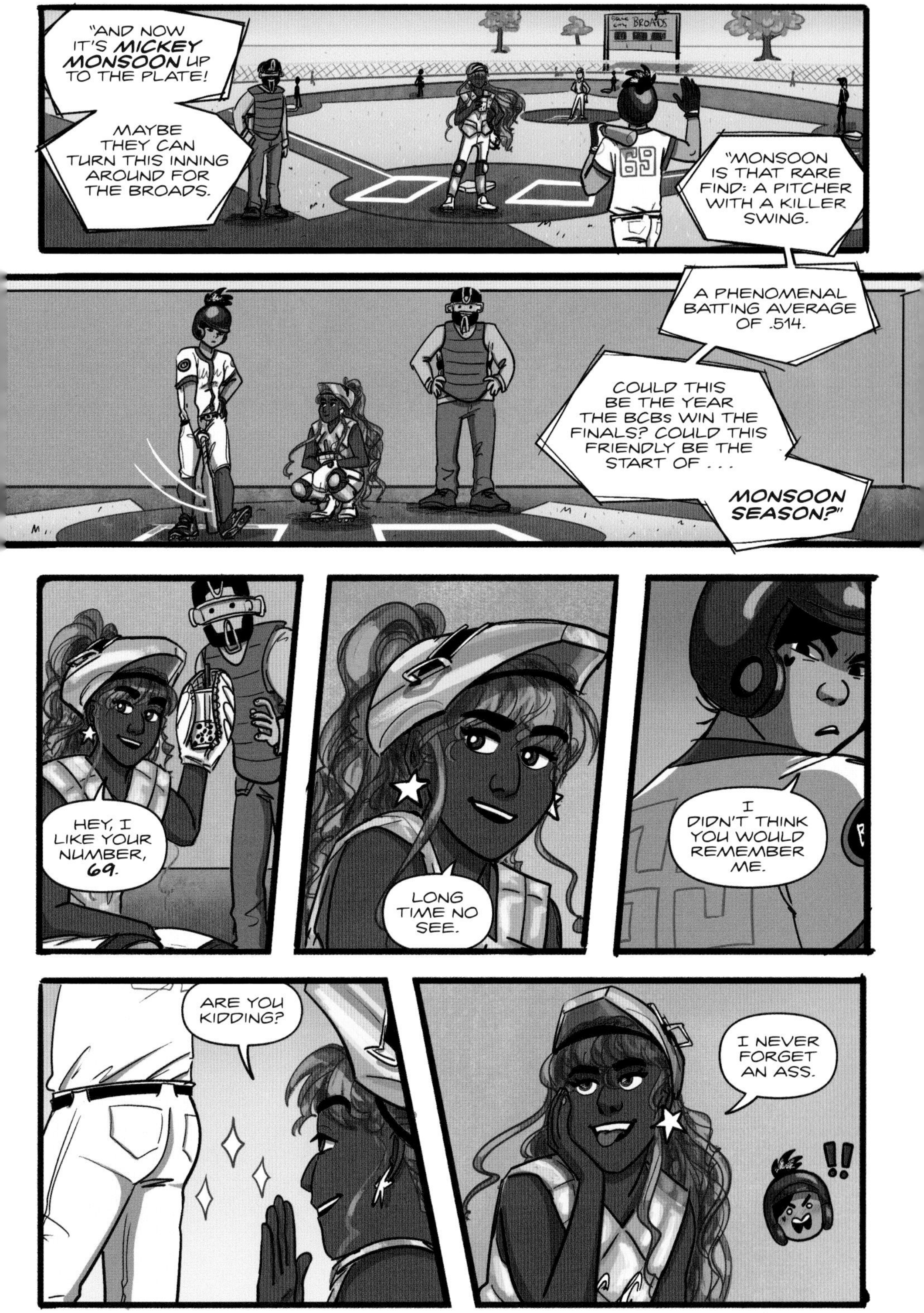
"AND NOW IT'S **MICKEY MONSOON** UP TO THE PLATE!
MAYBE THEY CAN TURN THIS INNING AROUND FOR THE BROADS.
BROADS
"MONSOON IS THAT RARE FIND: A PITCHER WITH A KILLER SWING.
A PHENOMENAL BATTING AVERAGE OF .514.
COULD THIS BE THE YEAR THE BCBs WIN THE FINALS? COULD THIS FRIENDLY BE THE START OF . . .
MONSOON SEASON?"
HEY, I LIKE YOUR NUMBER, **69**.
LONG TIME NO SEE.
I DIDN'T THINK YOU WOULD REMEMBER ME.
ARE YOU KIDDING?
I NEVER FORGET AN ASS.
!!

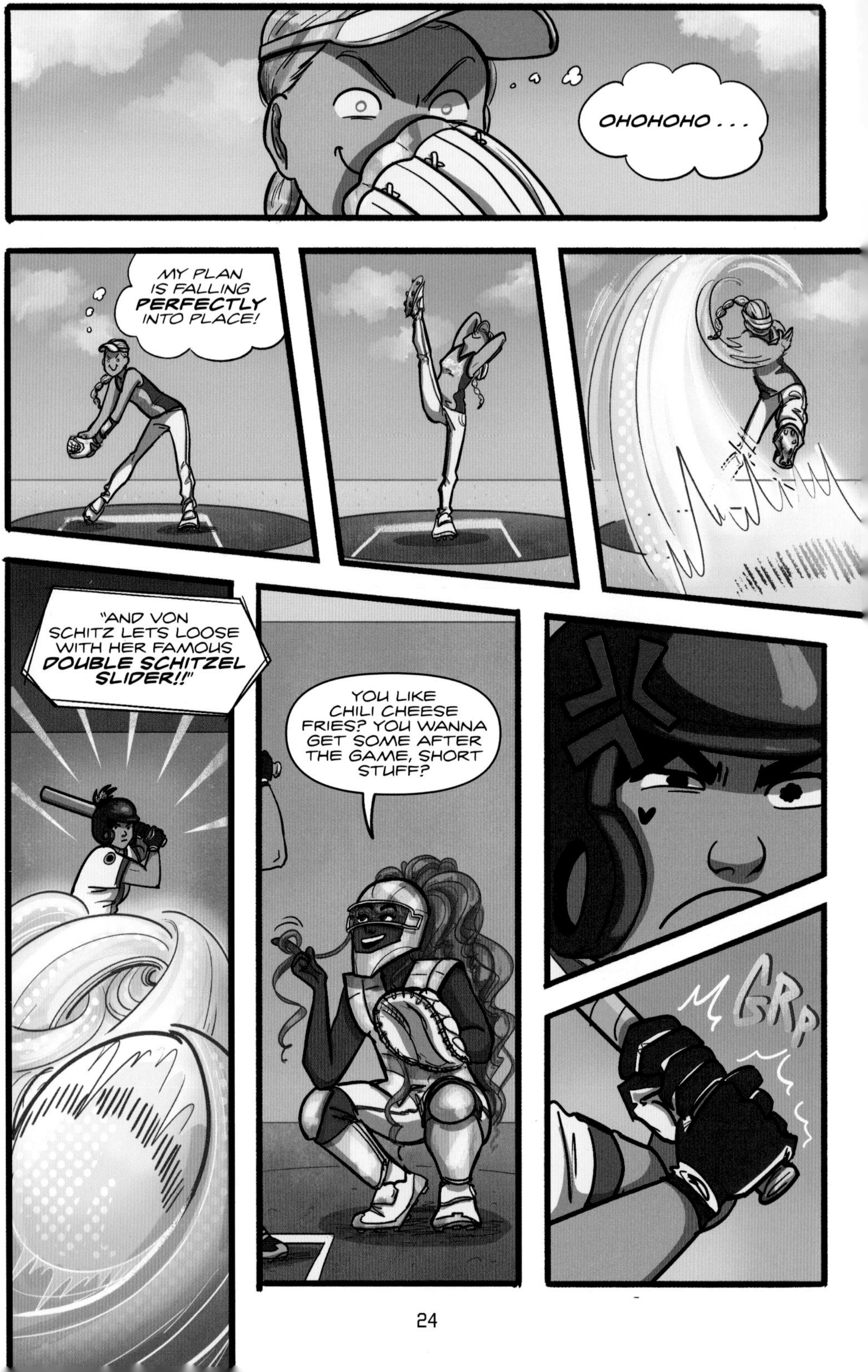
OHOHOHO . . .
MY PLAN IS FALLING **PERFECTLY** INTO PLACE!
"AND VON SCHITZ LETS LOOSE WITH HER FAMOUS **DOUBLE SCHITZEL SLIDER!!**"
YOU LIKE CHILI CHEESE FRIES? YOU WANNA GET SOME AFTER THE GAME, SHORT STUFF?
GRP

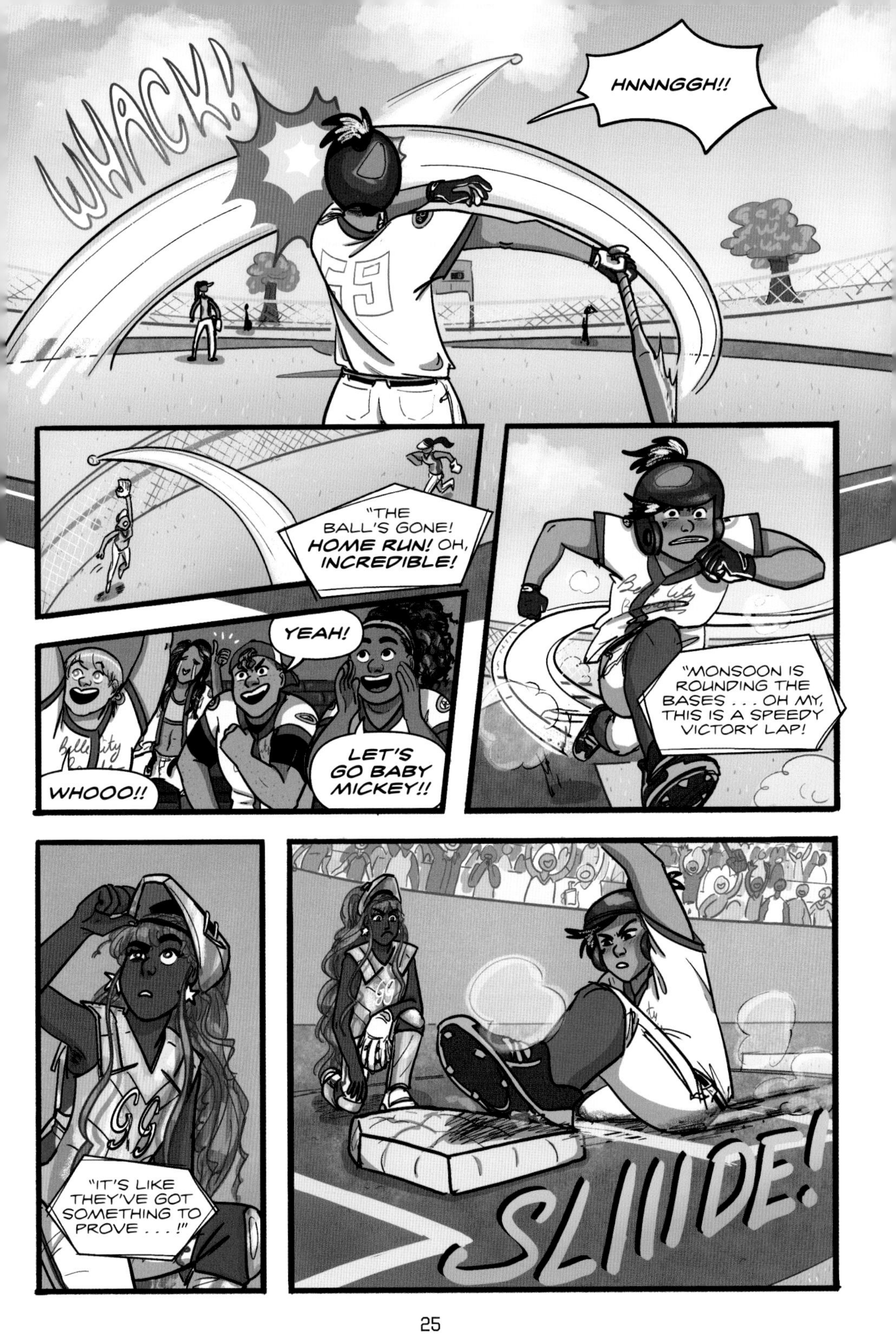
WHACK!
HNNNGGH!!
"THE BALL'S GONE! **HOME RUN!** OH, **INCREDIBLE!**
YEAH!
WHOOO!!
LET'S GO BABY MICKEY!!
"MONSOON IS ROUNDING THE BASES . . . OH MY, THIS IS A SPEEDY VICTORY LAP!
"IT'S LIKE THEY'VE GOT SOMETHING TO PROVE . . . !"
SLIIIDE!

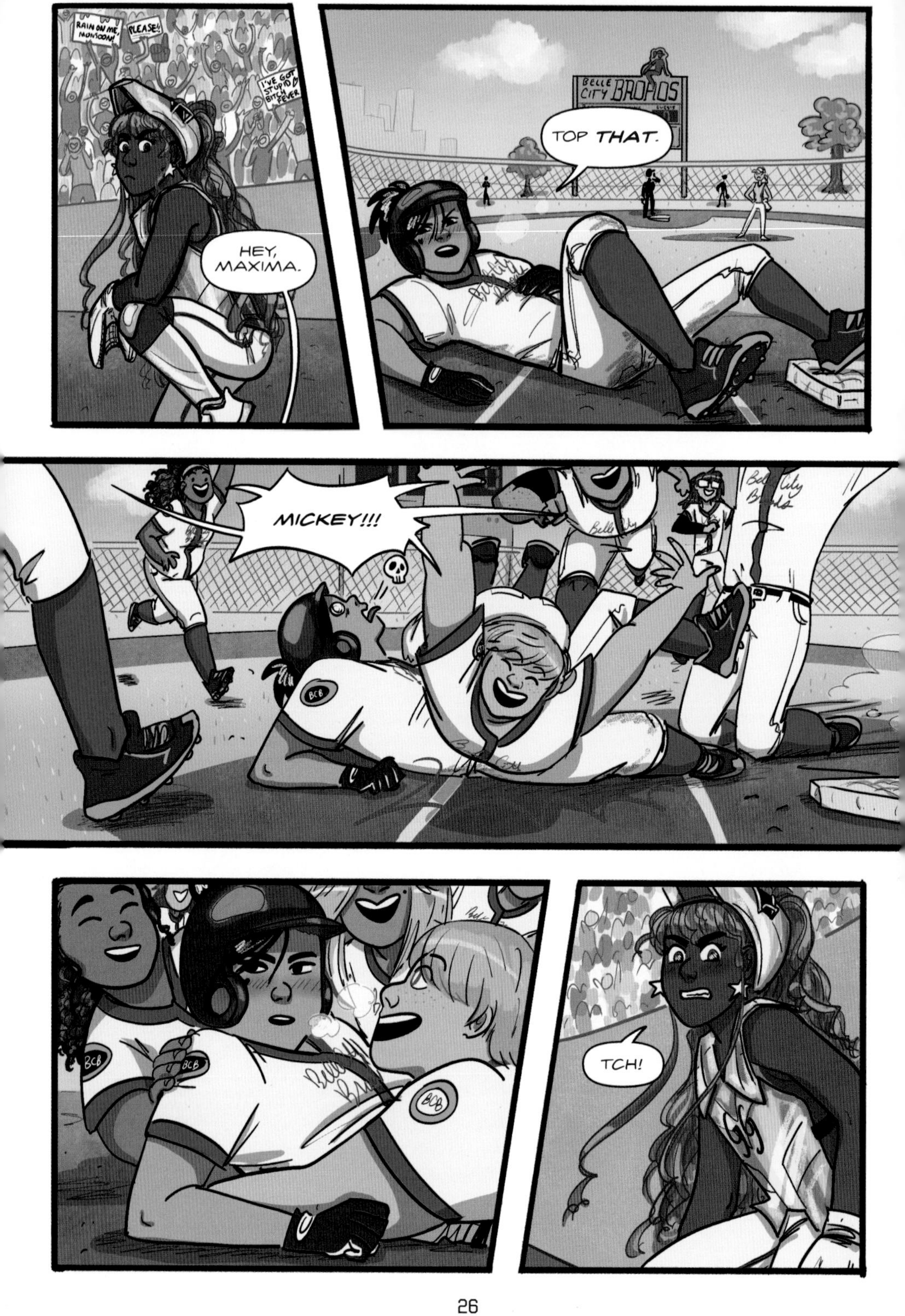
RAIN ON ME, MONSOON!
PLEASE!!
I'VE GOT STUPID BITCH FEVER
HEY, MAXIMA.
BELLE CITY BROADS
TOP THAT.
MICKEY!!!
TCH!

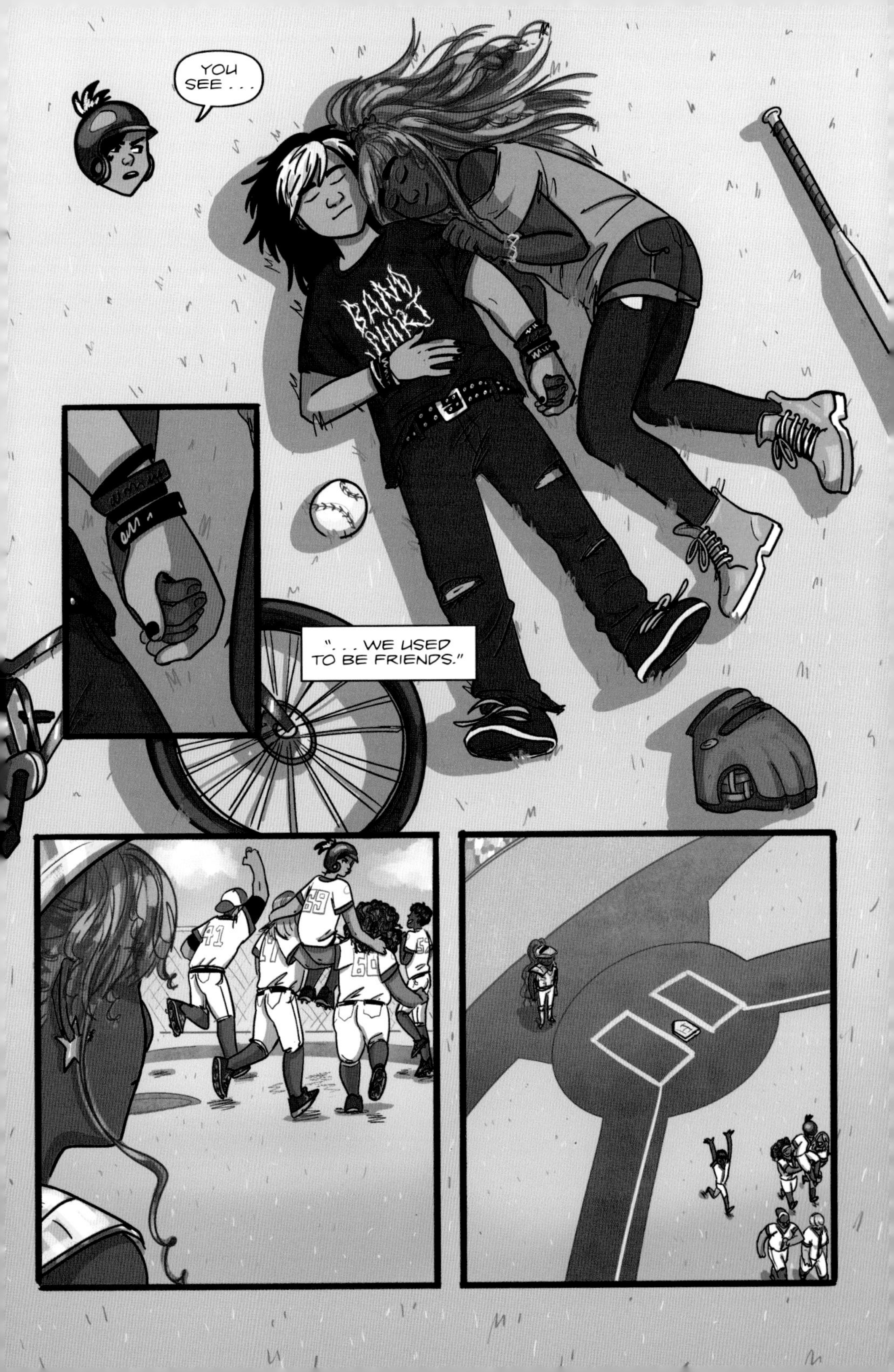

YOU SEE . . .
BAND SHIRT
". . . WE USED TO BE FRIENDS."

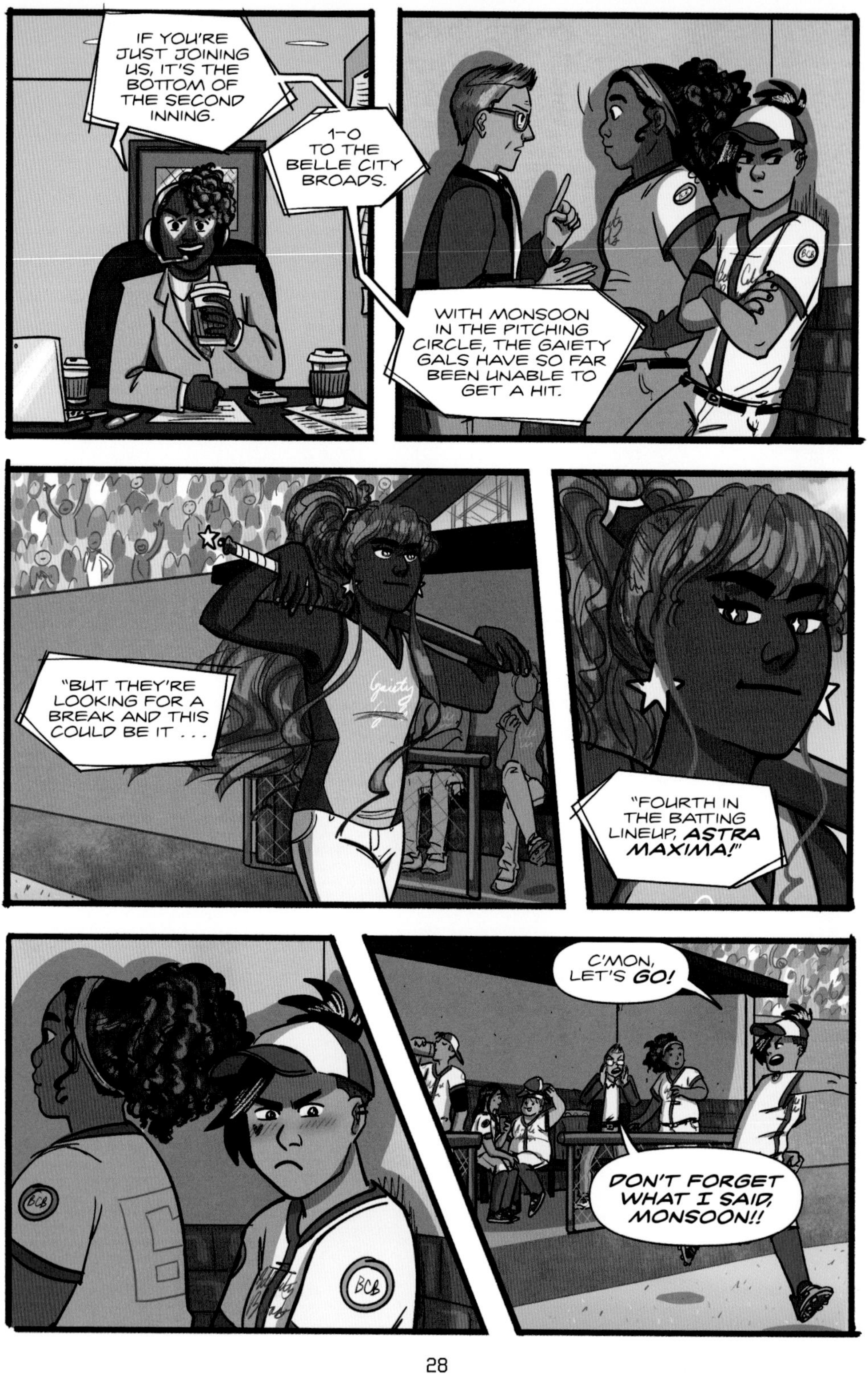
IF YOU'RE JUST JOINING US, IT'S THE BOTTOM OF THE SECOND INNING.
1-0 TO THE BELLE CITY BROADS.
WITH MONSOON IN THE PITCHING CIRCLE, THE GAIETY GALS HAVE SO FAR BEEN UNABLE TO GET A HIT.
"BUT THEY'RE LOOKING FOR A BREAK AND THIS COULD BE IT . . .
"FOURTH IN THE BATTING LINEUP, **ASTRA MAXIMA!**"
C'MON, LET'S **GO!**
DON'T FORGET WHAT I SAID, MONSOON!!

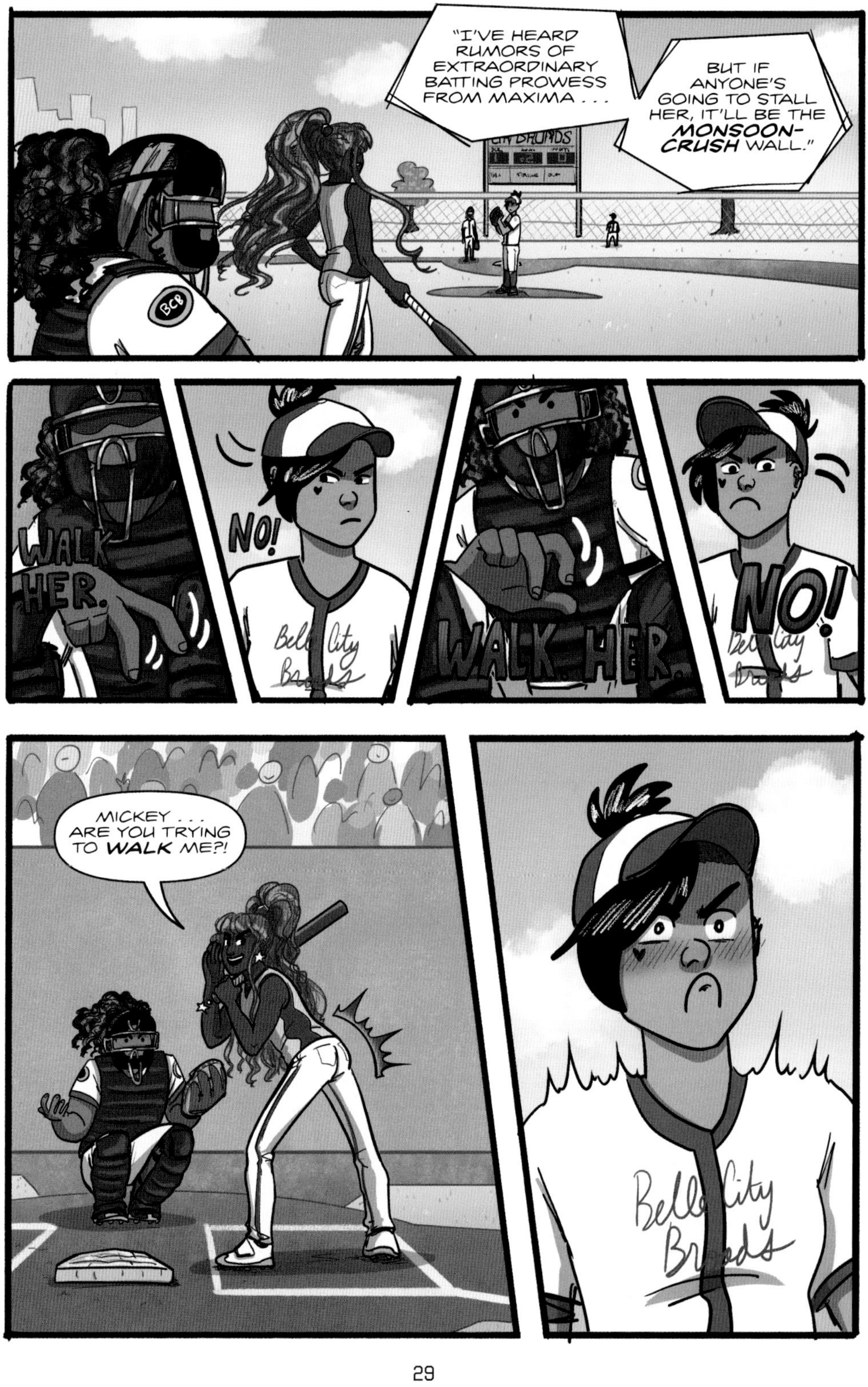
"I'VE HEARD RUMORS OF EXTRAORDINARY BATTING PROWESS FROM MAXIMA . . .
BUT IF ANYONE'S GOING TO STALL HER, IT'LL BE THE **MONSOON-CRUSH** WALL."
WALK HER.
NO!
WALK. HER.
NO!
MICKEY . . . ARE YOU TRYING TO **WALK** ME?!

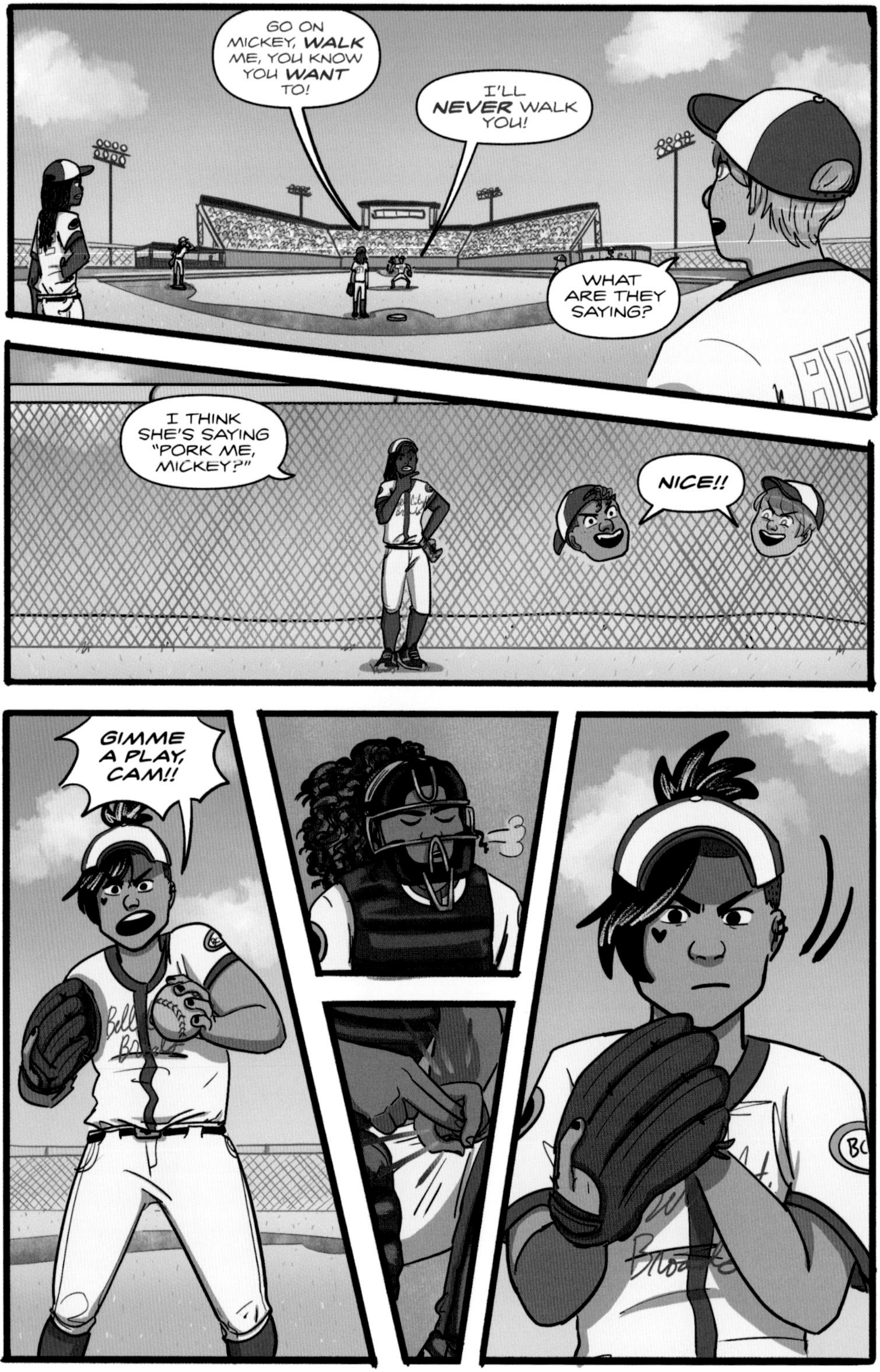
GO ON MICKEY, **WALK** ME, YOU KNOW YOU **WANT** TO!
I'LL **NEVER** WALK YOU!
WHAT ARE THEY SAYING?
I THINK SHE'S SAYING "PORK ME, MICKEY?"
NICE!!
GIMME A PLAY, CAM!!

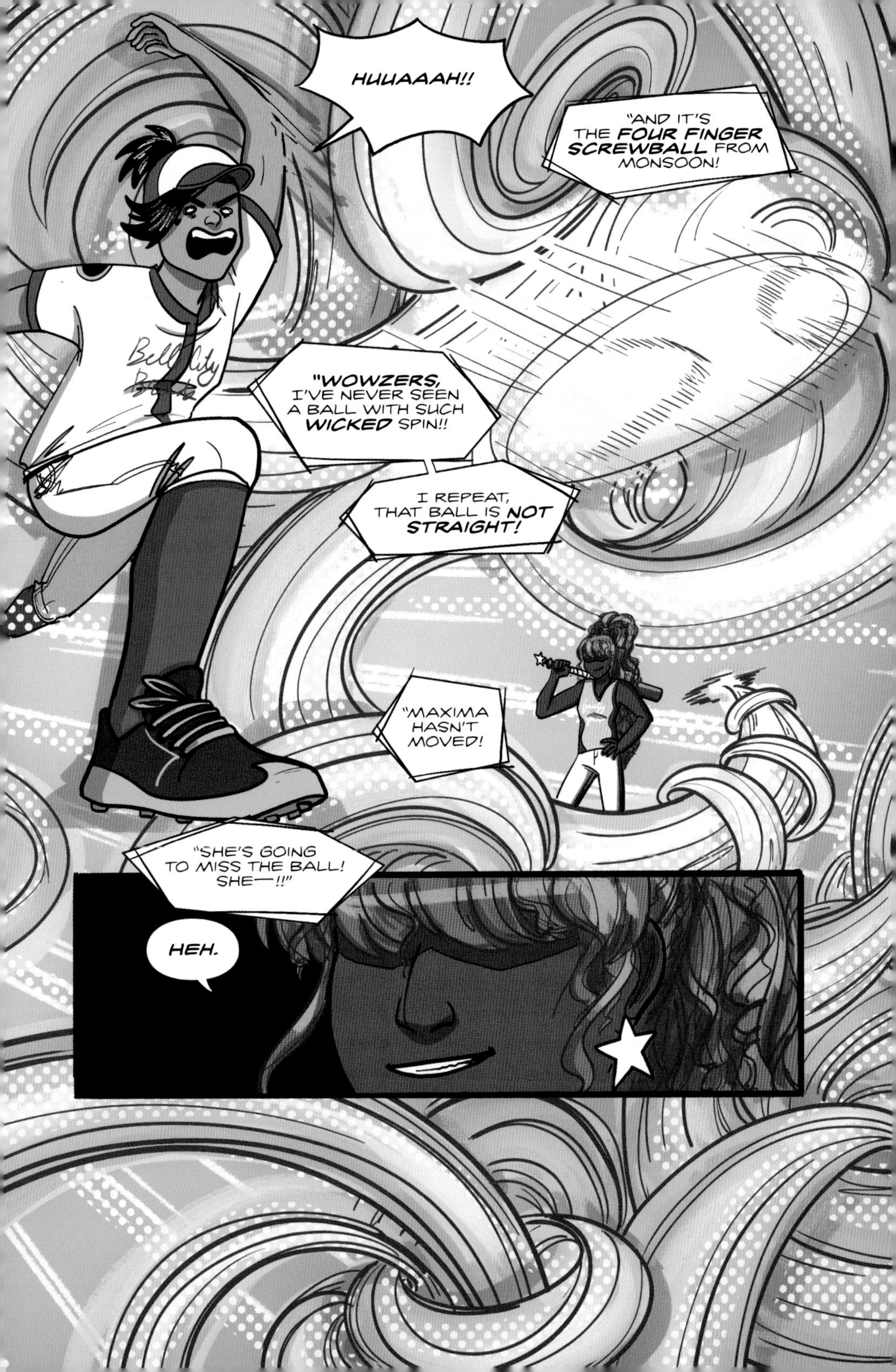
HUUAAAH!!
"AND IT'S THE FOUR FINGER SCREWBALL FROM MONSOON!
"WOWZERS, I'VE NEVER SEEN A BALL WITH SUCH WICKED SPIN!!
I REPEAT, THAT BALL IS NOT STRAIGHT!
"MAXIMA HASN'T MOVED!
"SHE'S GOING TO MISS THE BALL! SHE—!!"
HEH.

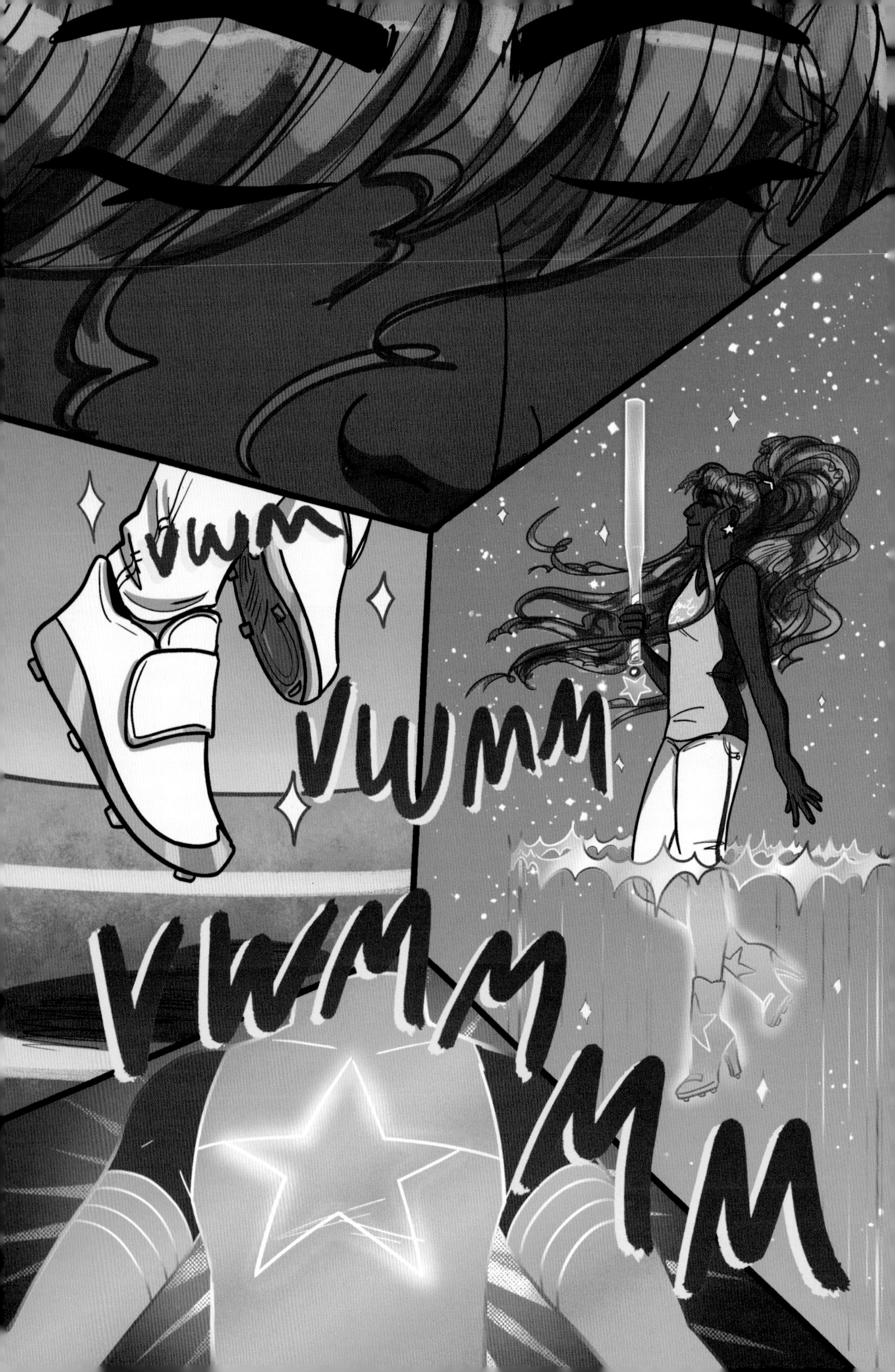
VWM
VWMM
VWMMMM

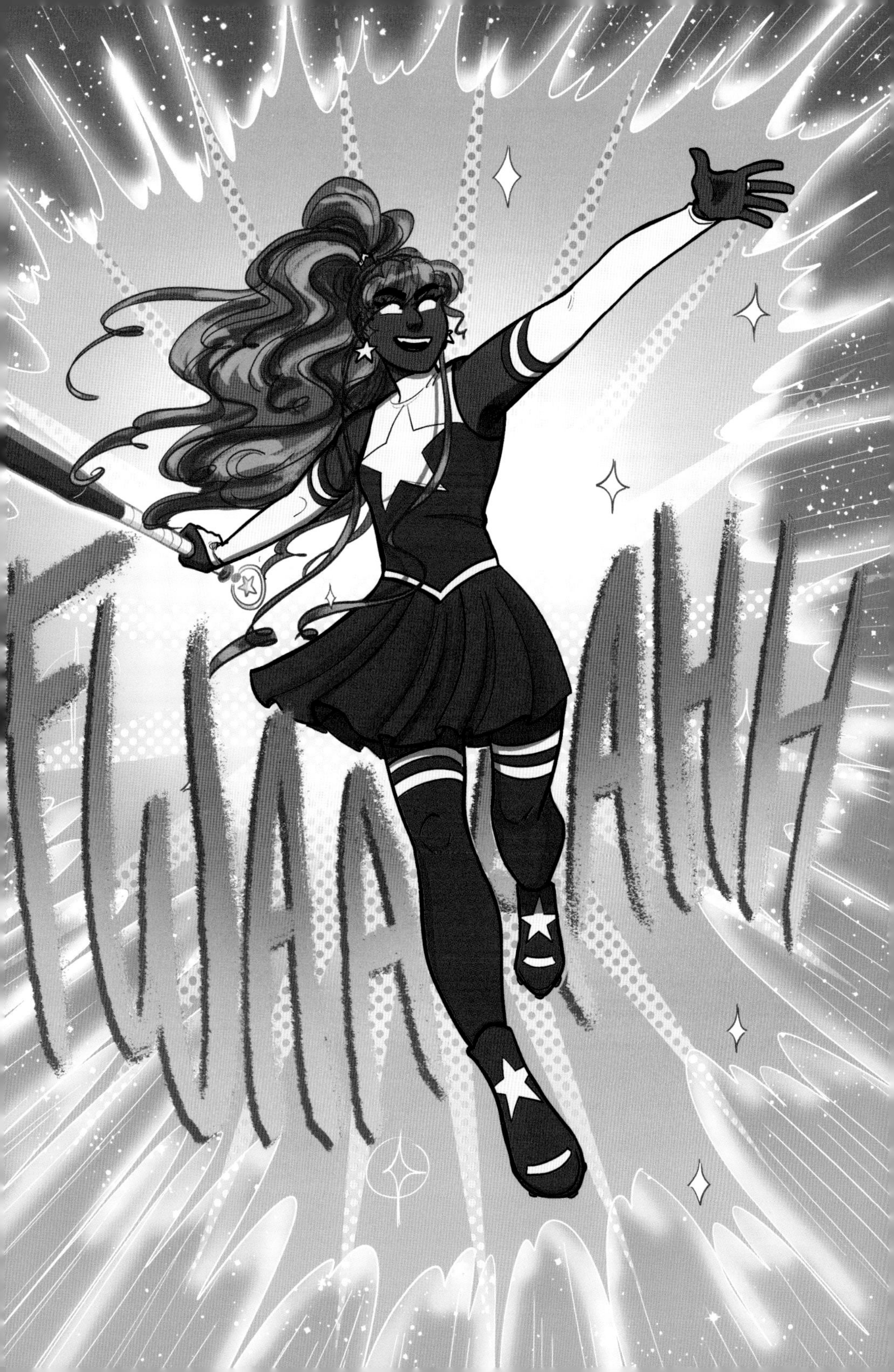
FWAAAHH

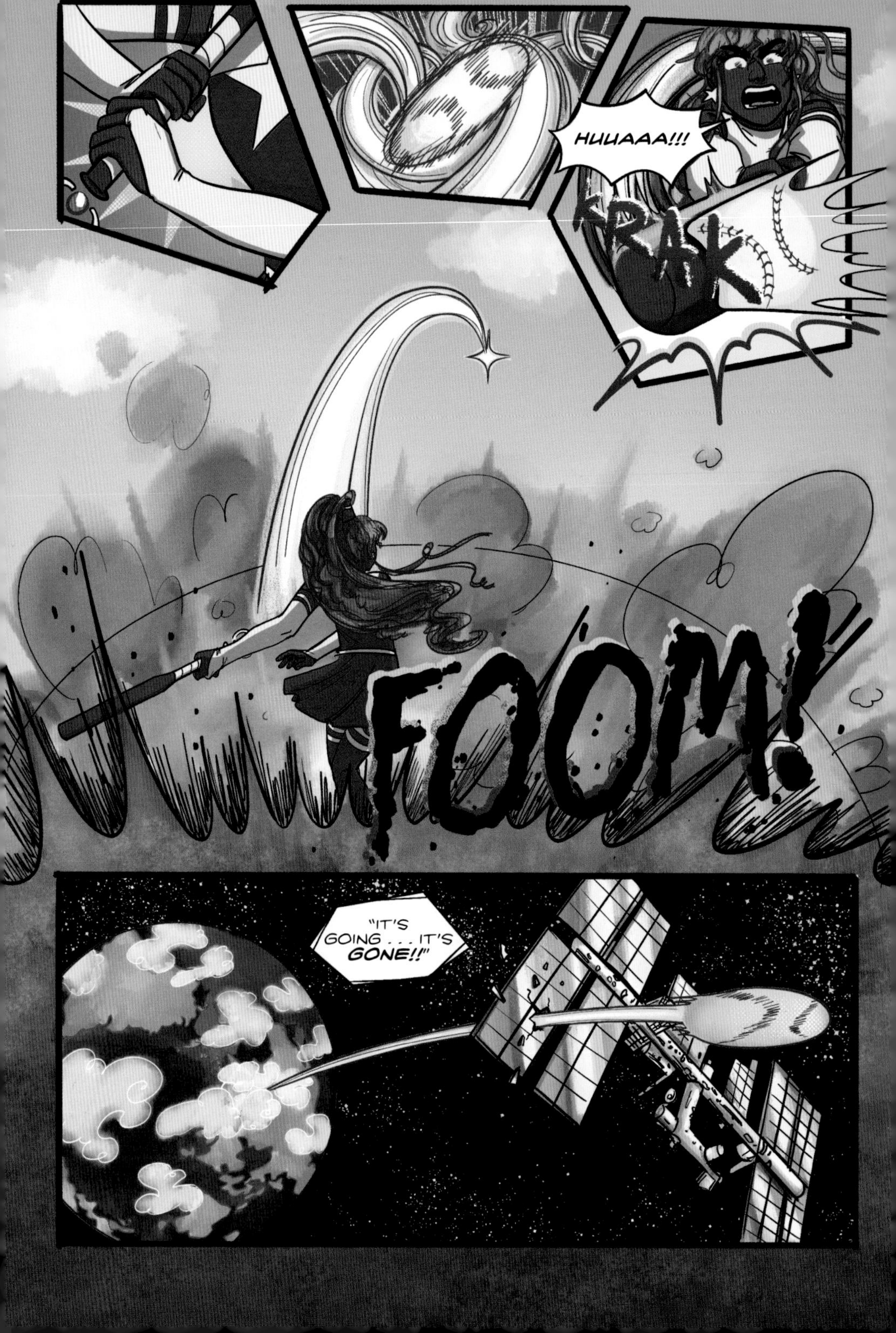
HUUAAA!!!
KRAK
FOOM!
"IT'S GOING . . . IT'S GONE!!"

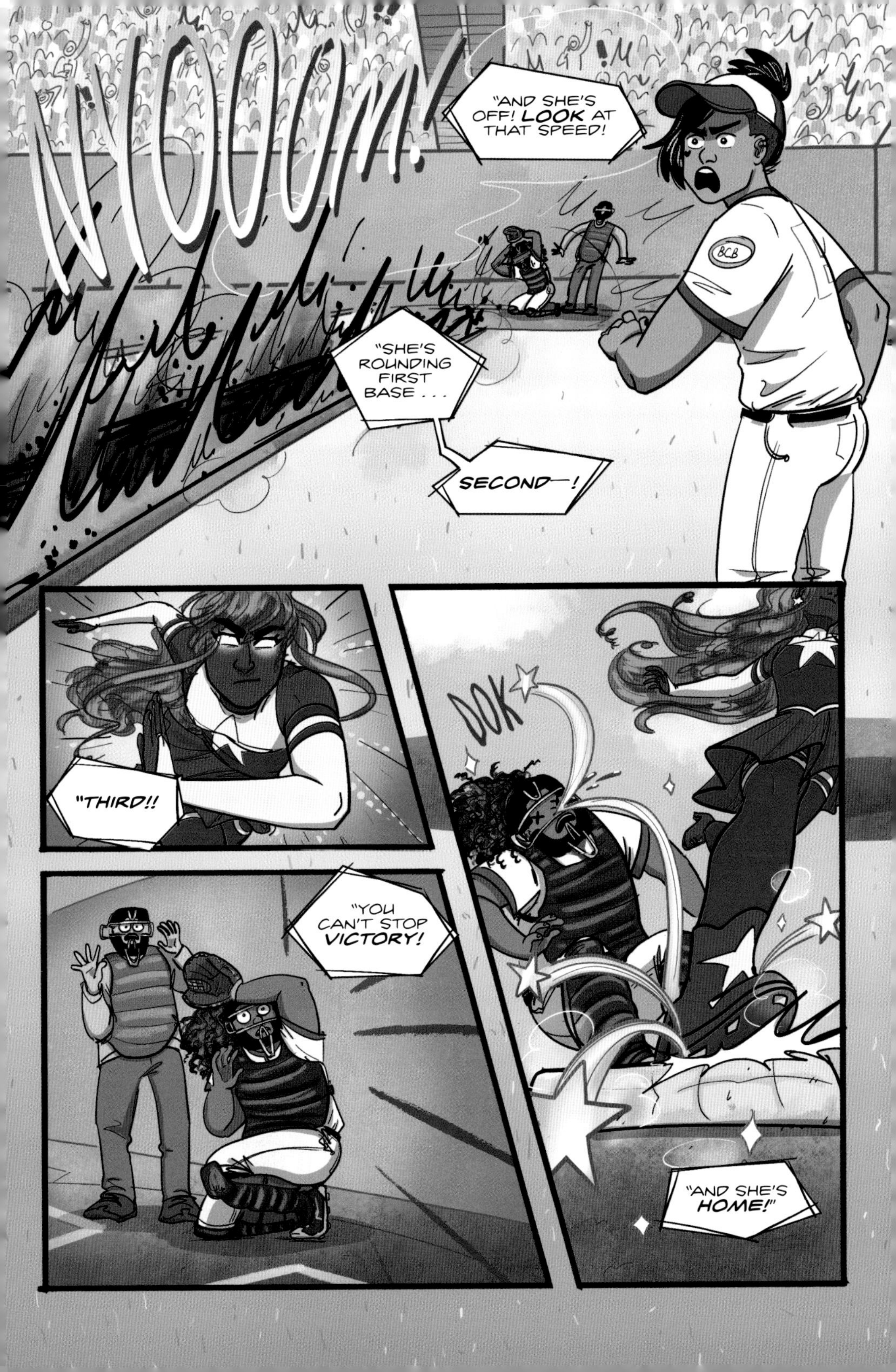
NYOOOM!
"AND SHE'S OFF! LOOK AT THAT SPEED!
"SHE'S ROUNDING FIRST BASE . . .
SECOND—!
"THIRD!!
DOK
"YOU CAN'T STOP VICTORY!
"AND SHE'S HOME!"

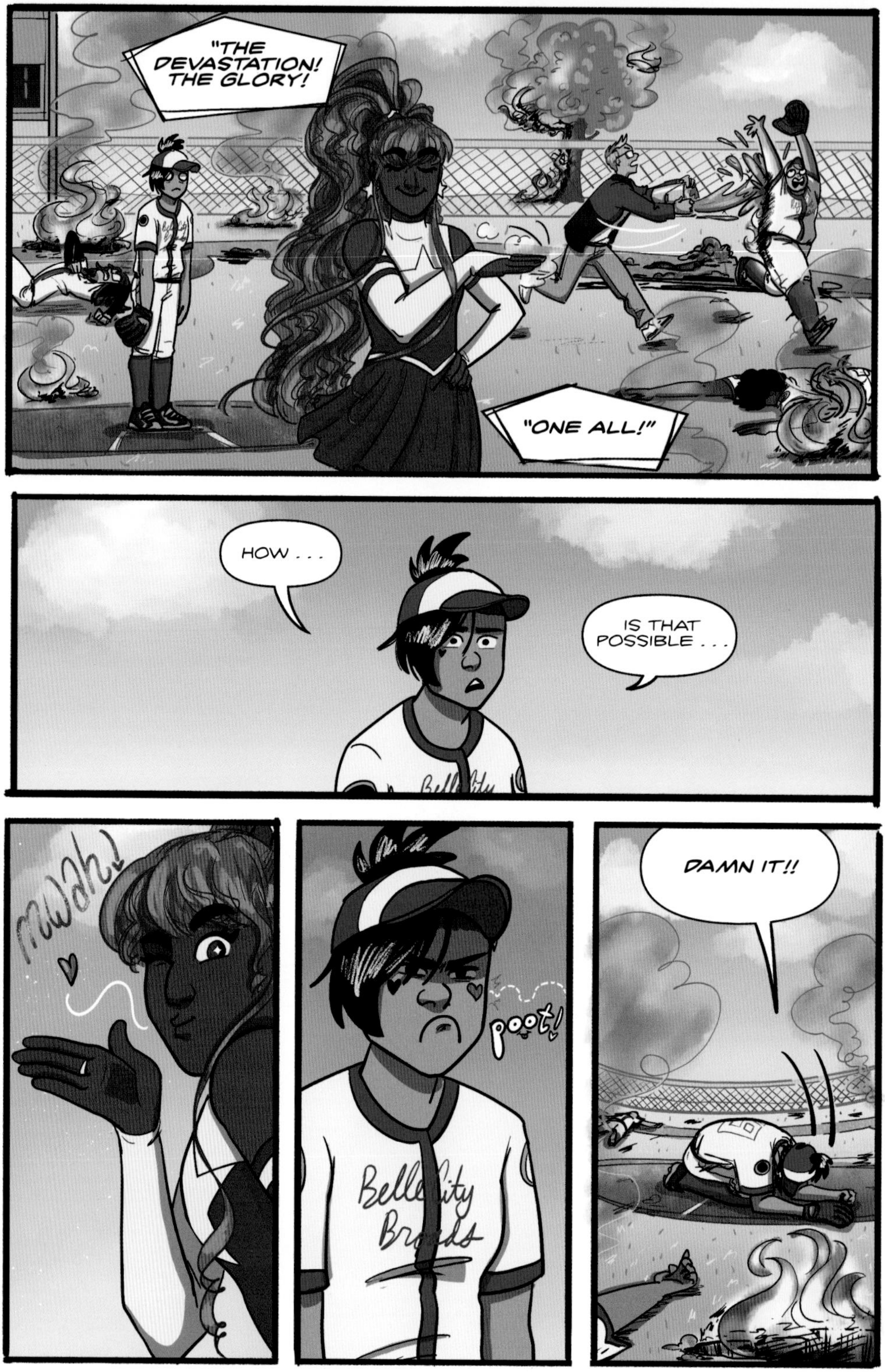
"THE DEVASTATION! THE GLORY!
"ONE ALL!"
HOW . . .
IS THAT POSSIBLE . . .
mwah!
poot!
DAMN IT!!

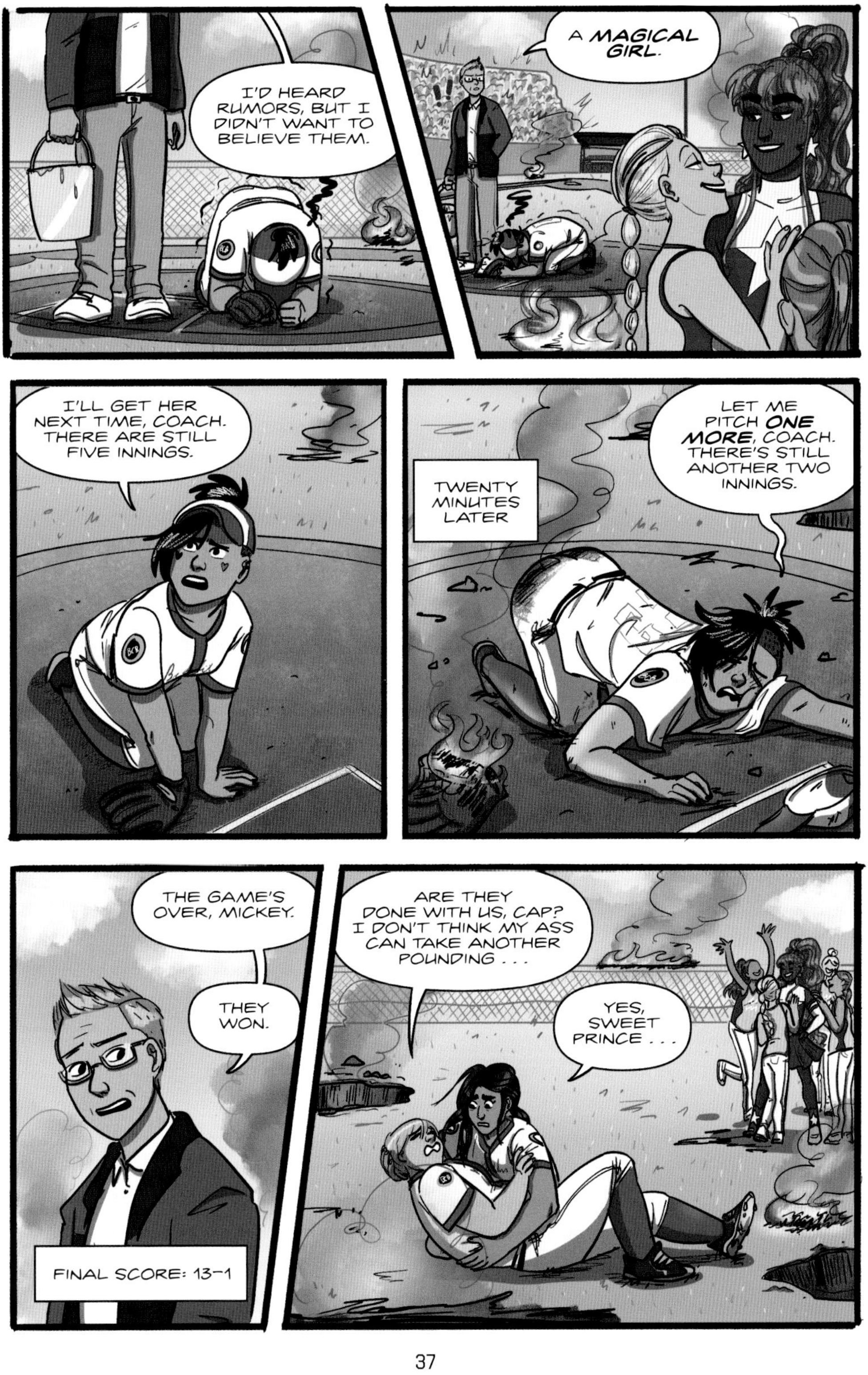

I'D HEARD RUMORS, BUT I DIDN'T WANT TO BELIEVE THEM.
A **MAGICAL GIRL**.
I'LL GET HER NEXT TIME, COACH. THERE ARE STILL FIVE INNINGS.
TWENTY MINUTES LATER
LET ME PITCH **ONE MORE**, COACH. THERE'S STILL ANOTHER TWO INNINGS.
THE GAME'S OVER, MICKEY.
THEY WON.
FINAL SCORE: 13–1
ARE THEY DONE WITH US, CAP? I DON'T THINK MY ASS CAN TAKE ANOTHER POUNDING . . .
YES, SWEET PRINCE . . .

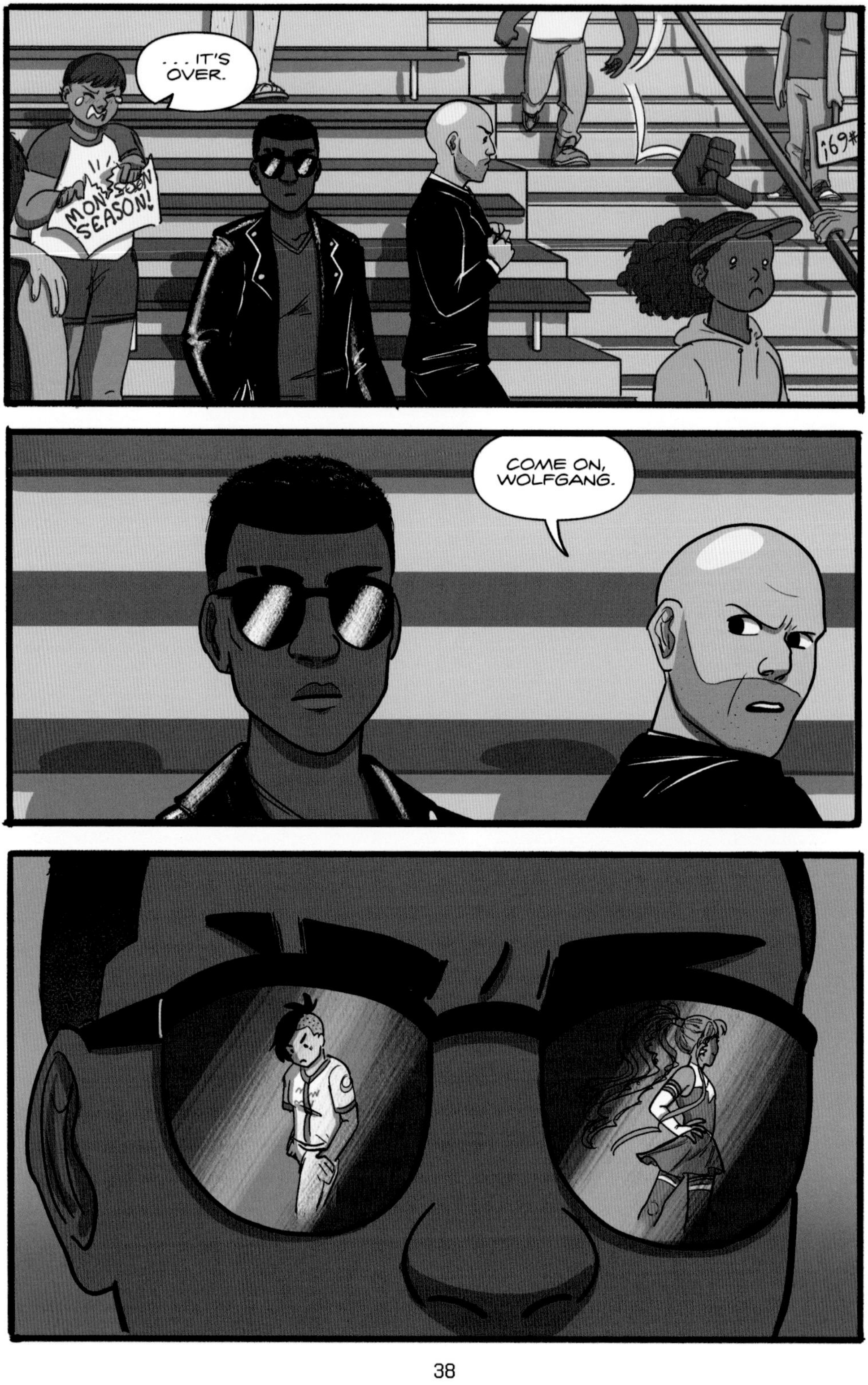
. . . IT'S OVER.
MONSOON SEASON!
COME ON, WOLFGANG.

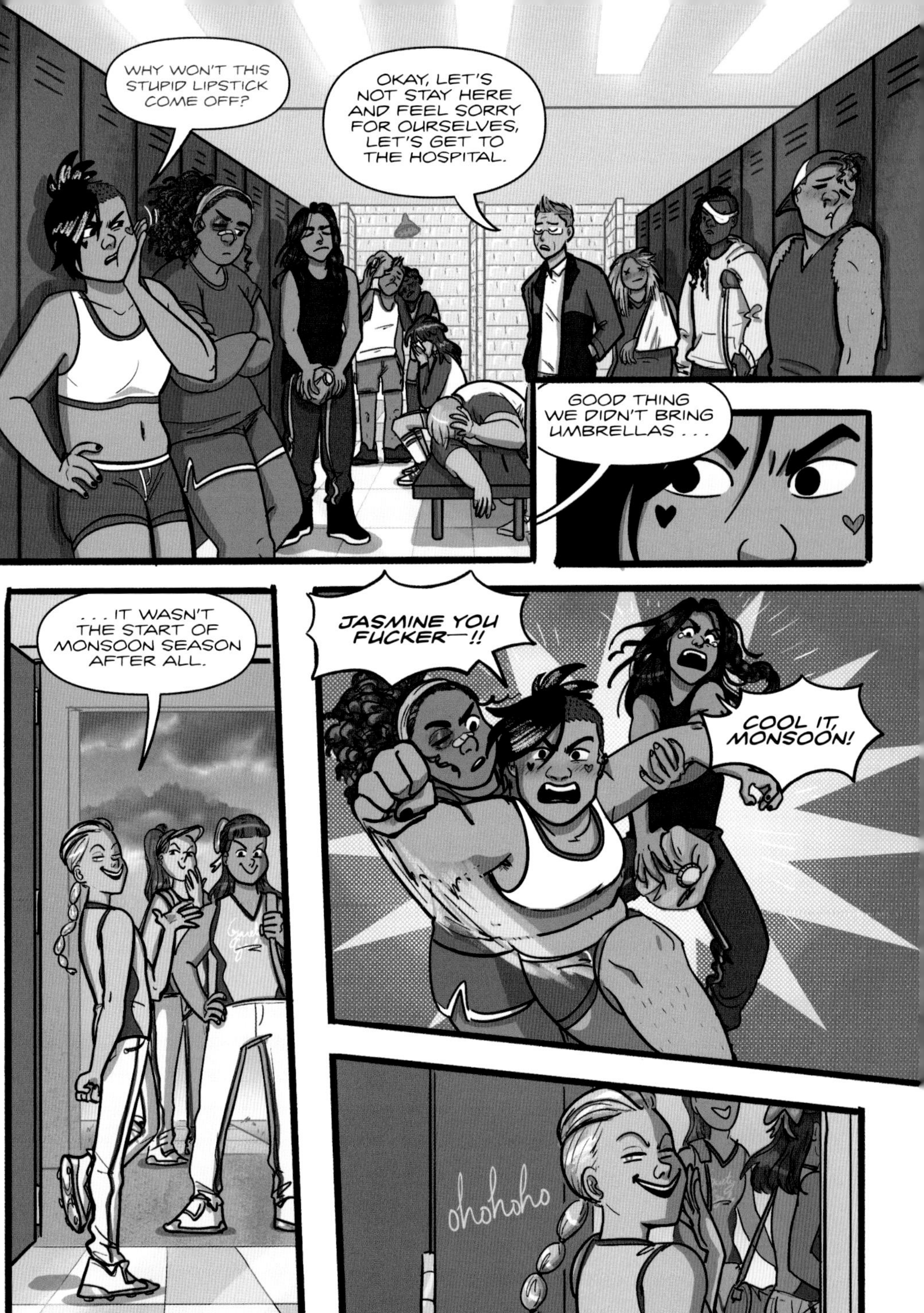
WHY WON'T THIS STUPID LIPSTICK COME OFF?
OKAY, LET'S NOT STAY HERE AND FEEL SORRY FOR OURSELVES, LET'S GET TO THE HOSPITAL.
GOOD THING WE DIDN'T BRING UMBRELLAS . . .
. . . IT WASN'T THE START OF MONSOON SEASON AFTER ALL.
JASMINE YOU FUCKER—!!
COOL IT, MONSOON!
ohohoho

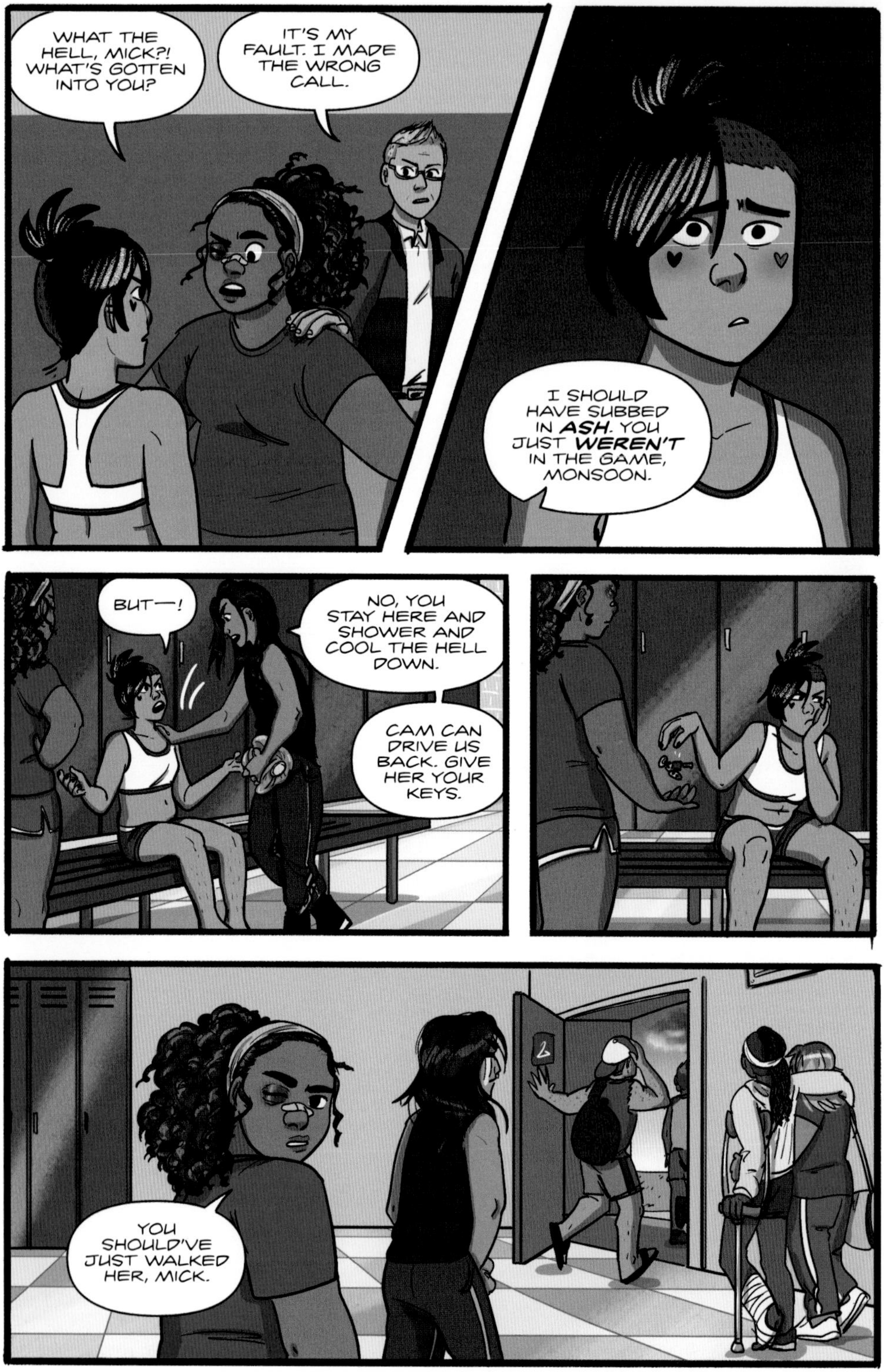
WHAT THE HELL, MICK?! WHAT'S GOTTEN INTO YOU?
IT'S MY FAULT. I MADE THE WRONG CALL.
I SHOULD HAVE SUBBED IN **ASH**. YOU JUST ***WEREN'T*** IN THE GAME, MONSOON.
BUT—!
NO, YOU STAY HERE AND SHOWER AND COOL THE HELL DOWN.
CAM CAN DRIVE US BACK. GIVE HER YOUR KEYS.
YOU SHOULD'VE JUST WALKED HER, MICK.

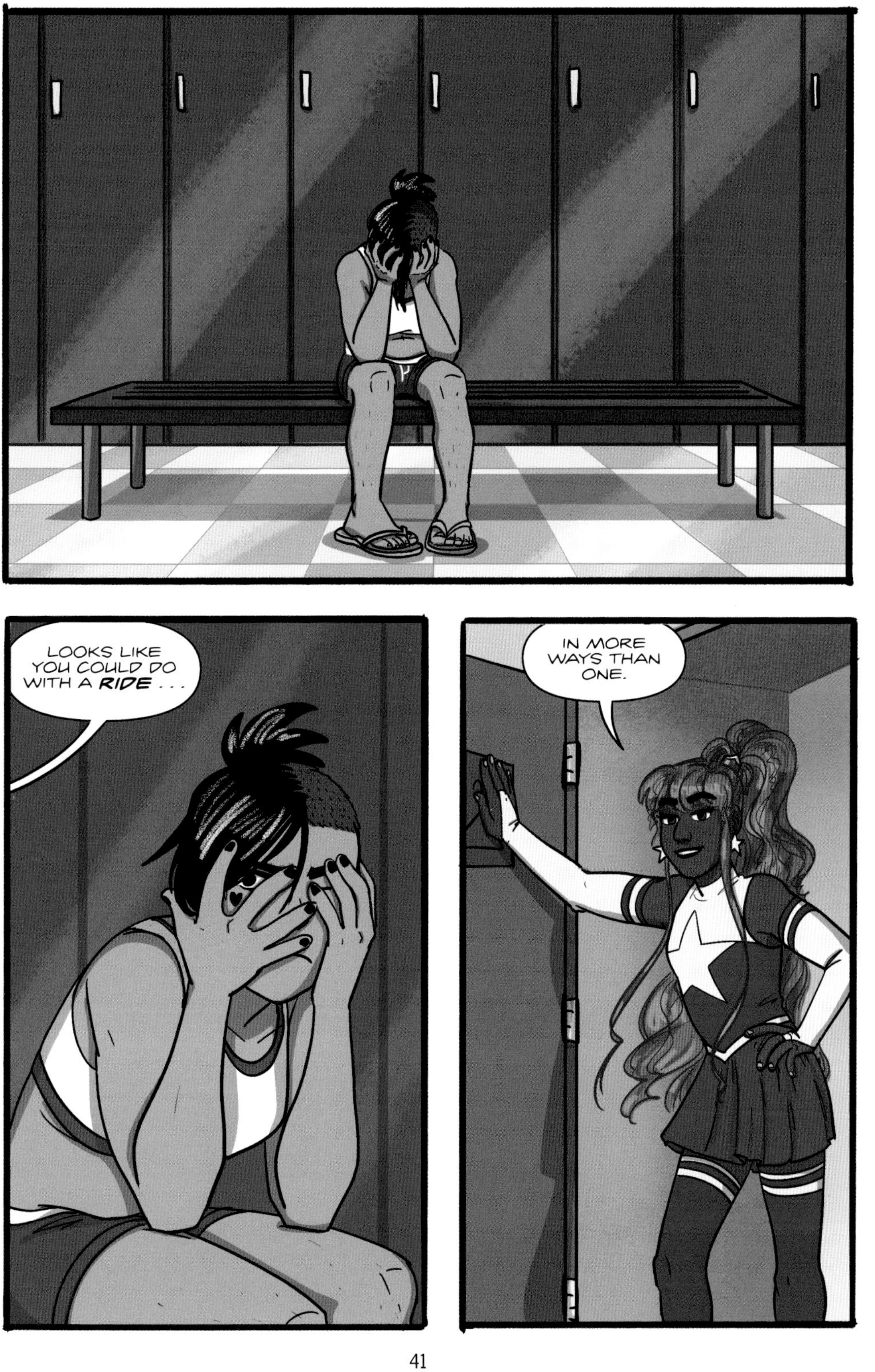
LOOKS LIKE YOU COULD DO WITH A *RIDE* . . .
IN MORE WAYS THAN ONE.

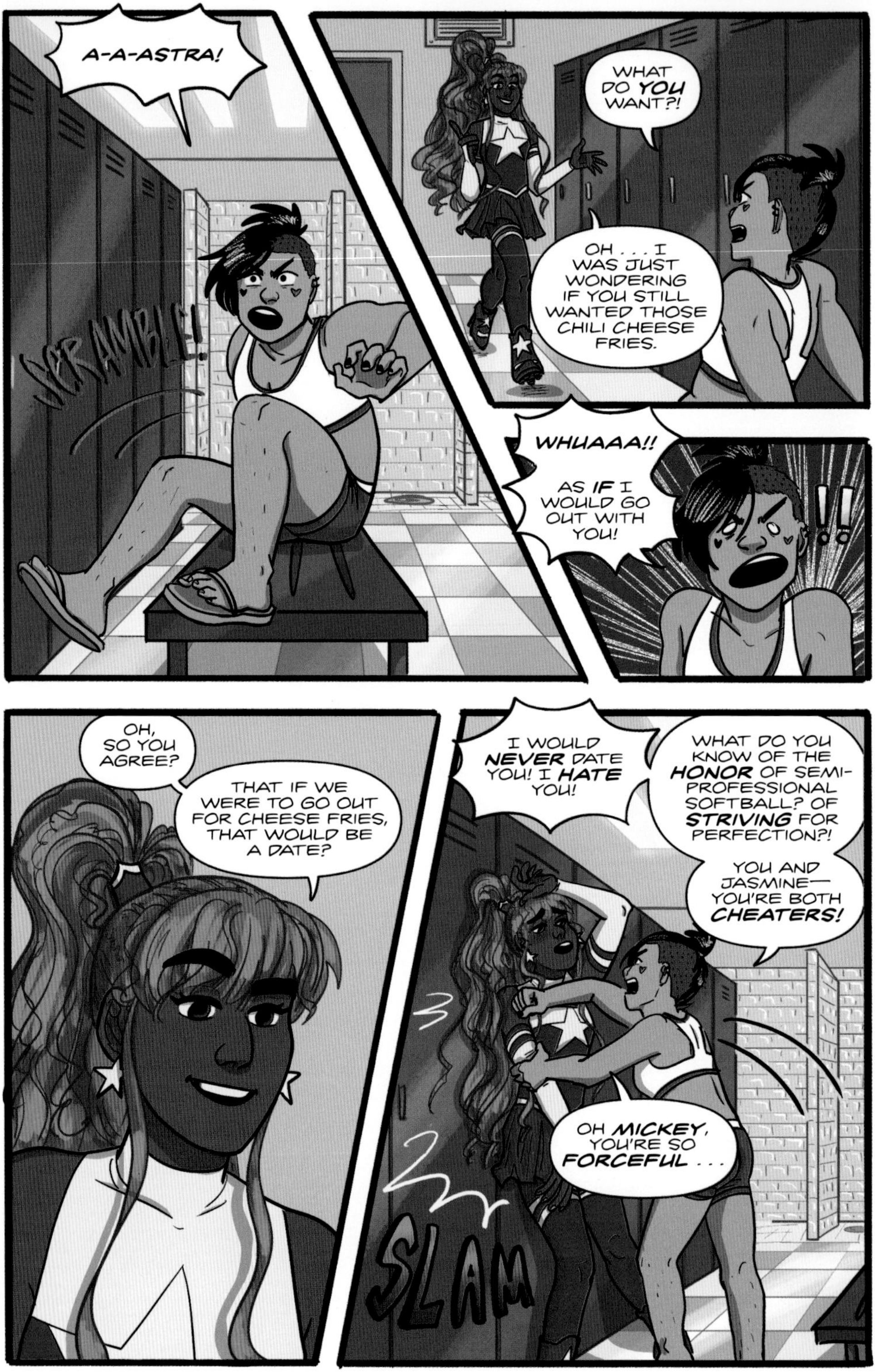
A-A-ASTRA!
SCRAMBLE!
WHAT DO YOU WANT?!
OH . . . I WAS JUST WONDERING IF YOU STILL WANTED THOSE CHILI CHEESE FRIES.
WHUAAA!!
AS IF I WOULD GO OUT WITH YOU!
!!
OH, SO YOU AGREE?
THAT IF WE WERE TO GO OUT FOR CHEESE FRIES, THAT WOULD BE A DATE?
I WOULD NEVER DATE YOU! I HATE YOU!
WHAT DO YOU KNOW OF THE HONOR OF SEMI-PROFESSIONAL SOFTBALL? OF STRIVING FOR PERFECTION?!
YOU AND JASMINE— YOU'RE BOTH CHEATERS!
OH MICKEY, YOU'RE SO FORCEFUL . . .
SLAM

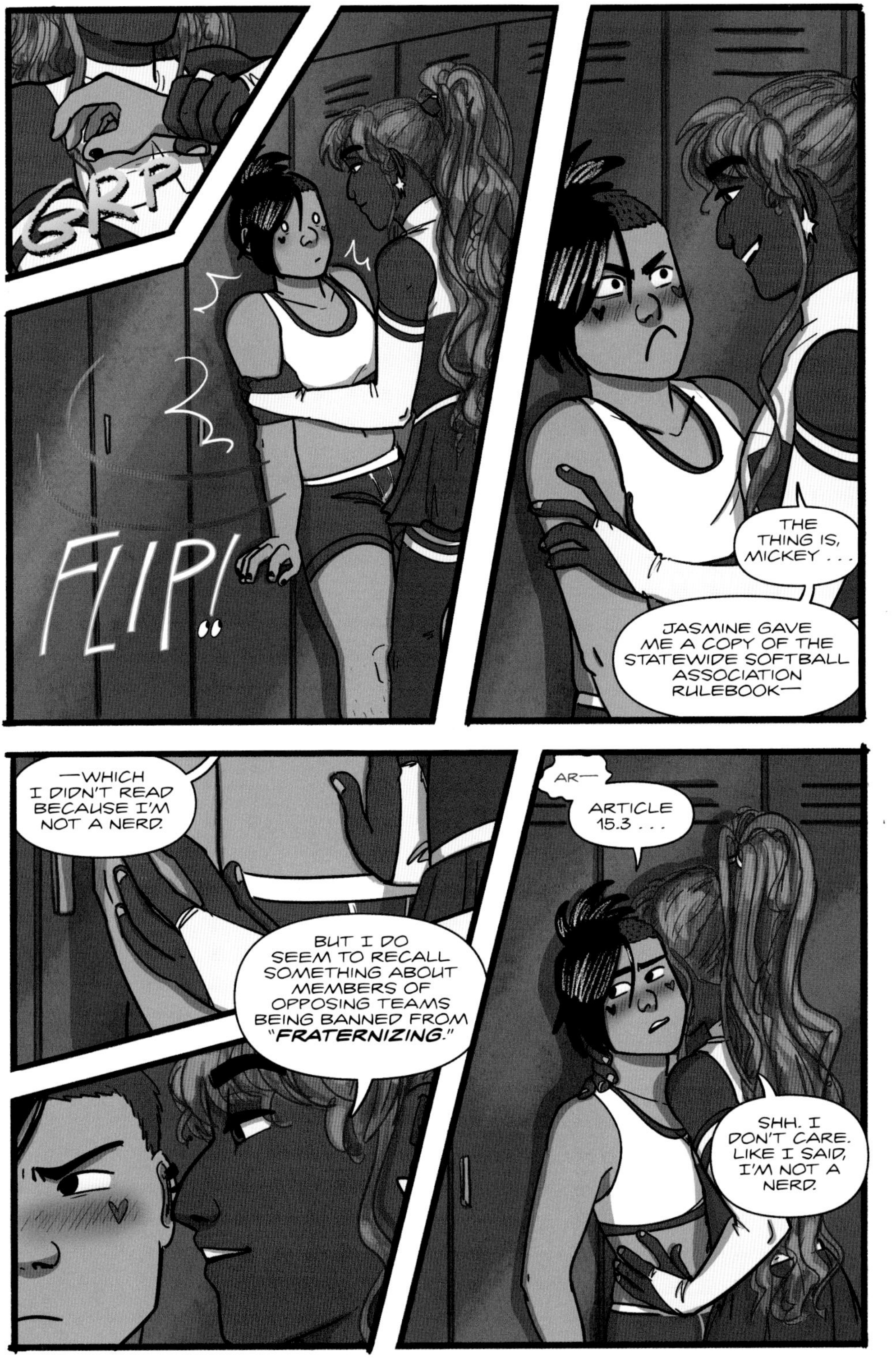
GRP
FLIP!
THE THING IS, MICKEY . . .
JASMINE GAVE ME A COPY OF THE STATEWIDE SOFTBALL ASSOCIATION RULEBOOK—
—WHICH I DIDN'T READ BECAUSE I'M NOT A NERD.
BUT I DO SEEM TO RECALL SOMETHING ABOUT MEMBERS OF OPPOSING TEAMS BEING BANNED FROM "FRATERNIZING."
AR—
ARTICLE 15.3 . . .
SHH. I DON'T CARE. LIKE I SAID, I'M NOT A NERD.

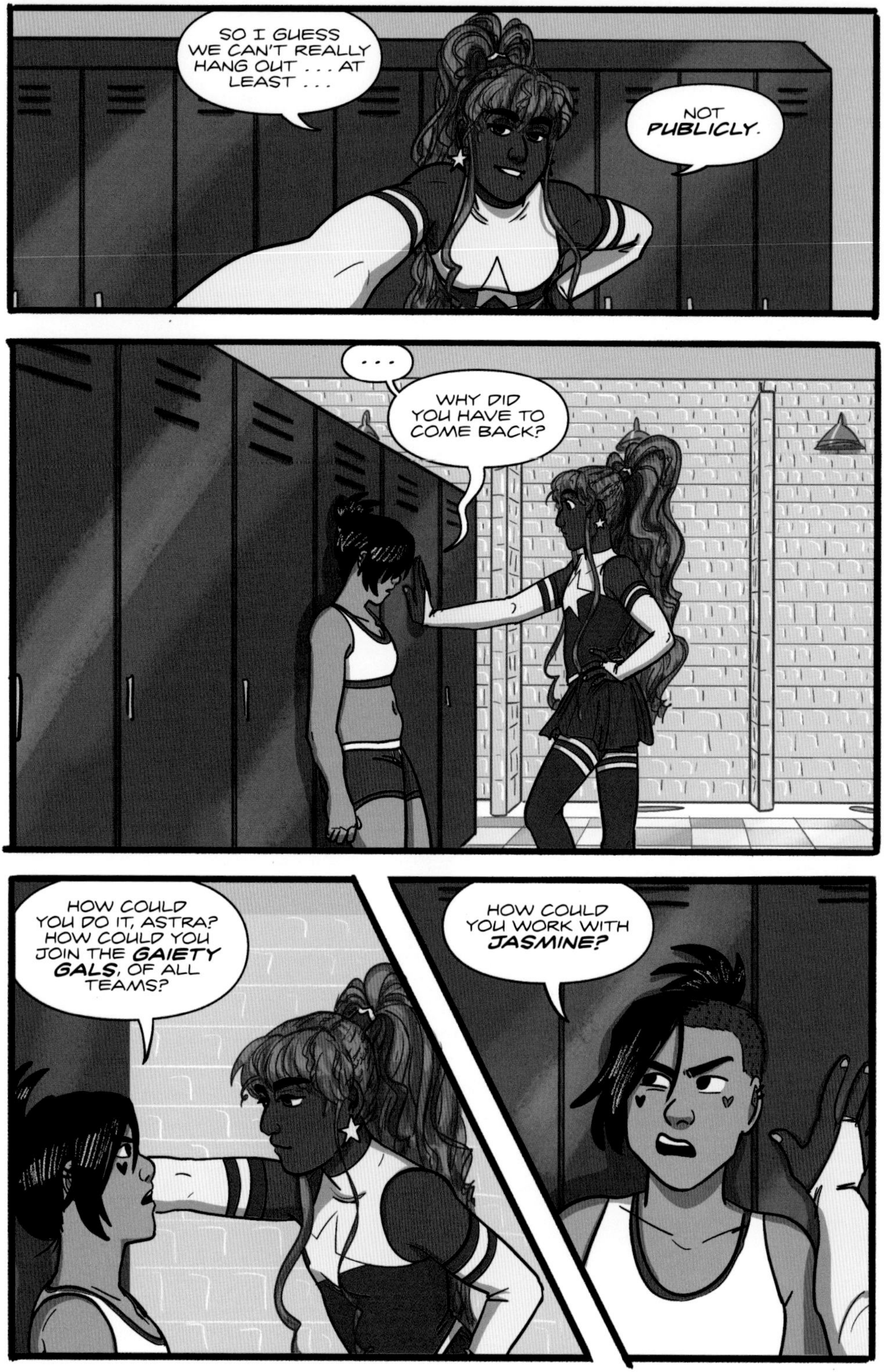
SO I GUESS WE CAN'T REALLY HANG OUT . . . AT LEAST . . .
NOT PUBLICLY.
. . .
WHY DID YOU HAVE TO COME BACK?
HOW COULD YOU DO IT, ASTRA? HOW COULD YOU JOIN THE GAIETY GALS, OF ALL TEAMS?
HOW COULD YOU WORK WITH JASMINE?

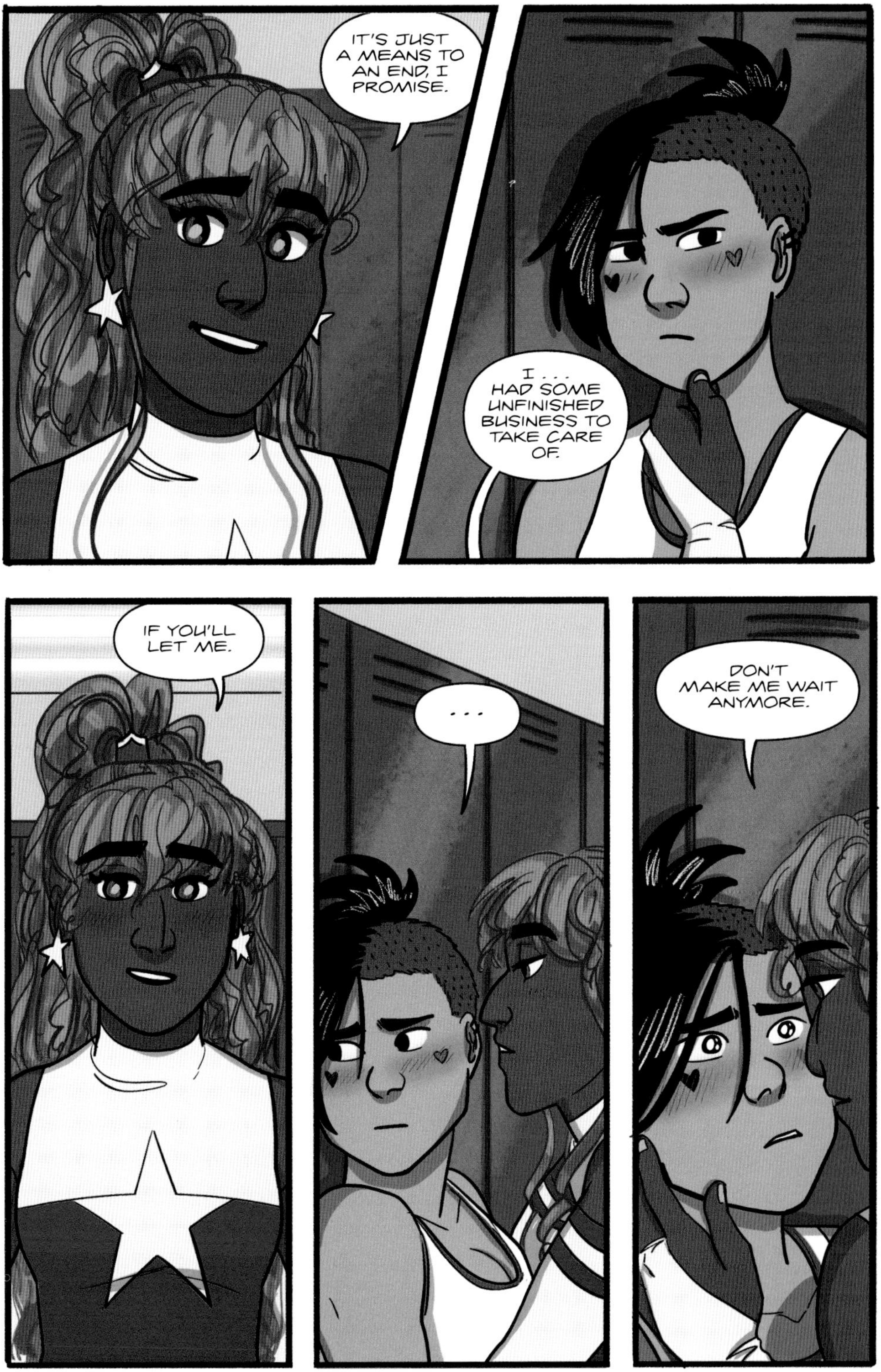
IT'S JUST A MEANS TO AN END, I PROMISE.
I . . . HAD SOME UNFINISHED BUSINESS TO TAKE CARE OF.
IF YOU'LL LET ME.
. . .
DON'T MAKE ME WAIT ANYMORE.

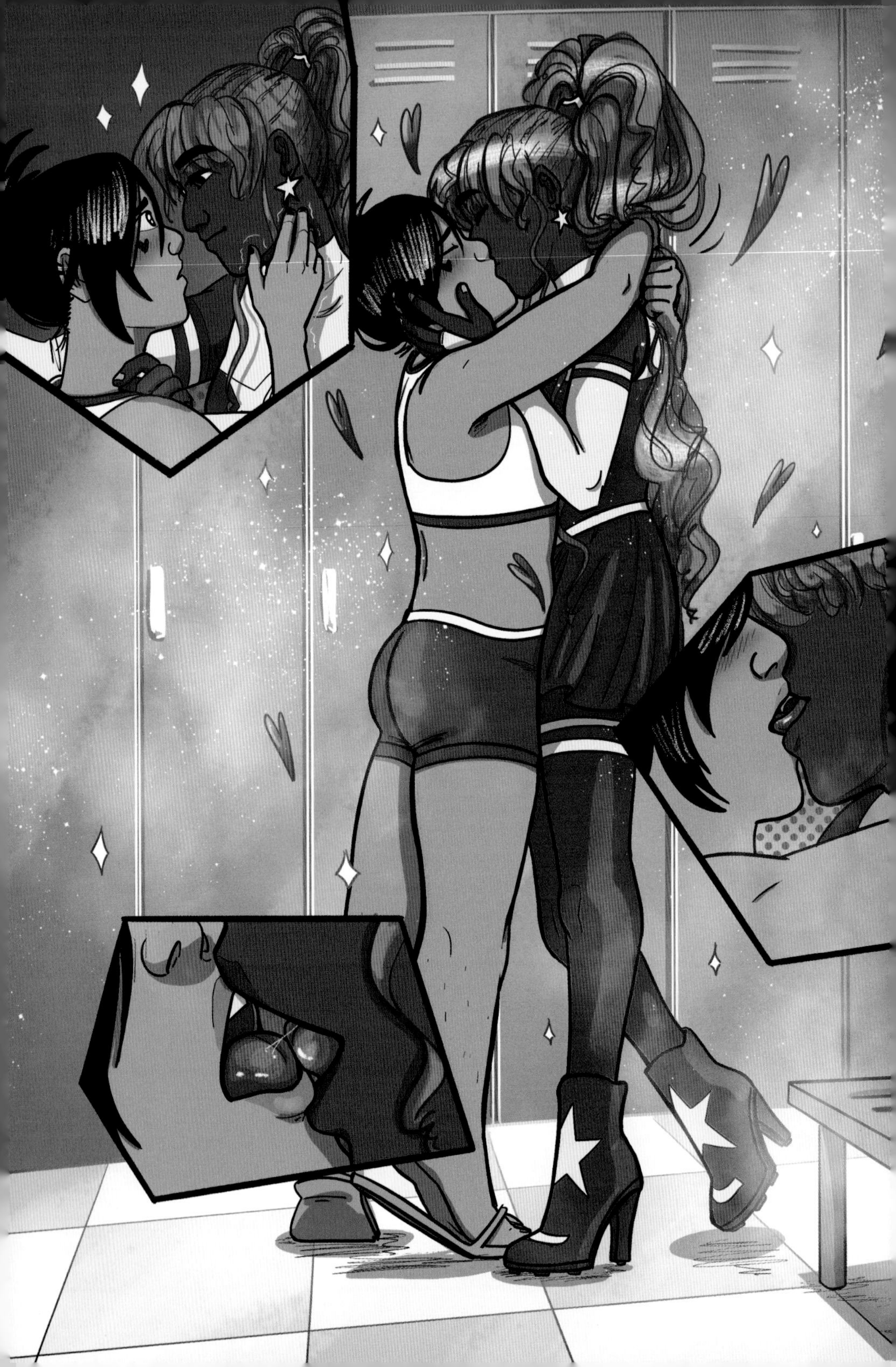

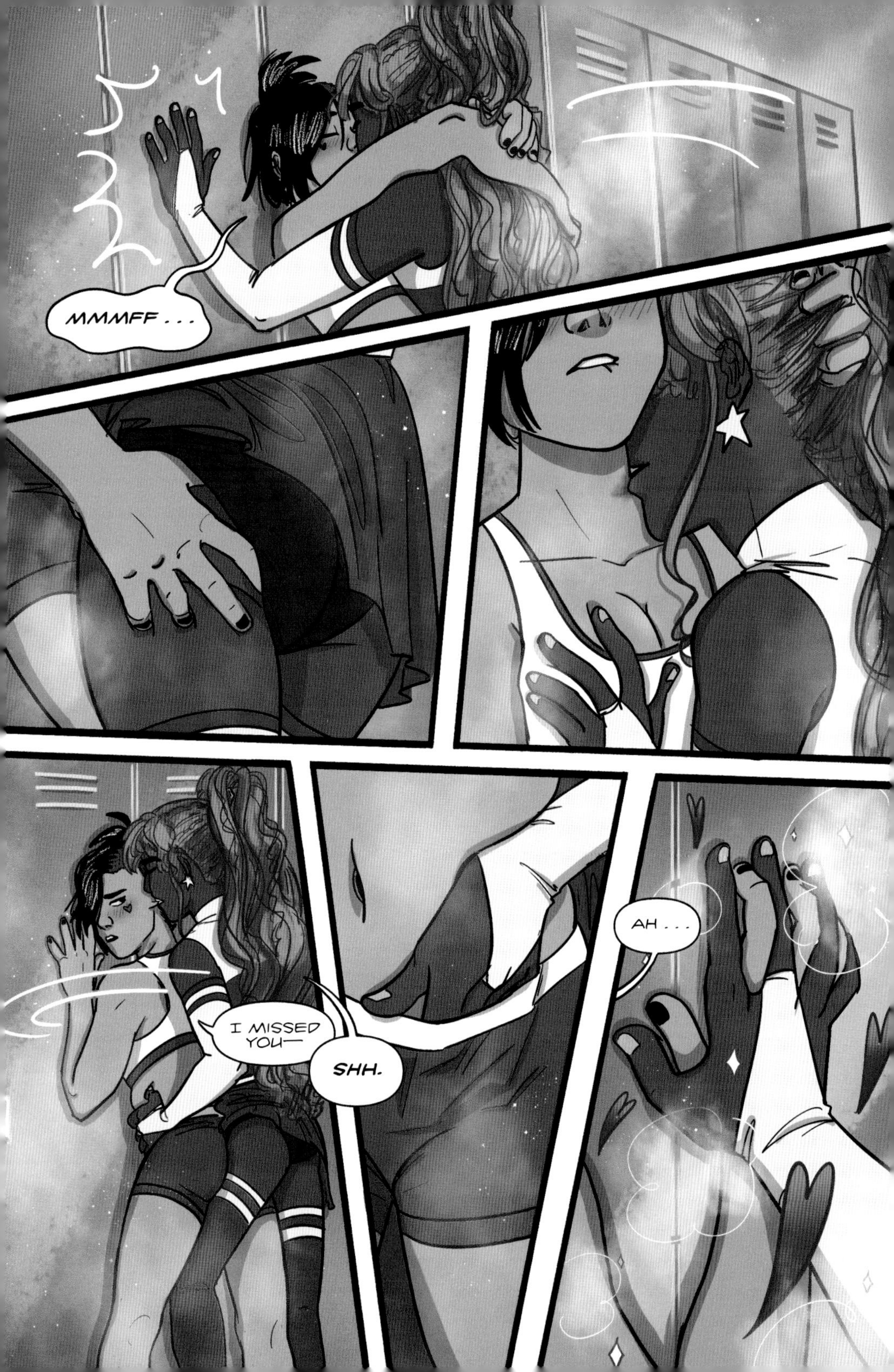
MMMFF . . .
I MISSED YOU—
SHH.
AH . . .

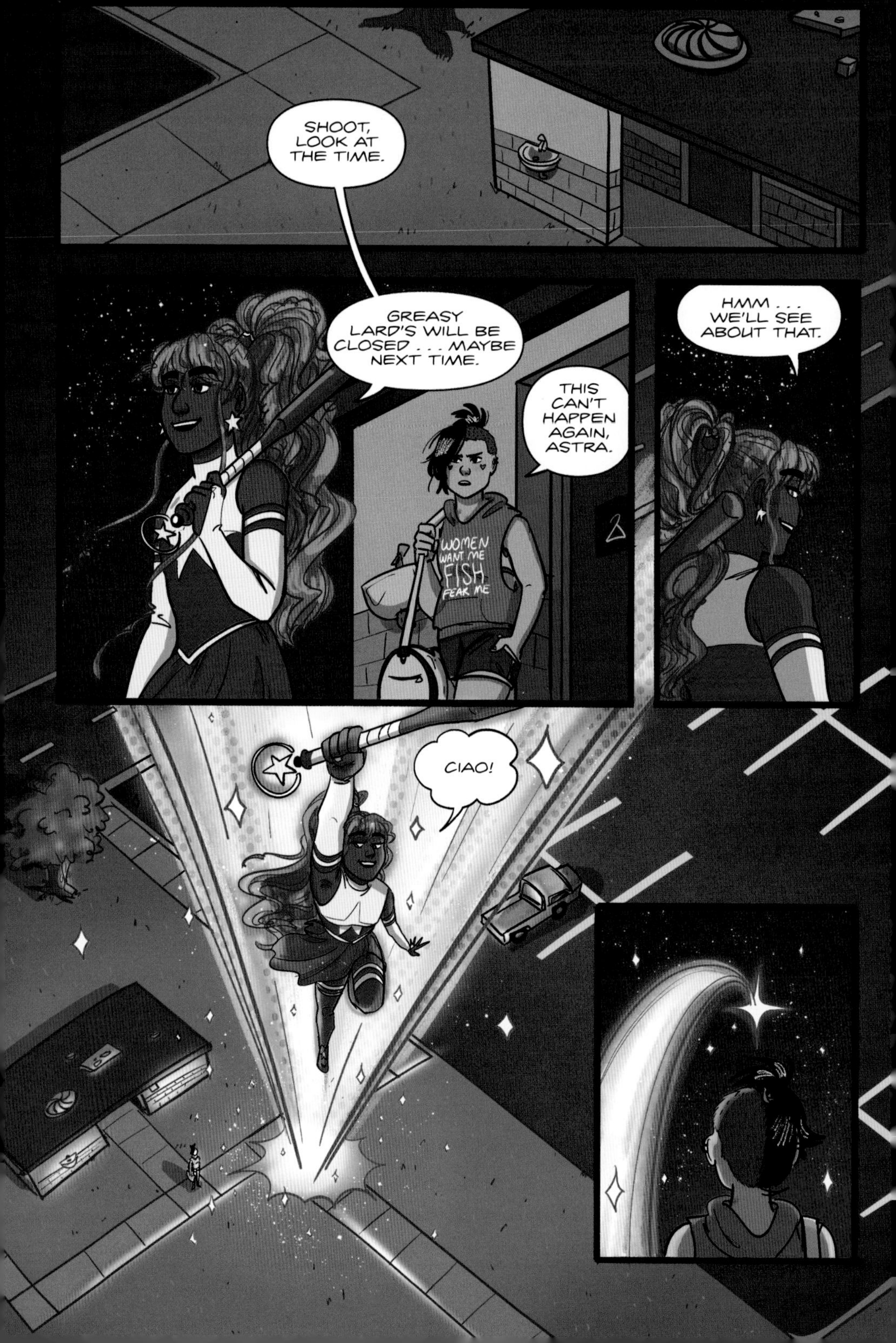
SHOOT, LOOK AT THE TIME.
GREASY LARD'S WILL BE CLOSED . . . MAYBE NEXT TIME.
THIS CAN'T HAPPEN AGAIN, ASTRA.
WOMEN WANT ME FISH FEAR ME
HMM . . . WE'LL SEE ABOUT THAT.
CIAO!

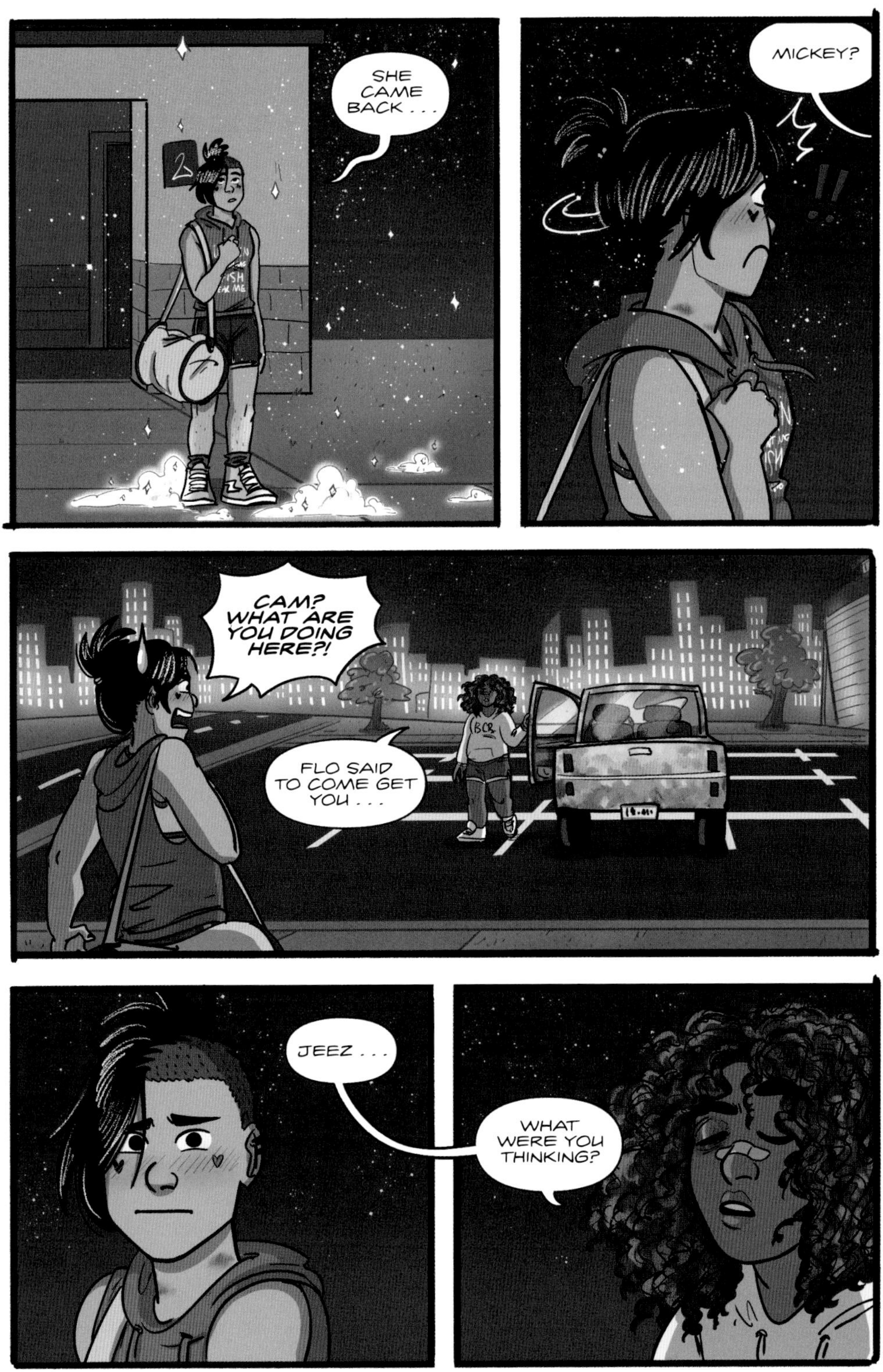
SHE CAME BACK . . .
MICKEY?
!!
CAM? WHAT ARE YOU DOING HERE?!
FLO SAID TO COME GET YOU . . .
JEEZ . . .
WHAT WERE YOU THINKING?

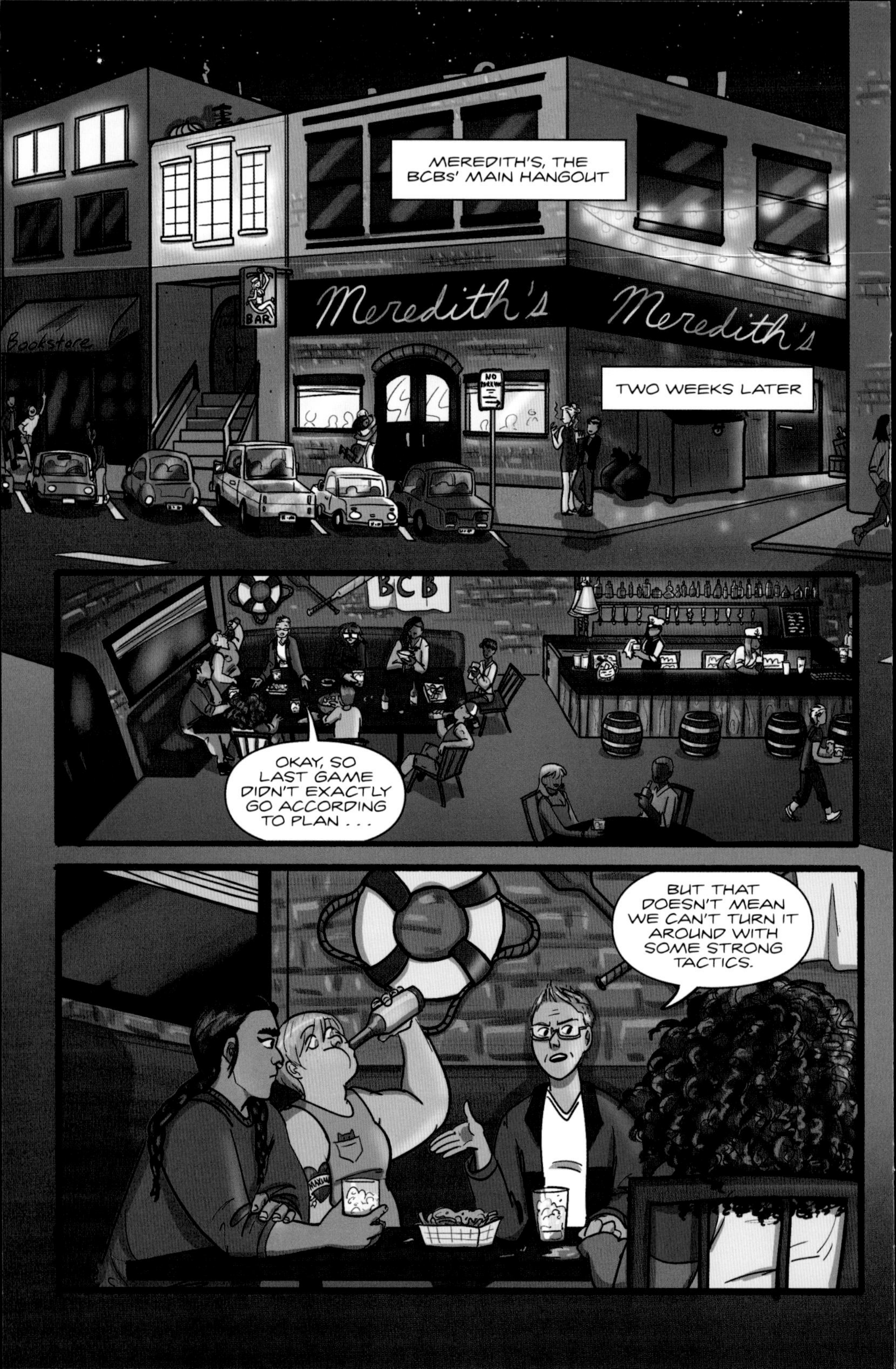
MEREDITH'S, THE BCBs' MAIN HANGOUT
Bookstore
BAR
Meredith's
Meredith's
TWO WEEKS LATER
BCB
OKAY, SO LAST GAME DIDN'T EXACTLY GO ACCORDING TO PLAN . . .
BUT THAT DOESN'T MEAN WE CAN'T TURN IT AROUND WITH SOME STRONG TACTICS.

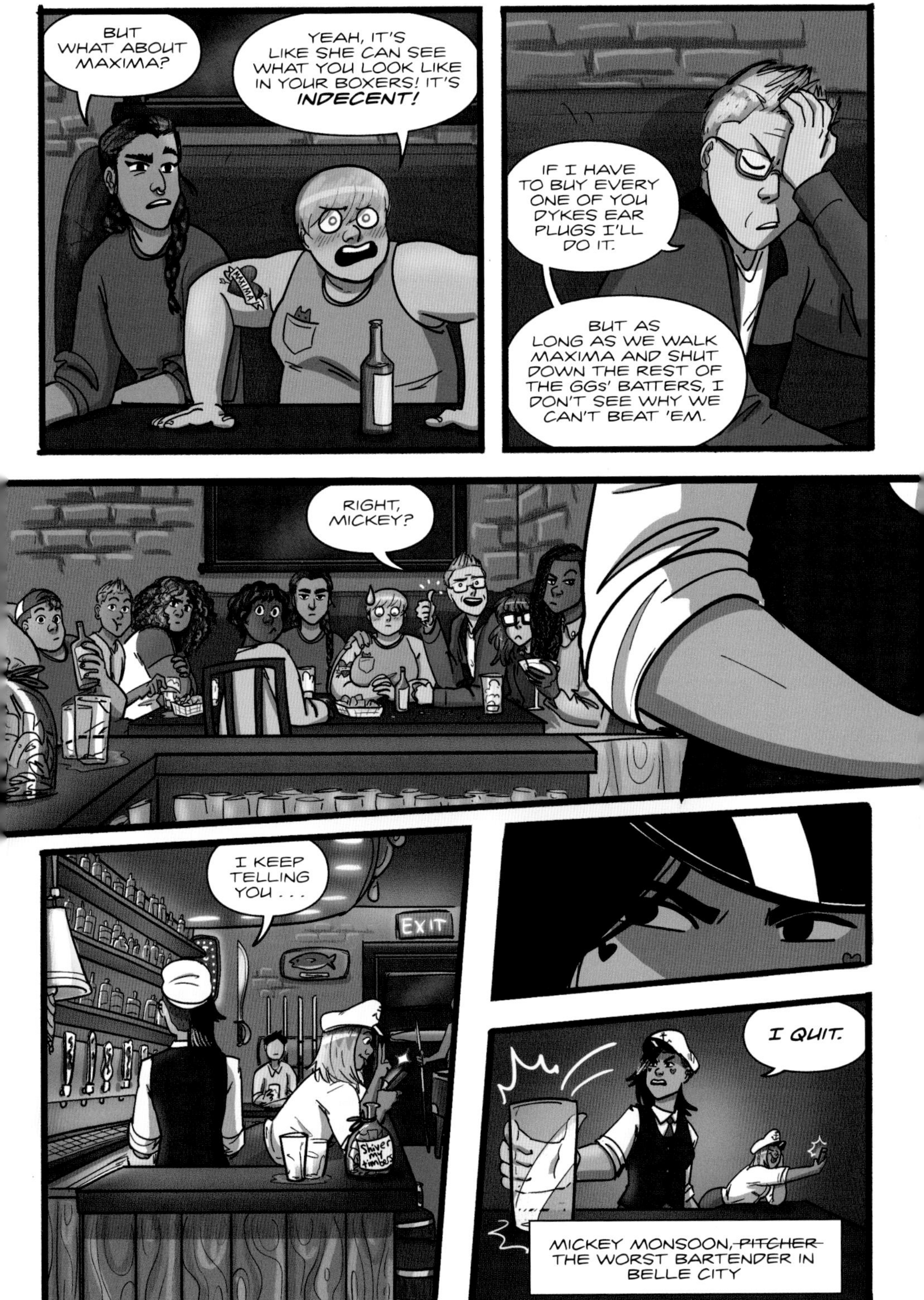
BUT WHAT ABOUT MAXIMA?
YEAH, IT'S LIKE SHE CAN SEE WHAT YOU LOOK LIKE IN YOUR BOXERS! IT'S *INDECENT!*
MAXIMA
IF I HAVE TO BUY EVERY ONE OF YOU DYKES EAR PLUGS I'LL DO IT.
BUT AS LONG AS WE WALK MAXIMA AND SHUT DOWN THE REST OF THE GGs' BATTERS, I DON'T SEE WHY WE CAN'T BEAT 'EM.
RIGHT, MICKEY?
I KEEP TELLING YOU . . .
EXIT
Shiver my timbers
I QUIT.
MICKEY MONSOON, ~~PITCHER~~ THE WORST BARTENDER IN BELLE CITY

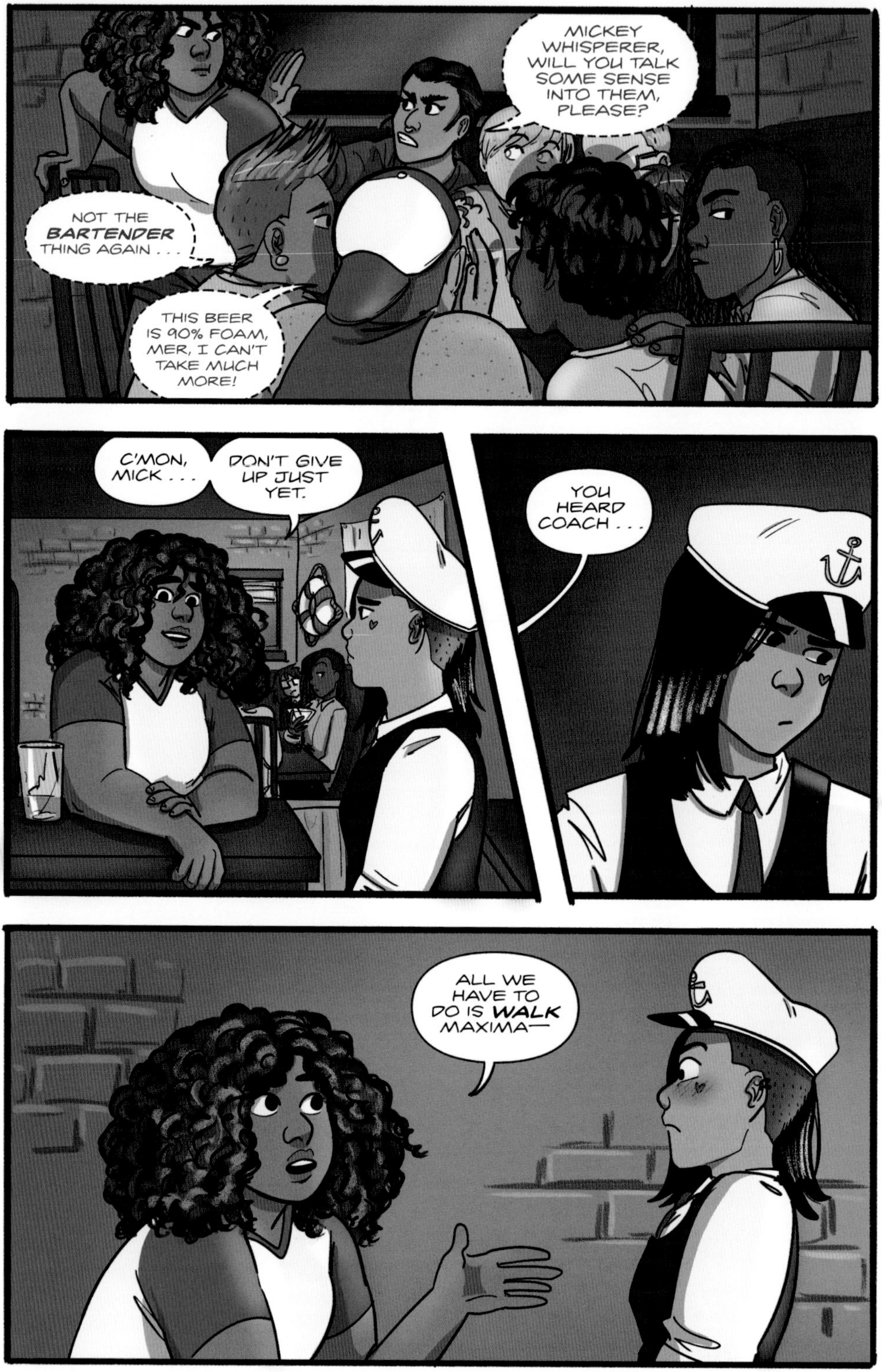
MICKEY WHISPERER, WILL YOU TALK SOME SENSE INTO THEM, PLEASE?
NOT THE **BARTENDER** THING AGAIN . . .
THIS BEER IS 90% FOAM, MER, I CAN'T TAKE MUCH MORE!
C'MON, MICK . . .
DON'T GIVE UP JUST YET.
YOU HEARD COACH . . .
ALL WE HAVE TO DO IS **WALK** MAXIMA—

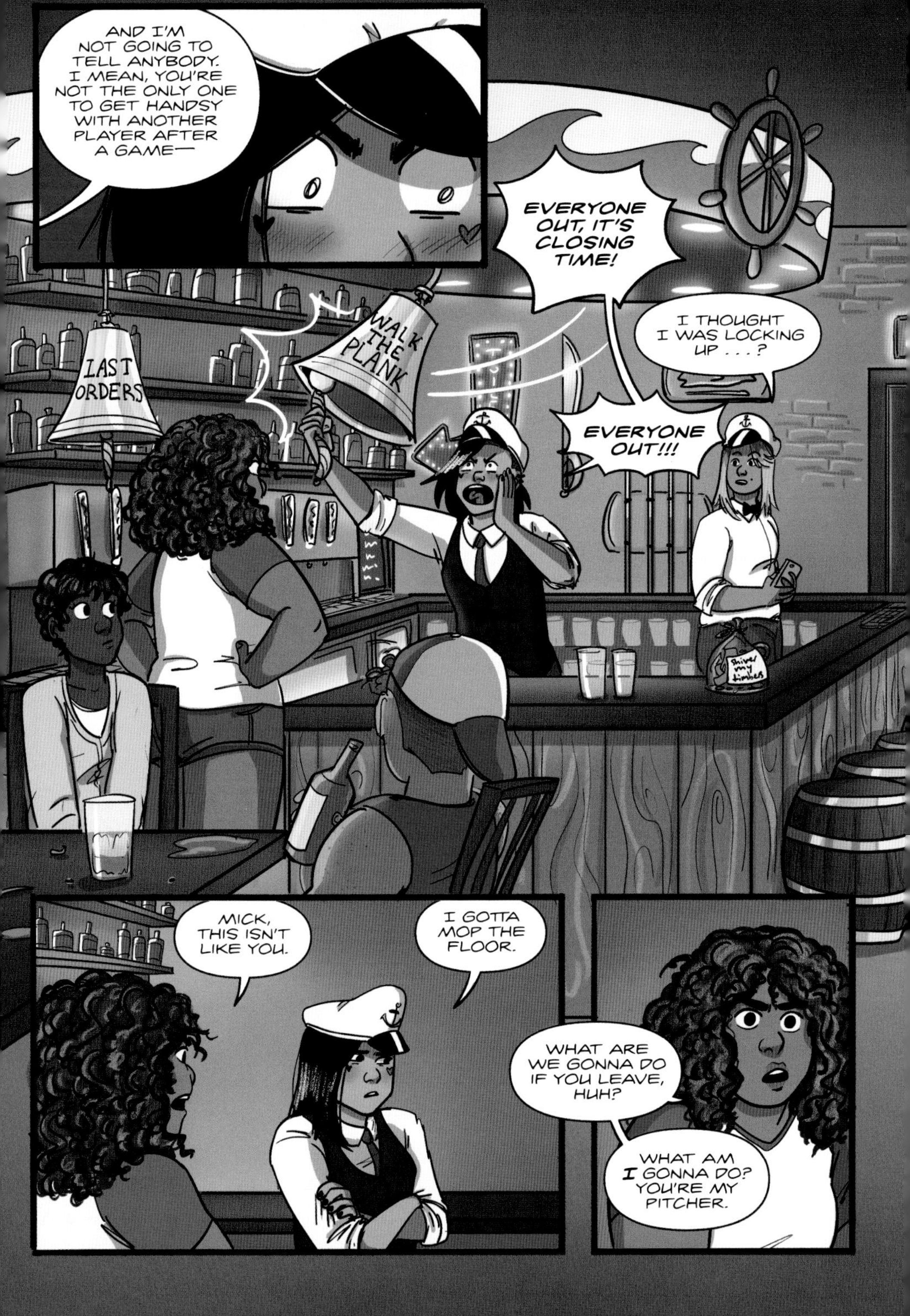
AND I'M NOT GOING TO TELL ANYBODY. I MEAN, YOU'RE NOT THE ONLY ONE TO GET HANDSY WITH ANOTHER PLAYER AFTER A GAME—
LAST ORDERS
WALK THE PLANK
EVERYONE OUT, IT'S CLOSING TIME!
I THOUGHT I WAS LOCKING UP . . . ?
EVERYONE OUT!!!
MICK, THIS ISN'T LIKE YOU.
I GOTTA MOP THE FLOOR.
WHAT ARE WE GONNA DO IF YOU LEAVE, HUH?
WHAT AM I GONNA DO? YOU'RE MY PITCHER.

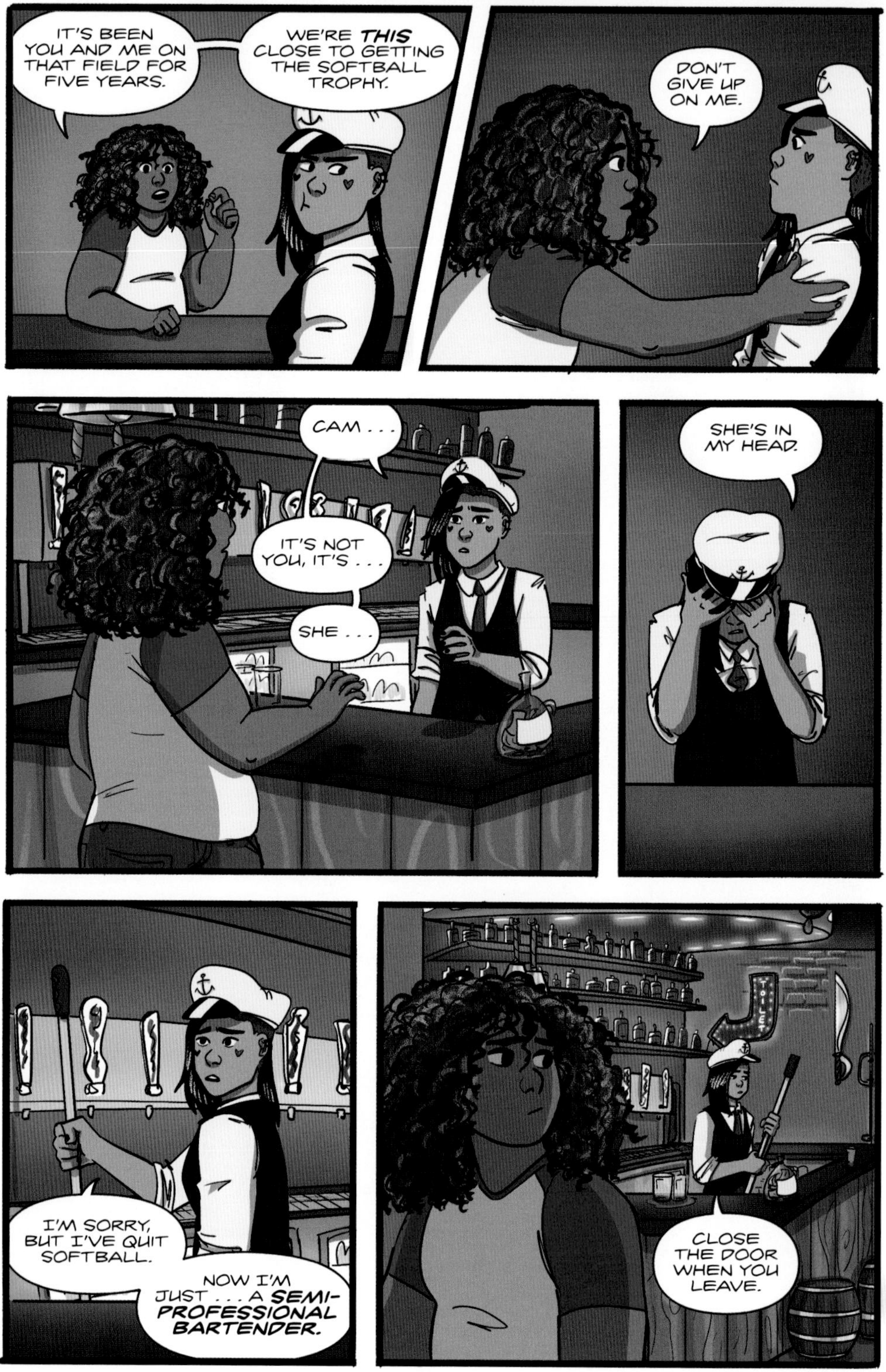
IT'S BEEN YOU AND ME ON THAT FIELD FOR FIVE YEARS.
WE'RE **THIS** CLOSE TO GETTING THE SOFTBALL TROPHY.
DON'T GIVE UP ON ME.
CAM . . .
IT'S NOT YOU, IT'S . . .
SHE . . .
SHE'S IN MY HEAD.
I'M SORRY, BUT I'VE QUIT SOFTBALL.
NOW I'M JUST . . . A **SEMI-PROFESSIONAL BARTENDER.**
TOILET
CLOSE THE DOOR WHEN YOU LEAVE.

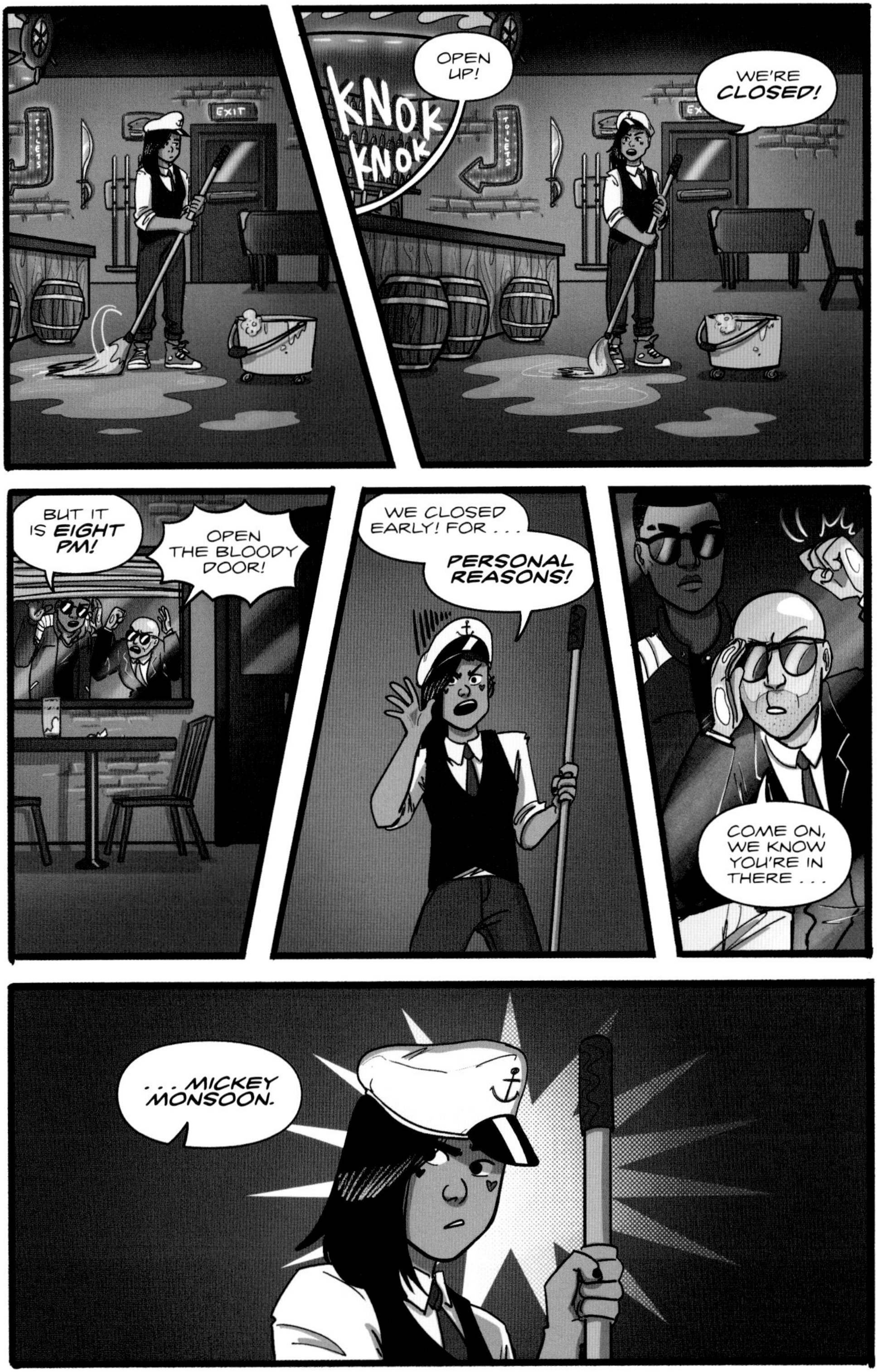

OPEN UP!
KNOK KNOK
WE'RE **CLOSED!**
BUT IT IS **EIGHT PM!**
OPEN THE BLOODY DOOR!
WE CLOSED EARLY! FOR . . .
PERSONAL REASONS!
COME ON, WE KNOW YOU'RE IN THERE . . .
. . . MICKEY MONSOON.

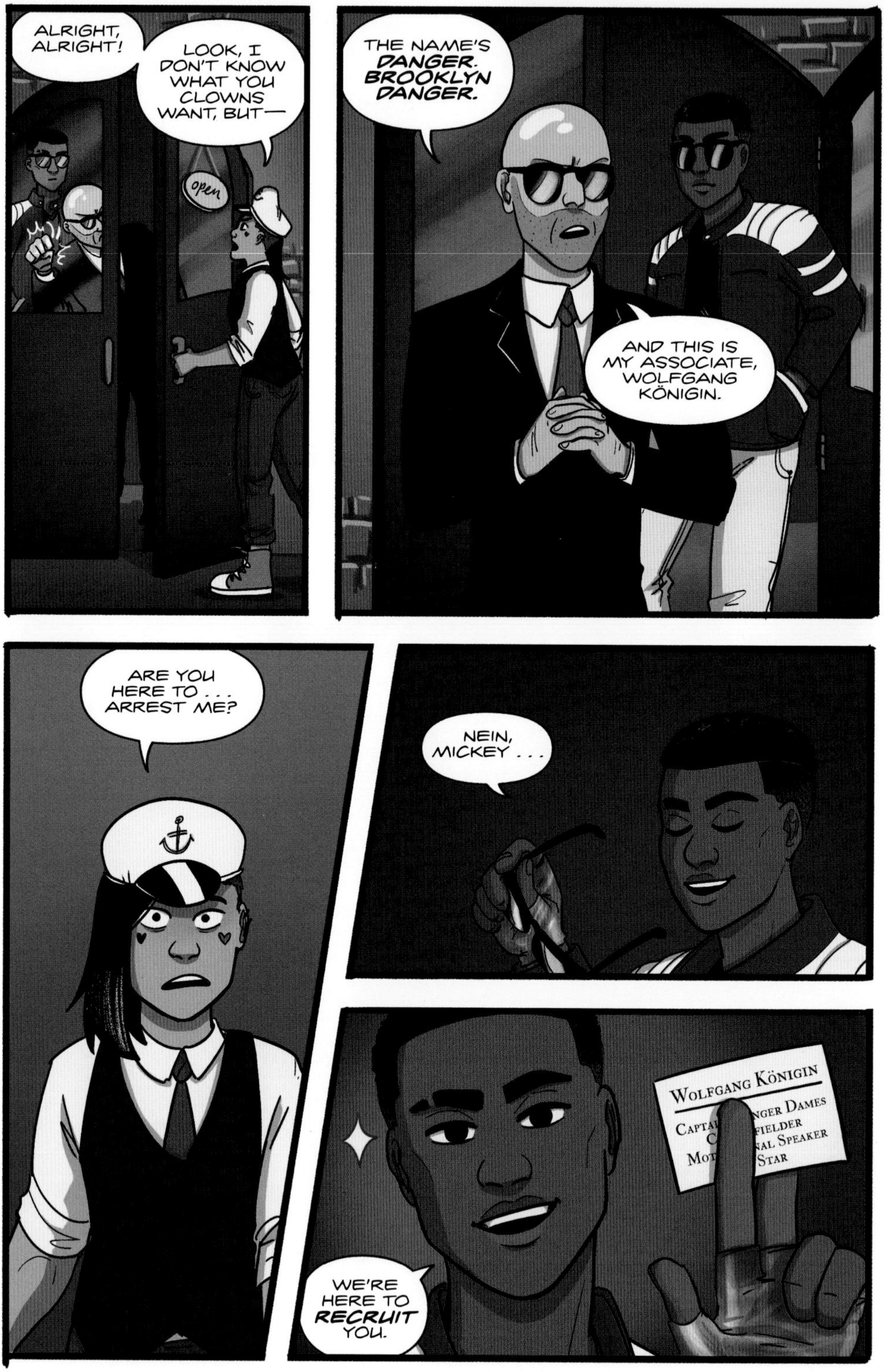
ALRIGHT, ALRIGHT!
LOOK, I DON'T KNOW WHAT YOU CLOWNS WANT, BUT—
open
THE NAME'S DANGER. BROOKLYN DANGER.
AND THIS IS MY ASSOCIATE, WOLFGANG KÖNIGIN.
ARE YOU HERE TO . . . ARREST ME?
NEIN, MICKEY . . .
WOLFGANG KÖNIGIN
CAPTAI NGER DAMES
C FIELDER
MOT NAL SPEAKER
STAR
WE'RE HERE TO RECRUIT YOU.

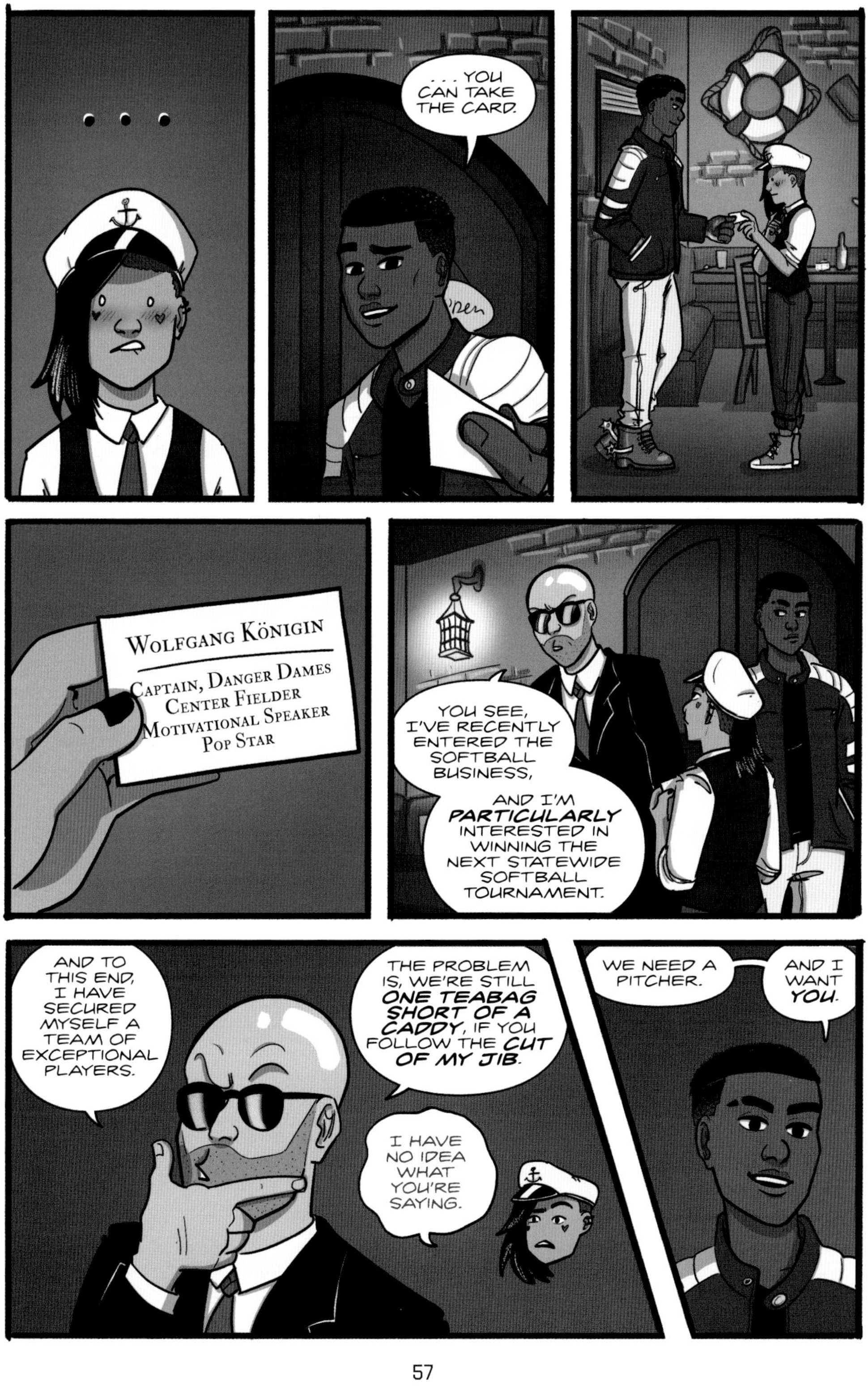
• • •
. . . YOU CAN TAKE THE CARD.
WOLFGANG KÖNIGIN
CAPTAIN, DANGER DAMES
CENTER FIELDER
MOTIVATIONAL SPEAKER
POP STAR
YOU SEE, I'VE RECENTLY ENTERED THE SOFTBALL BUSINESS,
AND I'M **PARTICULARLY** INTERESTED IN WINNING THE NEXT STATEWIDE SOFTBALL TOURNAMENT.
AND TO THIS END, I HAVE SECURED MYSELF A TEAM OF EXCEPTIONAL PLAYERS.
THE PROBLEM IS, WE'RE STILL ***ONE TEABAG SHORT OF A CADDY***, IF YOU FOLLOW THE ***CUT OF MY JIB***.
I HAVE NO IDEA WHAT YOU'RE SAYING.
WE NEED A PITCHER.
AND I WANT ***YOU***.

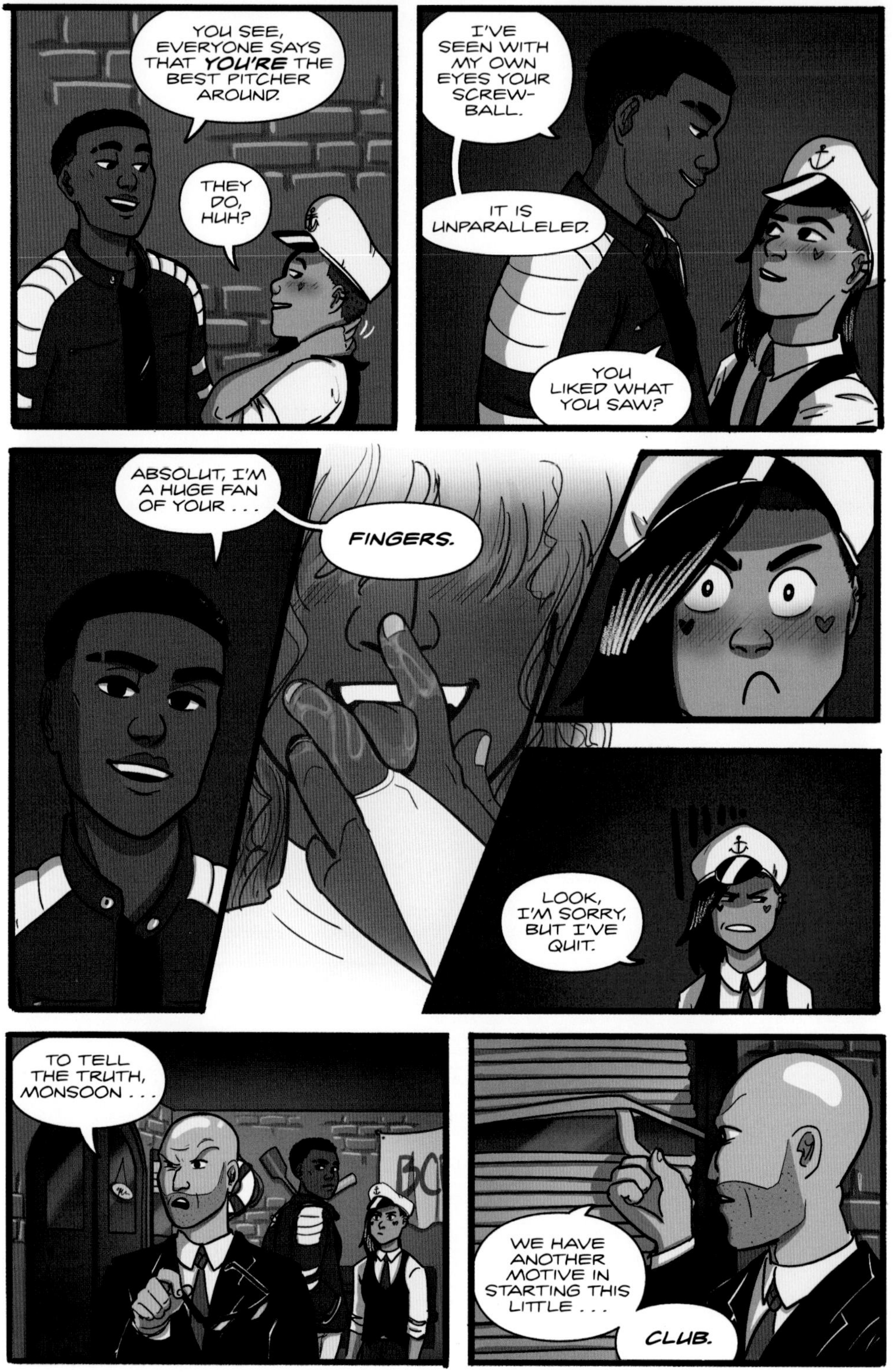
YOU SEE, EVERYONE SAYS THAT ***YOU'RE*** THE BEST PITCHER AROUND.
THEY DO, HUH?
I'VE SEEN WITH MY OWN EYES YOUR SCREW-BALL.
IT IS UNPARALLELED.
YOU LIKED WHAT YOU SAW?
ABSOLUT, I'M A HUGE FAN OF YOUR . . .
FINGERS.
LOOK, I'M SORRY, BUT I'VE QUIT.
TO TELL THE TRUTH, MONSOON . . .
WE HAVE ANOTHER MOTIVE IN STARTING THIS LITTLE . . .
CLUB.

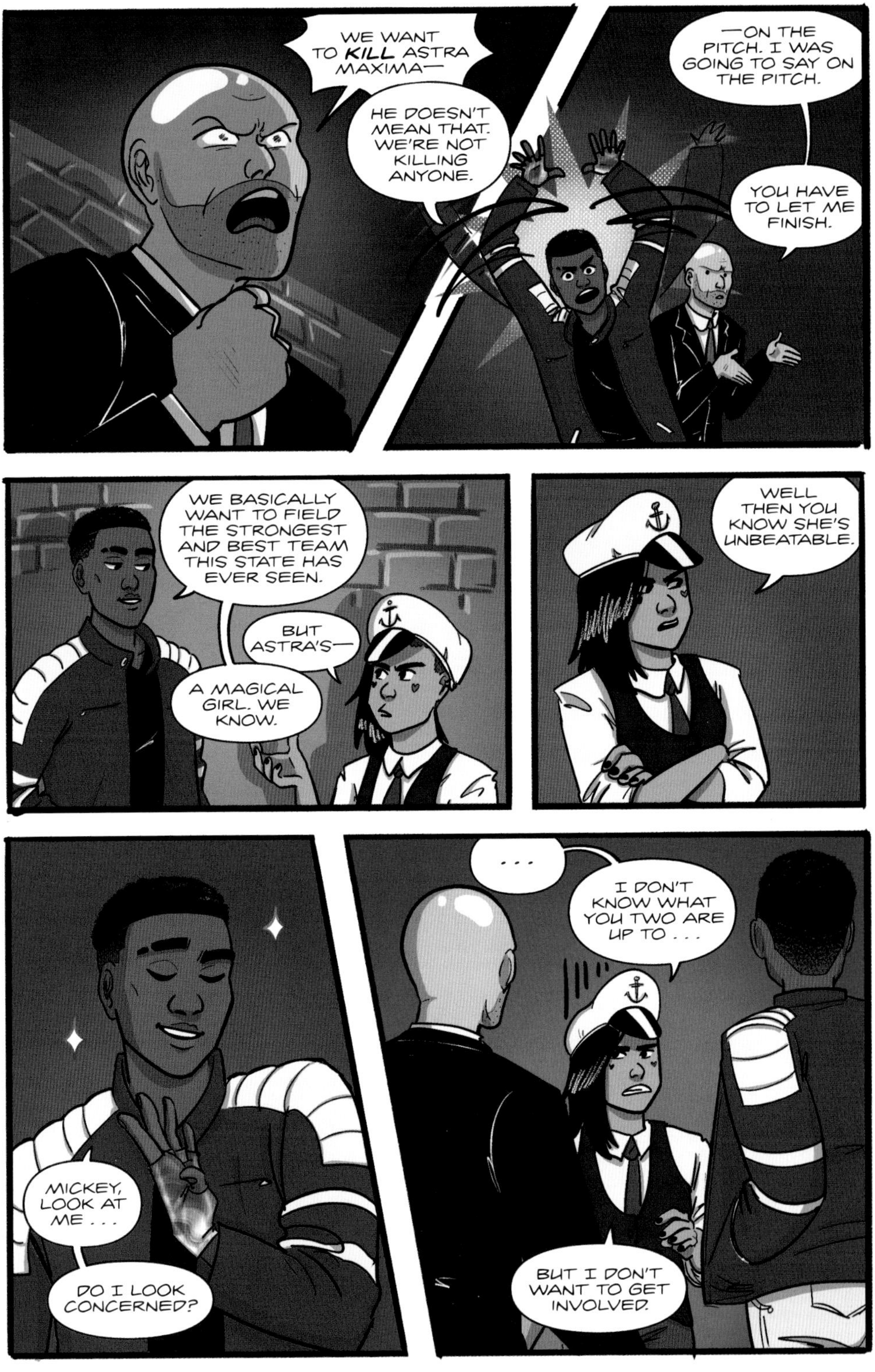
WE WANT TO KILL ASTRA MAXIMA—
HE DOESN'T MEAN THAT. WE'RE NOT KILLING ANYONE.
—ON THE PITCH. I WAS GOING TO SAY ON THE PITCH.
YOU HAVE TO LET ME FINISH.
WE BASICALLY WANT TO FIELD THE STRONGEST AND BEST TEAM THIS STATE HAS EVER SEEN.
BUT ASTRA'S—
A MAGICAL GIRL. WE KNOW.
WELL THEN YOU KNOW SHE'S UNBEATABLE.
MICKEY, LOOK AT ME . . .
DO I LOOK CONCERNED?
. . .
I DON'T KNOW WHAT YOU TWO ARE UP TO . . .
BUT I DON'T WANT TO GET INVOLVED.

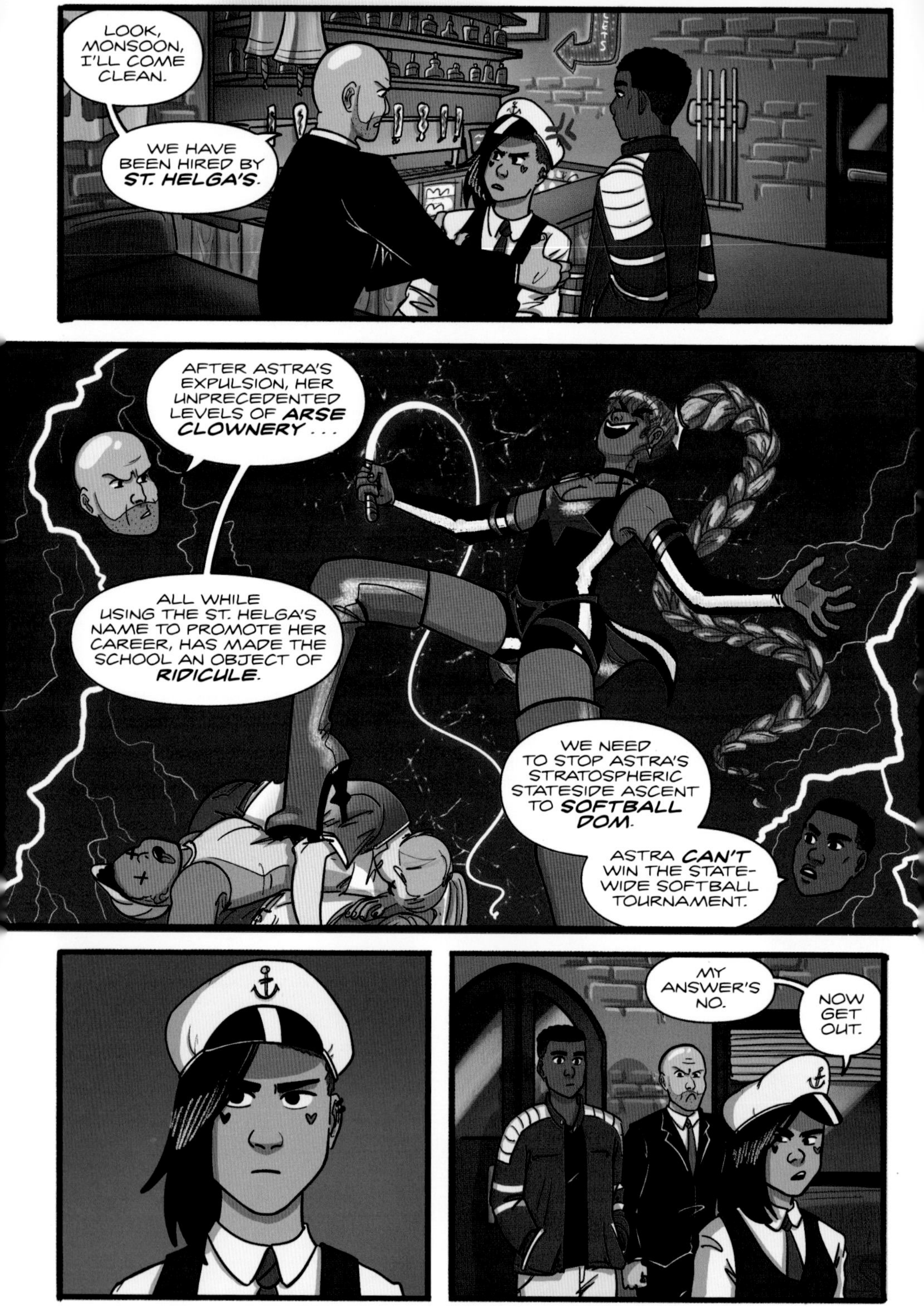
LOOK, MONSOON, I'LL COME CLEAN.
WE HAVE BEEN HIRED BY ST. HELGA'S.
AFTER ASTRA'S EXPULSION, HER UNPRECEDENTED LEVELS OF ARSE CLOWNERY . . .
ALL WHILE USING THE ST. HELGA'S NAME TO PROMOTE HER CAREER, HAS MADE THE SCHOOL AN OBJECT OF RIDICULE.
WE NEED TO STOP ASTRA'S STRATOSPHERIC STATESIDE ASCENT TO SOFTBALL DOM.
ASTRA CAN'T WIN THE STATE-WIDE SOFTBALL TOURNAMENT.
MY ANSWER'S NO.
NOW GET OUT.

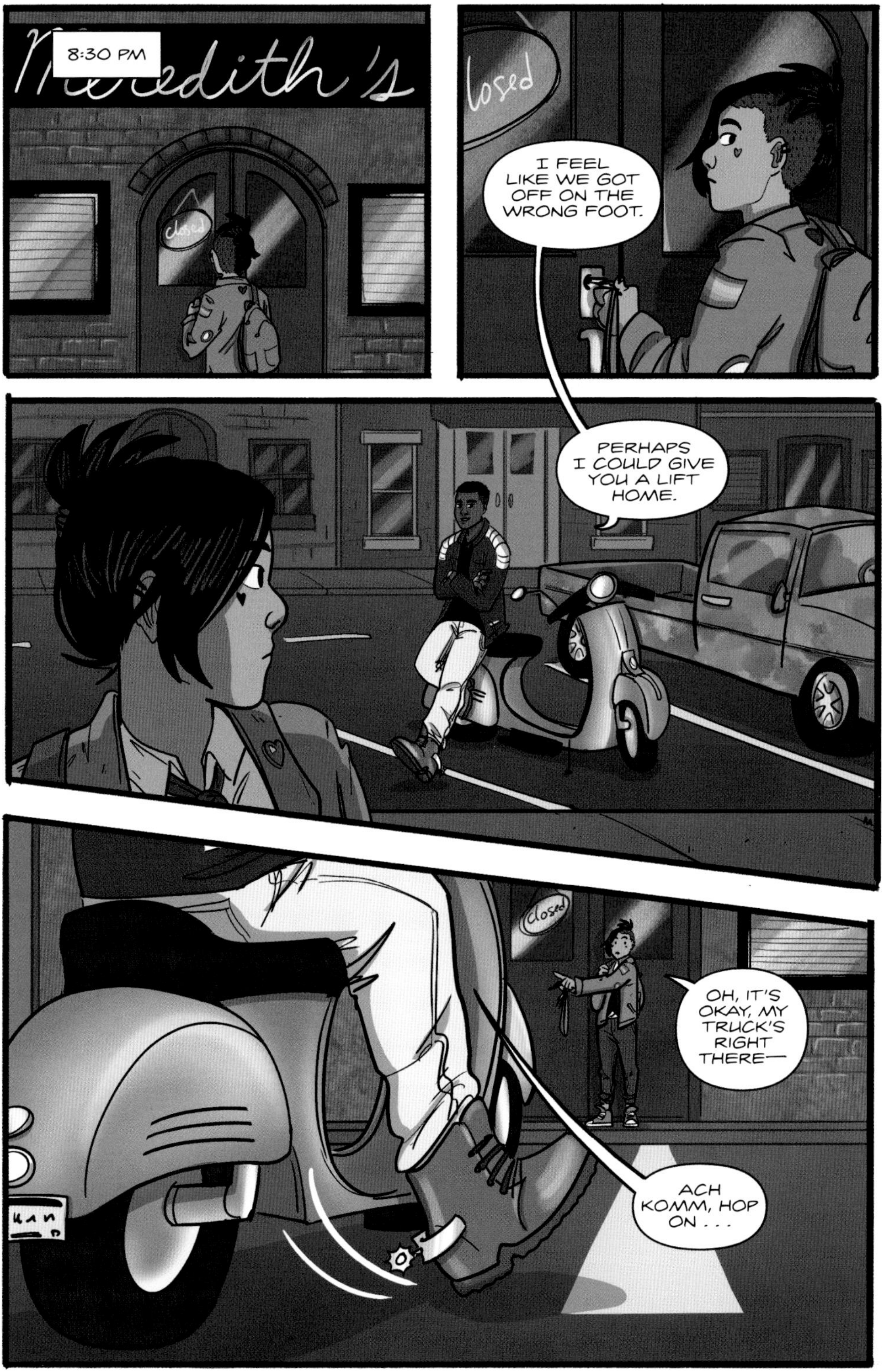
8:30 PM
Meredith's
closed
I FEEL LIKE WE GOT OFF ON THE WRONG FOOT.
PERHAPS I COULD GIVE YOU A LIFT HOME.
closed
OH, IT'S OKAY, MY TRUCK'S RIGHT THERE—
ACH KOMM, HOP ON . . .

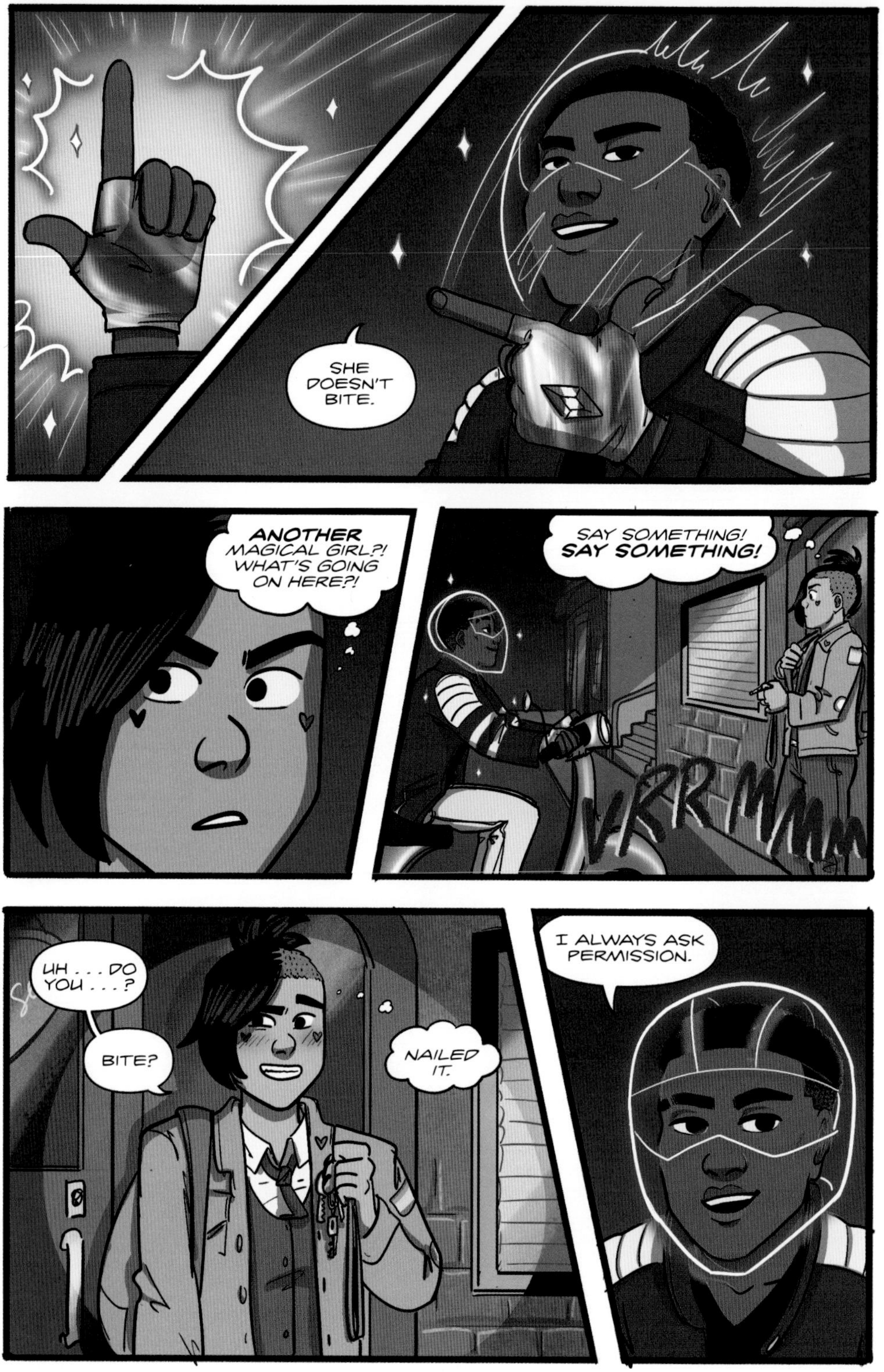

SHE DOESN'T BITE.
ANOTHER MAGICAL GIRL?! WHAT'S GOING ON HERE?!
SAY SOMETHING! SAY SOMETHING!
VRRMMMM
UH . . . DO YOU . . . ?
BITE?
NAILED IT.
I ALWAYS ASK PERMISSION.

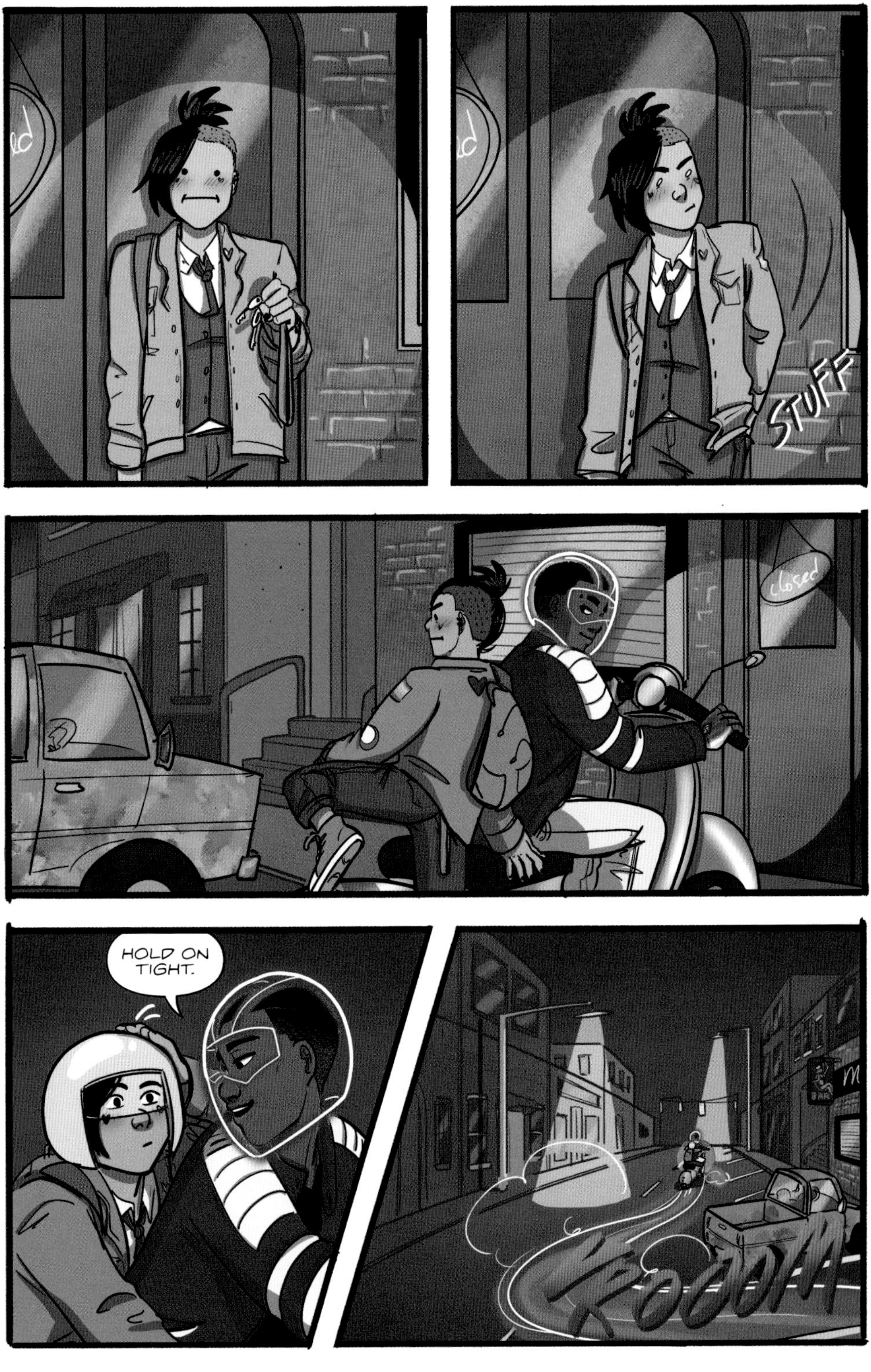
STUFF
closed
HOLD ON TIGHT.

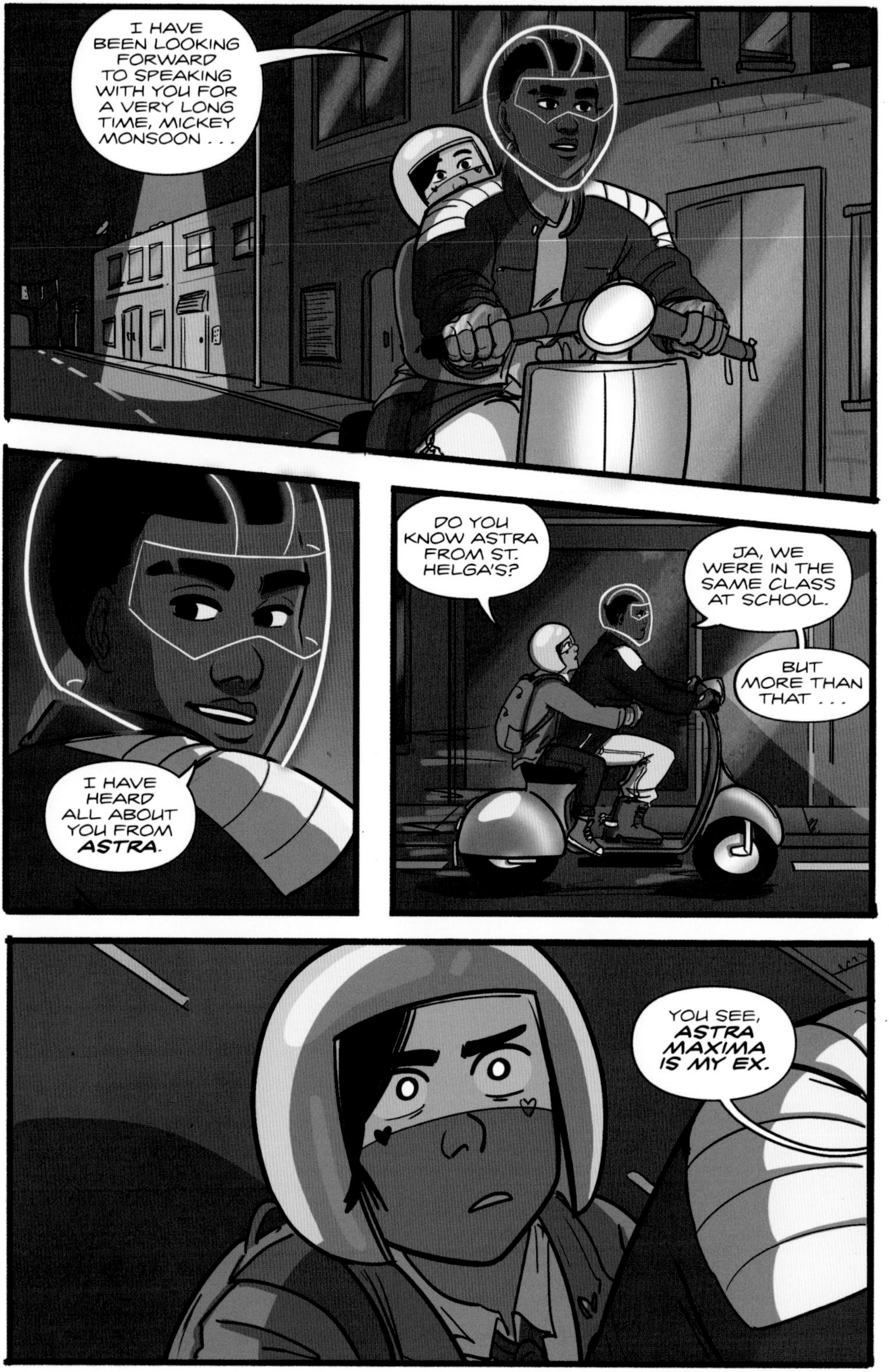
I HAVE BEEN LOOKING FORWARD TO SPEAKING WITH YOU FOR A VERY LONG TIME, MICKEY MONSOON . . .
I HAVE HEARD ALL ABOUT YOU FROM **ASTRA**.
DO YOU KNOW ASTRA FROM ST. HELGA'S?
JA, WE WERE IN THE SAME CLASS AT SCHOOL.
BUT MORE THAN THAT . . .
YOU SEE, **ASTRA MAXIMA IS MY EX.**

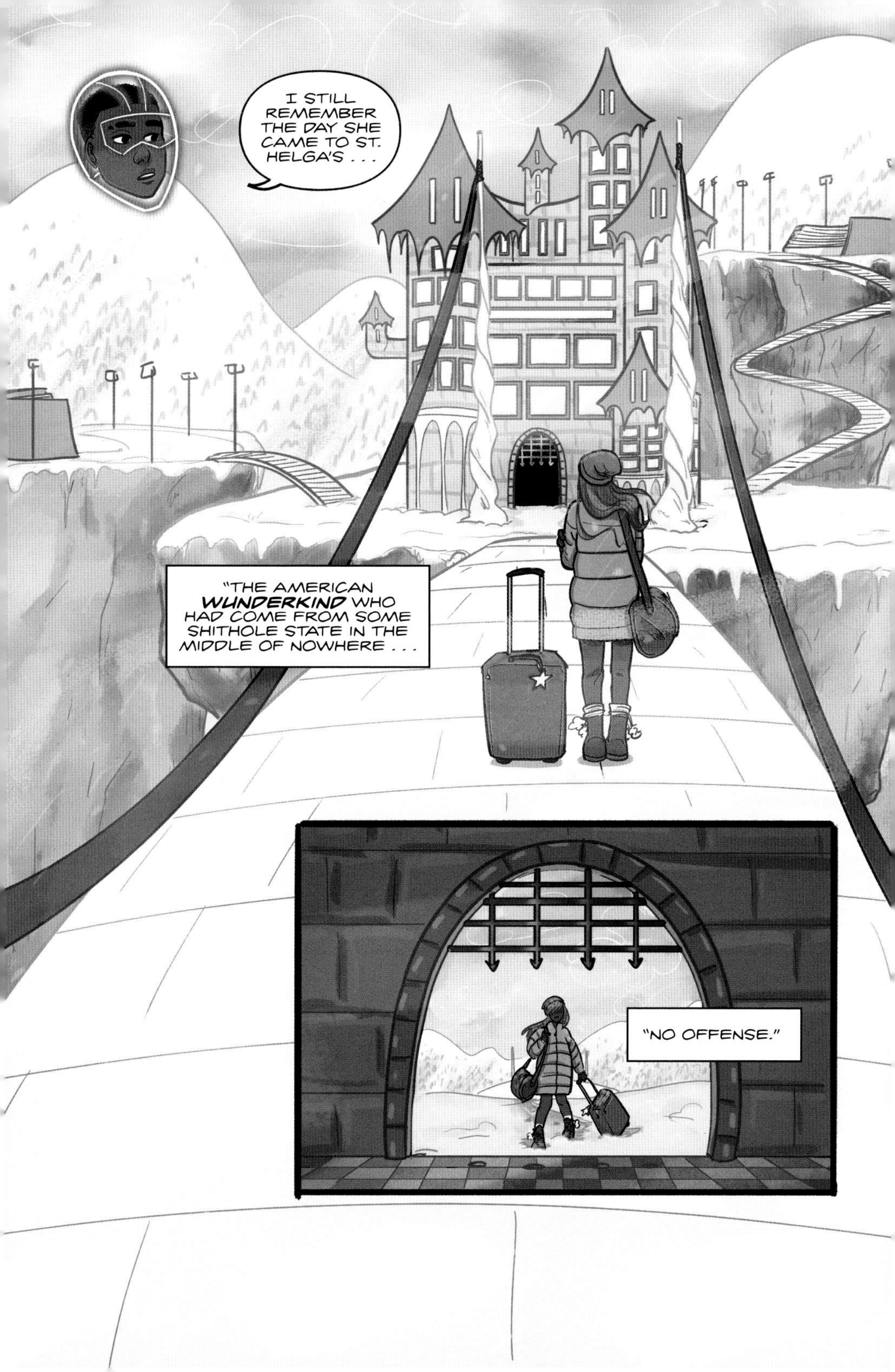
I STILL REMEMBER THE DAY SHE CAME TO ST. HELGA'S . . .
"THE AMERICAN **WUNDERKIND** WHO HAD COME FROM SOME SHITHOLE STATE IN THE MIDDLE OF NOWHERE . . .
"NO OFFENSE."

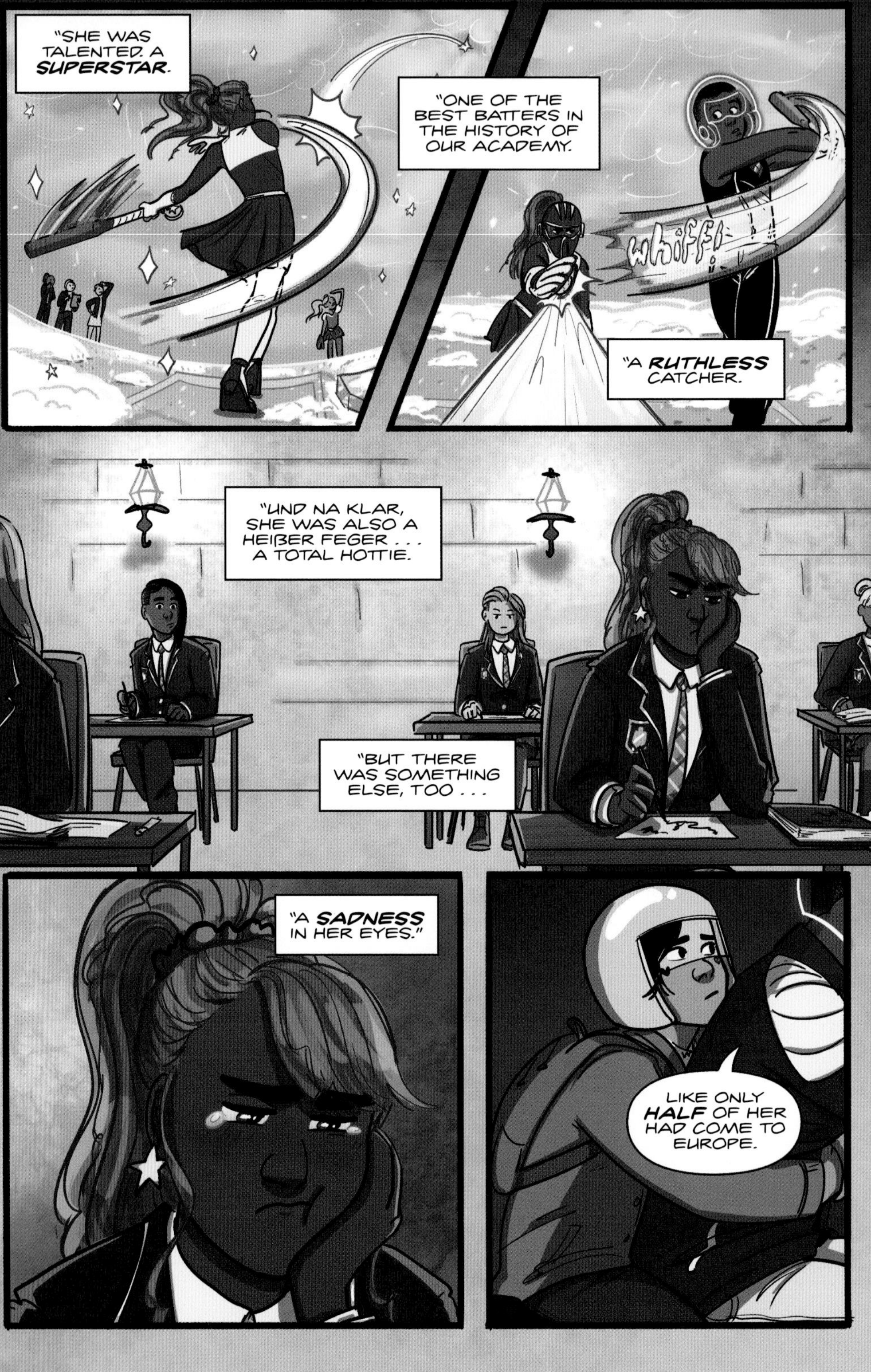
"SHE WAS TALENTED. A SUPERSTAR.
"ONE OF THE BEST BATTERS IN THE HISTORY OF OUR ACADEMY.
WHIFF!
"A RUTHLESS CATCHER.
"UND NA KLAR, SHE WAS ALSO A HEIẞER FEGER . . . A TOTAL HOTTIE.
"BUT THERE WAS SOMETHING ELSE, TOO . . .
"A SADNESS IN HER EYES."
LIKE ONLY HALF OF HER HAD COME TO EUROPE.

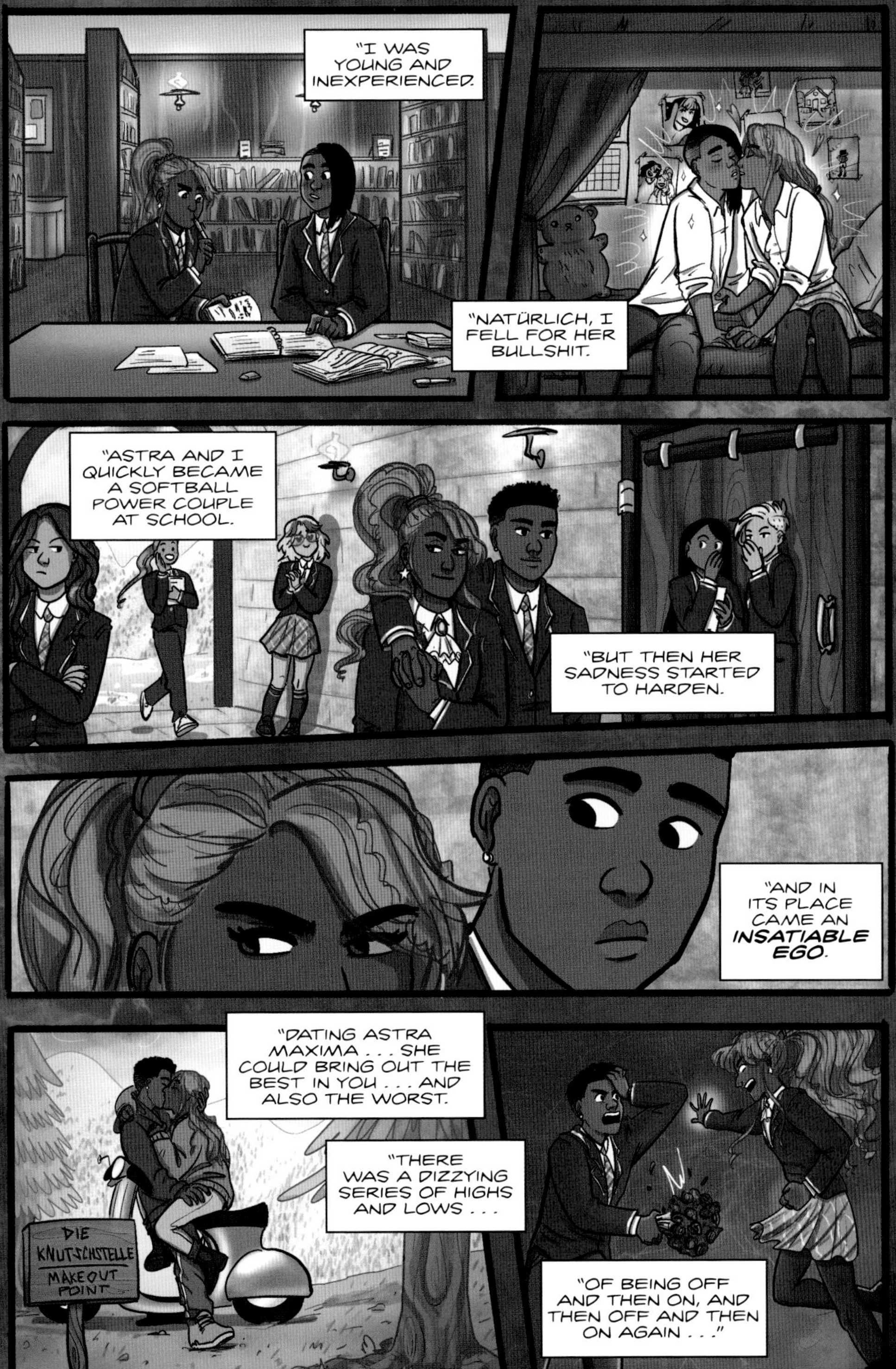
"I WAS YOUNG AND INEXPERIENCED.
"NATÜRLICH, I FELL FOR HER BULLSHIT.
"ASTRA AND I QUICKLY BECAME A SOFTBALL POWER COUPLE AT SCHOOL.
"BUT THEN HER SADNESS STARTED TO HARDEN.
"AND IN ITS PLACE CAME AN INSATIABLE EGO.
"DATING ASTRA MAXIMA . . . SHE COULD BRING OUT THE BEST IN YOU . . . AND ALSO THE WORST.
"THERE WAS A DIZZYING SERIES OF HIGHS AND LOWS . . .
DIE KNUTSCHSTELLE
MAKEOUT POINT
"OF BEING OFF AND THEN ON, AND THEN OFF AND THEN ON AGAIN . . ."

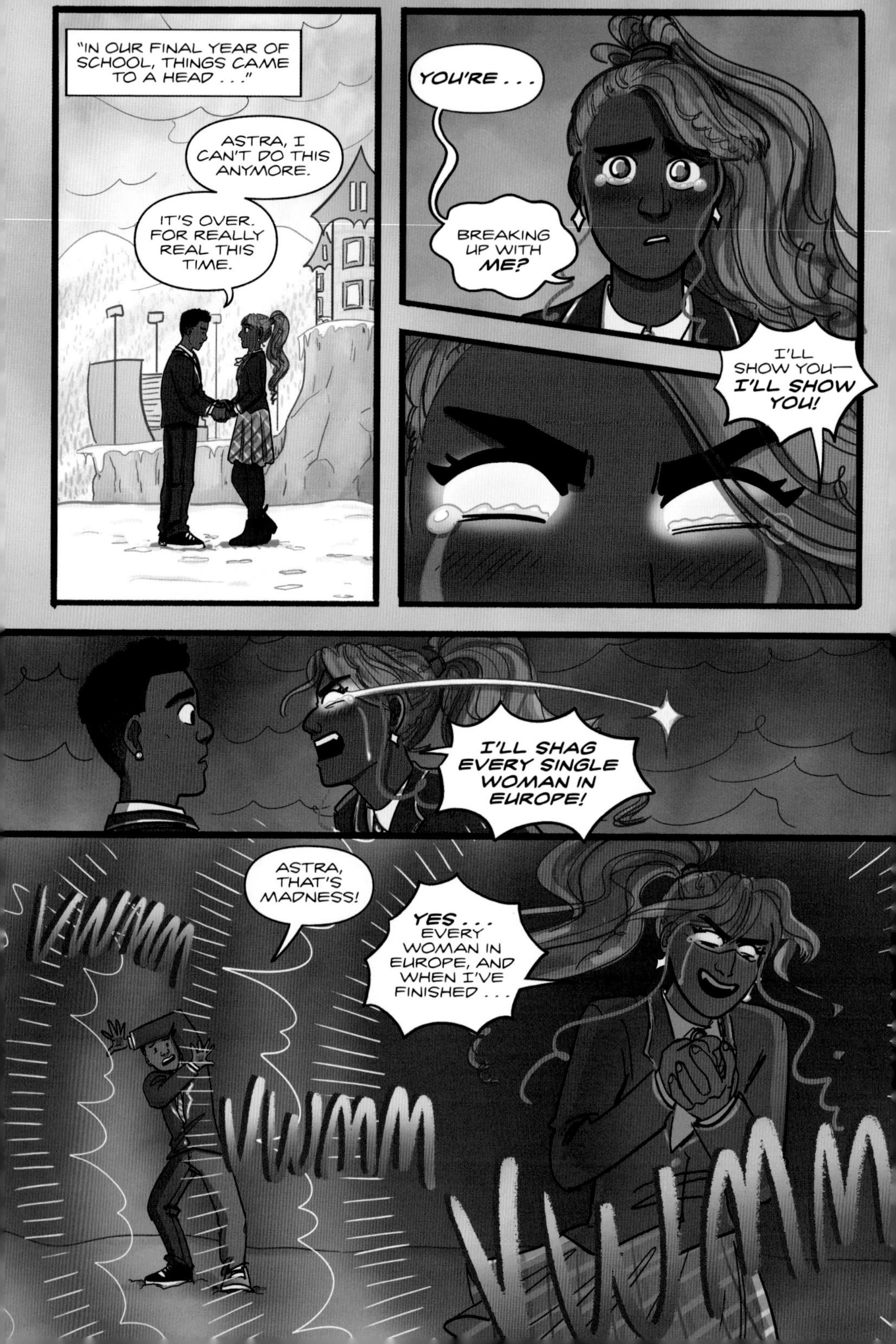

"IN OUR FINAL YEAR OF SCHOOL, THINGS CAME TO A HEAD . . ."
ASTRA, I CAN'T DO THIS ANYMORE.
IT'S OVER. FOR REALLY REAL THIS TIME.
YOU'RE . . .
BREAKING UP WITH ME?
I'LL SHOW YOU— I'LL SHOW YOU!
I'LL SHAG EVERY SINGLE WOMAN IN EUROPE!
VWMM
ASTRA, THAT'S MADNESS!
YES . . . EVERY WOMAN IN EUROPE, AND WHEN I'VE FINISHED . . .
VWMM
VWMM

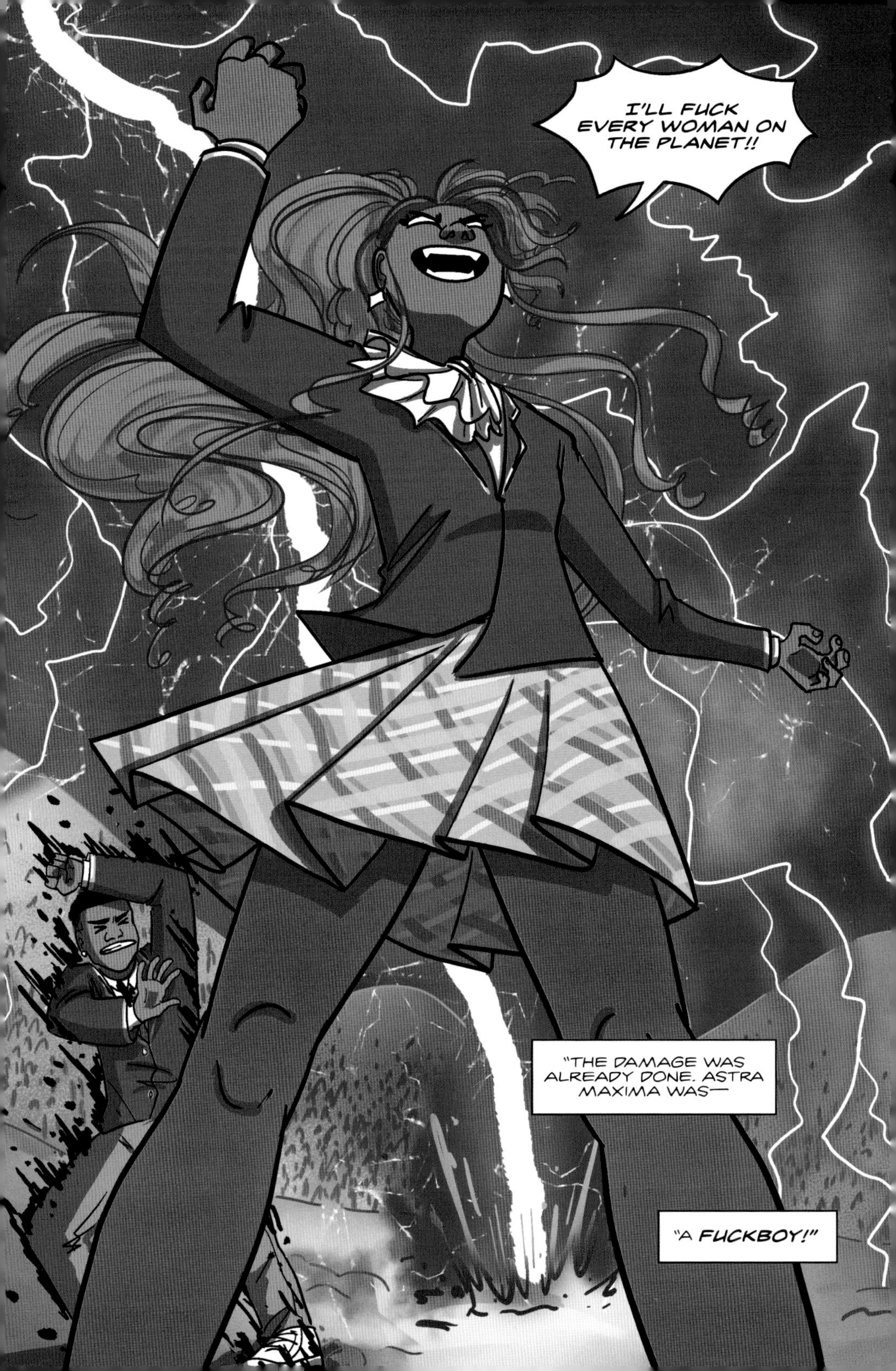
I'LL FUCK EVERY WOMAN ON THE PLANET!!
"THE DAMAGE WAS ALREADY DONE. ASTRA MAXIMA WAS—
"A FUCKBOY!"

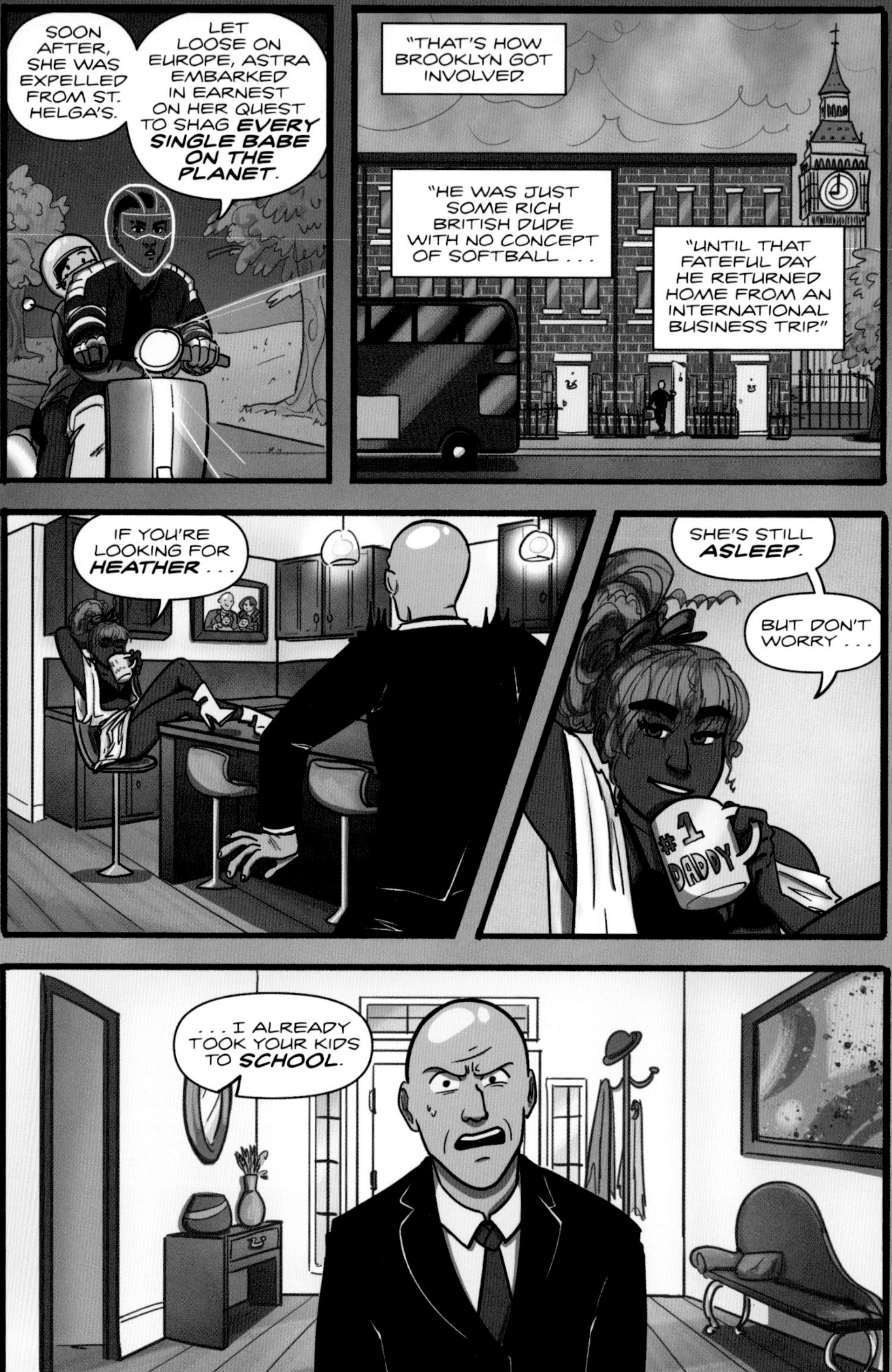
SOON AFTER, SHE WAS EXPELLED FROM ST. HELGA'S.
LET LOOSE ON EUROPE, ASTRA EMBARKED IN EARNEST ON HER QUEST TO SHAG **EVERY SINGLE BABE ON THE PLANET**.
"THAT'S HOW BROOKLYN GOT INVOLVED.
"HE WAS JUST SOME RICH BRITISH DUDE WITH NO CONCEPT OF SOFTBALL . . .
"UNTIL THAT FATEFUL DAY HE RETURNED HOME FROM AN INTERNATIONAL BUSINESS TRIP."
IF YOU'RE LOOKING FOR **HEATHER** . . .
SHE'S STILL **ASLEEP**.
BUT DON'T WORRY . . .
#1 DADDY
. . . I ALREADY TOOK YOUR KIDS TO **SCHOOL**.

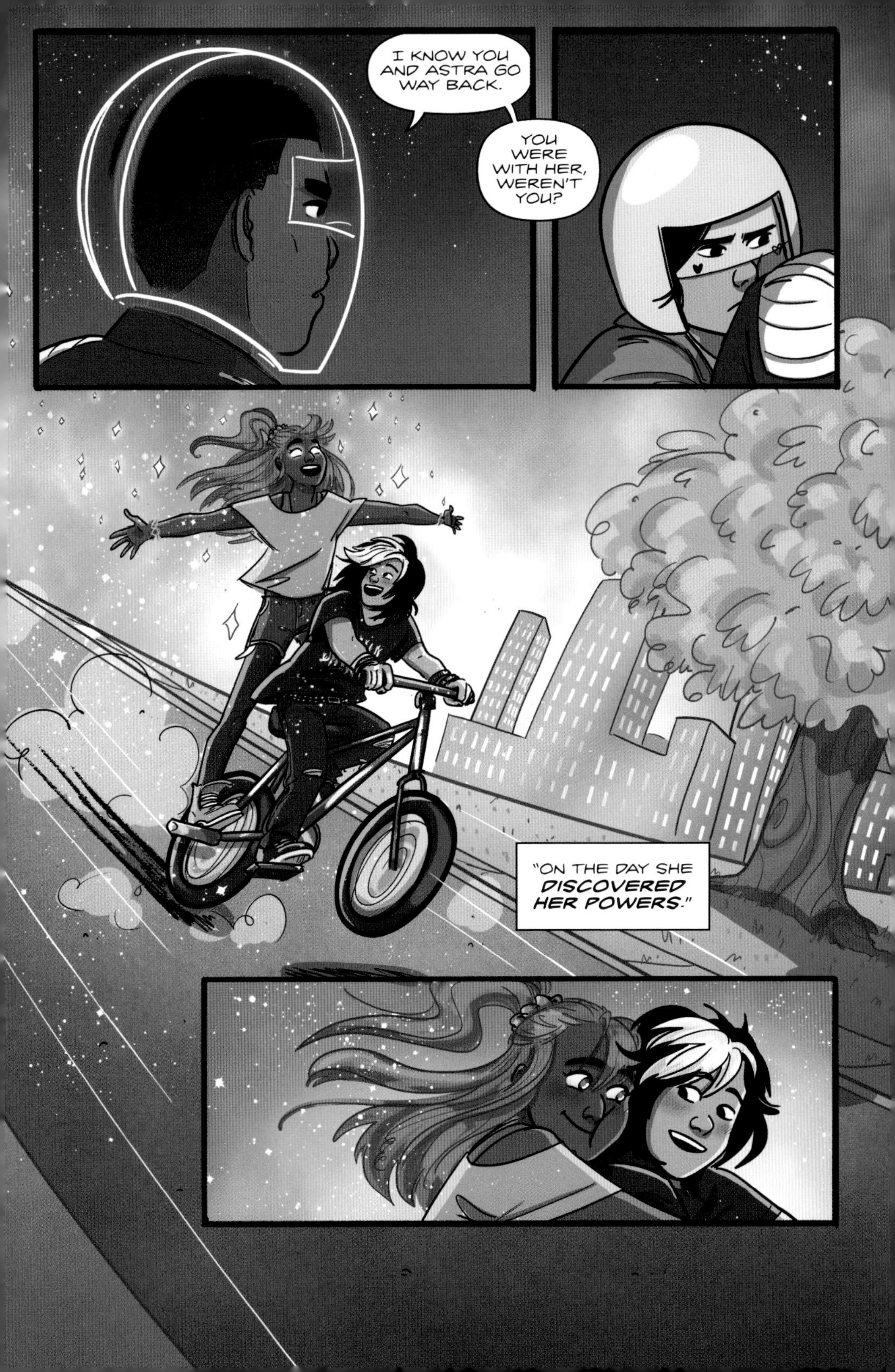
I KNOW YOU AND ASTRA GO WAY BACK.
YOU WERE WITH HER, WEREN'T YOU?
"ON THE DAY SHE *DISCOVERED HER POWERS*."

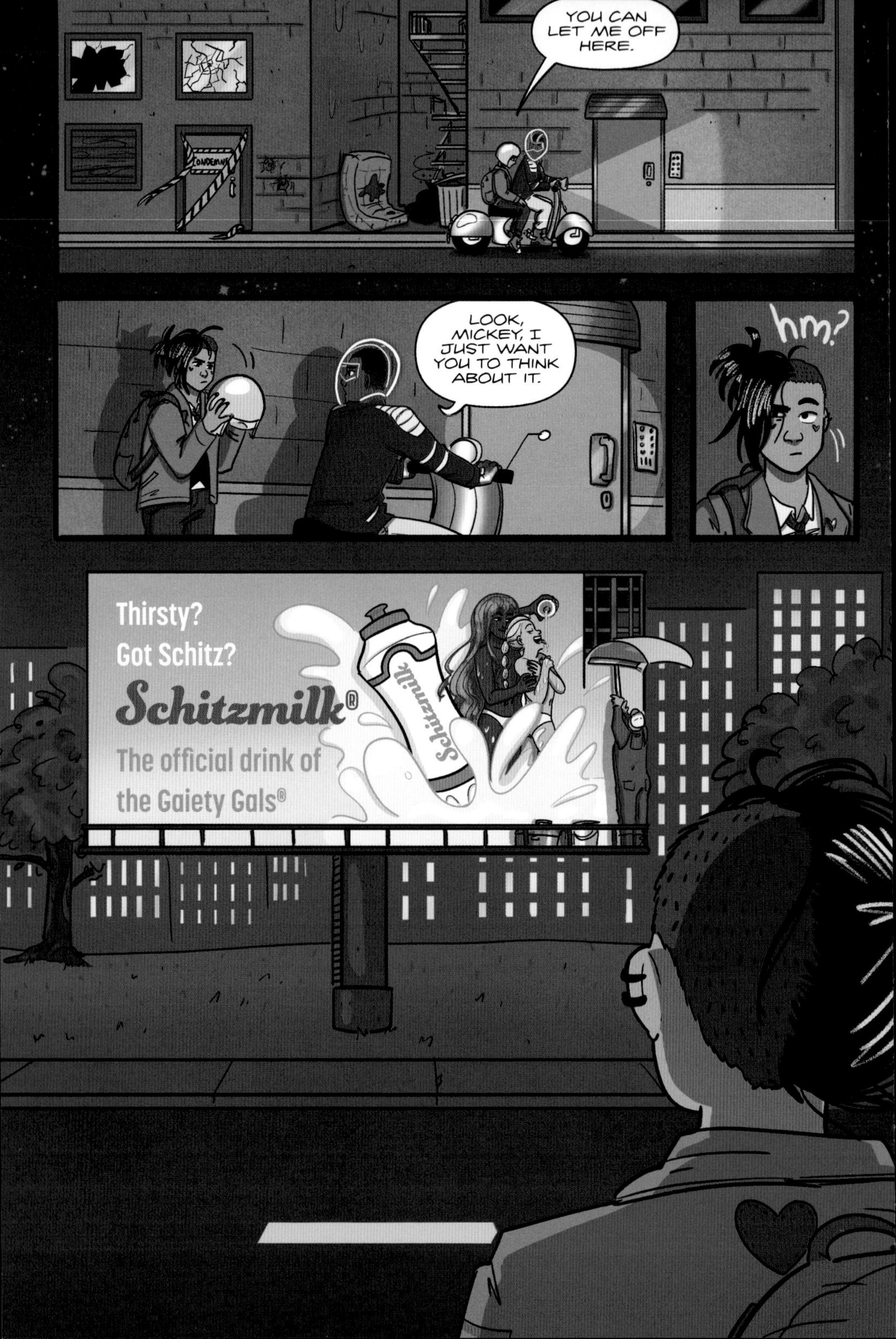
YOU CAN LET ME OFF HERE.
LOOK, MICKEY, I JUST WANT YOU TO THINK ABOUT IT.
hm?
Thirsty?
Got Schitz?
Schitzmilk®
The official drink of the Gaiety Gals®
Schitzmilk

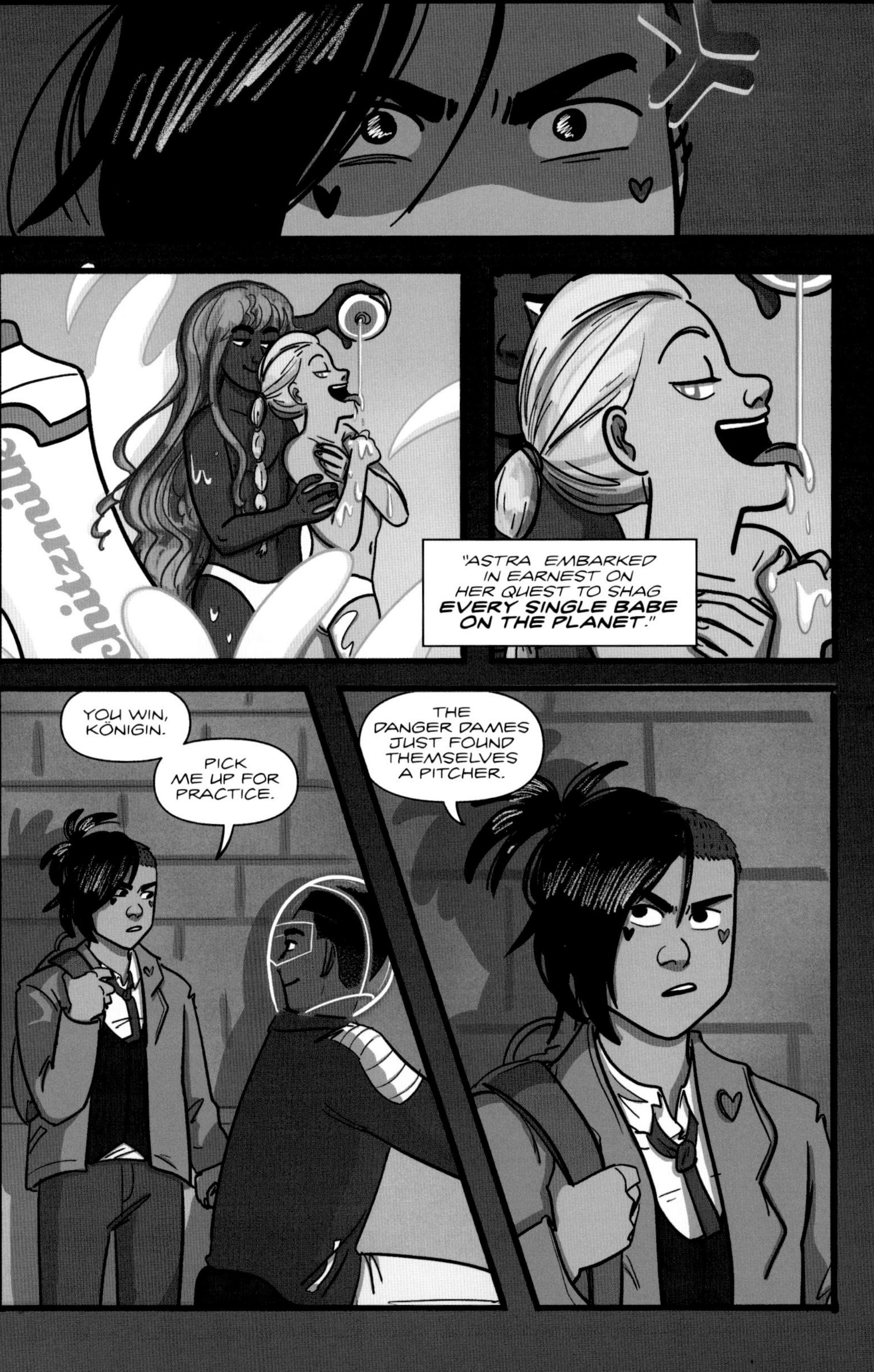
"ASTRA EMBARKED IN EARNEST ON HER QUEST TO SHAG **EVERY SINGLE BABE ON THE PLANET**."
YOU WIN, KÖNIGIN.
PICK ME UP FOR PRACTICE.
THE DANGER DAMES JUST FOUND THEMSELVES A PITCHER.

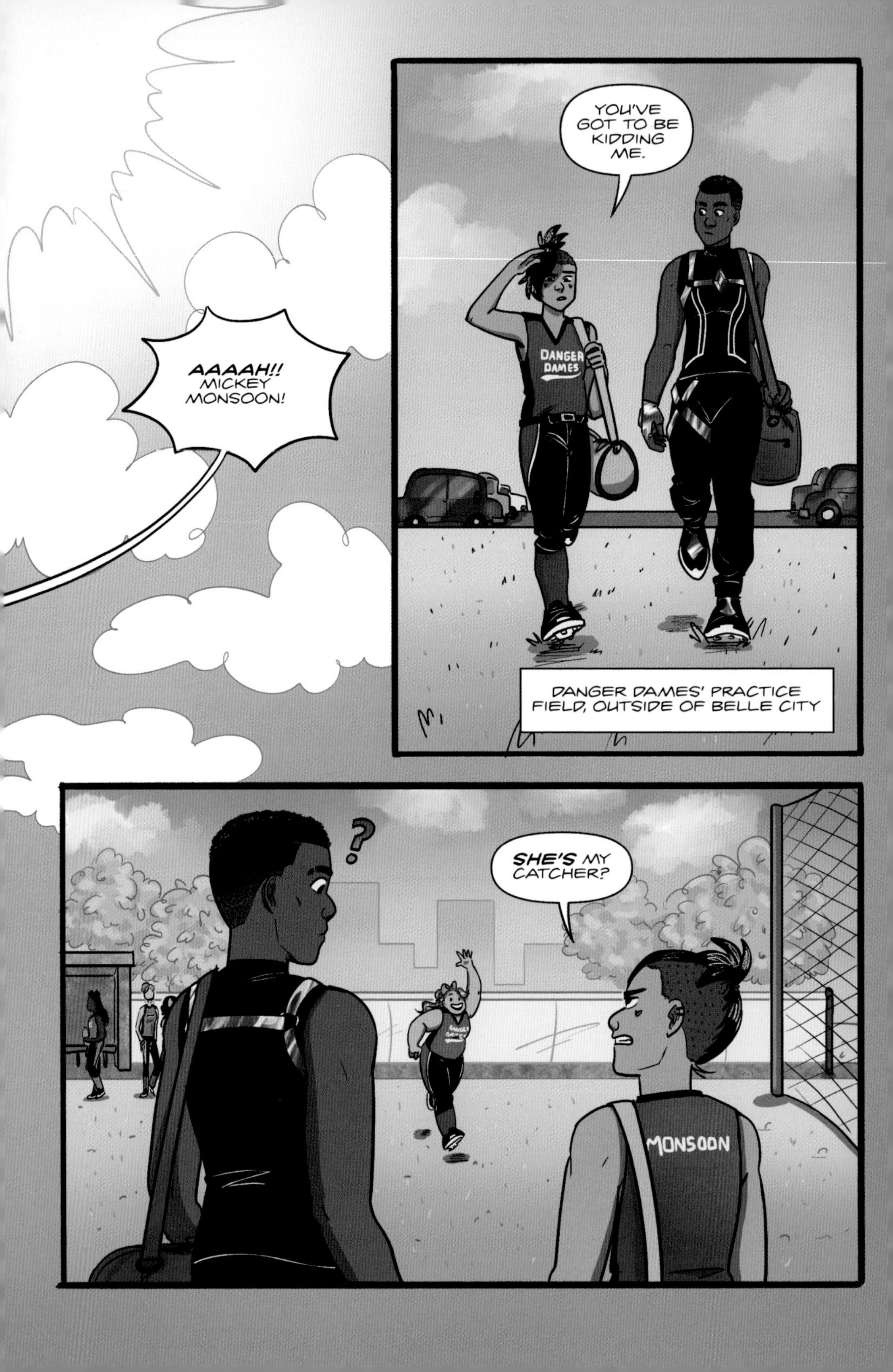
AAAAH!! MICKEY MONSOON!
YOU'VE GOT TO BE KIDDING ME.
DANGER DAMES' PRACTICE FIELD, OUTSIDE OF BELLE CITY
DANGER DAMES
?
SHE'S MY CATCHER?
MONSOON

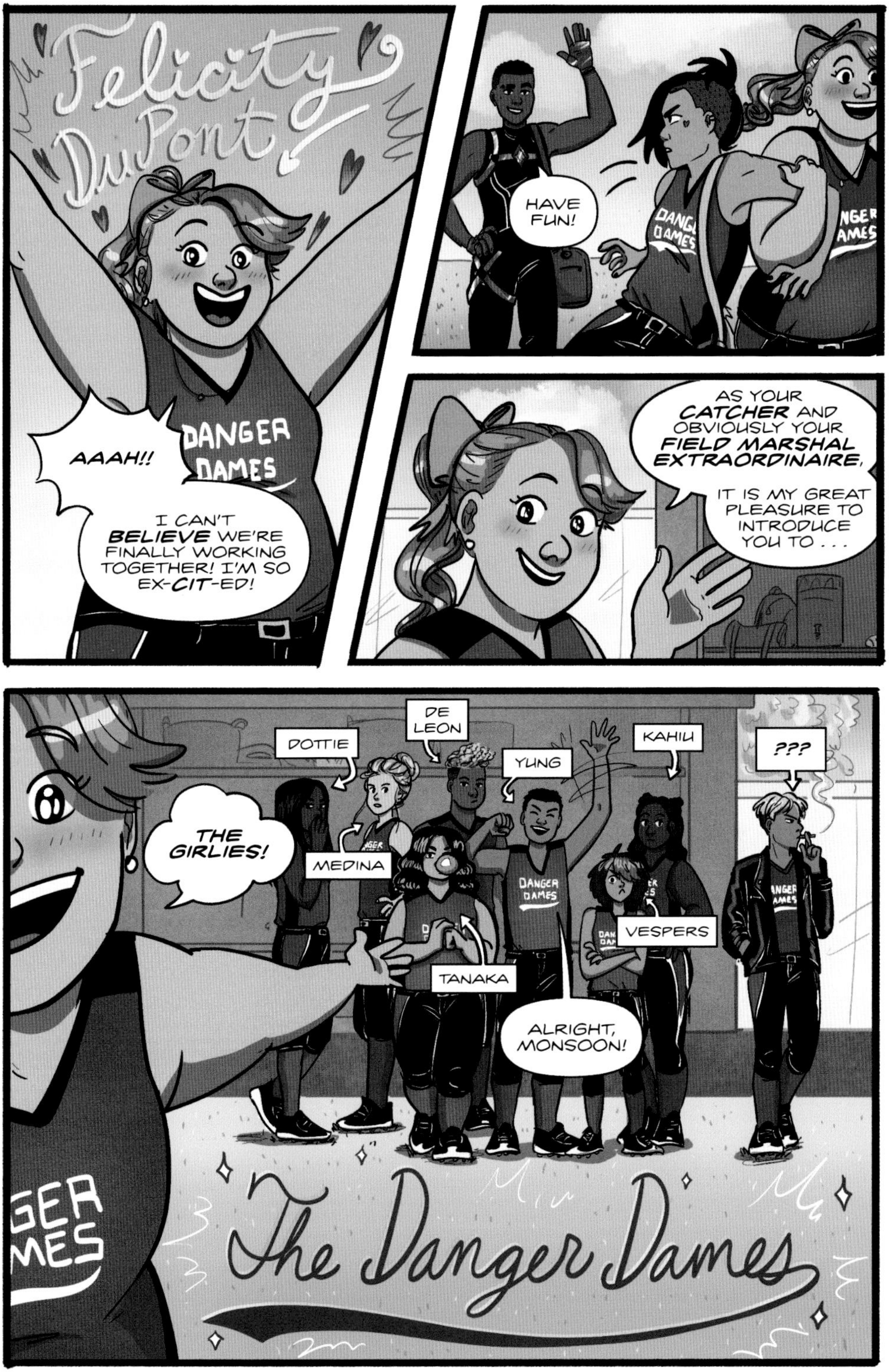
Felicity DuPont
AAAH!!
I CAN'T BELIEVE WE'RE FINALLY WORKING TOGETHER! I'M SO EX-CIT-ED!
HAVE FUN!
AS YOUR CATCHER AND OBVIOUSLY YOUR FIELD MARSHAL EXTRAORDINAIRE,
IT IS MY GREAT PLEASURE TO INTRODUCE YOU TO . . .
THE GIRLIES!
DOTTIE
DE LEON
YUNG
KAHIU
???
MEDINA
VESPERS
TANAKA
ALRIGHT, MONSOON!
The Danger Dames

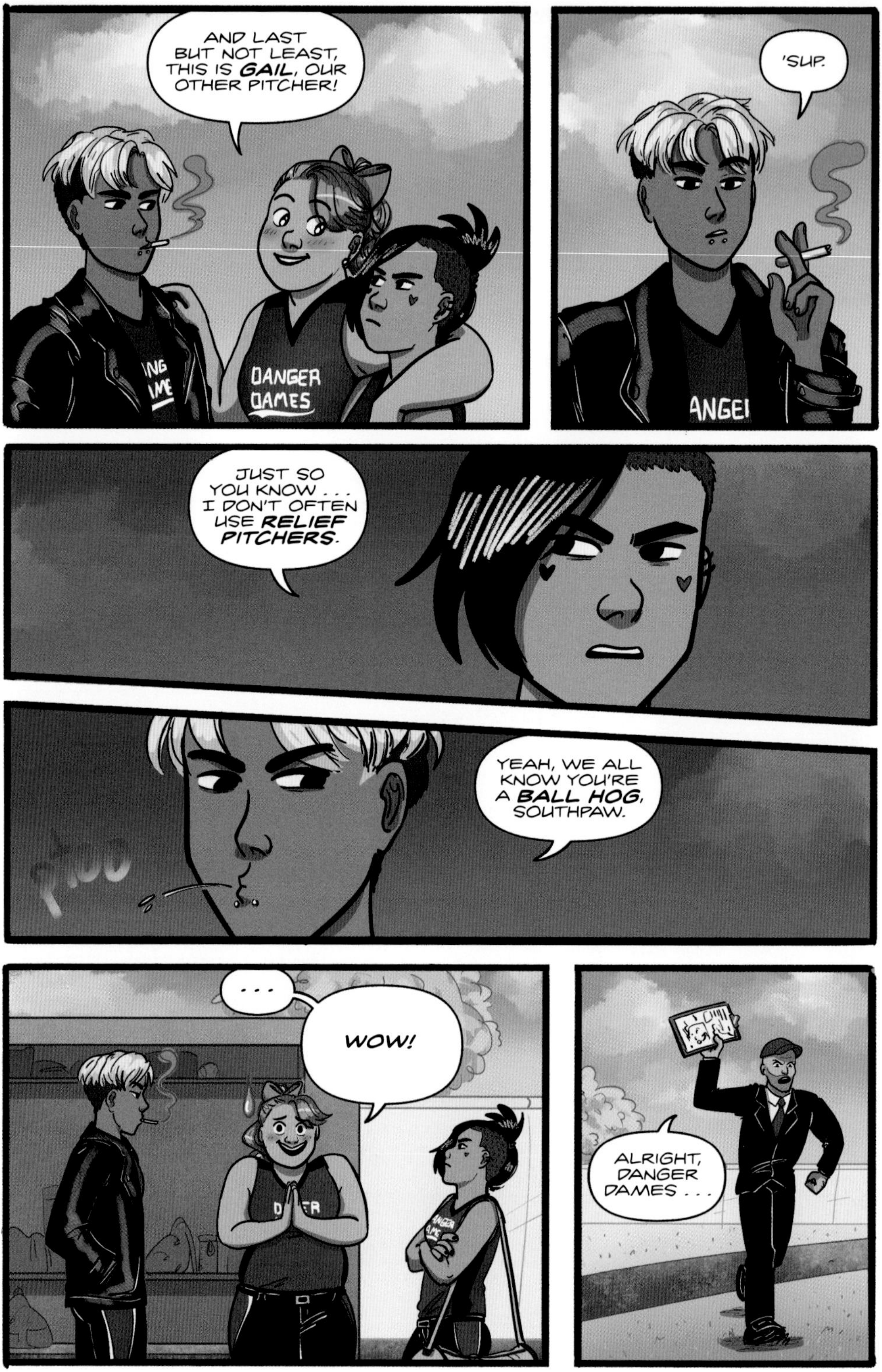
AND LAST BUT NOT LEAST, THIS IS **GAIL**, OUR OTHER PITCHER!
DANGER DAMES
'SUP.
JUST SO YOU KNOW . . . I DON'T OFTEN USE **RELIEF PITCHERS**.
YEAH, WE ALL KNOW YOU'RE A **BALL HOG**, SOUTHPAW.
. . .
WOW!
ALRIGHT, DANGER DAMES . . .

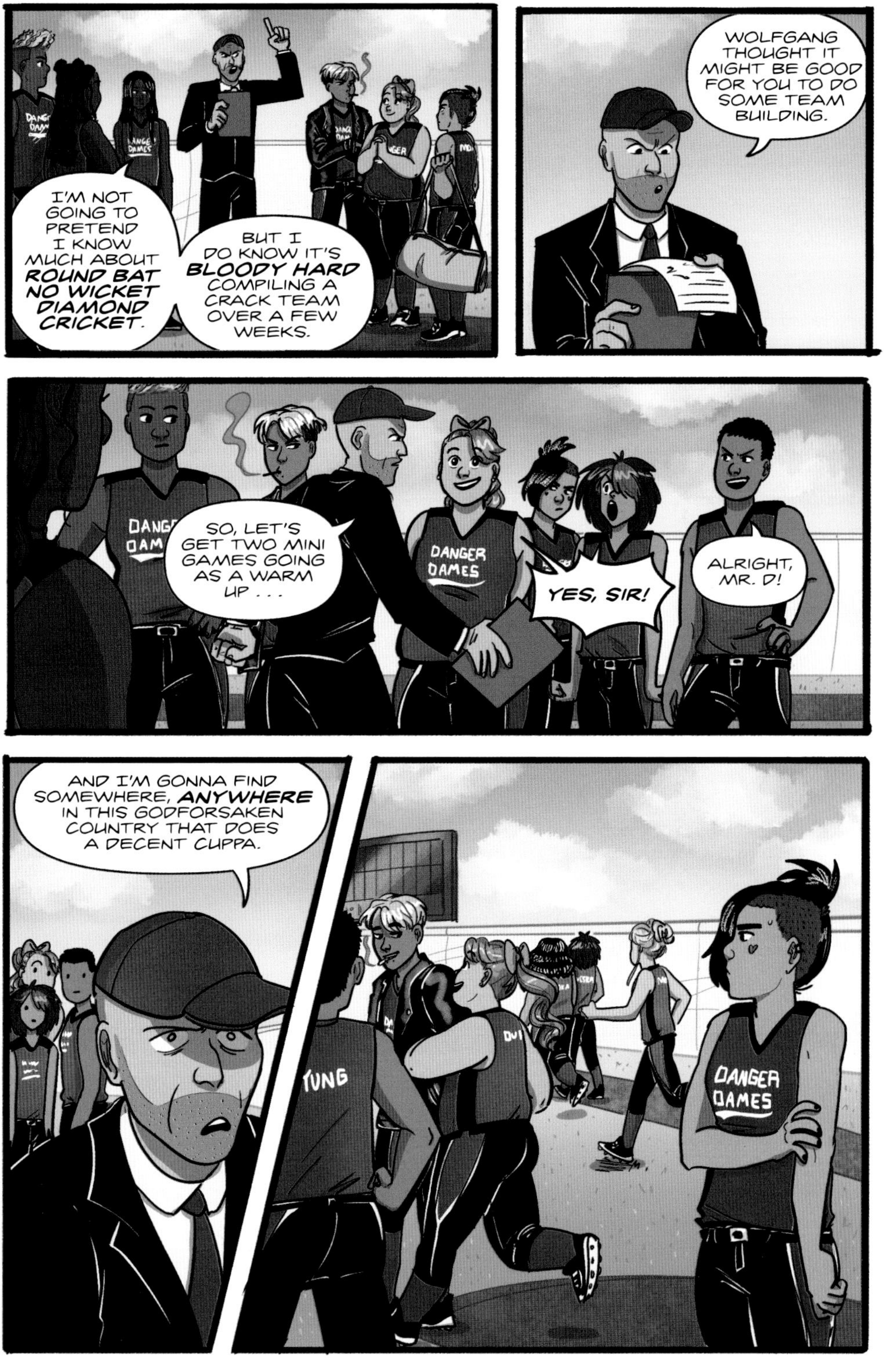
I'M NOT GOING TO PRETEND I KNOW MUCH ABOUT **ROUND BAT NO WICKET DIAMOND CRICKET**.
BUT I DO KNOW IT'S **BLOODY HARD** COMPILING A CRACK TEAM OVER A FEW WEEKS.
WOLFGANG THOUGHT IT MIGHT BE GOOD FOR YOU TO DO SOME TEAM BUILDING.
SO, LET'S GET TWO MINI GAMES GOING AS A WARM UP . . .
YES, SIR!
ALRIGHT, MR. D!
AND I'M GONNA FIND SOMEWHERE, **ANYWHERE** IN THIS GODFORSAKEN COUNTRY THAT DOES A DECENT CUPPA.

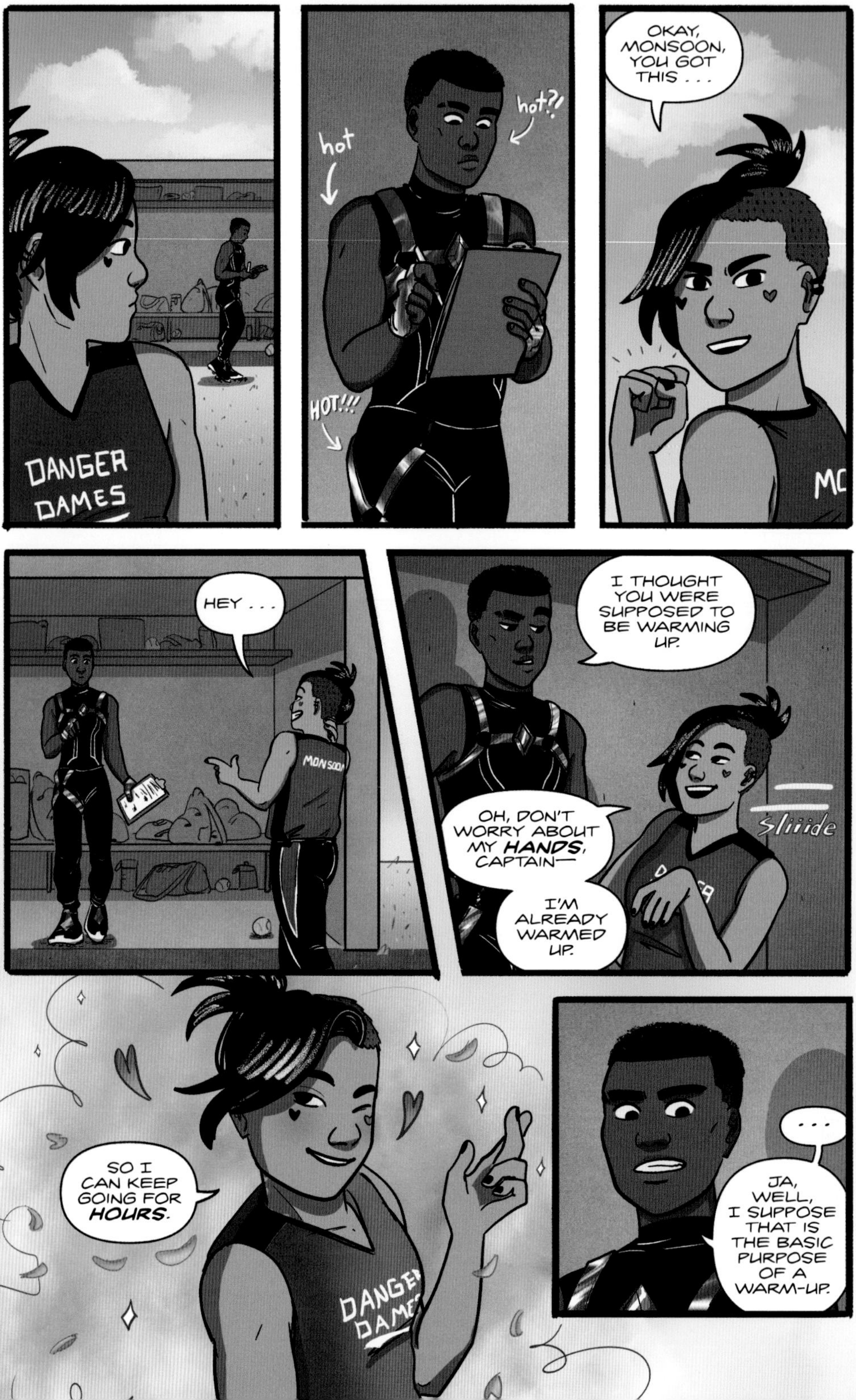

DANGER DAMES
hot
hot?!
HOT!!!
OKAY, MONSOON, YOU GOT THIS . . .
MO
HEY . . .
MONSOON
I THOUGHT YOU WERE SUPPOSED TO BE WARMING UP.
OH, DON'T WORRY ABOUT MY ***HANDS***, CAPTAIN—
I'M ALREADY WARMED UP.
Sliiide
SO I CAN KEEP GOING FOR ***HOURS***.
DANGER DAMES
. . .
JA, WELL, I SUPPOSE THAT IS THE BASIC PURPOSE OF A WARM-UP.

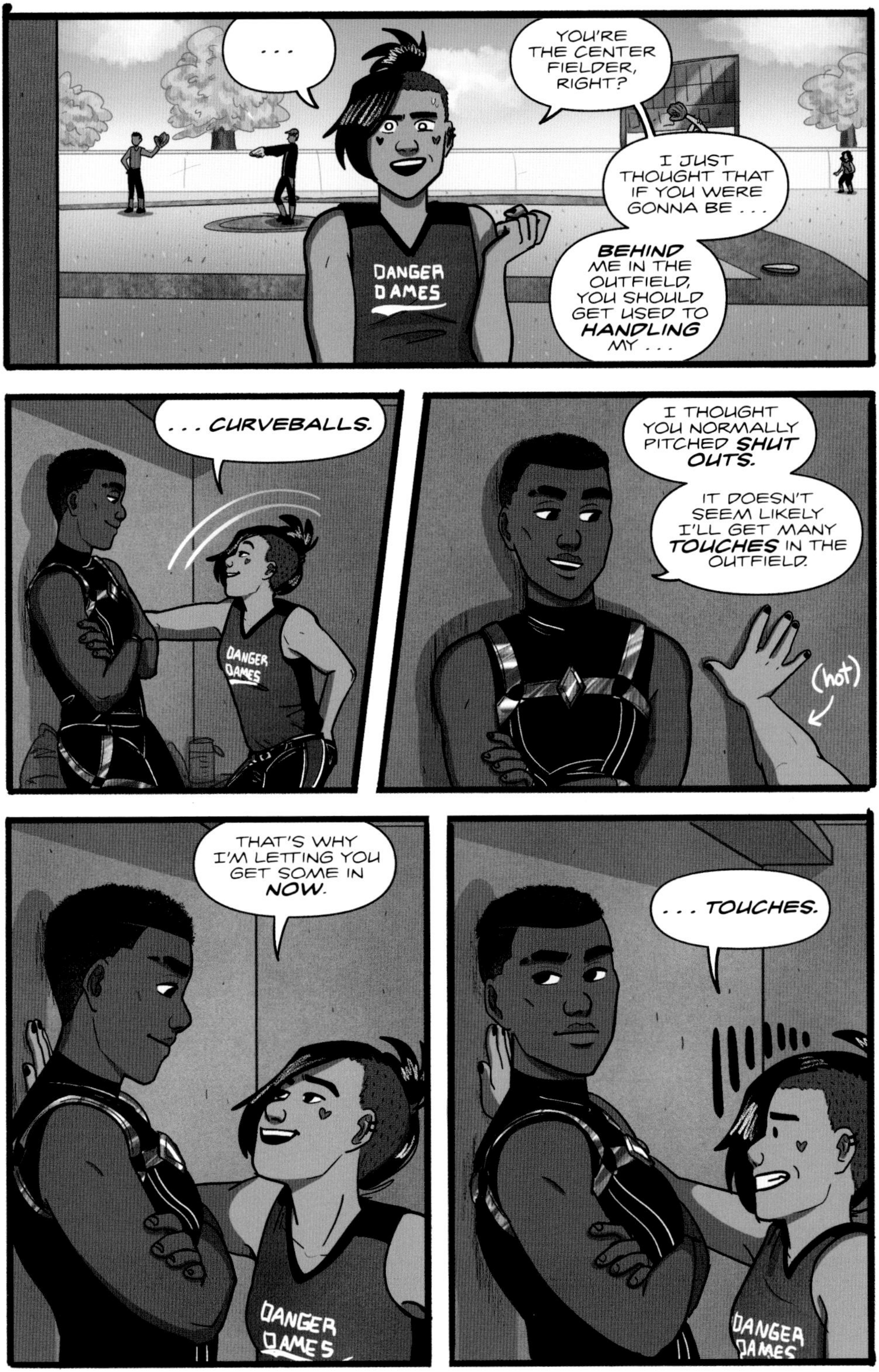
. . .
YOU'RE THE CENTER FIELDER, RIGHT?
I JUST THOUGHT THAT IF YOU WERE GONNA BE . . .
BEHIND ME IN THE OUTFIELD, YOU SHOULD GET USED TO HANDLING MY . . .
DANGER DAMES
. . . CURVEBALLS.
DANGER DAMES
I THOUGHT YOU NORMALLY PITCHED SHUT OUTS.
IT DOESN'T SEEM LIKELY I'LL GET MANY TOUCHES IN THE OUTFIELD.
(hot)
THAT'S WHY I'M LETTING YOU GET SOME IN NOW.
DANGER DAMES
. . . TOUCHES.
DANGER DAMES

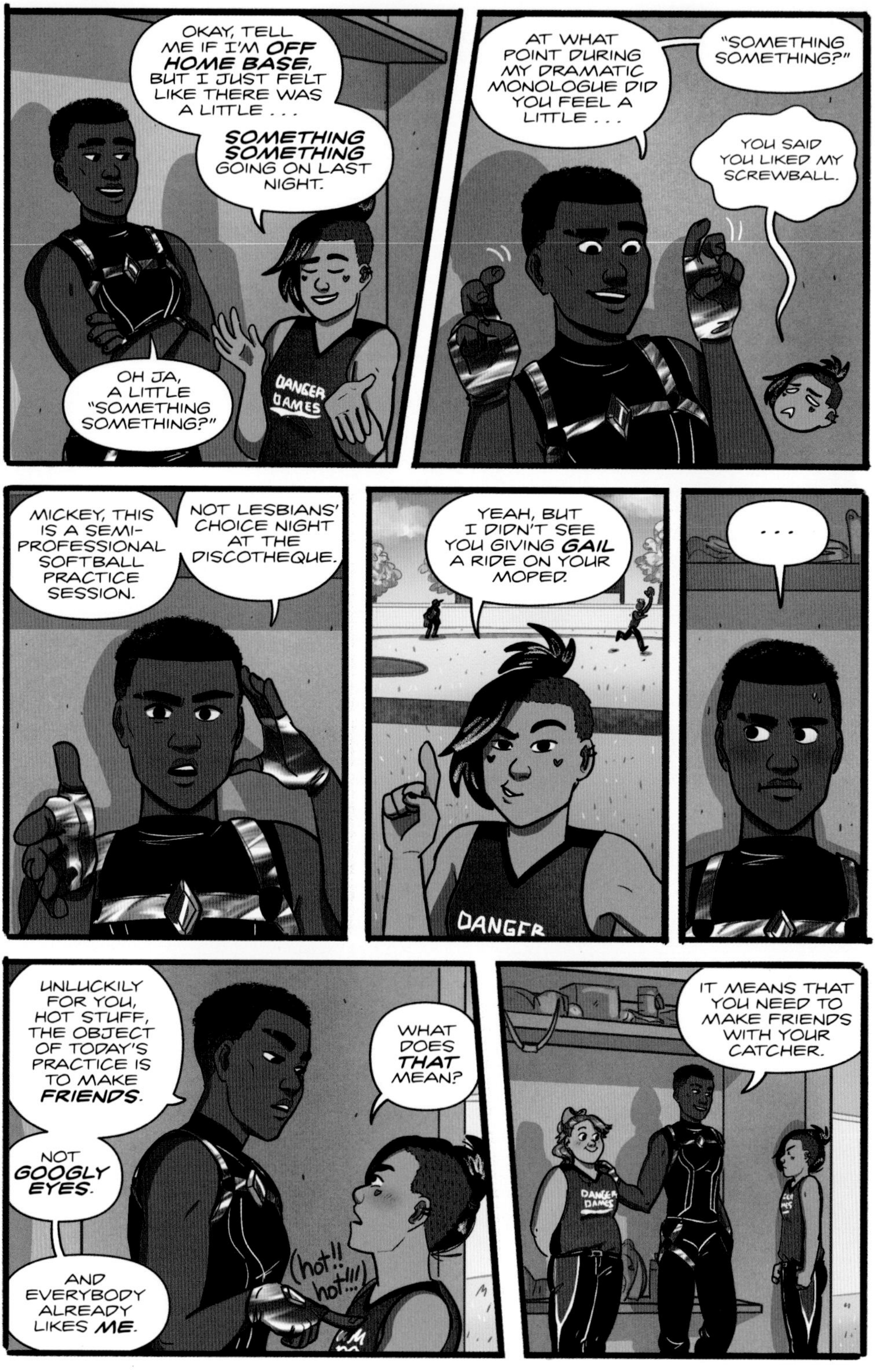
OKAY, TELL ME IF I'M ***OFF HOME BASE***, BUT I JUST FELT LIKE THERE WAS A LITTLE . . .
SOMETHING SOMETHING GOING ON LAST NIGHT.
OH JA, A LITTLE "SOMETHING SOMETHING?"
AT WHAT POINT DURING MY DRAMATIC MONOLOGUE DID YOU FEEL A LITTLE . . .
"SOMETHING SOMETHING?"
YOU SAID YOU LIKED MY SCREWBALL.
MICKEY, THIS IS A SEMI-PROFESSIONAL SOFTBALL PRACTICE SESSION.
NOT LESBIANS' CHOICE NIGHT AT THE DISCOTHEQUE.
YEAH, BUT I DIDN'T SEE YOU GIVING ***GAIL*** A RIDE ON YOUR MOPED.
. . .
UNLUCKILY FOR YOU, HOT STUFF, THE OBJECT OF TODAY'S PRACTICE IS TO MAKE ***FRIENDS***.
NOT ***GOOGLY EYES***.
AND EVERYBODY ALREADY LIKES ***ME***.
WHAT DOES ***THAT*** MEAN?
(hot!! hot!!!)
IT MEANS THAT YOU NEED TO MAKE FRIENDS WITH YOUR CATCHER.

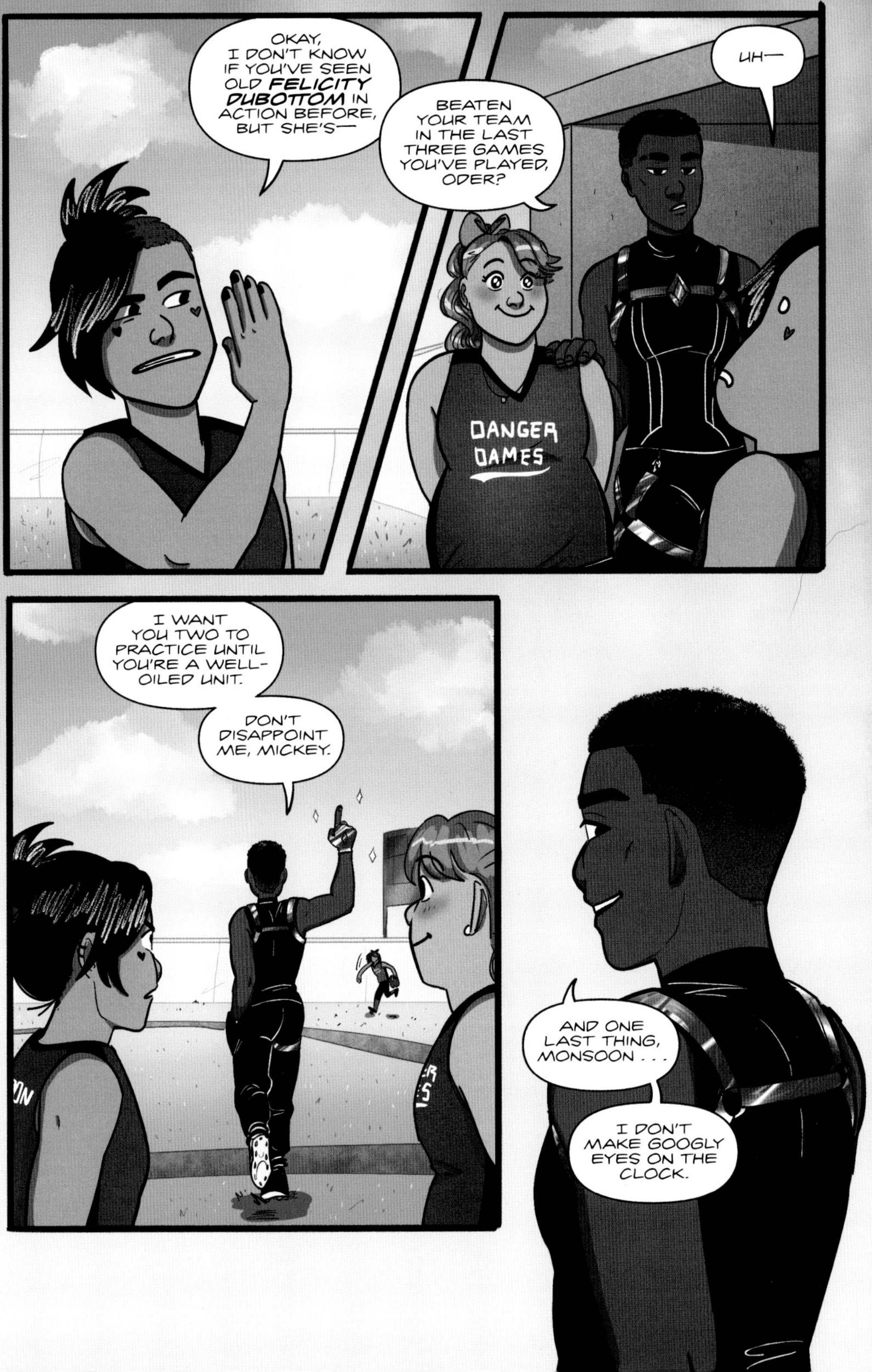
OKAY, I DON'T KNOW IF YOU'VE SEEN OLD **FELICITY DUBOTTOM** IN ACTION BEFORE, BUT SHE'S—
BEATEN YOUR TEAM IN THE LAST THREE GAMES YOU'VE PLAYED, ODER?
DANGER DAMES
UH—
I WANT YOU TWO TO PRACTICE UNTIL YOU'RE A WELL-OILED UNIT.
DON'T DISAPPOINT ME, MICKEY.
AND ONE LAST THING, MONSOON . . .
I DON'T MAKE GOOGLY EYES ON THE CLOCK.

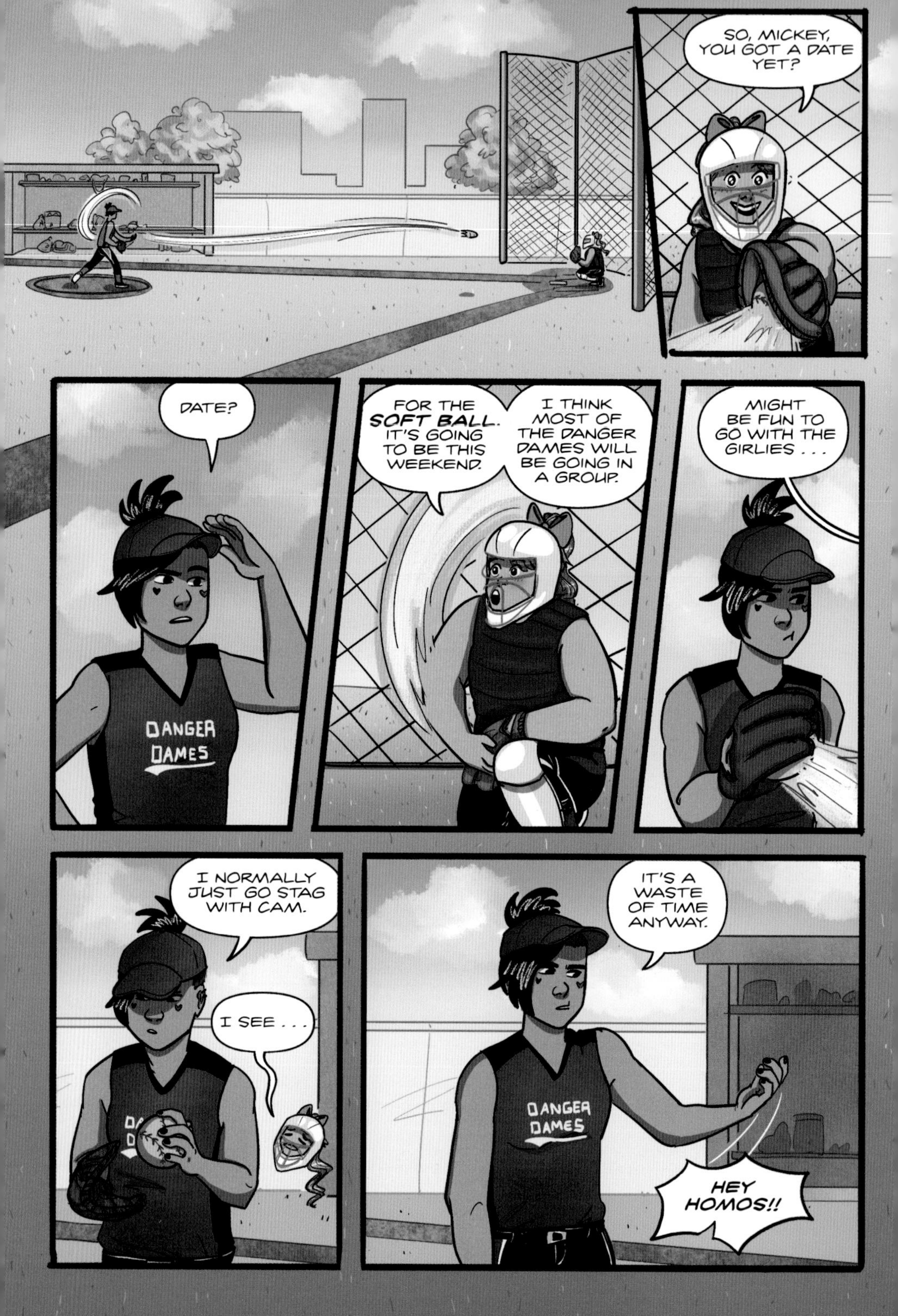
SO, MICKEY, YOU GOT A DATE YET?
DATE?
FOR THE SOFT BALL. IT'S GOING TO BE THIS WEEKEND.
I THINK MOST OF THE DANGER DAMES WILL BE GOING IN A GROUP.
DANGER DAMES
MIGHT BE FUN TO GO WITH THE GIRLIES . . .
I NORMALLY JUST GO STAG WITH CAM.
I SEE . . .
IT'S A WASTE OF TIME ANYWAY.
DANGER DAMES
HEY HOMOS!!

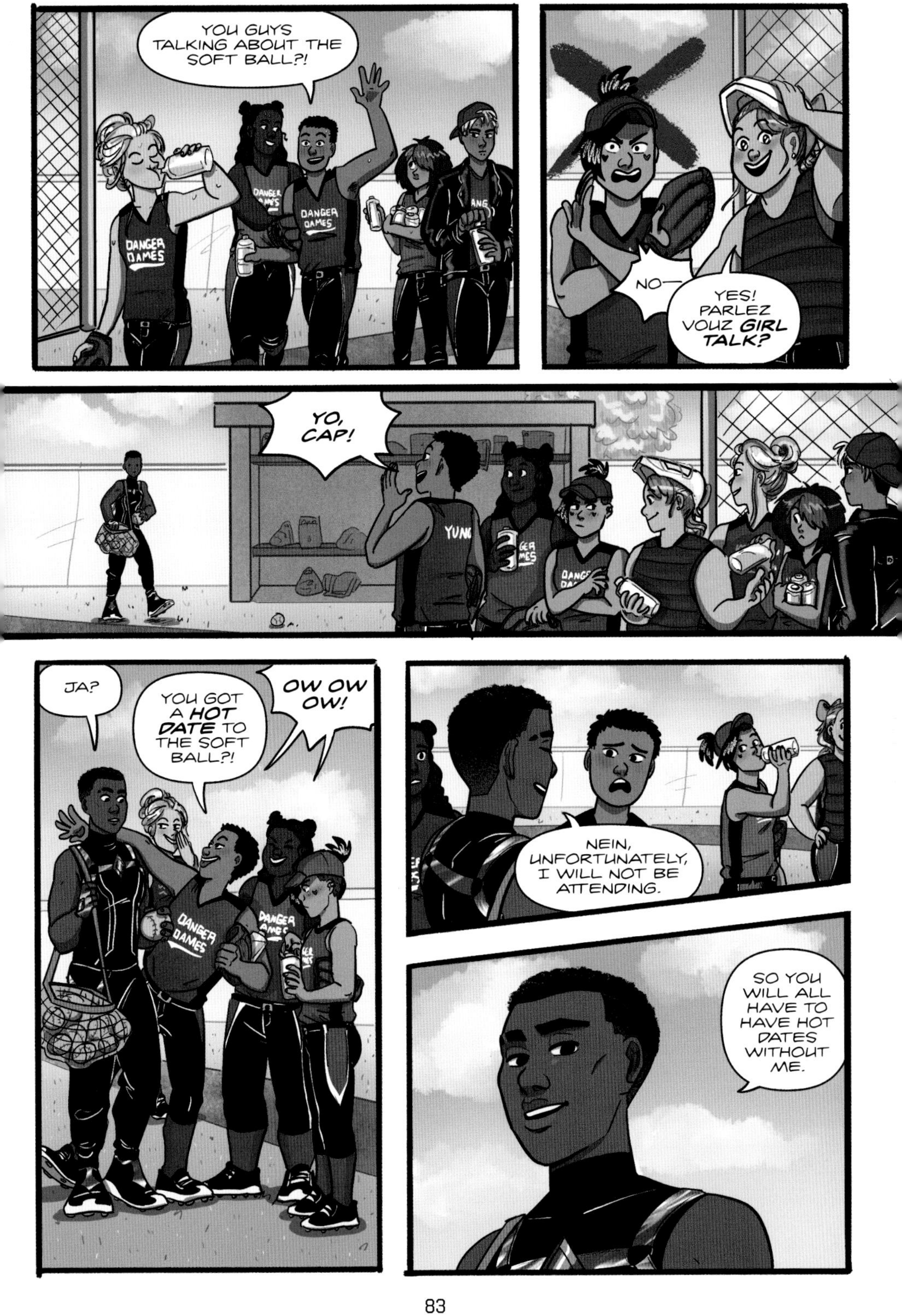
YOU GUYS TALKING ABOUT THE SOFT BALL?!
DANGER DAMES
NO—
YES! PARLEZ VOUZ **GIRL TALK?**
YO, CAP!
YUNG
JA?
YOU GOT A **HOT DATE** TO THE SOFT BALL?!
OW OW OW!
DANGER DAMES
NEIN, UNFORTUNATELY, I WILL NOT BE ATTENDING.
SO YOU WILL ALL HAVE TO HAVE HOT DATES WITHOUT ME.

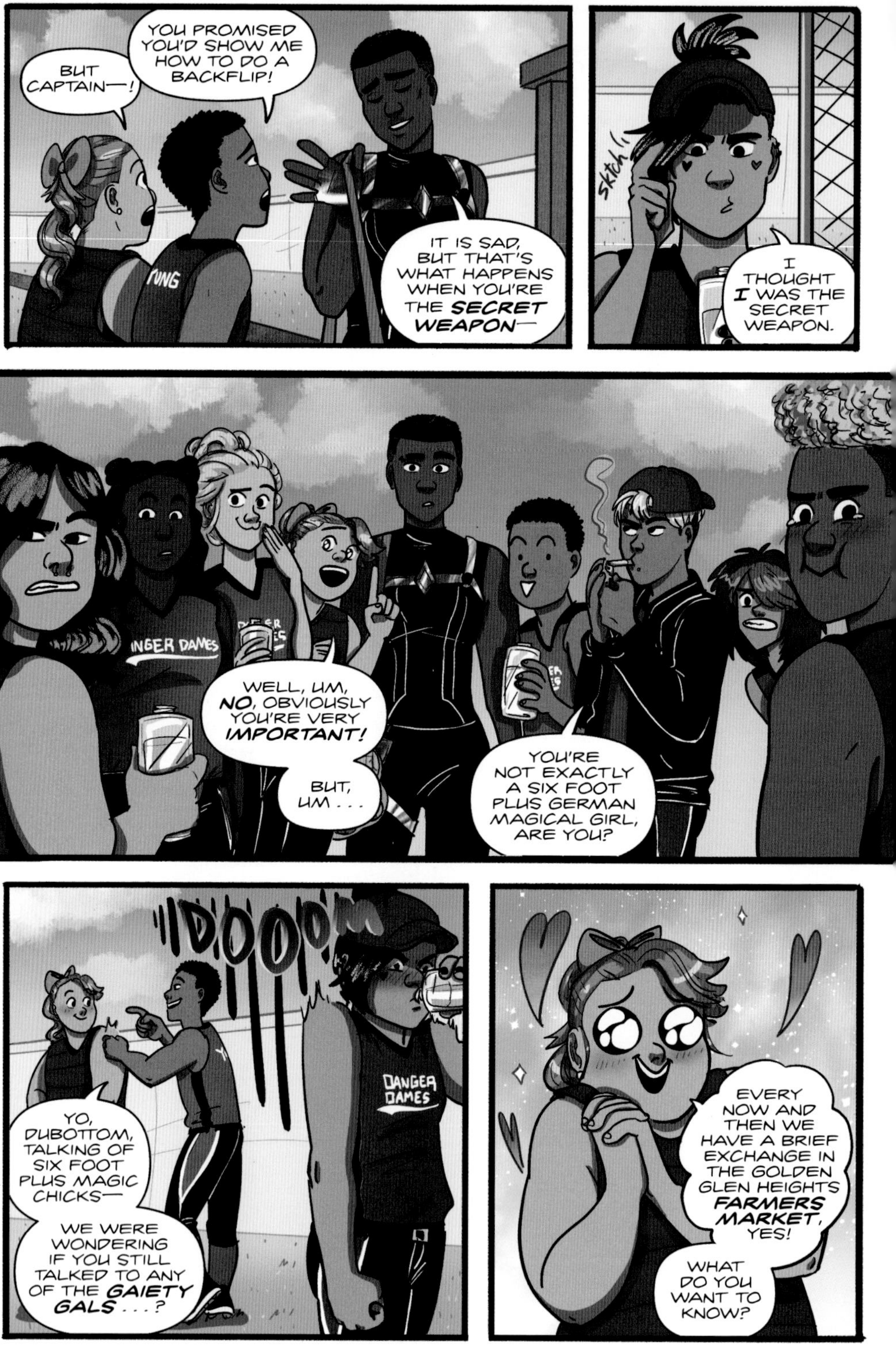
BUT CAPTAIN—!
YOU PROMISED YOU'D SHOW ME HOW TO DO A BACKFLIP!
IT IS SAD, BUT THAT'S WHAT HAPPENS WHEN YOU'RE THE *SECRET WEAPON*—
sktch
I THOUGHT *I* WAS THE SECRET WEAPON.
WELL, UM, *NO*, OBVIOUSLY YOU'RE VERY *IMPORTANT!*
BUT, UM . . .
YOU'RE NOT EXACTLY A SIX FOOT PLUS GERMAN MAGICAL GIRL, ARE YOU?
DOOOM
YO, DUBOTTOM, TALKING OF SIX FOOT PLUS MAGIC CHICKS—
WE WERE WONDERING IF YOU STILL TALKED TO ANY OF THE *GAIETY GALS* . . . ?
EVERY NOW AND THEN WE HAVE A BRIEF EXCHANGE IN THE GOLDEN GLEN HEIGHTS *FARMERS MARKET*, YES!
WHAT DO YOU WANT TO KNOW?

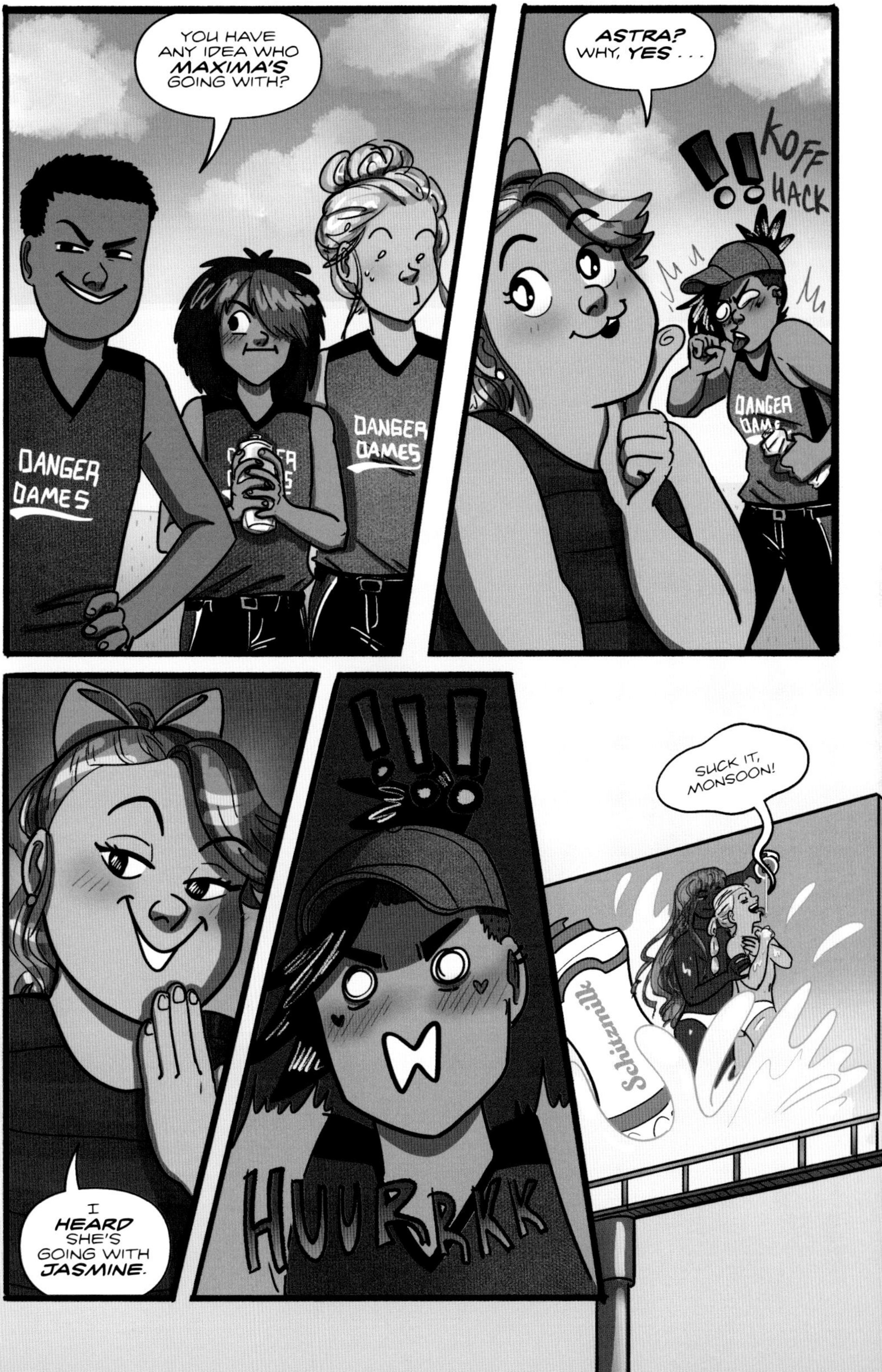
YOU HAVE ANY IDEA WHO MAXIMA'S GOING WITH?
DANGER DAMES
DANGER DAMES
ASTRA? WHY, YES . . .
!!
KOFF HACK
DANGER DAMES
I HEARD SHE'S GOING WITH JASMINE.
!!!
HUURRKK
SUCK IT, MONSOON!
Schitzmilk

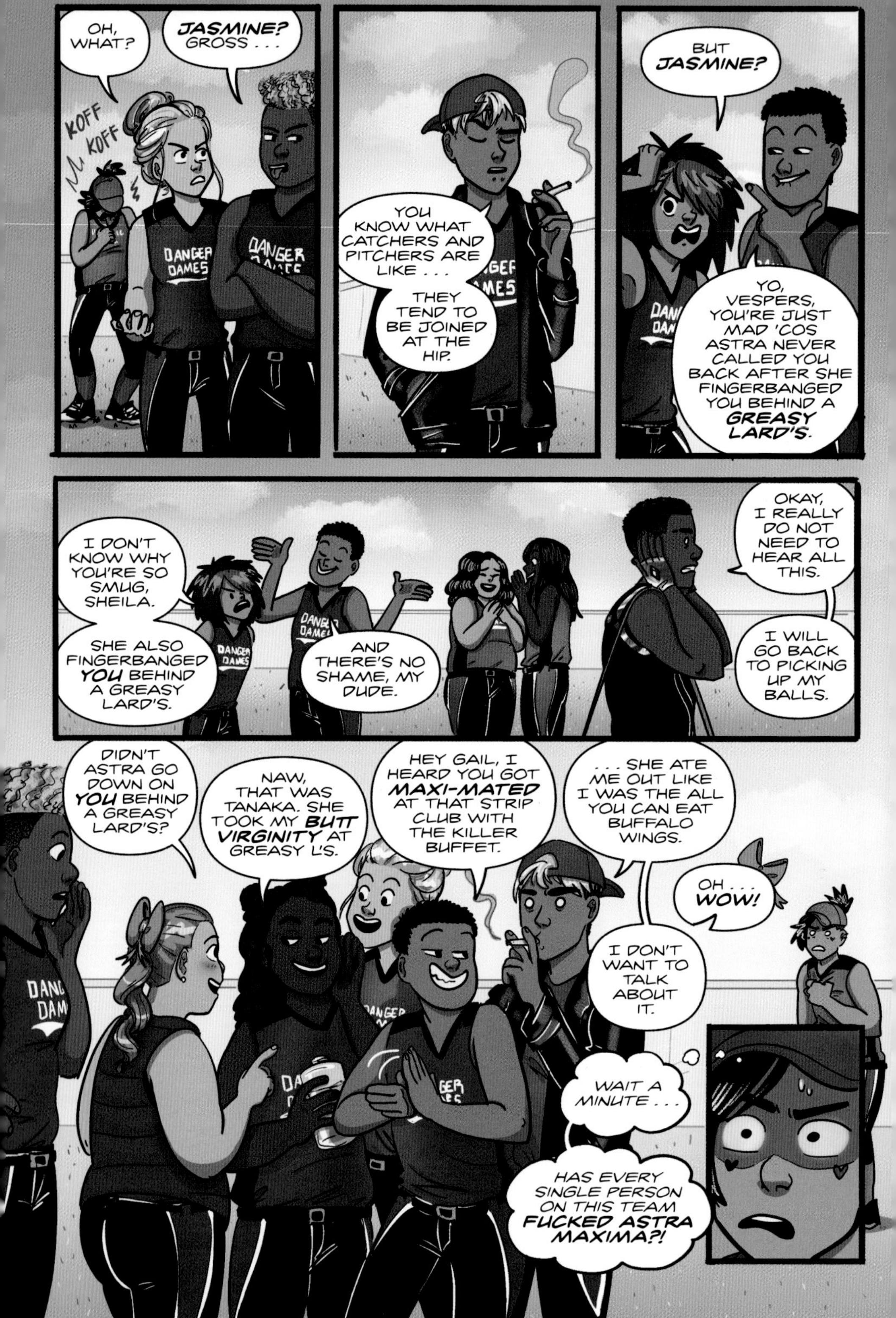
OH, WHAT?
JASMINE? GROSS . . .
KOFF KOFF
YOU KNOW WHAT CATCHERS AND PITCHERS ARE LIKE . . .
THEY TEND TO BE JOINED AT THE HIP.
BUT JASMINE?
YO, VESPERS, YOU'RE JUST MAD 'COS ASTRA NEVER CALLED YOU BACK AFTER SHE FINGERBANGED YOU BEHIND A GREASY LARD'S.
I DON'T KNOW WHY YOU'RE SO SMUG, SHEILA.
SHE ALSO FINGERBANGED YOU BEHIND A GREASY LARD'S.
AND THERE'S NO SHAME, MY DUDE.
OKAY, I REALLY DO NOT NEED TO HEAR ALL THIS.
I WILL GO BACK TO PICKING UP MY BALLS.
DIDN'T ASTRA GO DOWN ON YOU BEHIND A GREASY LARD'S?
NAW, THAT WAS TANAKA. SHE TOOK MY BUTT VIRGINITY AT GREASY L'S.
HEY GAIL, I HEARD YOU GOT MAXI-MATED AT THAT STRIP CLUB WITH THE KILLER BUFFET.
. . . SHE ATE ME OUT LIKE I WAS THE ALL YOU CAN EAT BUFFALO WINGS.
I DON'T WANT TO TALK ABOUT IT.
OH . . . WOW!
WAIT A MINUTE . . .
HAS EVERY SINGLE PERSON ON THIS TEAM FUCKED ASTRA MAXIMA?!

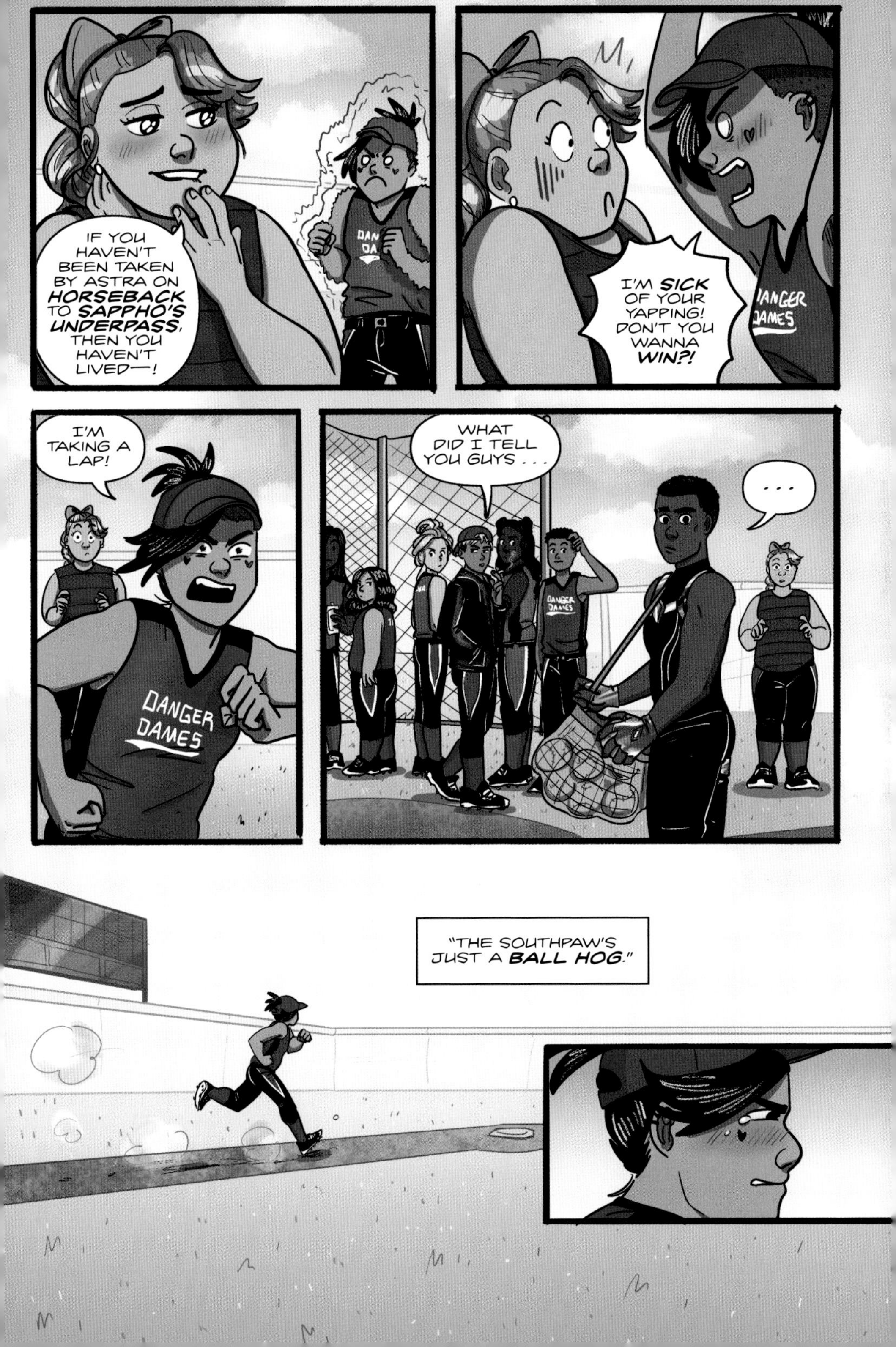
IF YOU HAVEN'T BEEN TAKEN BY ASTRA ON **HORSEBACK** TO **SAPPHO'S UNDERPASS**, THEN YOU HAVEN'T LIVED—!
DANGER DAMES
I'M **SICK** OF YOUR YAPPING! DON'T YOU WANNA **WIN?!**
I'M TAKING A LAP!
DANGER DAMES
WHAT DID I TELL YOU GUYS . . .
DANGER DAMES
. . .
"THE SOUTHPAW'S JUST A **BALL HOG**."

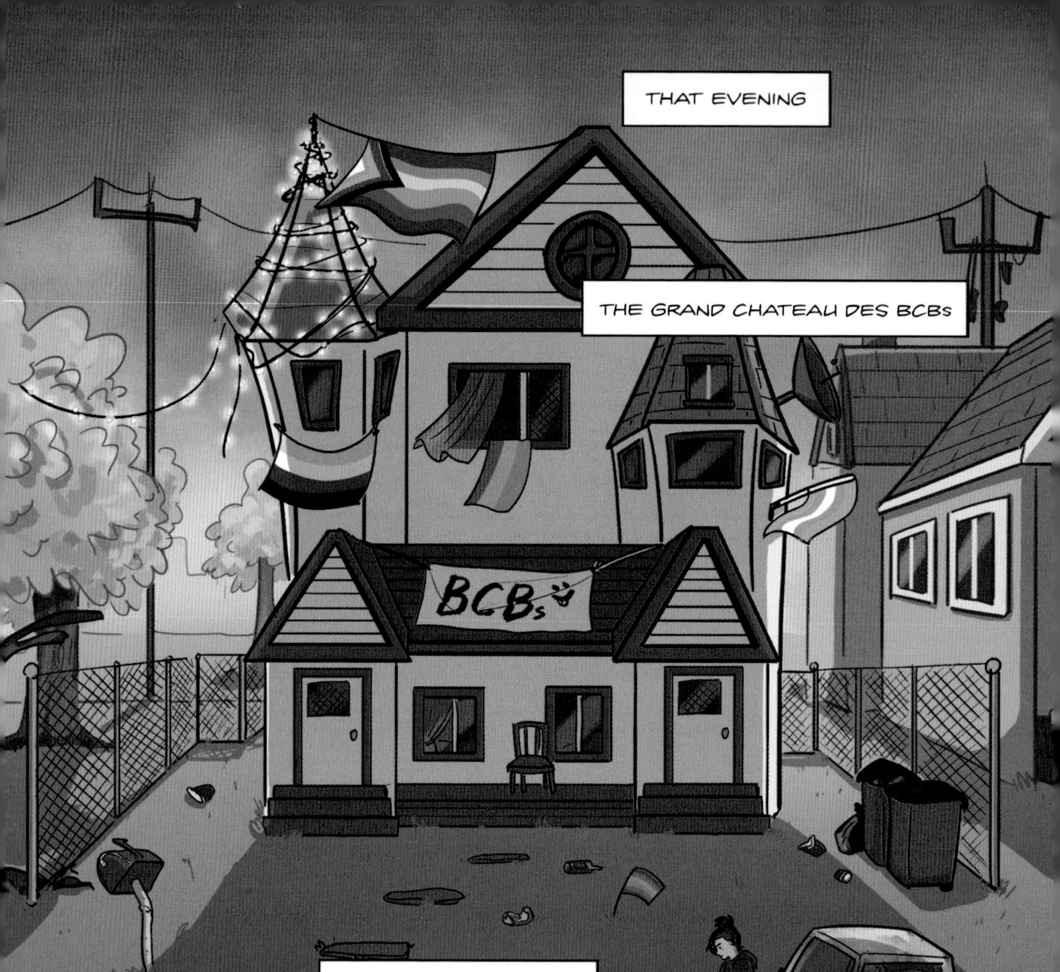
THAT EVENING
THE GRAND CHATEAU DES BCBs
BCBs
(CAM, FLO, BETH AND DUSTY'S PLACE)

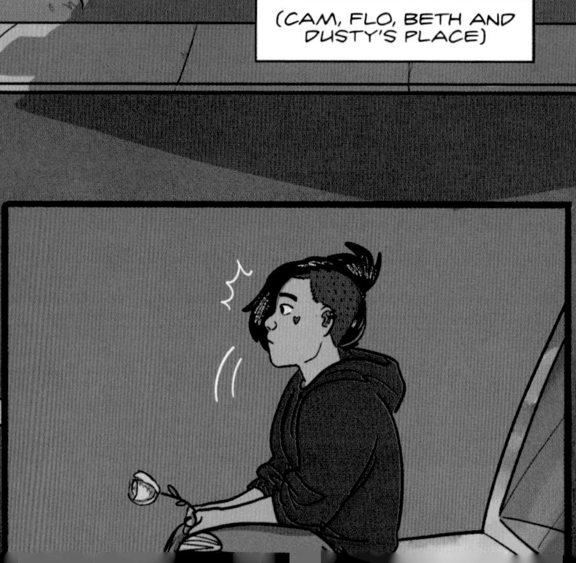

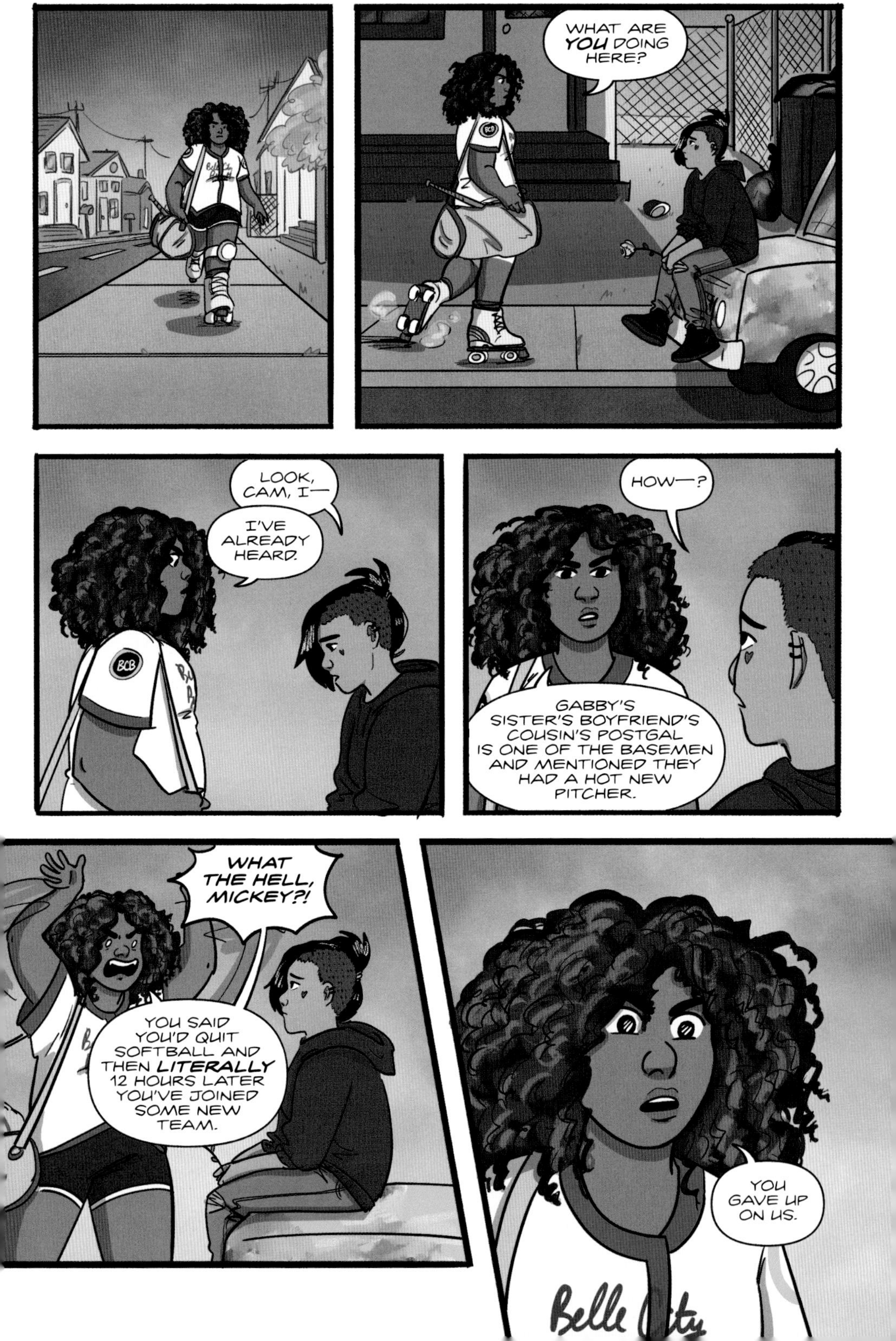
WHAT ARE YOU DOING HERE?
LOOK, CAM, I—
I'VE ALREADY HEARD.
HOW—?
GABBY'S SISTER'S BOYFRIEND'S COUSIN'S POSTGAL IS ONE OF THE BASEMEN AND MENTIONED THEY HAD A HOT NEW PITCHER.
WHAT THE HELL, MICKEY?!
YOU SAID YOU'D QUIT SOFTBALL AND THEN LITERALLY 12 HOURS LATER YOU'VE JOINED SOME NEW TEAM.
YOU GAVE UP ON US.

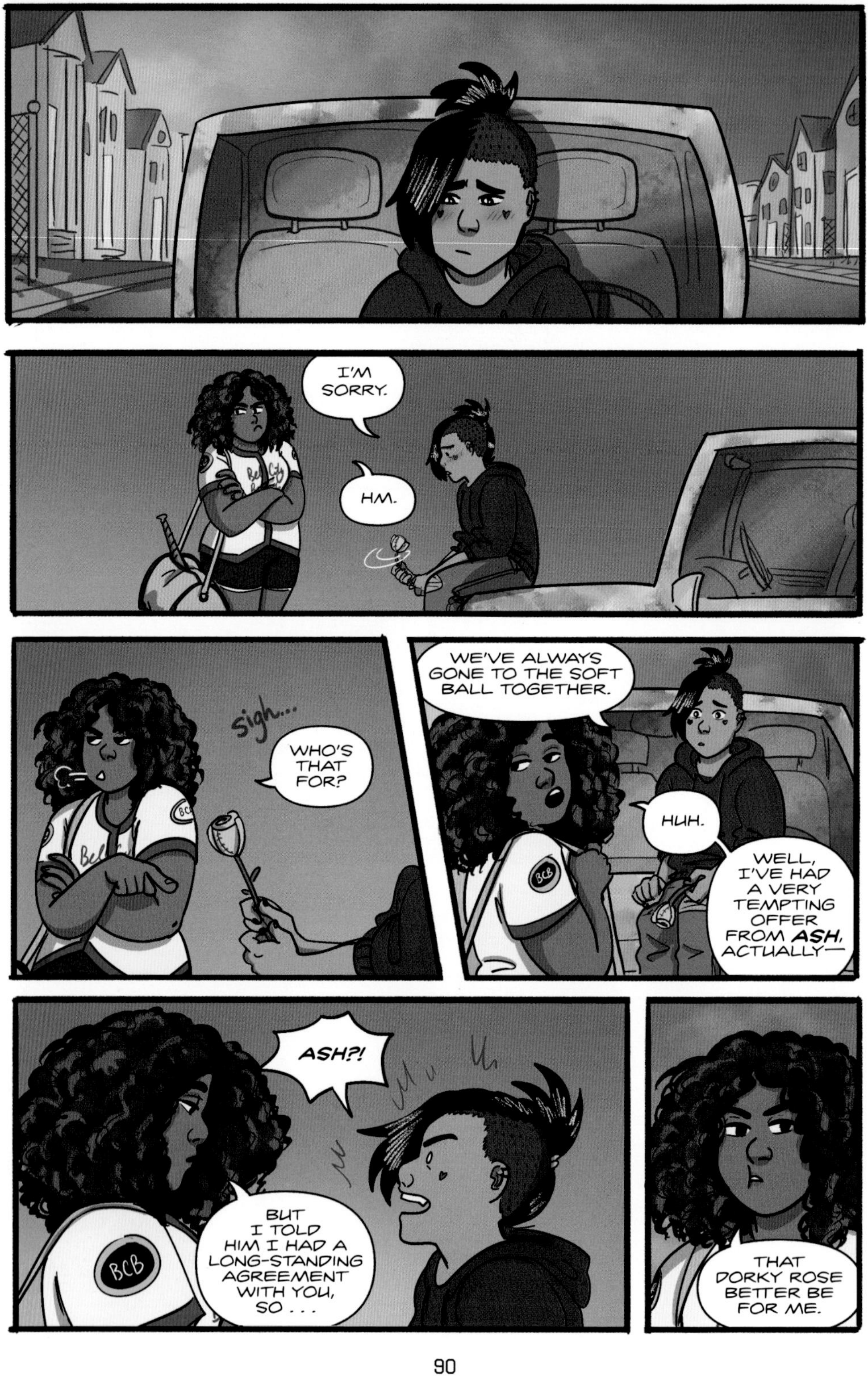
I'M SORRY.
HM.
sigh...
WHO'S THAT FOR?
WE'VE ALWAYS GONE TO THE SOFT BALL TOGETHER.
HUH.
WELL, I'VE HAD A VERY TEMPTING OFFER FROM ASH, ACTUALLY—
ASH?!
BUT I TOLD HIM I HAD A LONG-STANDING AGREEMENT WITH YOU, SO . . .
THAT DORKY ROSE BETTER BE FOR ME.

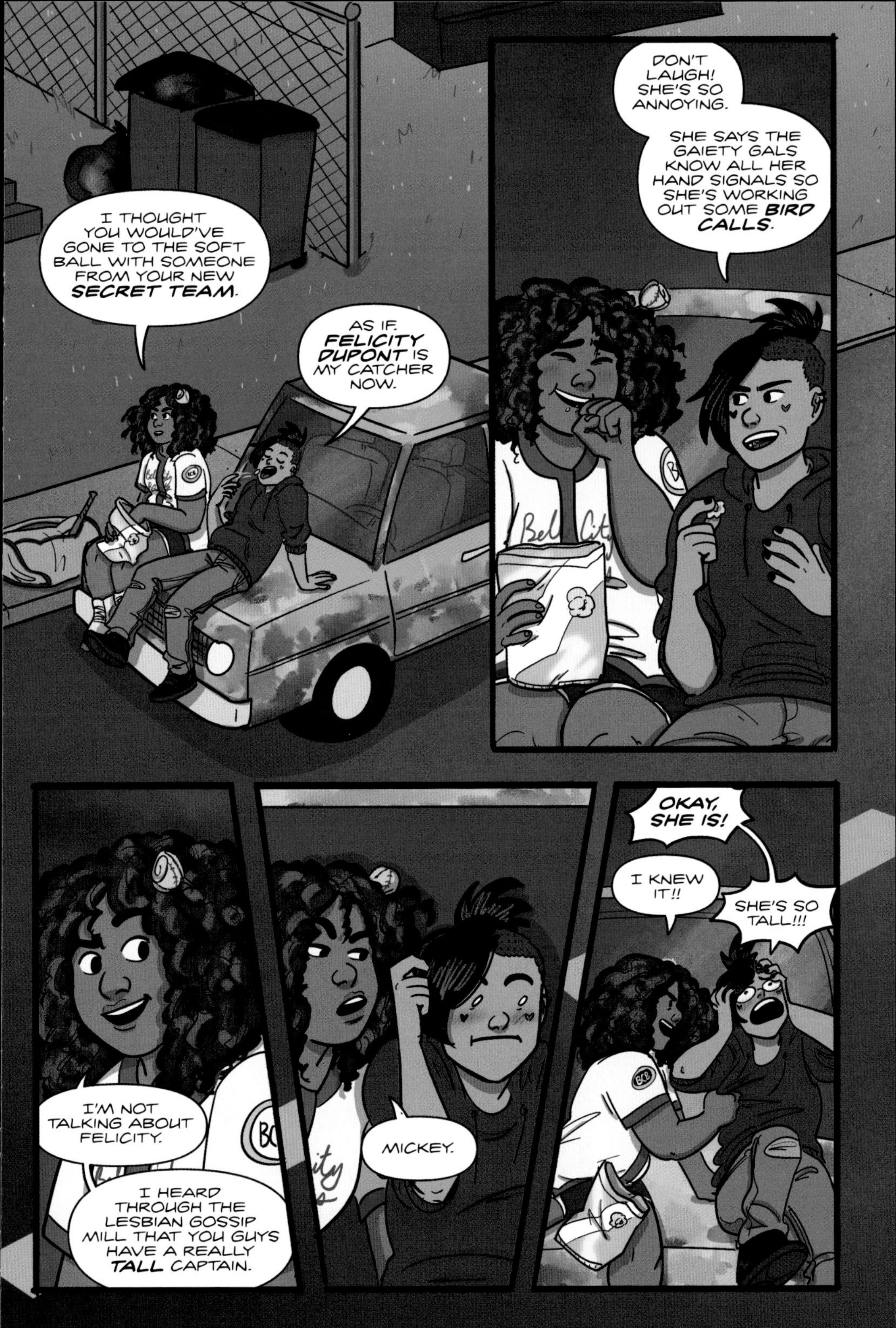
I THOUGHT YOU WOULD'VE GONE TO THE SOFT BALL WITH SOMEONE FROM YOUR NEW **SECRET TEAM**.
AS IF. **FELICITY DUPONT** IS MY CATCHER NOW.
DON'T LAUGH! SHE'S SO ANNOYING.
SHE SAYS THE GAIETY GALS KNOW ALL HER HAND SIGNALS SO SHE'S WORKING OUT SOME **BIRD CALLS**.
I'M NOT TALKING ABOUT FELICITY.
I HEARD THROUGH THE LESBIAN GOSSIP MILL THAT YOU GUYS HAVE A REALLY **TALL** CAPTAIN.
MICKEY.
OKAY, SHE IS!
I KNEW IT!!
SHE'S SO TALL!!!

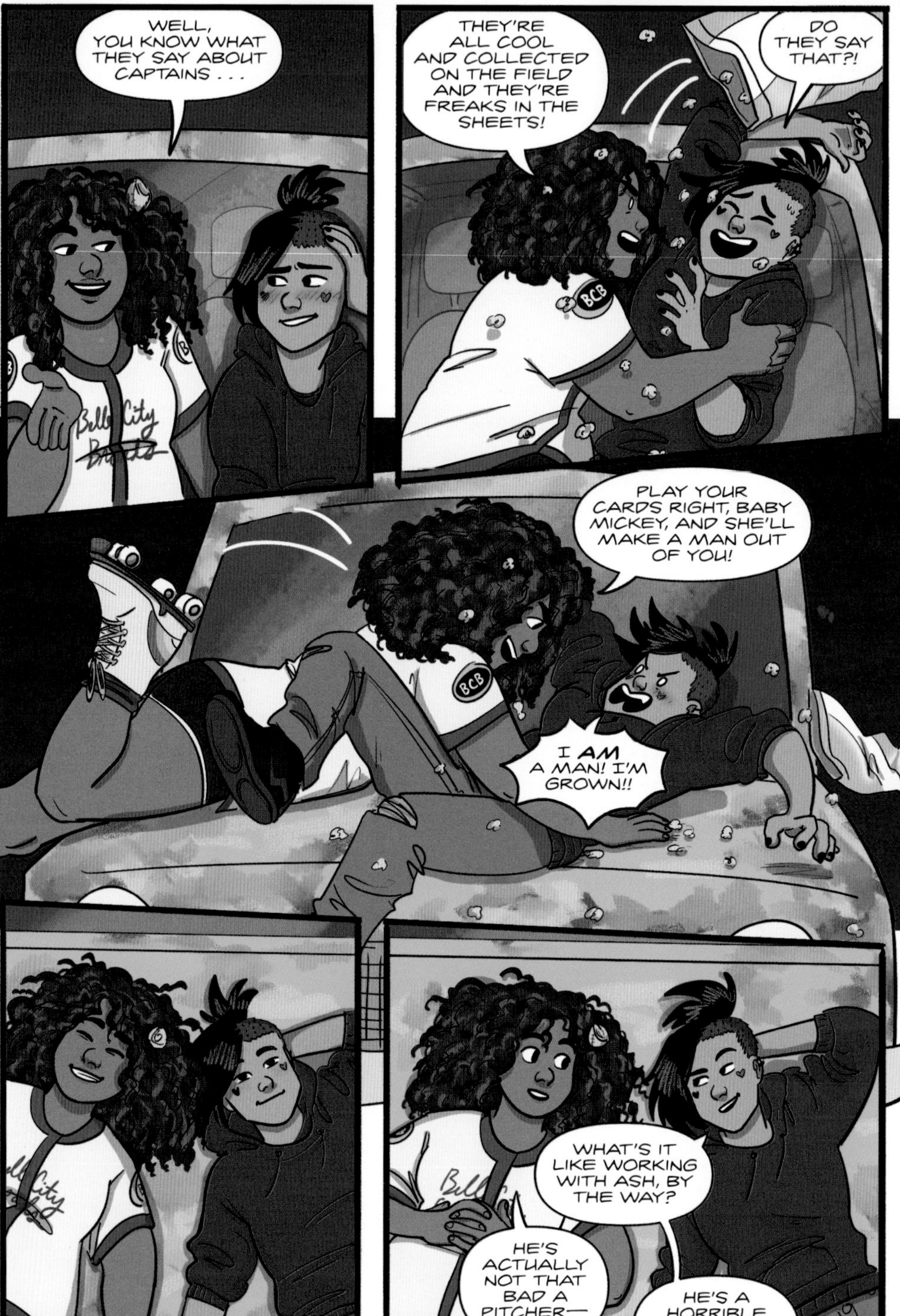

WELL, YOU KNOW WHAT THEY SAY ABOUT CAPTAINS . . .
THEY'RE ALL COOL AND COLLECTED ON THE FIELD AND THEY'RE FREAKS IN THE SHEETS!
DO THEY SAY THAT?!
PLAY YOUR CARDS RIGHT, BABY MICKEY, AND SHE'LL MAKE A MAN OUT OF YOU!
I **AM** A MAN! I'M GROWN!!
WHAT'S IT LIKE WORKING WITH ASH, BY THE WAY?
HE'S ACTUALLY NOT THAT BAD A PITCHER—
HE'S A HORRIBLE PITCHER, YOU'RE JUST ***GAY!***

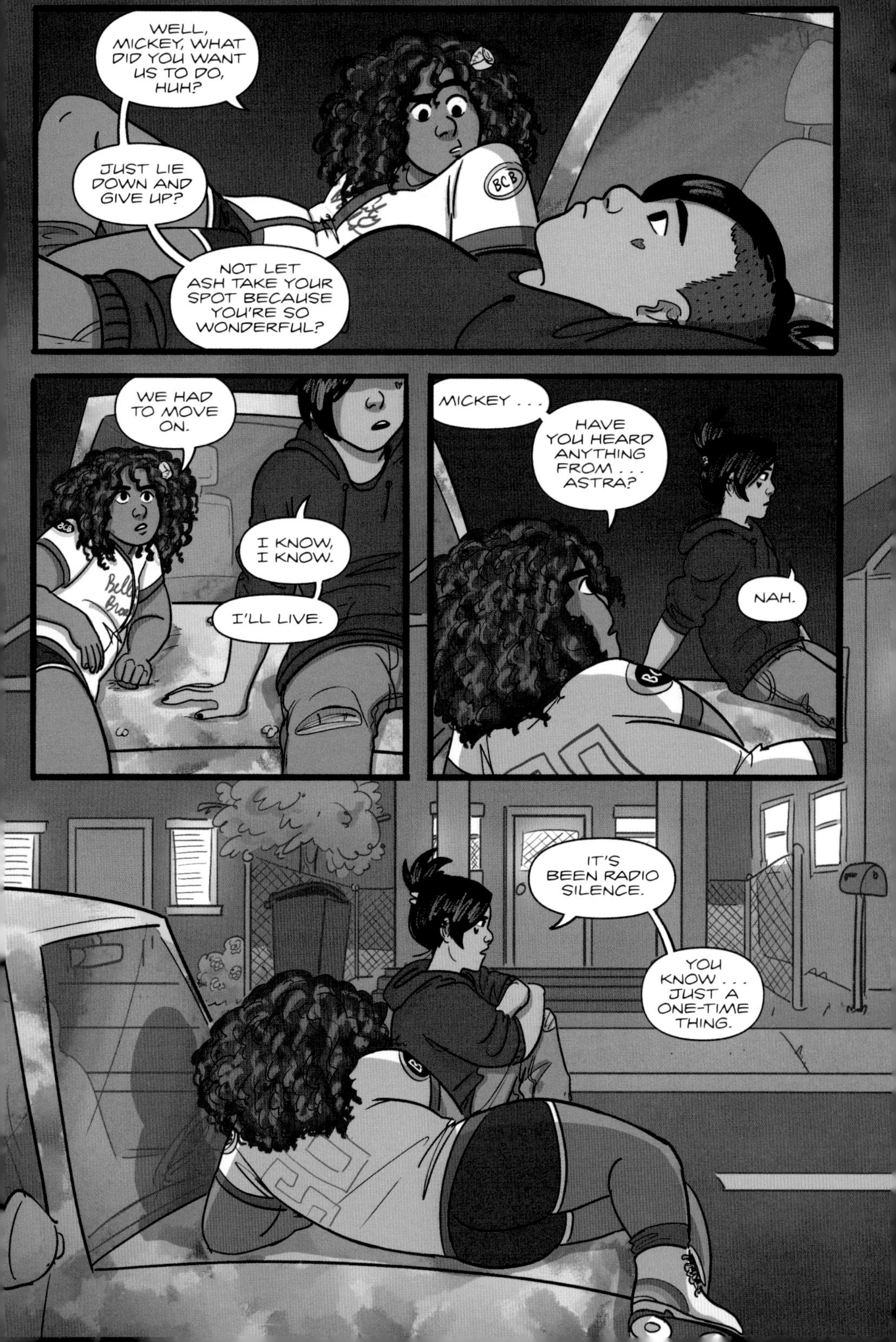
WELL, MICKEY, WHAT DID YOU WANT US TO DO, HUH?
JUST LIE DOWN AND GIVE UP?
NOT LET ASH TAKE YOUR SPOT BECAUSE YOU'RE SO WONDERFUL?
WE HAD TO MOVE ON.
I KNOW, I KNOW.
I'LL LIVE.
MICKEY . . .
HAVE YOU HEARD ANYTHING FROM . . . ASTRA?
NAH.
IT'S BEEN RADIO SILENCE.
YOU KNOW . . . JUST A ONE-TIME THING.

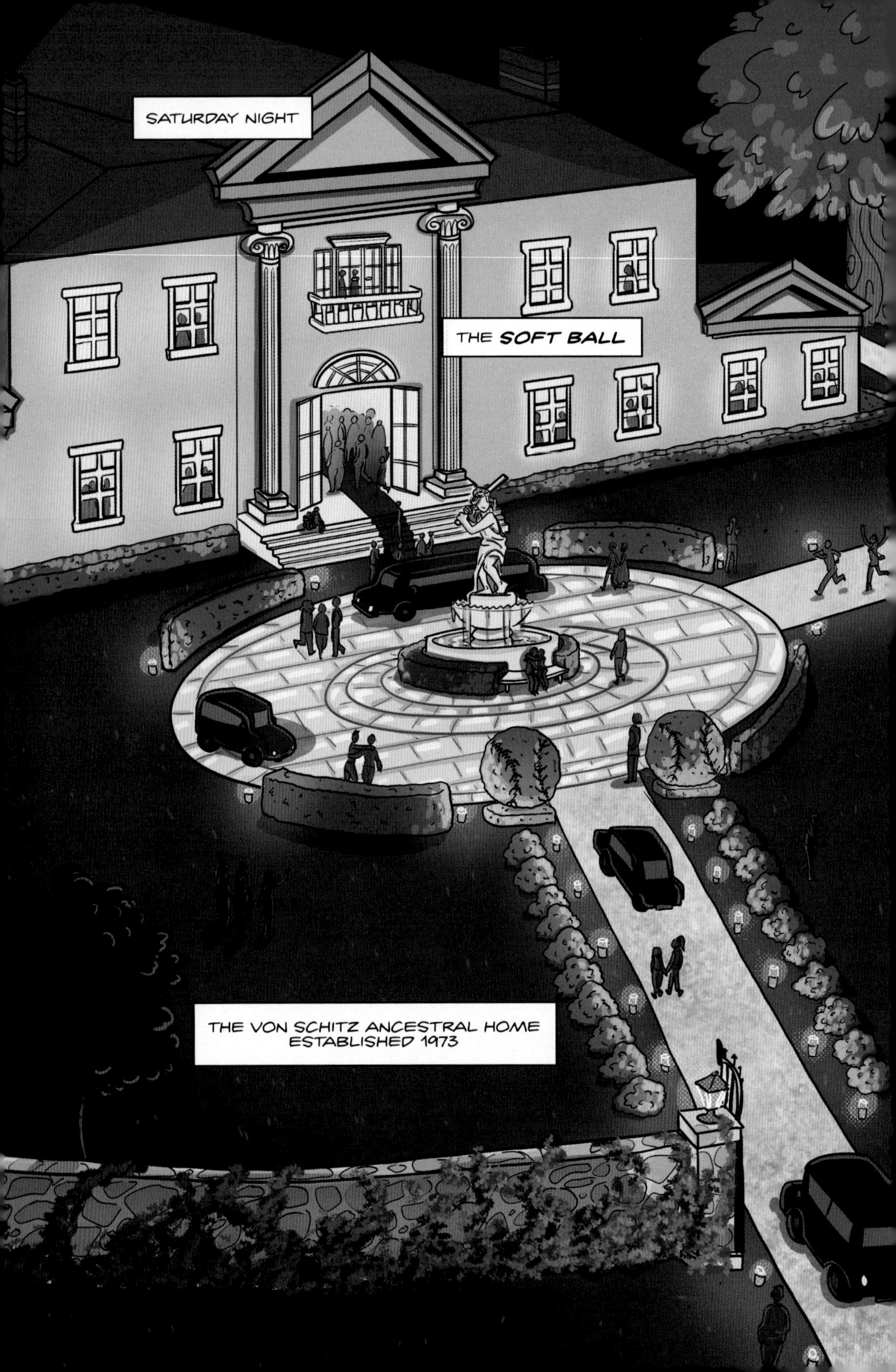
SATURDAY NIGHT
THE *SOFT BALL*
THE VON SCHITZ ANCESTRAL HOME
ESTABLISHED 1973

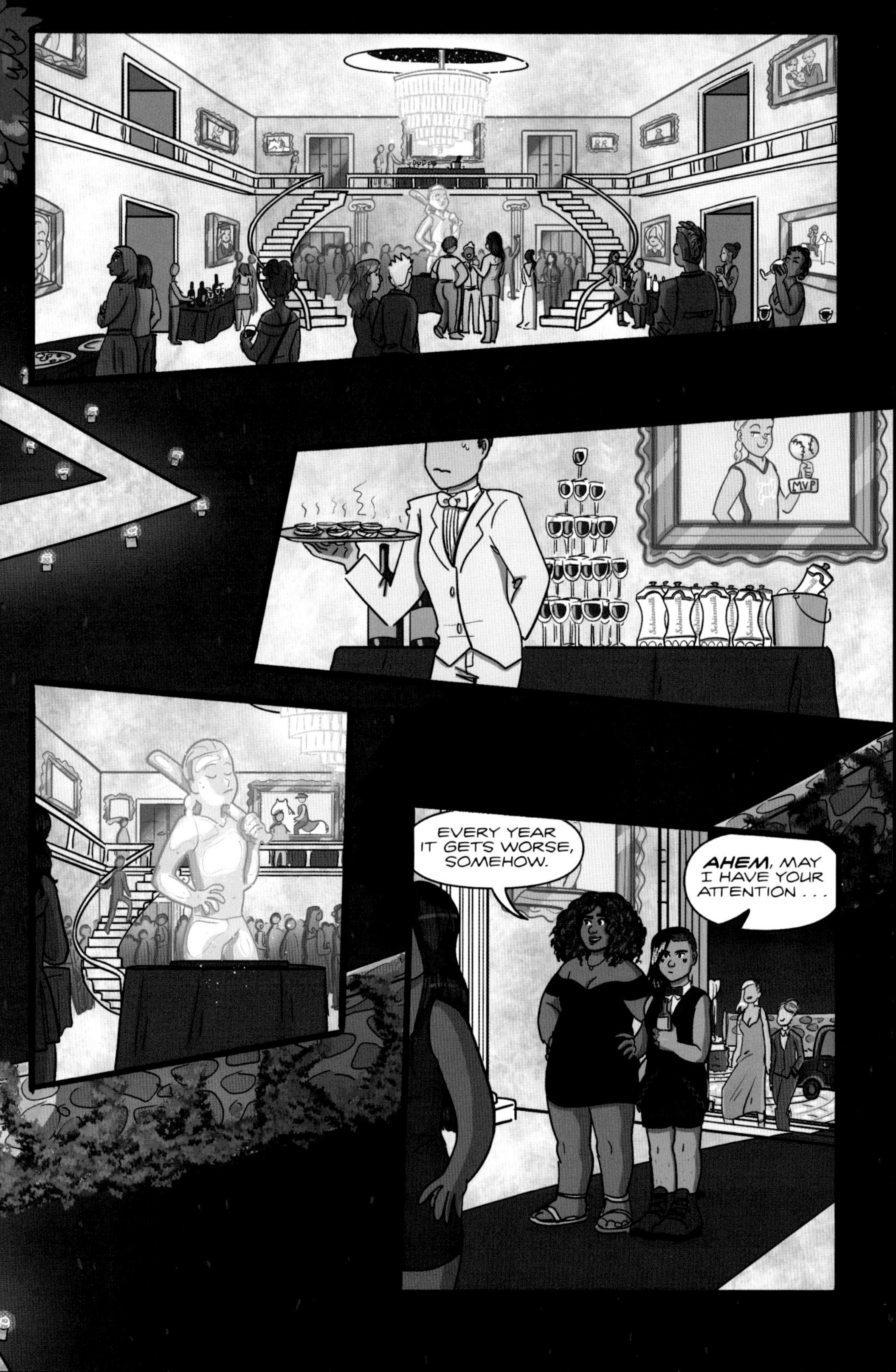
MVP
Schitzmilk
EVERY YEAR IT GETS WORSE, SOMEHOW.
AHEM, MAY I HAVE YOUR ATTENTION . . .

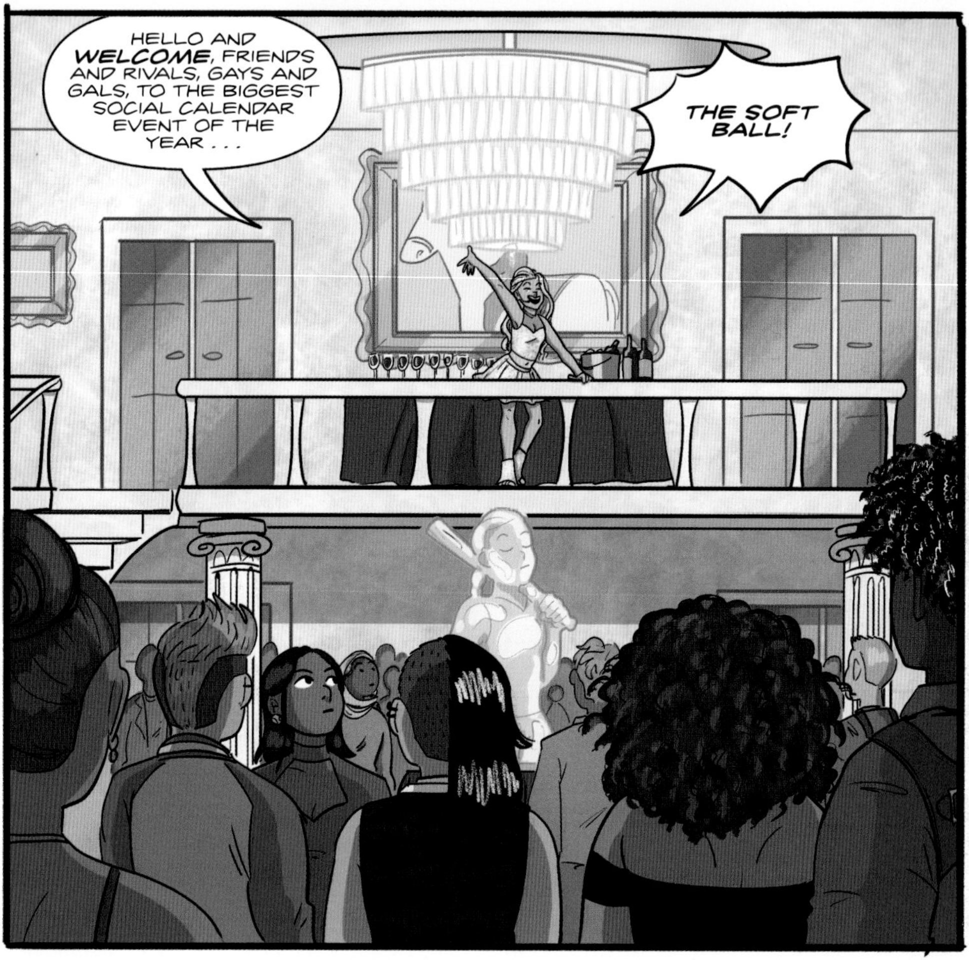
HELLO AND **WELCOME**, FRIENDS AND RIVALS, GAYS AND GALS, TO THE BIGGEST SOCIAL CALENDAR EVENT OF THE YEAR . . .
THE SOFT BALL!

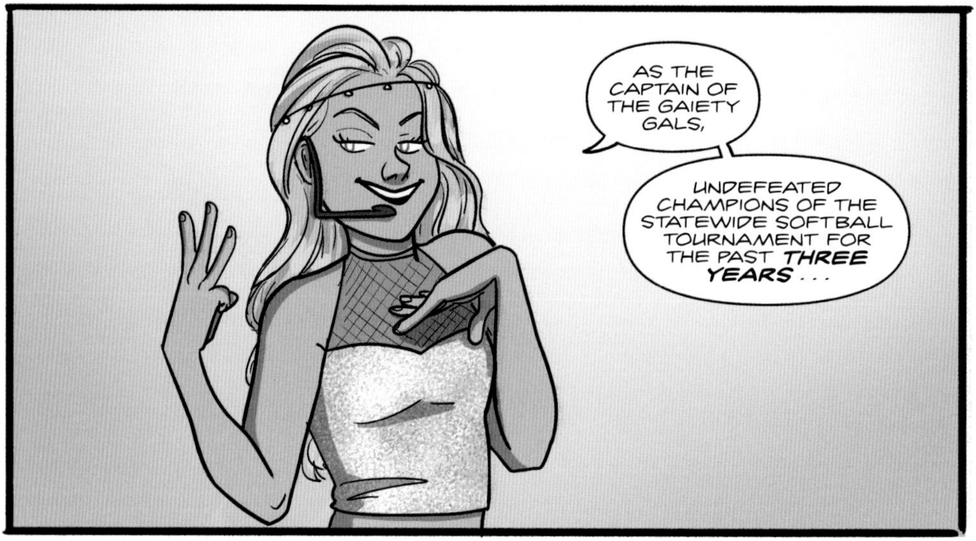
AS THE CAPTAIN OF THE GAIETY GALS,
UNDEFEATED CHAMPIONS OF THE STATEWIDE SOFTBALL TOURNAMENT FOR THE PAST ***THREE YEARS*** . . .

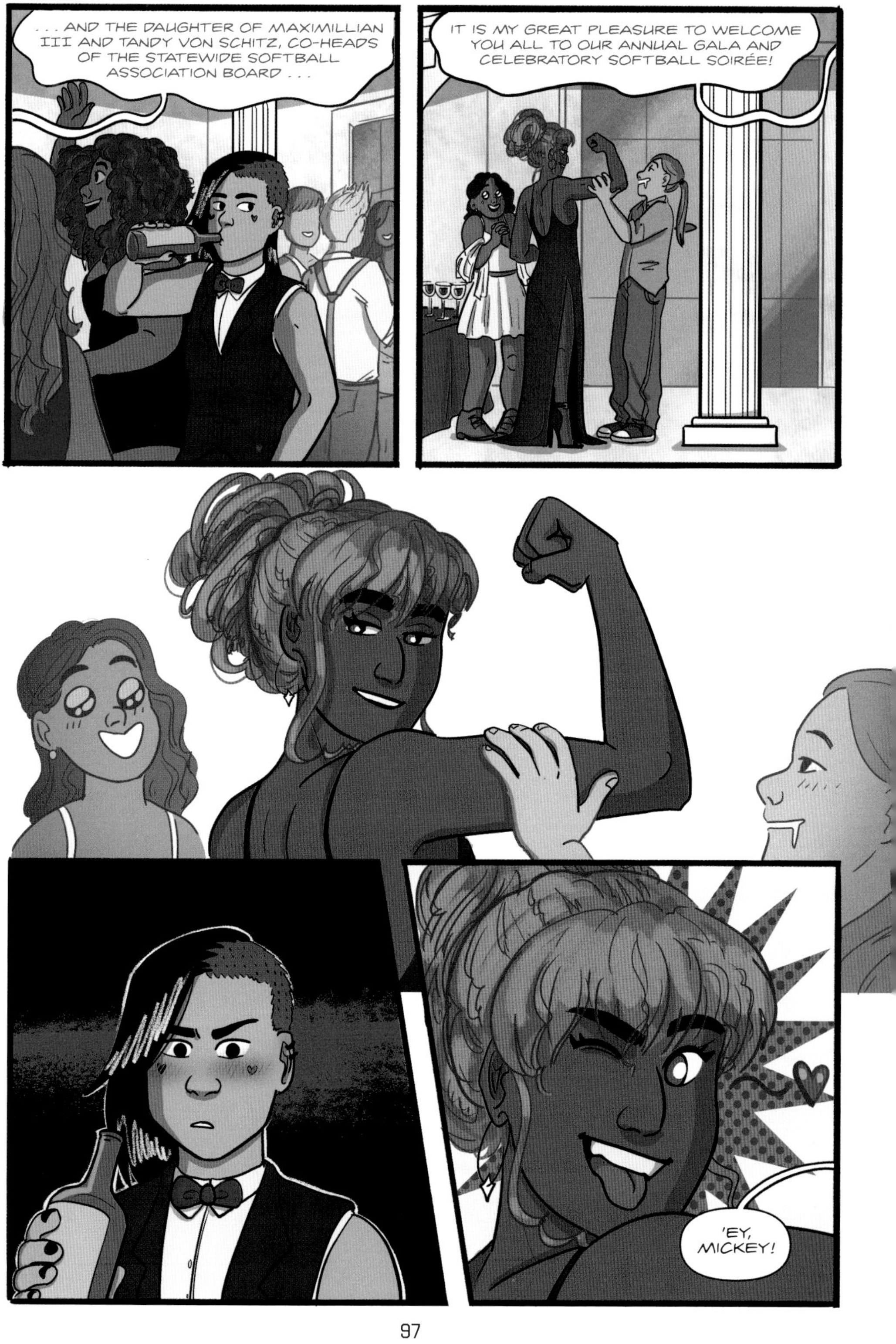
. . . AND THE DAUGHTER OF MAXIMILLIAN III AND TANDY VON SCHITZ, CO-HEADS OF THE STATEWIDE SOFTBALL ASSOCIATION BOARD . . .
IT IS MY GREAT PLEASURE TO WELCOME YOU ALL TO OUR ANNUAL GALA AND CELEBRATORY SOFTBALL SOIRÉE!
'EY, MICKEY!

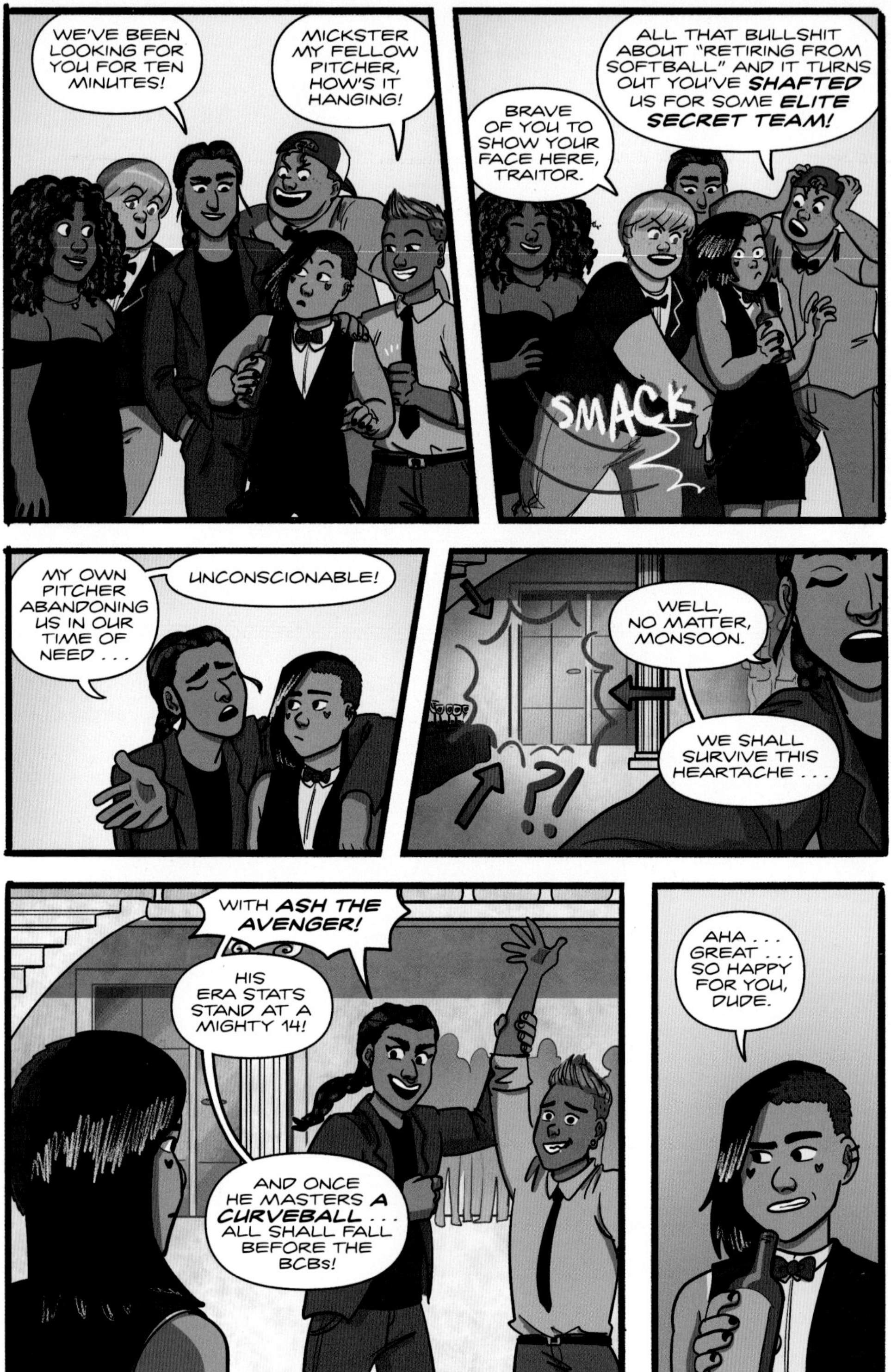
WE'VE BEEN LOOKING FOR YOU FOR TEN MINUTES!
MICKSTER MY FELLOW PITCHER, HOW'S IT HANGING!
BRAVE OF YOU TO SHOW YOUR FACE HERE, TRAITOR.
ALL THAT BULLSHIT ABOUT "RETIRING FROM SOFTBALL" AND IT TURNS OUT YOU'VE SHAFTED US FOR SOME ELITE SECRET TEAM!
SMACK
MY OWN PITCHER ABANDONING US IN OUR TIME OF NEED . . .
UNCONSCIONABLE!
?!
WELL, NO MATTER, MONSOON.
WE SHALL SURVIVE THIS HEARTACHE . . .
WITH ASH THE AVENGER!
HIS ERA STATS STAND AT A MIGHTY 14!
AND ONCE HE MASTERS A CURVEBALL . . . ALL SHALL FALL BEFORE THE BCBs!
AHA . . . GREAT . . . SO HAPPY FOR YOU, DUDE.

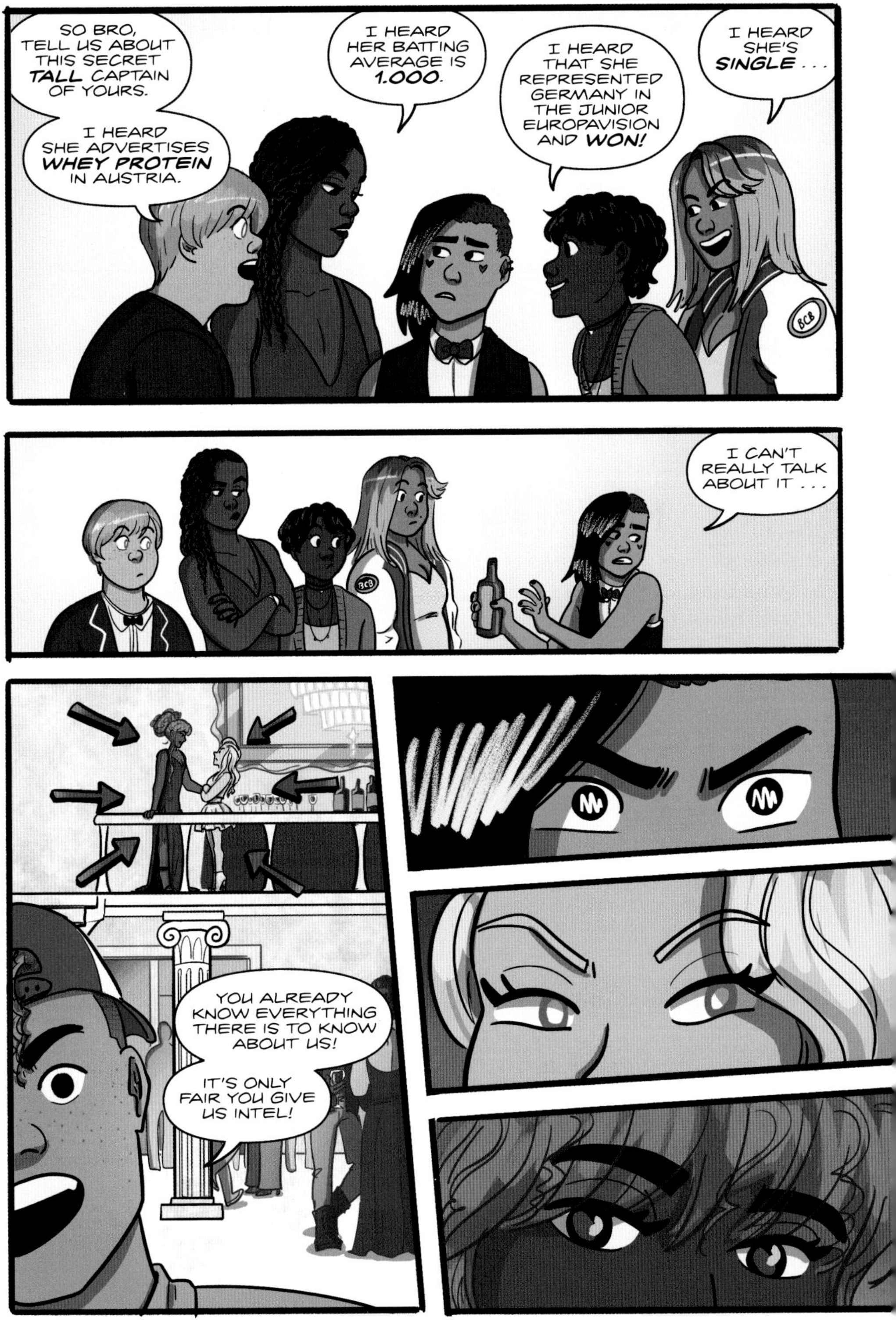

SO BRO, TELL US ABOUT THIS SECRET **TALL** CAPTAIN OF YOURS.
I HEARD SHE ADVERTISES **WHEY PROTEIN** IN AUSTRIA.
I HEARD HER BATTING AVERAGE IS **1.000**.
I HEARD THAT SHE REPRESENTED GERMANY IN THE JUNIOR EUROPAVISION AND **WON!**
I HEARD SHE'S **SINGLE** . . .
BCB
I CAN'T REALLY TALK ABOUT IT . . .
BCB
YOU ALREADY KNOW EVERYTHING THERE IS TO KNOW ABOUT US!
IT'S ONLY FAIR YOU GIVE US INTEL!

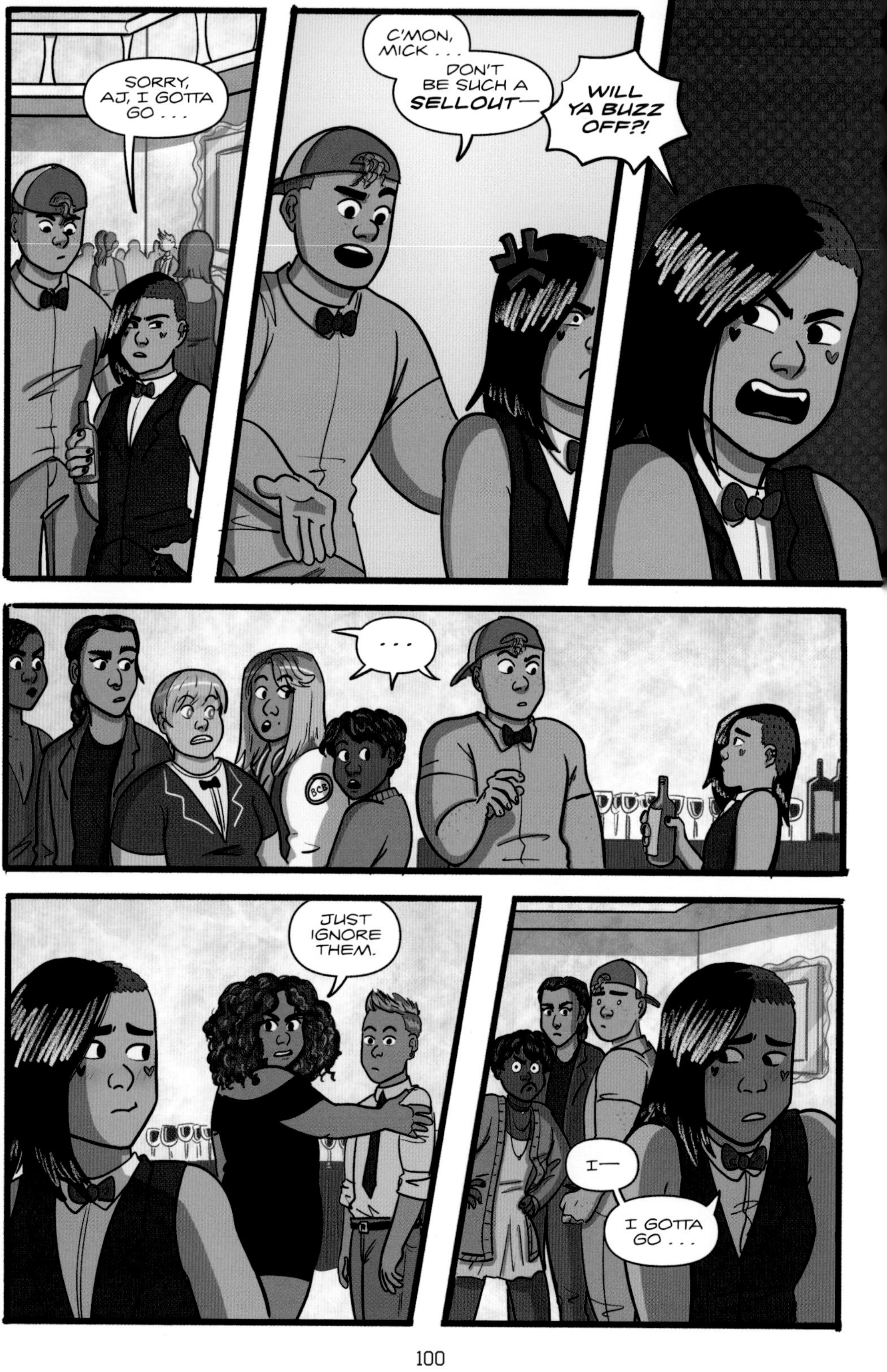
SORRY, AJ, I GOTTA GO . . .
C'MON, MICK . . .
DON'T BE SUCH A SELLOUT—
WILL YA BUZZ OFF?!
. . .
JUST IGNORE THEM.
I—
I GOTTA GO . . .

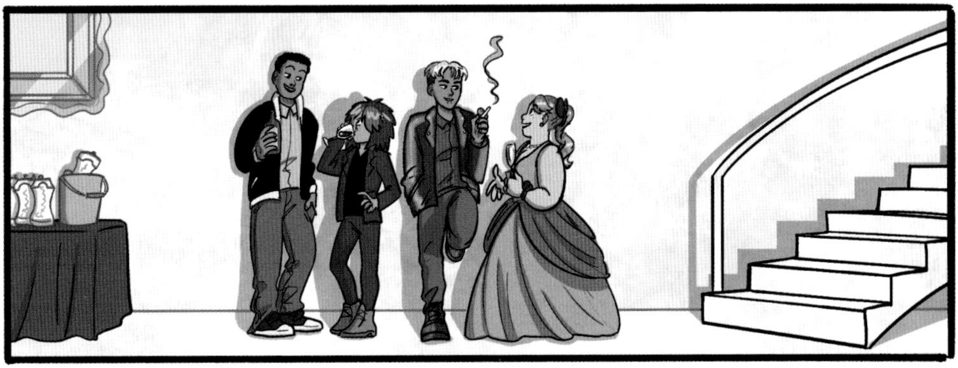

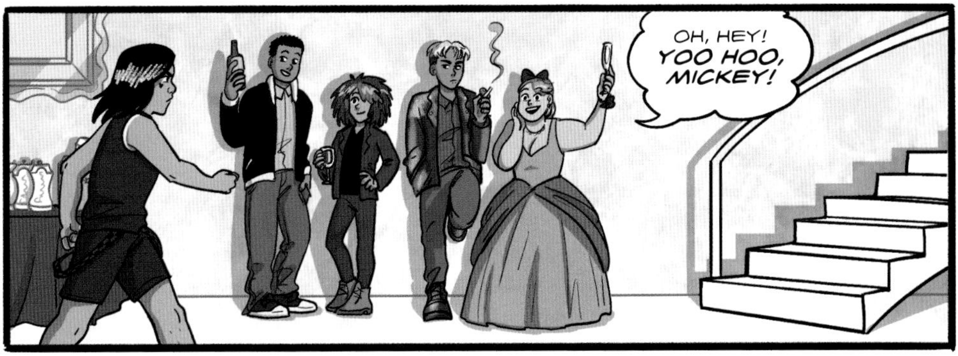
OH, HEY! YOO HOO, MICKEY!

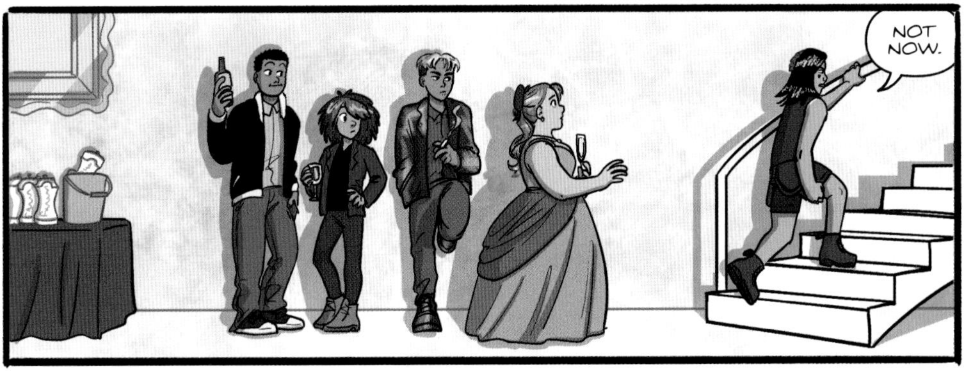
NOT NOW.

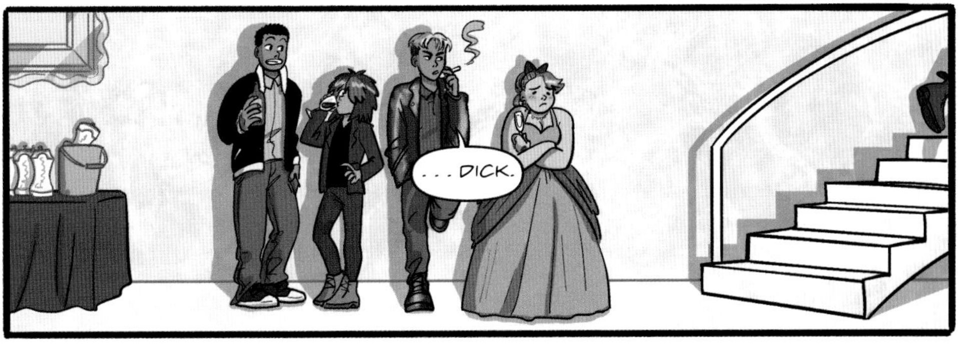
. . . DICK.

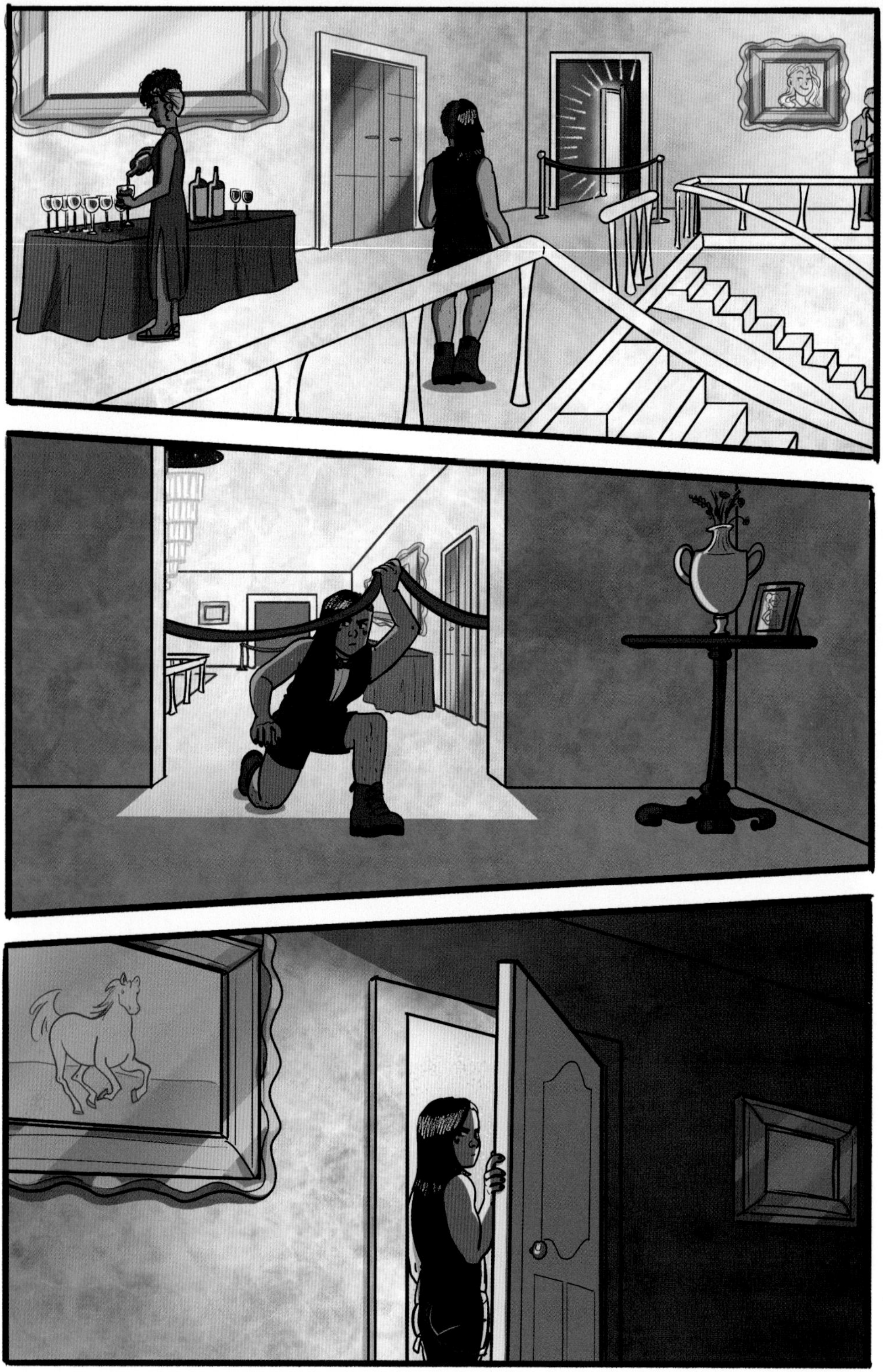

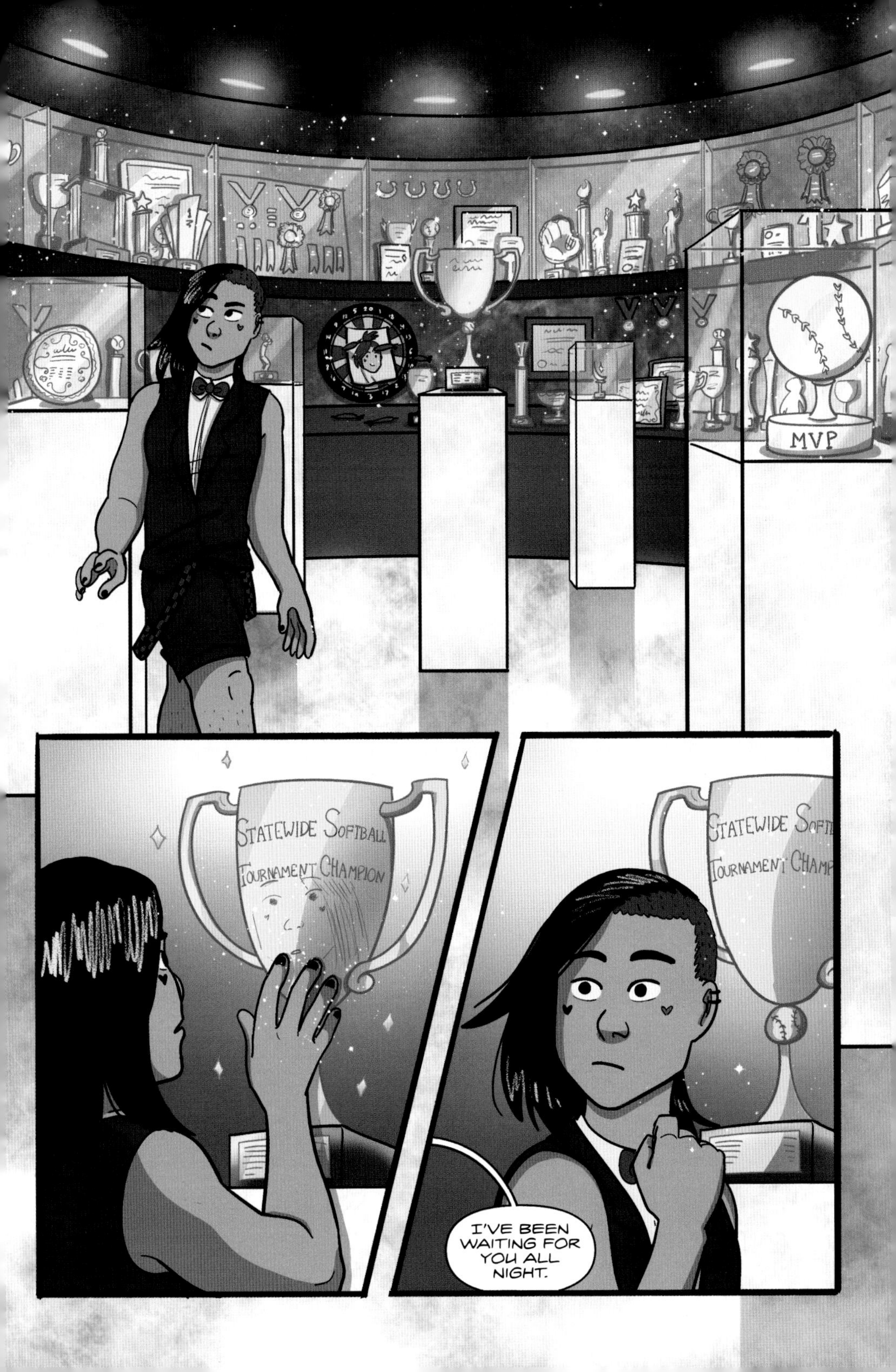
MVP
STATEWIDE SOFTBALL
TOURNAMENT CHAMPION
I'VE BEEN WAITING FOR YOU ALL NIGHT.

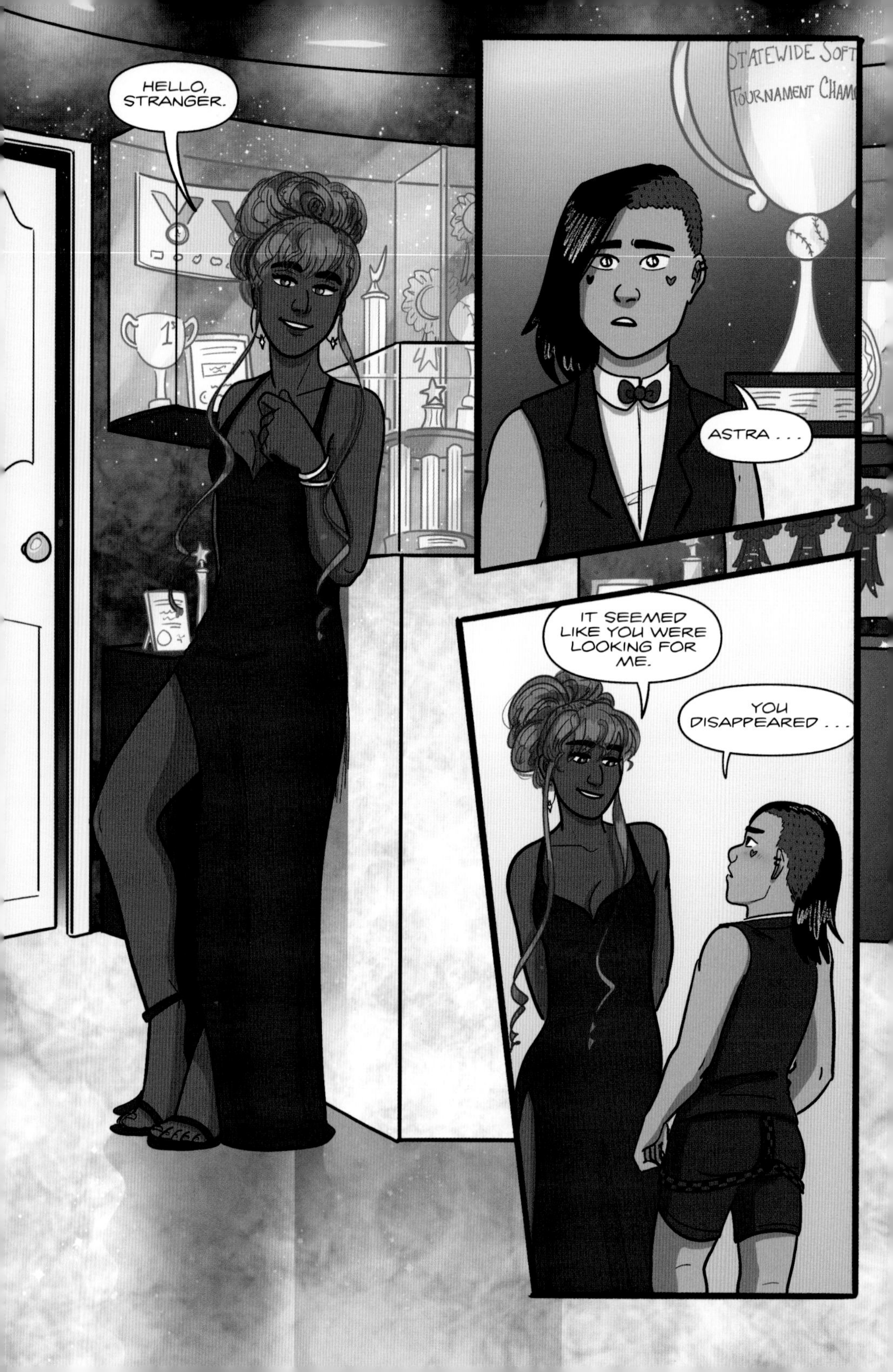
HELLO, STRANGER.
STATEWIDE SOFT
TOURNAMENT CHAM
ASTRA . . .
IT SEEMED LIKE YOU WERE LOOKING FOR ME.
YOU DISAPPEARED . . .

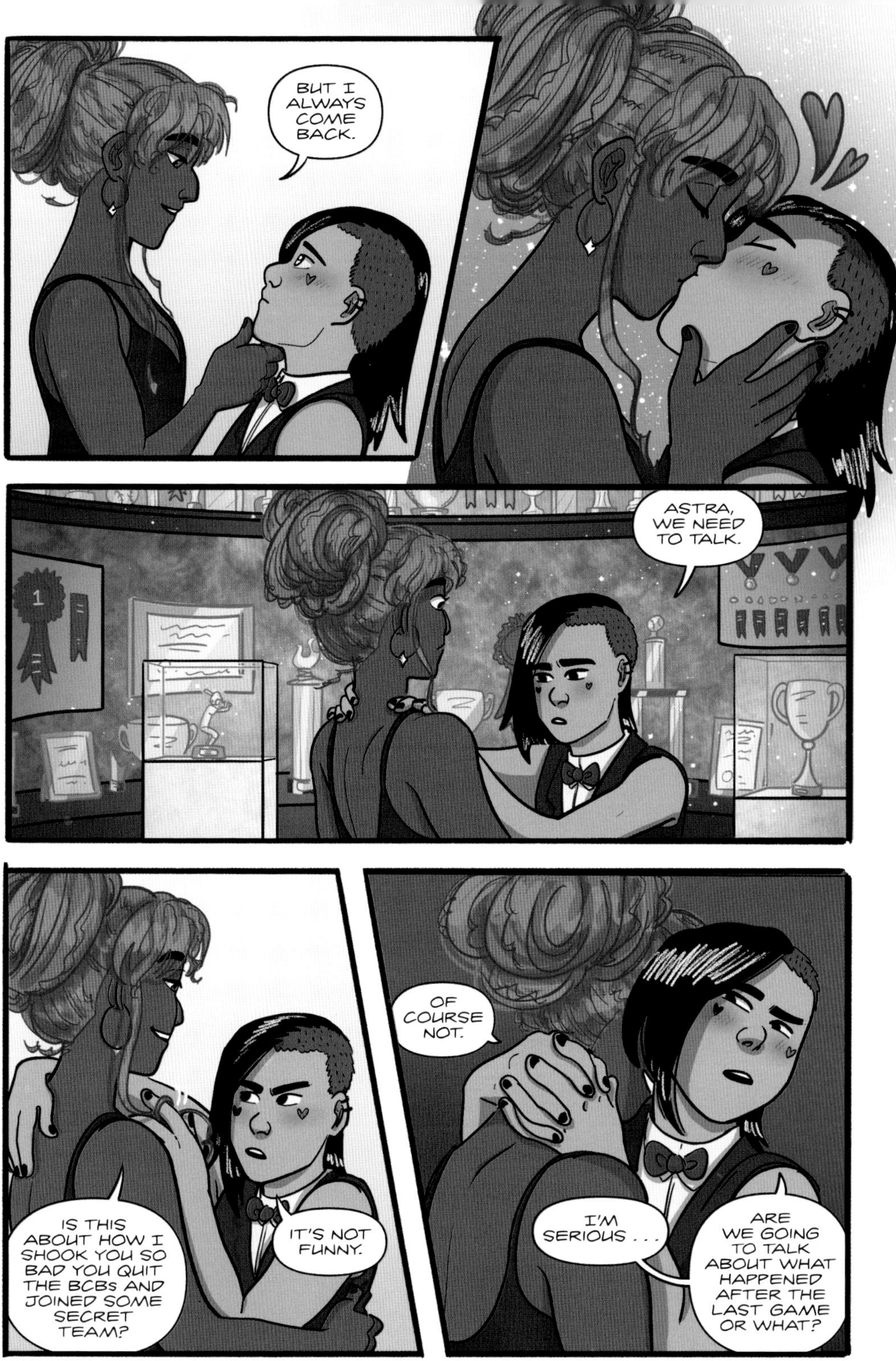

BUT I ALWAYS COME BACK.
ASTRA, WE NEED TO TALK.
IS THIS ABOUT HOW I SHOOK YOU SO BAD YOU QUIT THE BCBs AND JOINED SOME SECRET TEAM?
IT'S NOT FUNNY.
OF COURSE NOT.
I'M SERIOUS . . .
ARE WE GOING TO TALK ABOUT WHAT HAPPENED AFTER THE LAST GAME OR WHAT?

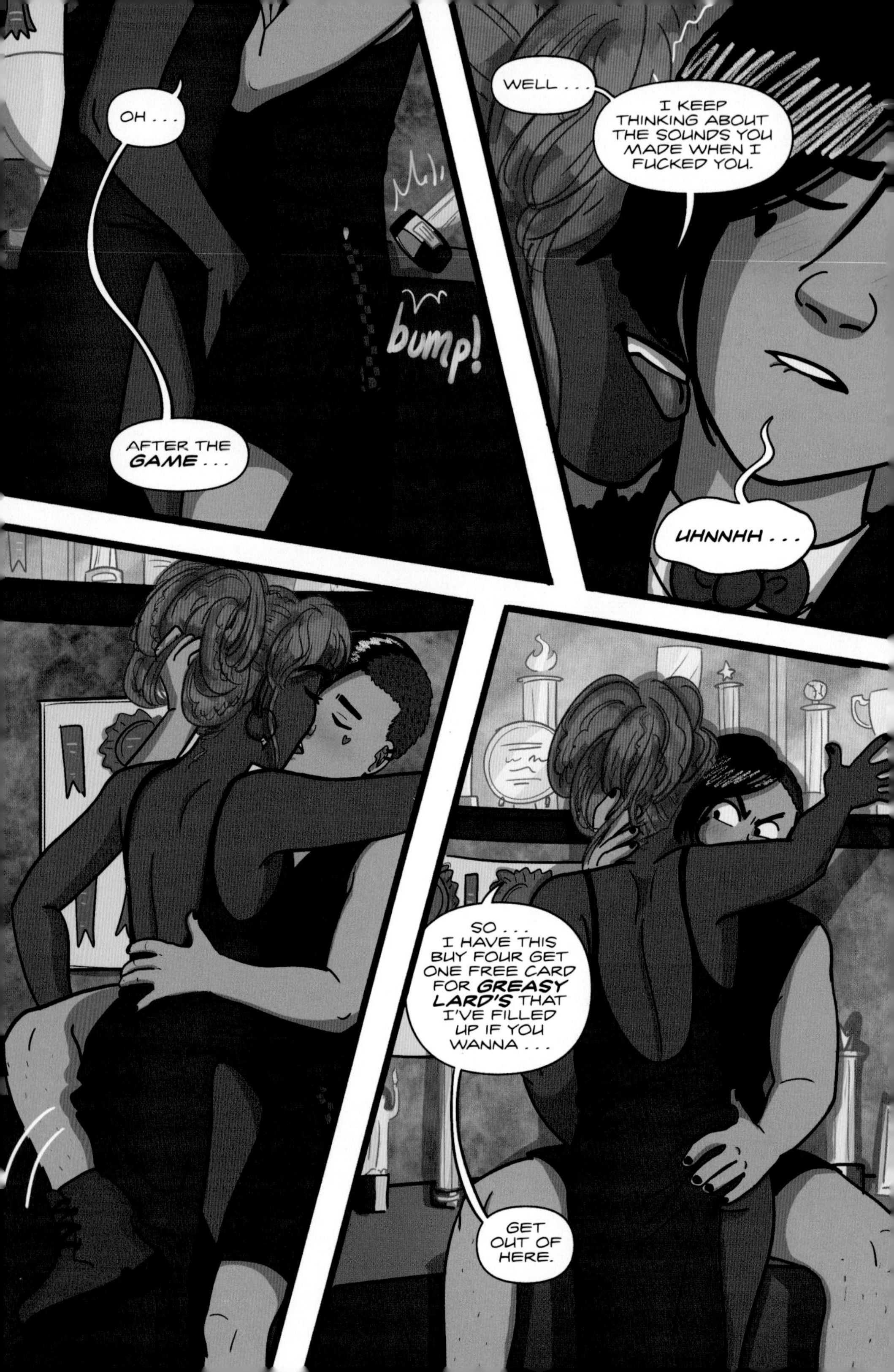
OH . . .
AFTER THE GAME . . .
bump!
WELL . . .
I KEEP THINKING ABOUT THE SOUNDS YOU MADE WHEN I FUCKED YOU.
UHNNHH . . .
SO . . . I HAVE THIS BUY FOUR GET ONE FREE CARD FOR GREASY LARD'S THAT I'VE FILLED UP IF YOU WANNA . . .
GET OUT OF HERE.

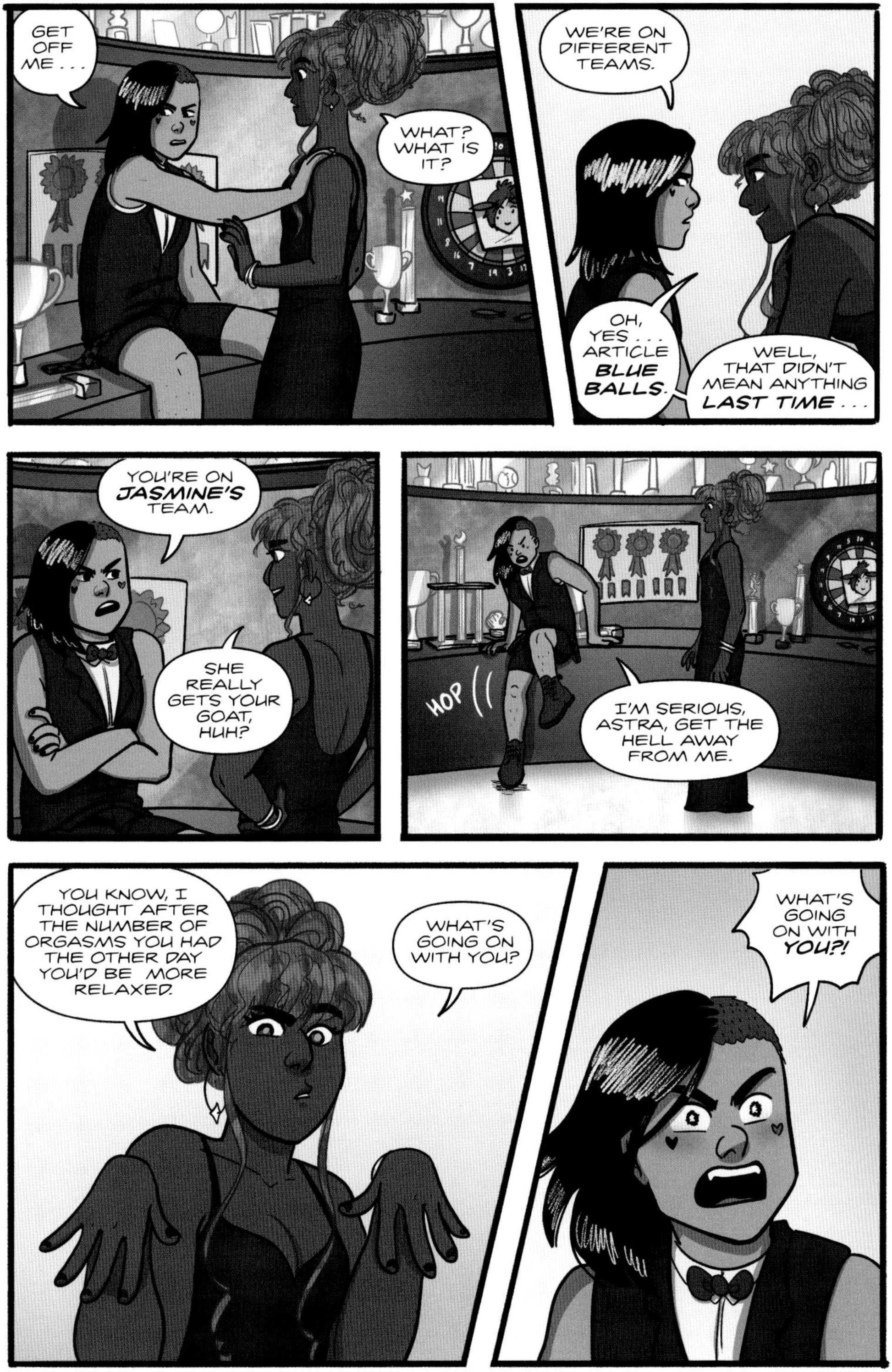

GET OFF ME . . .
WHAT? WHAT IS IT?
WE'RE ON DIFFERENT TEAMS.
OH, YES . . . ARTICLE **BLUE BALLS**.
WELL, THAT DIDN'T MEAN ANYTHING **LAST TIME** . . .
YOU'RE ON **JASMINE'S** TEAM.
SHE REALLY GETS YOUR GOAT, HUH?
HOP
I'M SERIOUS, ASTRA, GET THE HELL AWAY FROM ME.
YOU KNOW, I THOUGHT AFTER THE NUMBER OF ORGASMS YOU HAD THE OTHER DAY YOU'D BE MORE RELAXED.
WHAT'S GOING ON WITH YOU?
WHAT'S GOING ON WITH **YOU?!**

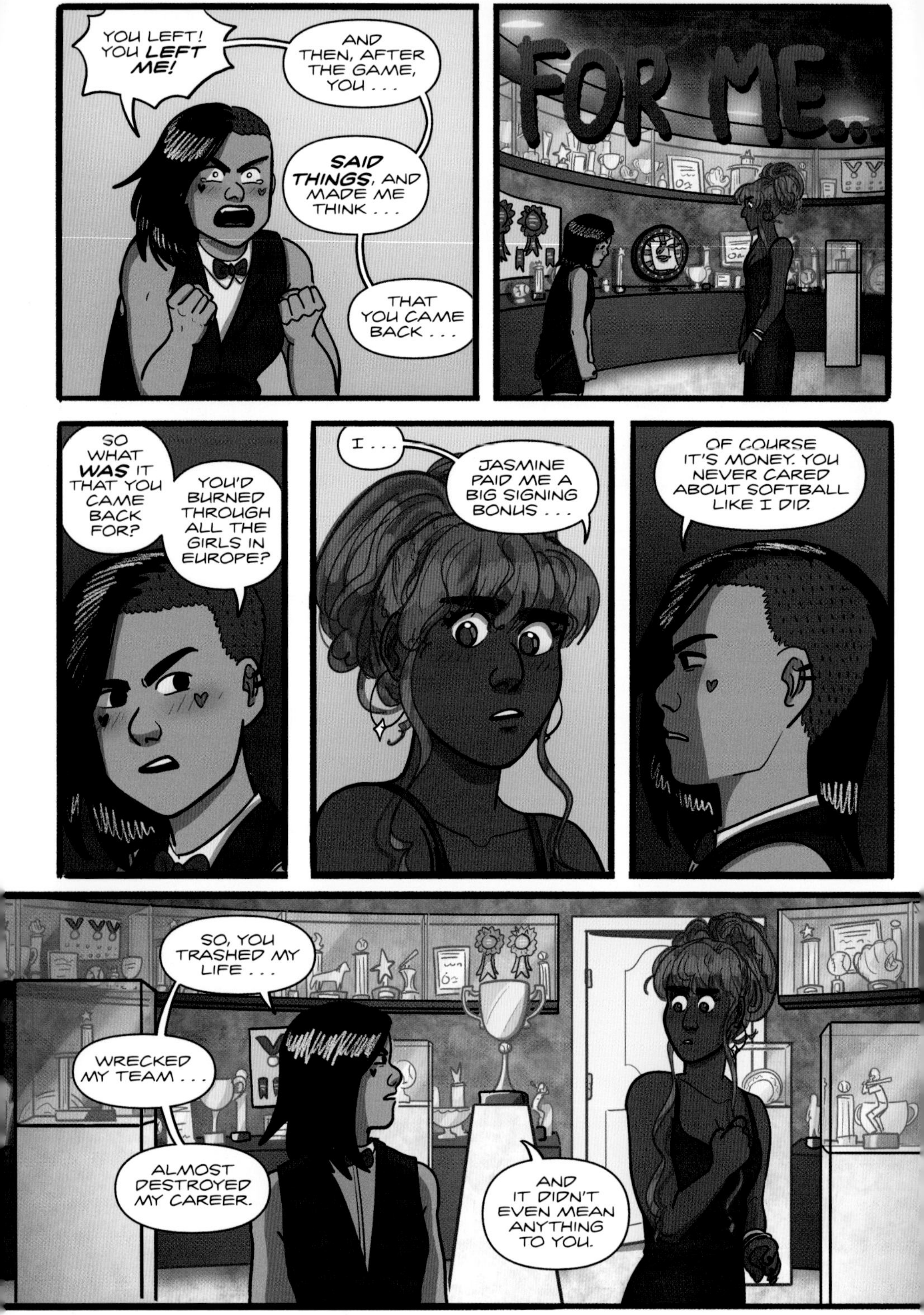
YOU LEFT! YOU **LEFT ME!**
AND THEN, AFTER THE GAME, YOU . . .
SAID THINGS, AND MADE ME THINK . . .
THAT YOU CAME BACK . . .
FOR ME...
SO WHAT **WAS** IT THAT YOU CAME BACK FOR?
YOU'D BURNED THROUGH ALL THE GIRLS IN EUROPE?
I . . .
JASMINE PAID ME A BIG SIGNING BONUS . . .
OF COURSE IT'S MONEY. YOU NEVER CARED ABOUT SOFTBALL LIKE I DID.
SO, YOU TRASHED MY LIFE . . .
WRECKED MY TEAM . . .
ALMOST DESTROYED MY CAREER.
AND IT DIDN'T EVEN MEAN ANYTHING TO YOU.

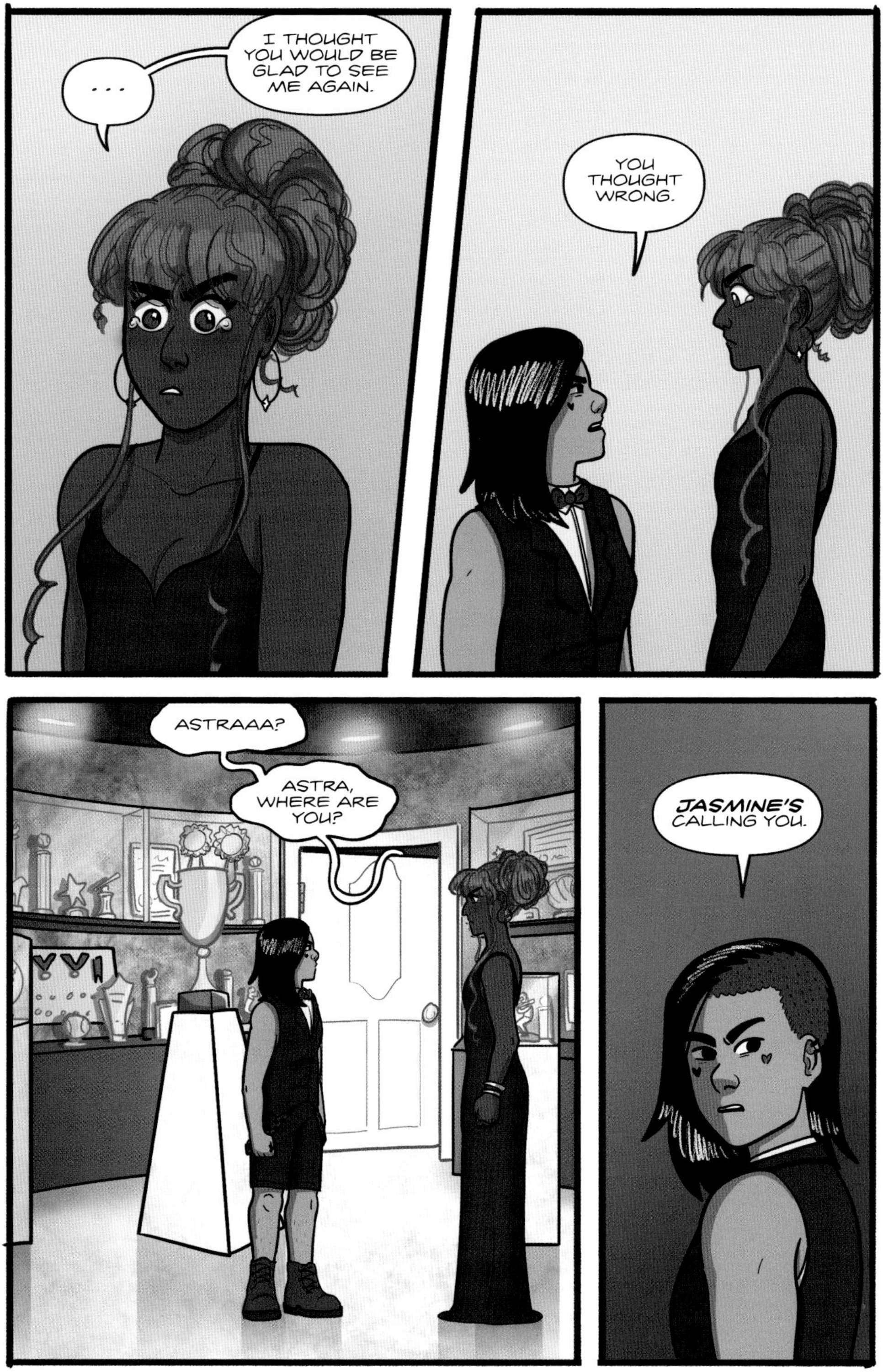
...
I THOUGHT YOU WOULD BE GLAD TO SEE ME AGAIN.
YOU THOUGHT WRONG.
ASTRAAA?
ASTRA, WHERE ARE YOU?
JASMINE'S CALLING YOU.

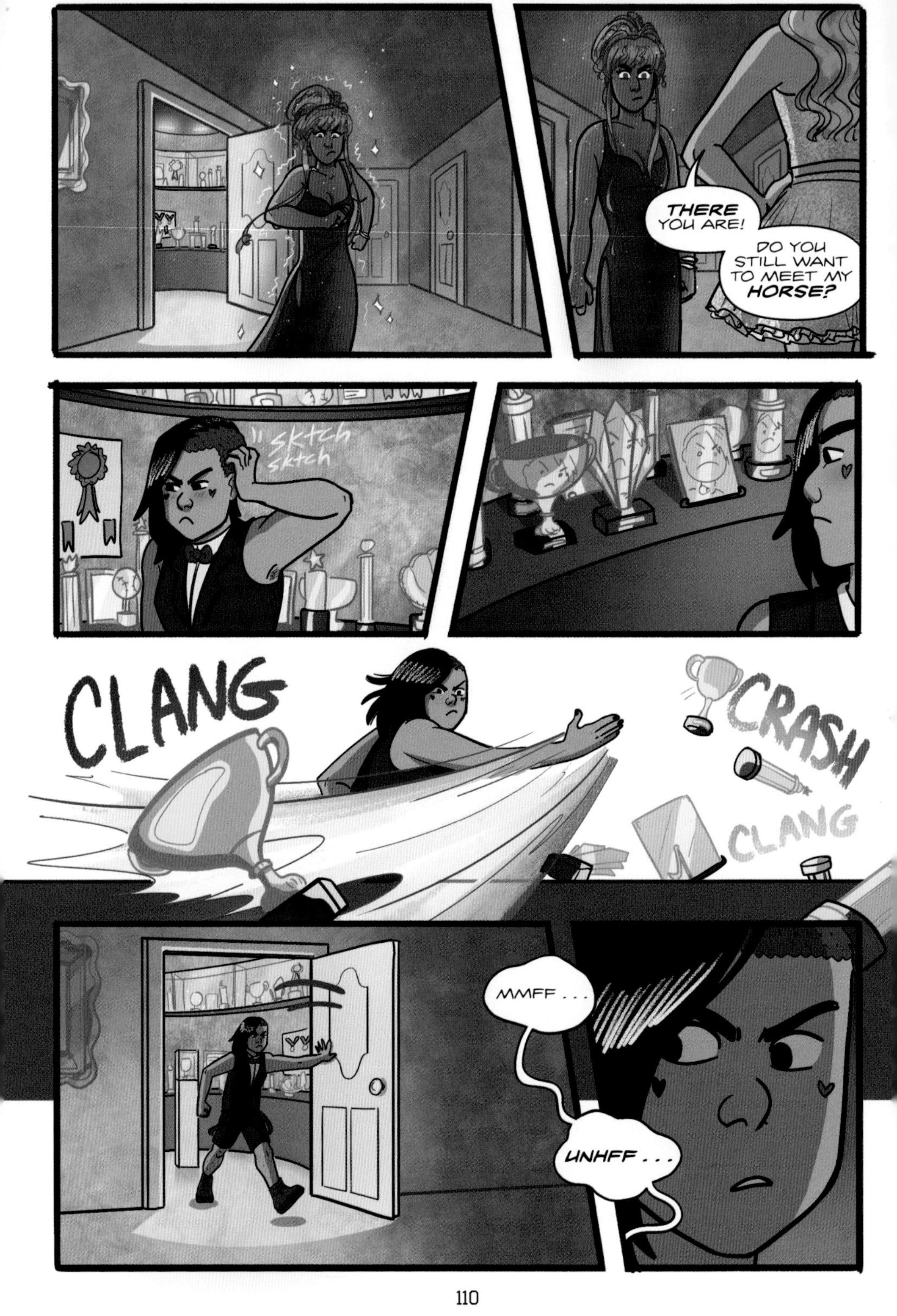
THERE YOU ARE!
DO YOU STILL WANT TO MEET MY HORSE?
sktch sktch
CLANG
CRASH
CLANG
MMFF . . .
UNHFF . . .

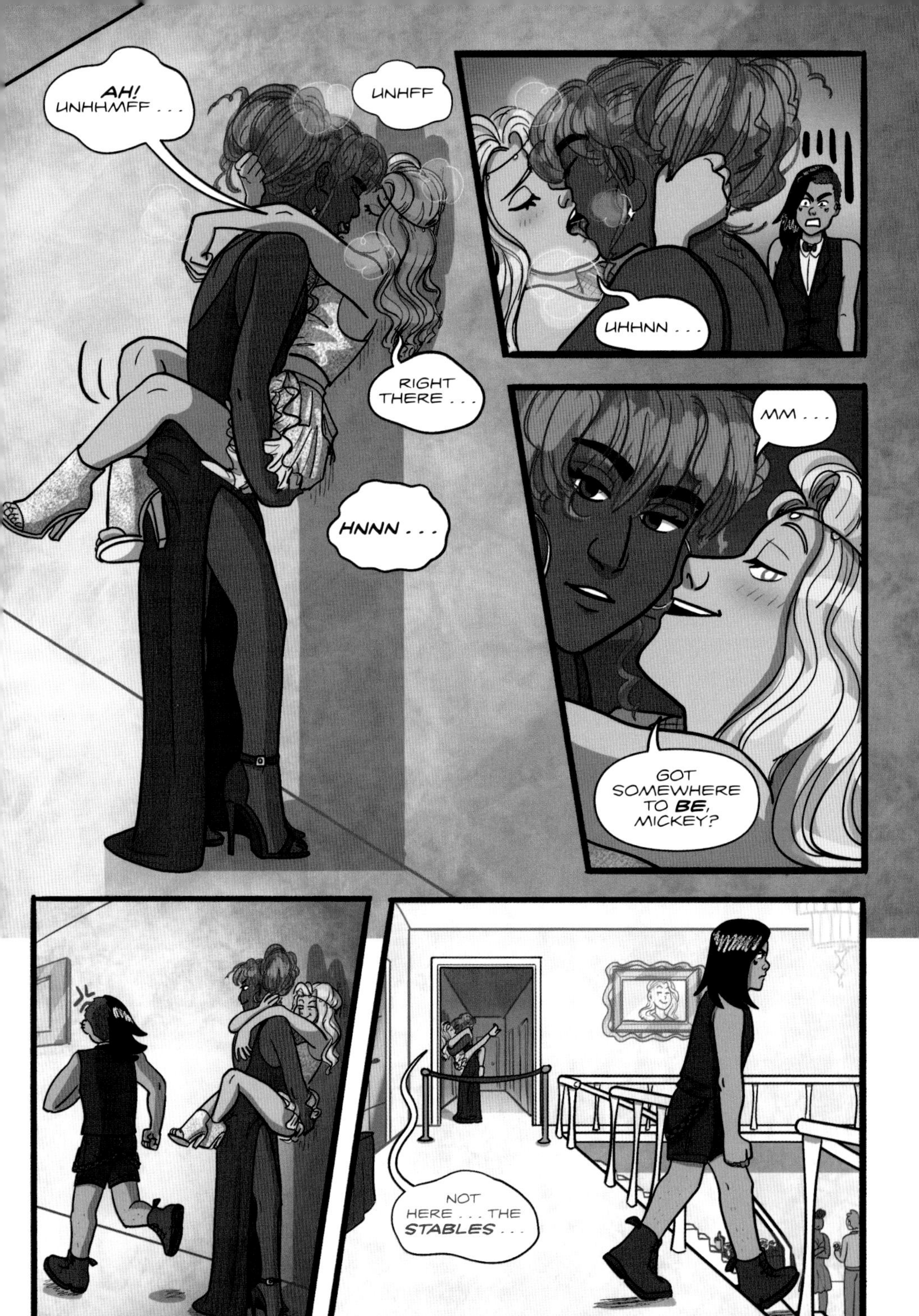

AH! UNHHMFF . . .
UNHFF
RIGHT THERE . . .
HNNN . . .
UHHNN . . .
MM . . .
GOT SOMEWHERE TO BE, MICKEY?
NOT HERE . . . THE STABLES . . .

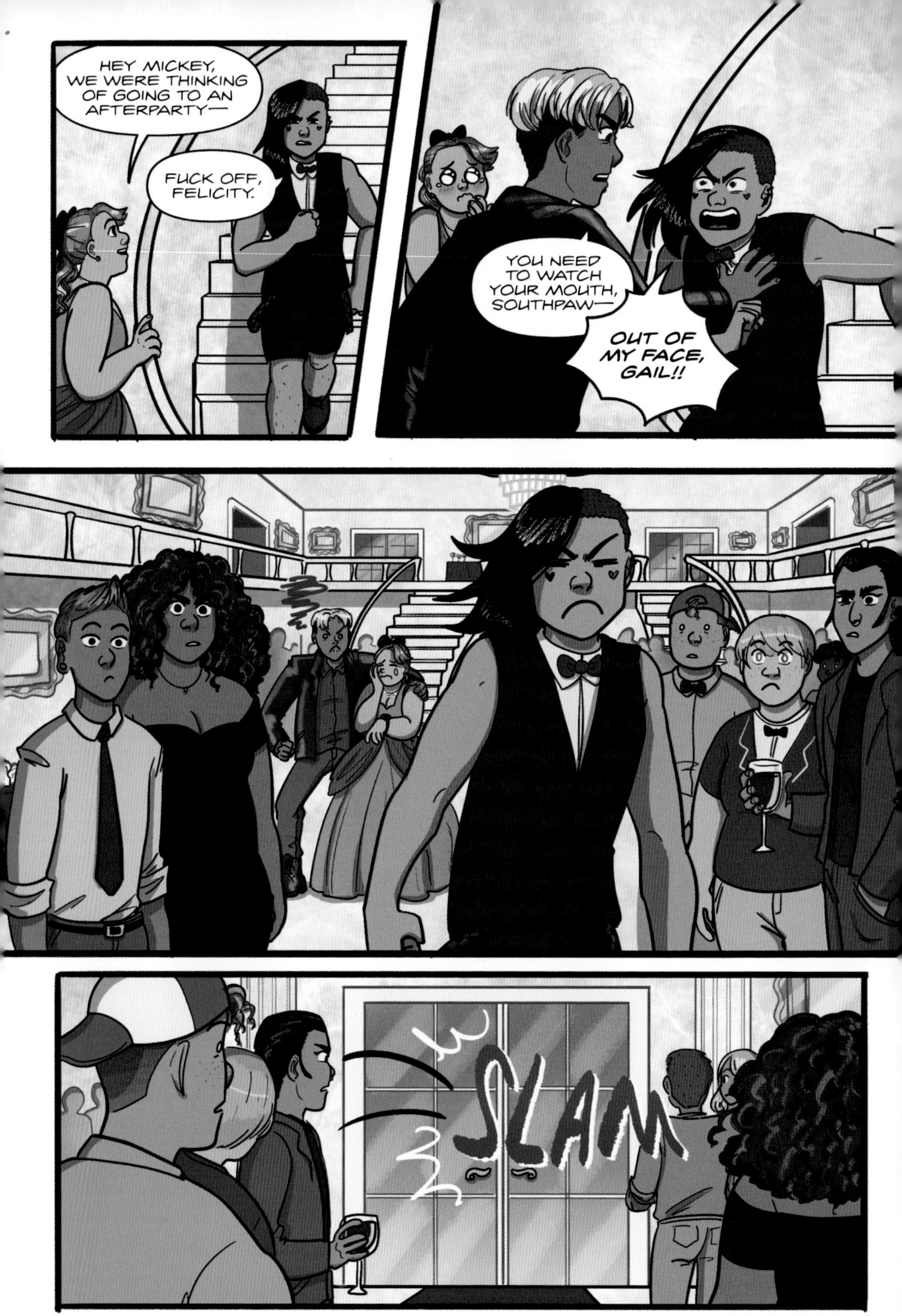
HEY MICKEY, WE WERE THINKING OF GOING TO AN AFTERPARTY—
FUCK OFF, FELICITY.
YOU NEED TO WATCH YOUR MOUTH, SOUTHPAW—
OUT OF MY FACE, GAIL!!
SLAM

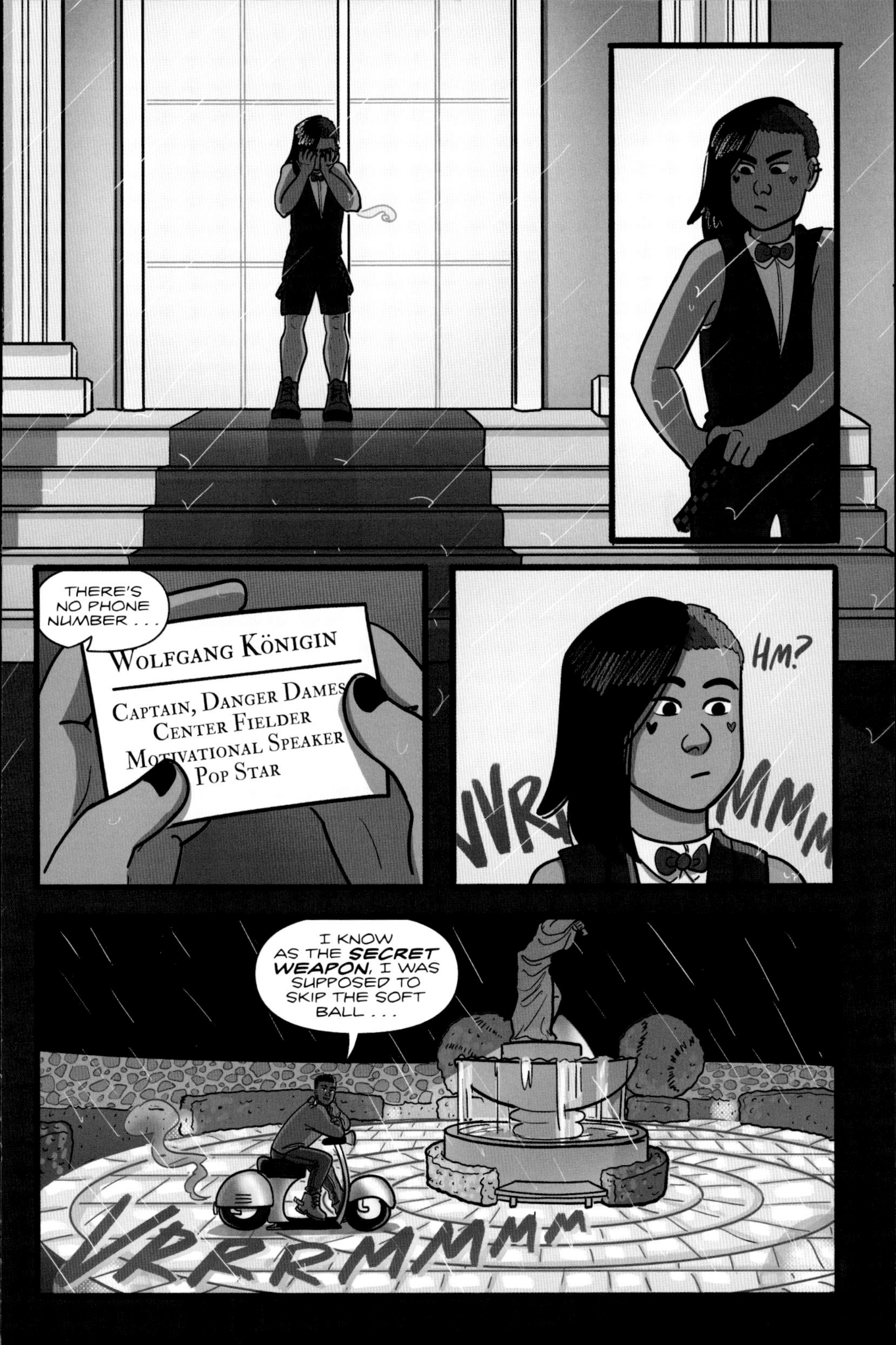
THERE'S NO PHONE NUMBER . . .
WOLFGANG KÖNIGIN
CAPTAIN, DANGER DAMES
CENTER FIELDER
MOTIVATIONAL SPEAKER
POP STAR
HM?
VVRRMMM
I KNOW AS THE SECRET WEAPON, I WAS SUPPOSED TO SKIP THE SOFT BALL . . .
VRRRMMMM

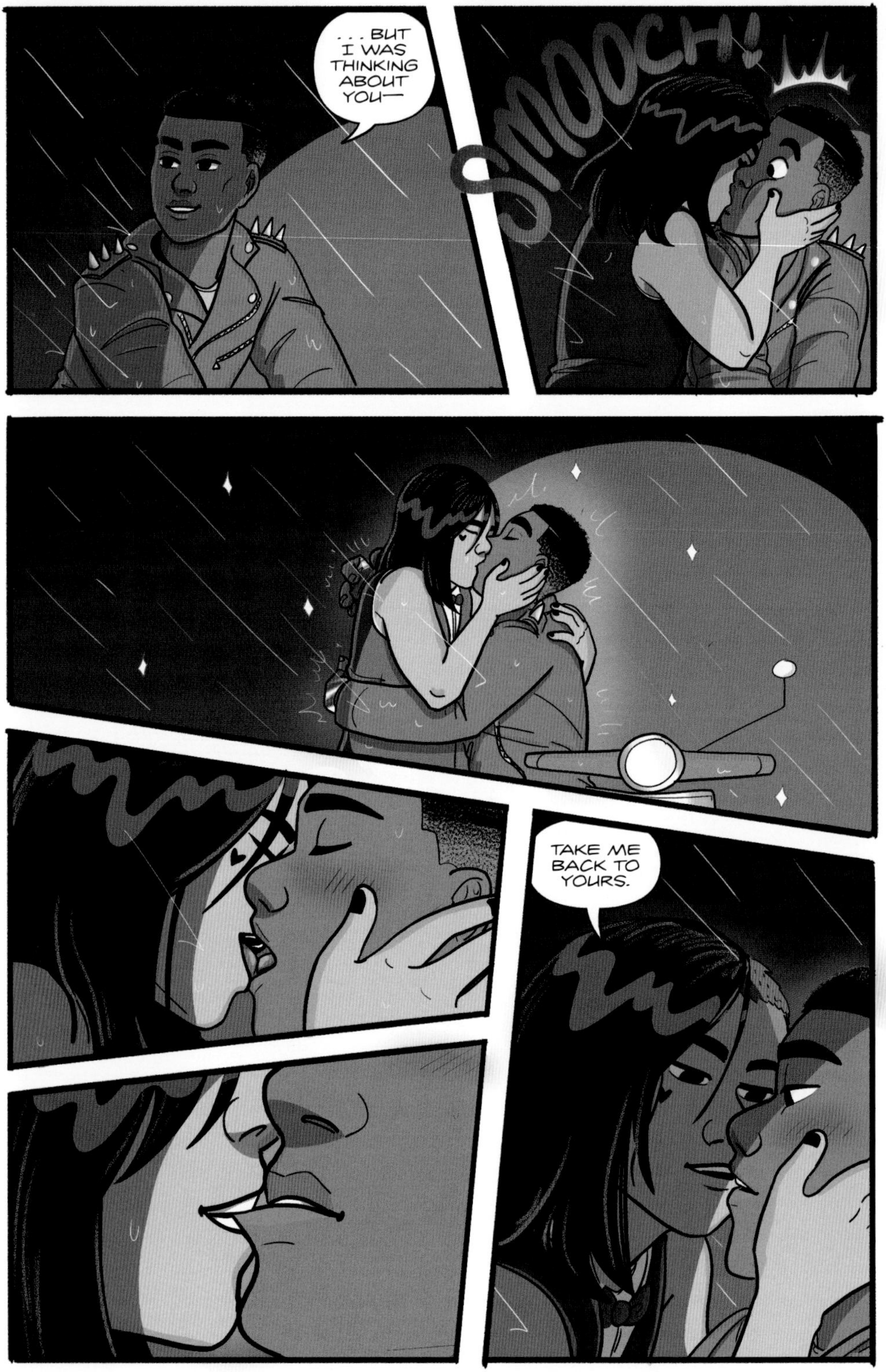
. . . BUT I WAS THINKING ABOUT YOU—
SMOOCH!
TAKE ME BACK TO YOURS.

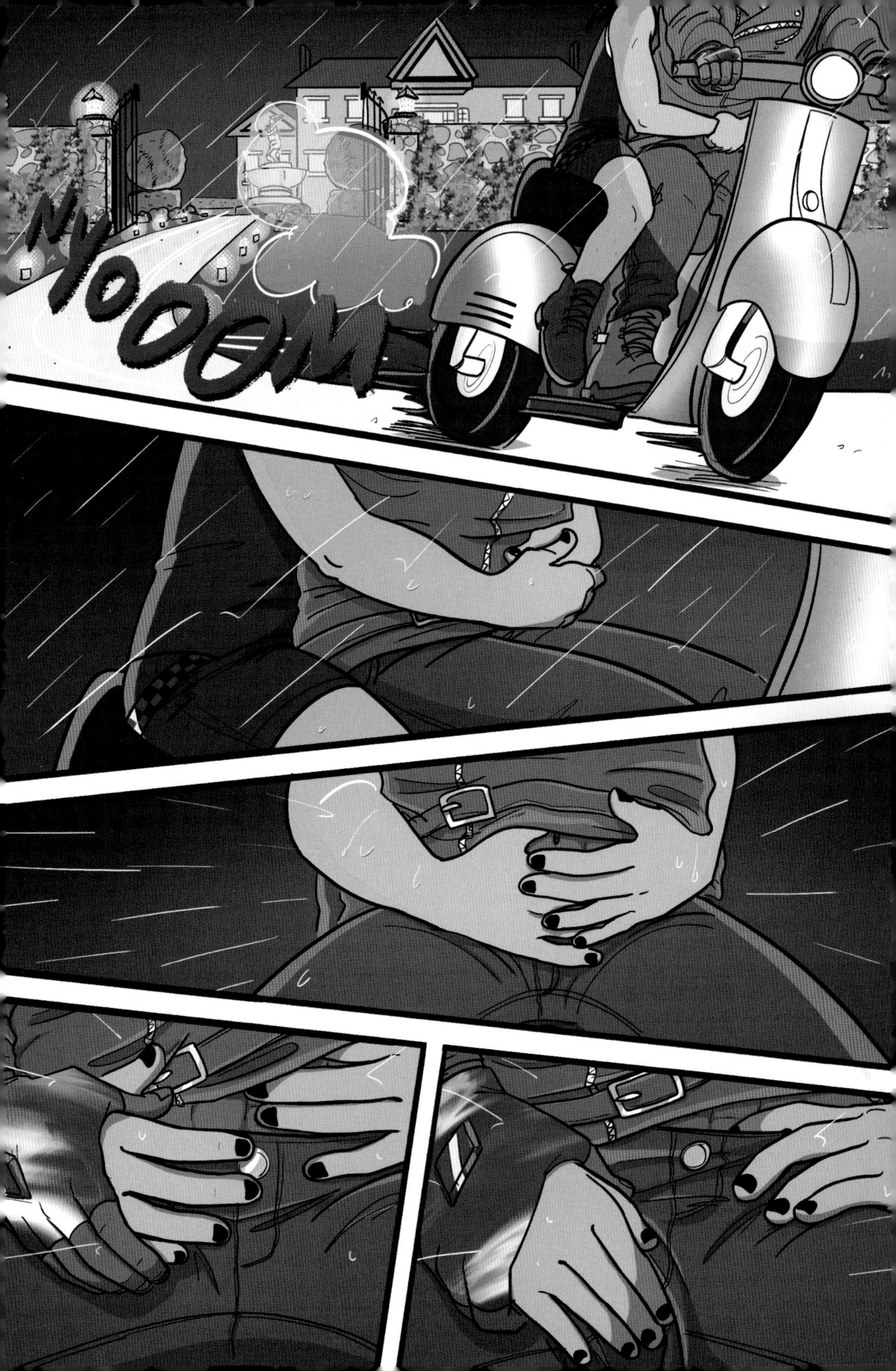
NYOOOM

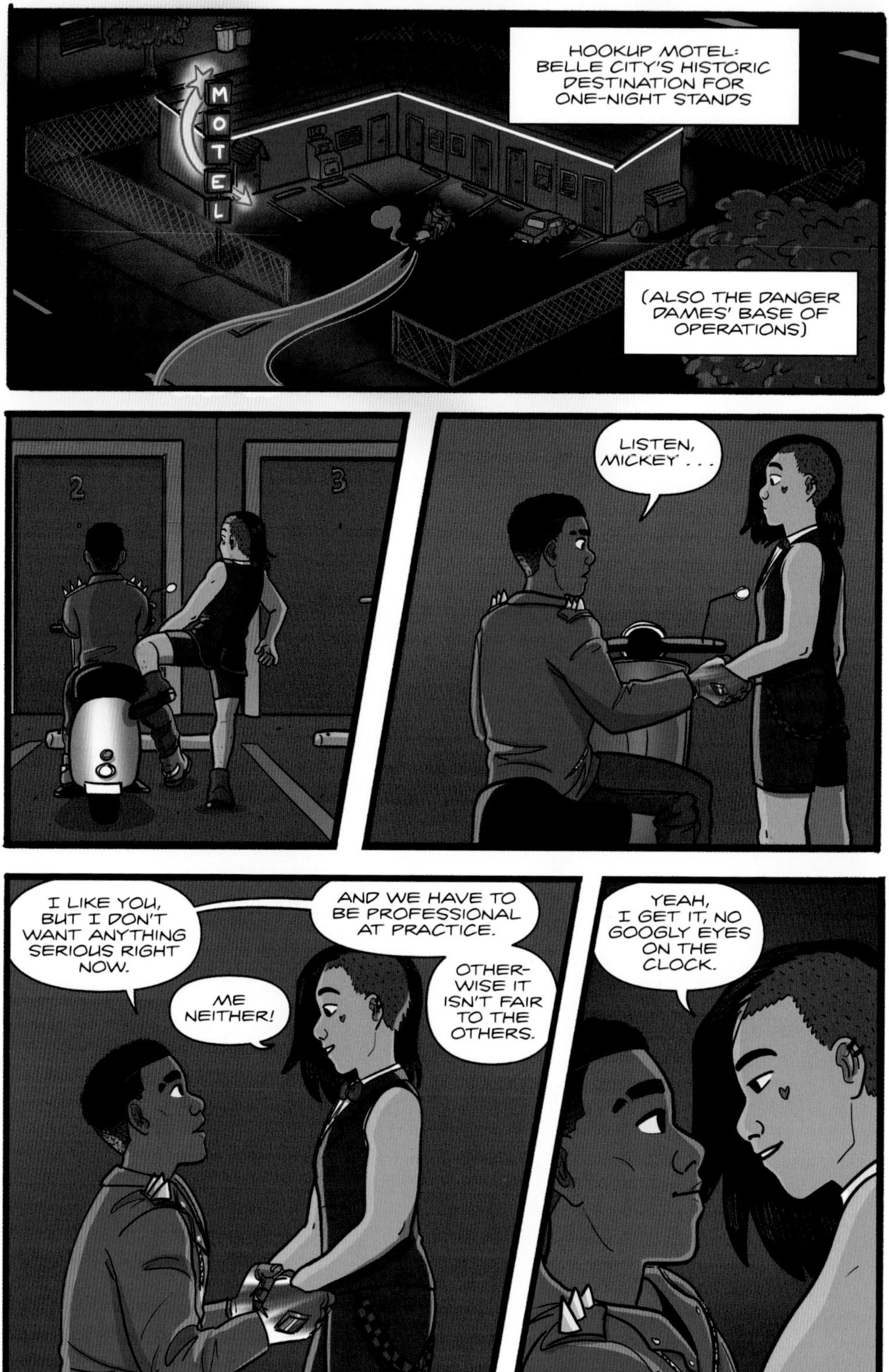
HOOKUP MOTEL: BELLE CITY'S HISTORIC DESTINATION FOR ONE-NIGHT STANDS
MOTEL
(ALSO THE DANGER DAMES' BASE OF OPERATIONS)
2
3
LISTEN, MICKEY . . .
I LIKE YOU, BUT I DON'T WANT ANYTHING SERIOUS RIGHT NOW.
ME NEITHER!
AND WE HAVE TO BE PROFESSIONAL AT PRACTICE.
OTHER-WISE IT ISN'T FAIR TO THE OTHERS.
YEAH, I GET IT, NO GOOGLY EYES ON THE CLOCK.

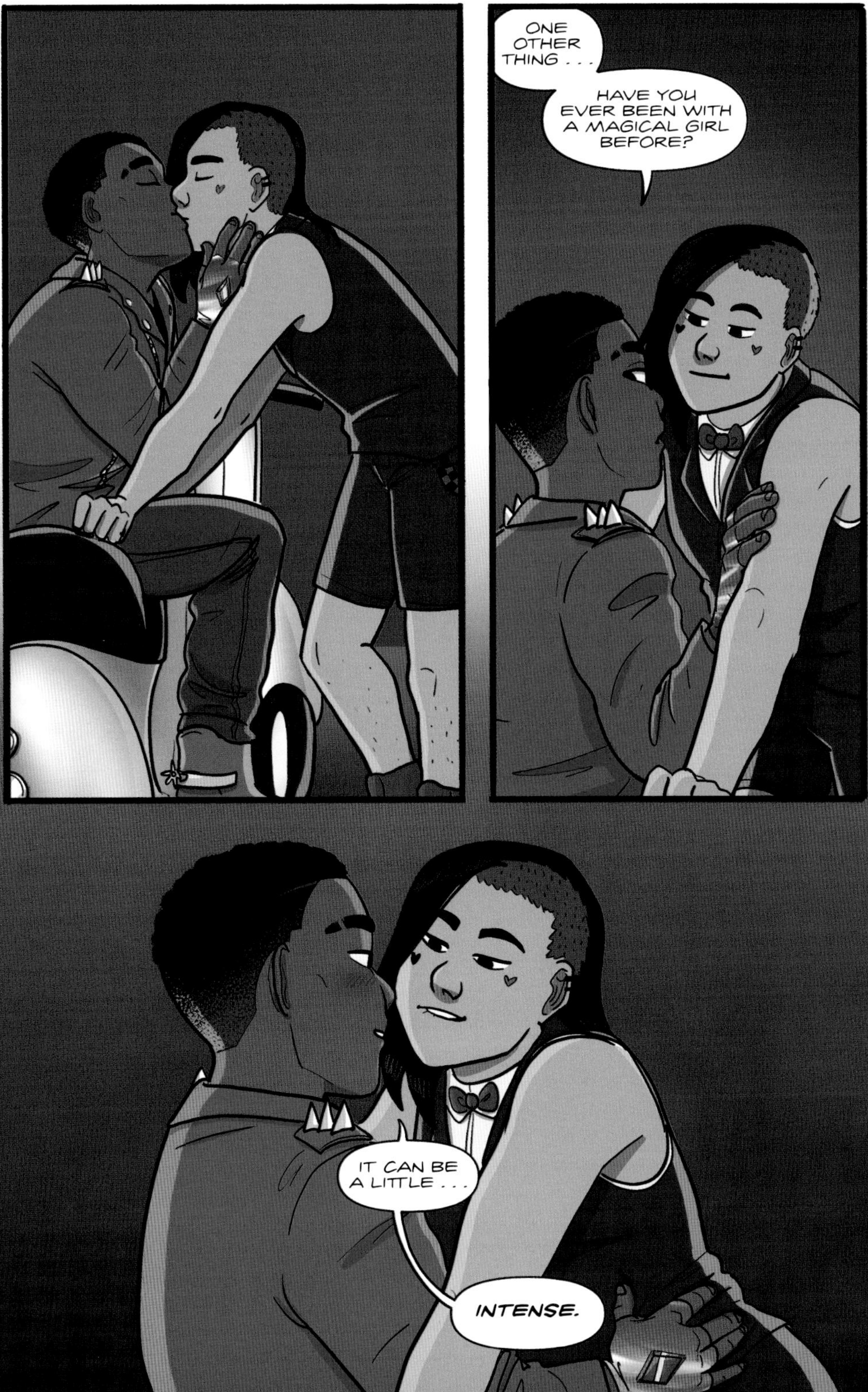
ONE OTHER THING . . .
HAVE YOU EVER BEEN WITH A MAGICAL GIRL BEFORE?
IT CAN BE A LITTLE . . .
INTENSE.

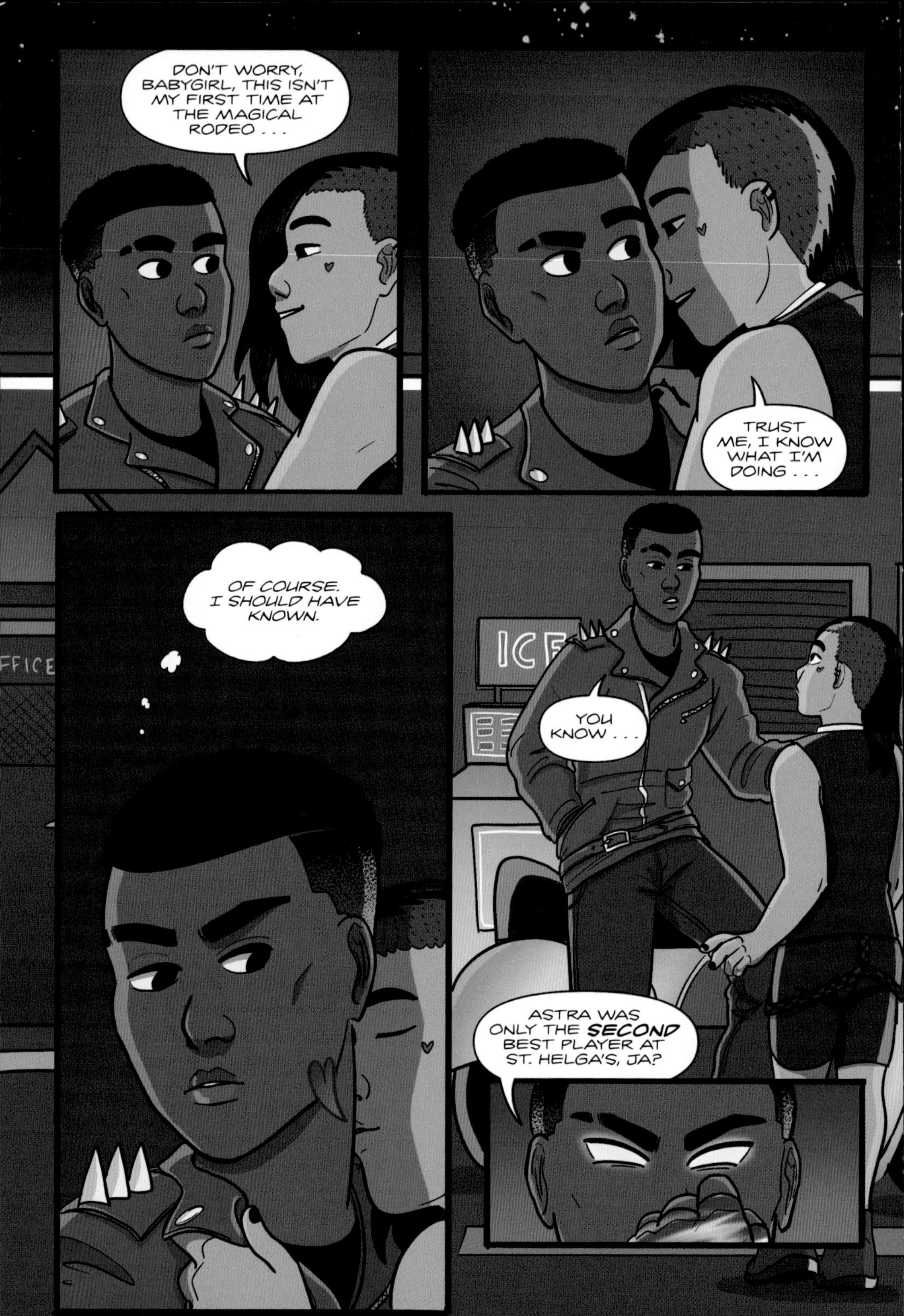
DON'T WORRY, BABYGIRL, THIS ISN'T MY FIRST TIME AT THE MAGICAL RODEO . . .
TRUST ME, I KNOW WHAT I'M DOING . . .
OF COURSE. I SHOULD HAVE KNOWN.
ICE
YOU KNOW . . .
ASTRA WAS ONLY THE **SECOND** BEST PLAYER AT ST. HELGA'S, JA?

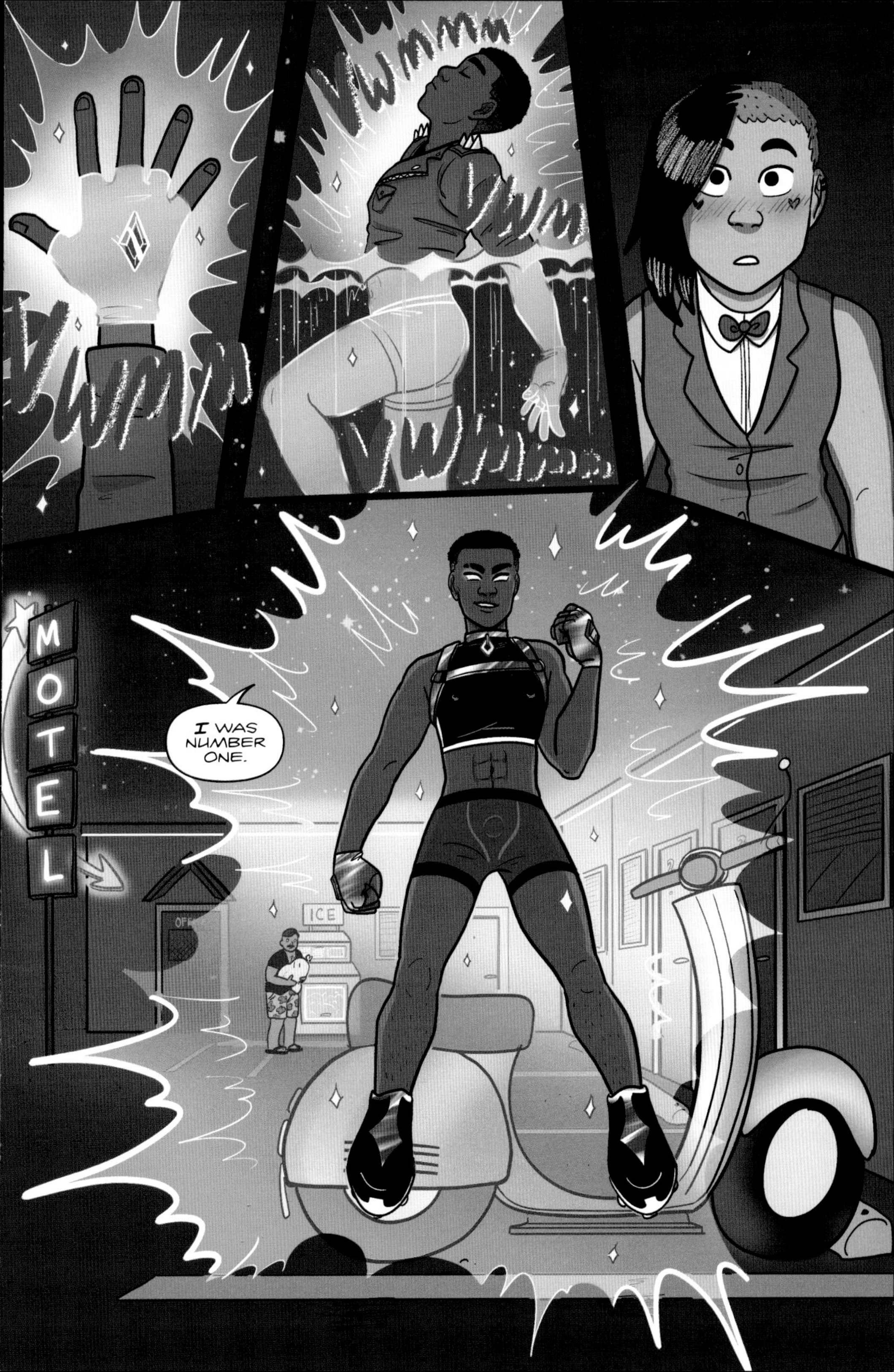
VWMMM
VWMMM
VWMM
VWMMM
I WAS NUMBER ONE.
MOTEL
ICE

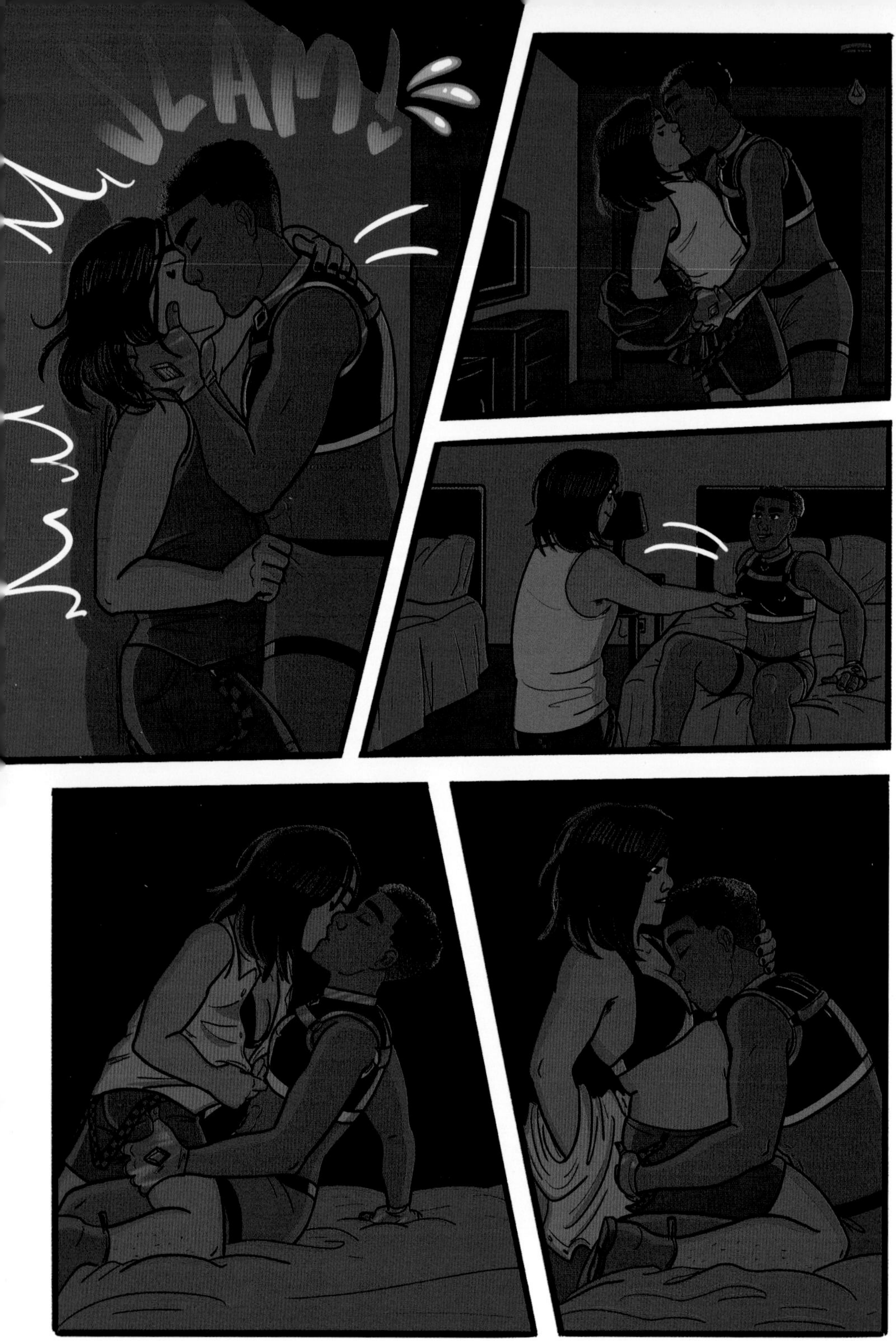
SLAM!

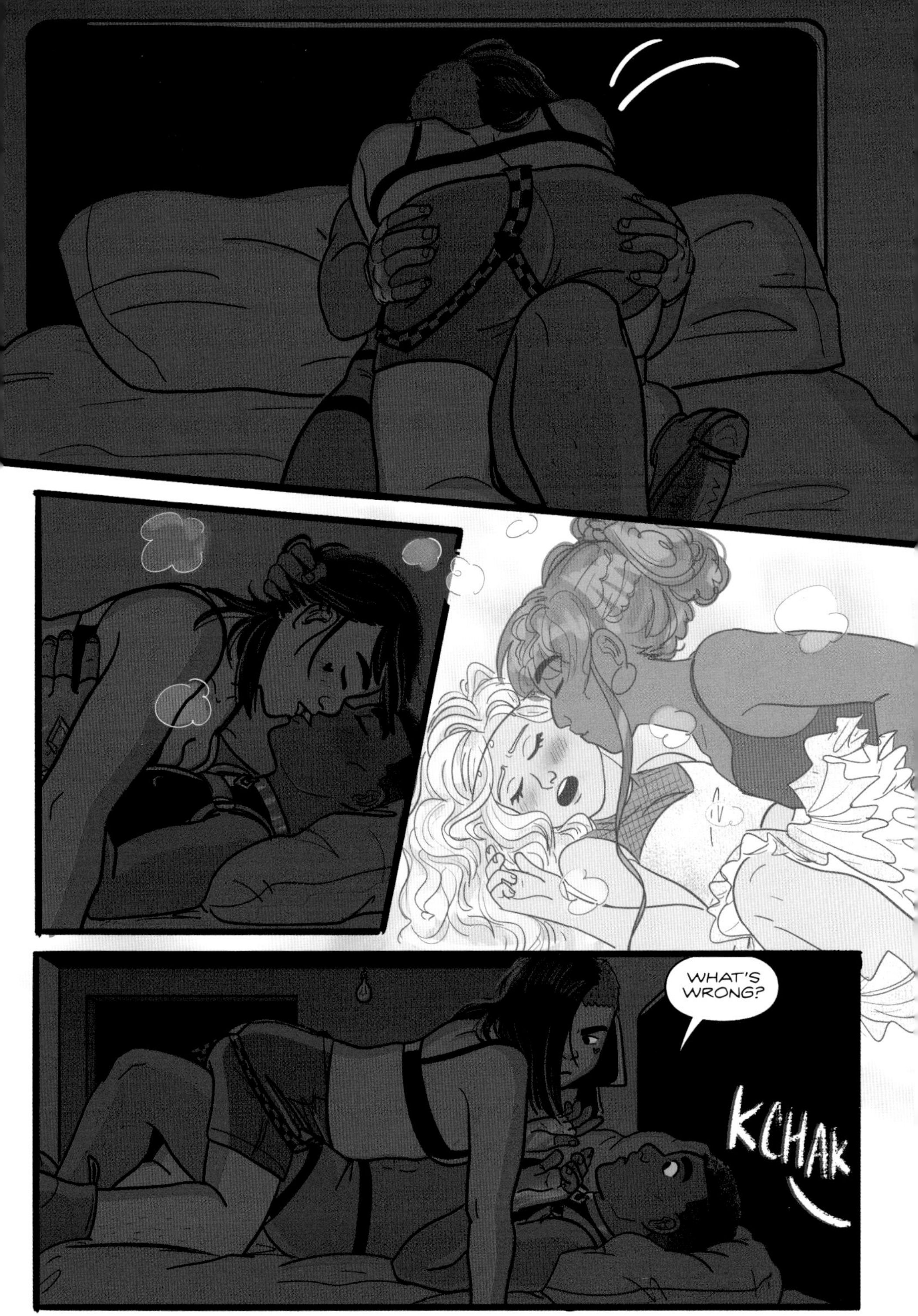
WHAT'S WRONG?
KCHAK

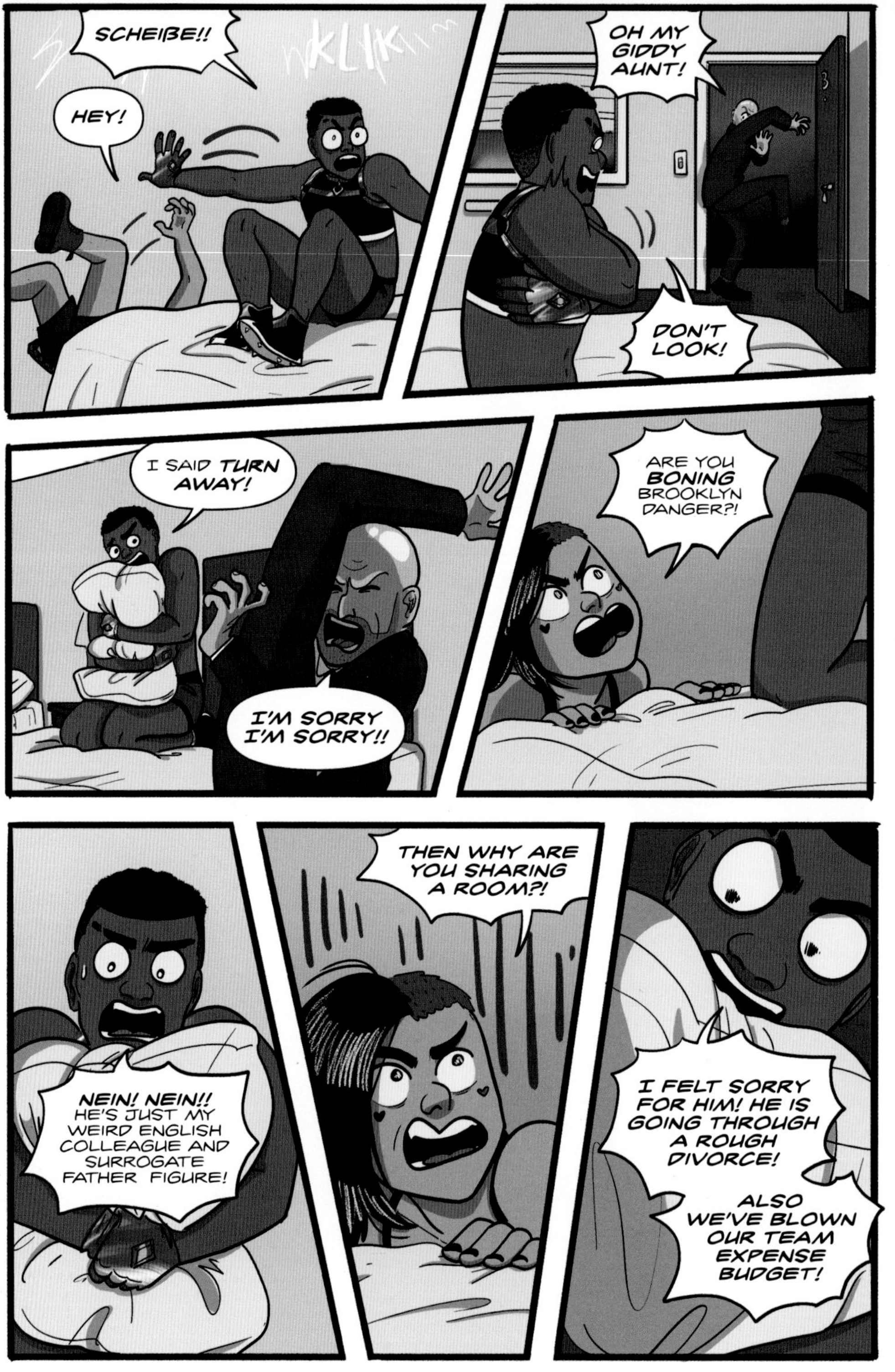
SCHEIßE!!
KLIK
HEY!
OH MY GIDDY AUNT!
DON'T LOOK!
I SAID **TURN AWAY!**
I'M SORRY I'M SORRY!!
ARE YOU **BONING** BROOKLYN DANGER?!
NEIN! NEIN!! HE'S JUST MY WEIRD ENGLISH COLLEAGUE AND SURROGATE FATHER FIGURE!
THEN WHY ARE YOU SHARING A ROOM?!
I FELT SORRY FOR HIM! HE IS GOING THROUGH A ROUGH DIVORCE!
ALSO WE'VE BLOWN OUR TEAM EXPENSE BUDGET!

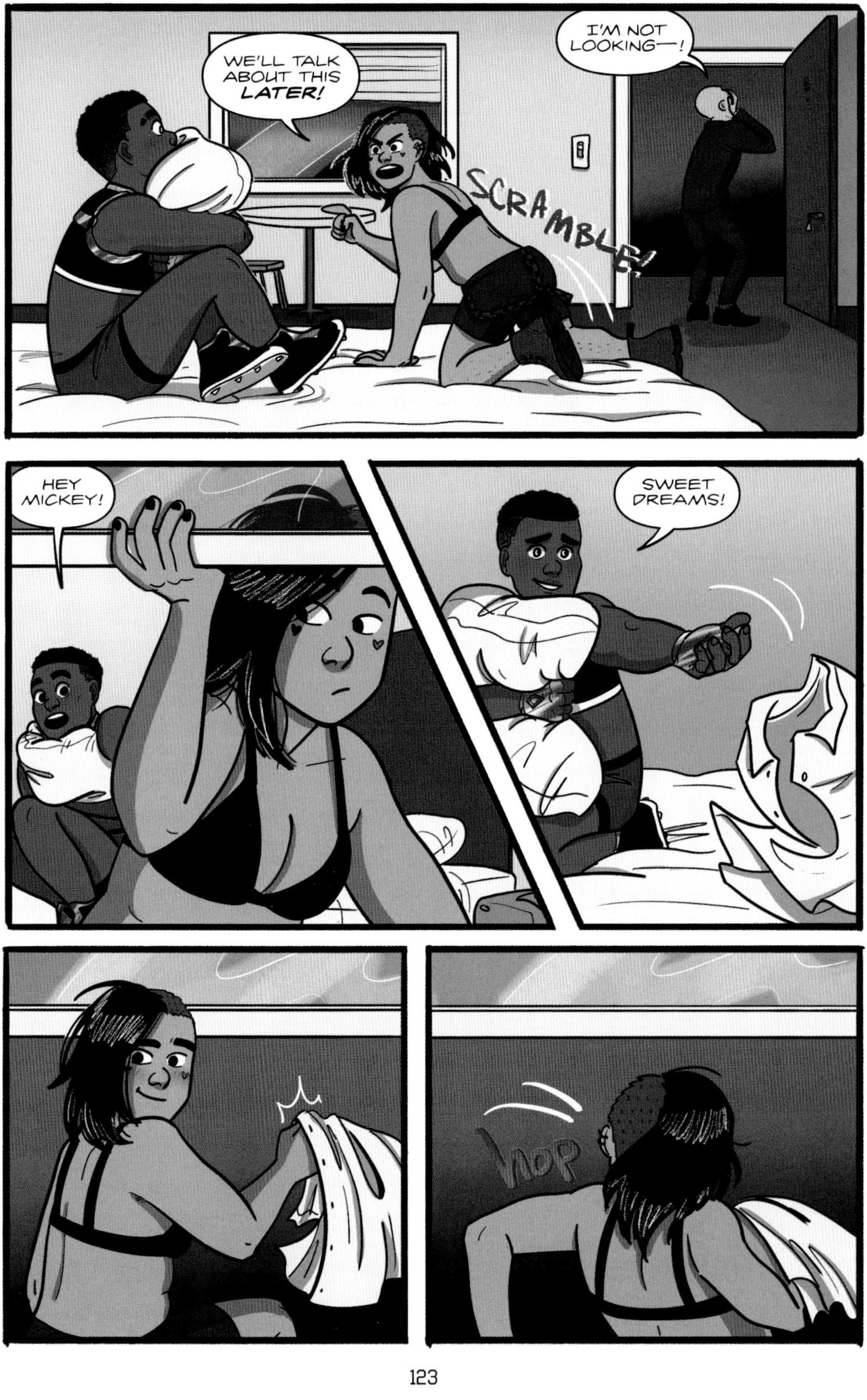
WE'LL TALK ABOUT THIS LATER!
I'M NOT LOOKING—!
SCRAMBLE!
HEY MICKEY!
SWEET DREAMS!

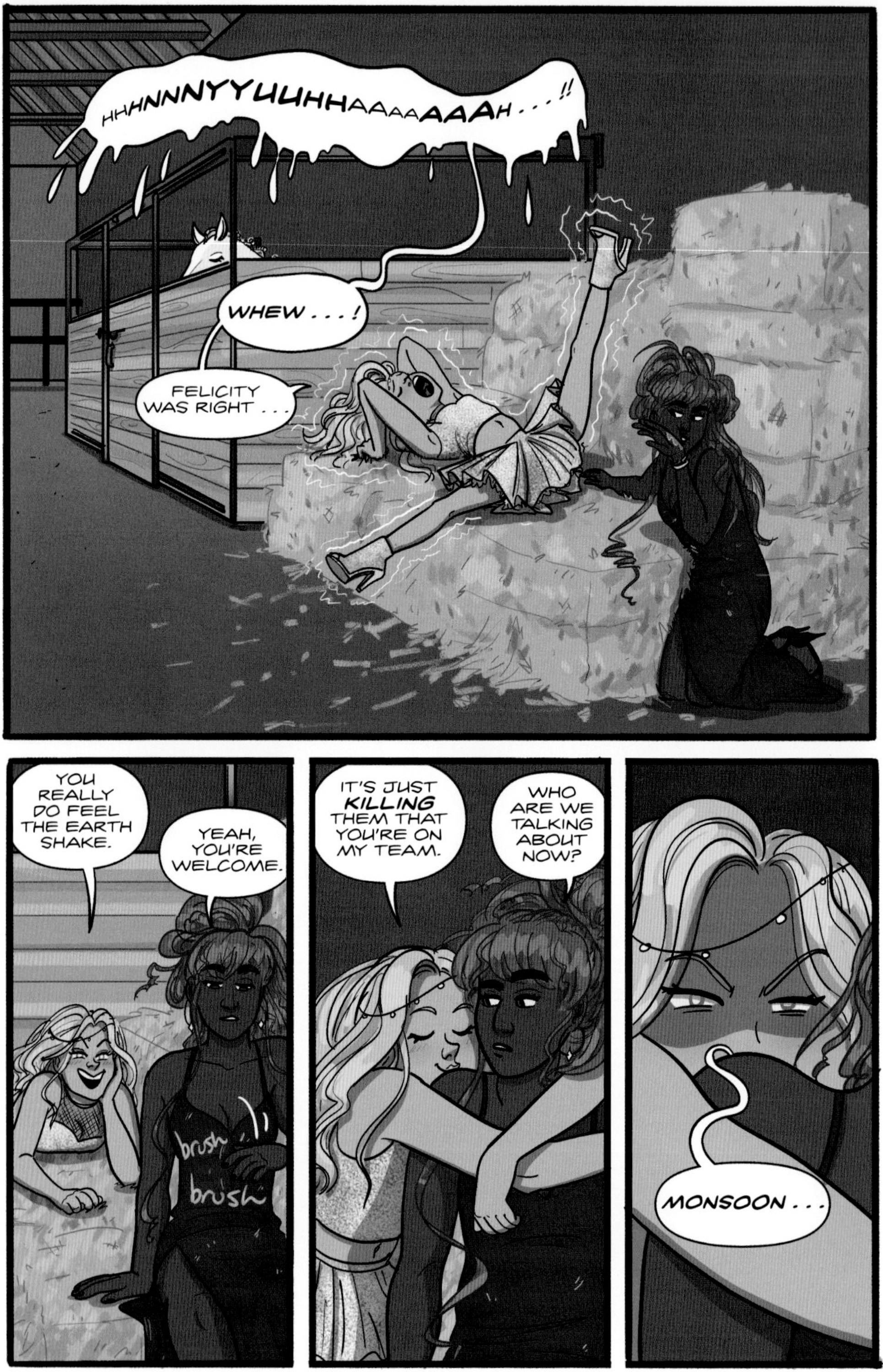
HHHNNNYYUUHHAAAAAAAH . . . !!
WHEW . . . !
FELICITY WAS RIGHT . . .
YOU REALLY DO FEEL THE EARTH SHAKE.
YEAH, YOU'RE WELCOME.
brush brush
IT'S JUST **KILLING** THEM THAT YOU'RE ON MY TEAM.
WHO ARE WE TALKING ABOUT NOW?
MONSOON . . .

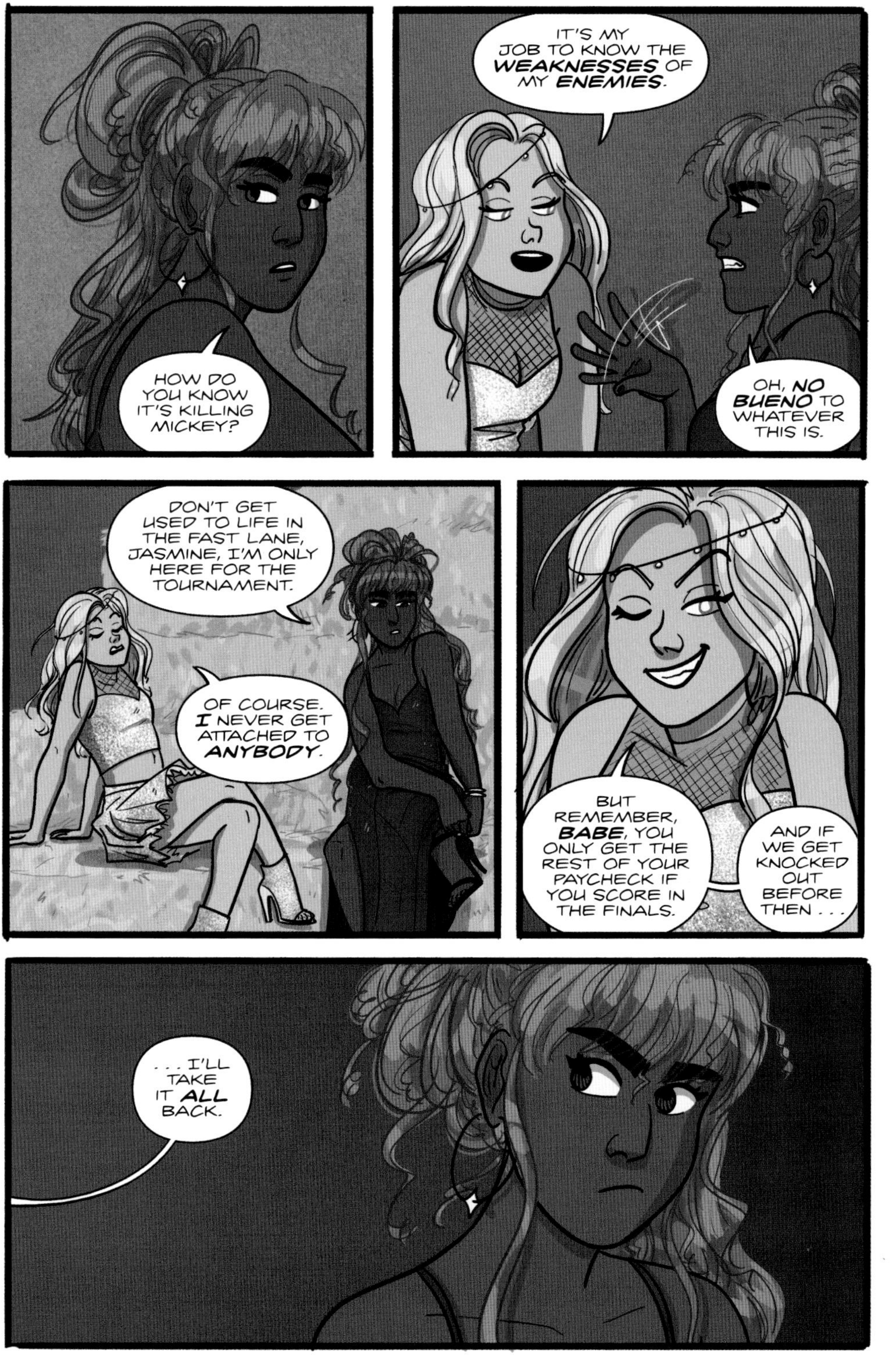
HOW DO YOU KNOW IT'S KILLING MICKEY?
IT'S MY JOB TO KNOW THE **WEAKNESSES** OF MY **ENEMIES**.
OH, **NO BUENO** TO WHATEVER THIS IS.
DON'T GET USED TO LIFE IN THE FAST LANE, JASMINE, I'M ONLY HERE FOR THE TOURNAMENT.
OF COURSE. ***I*** NEVER GET ATTACHED TO ***ANYBODY***.
BUT REMEMBER, **BABE**, YOU ONLY GET THE REST OF YOUR PAYCHECK IF YOU SCORE IN THE FINALS.
AND IF WE GET KNOCKED OUT BEFORE THEN . . .
. . . I'LL TAKE IT **ALL** BACK.

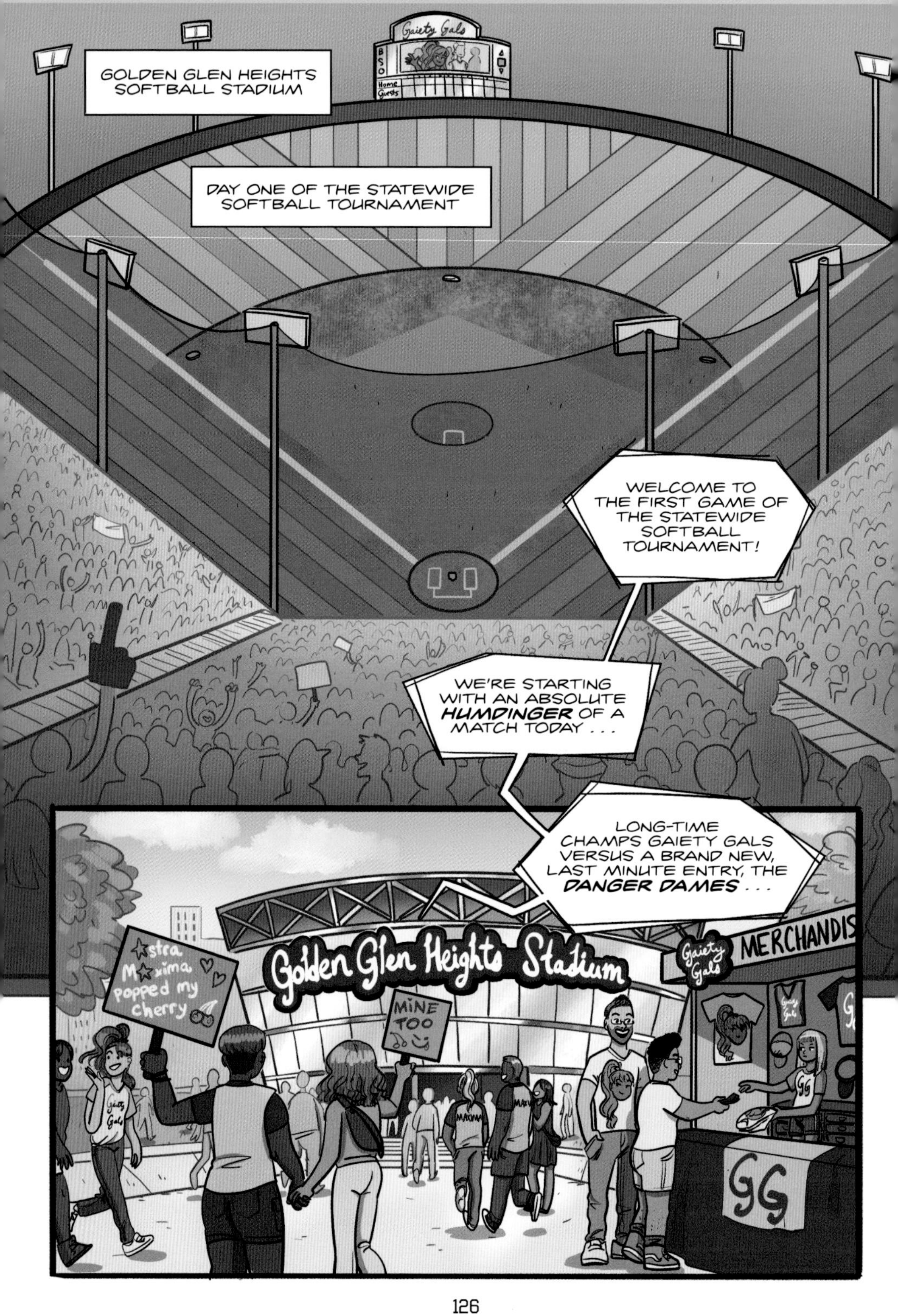
GOLDEN GLEN HEIGHTS SOFTBALL STADIUM
Gaiety Gals
Home
Guests
DAY ONE OF THE STATEWIDE SOFTBALL TOURNAMENT
WELCOME TO THE FIRST GAME OF THE STATEWIDE SOFTBALL TOURNAMENT!
WE'RE STARTING WITH AN ABSOLUTE ***HUMDINGER*** OF A MATCH TODAY . . .
LONG-TIME CHAMPS GAIETY GALS VERSUS A BRAND NEW, LAST MINUTE ENTRY, THE ***DANGER DAMES*** . . .
Golden Glen Heights Stadium
Gaiety Gals
MERCHANDIS
stra M xima popped my cherry
MINE TOO
Gaiety Gals
GG

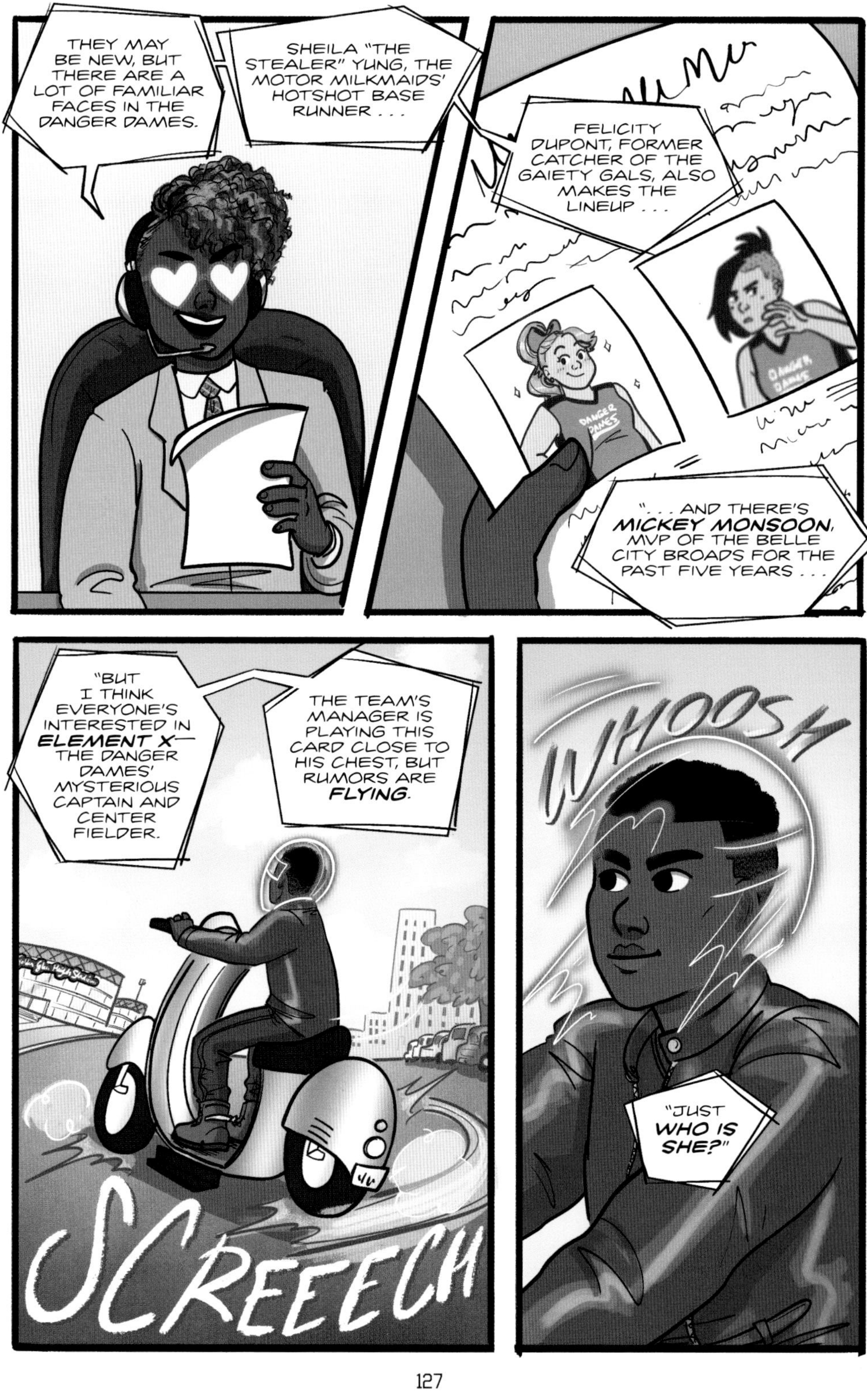

THEY MAY BE NEW, BUT THERE ARE A LOT OF FAMILIAR FACES IN THE DANGER DAMES.
SHEILA "THE STEALER" YUNG, THE MOTOR MILKMAIDS' HOTSHOT BASE RUNNER . . .
FELICITY DUPONT, FORMER CATCHER OF THE GAIETY GALS, ALSO MAKES THE LINEUP . . .
DANGER DAMES
DANGER DAMES
". . . AND THERE'S **MICKEY MONSOON**, MVP OF THE BELLE CITY BROADS FOR THE PAST FIVE YEARS . . .
"BUT I THINK EVERYONE'S INTERESTED IN **ELEMENT X**— THE DANGER DAMES' MYSTERIOUS CAPTAIN AND CENTER FIELDER.
THE TEAM'S MANAGER IS PLAYING THIS CARD CLOSE TO HIS CHEST, BUT RUMORS ARE **FLYING**.
SCREEECH
WHOOSH
"JUST **WHO IS SHE?**"

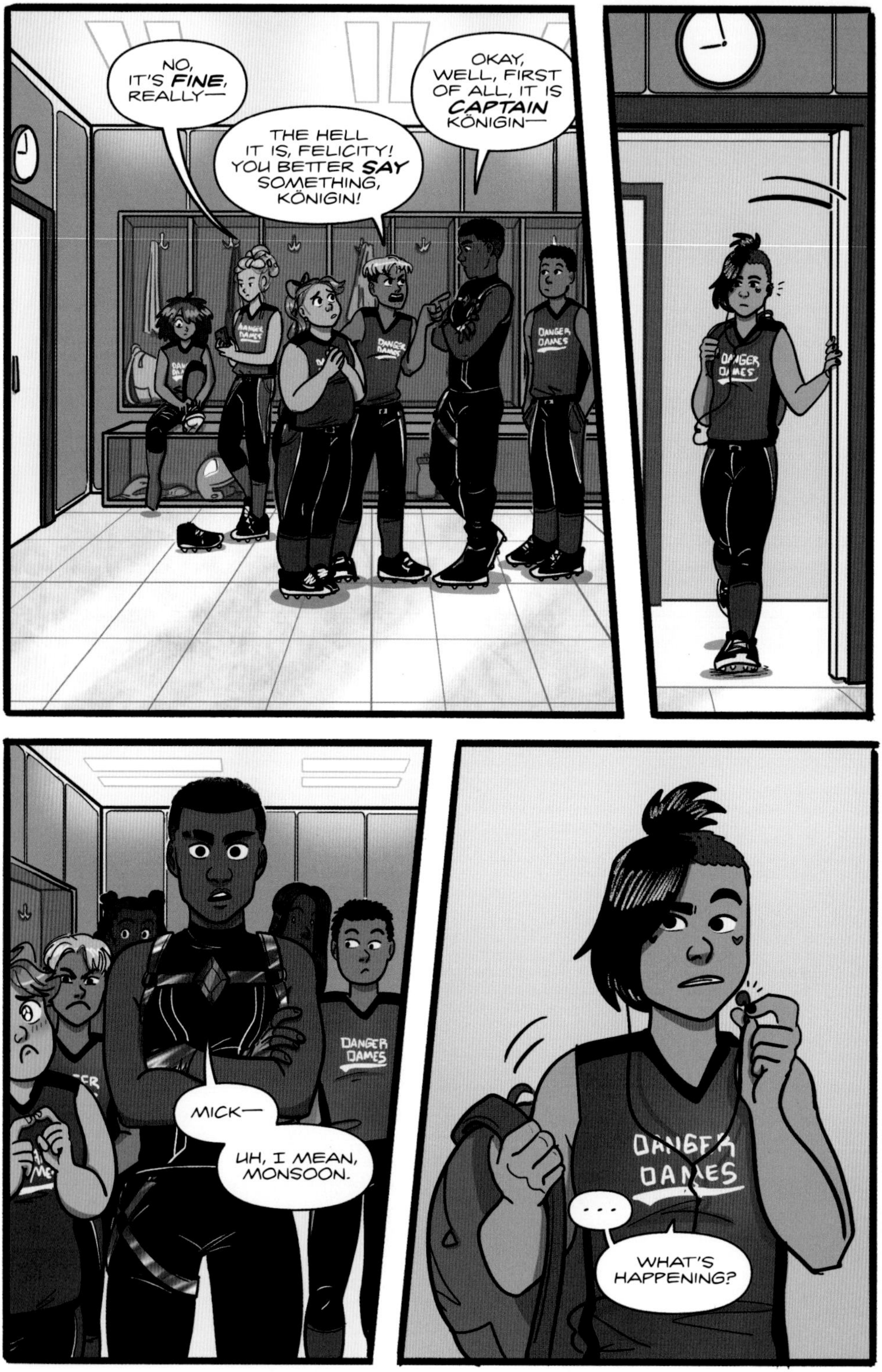
NO, IT'S **FINE**, REALLY—
THE HELL IT IS, FELICITY! YOU BETTER **SAY** SOMETHING, KÖNIGIN!
OKAY, WELL, FIRST OF ALL, IT IS **CAPTAIN** KÖNIGIN—
DANGER DAMES
MICK—
UH, I MEAN, MONSOON.
...
WHAT'S HAPPENING?

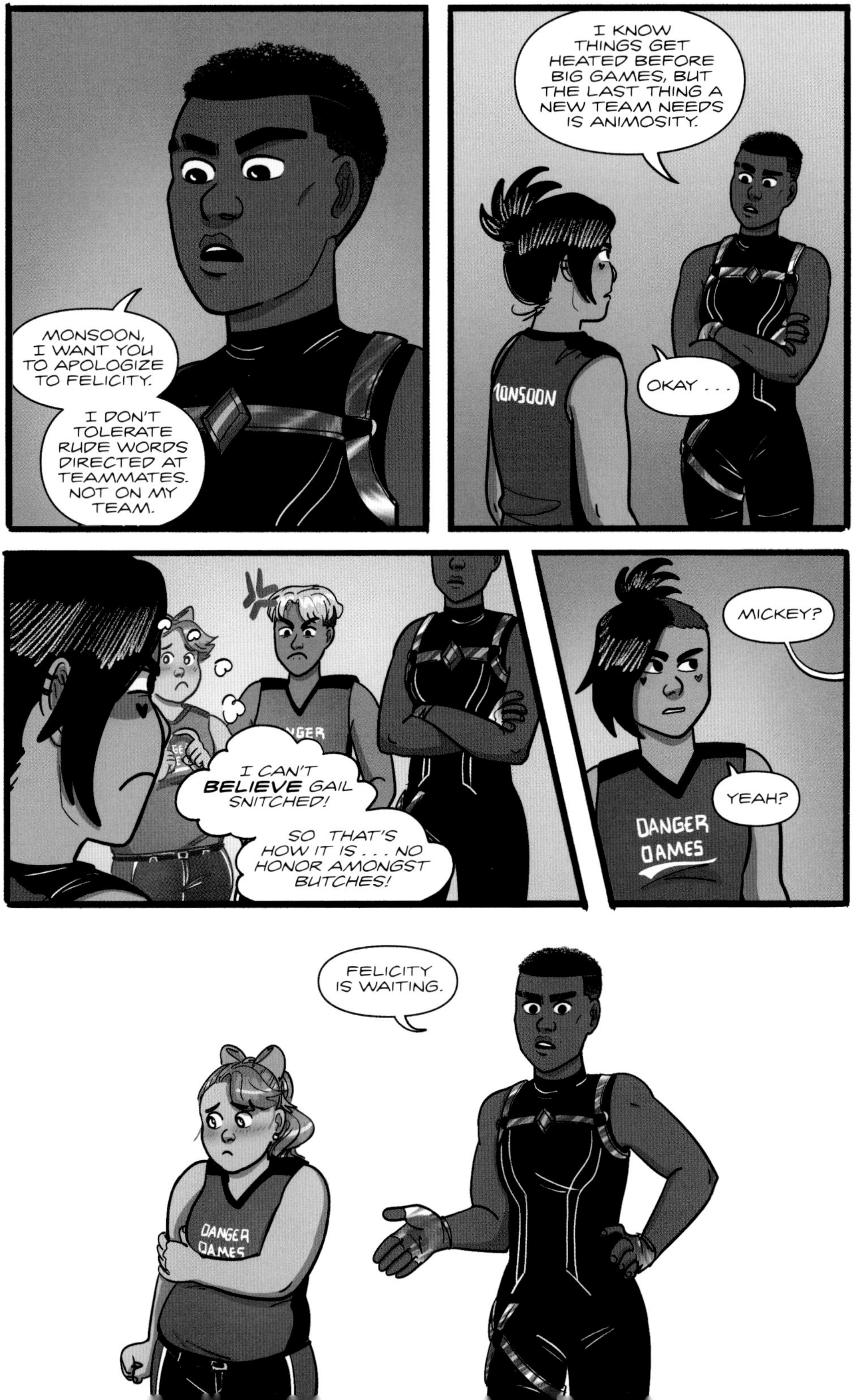
MONSOON, I WANT YOU TO APOLOGIZE TO FELICITY.
I DON'T TOLERATE RUDE WORDS DIRECTED AT TEAMMATES. NOT ON MY TEAM.
I KNOW THINGS GET HEATED BEFORE BIG GAMES, BUT THE LAST THING A NEW TEAM NEEDS IS ANIMOSITY.
MONSOON
OKAY . . .
I CAN'T **BELIEVE** GAIL SNITCHED!
SO THAT'S HOW IT IS . . . NO HONOR AMONGST BUTCHES!
MICKEY?
YEAH?
DANGER DAMES
FELICITY IS WAITING.
DANGER DAMES

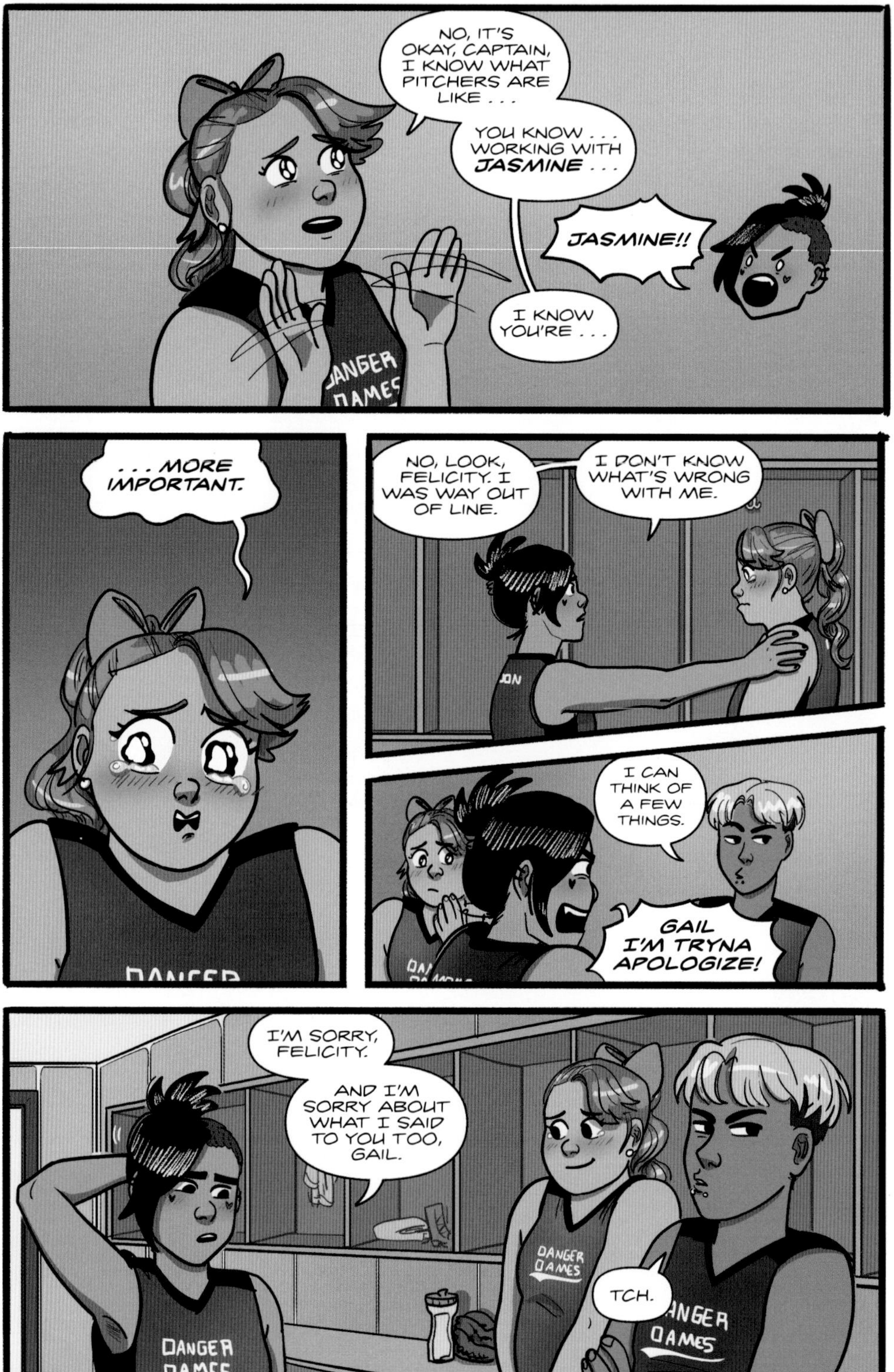
NO, IT'S OKAY, CAPTAIN, I KNOW WHAT PITCHERS ARE LIKE . . .
YOU KNOW . . . WORKING WITH JASMINE . . .
I KNOW YOU'RE . . .
JASMINE!!
DANGER DAMES
. . . MORE IMPORTANT.
DANGER
NO, LOOK, FELICITY. I WAS WAY OUT OF LINE.
I DON'T KNOW WHAT'S WRONG WITH ME.
I CAN THINK OF A FEW THINGS.
GAIL I'M TRYNA APOLOGIZE!
I'M SORRY, FELICITY.
AND I'M SORRY ABOUT WHAT I SAID TO YOU TOO, GAIL.
DANGER DAMES
DANGER DAMES
TCH.
DANGER DAMES

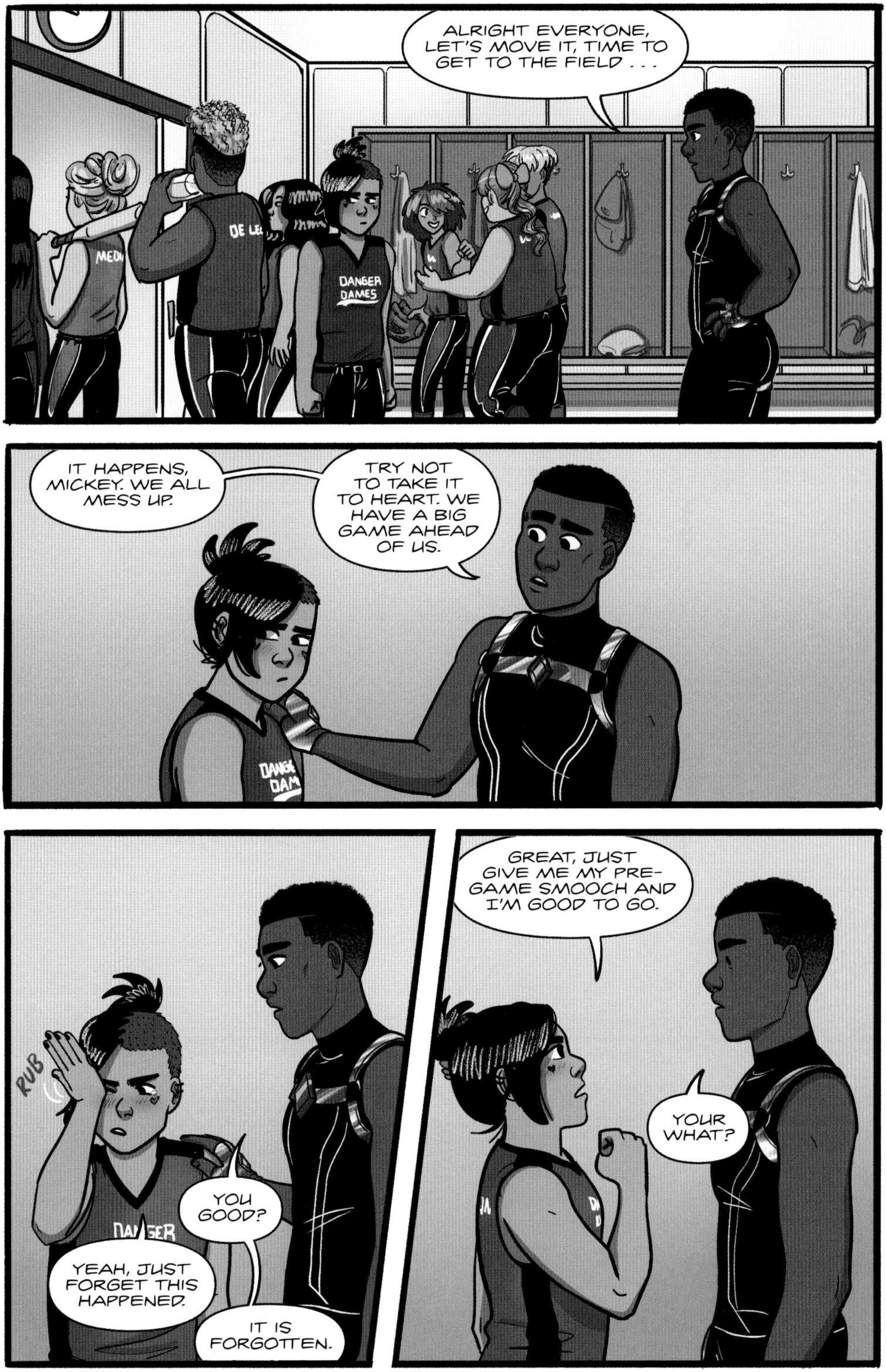
ALRIGHT EVERYONE, LET'S MOVE IT, TIME TO GET TO THE FIELD . . .
DANGER DAMES
IT HAPPENS, MICKEY. WE ALL MESS UP.
TRY NOT TO TAKE IT TO HEART. WE HAVE A BIG GAME AHEAD OF US.
RUB
YOU GOOD?
YEAH, JUST FORGET THIS HAPPENED.
IT IS FORGOTTEN.
GREAT, JUST GIVE ME MY PRE-GAME SMOOCH AND I'M GOOD TO GO.
YOUR WHAT?

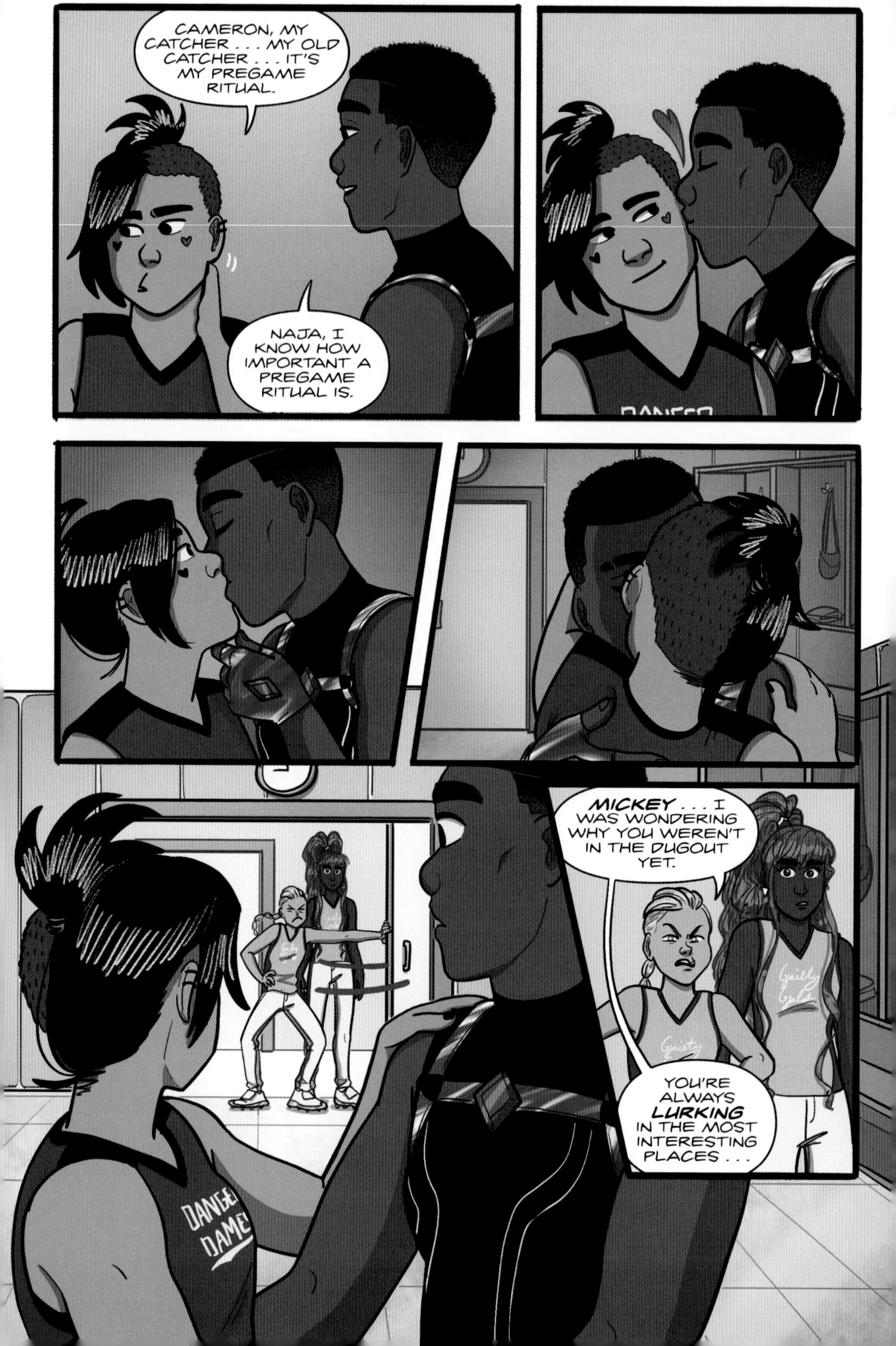
CAMERON, MY CATCHER . . . MY OLD CATCHER . . . IT'S MY PREGAME RITUAL.
NAJA, I KNOW HOW IMPORTANT A PREGAME RITUAL IS.
MICKEY . . . I WAS WONDERING WHY YOU WEREN'T IN THE DUGOUT YET.
YOU'RE ALWAYS **LURKING** IN THE MOST INTERESTING PLACES . . .

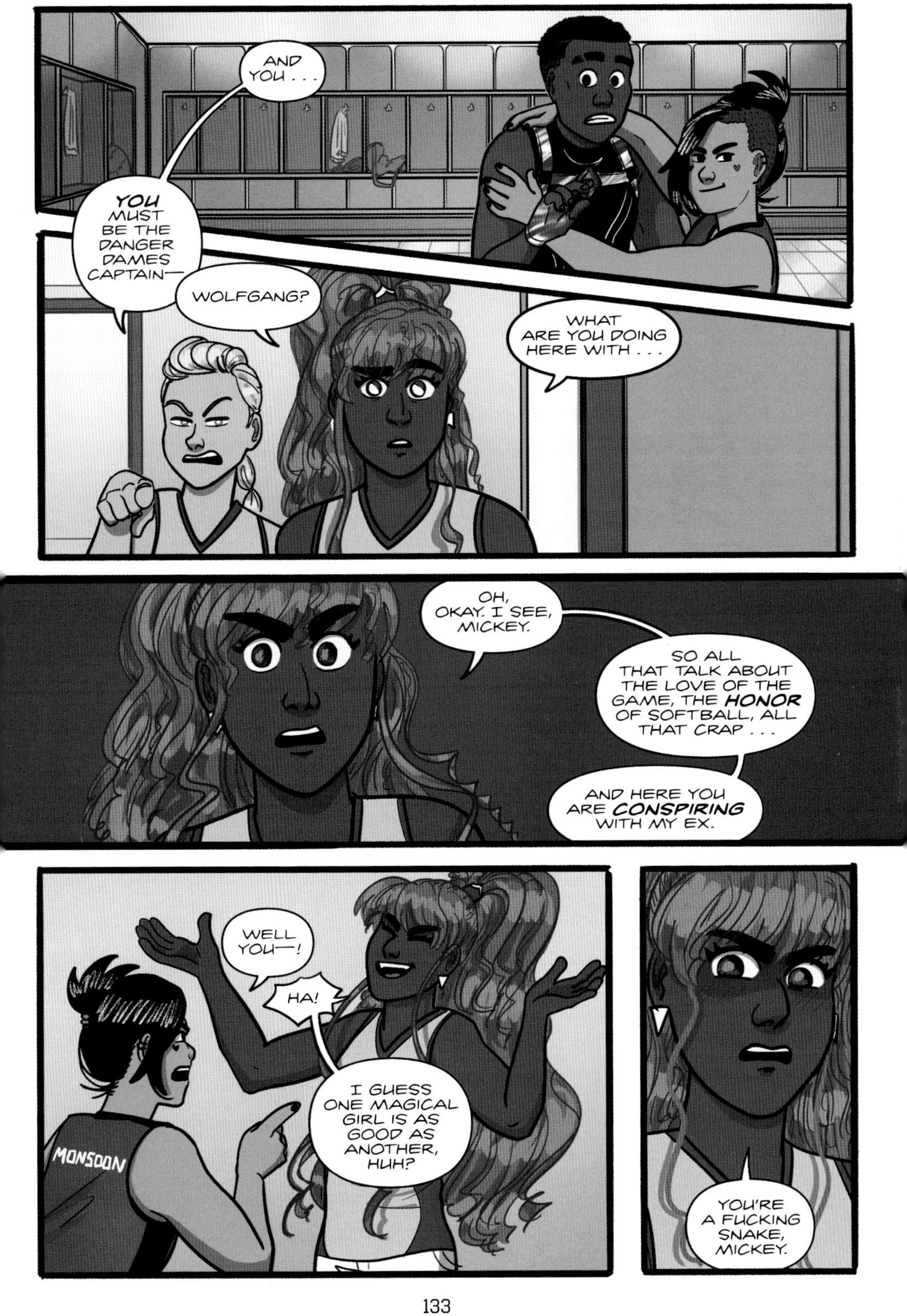

AND YOU . . .
YOU MUST BE THE DANGER DAMES CAPTAIN—
WOLFGANG?
WHAT ARE YOU DOING HERE WITH . . .
OH, OKAY. I SEE, MICKEY.
SO ALL THAT TALK ABOUT THE LOVE OF THE GAME, THE HONOR OF SOFTBALL, ALL THAT CRAP . . .
AND HERE YOU ARE CONSPIRING WITH MY EX.
WELL YOU—!
HA!
I GUESS ONE MAGICAL GIRL IS AS GOOD AS ANOTHER, HUH?
MONSOON
YOU'RE A FUCKING SNAKE, MICKEY.

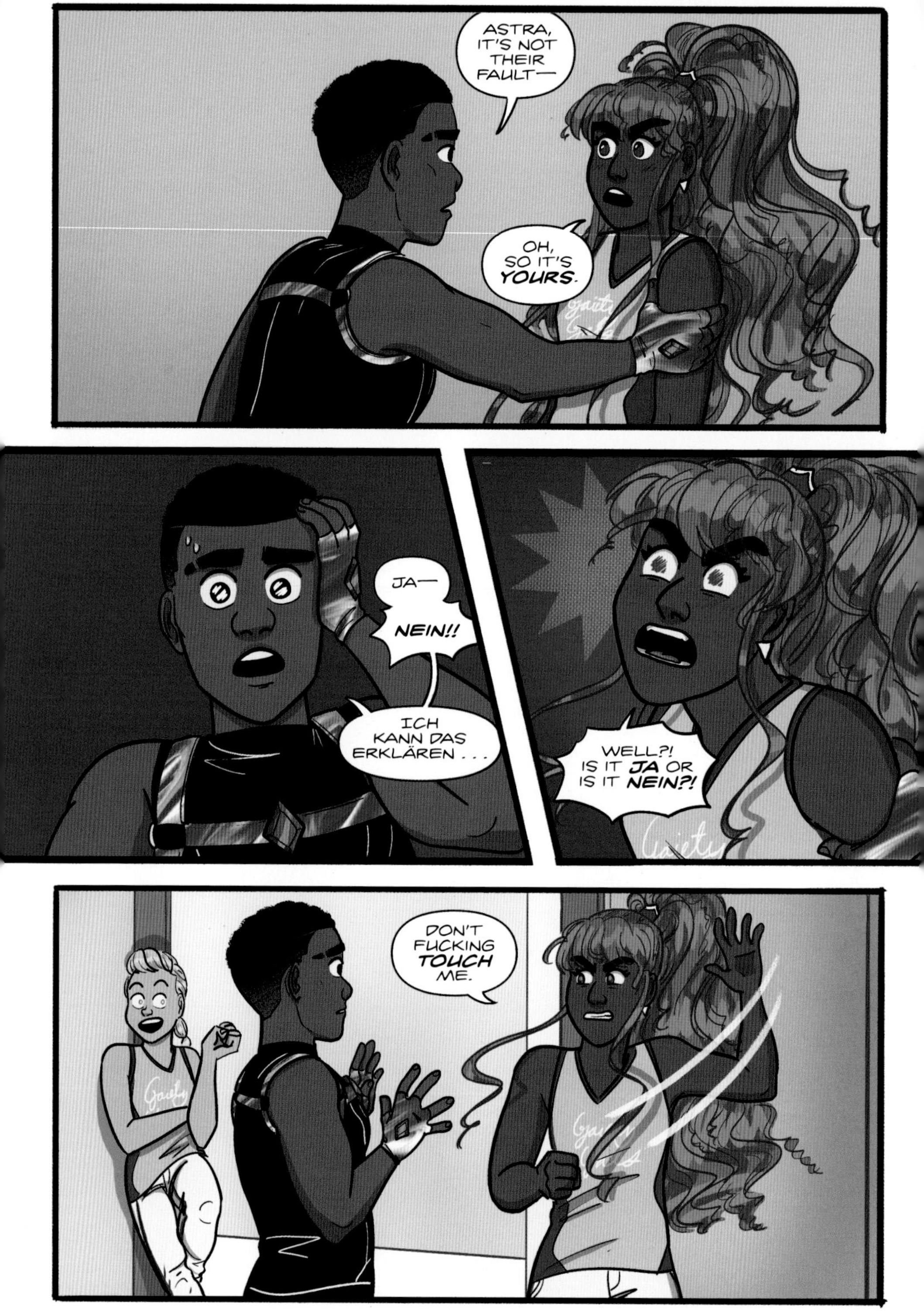
ASTRA, IT'S NOT THEIR FAULT—
OH, SO IT'S **YOURS**.
JA—
NEIN!!
ICH KANN DAS ERKLÄREN . . .
WELL?! IS IT **JA** OR IS IT **NEIN?!**
DON'T FUCKING **TOUCH** ME.

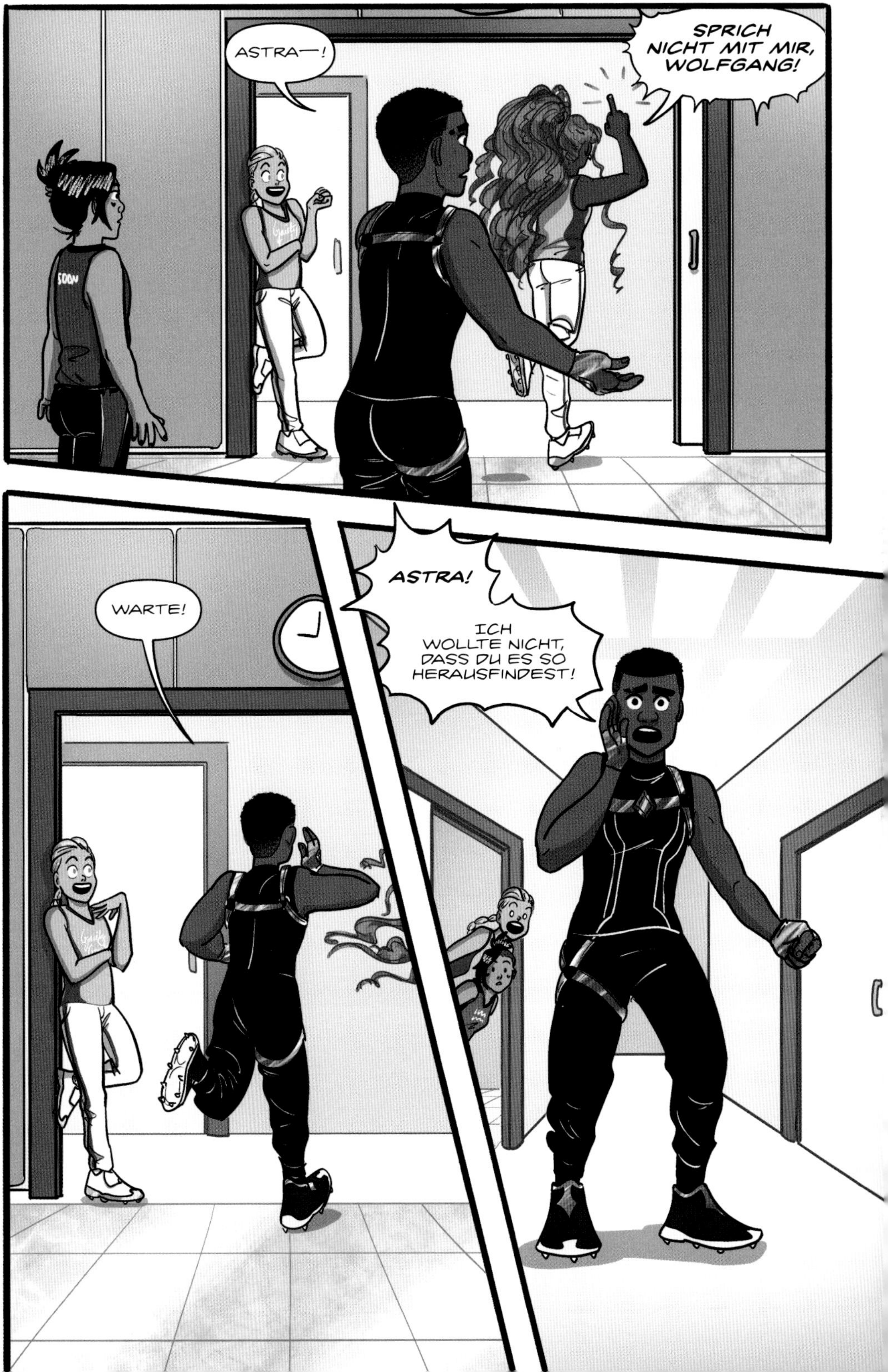
ASTRA—!
SPRICH NICHT MIT MIR, WOLFGANG!
WARTE!
ASTRA!
ICH WOLLTE NICHT, DASS DU ES SO HERAUSFINDEST!

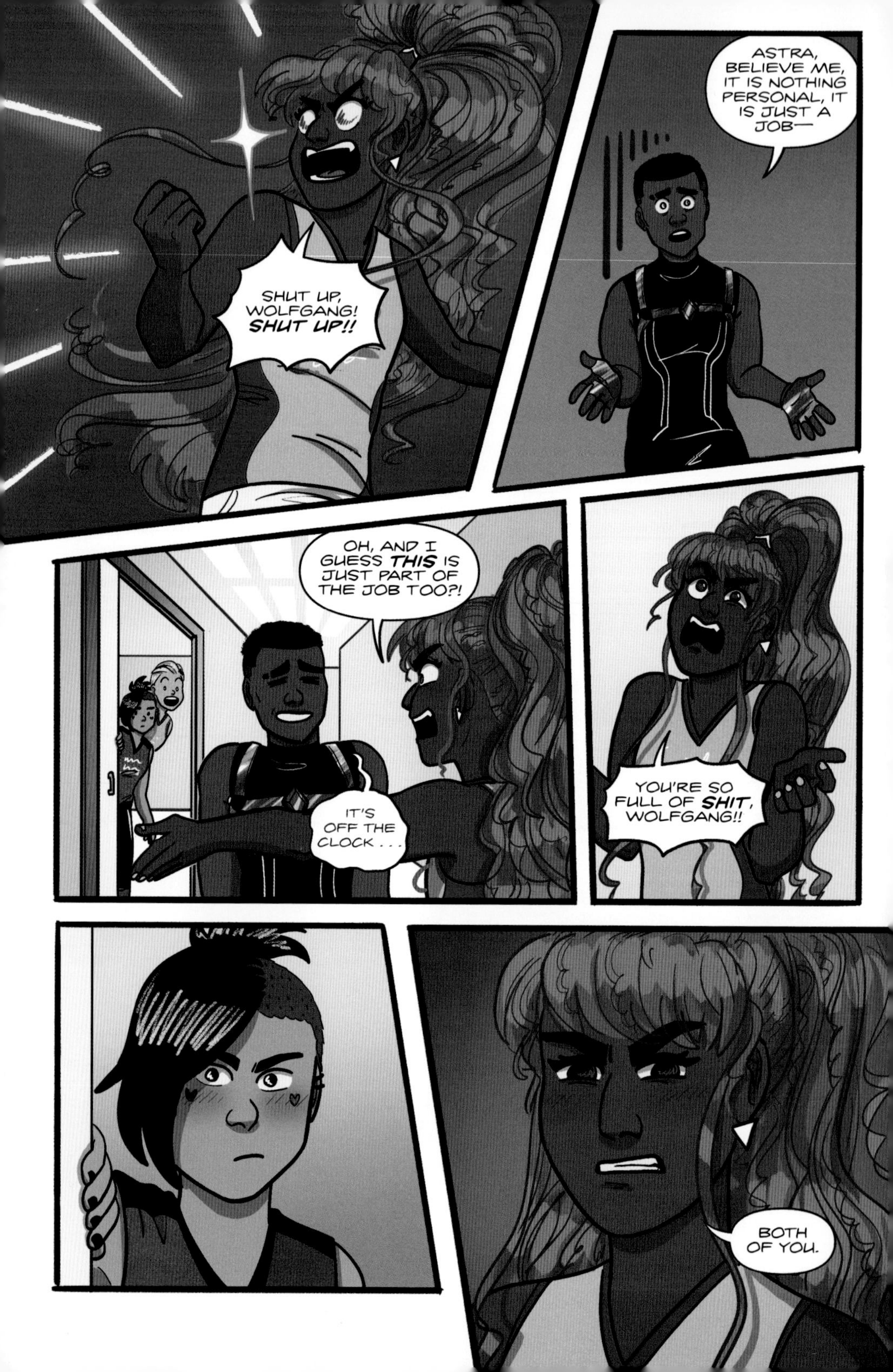
SHUT UP, WOLFGANG! ***SHUT UP!!***
ASTRA, BELIEVE ME, IT IS NOTHING PERSONAL, IT IS JUST A JOB—
OH, AND I GUESS ***THIS*** IS JUST PART OF THE JOB TOO?!
IT'S OFF THE CLOCK . . .
YOU'RE SO FULL OF ***SHIT***, WOLFGANG!!
BOTH OF YOU.

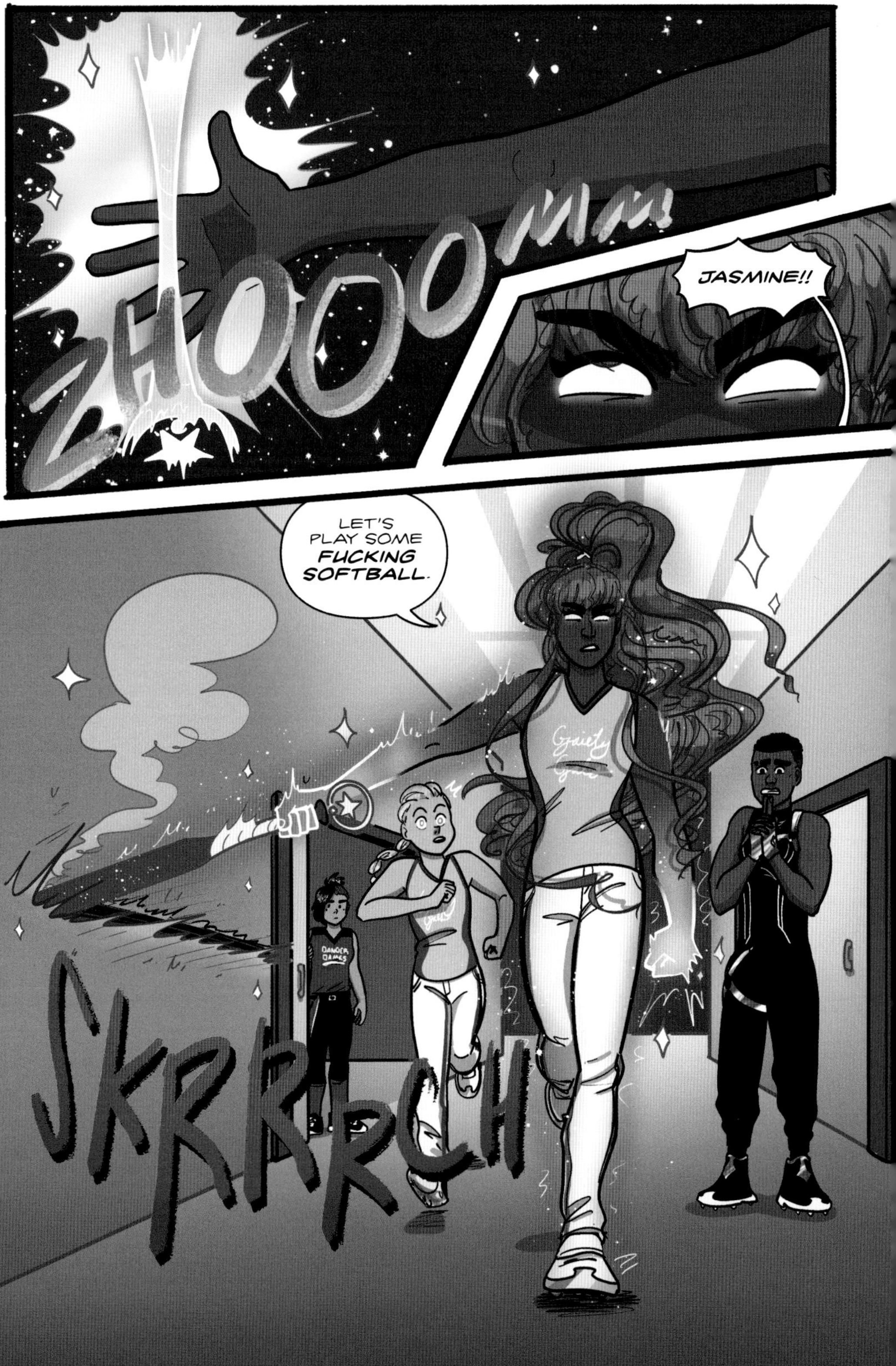
ZHOOOMM!
JASMINE!!
LET'S PLAY SOME FUCKING SOFTBALL.
SKRRRCH

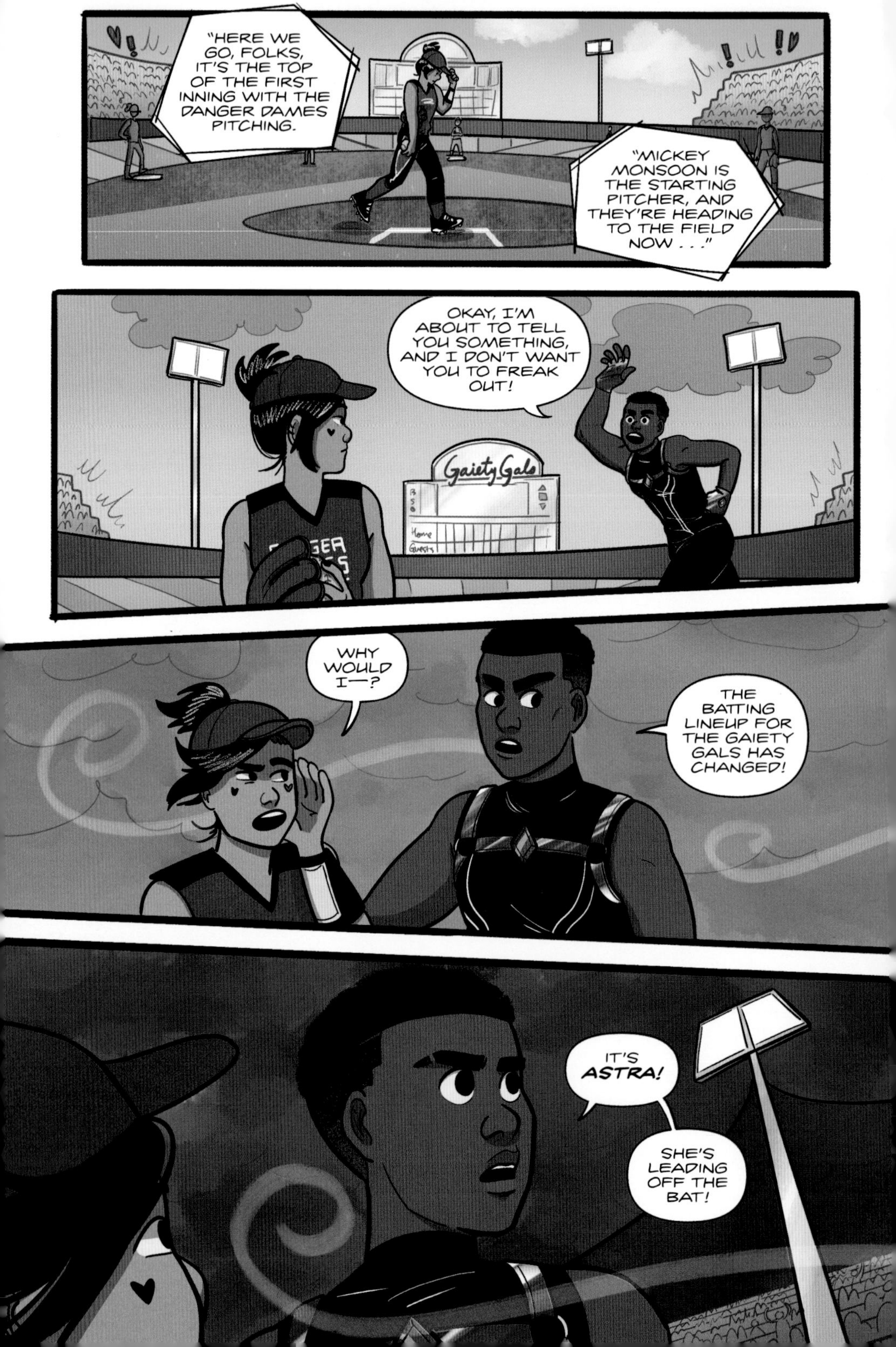
"HERE WE GO, FOLKS, IT'S THE TOP OF THE FIRST INNING WITH THE DANGER DAMES PITCHING.
"MICKEY MONSOON IS THE STARTING PITCHER, AND THEY'RE HEADING TO THE FIELD NOW . . ."
OKAY, I'M ABOUT TO TELL YOU SOMETHING, AND I DON'T WANT YOU TO FREAK OUT!
Gaiety Gals
Home
Guests
WHY WOULD I—?
THE BATTING LINEUP FOR THE GAIETY GALS HAS CHANGED!
IT'S ASTRA!
SHE'S LEADING OFF THE BAT!

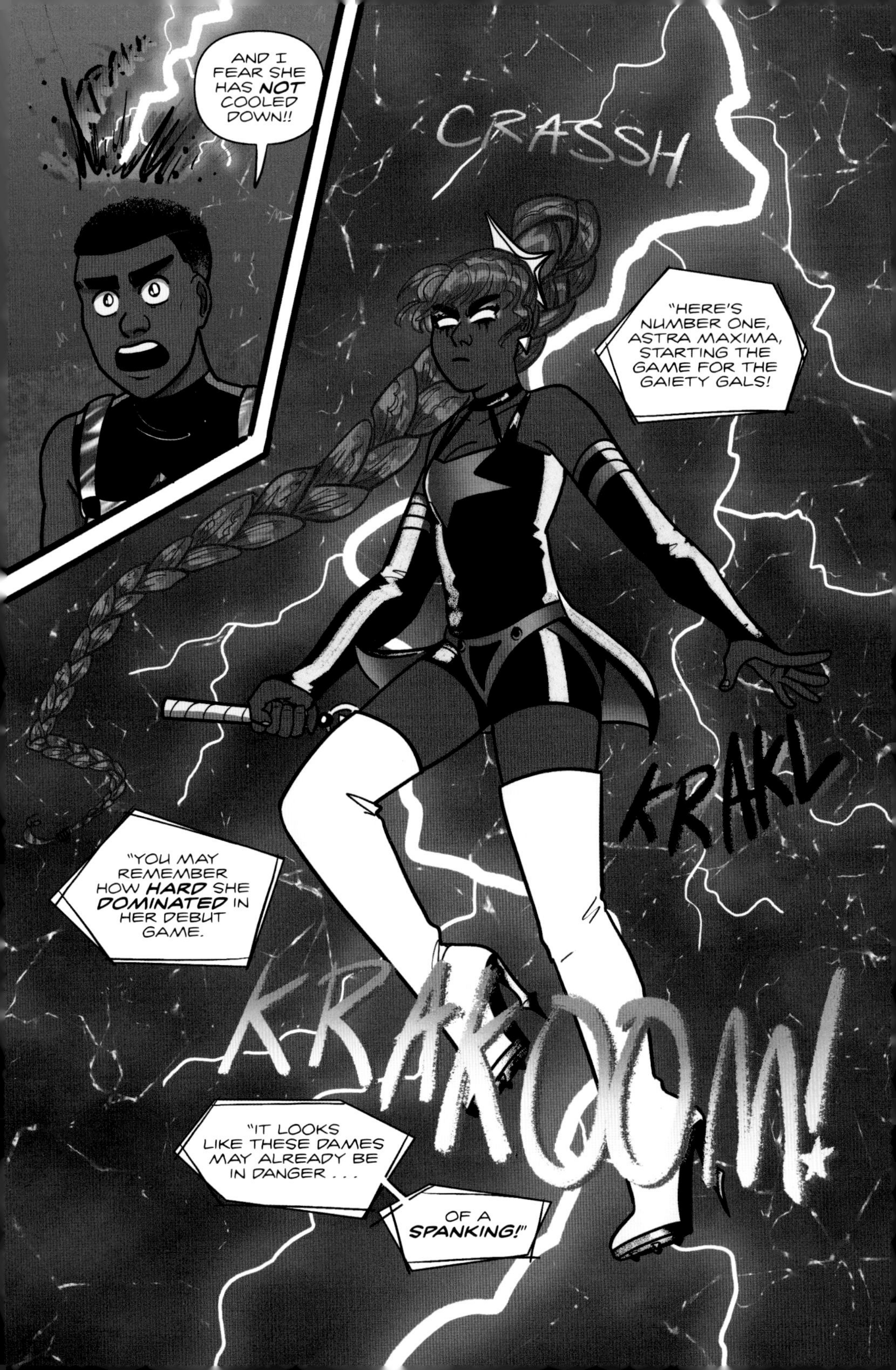
KRAKL
AND I FEAR SHE HAS **NOT** COOLED DOWN!!
CRASSH
"HERE'S NUMBER ONE, ASTRA MAXIMA, STARTING THE GAME FOR THE GAIETY GALS!
KRAKL
"YOU MAY REMEMBER HOW **HARD** SHE **DOMINATED** IN HER DEBUT GAME.
KRAKOOM!
"IT LOOKS LIKE THESE DAMES MAY ALREADY BE IN DANGER . . .
OF A **SPANKING!**"

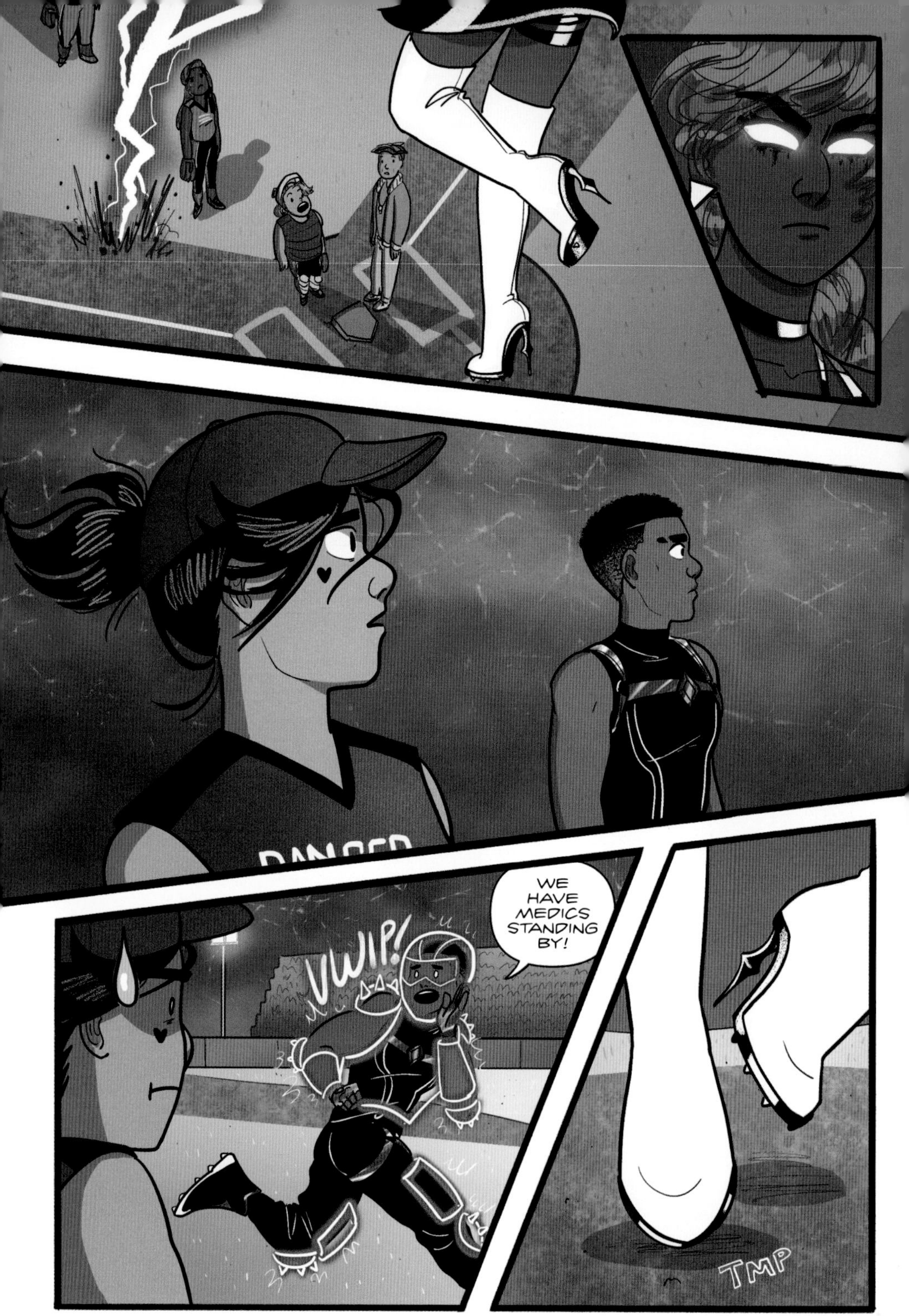
VWIP!
WE HAVE MEDICS STANDING BY!
TMP

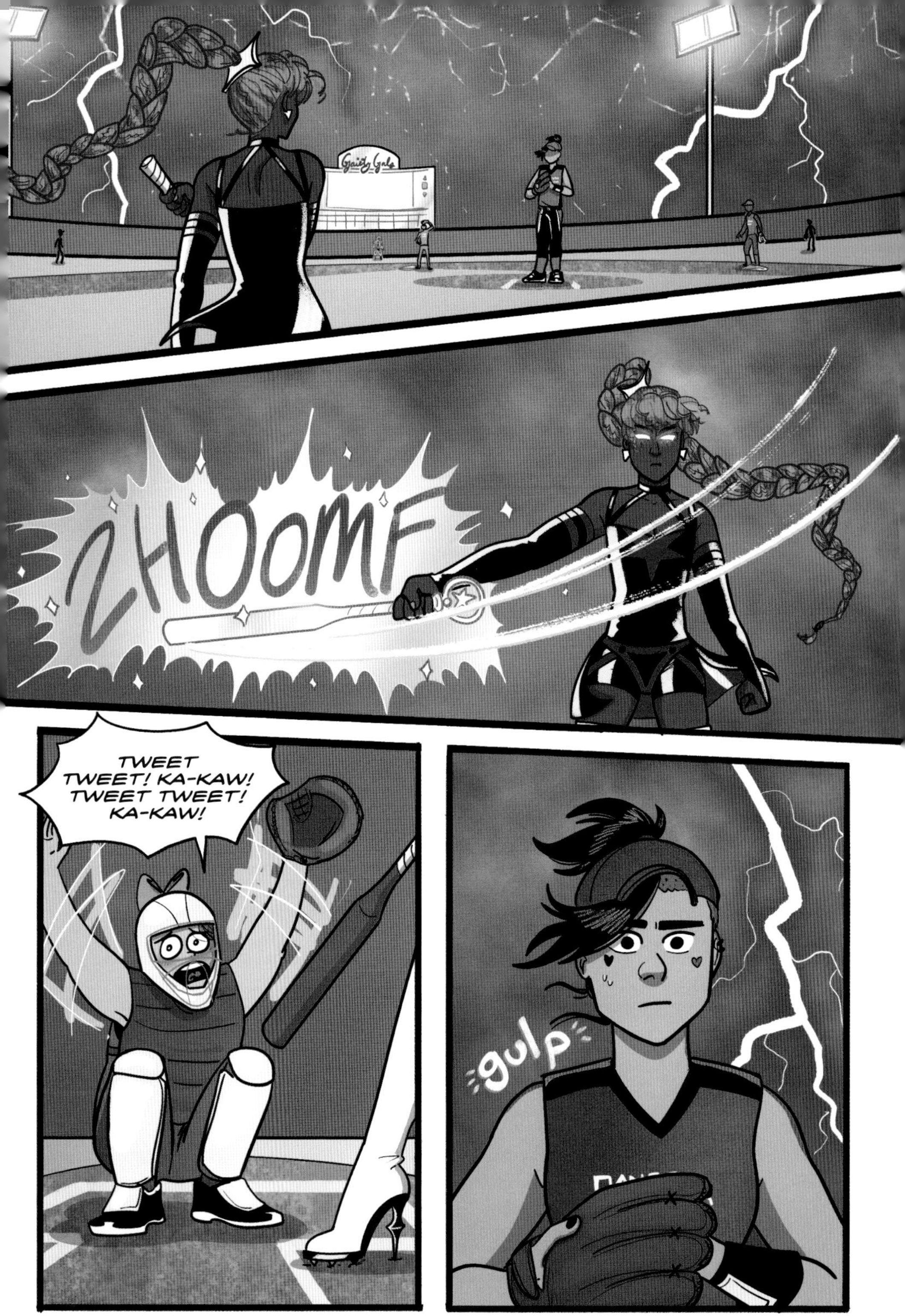
ZHOOMF
TWEET TWEET! KA-KAW! TWEET TWEET! KA-KAW!
gulp

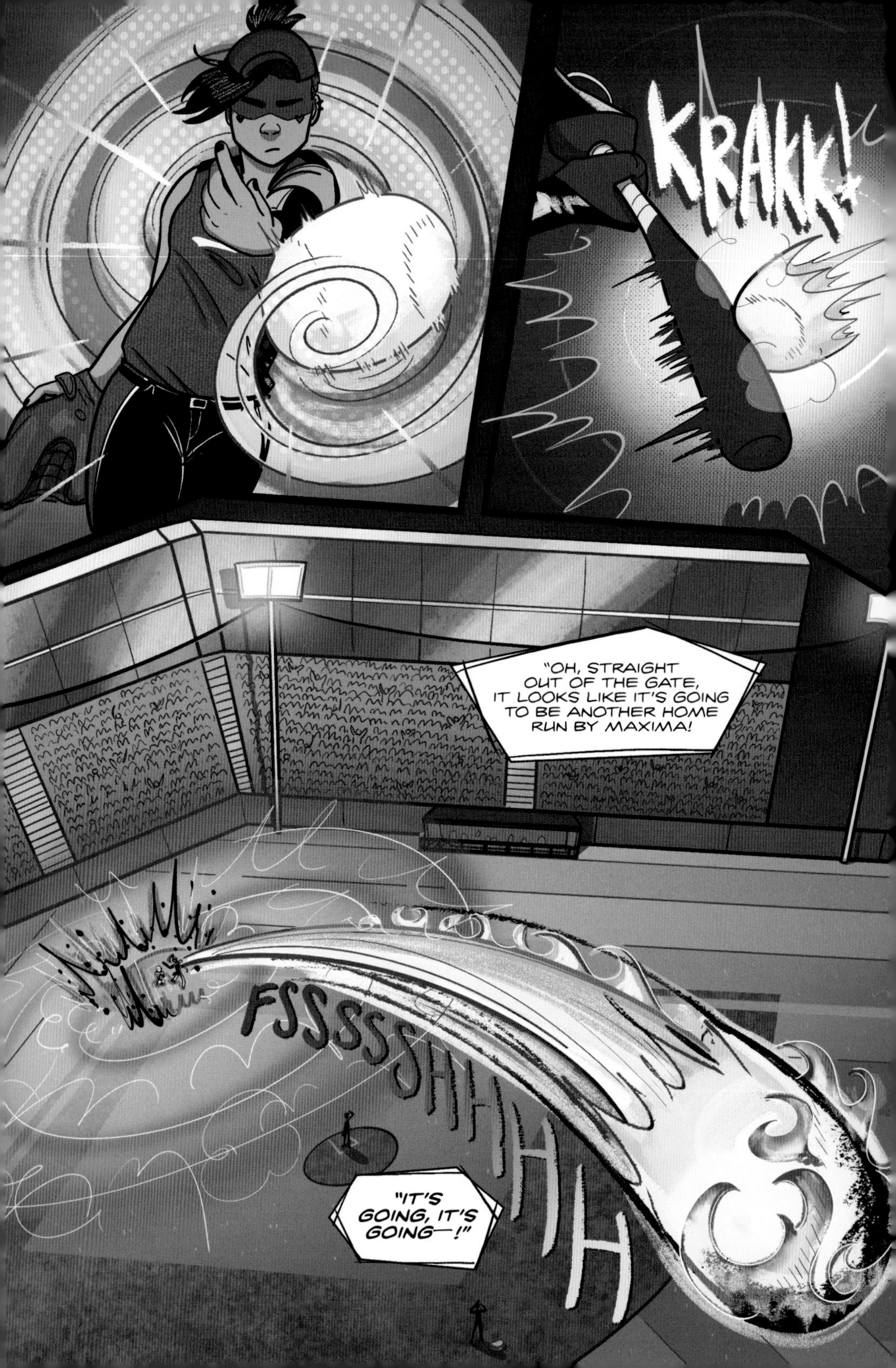
KRAKK!
"OH, STRAIGHT OUT OF THE GATE, IT LOOKS LIKE IT'S GOING TO BE ANOTHER HOME RUN BY MAXIMA!
FSSSSSHHHHH
"IT'S GOING, IT'S GOING—!"

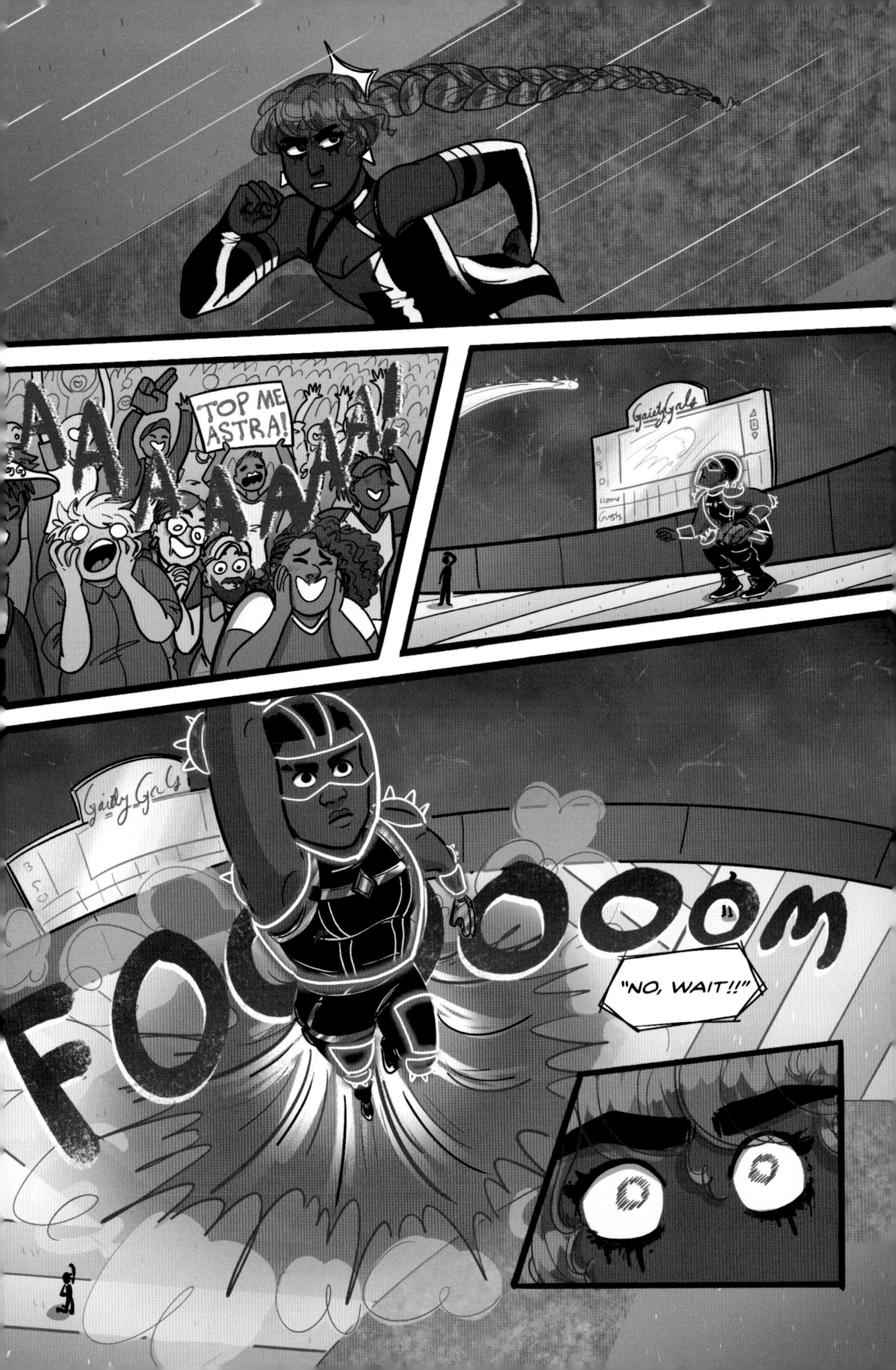
TOP ME ASTRA!
AAAAAAA!
Gaiety Gals
Home
Guests
Gaiety Gals
FOOOOOM
"NO, WAIT!!"

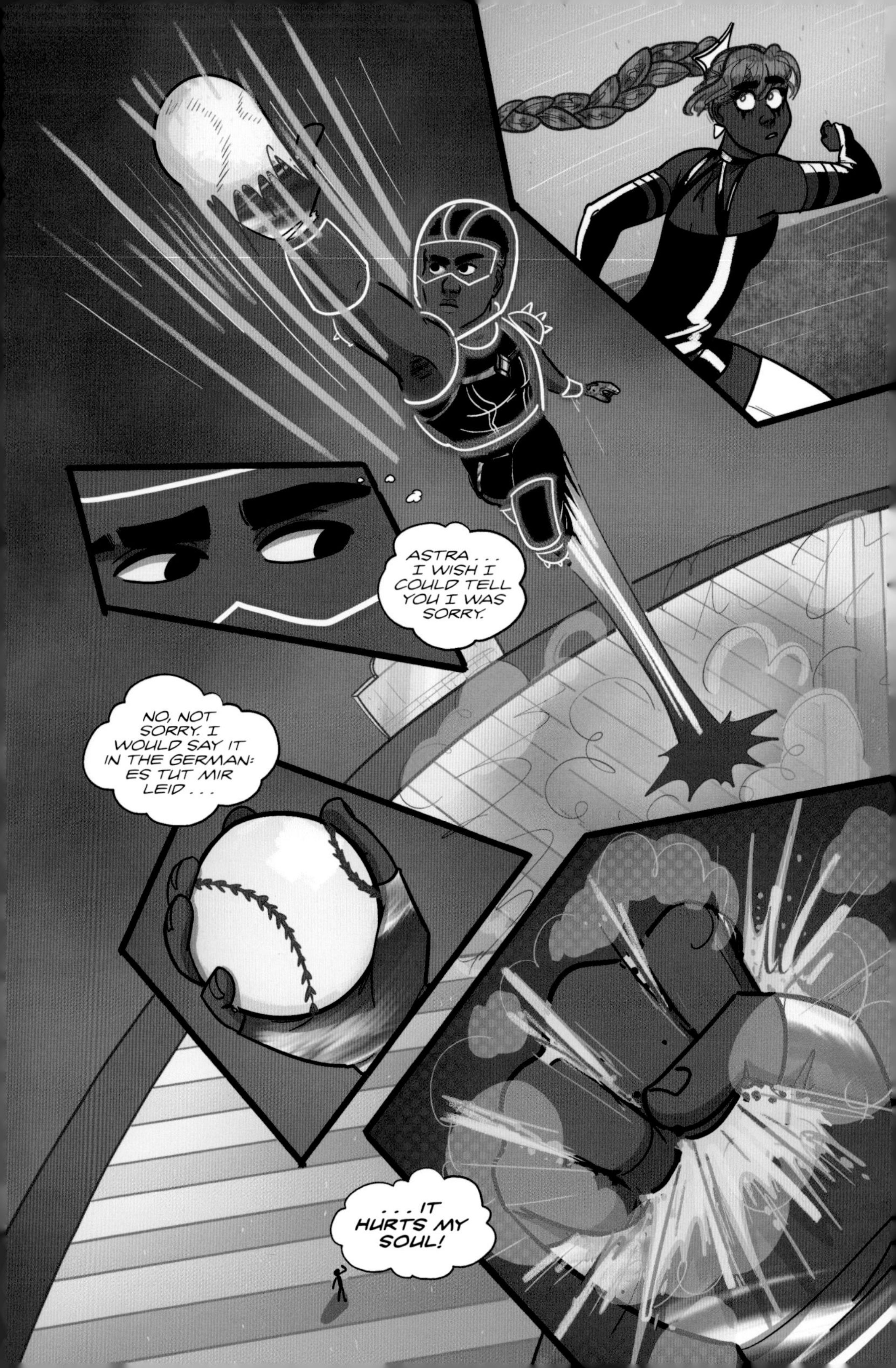
ASTRA . . . I WISH I COULD TELL YOU I WAS SORRY.
NO, NOT SORRY. I WOULD SAY IT IN THE GERMAN: ES TUT MIR LEID . . .
. . . IT HURTS MY SOUL!

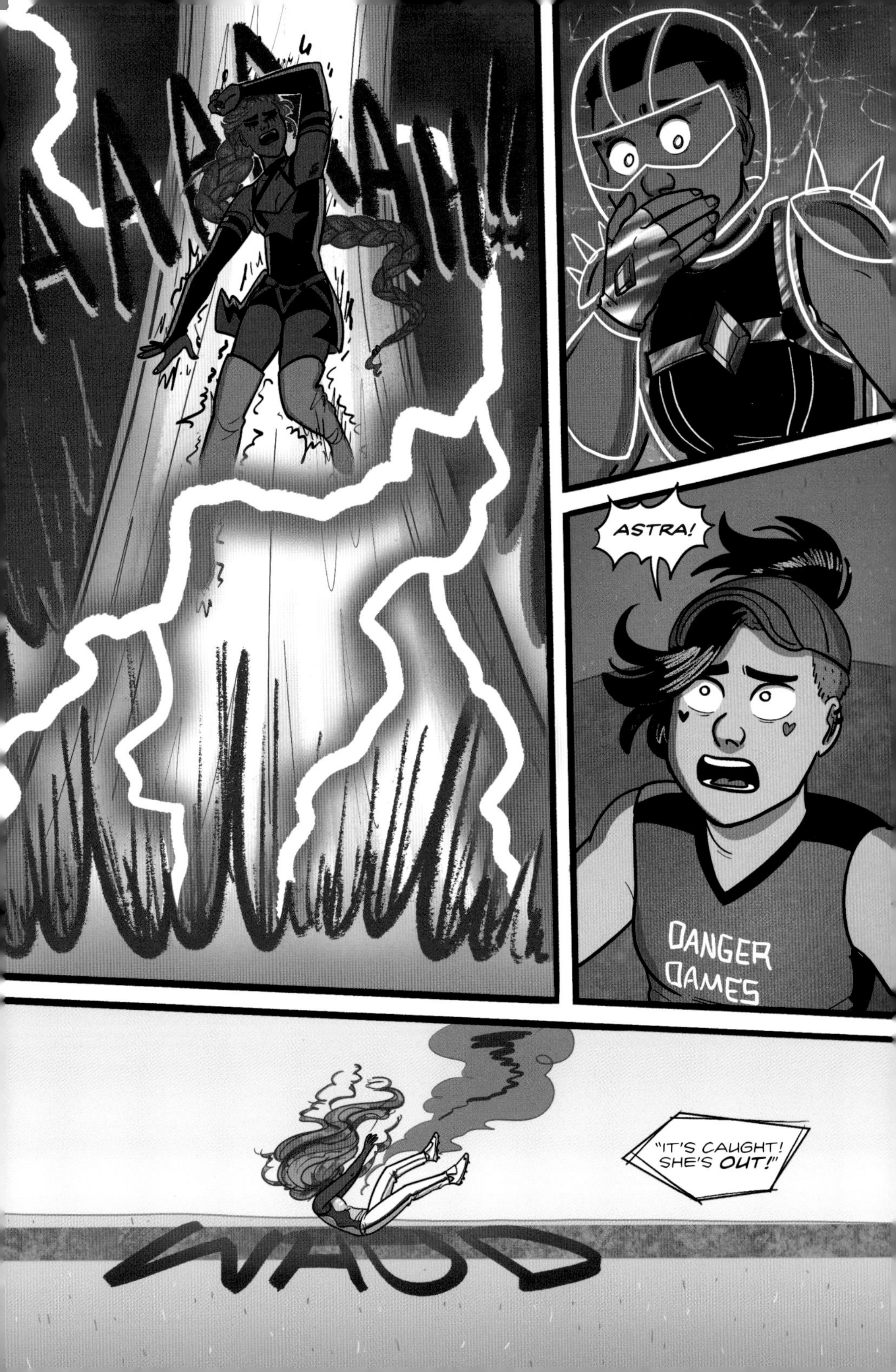
AAAAAHH!!
ASTRA!
DANGER DAMES
"IT'S CAUGHT! SHE'S **OUT!**"
WAUD

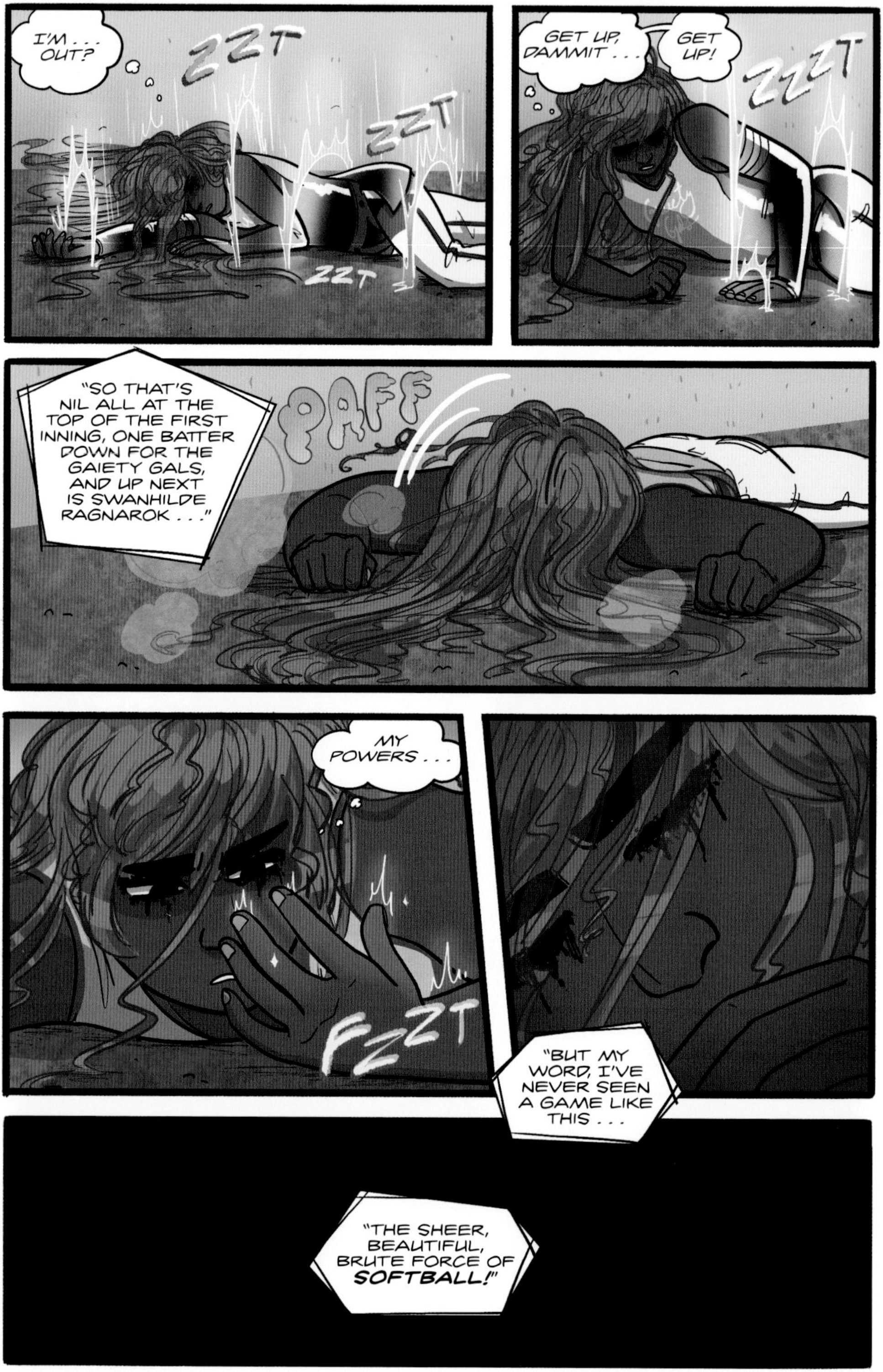
I'M . . . OUT?
ZZT
ZZT
ZZT
GET UP, DAMMIT . . .
GET UP!
ZZZT
"SO THAT'S NIL ALL AT THE TOP OF THE FIRST INNING, ONE BATTER DOWN FOR THE GAIETY GALS, AND UP NEXT IS SWANHILDE RAGNAROK . . ."
PAFF
MY POWERS . . .
FZZT
"BUT MY WORD, I'VE NEVER SEEN A GAME LIKE THIS . . .
"THE SHEER, BEAUTIFUL, BRUTE FORCE OF **SOFTBALL!**"

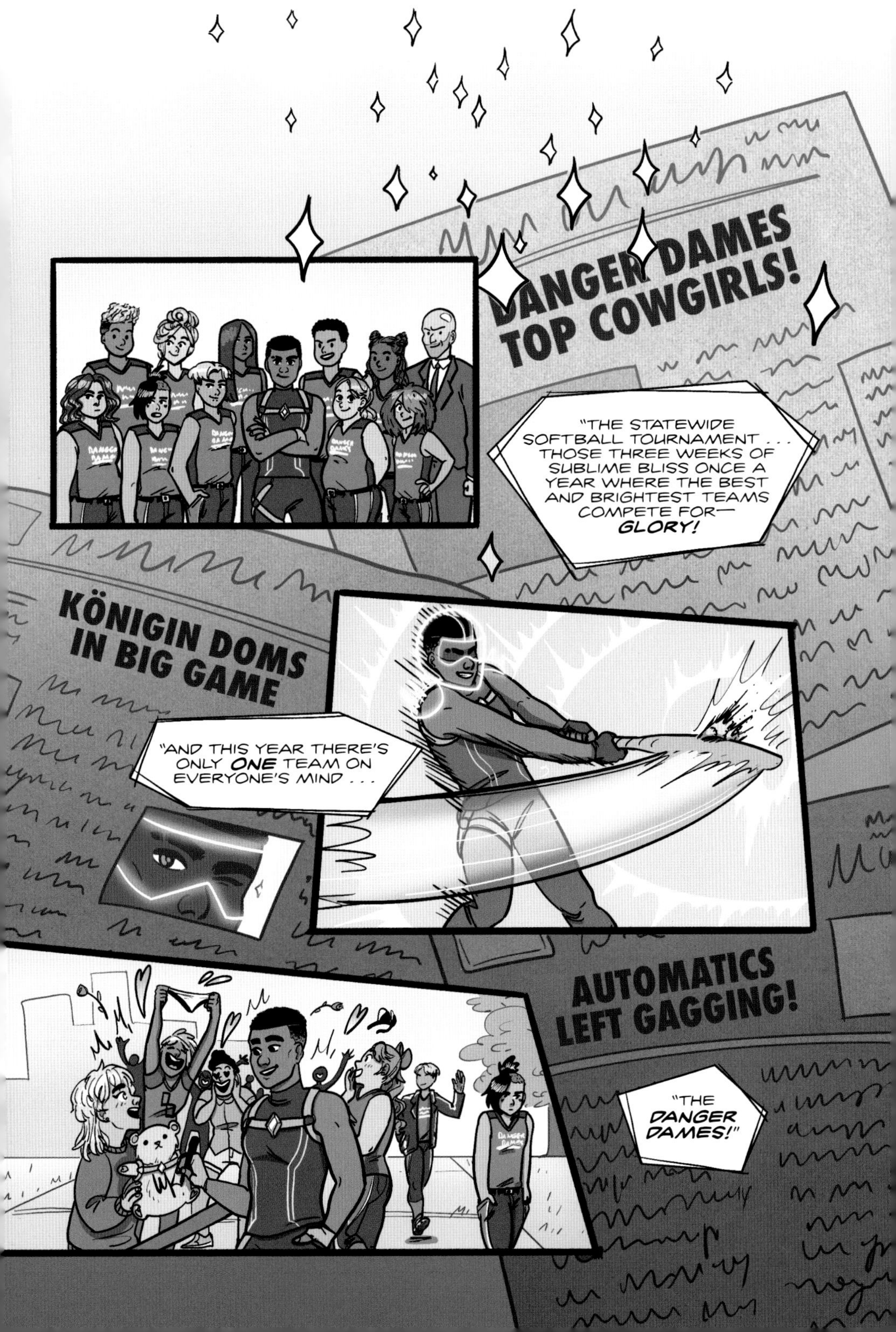
DANGER DAMES TOP COWGIRLS!
"THE STATEWIDE SOFTBALL TOURNAMENT . . . THOSE THREE WEEKS OF SUBLIME BLISS ONCE A YEAR WHERE THE BEST AND BRIGHTEST TEAMS COMPETE FOR— *GLORY!*
KÖNIGIN DOMS IN BIG GAME
"AND THIS YEAR THERE'S ONLY *ONE* TEAM ON EVERYONE'S MIND . . .
AUTOMATICS LEFT GAGGING!
"THE *DANGER DAMES!*"

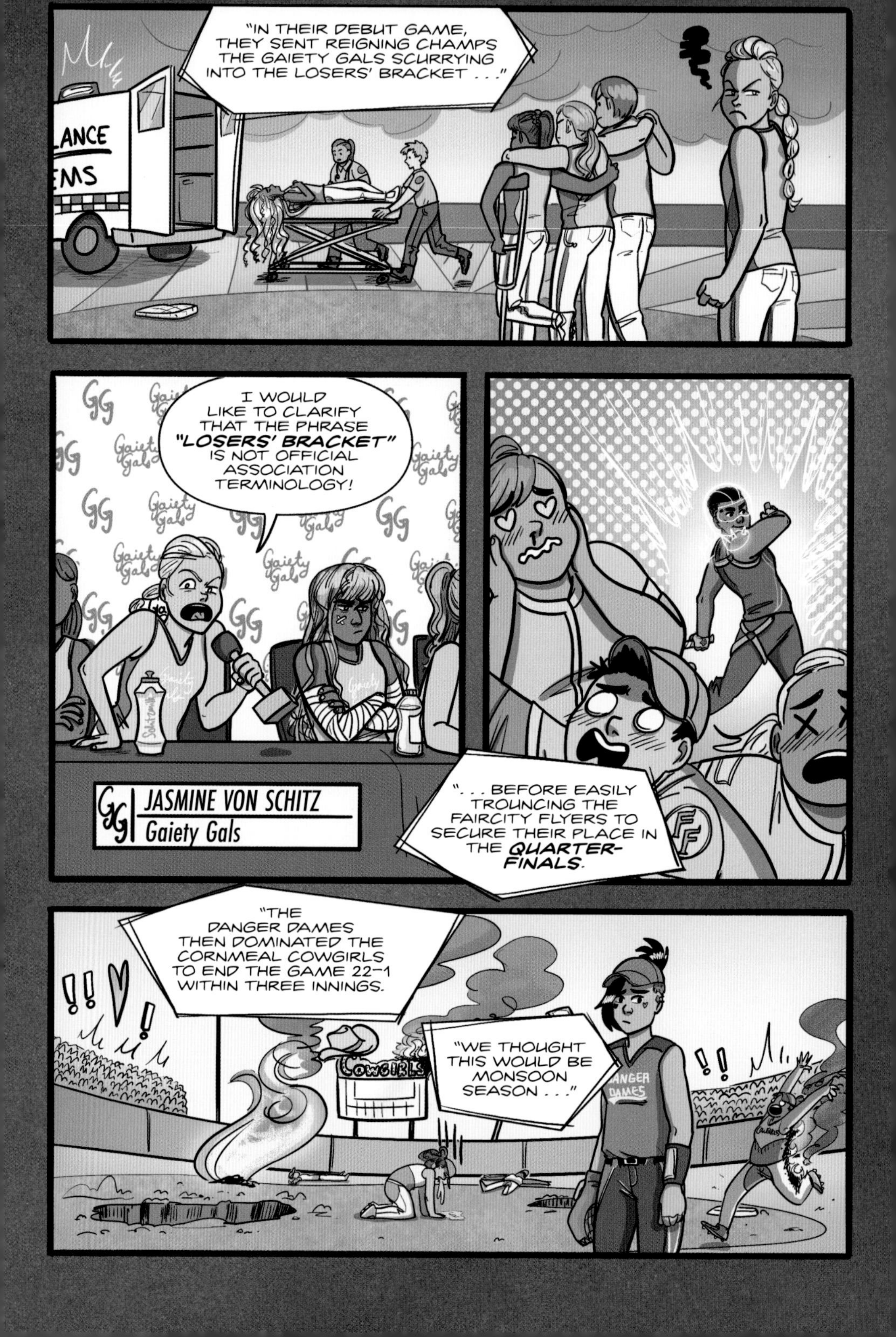
"IN THEIR DEBUT GAME, THEY SENT REIGNING CHAMPS THE GAIETY GALS SCURRYING INTO THE LOSERS' BRACKET . . ."
LANCE
EMS
I WOULD LIKE TO CLARIFY THAT THE PHRASE **"LOSERS' BRACKET"** IS NOT OFFICIAL ASSOCIATION TERMINOLOGY!
JASMINE VON SCHITZ
Gaiety Gals
". . . BEFORE EASILY TROUNCING THE FAIRCITY FLYERS TO SECURE THEIR PLACE IN THE ***QUARTER-FINALS***.
"THE DANGER DAMES THEN DOMINATED THE CORNMEAL COWGIRLS TO END THE GAME 22-1 WITHIN THREE INNINGS.
COWGIRLS
"WE THOUGHT THIS WOULD BE MONSOON SEASON . . ."
DANGER DAMES

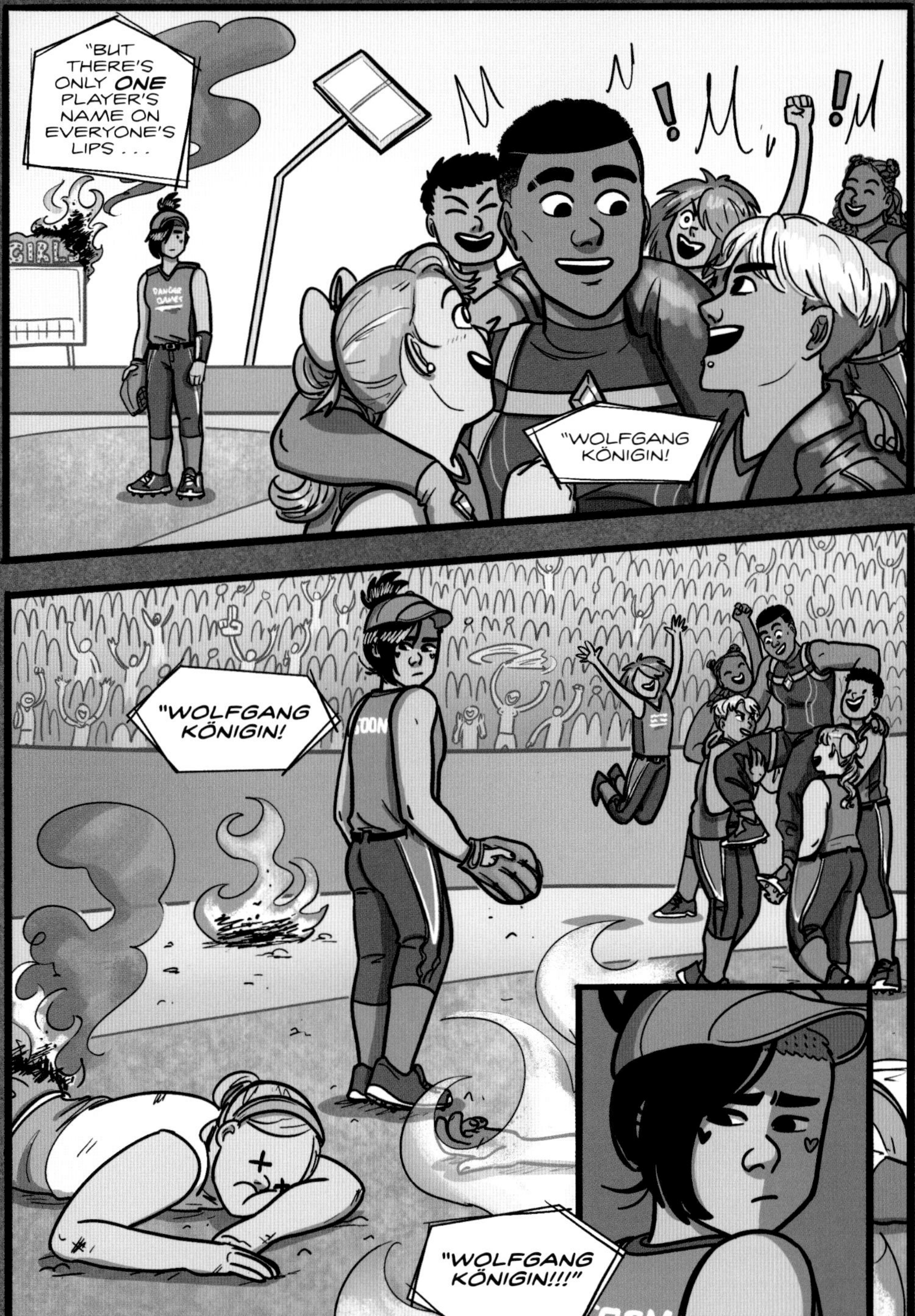
"BUT THERE'S ONLY ONE PLAYER'S NAME ON EVERYONE'S LIPS . . .
M N ! M ! M
"WOLFGANG KÖNIGIN!
"WOLFGANG KÖNIGIN!
"WOLFGANG KÖNIGIN!!!"

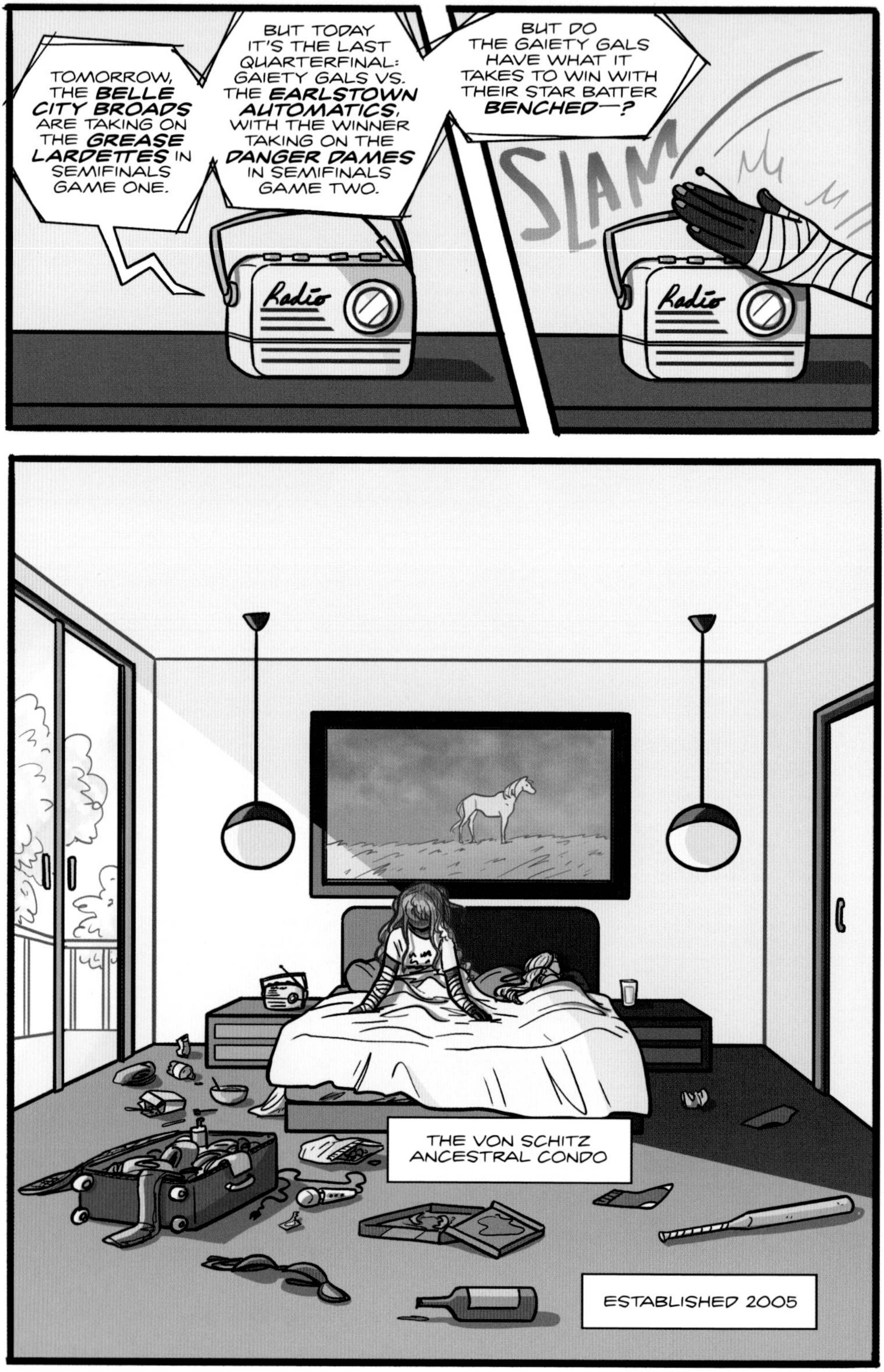
TOMORROW, THE **BELLE CITY BROADS** ARE TAKING ON THE **GREASE LARDETTES** IN SEMIFINALS GAME ONE.
BUT TODAY IT'S THE LAST QUARTERFINAL: GAIETY GALS VS. THE **EARLSTOWN AUTOMATICS**, WITH THE WINNER TAKING ON THE **DANGER DAMES** IN SEMIFINALS GAME TWO.
Radio
BUT DO THE GAIETY GALS HAVE WHAT IT TAKES TO WIN WITH THEIR STAR BATTER **BENCHED—?**
SLAM
Radio
THE VON SCHITZ ANCESTRAL CONDO
ESTABLISHED 2005

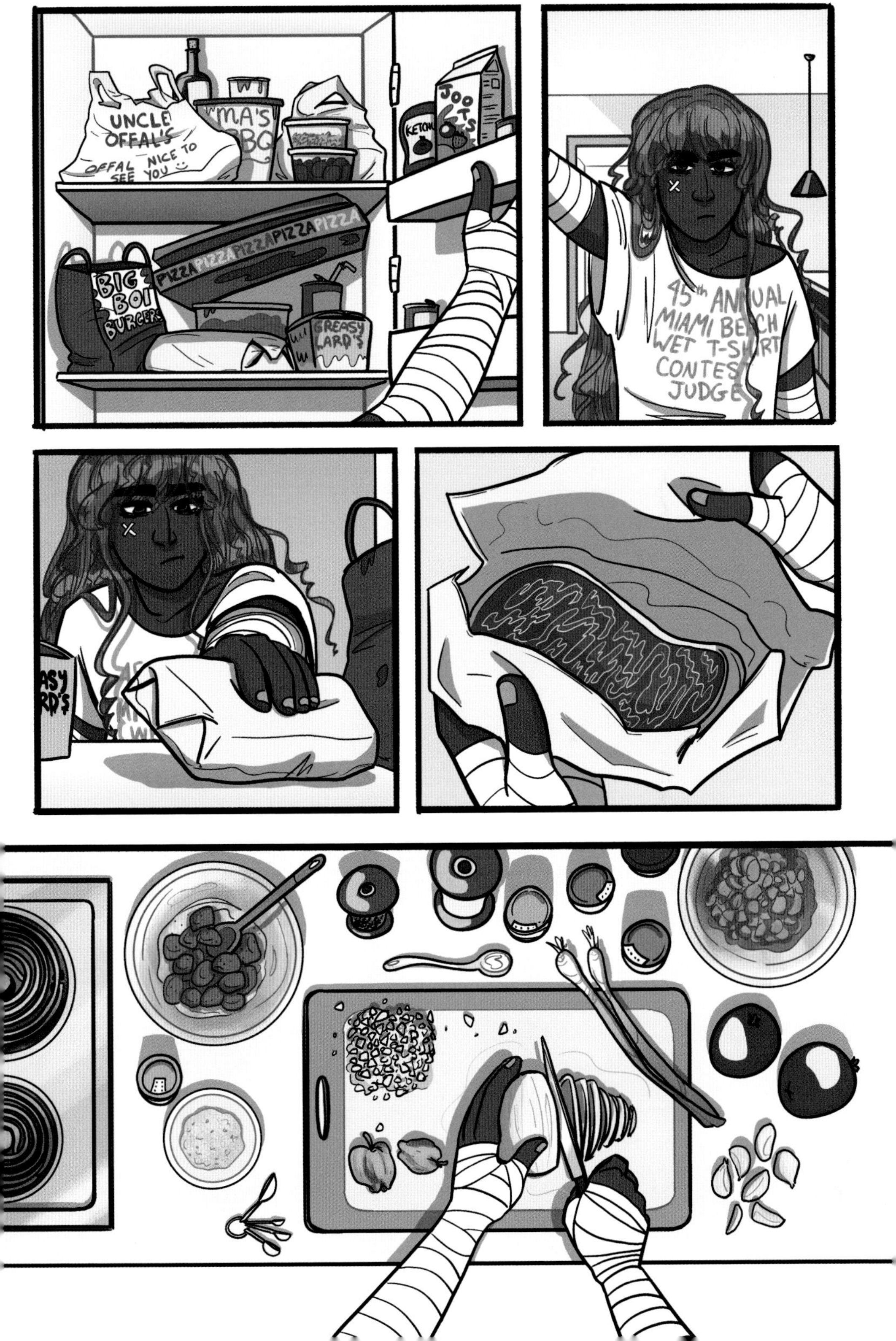

UNCLE OFFAL'S
OFFAL NICE TO SEE YOU
MA'S BBQ
PIZZA PIZZA PIZZA PIZZA PIZZA
BIG BOI BURGERS
GREASY LARD'S
45th ANNUAL MIAMI BEACH WET T-SHIRT CONTEST JUDGE

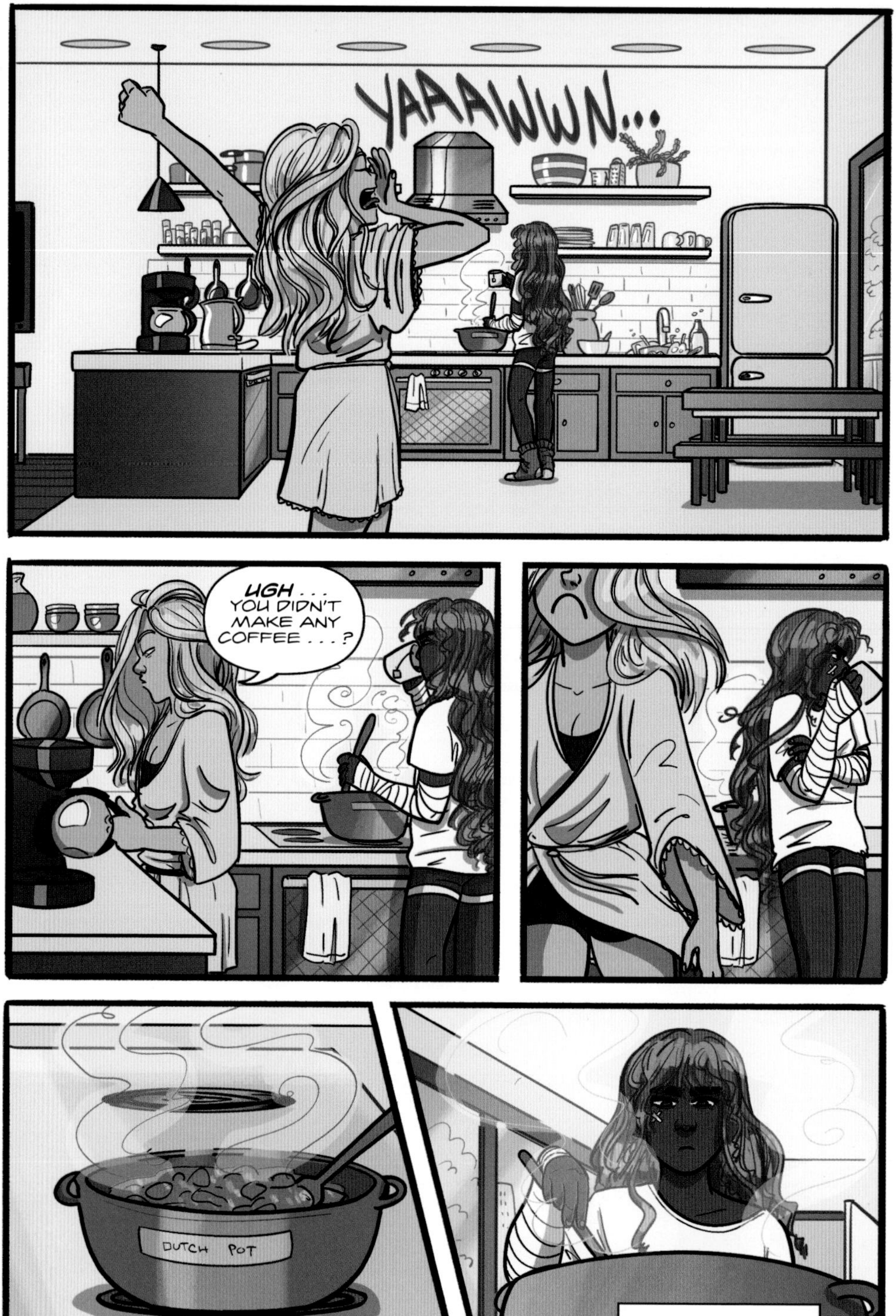
YAAAWWN...
UGH . . . YOU DIDN'T MAKE ANY COFFEE . . . ?
DUTCH POT
"HEY, PINK HAIR!"

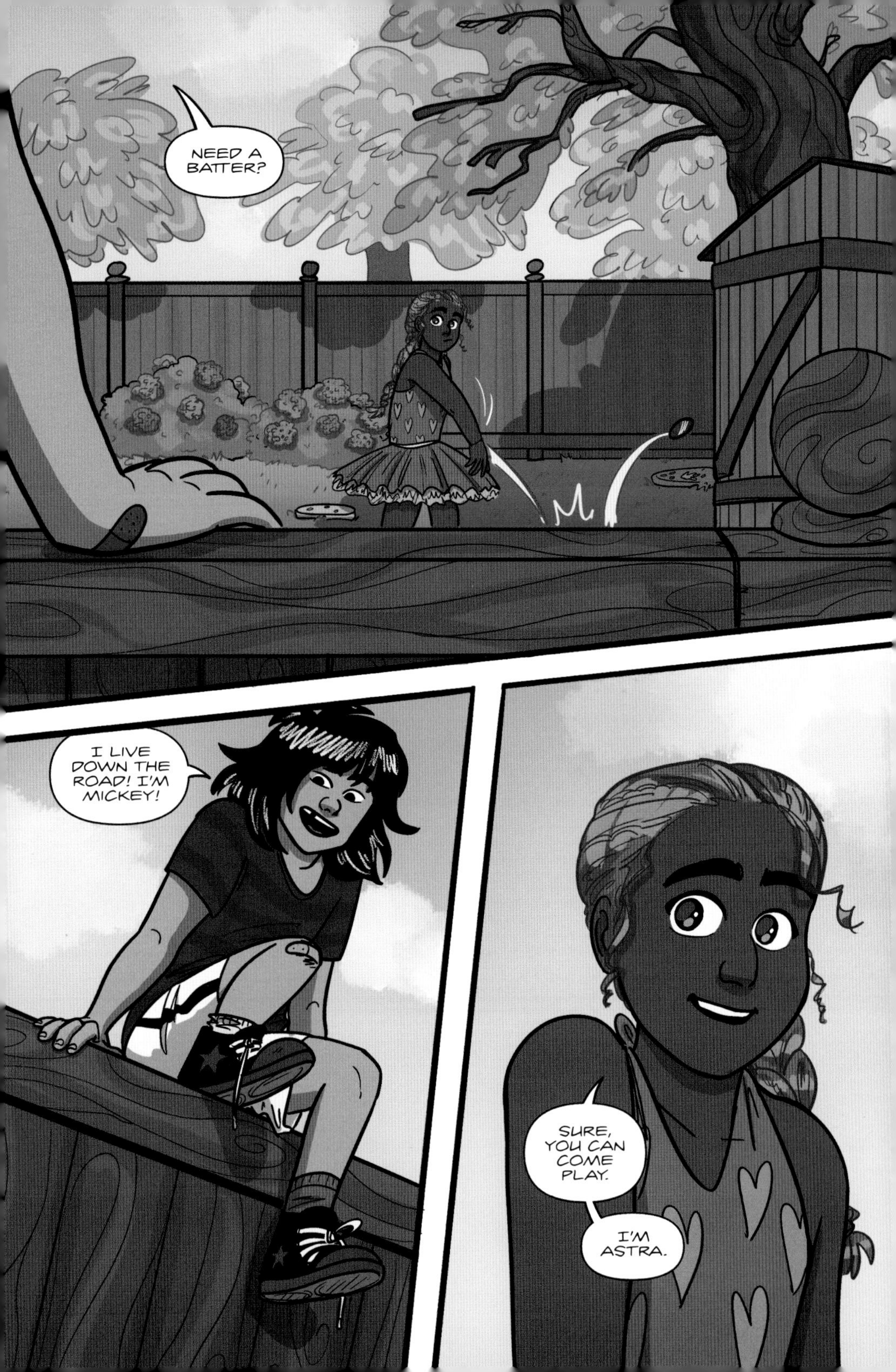
NEED A BATTER?
I LIVE DOWN THE ROAD! I'M MICKEY!
SURE, YOU CAN COME PLAY.
I'M ASTRA.

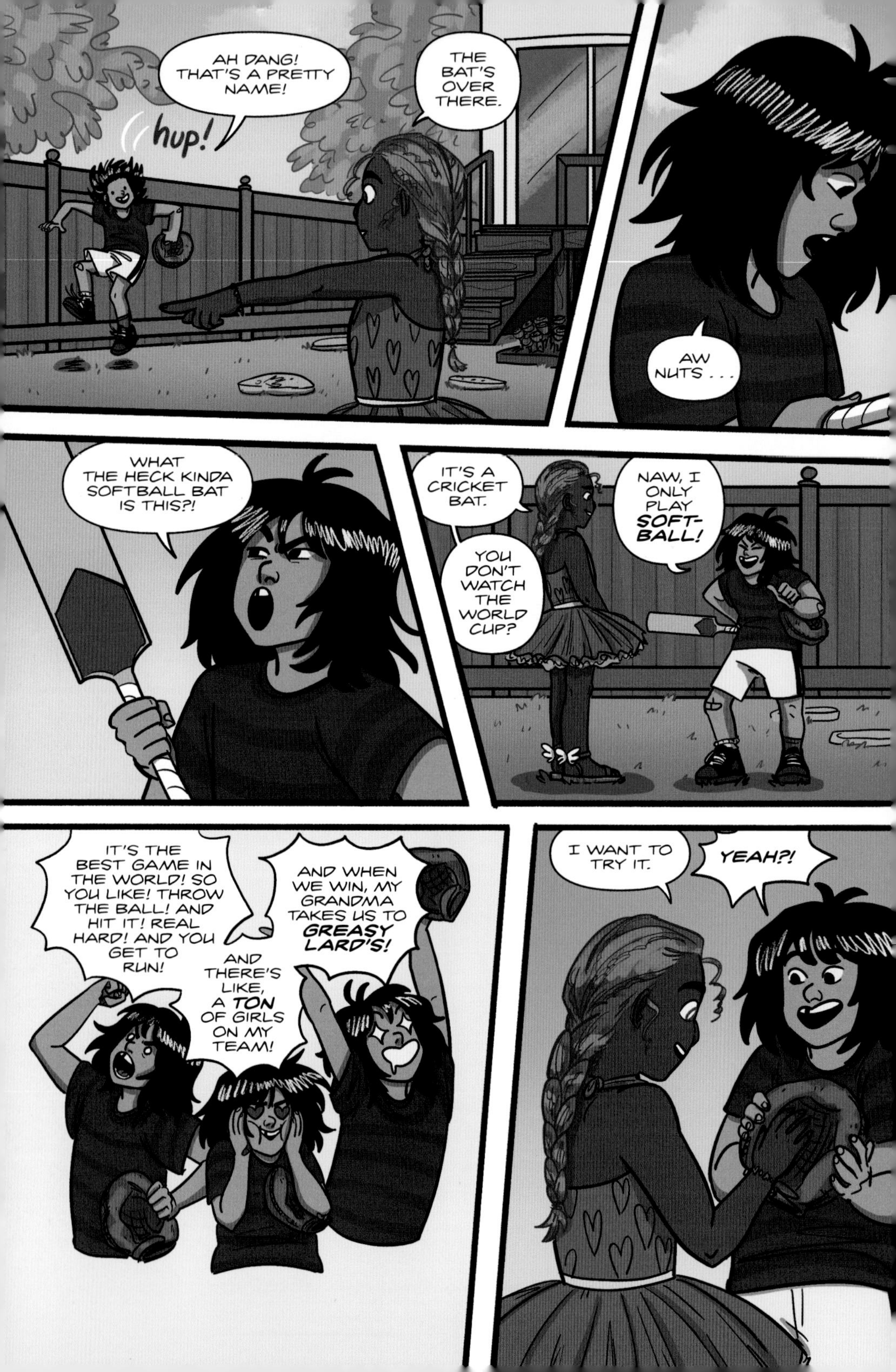

hup!
AH DANG! THAT'S A PRETTY NAME!
THE BAT'S OVER THERE.
AW NUTS . . .
WHAT THE HECK KINDA SOFTBALL BAT IS THIS?!
IT'S A CRICKET BAT.
YOU DON'T WATCH THE WORLD CUP?
NAW, I ONLY PLAY **SOFT-BALL!**
IT'S THE BEST GAME IN THE WORLD! SO YOU LIKE! THROW THE BALL! AND HIT IT! REAL HARD! AND YOU GET TO RUN!
AND THERE'S LIKE, A **TON** OF GIRLS ON MY TEAM!
AND WHEN WE WIN, MY GRANDMA TAKES US TO **GREASY LARD'S!**
I WANT TO TRY IT.
YEAH?!

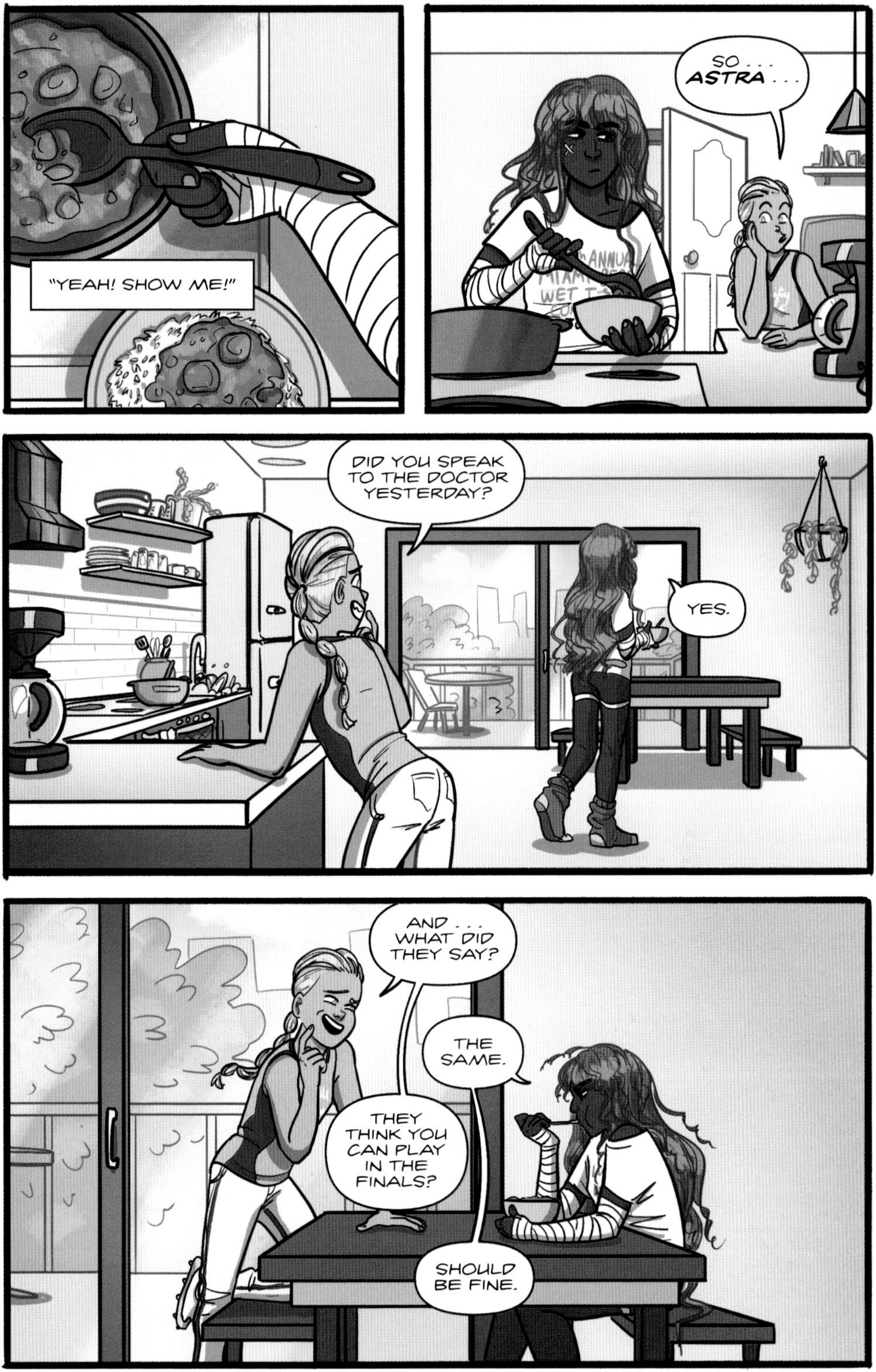
"YEAH! SHOW ME!"
SO . . . ASTRA . . .
DID YOU SPEAK TO THE DOCTOR YESTERDAY?
YES.
AND . . . WHAT DID THEY SAY?
THE SAME.
THEY THINK YOU CAN PLAY IN THE FINALS?
SHOULD BE FINE.

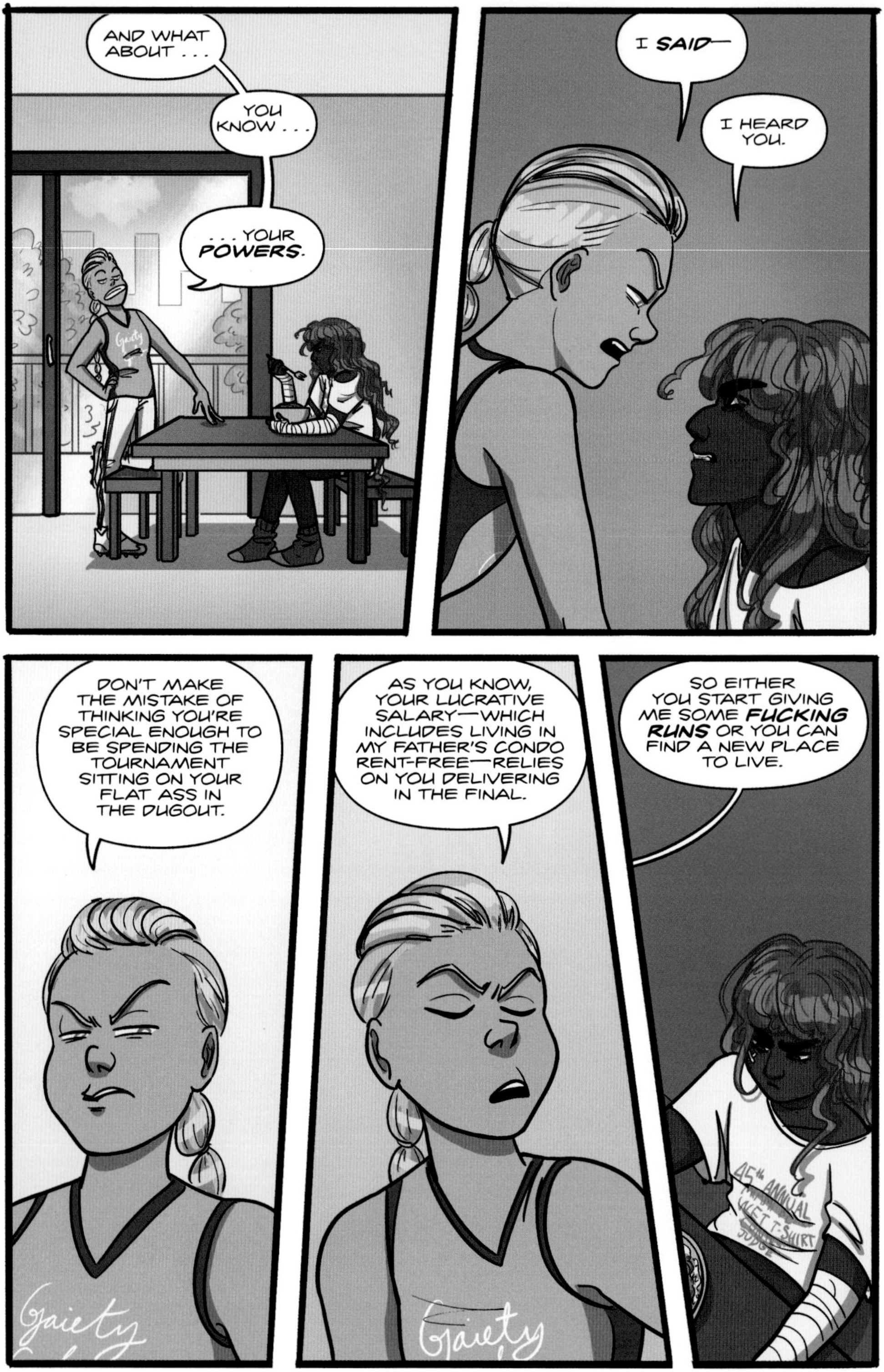
AND WHAT ABOUT . . .
YOU KNOW . . .
. . . YOUR POWERS.
I SAID—
I HEARD YOU.
DON'T MAKE THE MISTAKE OF THINKING YOU'RE SPECIAL ENOUGH TO BE SPENDING THE TOURNAMENT SITTING ON YOUR FLAT ASS IN THE DUGOUT.
Gaiety
AS YOU KNOW, YOUR LUCRATIVE SALARY—WHICH INCLUDES LIVING IN MY FATHER'S CONDO RENT-FREE—RELIES ON YOU DELIVERING IN THE FINAL.
Gaiety
SO EITHER YOU START GIVING ME SOME FUCKING RUNS OR YOU CAN FIND A NEW PLACE TO LIVE.

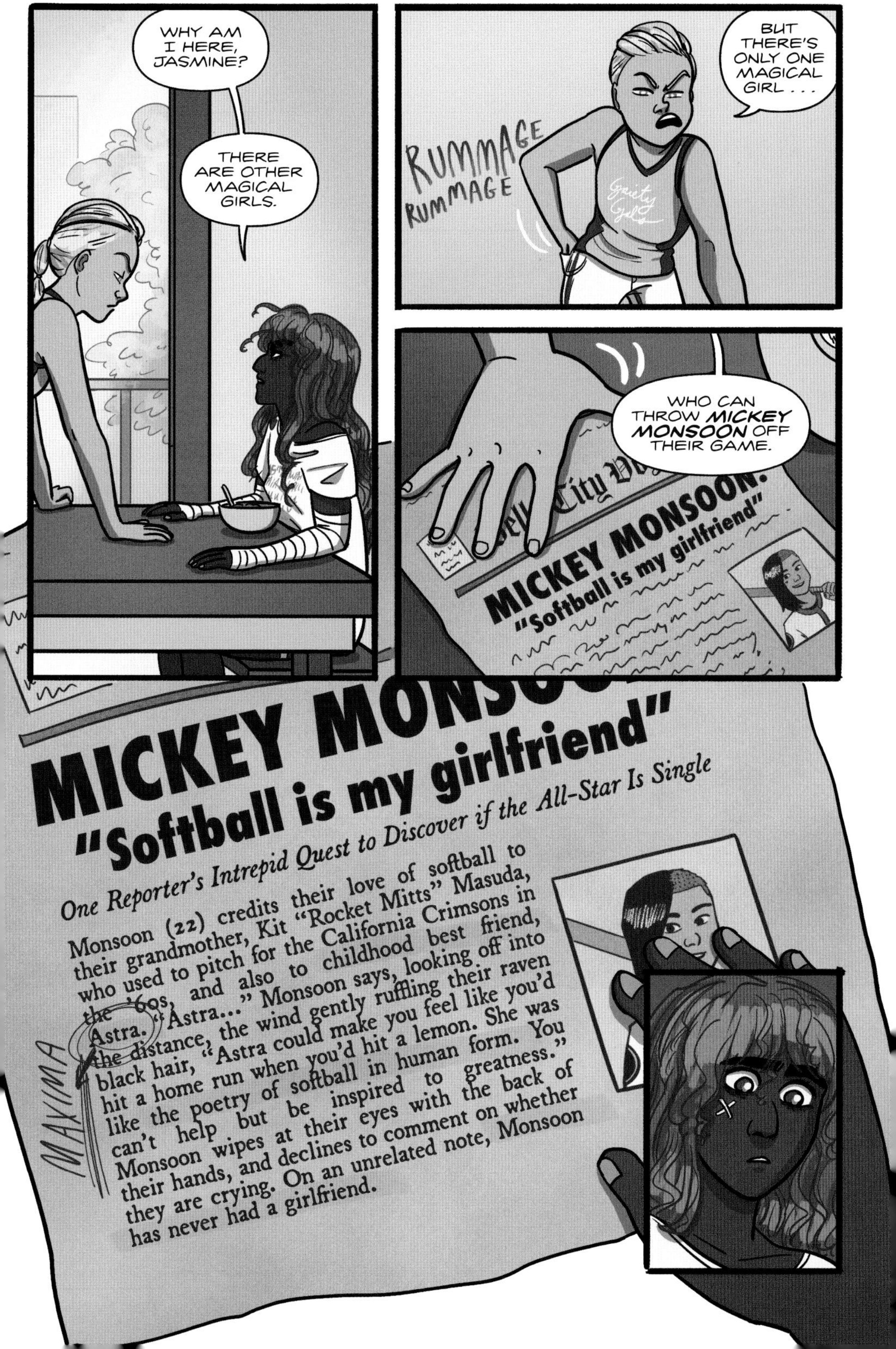
WHY AM I HERE, JASMINE?
THERE ARE OTHER MAGICAL GIRLS.
RUMMAGE
RUMMAGE
BUT THERE'S ONLY ONE MAGICAL GIRL . . .
WHO CAN THROW MICKEY MONSOON OFF THEIR GAME.
MICKEY MONSOON:
"Softball is my girlfriend"
MICKEY MONSO
"Softball is my girlfriend"
One Reporter's Intrepid Quest to Discover if the All-Star Is Single
Monsoon (22) credits their love of softball to their grandmother, Kit "Rocket Mitts" Masuda, who used to pitch for the California Crimsons in the '60s, and also to childhood best friend, Astra. "Astra..." Monsoon says, looking off into the distance, the wind gently ruffling their raven black hair, "Astra could make you feel like you'd hit a home run when you'd hit a lemon. She was like the poetry of softball in human form. You can't help but be inspired to greatness." Monsoon wipes at their eyes with the back of their hands, and declines to comment on whether they are crying. On an unrelated note, Monsoon has never had a girlfriend.
MAXIMA

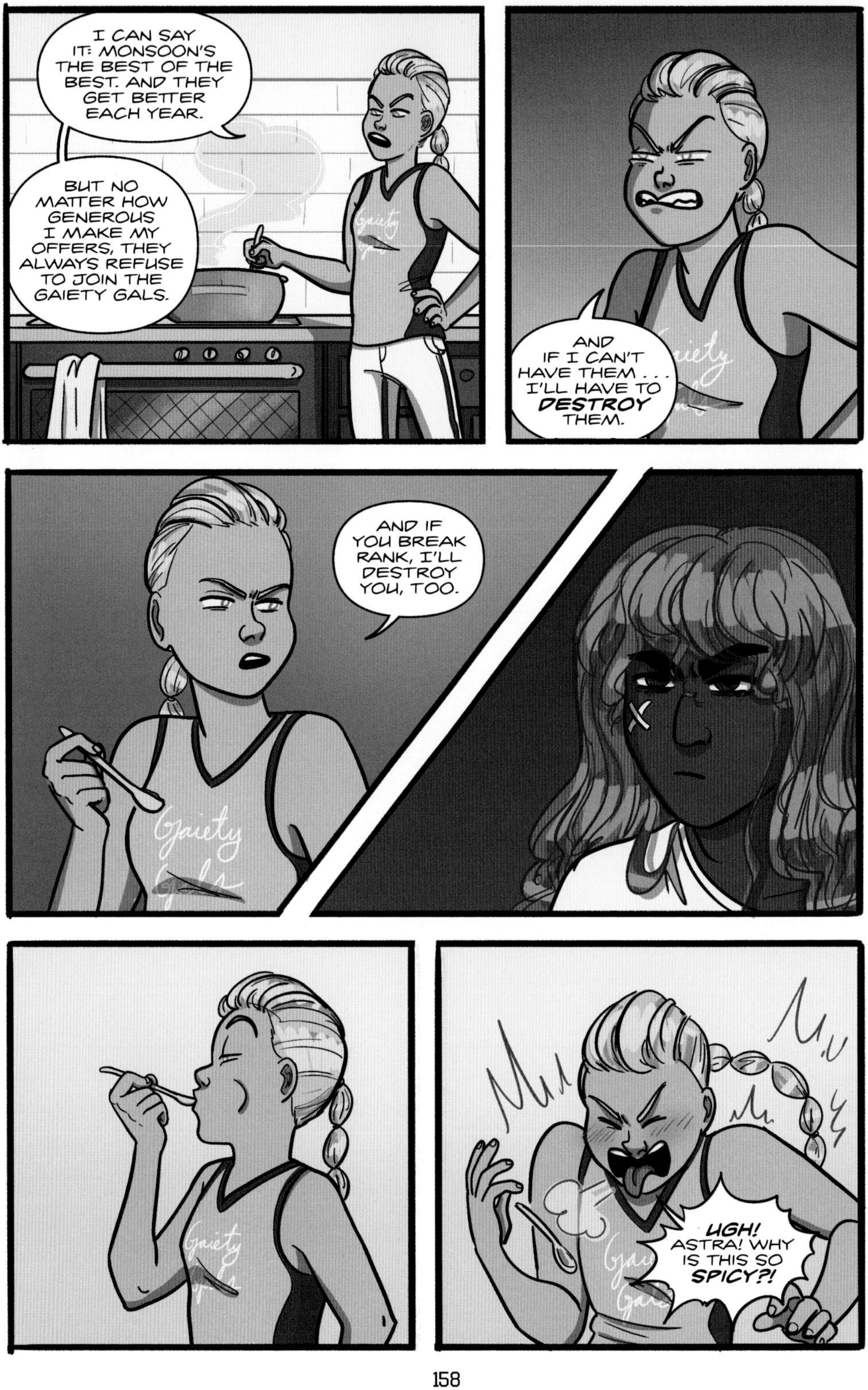
I CAN SAY IT: MONSOON'S THE BEST OF THE BEST. AND THEY GET BETTER EACH YEAR.
BUT NO MATTER HOW GENEROUS I MAKE MY OFFERS, THEY ALWAYS REFUSE TO JOIN THE GAIETY GALS.
AND IF I CAN'T HAVE THEM . . . I'LL HAVE TO **DESTROY** THEM.
AND IF YOU BREAK RANK, I'LL DESTROY YOU, TOO.
UGH! ASTRA! WHY IS THIS SO **SPICY?!**

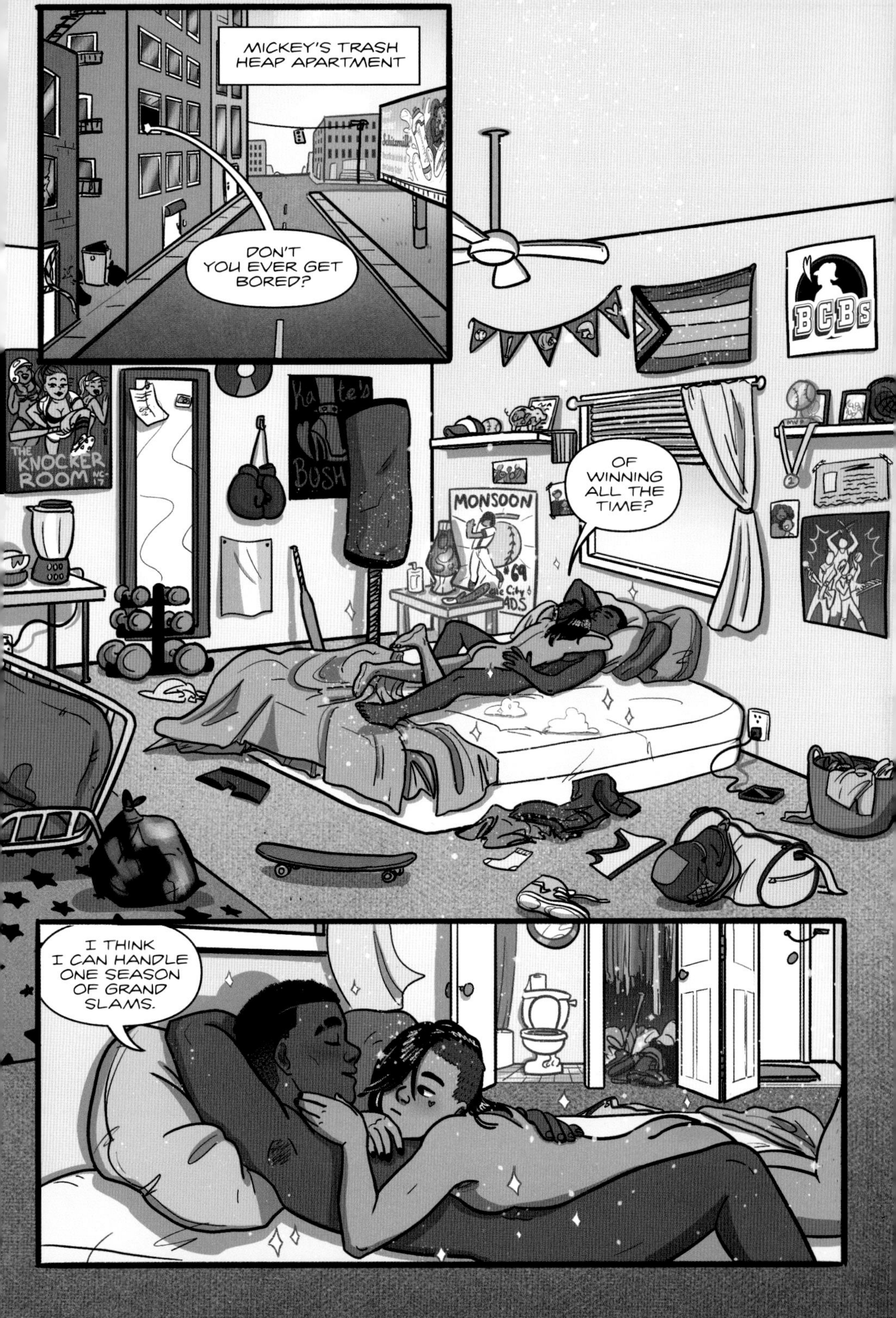
MICKEY'S TRASH HEAP APARTMENT
DON'T YOU EVER GET BORED?
THE KNOCKER ROOM NC-17
BCBs
MONSOON
#69
OF WINNING ALL THE TIME?
I THINK I CAN HANDLE ONE SEASON OF GRAND SLAMS.

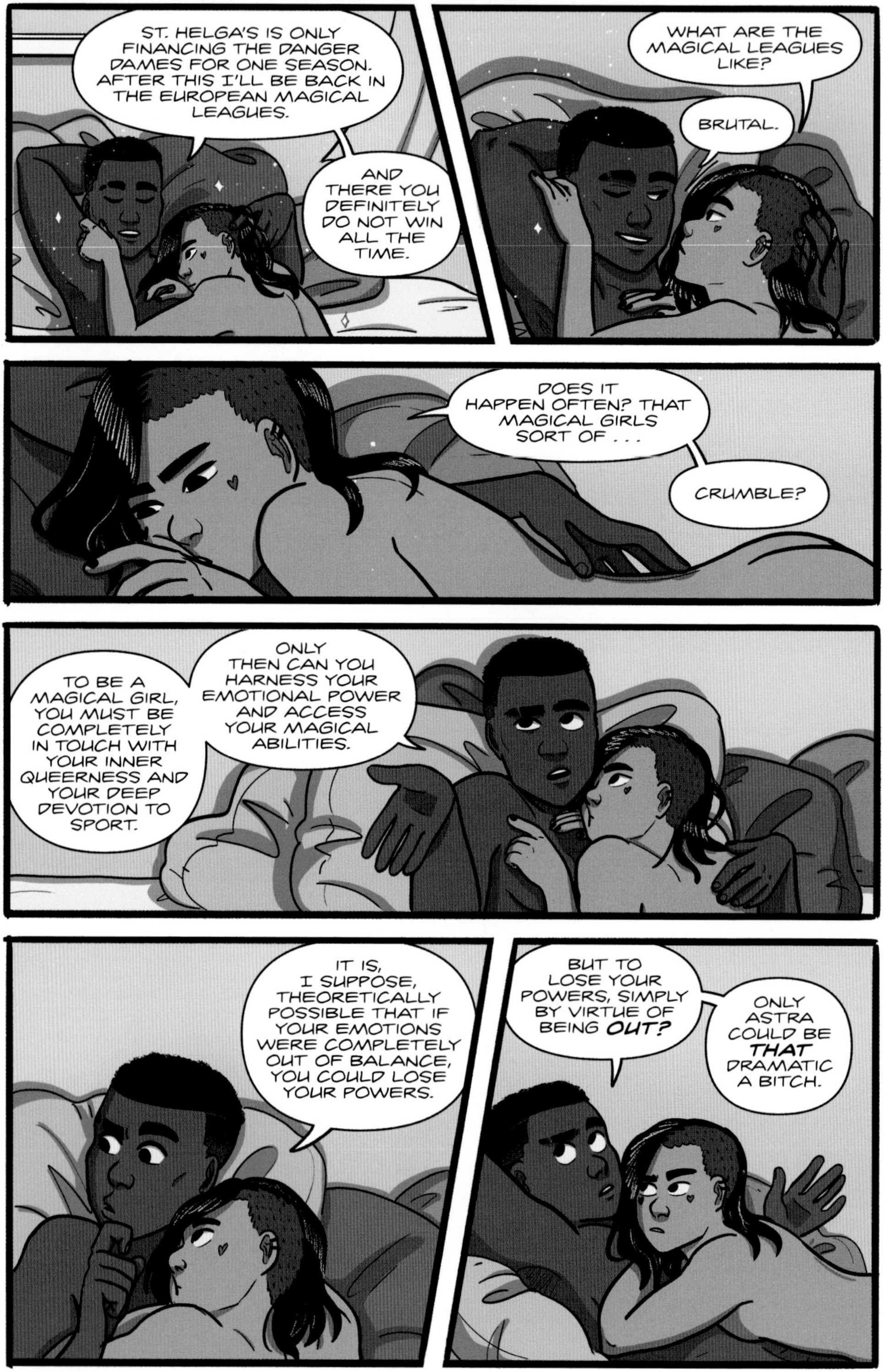
ST. HELGA'S IS ONLY FINANCING THE DANGER DAMES FOR ONE SEASON. AFTER THIS I'LL BE BACK IN THE EUROPEAN MAGICAL LEAGUES.
AND THERE YOU DEFINITELY DO NOT WIN ALL THE TIME.
WHAT ARE THE MAGICAL LEAGUES LIKE?
BRUTAL.
DOES IT HAPPEN OFTEN? THAT MAGICAL GIRLS SORT OF . . .
CRUMBLE?
TO BE A MAGICAL GIRL, YOU MUST BE COMPLETELY IN TOUCH WITH YOUR INNER QUEERNESS AND YOUR DEEP DEVOTION TO SPORT.
ONLY THEN CAN YOU HARNESS YOUR EMOTIONAL POWER AND ACCESS YOUR MAGICAL ABILITIES.
IT IS, I SUPPOSE, THEORETICALLY POSSIBLE THAT IF YOUR EMOTIONS WERE COMPLETELY OUT OF BALANCE, YOU COULD LOSE YOUR POWERS.
BUT TO LOSE YOUR POWERS, SIMPLY BY VIRTUE OF BEING ***OUT?***
ONLY ASTRA COULD BE ***THAT*** DRAMATIC A BITCH.

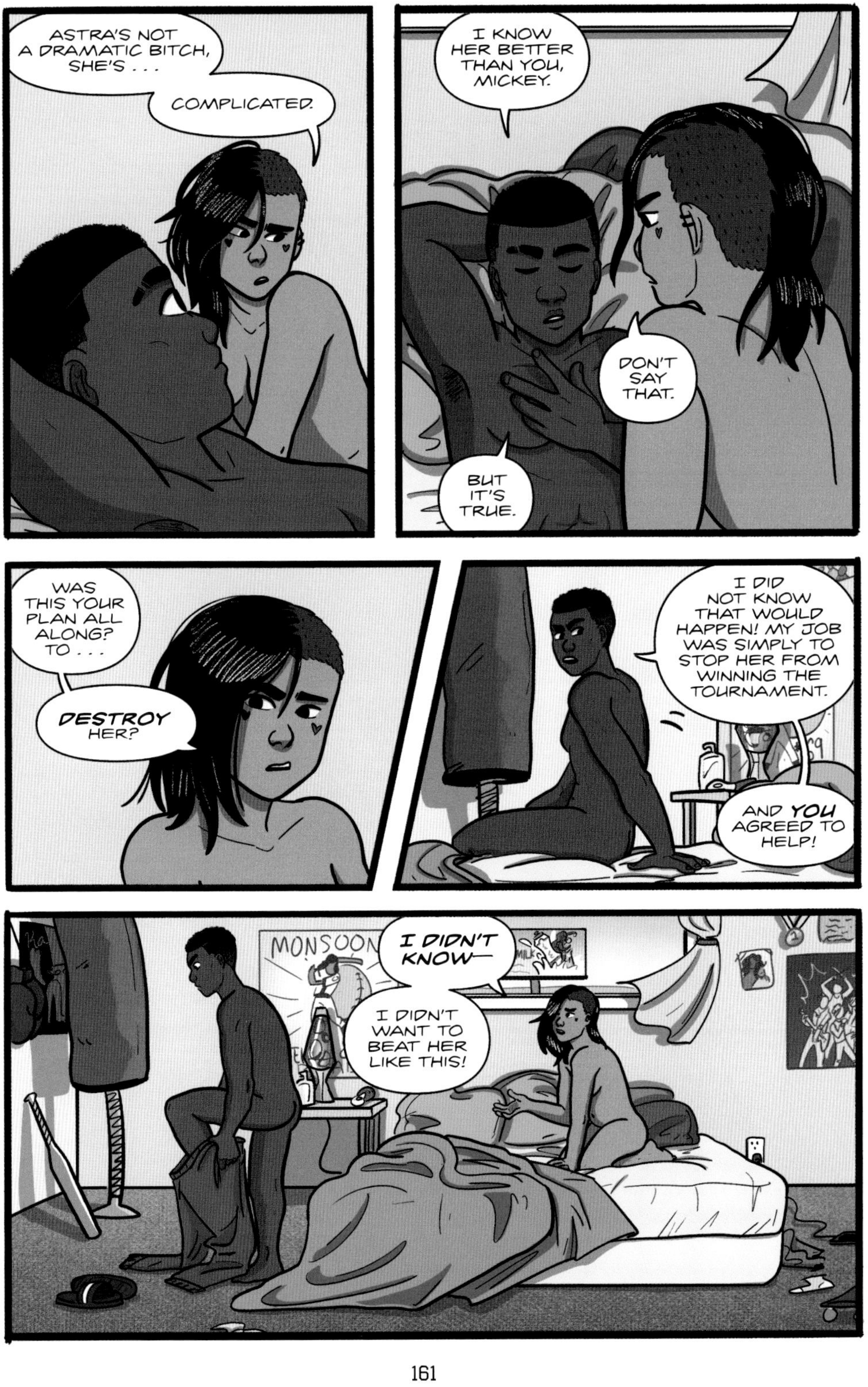
ASTRA'S NOT A DRAMATIC BITCH, SHE'S . . .
COMPLICATED.
I KNOW HER BETTER THAN YOU, MICKEY.
DON'T SAY THAT.
BUT IT'S TRUE.
WAS THIS YOUR PLAN ALL ALONG? TO . . .
DESTROY HER?
I DID NOT KNOW THAT WOULD HAPPEN! MY JOB WAS SIMPLY TO STOP HER FROM WINNING THE TOURNAMENT.
AND ***YOU*** AGREED TO HELP!
MONSOON
I DIDN'T KNOW—
I DIDN'T WANT TO BEAT HER LIKE THIS!

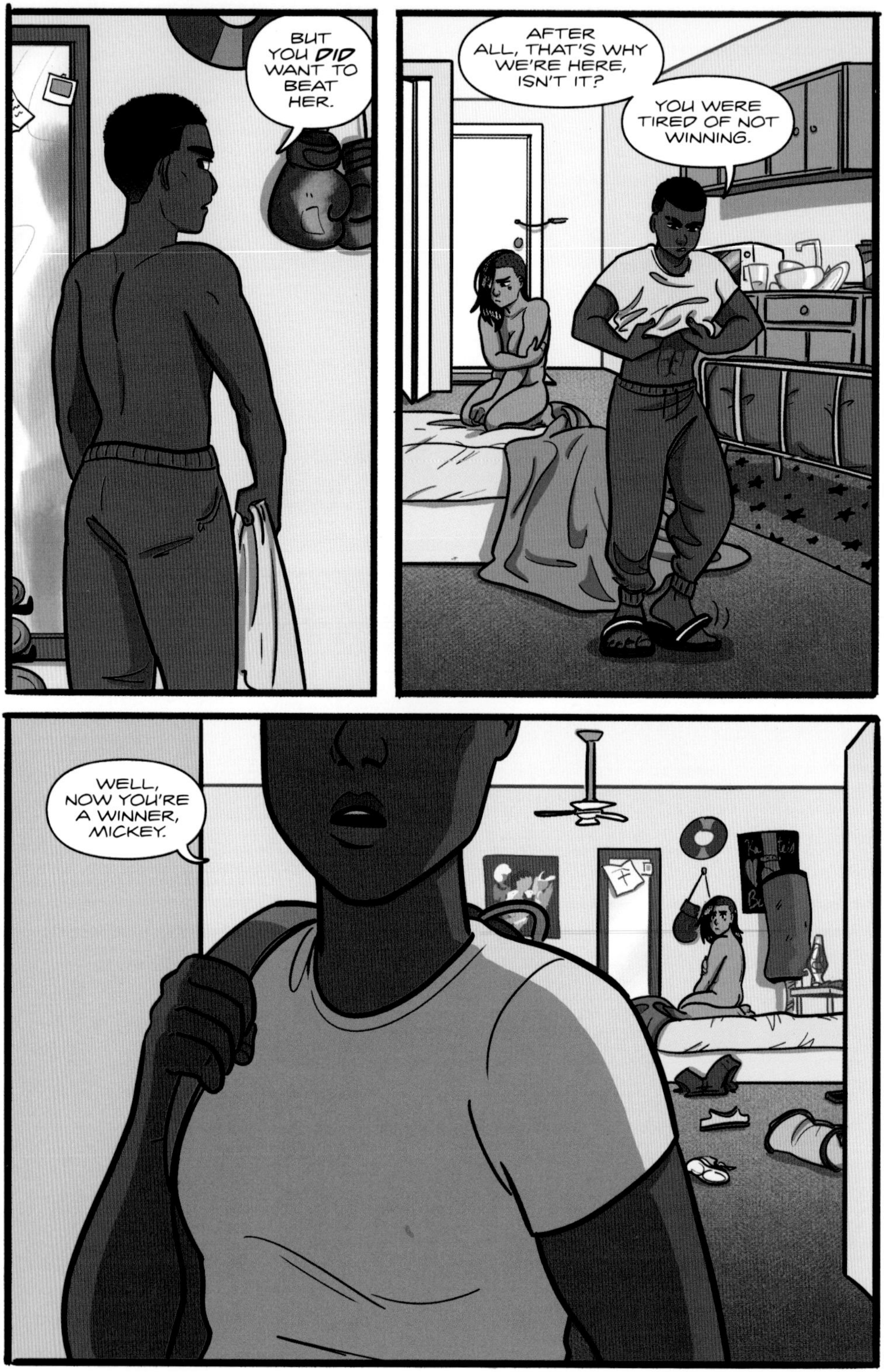
BUT YOU ***DID*** WANT TO BEAT HER.
AFTER ALL, THAT'S WHY WE'RE HERE, ISN'T IT?
YOU WERE TIRED OF NOT WINNING.
WELL, NOW YOU'RE A WINNER, MICKEY.

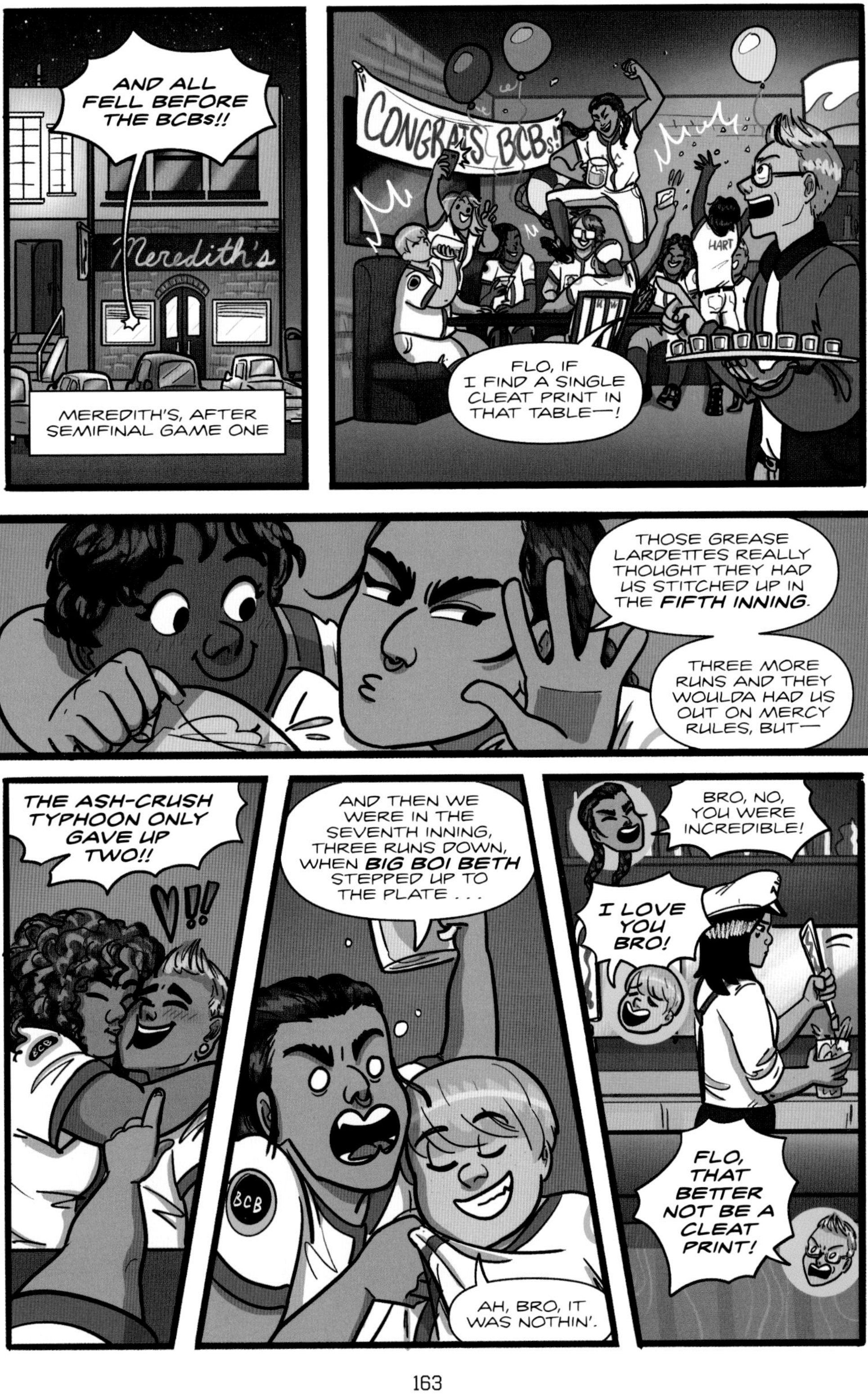
AND ALL FELL BEFORE THE BCBs!!
Meredith's
MEREDITH'S, AFTER SEMIFINAL GAME ONE
CONGRATS BCBs!
HART
FLO, IF I FIND A SINGLE CLEAT PRINT IN THAT TABLE—!
THOSE GREASE LARDETTES REALLY THOUGHT THEY HAD US STITCHED UP IN THE FIFTH INNING.
THREE MORE RUNS AND THEY WOULDA HAD US OUT ON MERCY RULES, BUT—
THE ASH-CRUSH TYPHOON ONLY GAVE UP TWO!!
BCB
AND THEN WE WERE IN THE SEVENTH INNING, THREE RUNS DOWN, WHEN BIG BOI BETH STEPPED UP TO THE PLATE . . .
BCB
AH, BRO, IT WAS NOTHIN'.
BRO, NO, YOU WERE INCREDIBLE!
I LOVE YOU BRO!
FLO, THAT BETTER NOT BE A CLEAT PRINT!

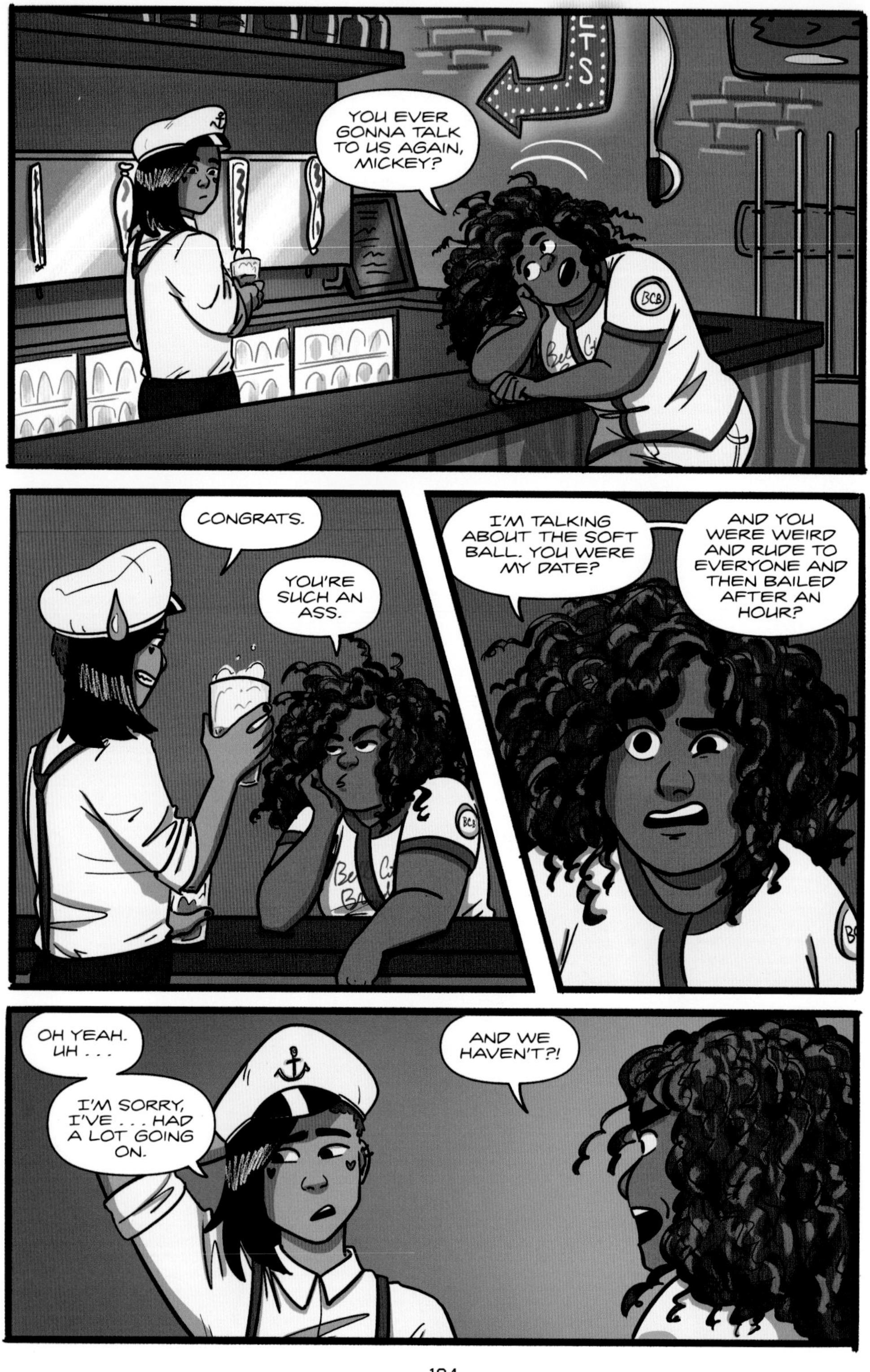
YOU EVER GONNA TALK TO US AGAIN, MICKEY?
CONGRATS.
YOU'RE SUCH AN ASS.
I'M TALKING ABOUT THE SOFT BALL. YOU WERE MY DATE?
AND YOU WERE WEIRD AND RUDE TO EVERYONE AND THEN BAILED AFTER AN HOUR?
OH YEAH. UH . . .
I'M SORRY, I'VE . . . HAD A LOT GOING ON.
AND WE HAVEN'T?!

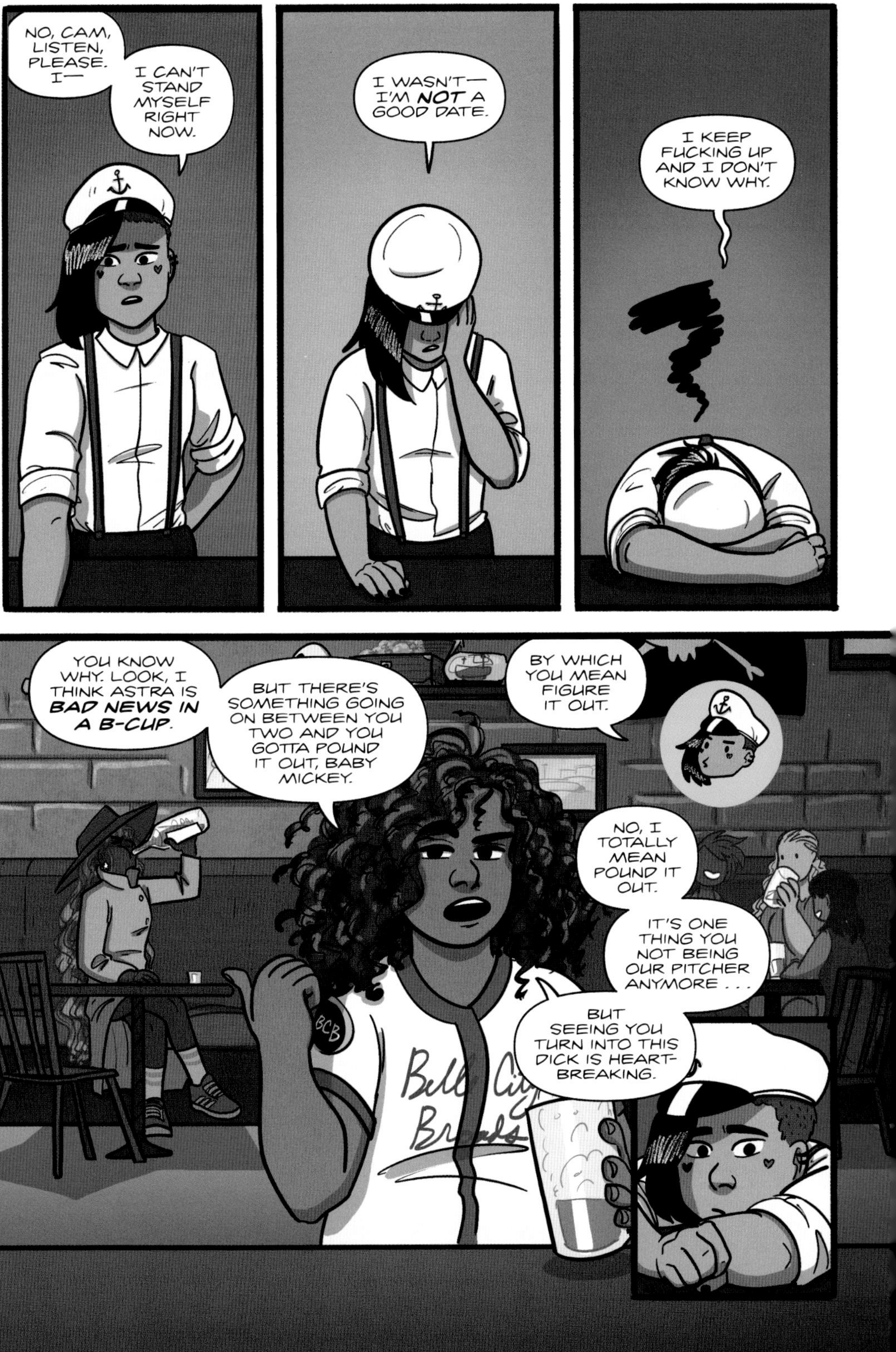
NO, CAM, LISTEN, PLEASE. I—
I CAN'T STAND MYSELF RIGHT NOW.
I WASN'T— I'M **NOT** A GOOD DATE.
I KEEP FUCKING UP AND I DON'T KNOW WHY.
YOU KNOW WHY. LOOK, I THINK ASTRA IS ***BAD NEWS IN A B-CUP***.
BUT THERE'S SOMETHING GOING ON BETWEEN YOU TWO AND YOU GOTTA POUND IT OUT, BABY MICKEY.
BY WHICH YOU MEAN FIGURE IT OUT.
NO, I TOTALLY MEAN POUND IT OUT.
IT'S ONE THING YOU NOT BEING OUR PITCHER ANYMORE . . .
BUT SEEING YOU TURN INTO THIS DICK IS HEART-BREAKING.
BCB

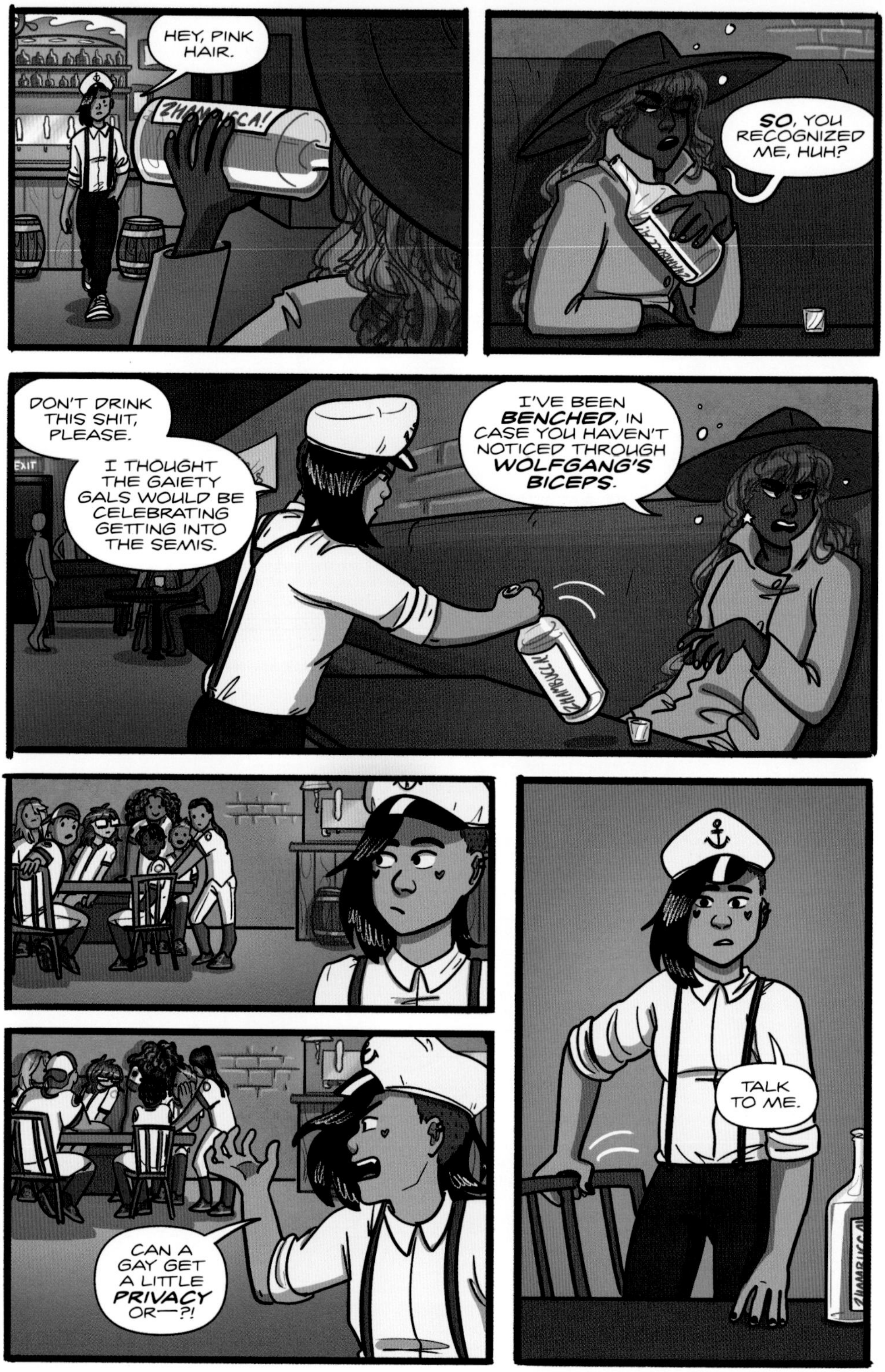
HEY, PINK HAIR.
ZHAMBUSCA!
SO, YOU RECOGNIZED ME, HUH?
DON'T DRINK THIS SHIT, PLEASE.
I THOUGHT THE GAIETY GALS WOULD BE CELEBRATING GETTING INTO THE SEMIS.
I'VE BEEN BENCHED, IN CASE YOU HAVEN'T NOTICED THROUGH WOLFGANG'S BICEPS.
EXIT
CAN A GAY GET A LITTLE PRIVACY OR—?!
TALK TO ME.

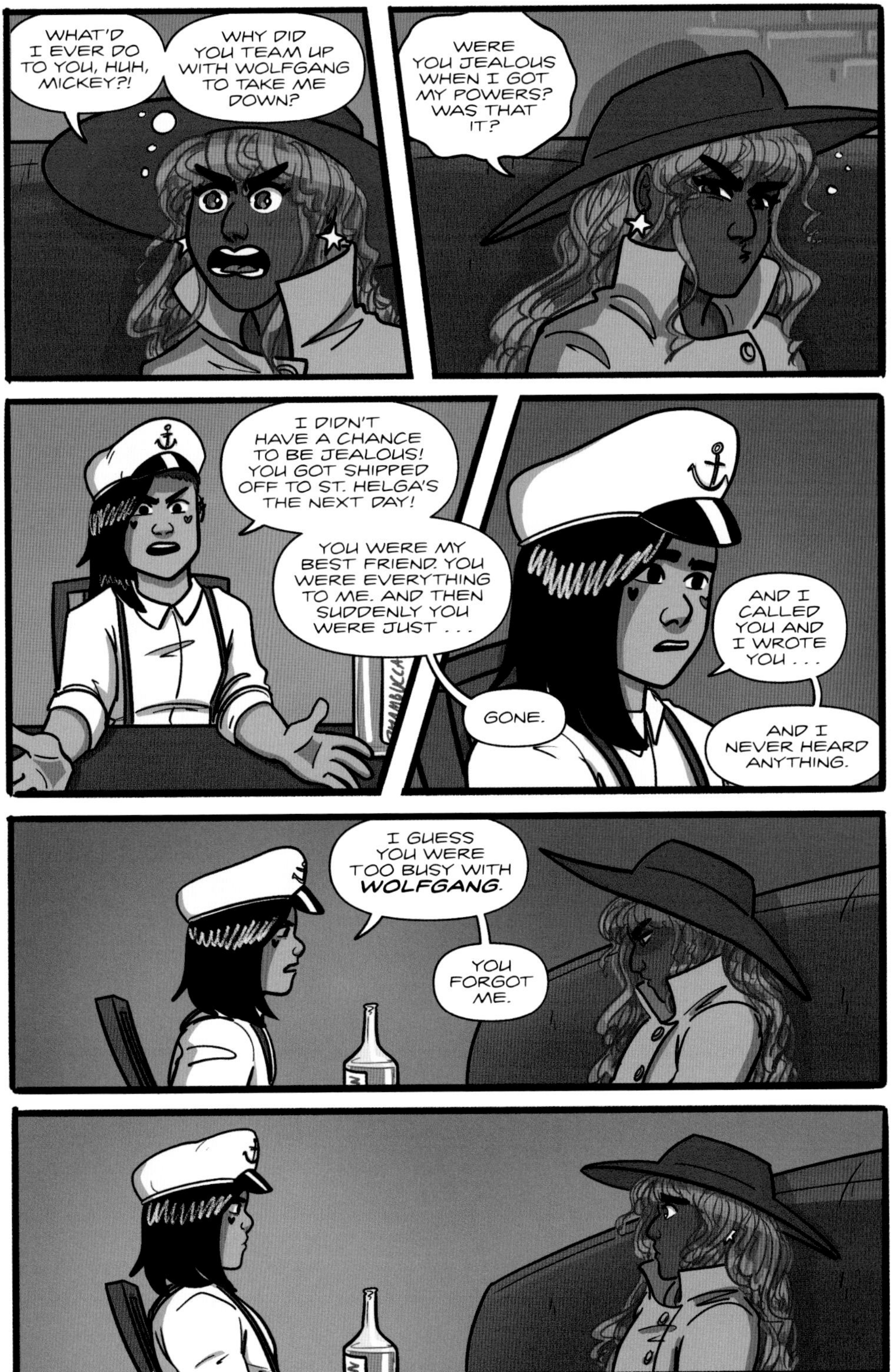
WHAT'D I EVER DO TO YOU, HUH, MICKEY?!
WHY DID YOU TEAM UP WITH WOLFGANG TO TAKE ME DOWN?
WERE YOU JEALOUS WHEN I GOT MY POWERS? WAS THAT IT?
I DIDN'T HAVE A CHANCE TO BE JEALOUS! YOU GOT SHIPPED OFF TO ST. HELGA'S THE NEXT DAY!
YOU WERE MY BEST FRIEND. YOU WERE EVERYTHING TO ME. AND THEN SUDDENLY YOU WERE JUST . . .
GONE.
AND I CALLED YOU AND I WROTE YOU . . .
AND I NEVER HEARD ANYTHING.
I GUESS YOU WERE TOO BUSY WITH **WOLFGANG**.
YOU FORGOT ME.

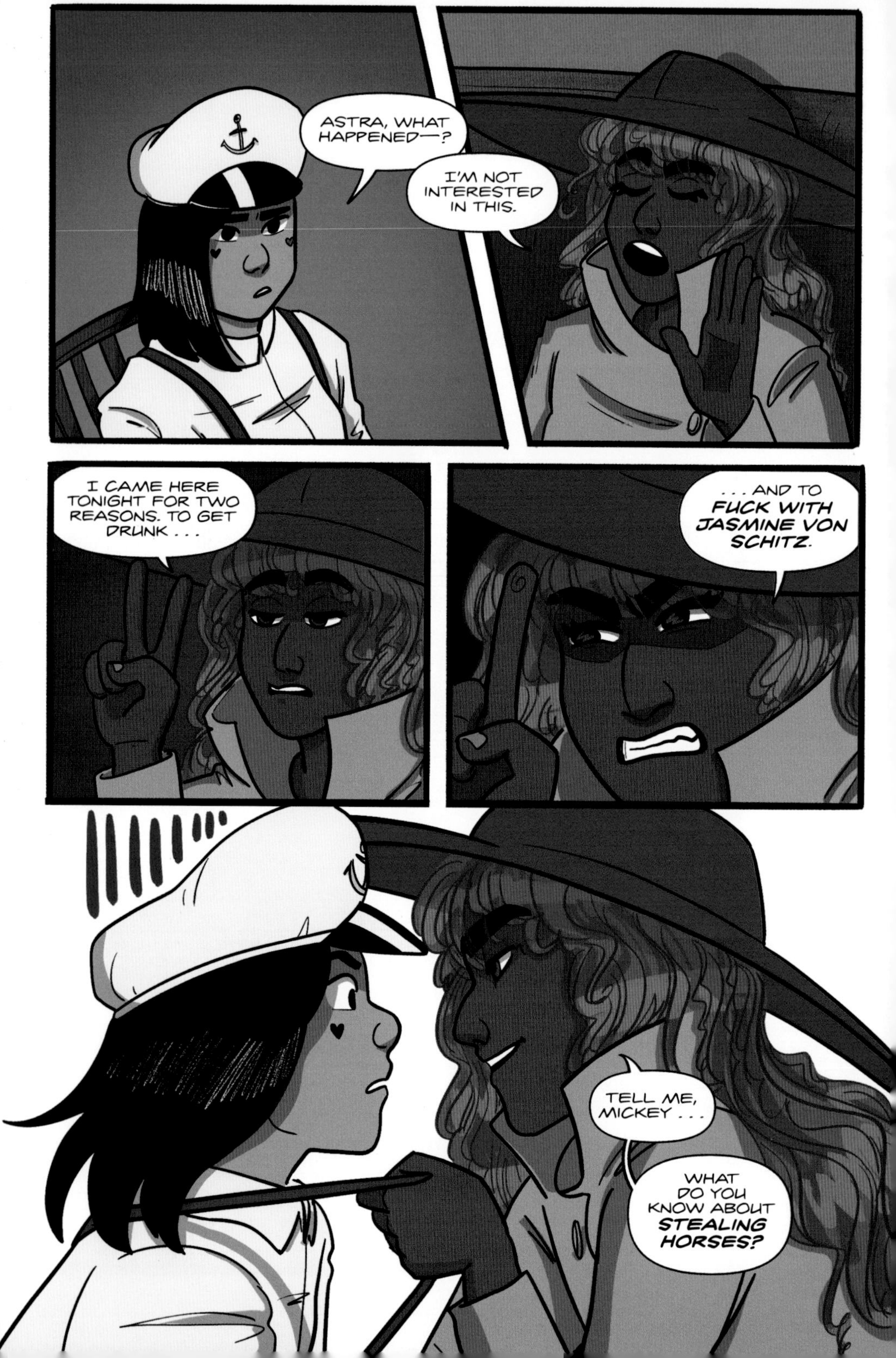
ASTRA, WHAT HAPPENED—?
I'M NOT INTERESTED IN THIS.
I CAME HERE TONIGHT FOR TWO REASONS. TO GET DRUNK . . .
. . . AND TO **FUCK WITH JASMINE VON SCHITZ**.
TELL ME, MICKEY . . .
WHAT DO YOU KNOW ABOUT **STEALING HORSES?**

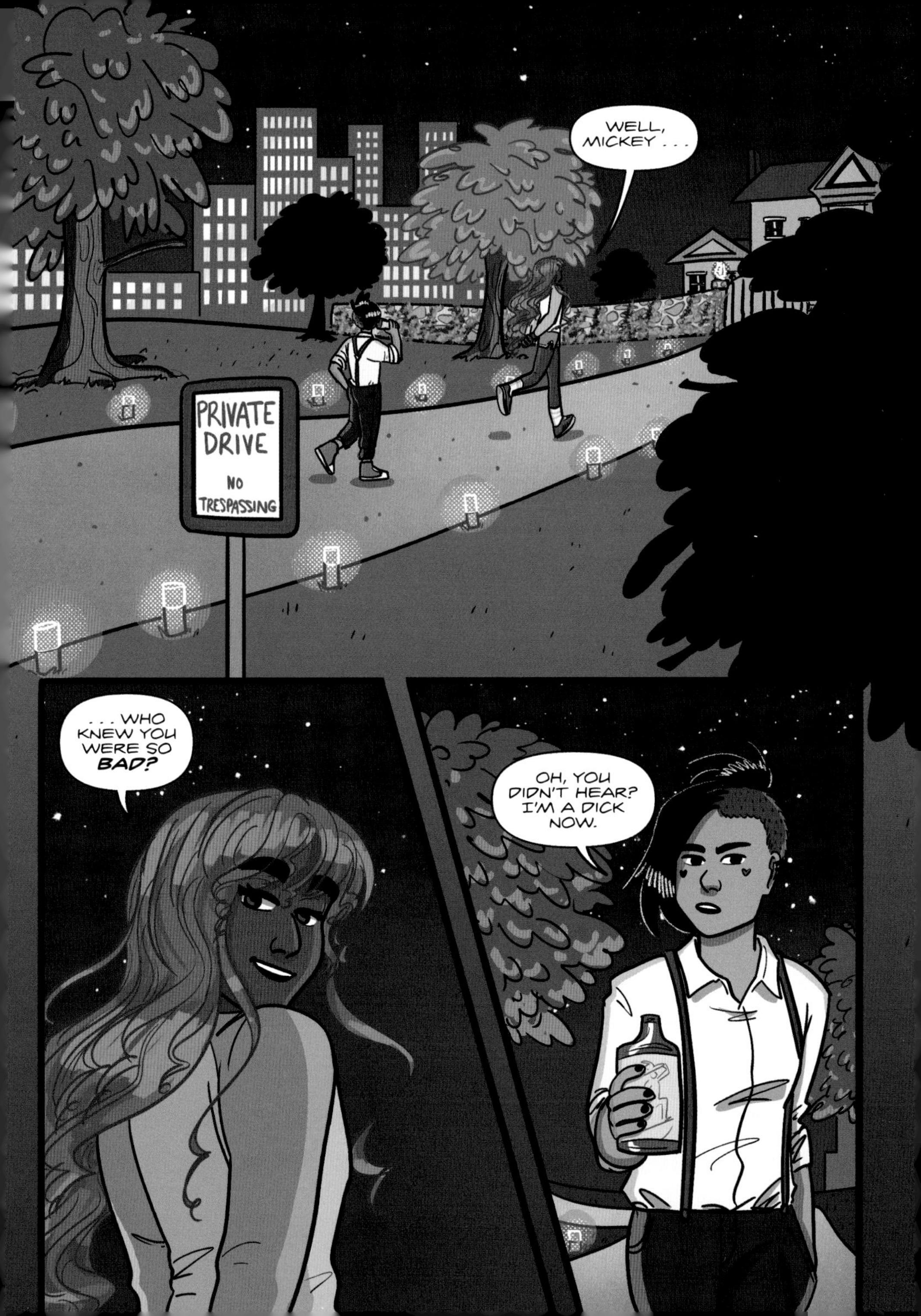
WELL, MICKEY . . .
PRIVATE DRIVE
NO TRESPASSING
. . . WHO KNEW YOU WERE SO *BAD?*
OH, YOU DIDN'T HEAR? I'M A DICK NOW.

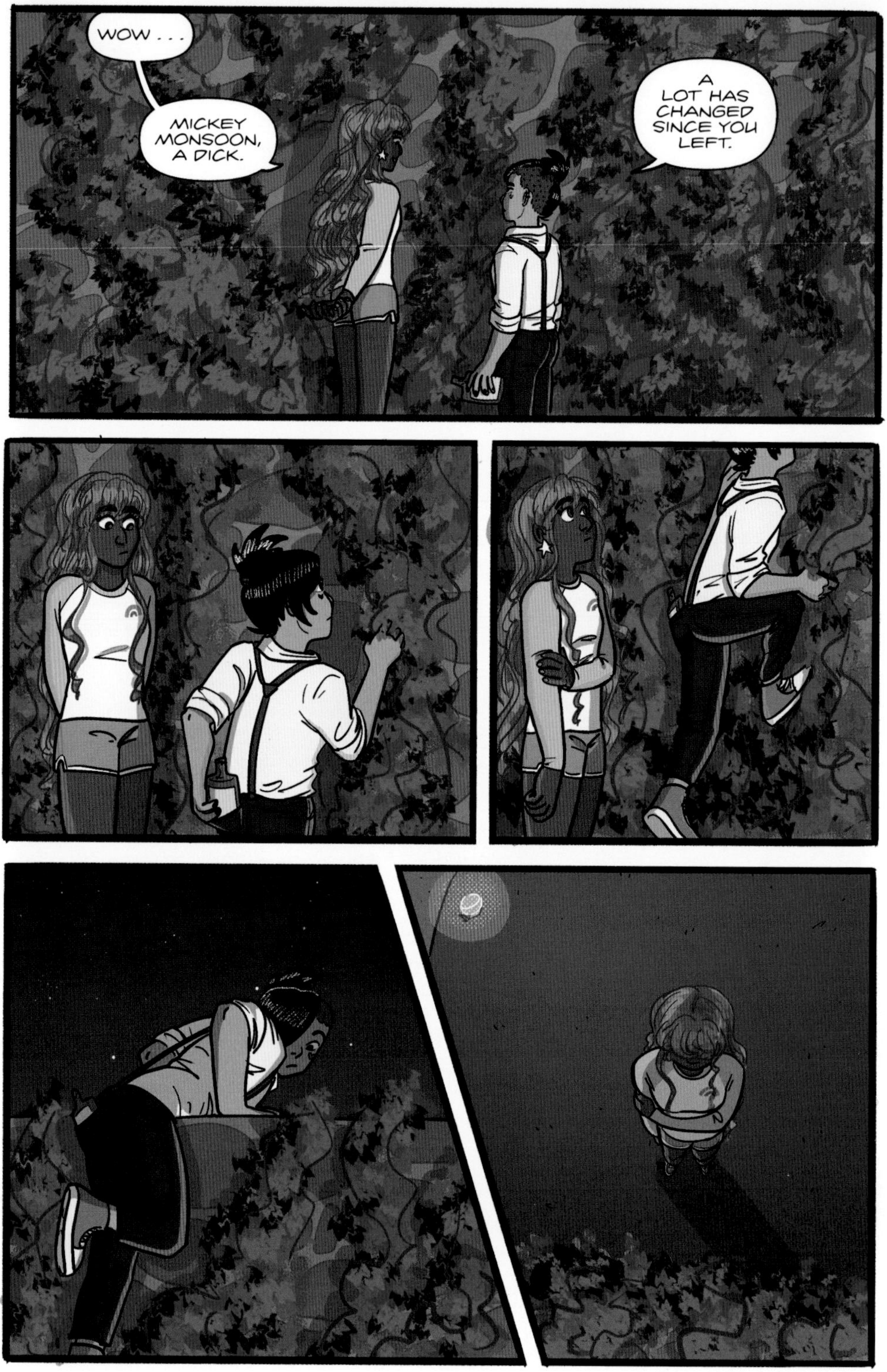
WOW . . .
MICKEY MONSOON, A DICK.
A LOT HAS CHANGED SINCE YOU LEFT.

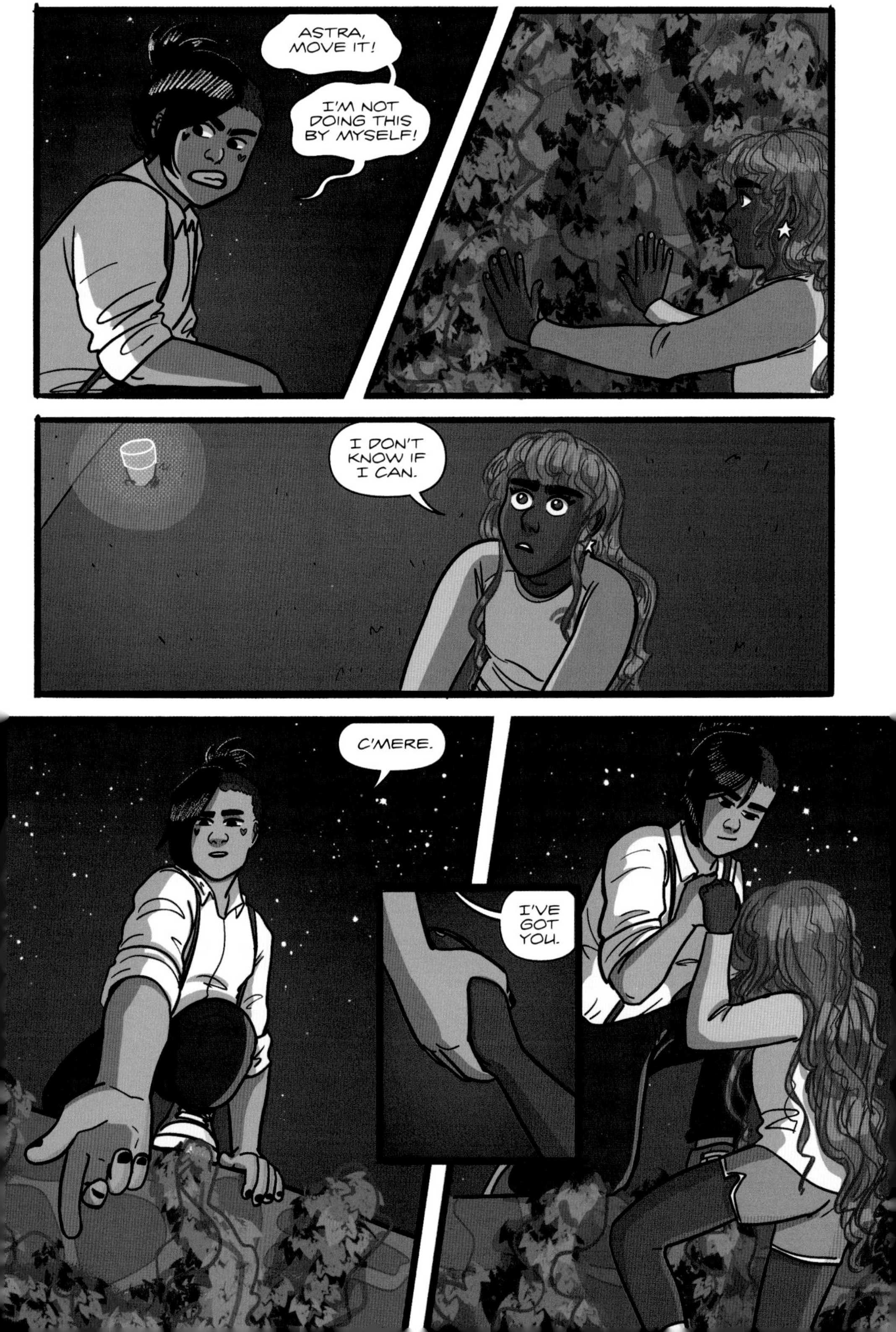
ASTRA, MOVE IT!
I'M NOT DOING THIS BY MYSELF!
I DON'T KNOW IF I CAN.
C'MERE.
I'VE GOT YOU.

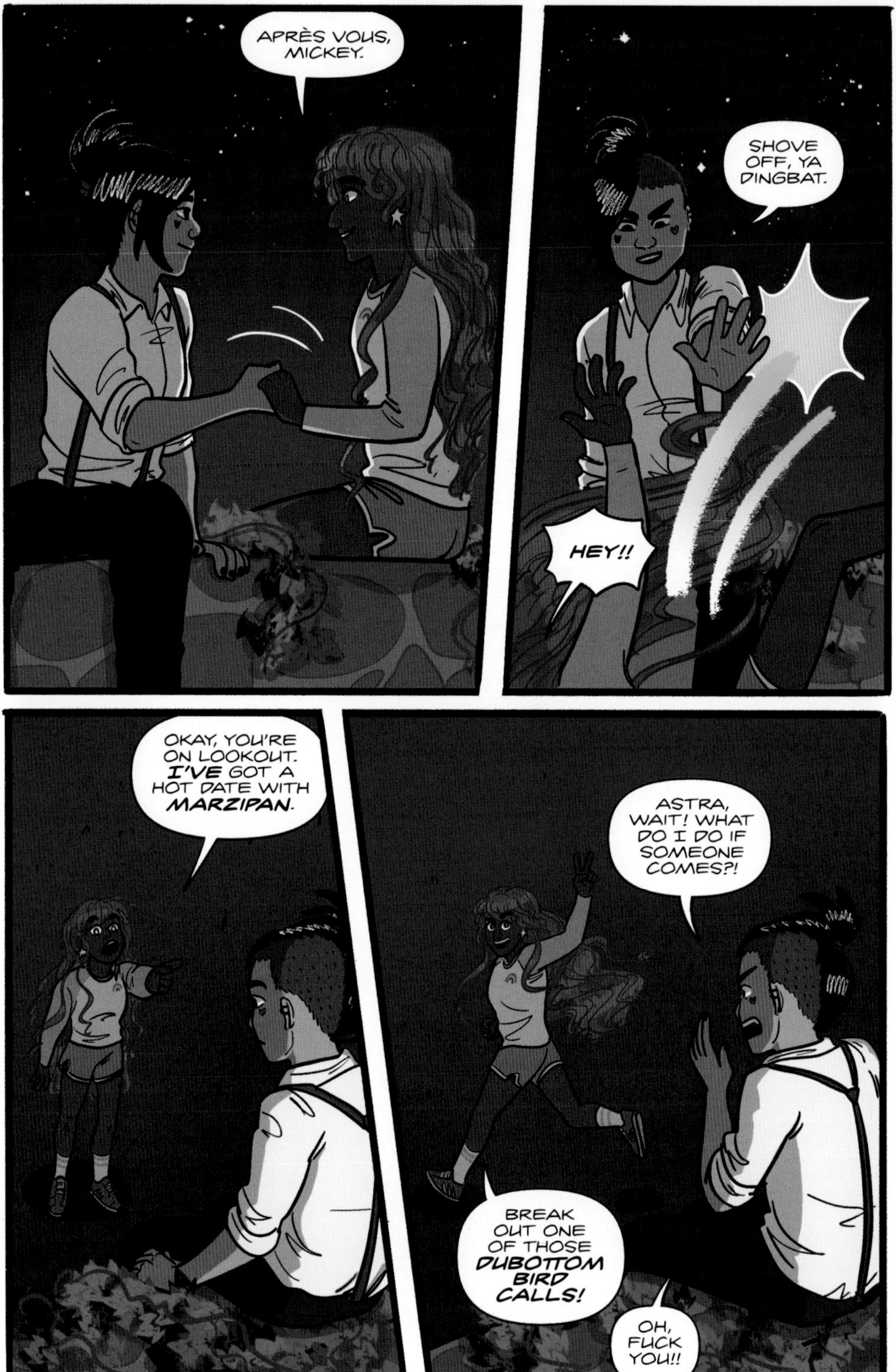
APRÈS VOUS, MICKEY.
SHOVE OFF, YA DINGBAT.
HEY!!
OKAY, YOU'RE ON LOOKOUT. ***I'VE*** GOT A HOT DATE WITH ***MARZIPAN***.
ASTRA, WAIT! WHAT DO I DO IF SOMEONE COMES?!
BREAK OUT ONE OF THOSE ***DUBOTTOM BIRD CALLS!***
OH, FUCK YOU!!

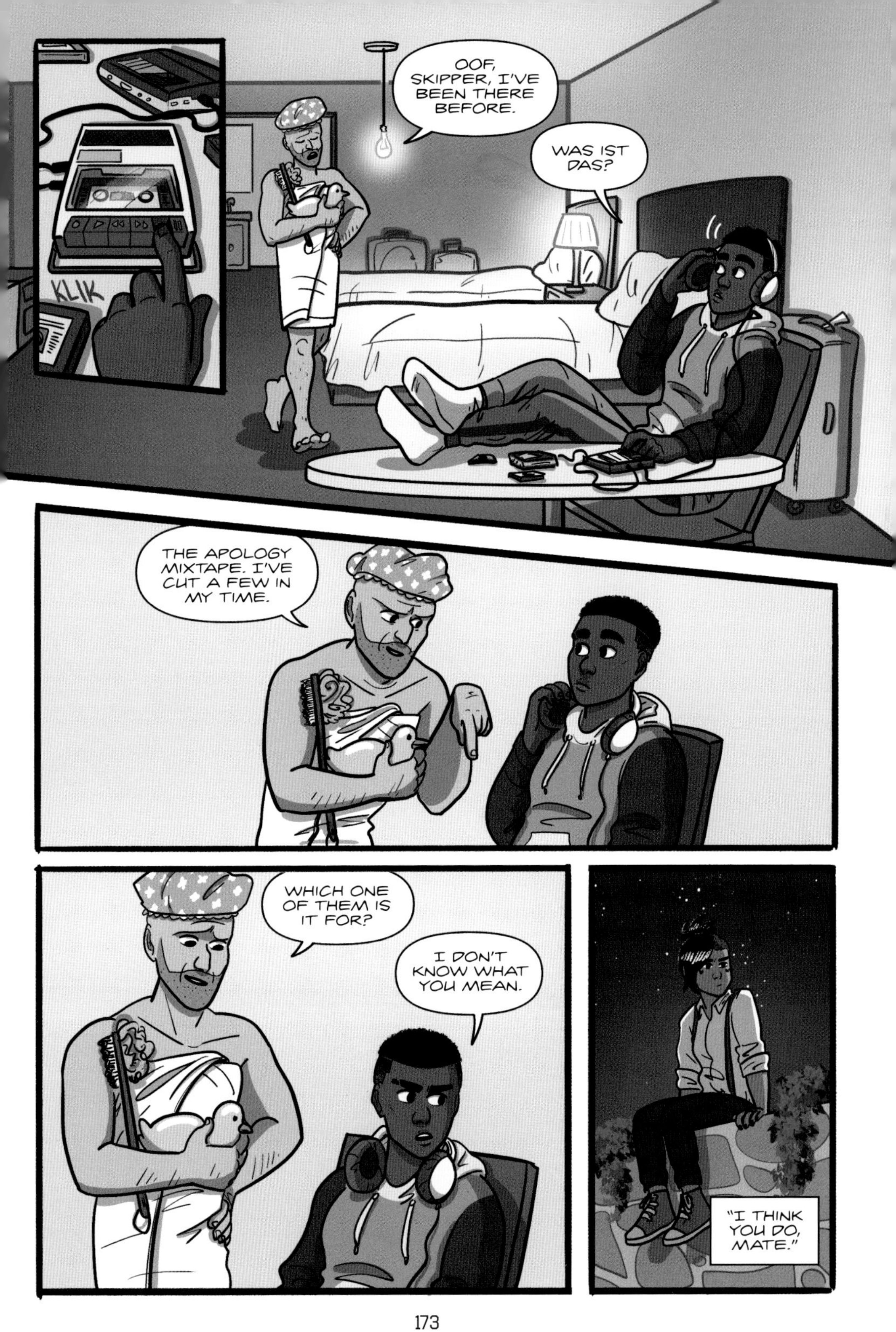
KLIK
OOF, SKIPPER, I'VE BEEN THERE BEFORE.
WAS IST DAS?
THE APOLOGY MIXTAPE. I'VE CUT A FEW IN MY TIME.
WHICH ONE OF THEM IS IT FOR?
I DON'T KNOW WHAT YOU MEAN.
"I THINK YOU DO, MATE."

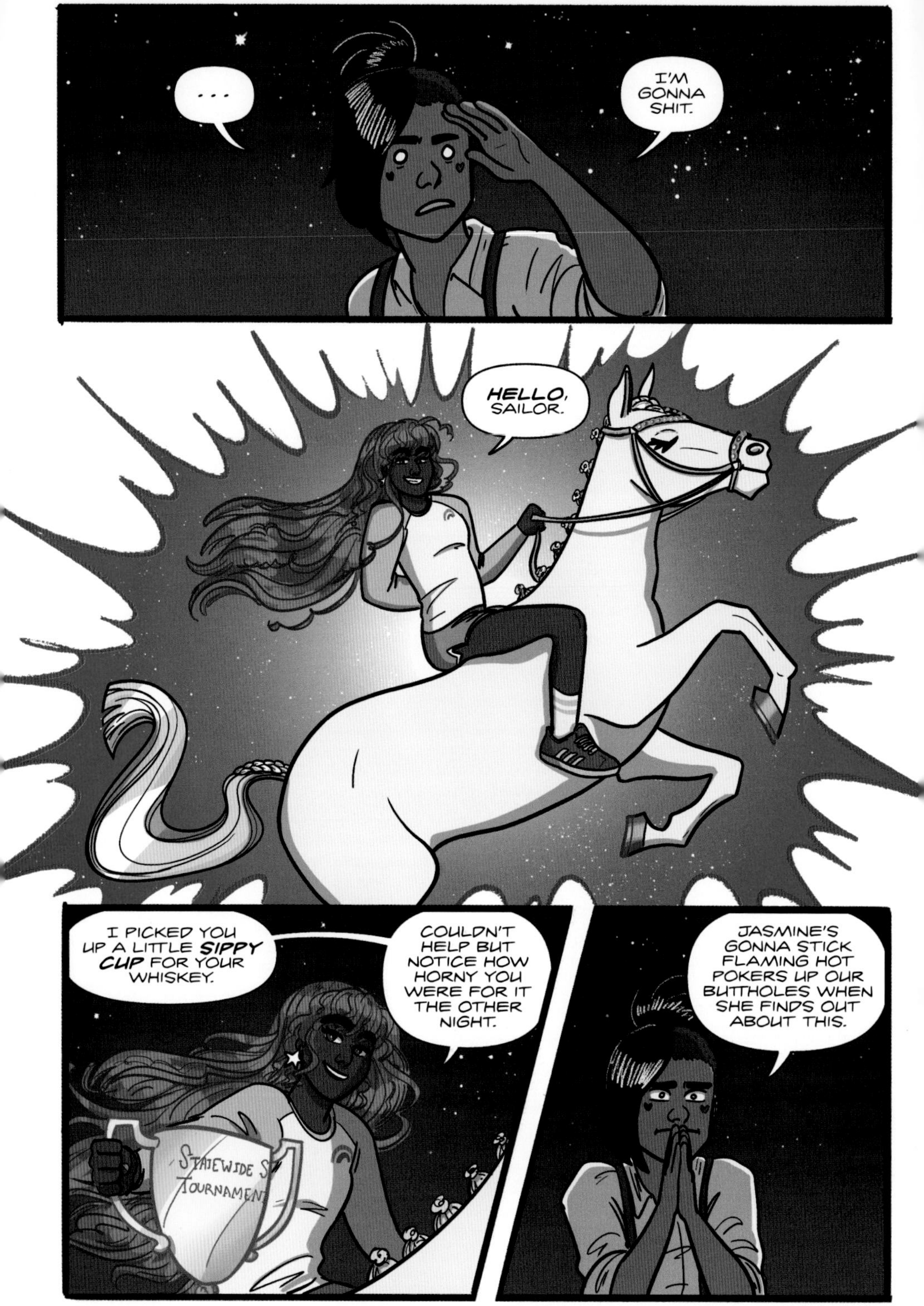
...
I'M GONNA SHIT.
HELLO, SAILOR.
I PICKED YOU UP A LITTLE ***SIPPY CUP*** FOR YOUR WHISKEY.
COULDN'T HELP BUT NOTICE HOW HORNY YOU WERE FOR IT THE OTHER NIGHT.
STATEWIDE S TOURNAMENT
JASMINE'S GONNA STICK FLAMING HOT POKERS UP OUR BUTTHOLES WHEN SHE FINDS OUT ABOUT THIS.

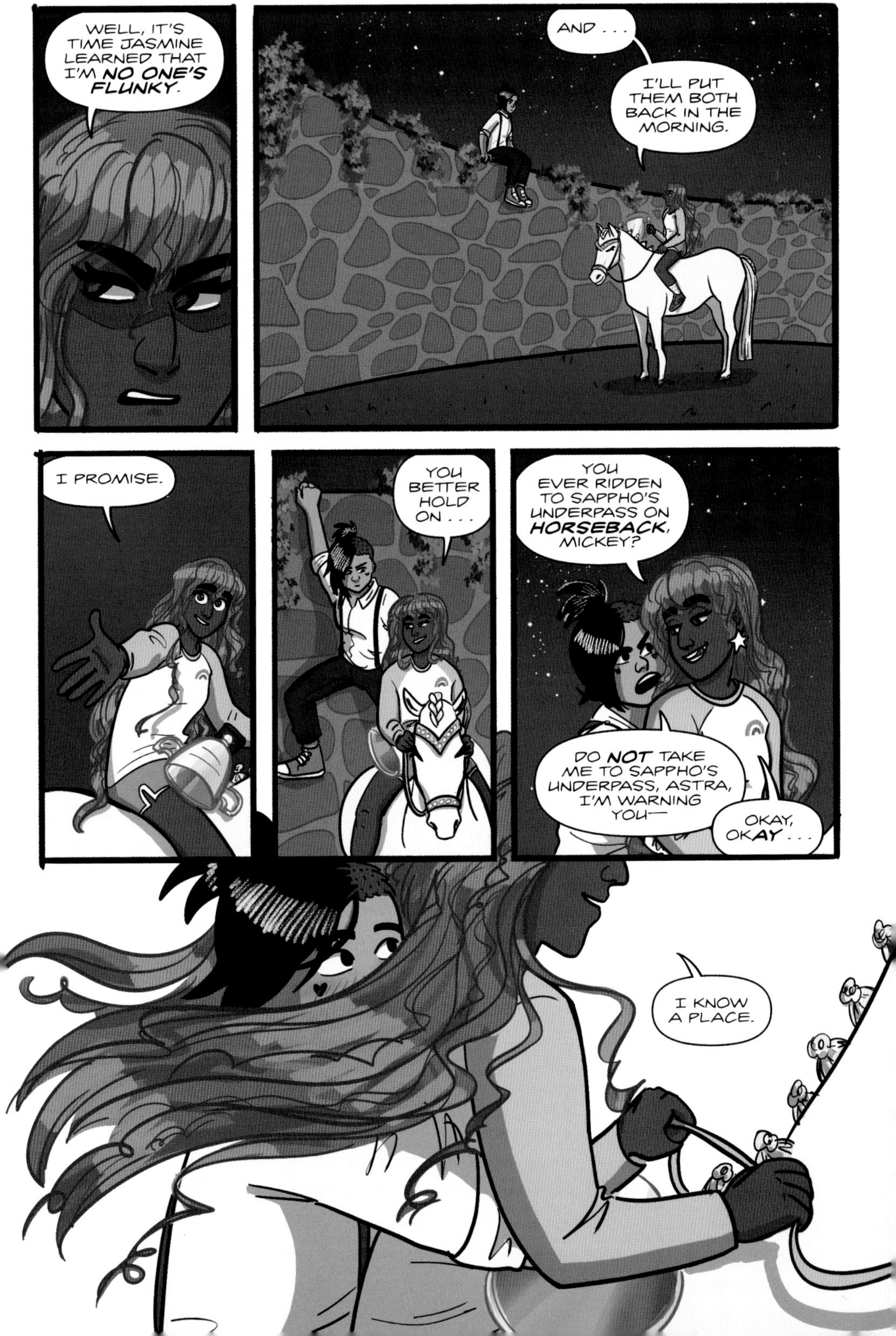
WELL, IT'S TIME JASMINE LEARNED THAT I'M **NO ONE'S FLUNKY**.
AND . . .
I'LL PUT THEM BOTH BACK IN THE MORNING.
I PROMISE.
YOU BETTER HOLD ON . . .
YOU EVER RIDDEN TO SAPPHO'S UNDERPASS ON **HORSEBACK**, MICKEY?
DO **NOT** TAKE ME TO SAPPHO'S UNDERPASS, ASTRA, I'M WARNING YOU—
OKAY, OK**AY** . . .
I KNOW A PLACE.

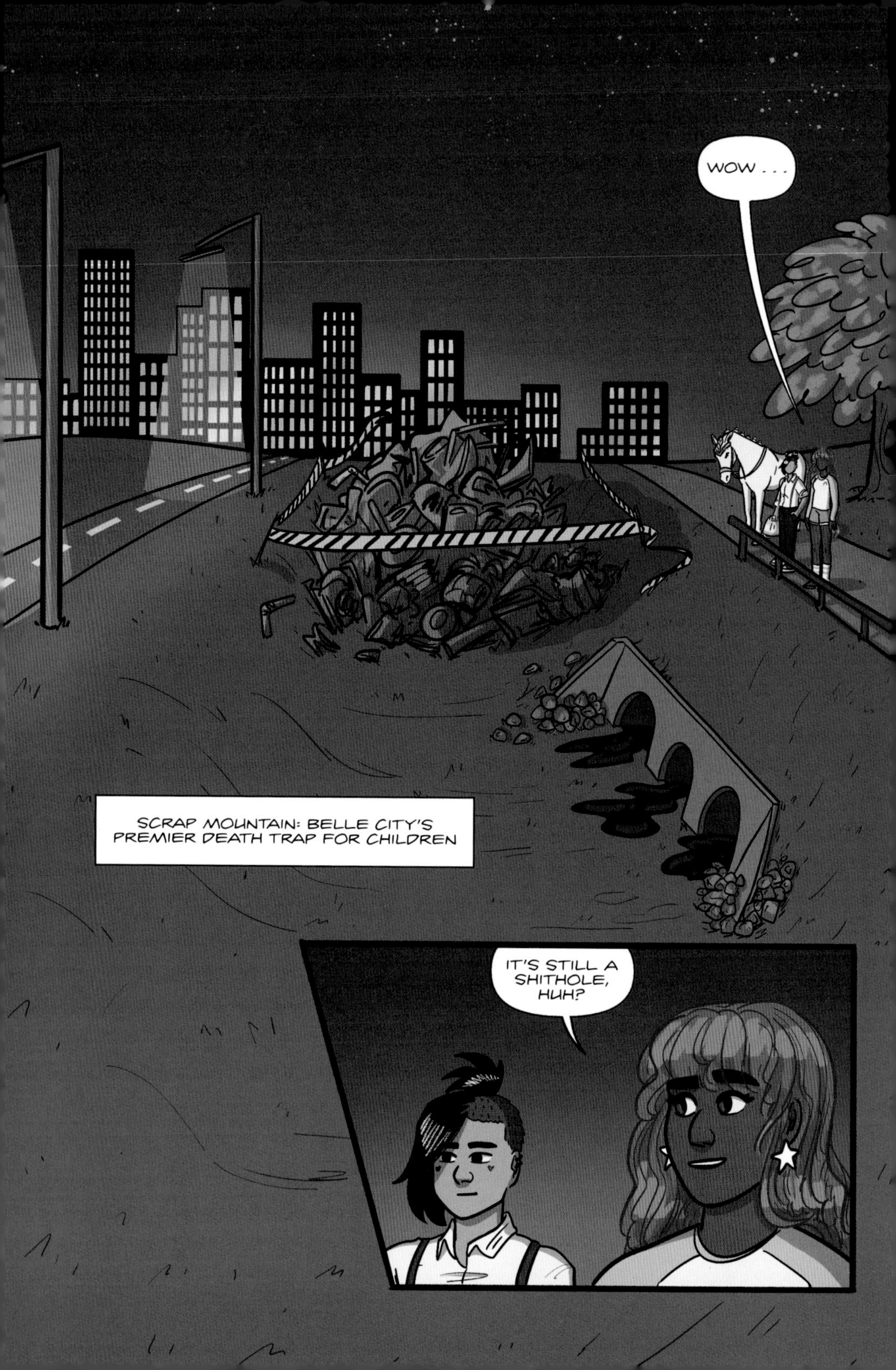
WOW . . .
SCRAP MOUNTAIN: BELLE CITY'S PREMIER DEATH TRAP FOR CHILDREN
IT'S STILL A SHITHOLE, HUH?

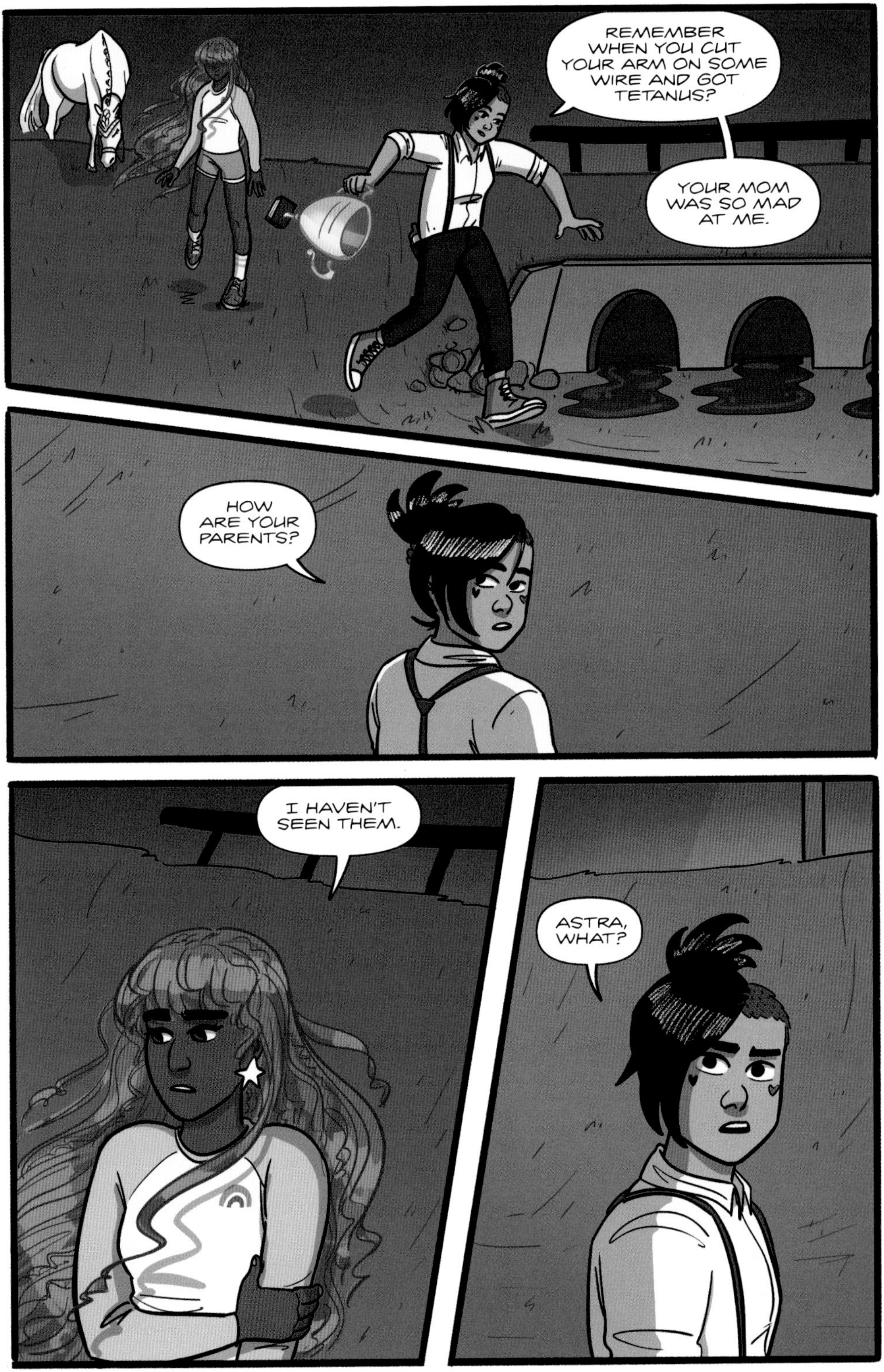
REMEMBER WHEN YOU CUT YOUR ARM ON SOME WIRE AND GOT TETANUS?
YOUR MOM WAS SO MAD AT ME.
HOW ARE YOUR PARENTS?
I HAVEN'T SEEN THEM.
ASTRA, WHAT?

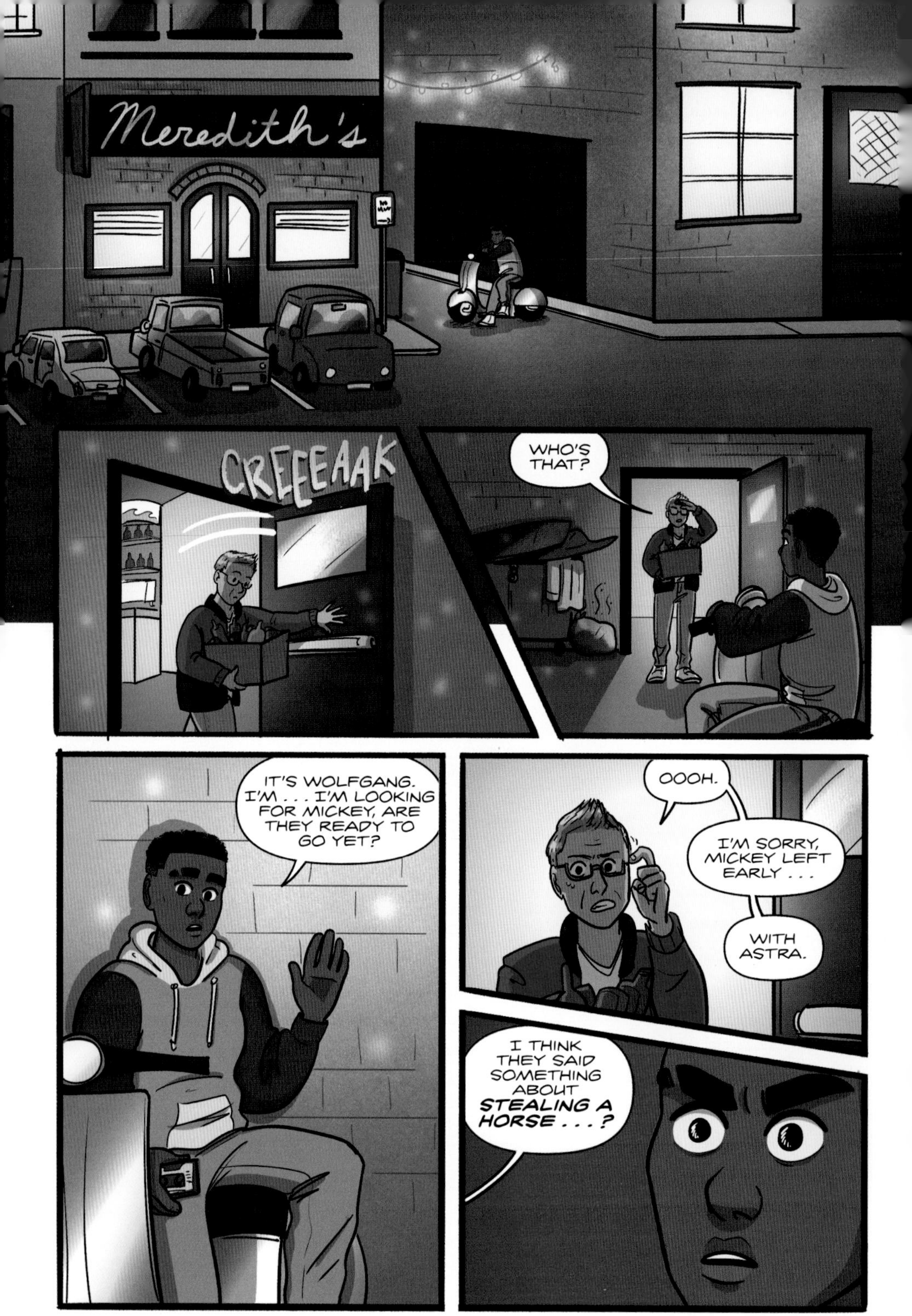
Meredith's
CREEEAAK
WHO'S THAT?
IT'S WOLFGANG. I'M . . . I'M LOOKING FOR MICKEY, ARE THEY READY TO GO YET?
OOOH.
I'M SORRY, MICKEY LEFT EARLY . . .
WITH ASTRA.
I THINK THEY SAID SOMETHING ABOUT ***STEALING A HORSE . . .?***

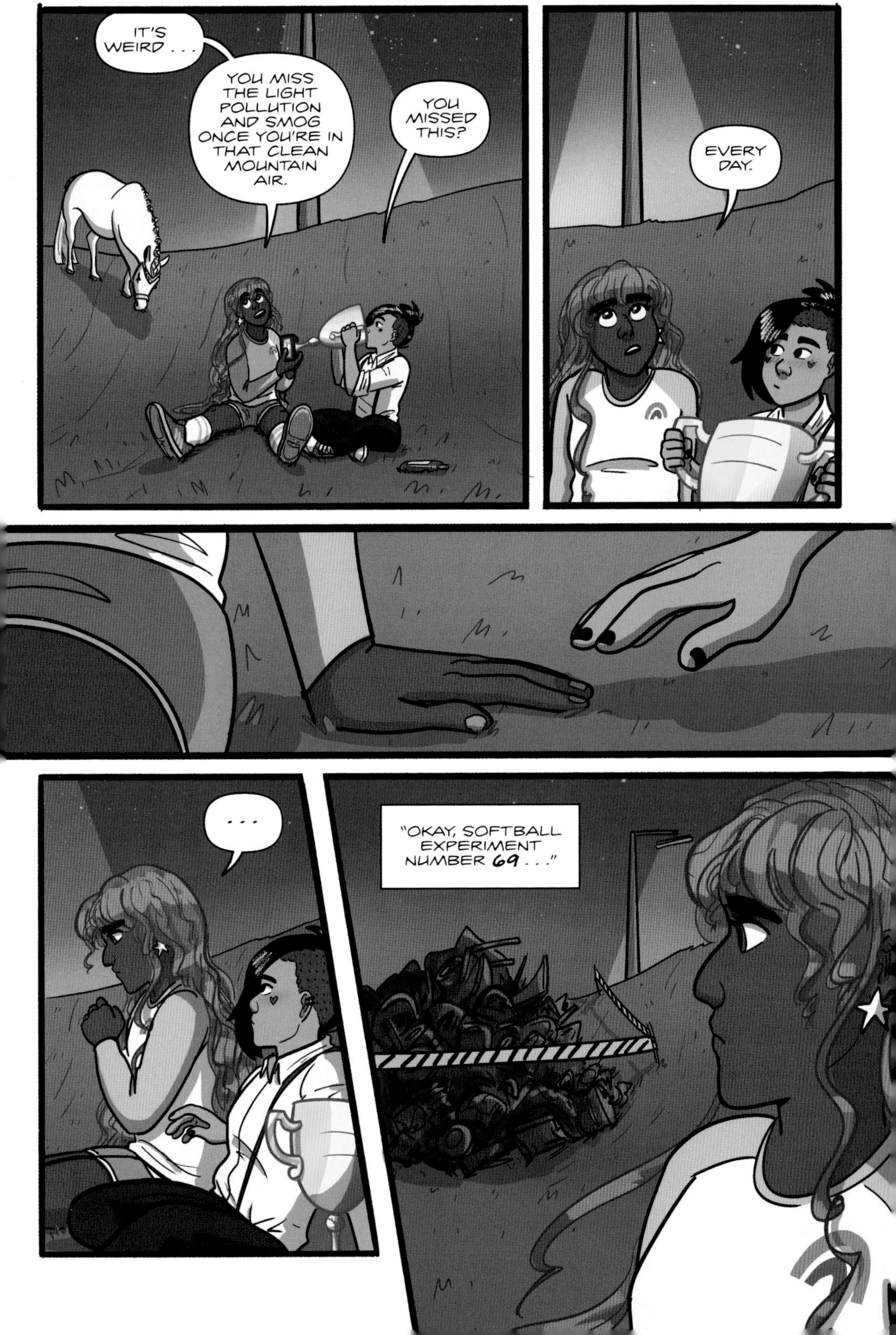
IT'S WEIRD . . .
YOU MISS THE LIGHT POLLUTION AND SMOG ONCE YOU'RE IN THAT CLEAN MOUNTAIN AIR.
YOU MISSED THIS?
EVERY DAY.
. . .
"OKAY, SOFTBALL EXPERIMENT NUMBER 69 . . ."

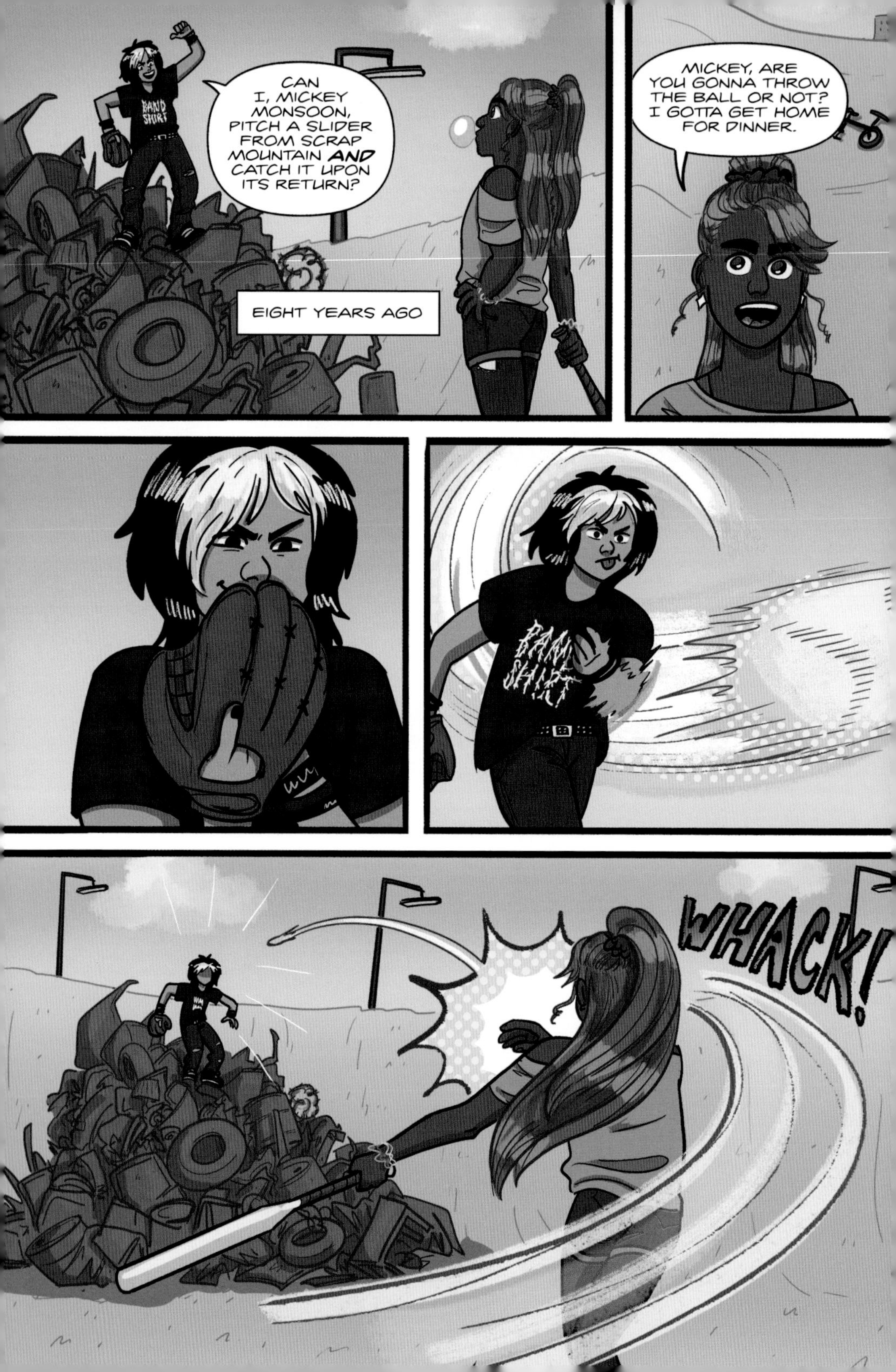
CAN I, MICKEY MONSOON, PITCH A SLIDER FROM SCRAP MOUNTAIN AND CATCH IT UPON ITS RETURN?
BAND SHIRT
EIGHT YEARS AGO
MICKEY, ARE YOU GONNA THROW THE BALL OR NOT? I GOTTA GET HOME FOR DINNER.
BAND SHIRT
WHACK!

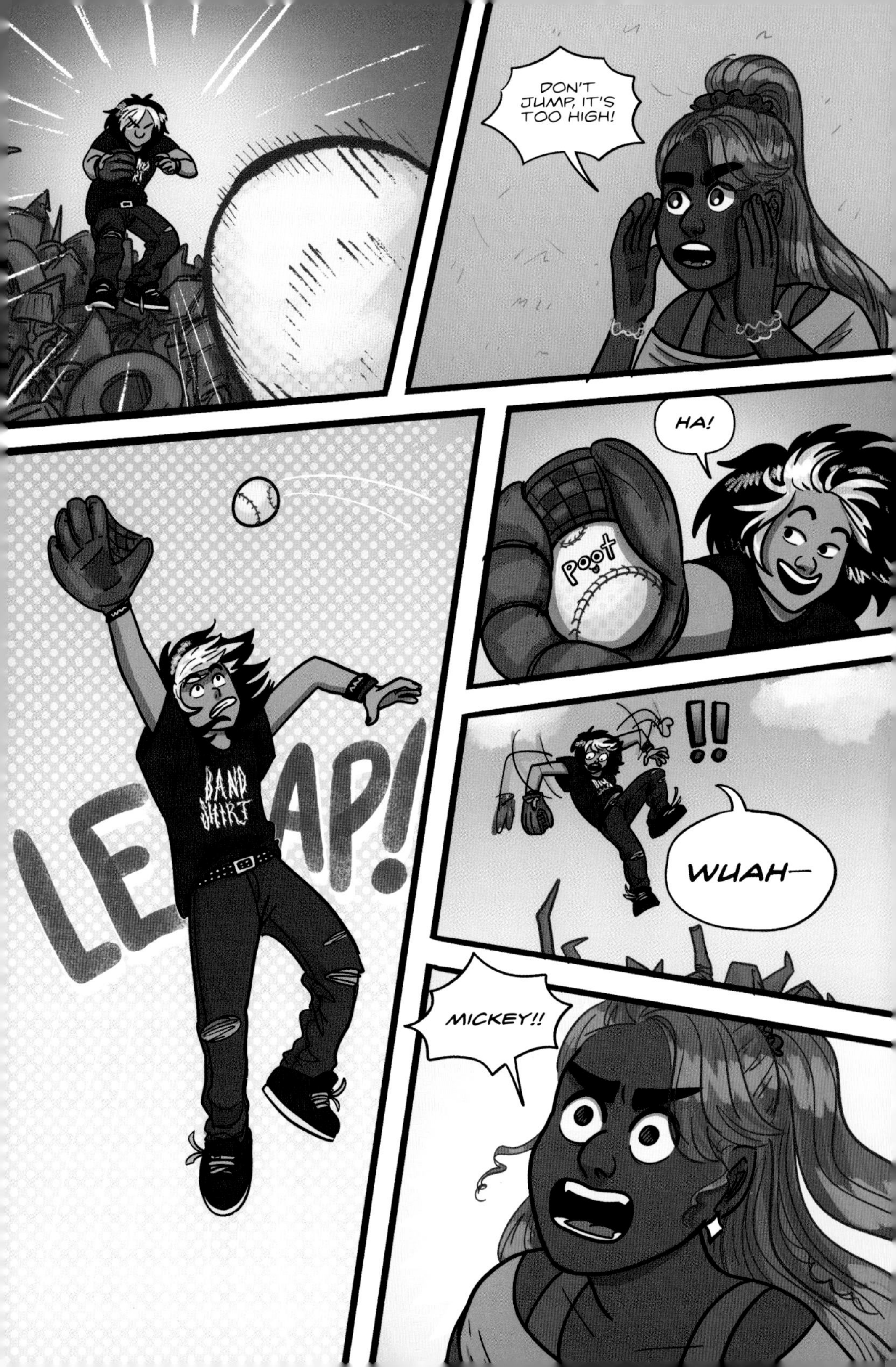
DON'T JUMP, IT'S TOO HIGH!
LEAP!
BAND SHIRT
HA!
poot
!!
WUAH—
MICKEY!!

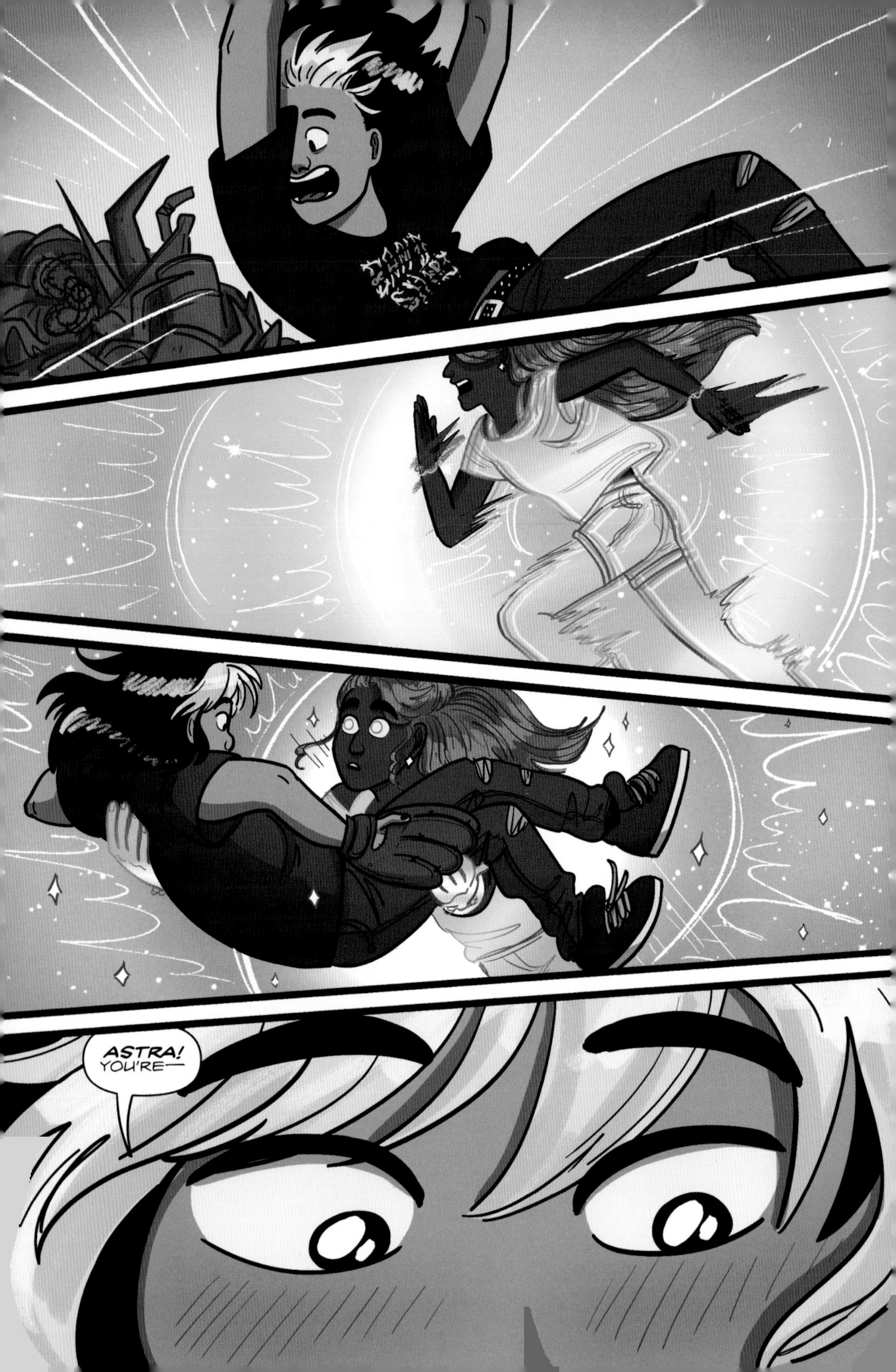
ASTRA! YOU'RE—

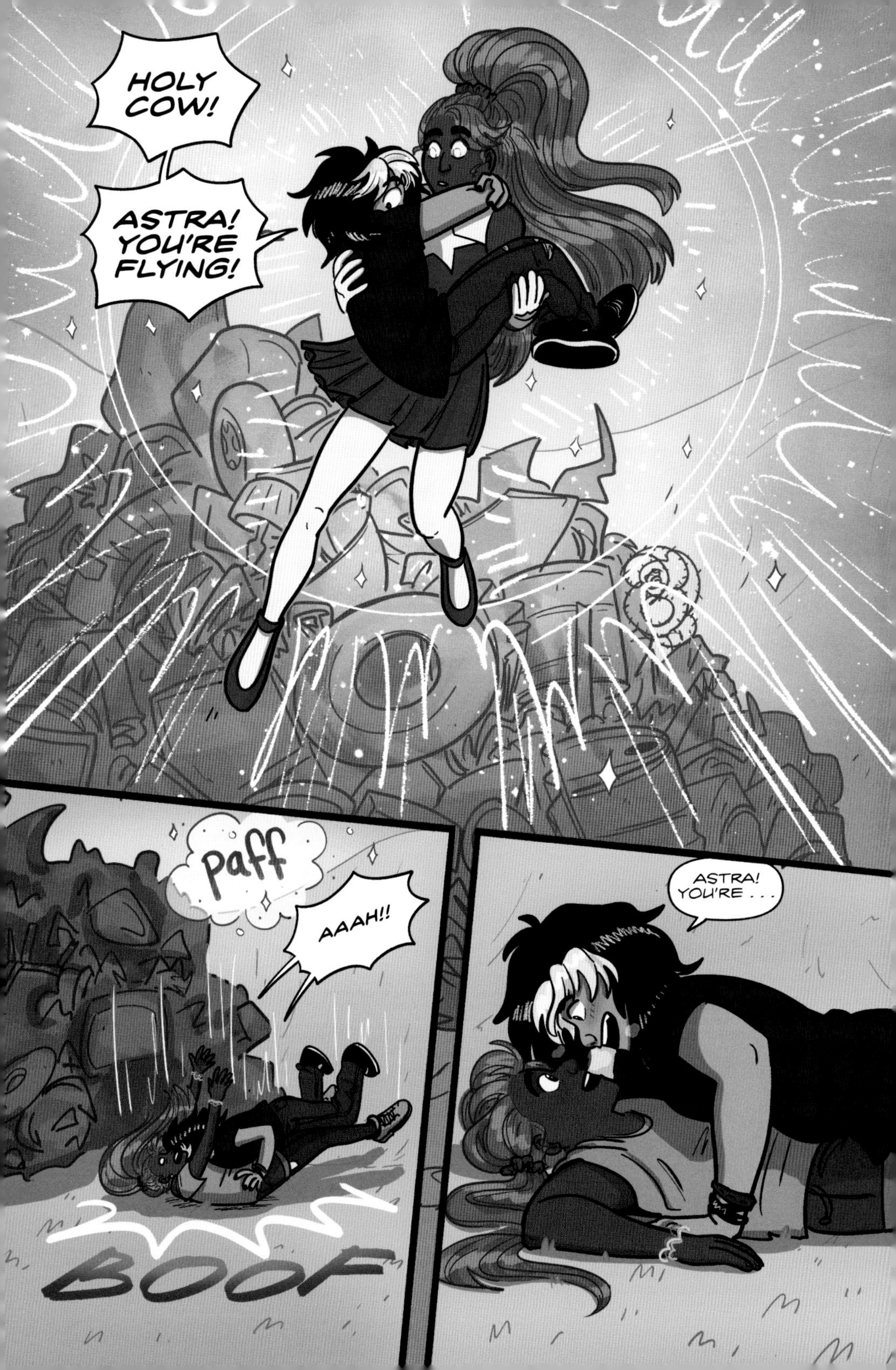
HOLY COW!
ASTRA! YOU'RE FLYING!
Paff
AAAH!!
BOOF
ASTRA! YOU'RE . . .

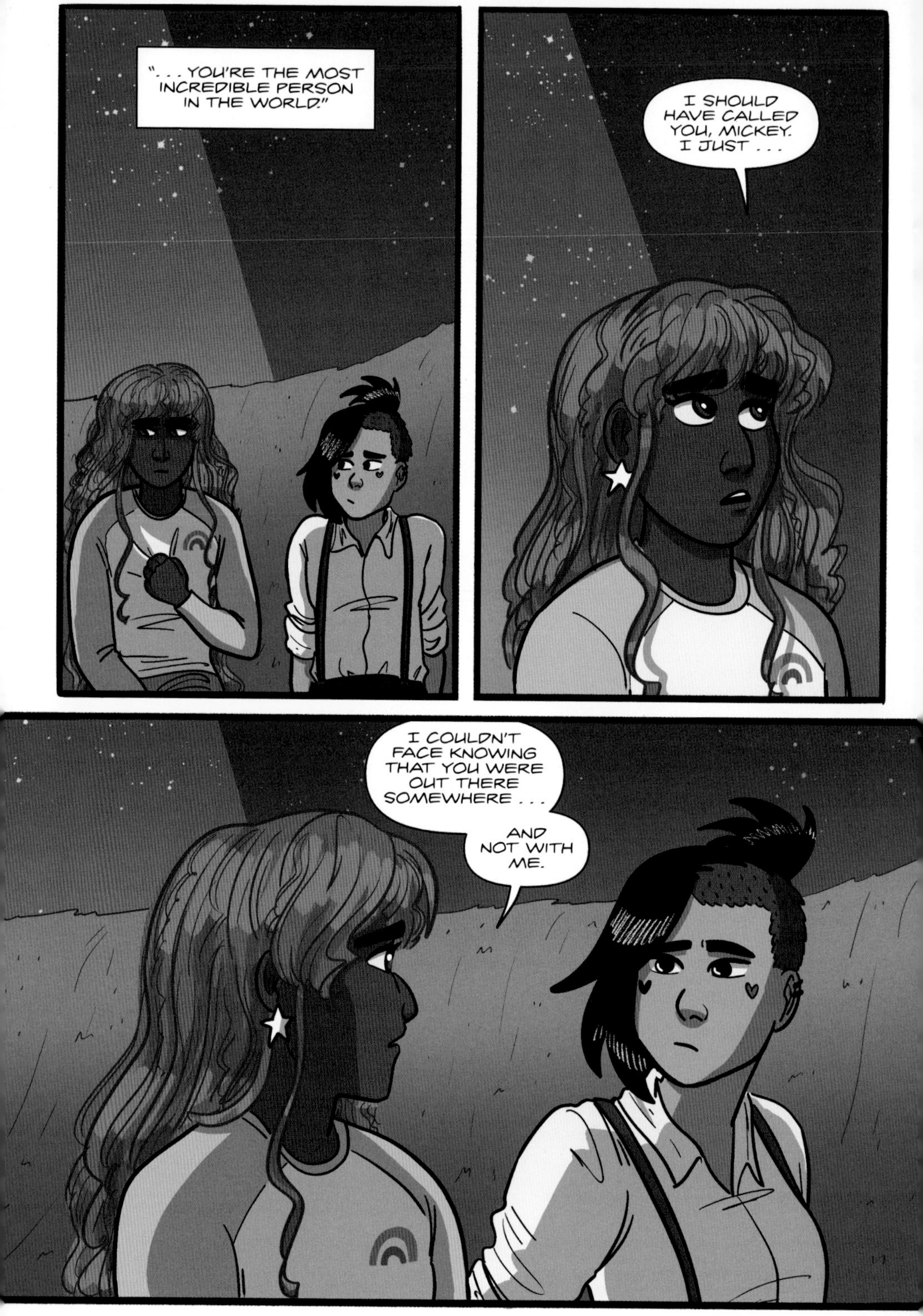
". . . YOU'RE THE MOST INCREDIBLE PERSON IN THE WORLD."
I SHOULD HAVE CALLED YOU, MICKEY. I JUST . . .
I COULDN'T FACE KNOWING THAT YOU WERE OUT THERE SOMEWHERE . . .
AND NOT WITH ME.

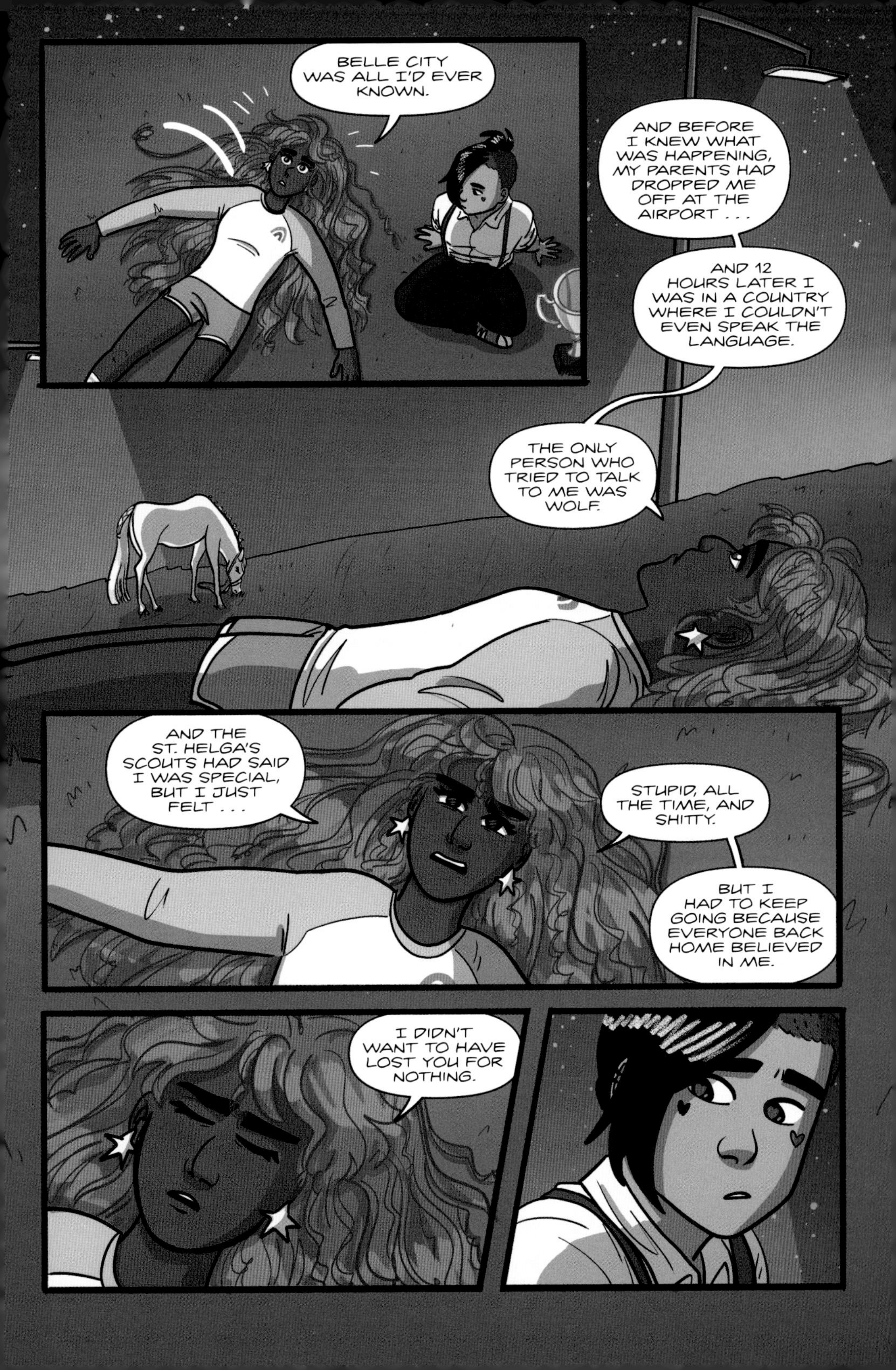
BELLE CITY WAS ALL I'D EVER KNOWN.
AND BEFORE I KNEW WHAT WAS HAPPENING, MY PARENTS HAD DROPPED ME OFF AT THE AIRPORT . . .
AND 12 HOURS LATER I WAS IN A COUNTRY WHERE I COULDN'T EVEN SPEAK THE LANGUAGE.
THE ONLY PERSON WHO TRIED TO TALK TO ME WAS WOLF.
AND THE ST. HELGA'S SCOUTS HAD SAID I WAS SPECIAL, BUT I JUST FELT . . .
STUPID, ALL THE TIME, AND SHITTY.
BUT I HAD TO KEEP GOING BECAUSE EVERYONE BACK HOME BELIEVED IN ME.
I DIDN'T WANT TO HAVE LOST YOU FOR NOTHING.

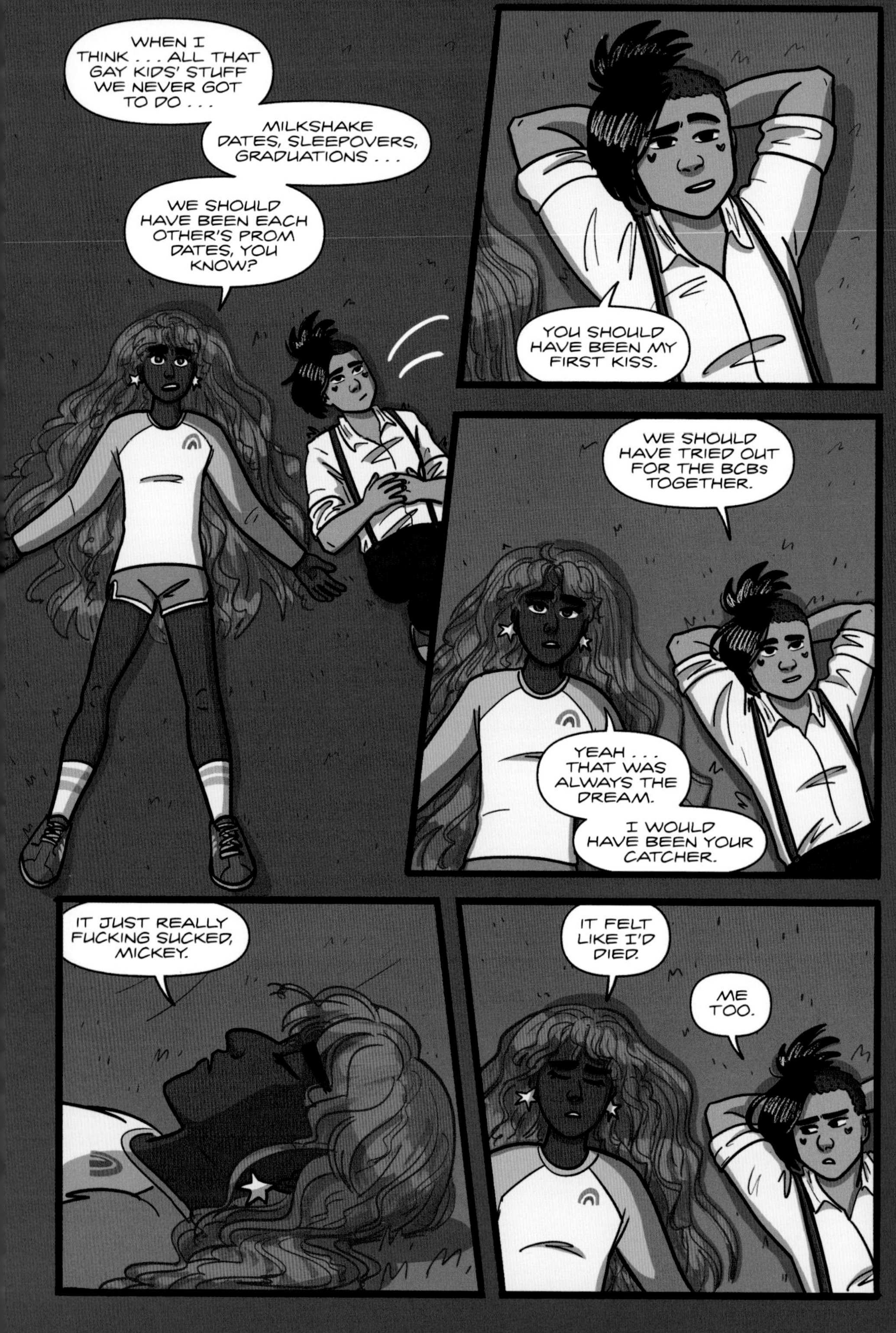
WHEN I THINK . . . ALL THAT GAY KIDS' STUFF WE NEVER GOT TO DO . . .
MILKSHAKE DATES, SLEEPOVERS, GRADUATIONS . . .
WE SHOULD HAVE BEEN EACH OTHER'S PROM DATES, YOU KNOW?
YOU SHOULD HAVE BEEN MY FIRST KISS.
WE SHOULD HAVE TRIED OUT FOR THE BCBs TOGETHER.
YEAH . . . THAT WAS ALWAYS THE DREAM.
I WOULD HAVE BEEN YOUR CATCHER.
IT JUST REALLY FUCKING SUCKED, MICKEY.
IT FELT LIKE I'D DIED.
ME TOO.

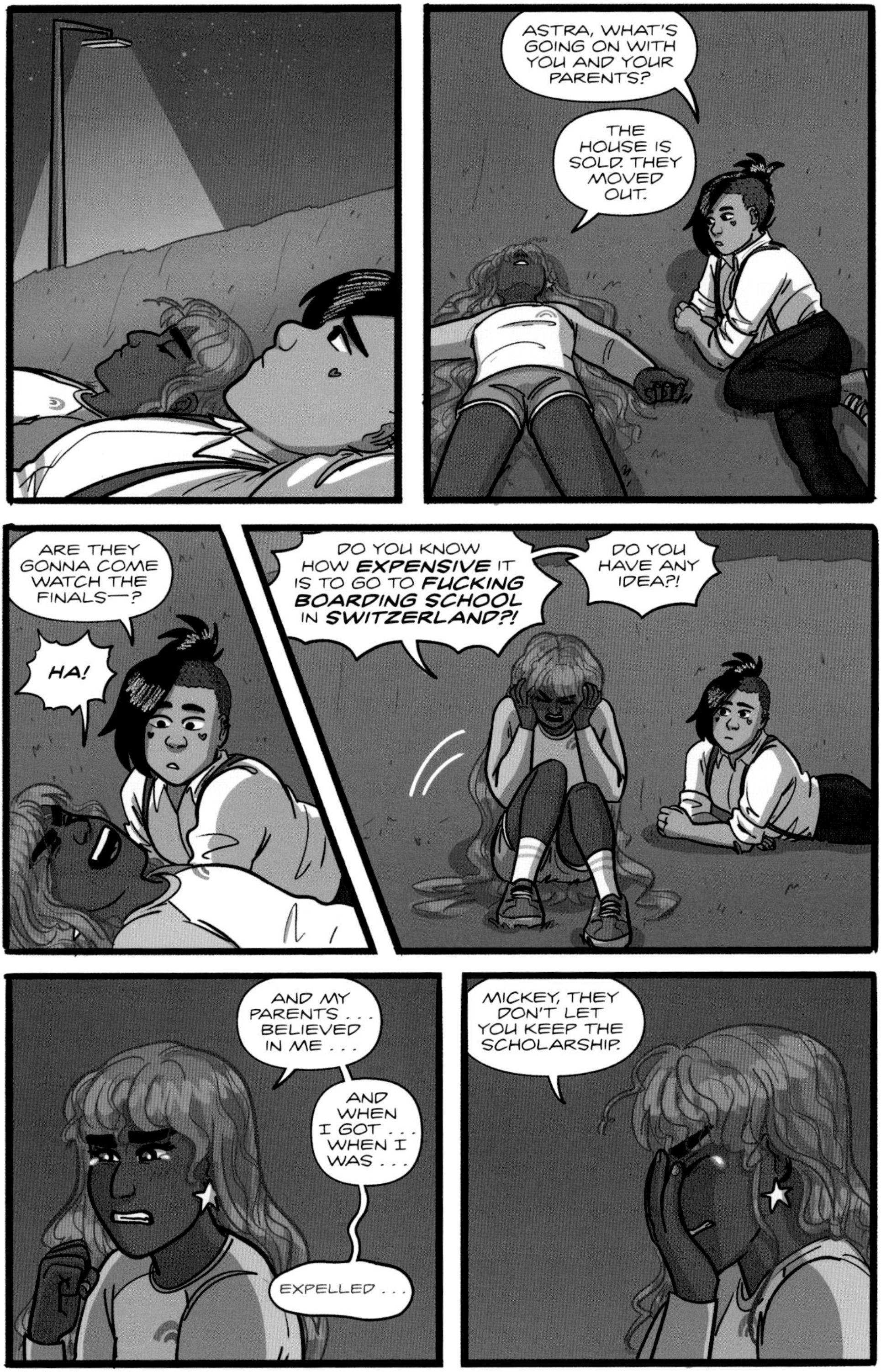

ASTRA, WHAT'S GOING ON WITH YOU AND YOUR PARENTS?
THE HOUSE IS SOLD. THEY MOVED OUT.
ARE THEY GONNA COME WATCH THE FINALS—?
HA!
DO YOU KNOW HOW EXPENSIVE IT IS TO GO TO FUCKING BOARDING SCHOOL IN SWITZERLAND?!
DO YOU HAVE ANY IDEA?!
AND MY PARENTS . . . BELIEVED IN ME . . .
AND WHEN I GOT . . . WHEN I WAS . . .
EXPELLED . . .
MICKEY, THEY DON'T LET YOU KEEP THE SCHOLARSHIP.

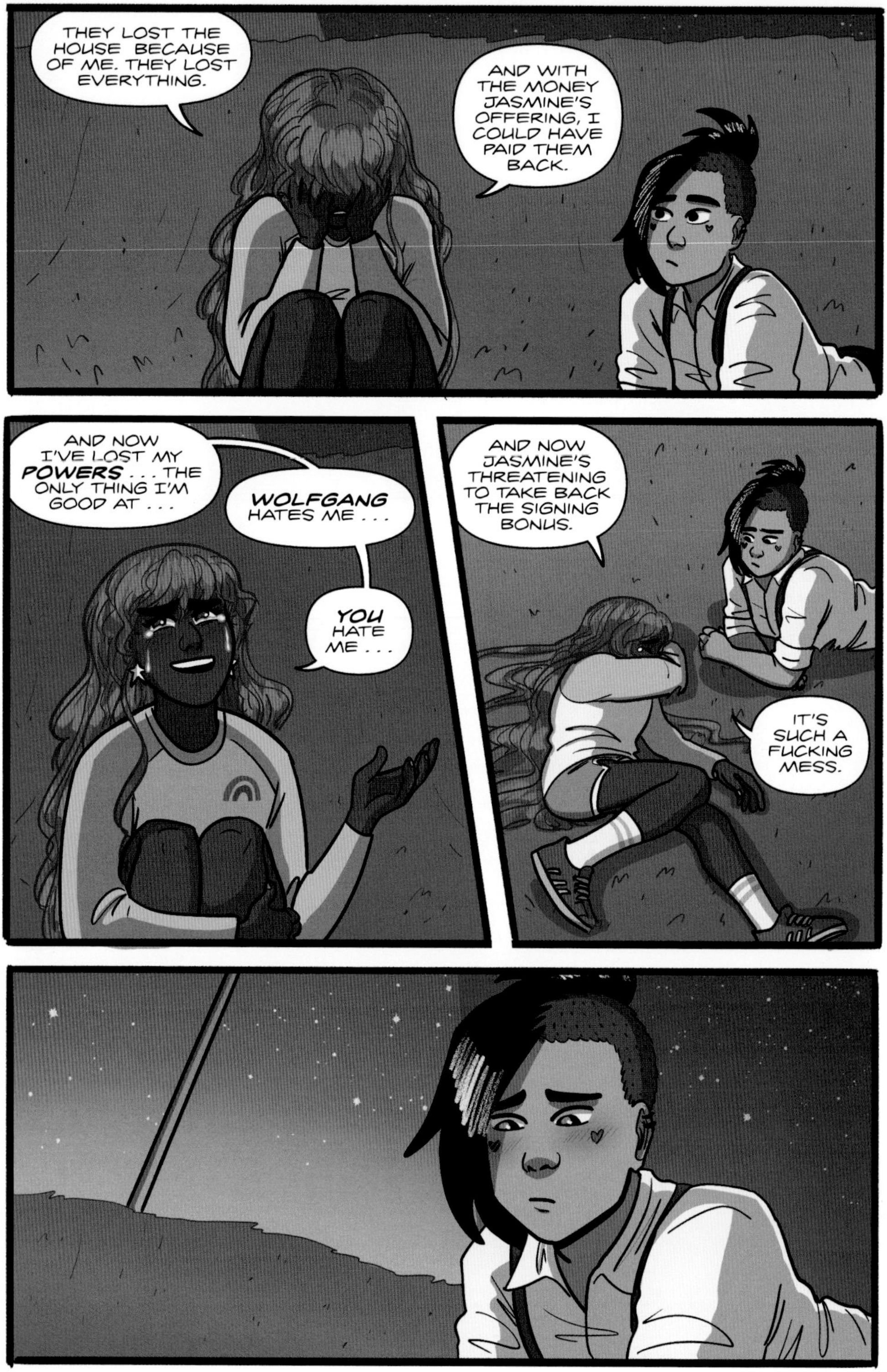

THEY LOST THE HOUSE BECAUSE OF ME. THEY LOST EVERYTHING.
AND WITH THE MONEY JASMINE'S OFFERING, I COULD HAVE PAID THEM BACK.
AND NOW I'VE LOST MY POWERS . . . THE ONLY THING I'M GOOD AT . . .
WOLFGANG HATES ME . . .
YOU HATE ME . . .
AND NOW JASMINE'S THREATENING TO TAKE BACK THE SIGNING BONUS.
IT'S SUCH A FUCKING MESS.

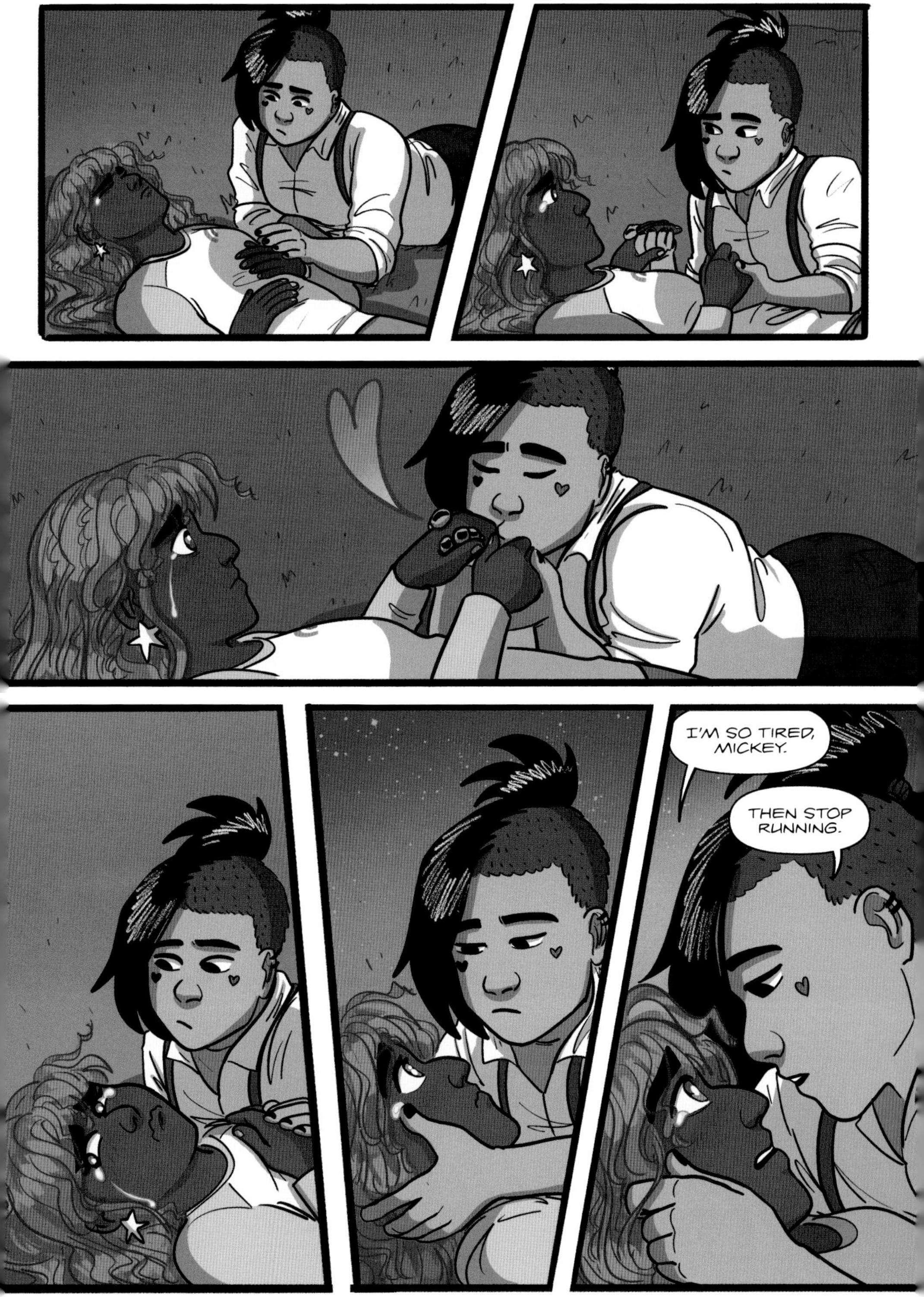
I'M SO TIRED, MICKEY.
THEN STOP RUNNING.

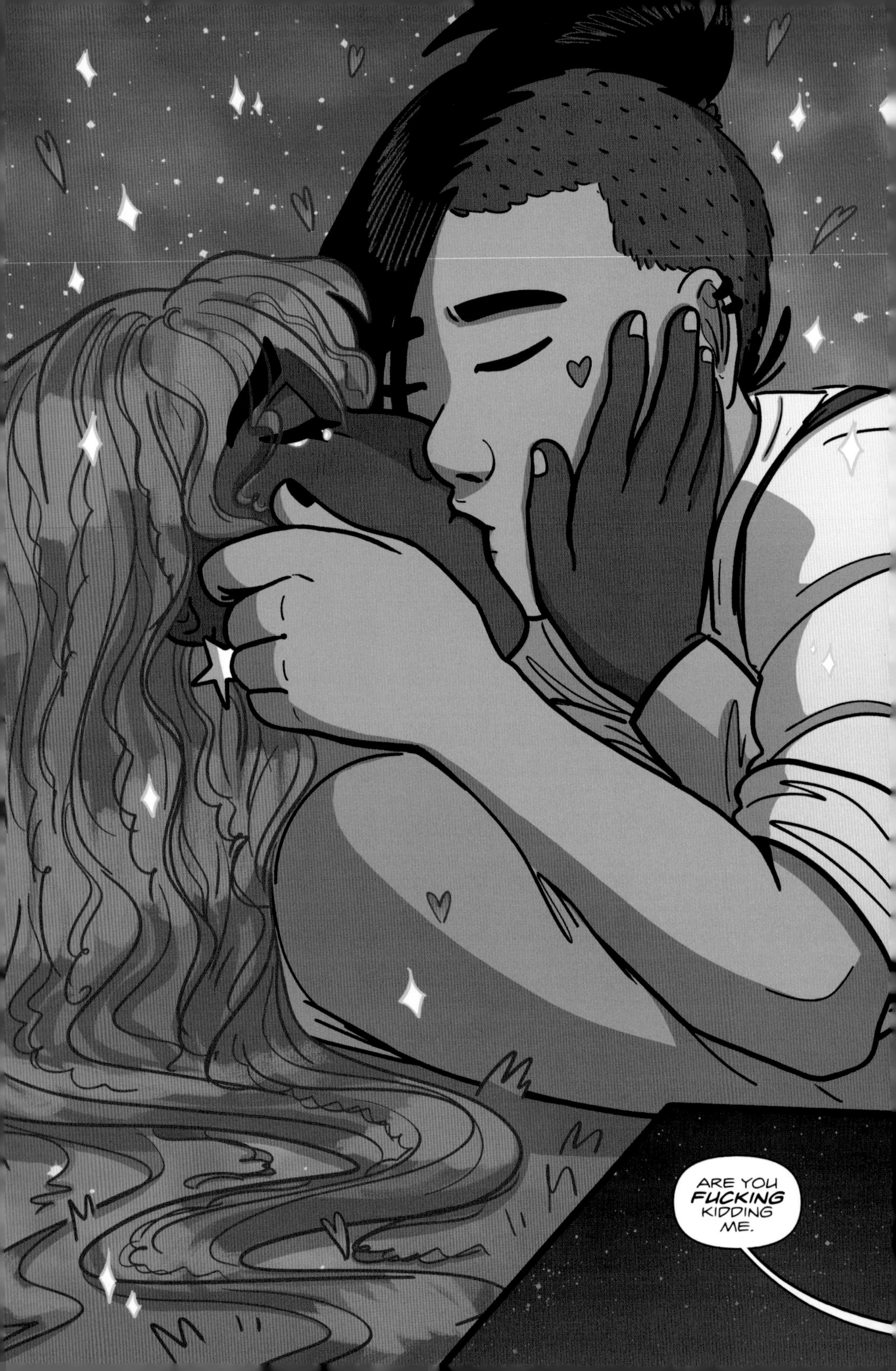
ARE YOU ***FUCKING*** KIDDING ME.

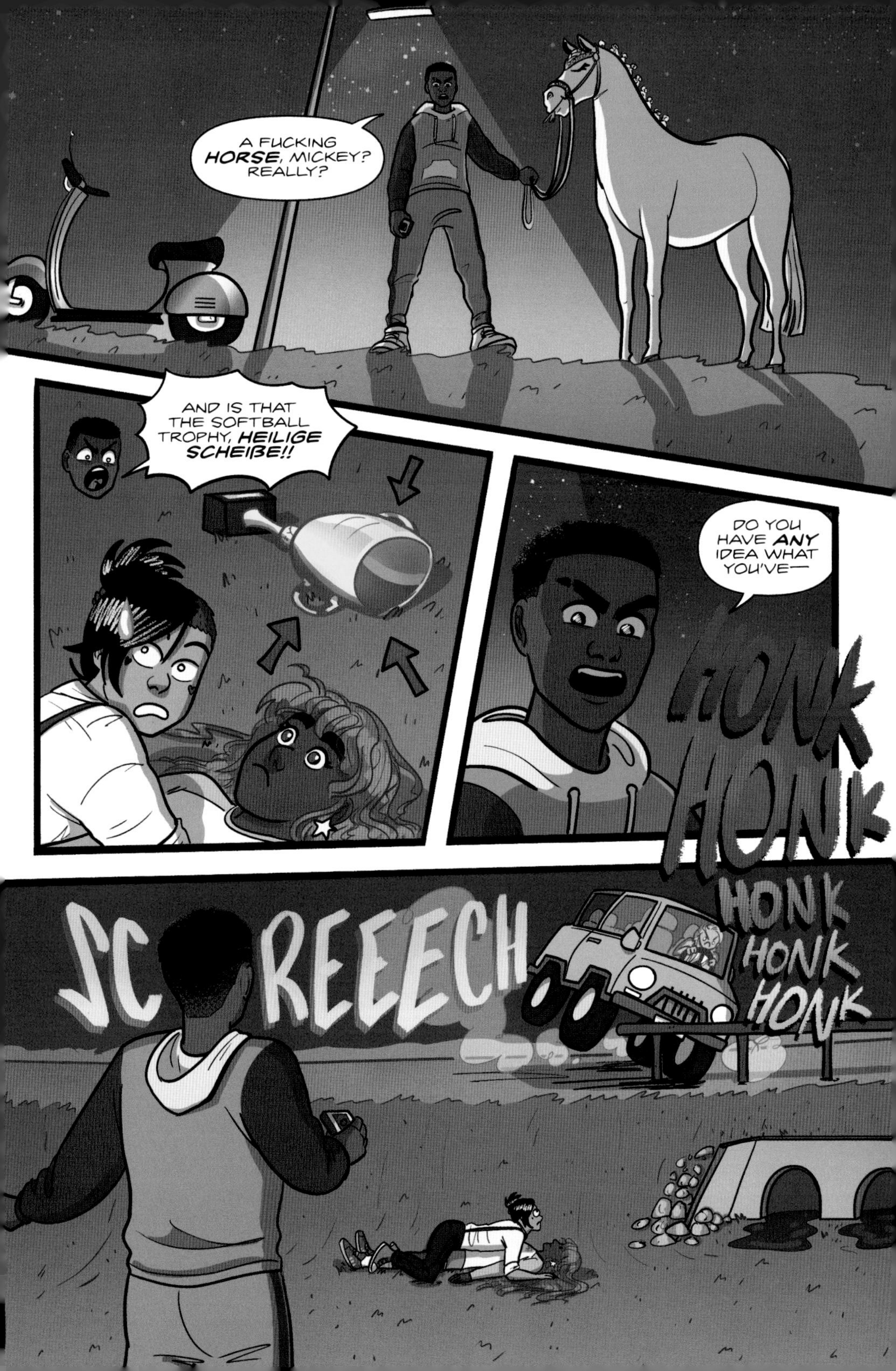
A FUCKING HORSE, MICKEY? REALLY?
AND IS THAT THE SOFTBALL TROPHY, HEILIGE SCHEIßE!!
DO YOU HAVE ANY IDEA WHAT YOU'VE—
HONK HONK
SCREEECH
HONK HONK HONK

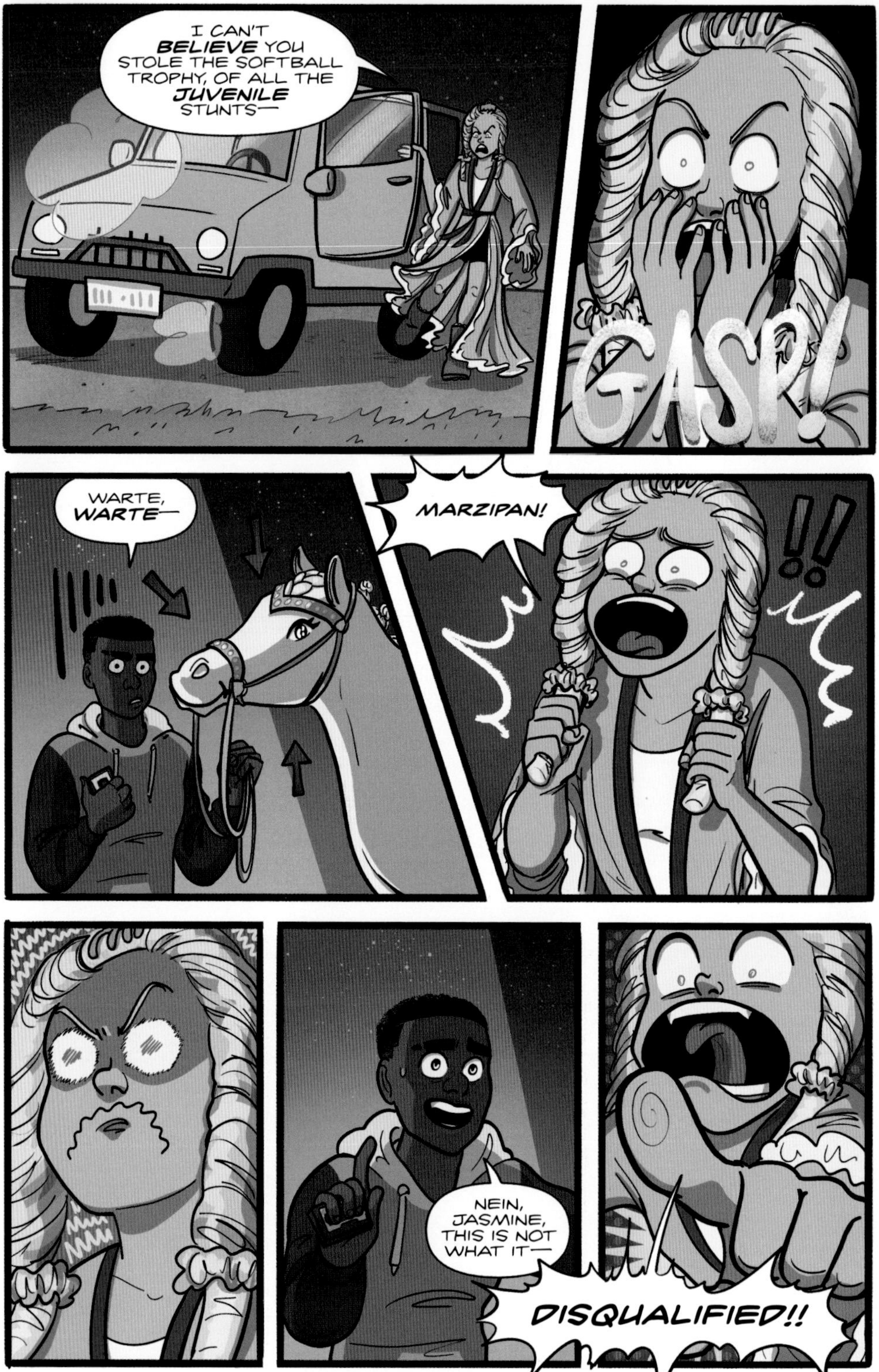

I CAN'T **BELIEVE** YOU STOLE THE SOFTBALL TROPHY, OF ALL THE **JUVENILE** STUNTS—
GASP!
WARTE, **WARTE**—
MARZIPAN!
!!
NEIN, JASMINE, THIS IS NOT WHAT IT—
DISQUALIFIED!!

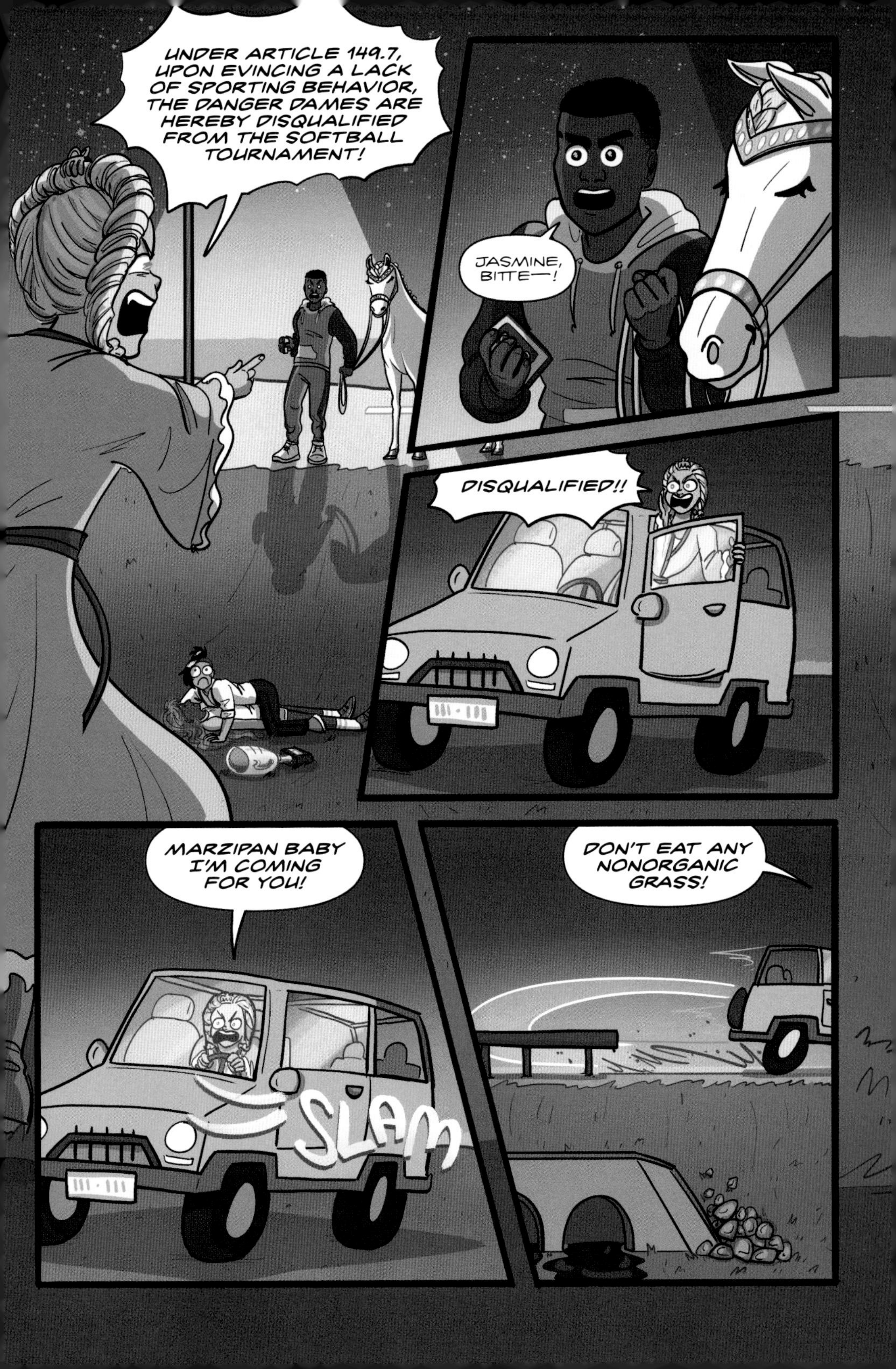
UNDER ARTICLE 149.7, UPON EVINCING A LACK OF SPORTING BEHAVIOR, THE DANGER DAMES ARE HEREBY DISQUALIFIED FROM THE SOFTBALL TOURNAMENT!
JASMINE, BITTE—!
DISQUALIFIED!!
MARZIPAN BABY I'M COMING FOR YOU!
SLAM
DON'T EAT ANY NONORGANIC GRASS!

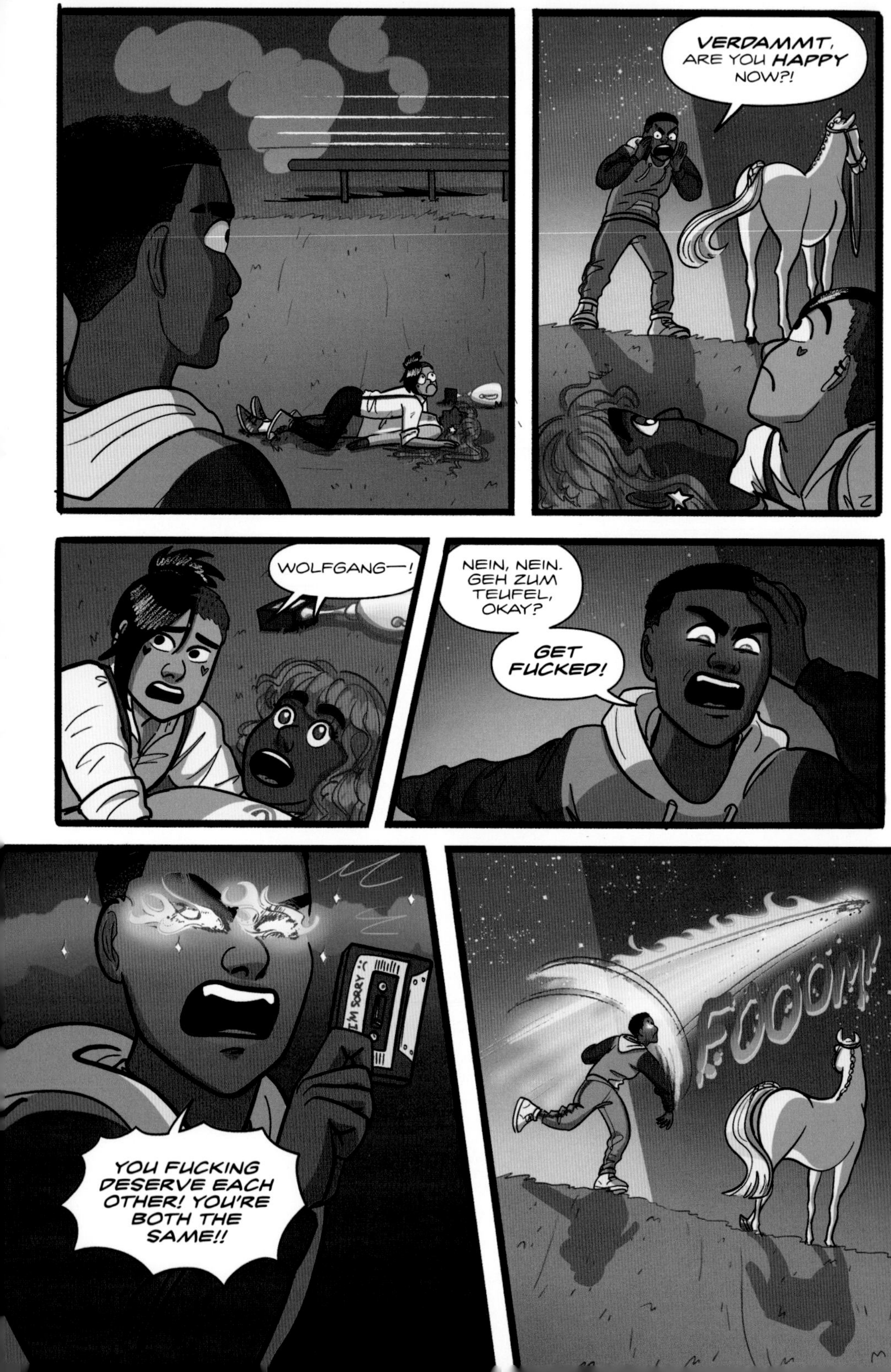
VERDAMMT, ARE YOU HAPPY NOW?!
WOLFGANG—!
NEIN, NEIN. GEH ZUM TEUFEL, OKAY?
GET FUCKED!
I'M SORRY
YOU FUCKING DESERVE EACH OTHER! YOU'RE BOTH THE SAME!!
FOOOM!

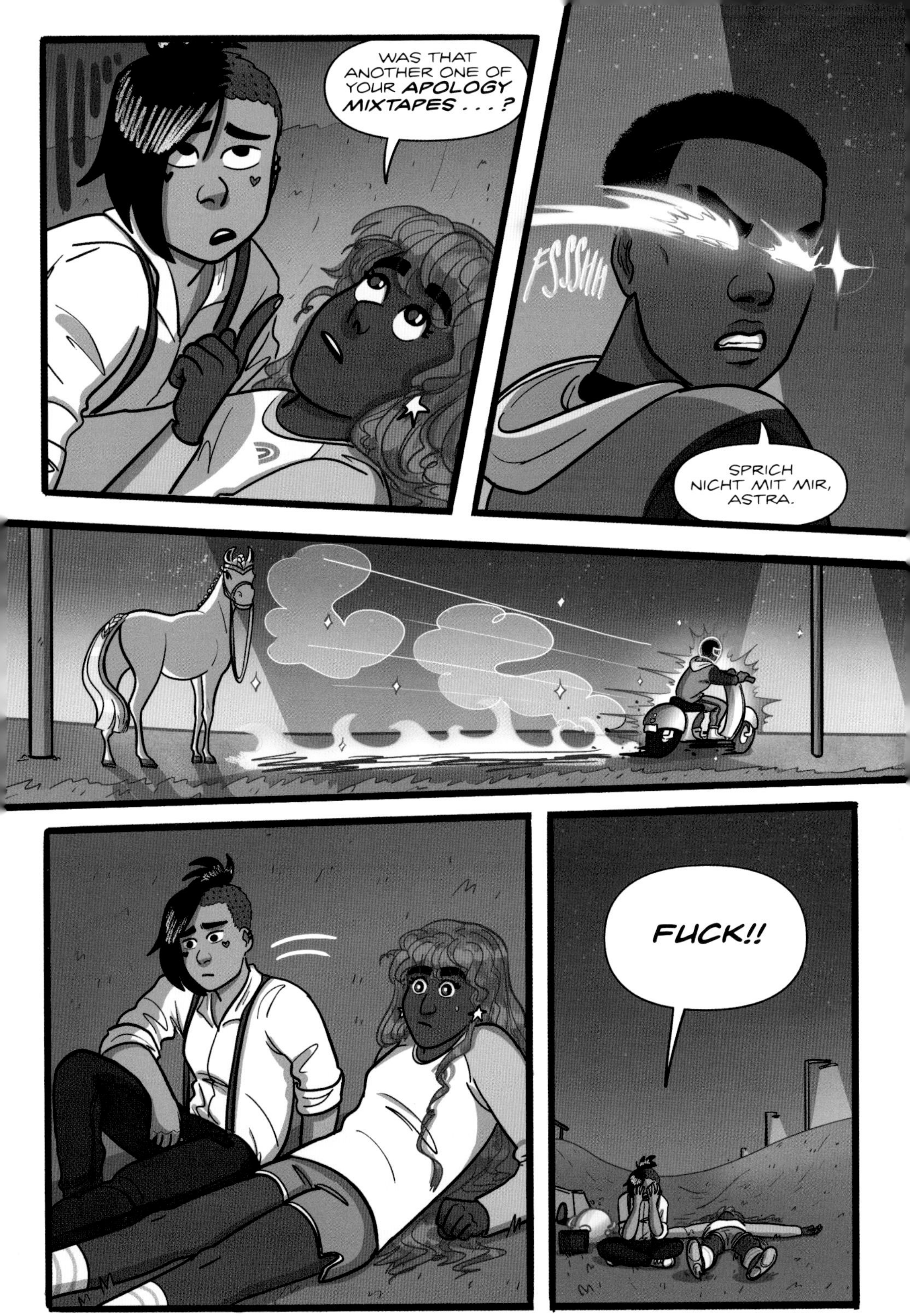
WAS THAT ANOTHER ONE OF YOUR APOLOGY MIXTAPES . . . ?
FSSSHH
SPRICH NICHT MIT MIR, ASTRA.
FUCK!!

THE NEXT DAY

'EY, MICK . . .

WE HEARD WHAT HAPPENED LAST NIGHT. TOUGH BREAK.

THANKS, FLO. I APPRECIATE THAT.

IT'S *SLANDER* IS WHAT IT IS!

JASMINE KNEW SHE WAS GOING TO LOSE AGAINST YOU IN THE SEMIS, SO SHE MADE UP SOME BULLSHIT ABOUT YOU STEALING THE TROPHY.

AND ALSO HER *HORSE*.

RIGHT, WHAT KIND OF *HORRIBLE* PERSON WOULD DO THAT?!

196

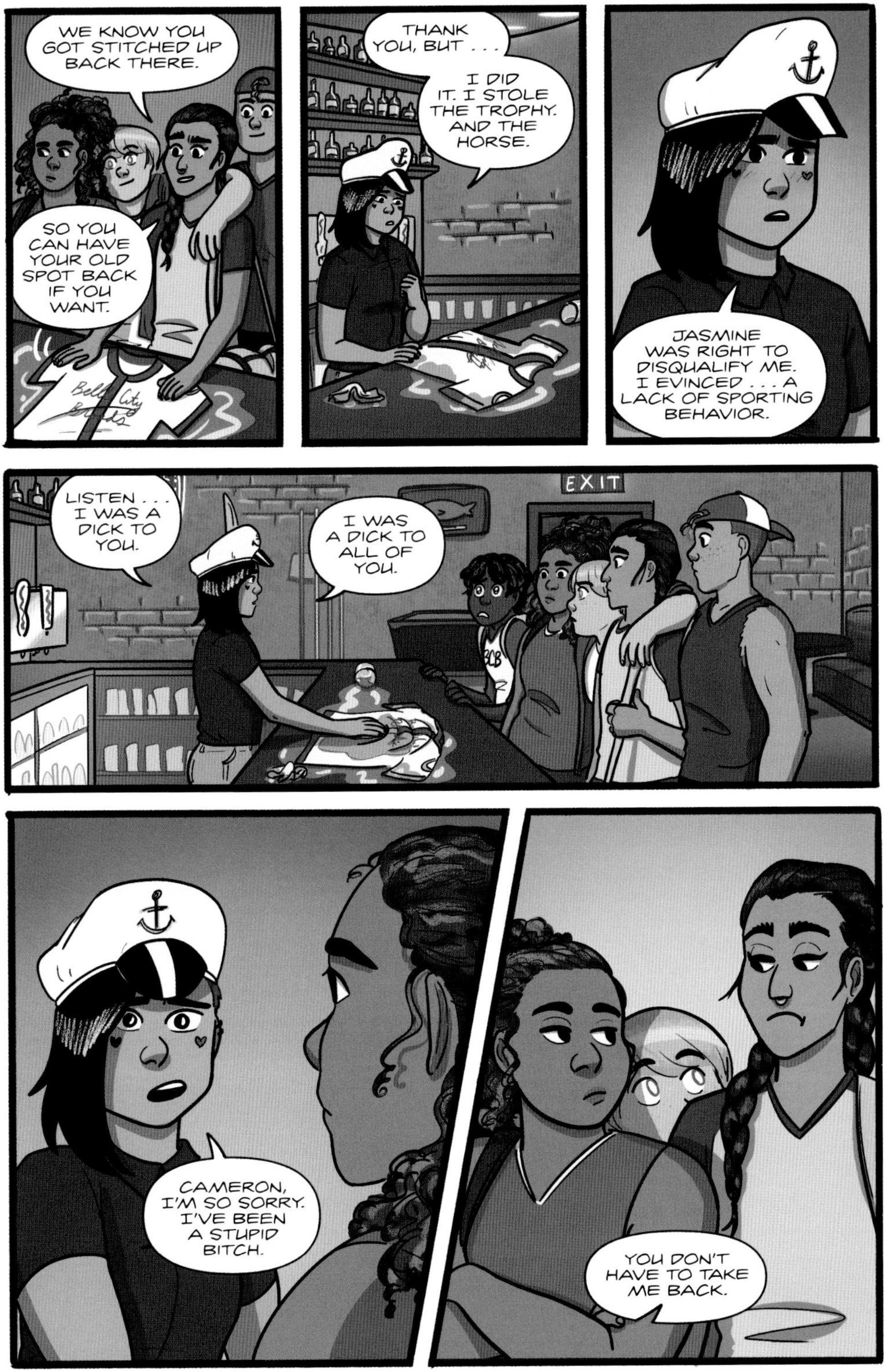
WE KNOW YOU GOT STITCHED UP BACK THERE.
SO YOU CAN HAVE YOUR OLD SPOT BACK IF YOU WANT.
THANK YOU, BUT . . .
I DID IT. I STOLE THE TROPHY. AND THE HORSE.
JASMINE WAS RIGHT TO DISQUALIFY ME. I EVINCED . . . A LACK OF SPORTING BEHAVIOR.
EXIT
LISTEN . . . I WAS A DICK TO YOU.
I WAS A DICK TO ALL OF YOU.
CAMERON, I'M SO SORRY. I'VE BEEN A STUPID BITCH.
YOU DON'T HAVE TO TAKE ME BACK.

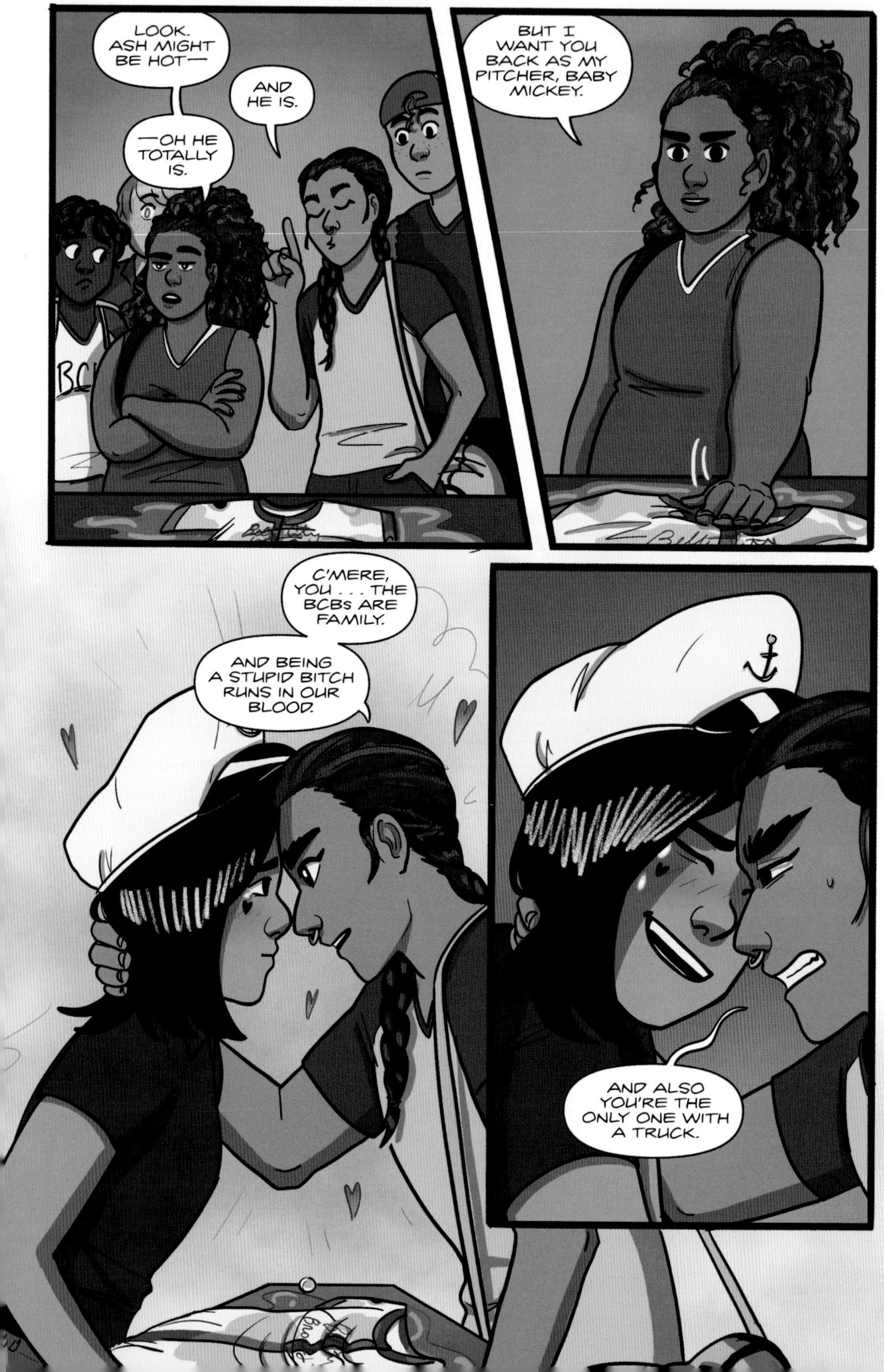
LOOK. ASH MIGHT BE HOT—
AND HE IS.
—OH HE TOTALLY IS.
BUT I WANT YOU BACK AS MY PITCHER, BABY MICKEY.
C'MERE, YOU . . . THE BCBs ARE FAMILY.
AND BEING A STUPID BITCH RUNS IN OUR BLOOD.
AND ALSO YOU'RE THE ONLY ONE WITH A TRUCK.

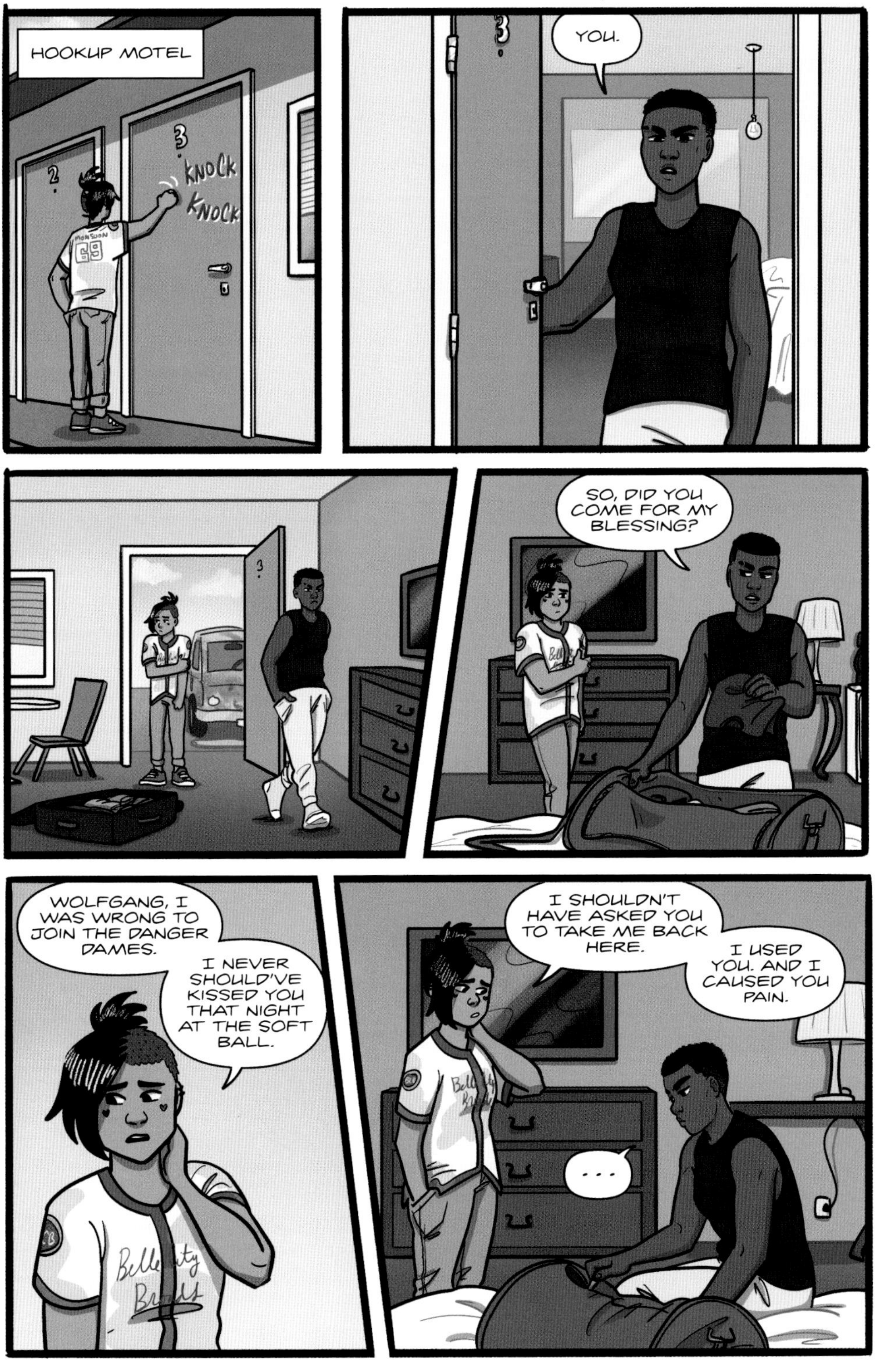
HOOKUP MOTEL
3
KNOCK
KNOCK
YOU.
SO, DID YOU COME FOR MY BLESSING?
WOLFGANG, I WAS WRONG TO JOIN THE DANGER DAMES.
I NEVER SHOULD'VE KISSED YOU THAT NIGHT AT THE SOFT BALL.
I SHOULDN'T HAVE ASKED YOU TO TAKE ME BACK HERE.
I USED YOU. AND I CAUSED YOU PAIN.
...

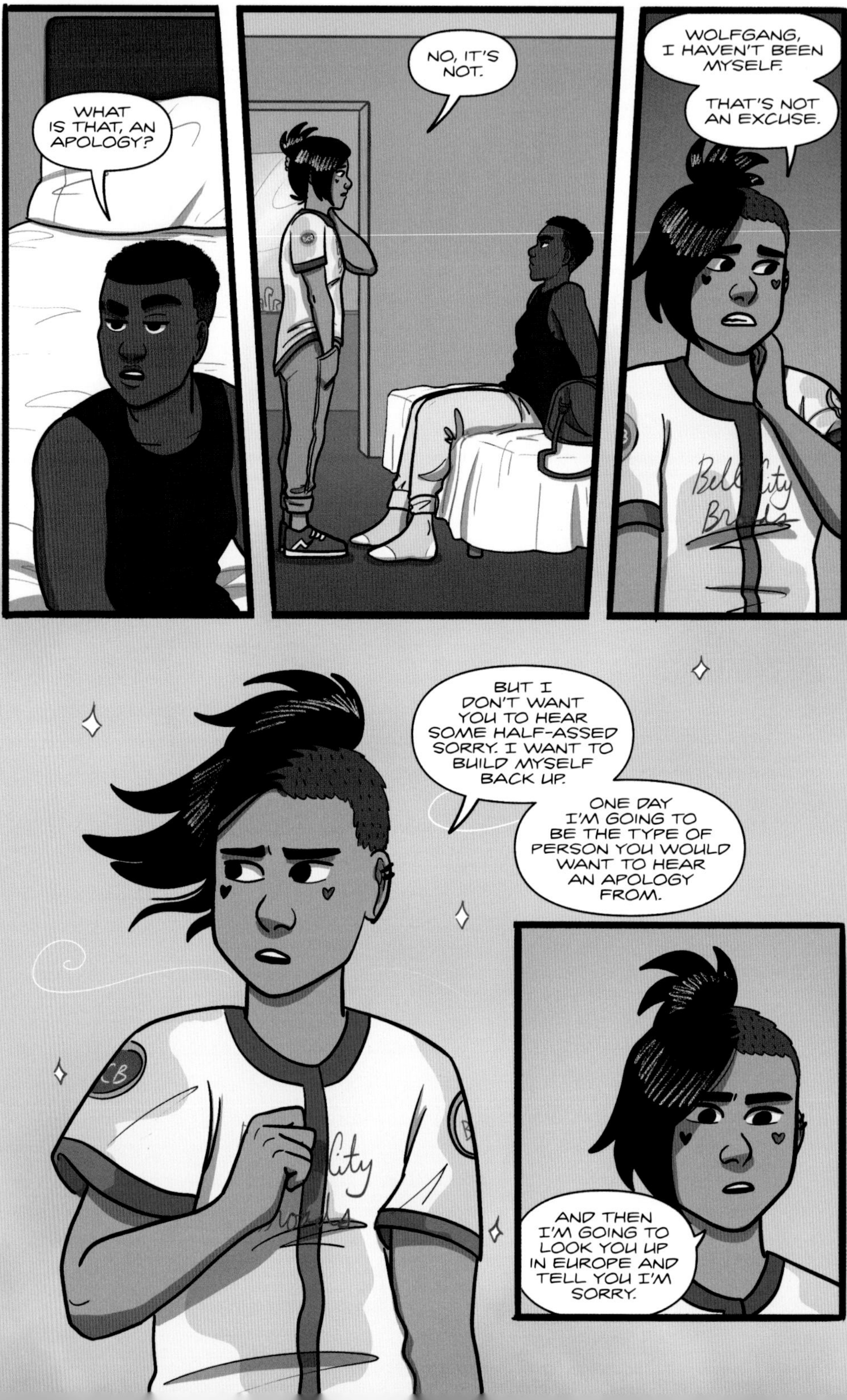

WHAT IS THAT, AN APOLOGY?
NO, IT'S NOT.
WOLFGANG, I HAVEN'T BEEN MYSELF.
THAT'S NOT AN EXCUSE.
Bell City Bruds
BUT I DON'T WANT YOU TO HEAR SOME HALF-ASSED SORRY. I WANT TO BUILD MYSELF BACK UP.
ONE DAY I'M GOING TO BE THE TYPE OF PERSON YOU WOULD WANT TO HEAR AN APOLOGY FROM.
CB
AND THEN I'M GOING TO LOOK YOU UP IN EUROPE AND TELL YOU I'M SORRY.

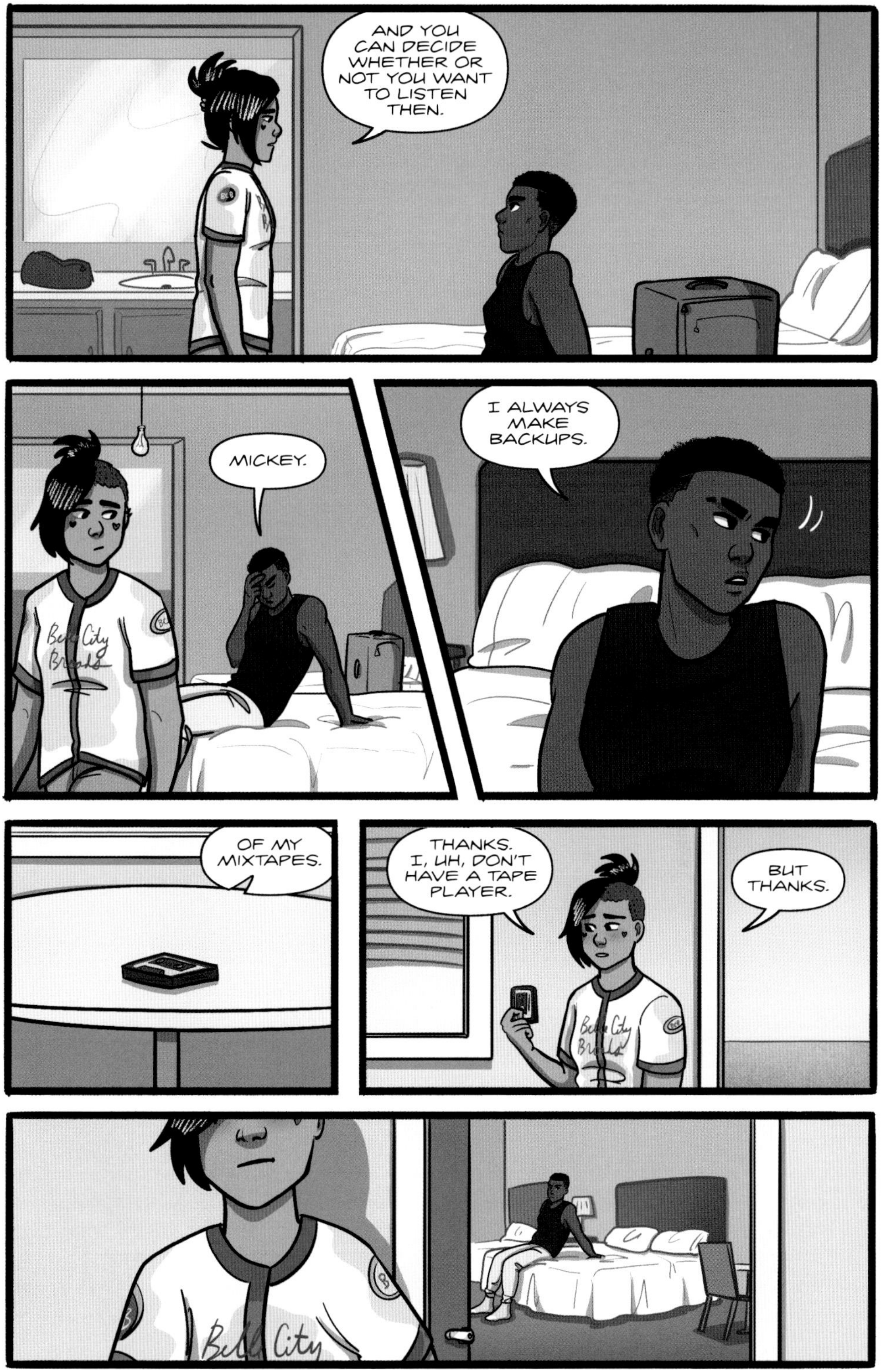
AND YOU CAN DECIDE WHETHER OR NOT YOU WANT TO LISTEN THEN.
MICKEY.
I ALWAYS MAKE BACKUPS.
OF MY MIXTAPES.
THANKS. I, UH, DON'T HAVE A TAPE PLAYER.
BUT THANKS.

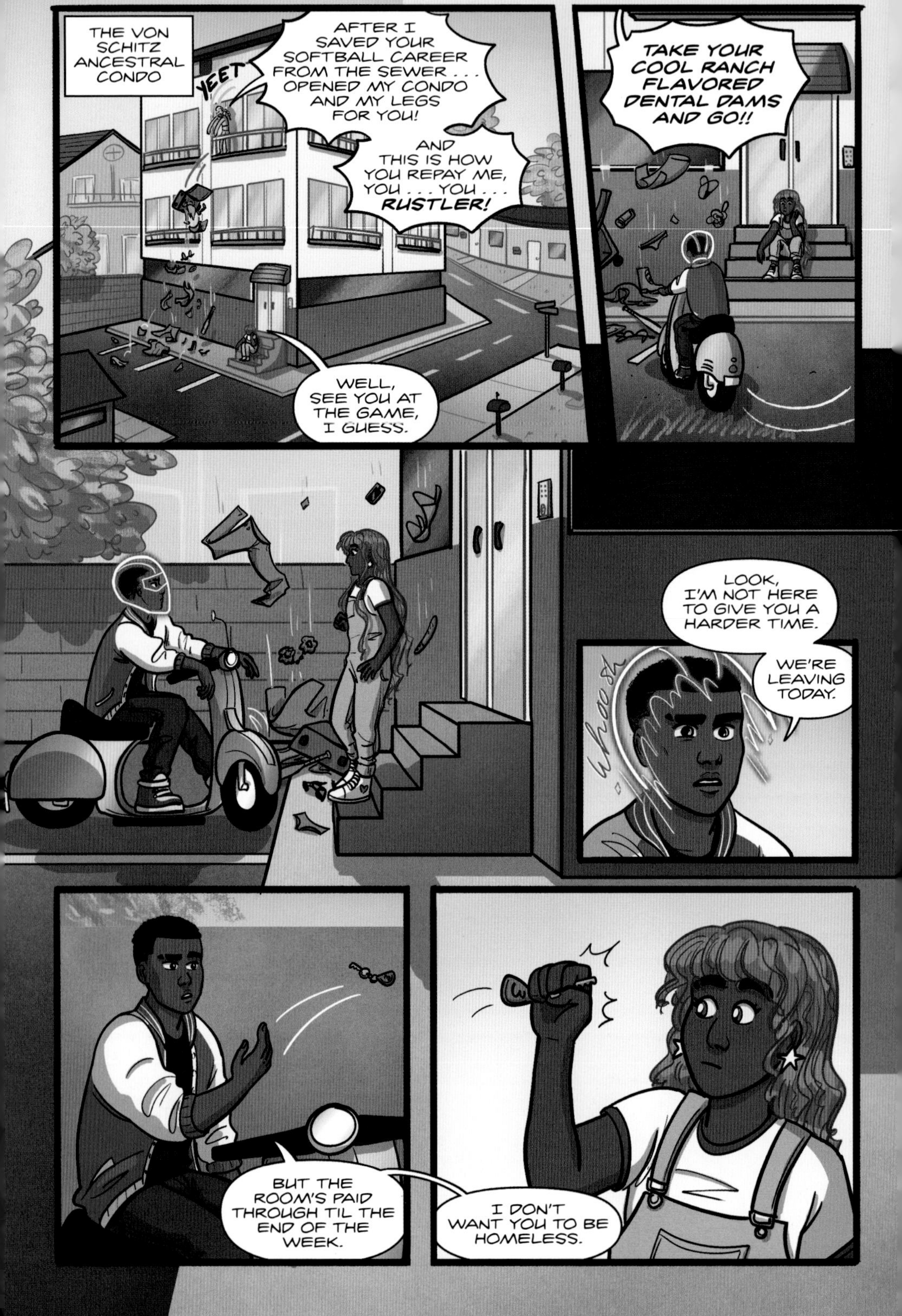
THE VON SCHITZ ANCESTRAL CONDO
YEET
AFTER I SAVED YOUR SOFTBALL CAREER FROM THE SEWER . . . OPENED MY CONDO AND MY LEGS FOR YOU!
AND THIS IS HOW YOU REPAY ME, YOU . . . YOU . . . RUSTLER!
WELL, SEE YOU AT THE GAME, I GUESS.
TAKE YOUR COOL RANCH FLAVORED DENTAL DAMS AND GO!!
LOOK, I'M NOT HERE TO GIVE YOU A HARDER TIME.
WE'RE LEAVING TODAY.
whoosh
BUT THE ROOM'S PAID THROUGH TIL THE END OF THE WEEK.
I DON'T WANT YOU TO BE HOMELESS.

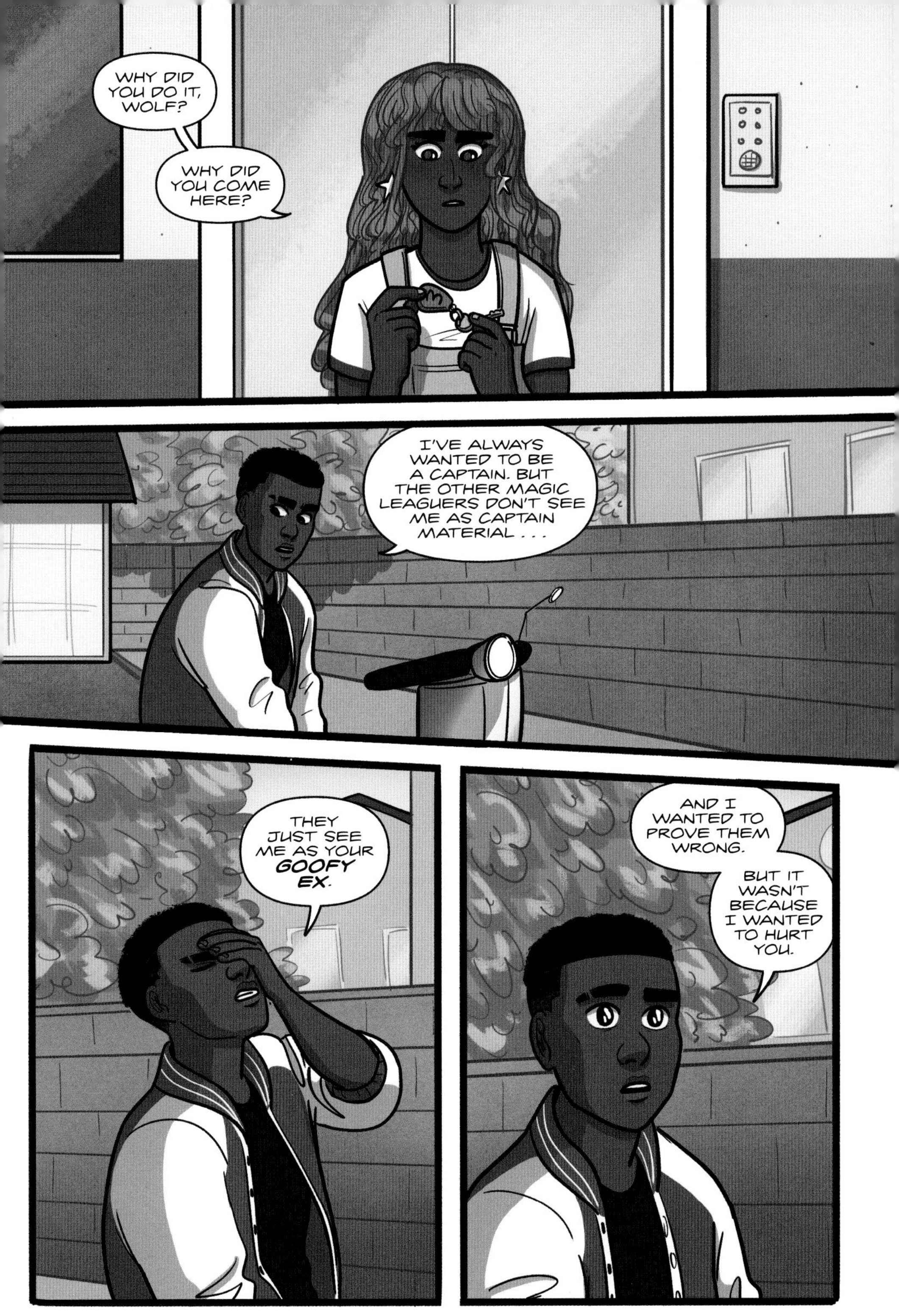
WHY DID YOU DO IT, WOLF?
WHY DID YOU COME HERE?
I'VE ALWAYS WANTED TO BE A CAPTAIN. BUT THE OTHER MAGIC LEAGUERS DON'T SEE ME AS CAPTAIN MATERIAL . . .
THEY JUST SEE ME AS YOUR **GOOFY EX**.
AND I WANTED TO PROVE THEM WRONG.
BUT IT WASN'T BECAUSE I WANTED TO HURT YOU.

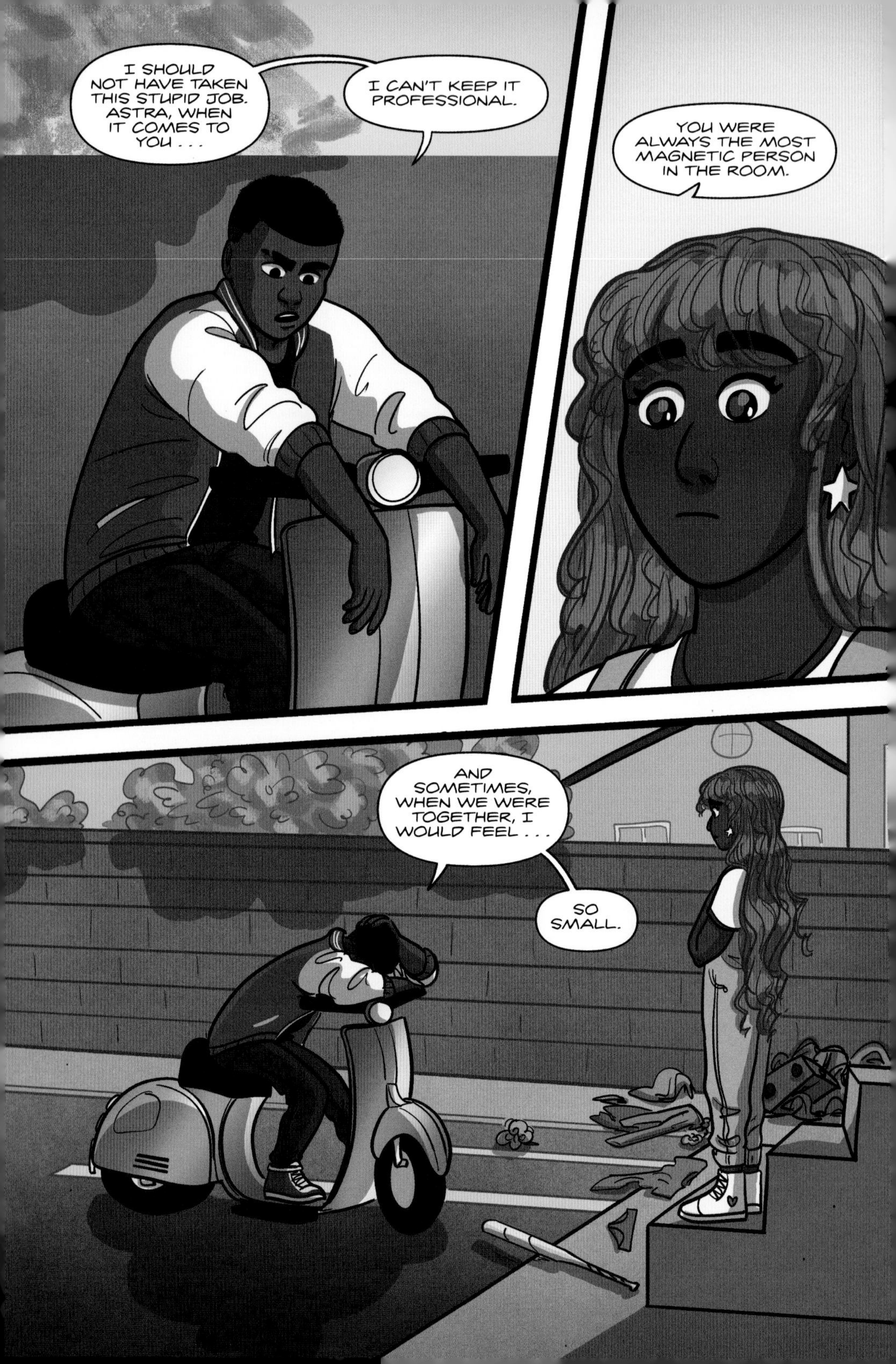
I SHOULD NOT HAVE TAKEN THIS STUPID JOB. ASTRA, WHEN IT COMES TO YOU . . .
I CAN'T KEEP IT PROFESSIONAL.
YOU WERE ALWAYS THE MOST MAGNETIC PERSON IN THE ROOM.
AND SOMETIMES, WHEN WE WERE TOGETHER, I WOULD FEEL . . .
SO SMALL.

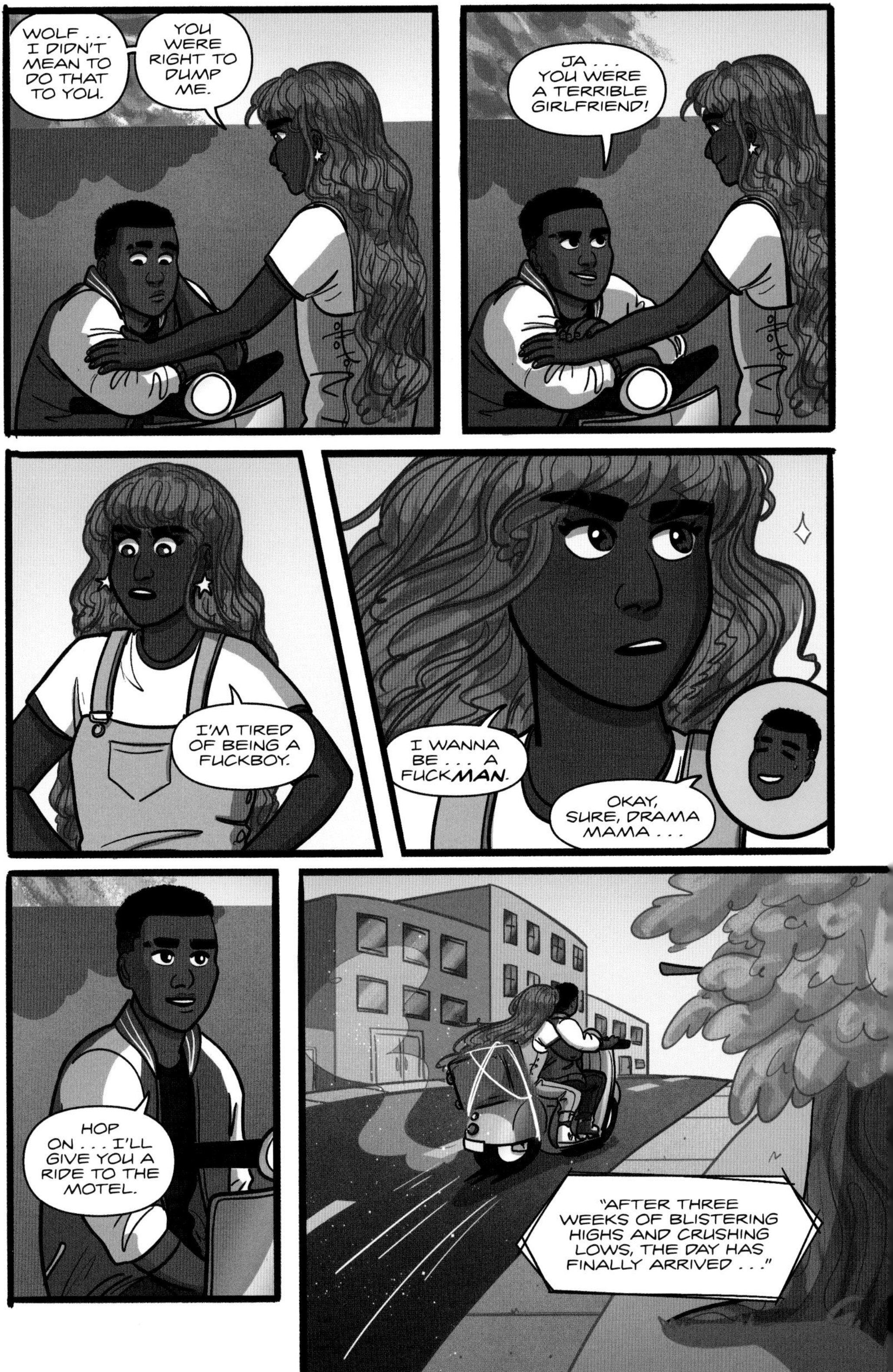
WOLF . . . I DIDN'T MEAN TO DO THAT TO YOU.
YOU WERE RIGHT TO DUMP ME.
JA . . . YOU WERE A TERRIBLE GIRLFRIEND!
I'M TIRED OF BEING A FUCKBOY.
I WANNA BE . . . A FUCK*MAN*.
OKAY, SURE, DRAMA MAMA . . .
HOP ON . . . I'LL GIVE YOU A RIDE TO THE MOTEL.
"AFTER THREE WEEKS OF BLISTERING HIGHS AND CRUSHING LOWS, THE DAY HAS FINALLY ARRIVED . . ."

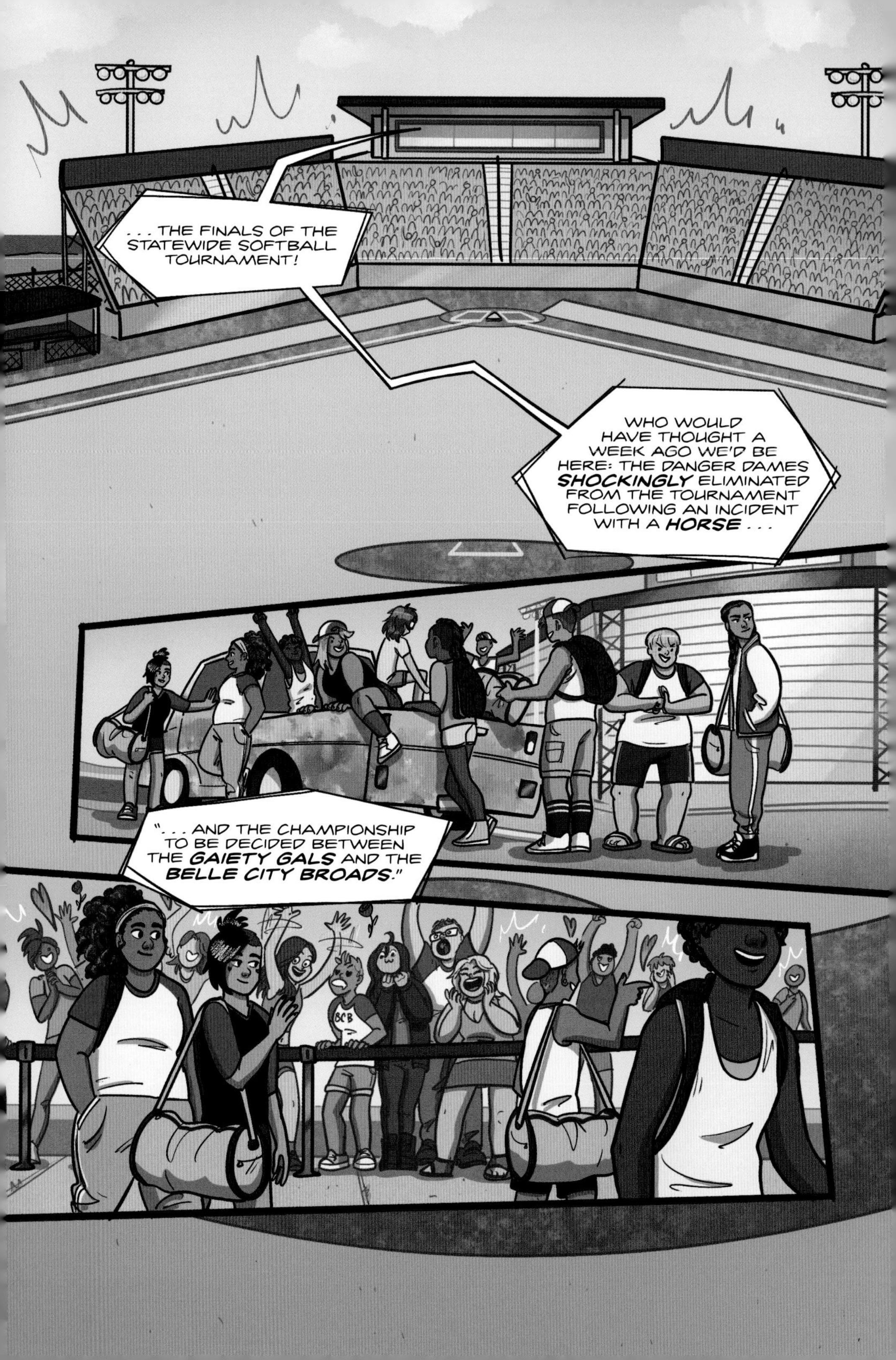
. . . THE FINALS OF THE STATEWIDE SOFTBALL TOURNAMENT!
WHO WOULD HAVE THOUGHT A WEEK AGO WE'D BE HERE: THE DANGER DAMES **SHOCKINGLY** ELIMINATED FROM THE TOURNAMENT FOLLOWING AN INCIDENT WITH A **HORSE** . . .
". . . AND THE CHAMPIONSHIP TO BE DECIDED BETWEEN THE **GAIETY GALS** AND THE **BELLE CITY BROADS**."
BCB

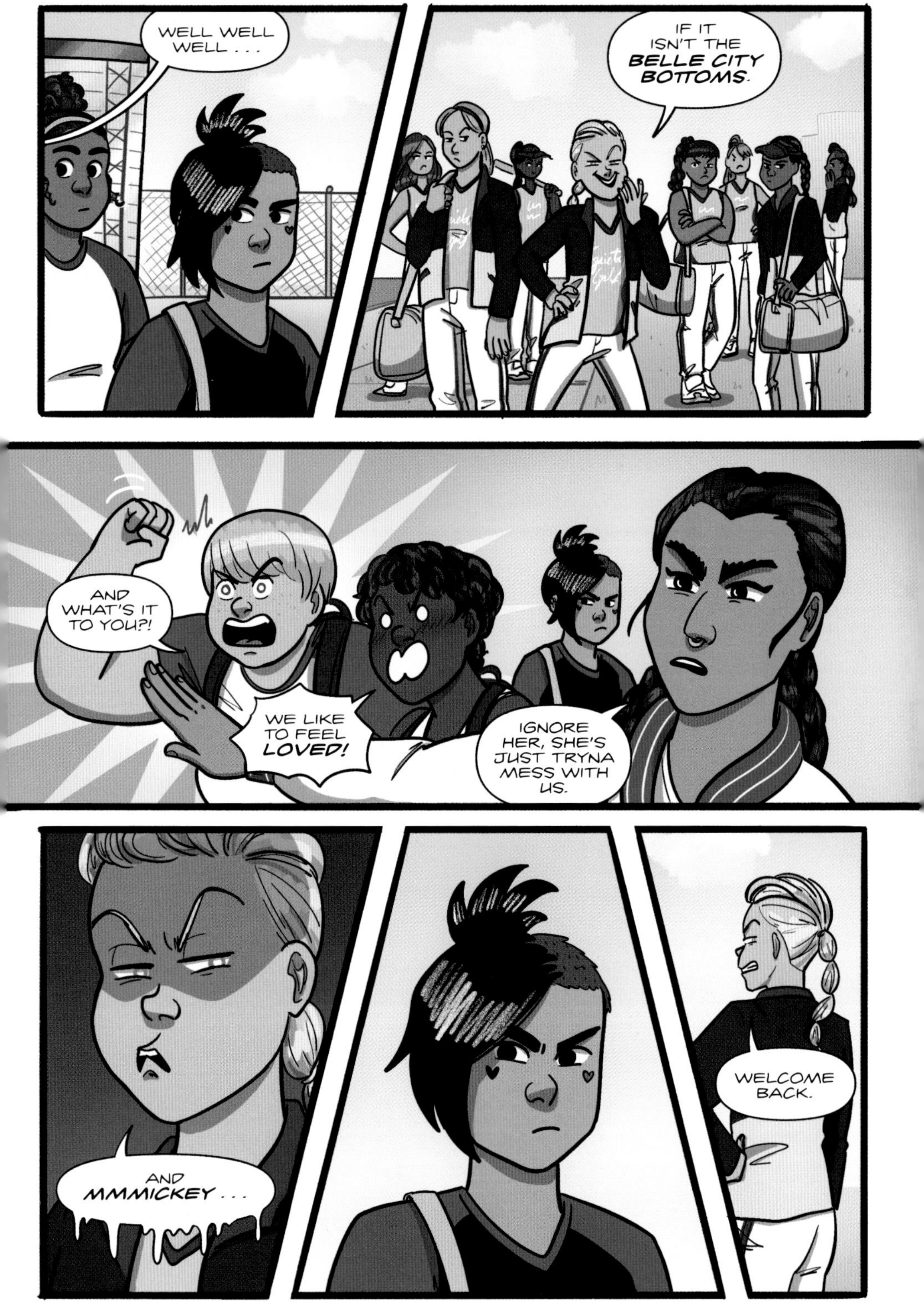
WELL WELL WELL . . .
IF IT ISN'T THE BELLE CITY BOTTOMS.
AND WHAT'S IT TO YOU?!
WE LIKE TO FEEL LOVED!
IGNORE HER, SHE'S JUST TRYNA MESS WITH US.
AND MMMICKEY . . .
WELCOME BACK.

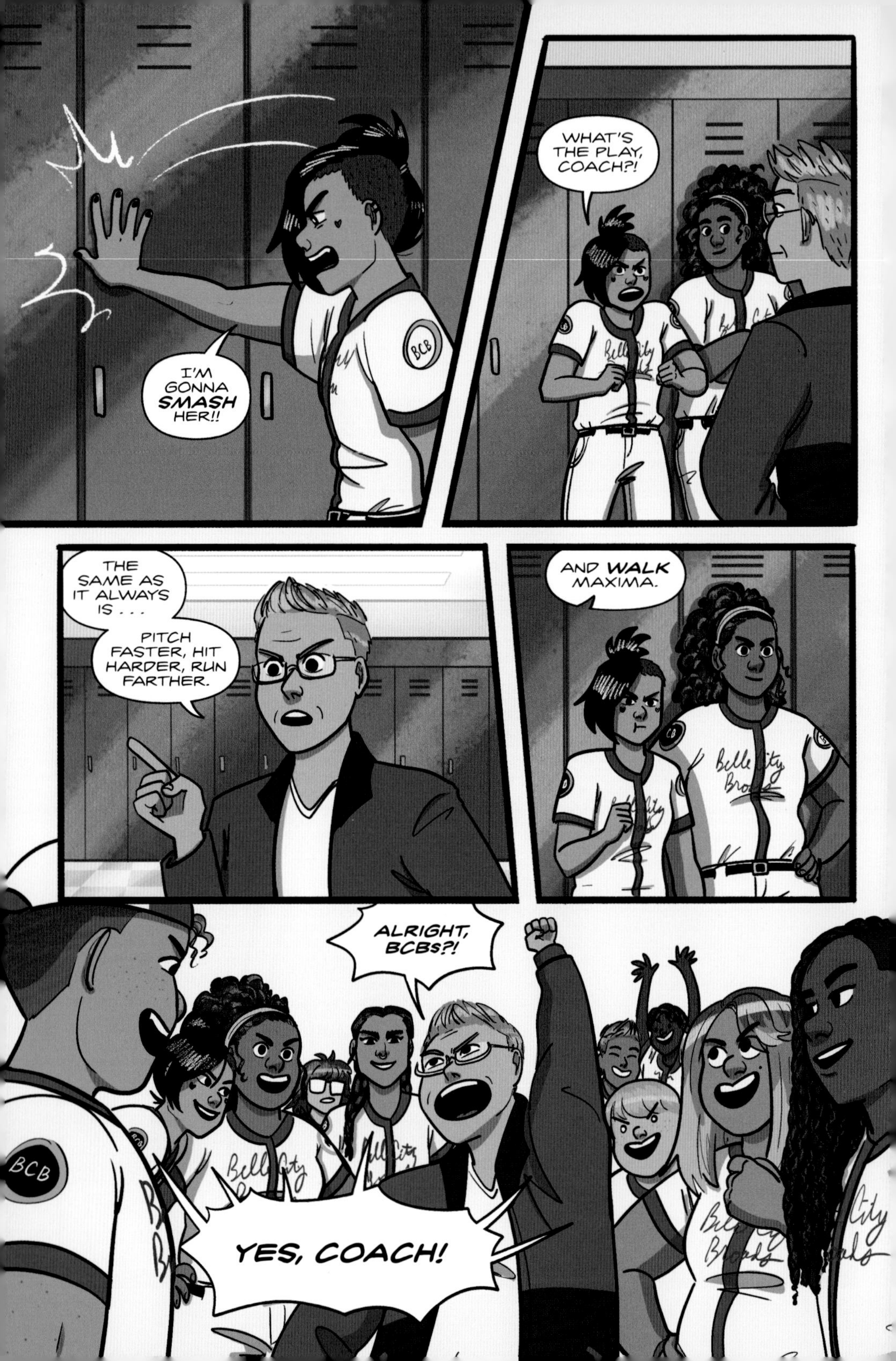
I'M GONNA **SMASH** HER!!
WHAT'S THE PLAY, COACH?!
THE SAME AS IT ALWAYS IS . . .
PITCH FASTER, HIT HARDER, RUN FARTHER.
AND **WALK** MAXIMA.
ALRIGHT, BCBs?!
YES, COACH!

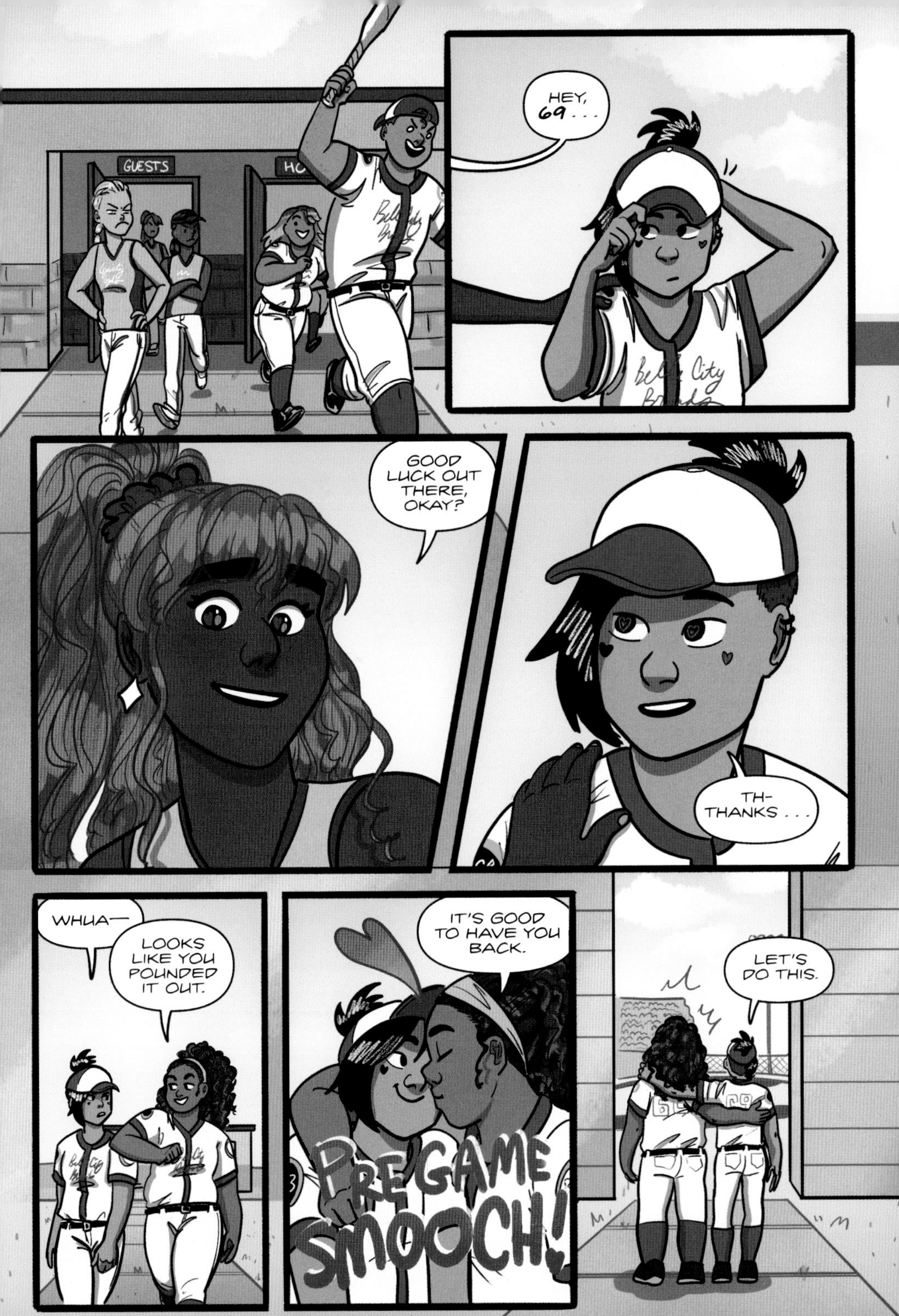
GUESTS
HEY, 69 . . .
GOOD LUCK OUT THERE, OKAY?
TH- THANKS . . .
WHUA—
LOOKS LIKE YOU POUNDED IT OUT.
IT'S GOOD TO HAVE YOU BACK.
PRE GAME SMOOCH!
LET'S DO THIS.

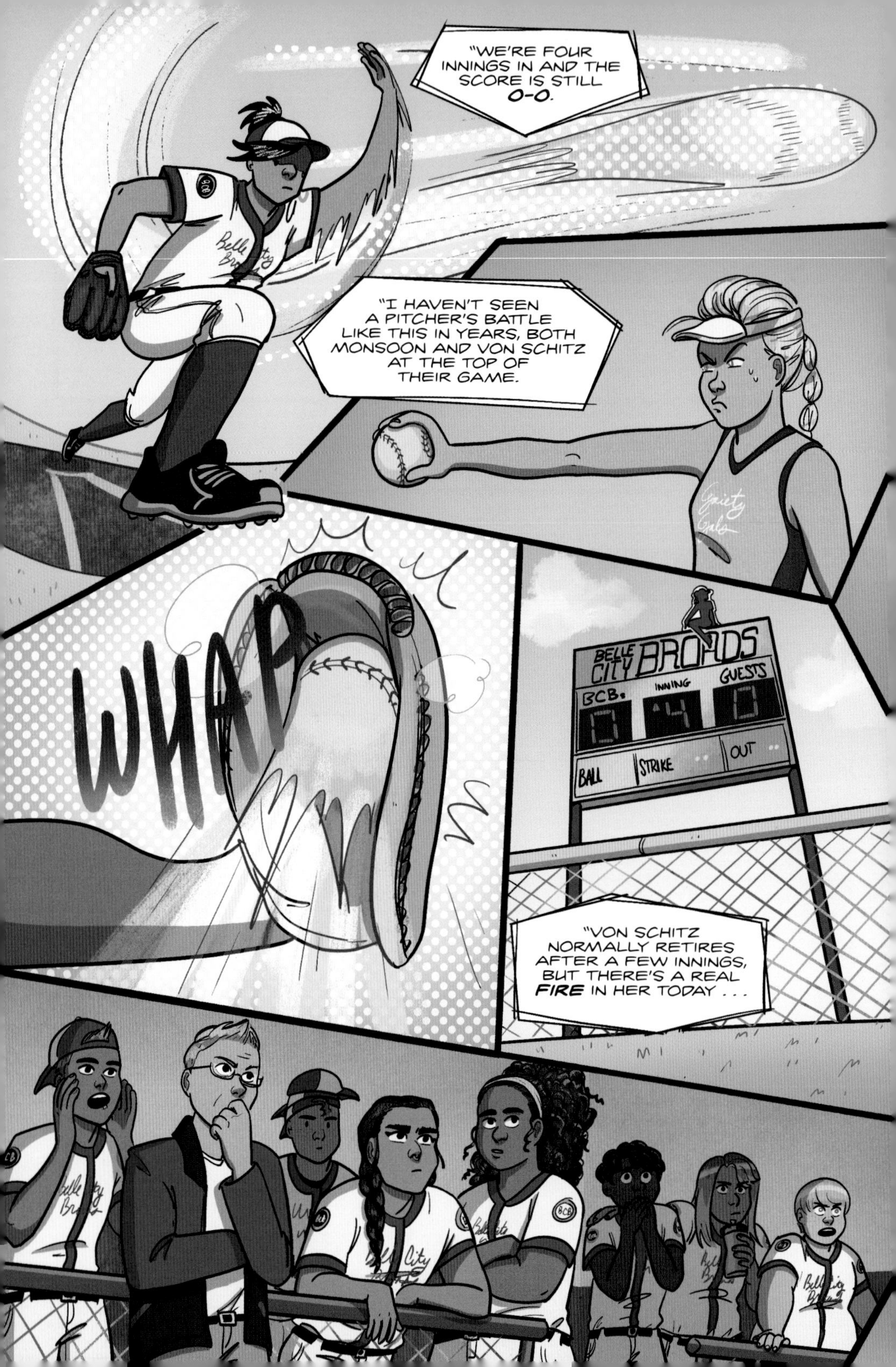
"WE'RE FOUR INNINGS IN AND THE SCORE IS STILL **0-0**.
"I HAVEN'T SEEN A PITCHER'S BATTLE LIKE THIS IN YEARS, BOTH MONSOON AND VON SCHITZ AT THE TOP OF THEIR GAME.
WHAP
BELLE CITY BROADS
BCB.
INNING
GUESTS
BALL
STRIKE
OUT
"VON SCHITZ NORMALLY RETIRES AFTER A FEW INNINGS, BUT THERE'S A REAL ***FIRE*** IN HER TODAY . . .

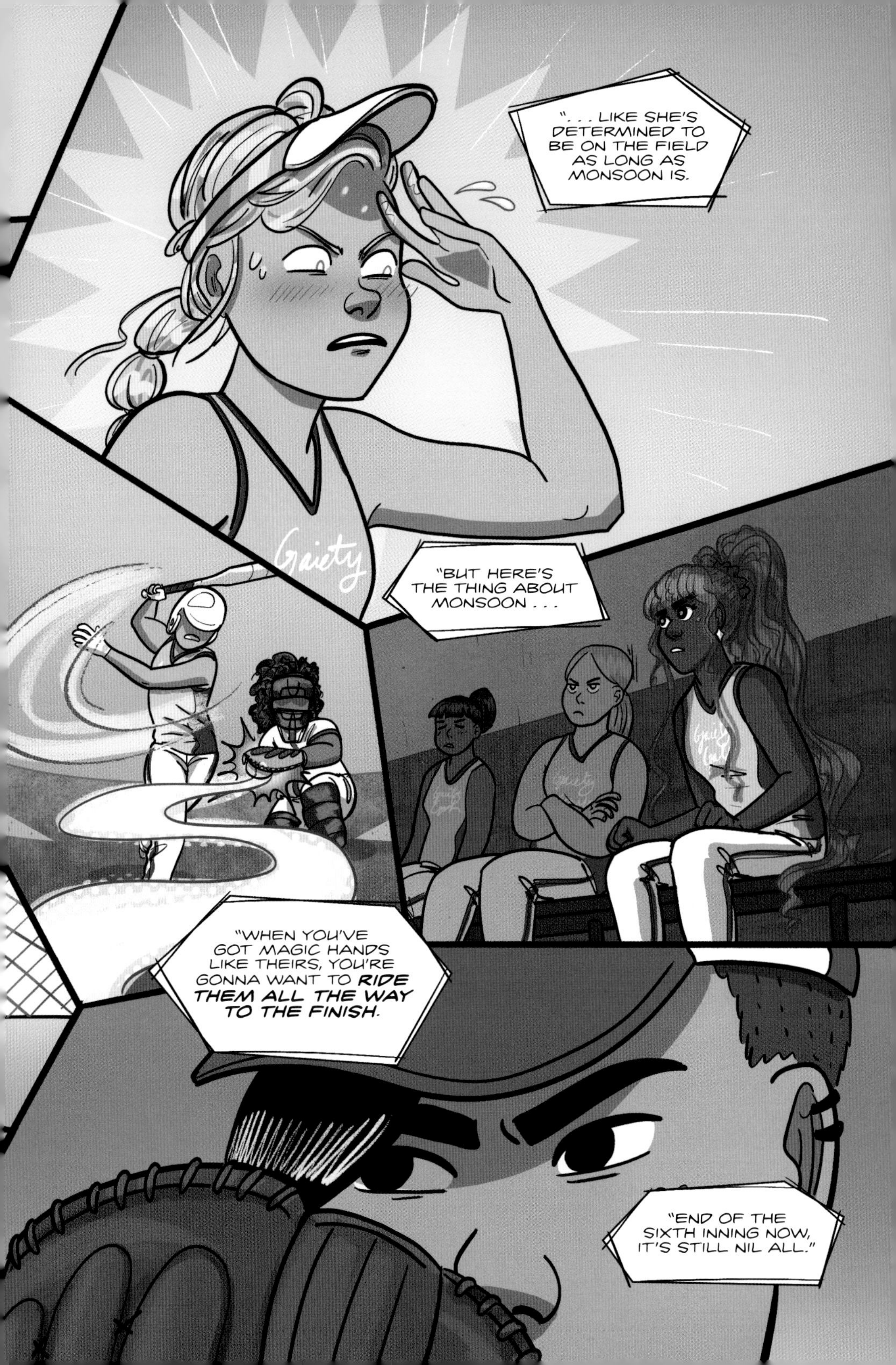
". . . LIKE SHE'S DETERMINED TO BE ON THE FIELD AS LONG AS MONSOON IS.
"BUT HERE'S THE THING ABOUT MONSOON . . .
Gaiety
"WHEN YOU'VE GOT MAGIC HANDS LIKE THEIRS, YOU'RE GONNA WANT TO ***RIDE THEM ALL THE WAY TO THE FINISH***.
"END OF THE SIXTH INNING NOW, IT'S STILL NIL ALL."

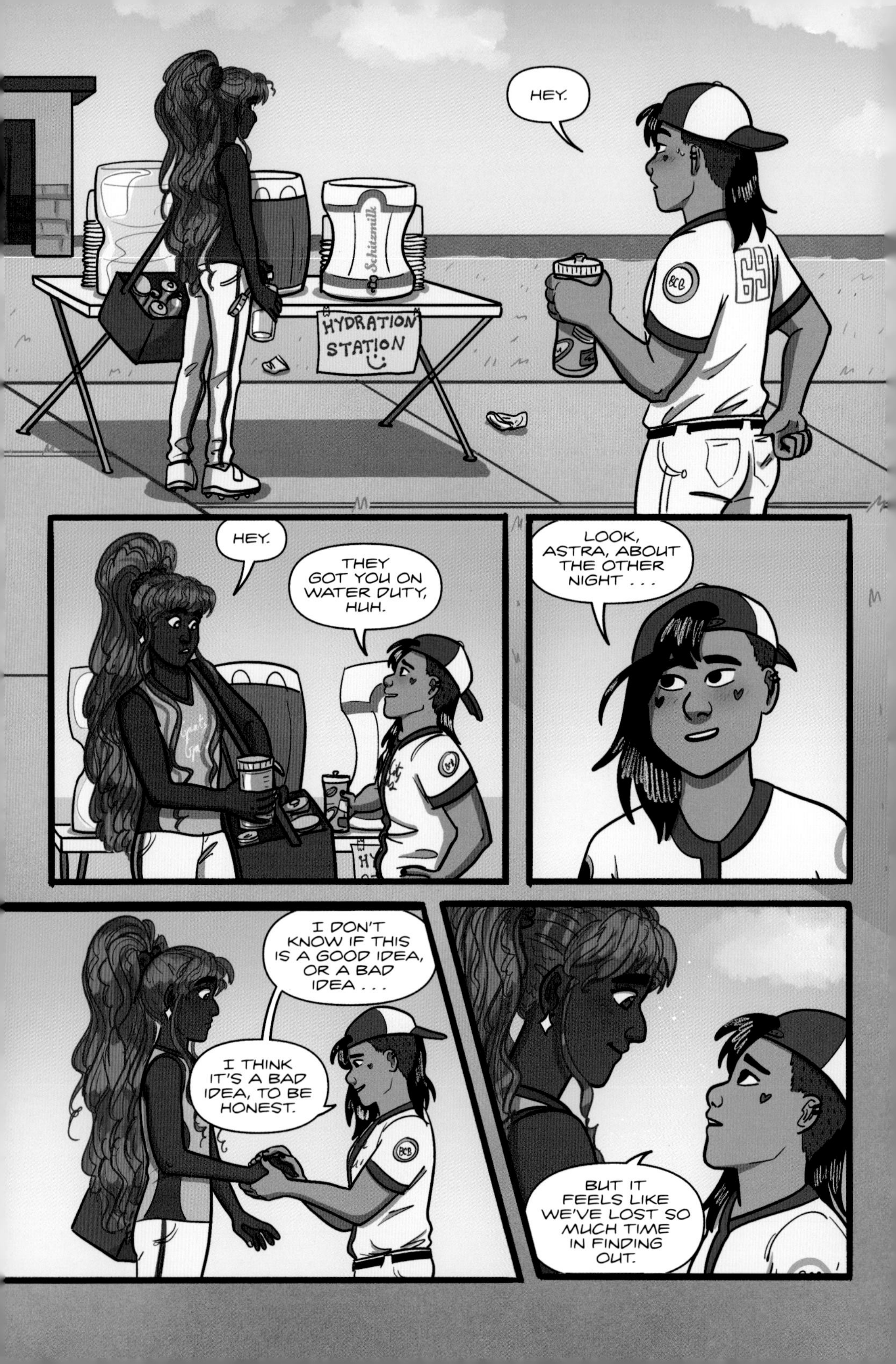
HEY.
HYDRATION STATION
Schitzmilk
69
BCB
HEY.
THEY GOT YOU ON WATER DUTY, HUH.
LOOK, ASTRA, ABOUT THE OTHER NIGHT . . .
I DON'T KNOW IF THIS IS A GOOD IDEA, OR A BAD IDEA . . .
I THINK IT'S A BAD IDEA, TO BE HONEST.
BCB
BUT IT FEELS LIKE WE'VE LOST SO MUCH TIME IN FINDING OUT.

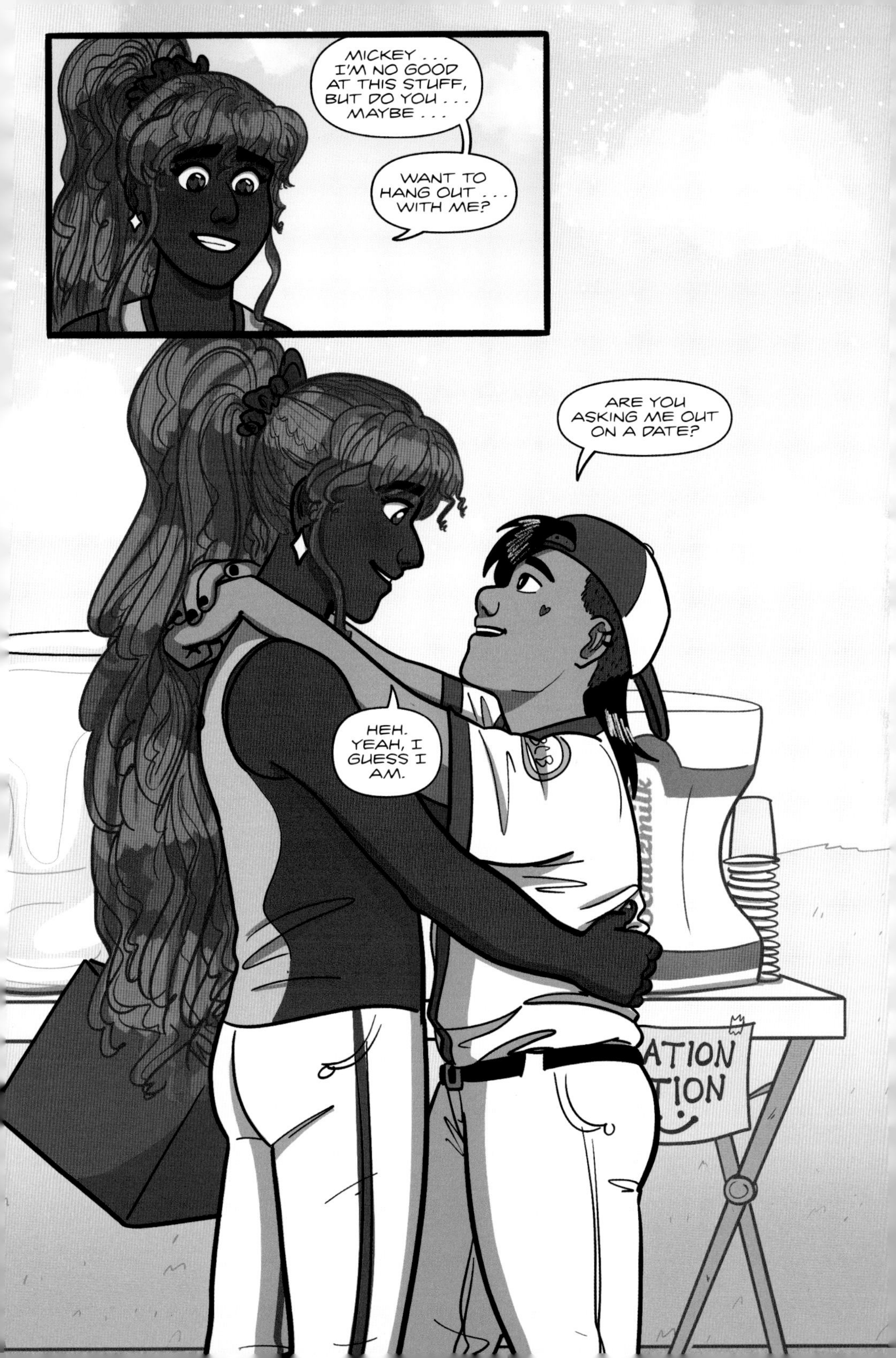
MICKEY . . . I'M NO GOOD AT THIS STUFF, BUT DO YOU . . . MAYBE . . .
WANT TO HANG OUT . . . WITH ME?
ARE YOU ASKING ME OUT ON A DATE?
HEH. YEAH, I GUESS I AM.
ATION
TION

JUST WHEN I THINK YOU CLOWNS CAN'T GET ANY STUPIDER IN YOUR CHOICE OF **RENDEZVOUS-ZES**.

SO HERE'S HOW THIS IS GOING TO GO. ASTRA, YOU'RE UP TO BAT.

I'M GOING TO GIVE YOU ONE MORE CHANCE TO SCORE A FUCKING RUN AND EARN THAT TRANSFER FEE.

AND **MICKEY** . . .

I HAVE ENOUGH EVIDENCE OF YOU BREAKING ARTICLE BLUE BALLS TO GET YOU THROWN OUT OF SEMI-PROFESSIONAL REGIONAL SOFTBALL FOR AN **EXTREMELY** LONG TIME.

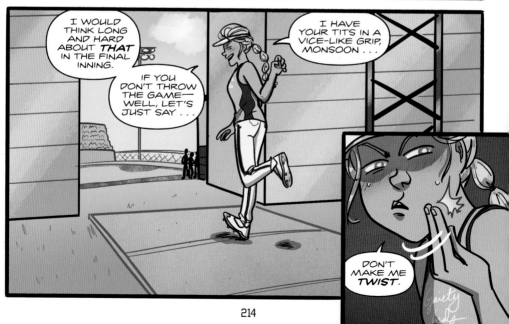

I WOULD THINK LONG AND HARD ABOUT **THAT** IN THE FINAL INNING.

IF YOU DON'T THROW THE GAME— WELL, LET'S JUST SAY . . .

I HAVE YOUR TITS IN A VICE-LIKE GRIP, MONSOON . . .

DON'T MAKE ME **TWIST**.

214

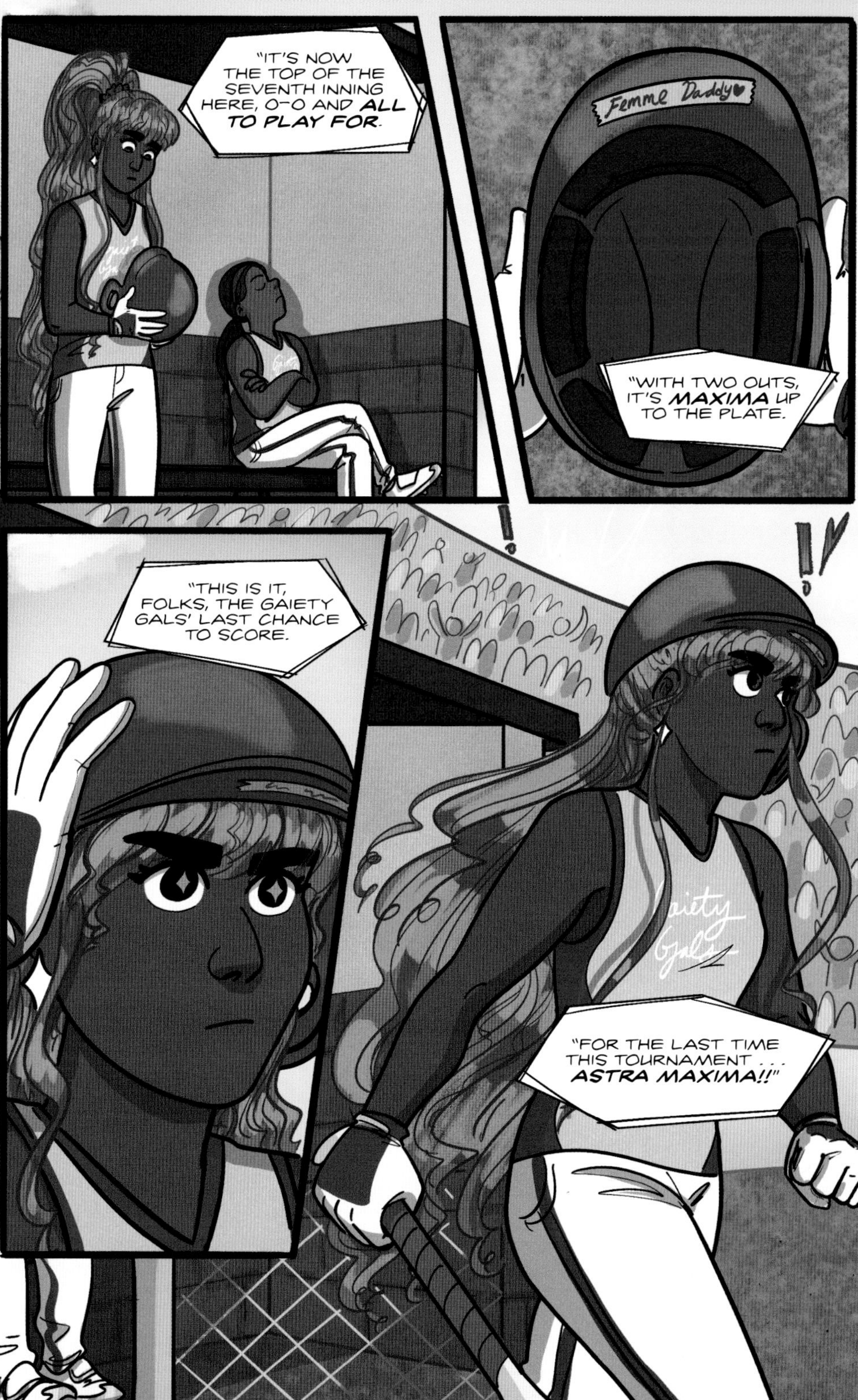
"IT'S NOW THE TOP OF THE SEVENTH INNING HERE, 0-0 AND **ALL TO PLAY FOR.**
Femme Daddy♥
"WITH TWO OUTS, IT'S **MAXIMA** UP TO THE PLATE.
"THIS IS IT, FOLKS, THE GAIETY GALS' LAST CHANCE TO SCORE.
Gaiety Gals
"FOR THE LAST TIME THIS TOURNAMENT . . . **ASTRA MAXIMA!!"**

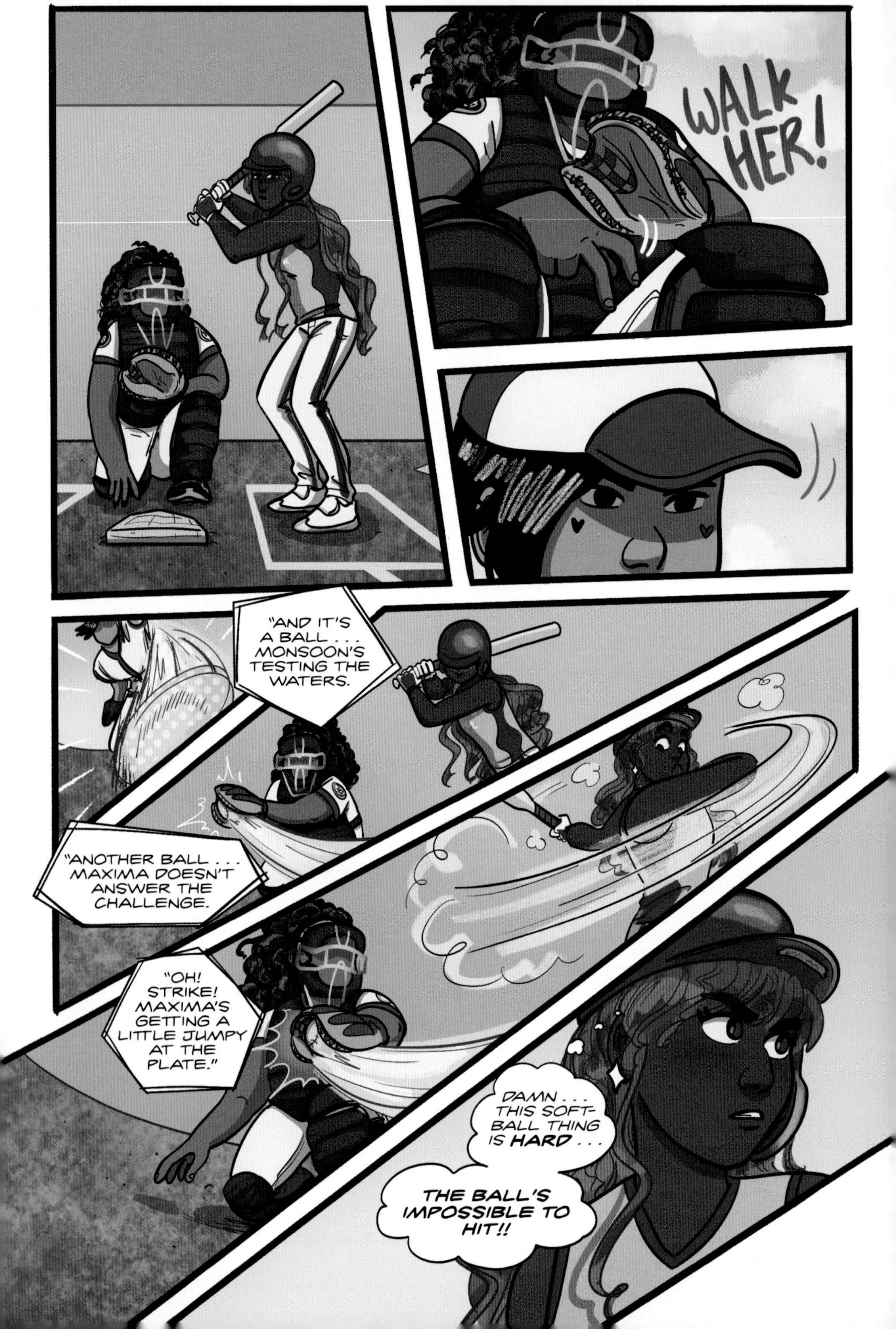
WALK HER!
"AND IT'S A BALL . . . MONSOON'S TESTING THE WATERS.
"ANOTHER BALL . . . MAXIMA DOESN'T ANSWER THE CHALLENGE.
"OH! STRIKE! MAXIMA'S GETTING A LITTLE JUMPY AT THE PLATE."
DAMN . . . THIS SOFT-BALL THING IS **HARD** . . .
THE BALL'S IMPOSSIBLE TO HIT!!

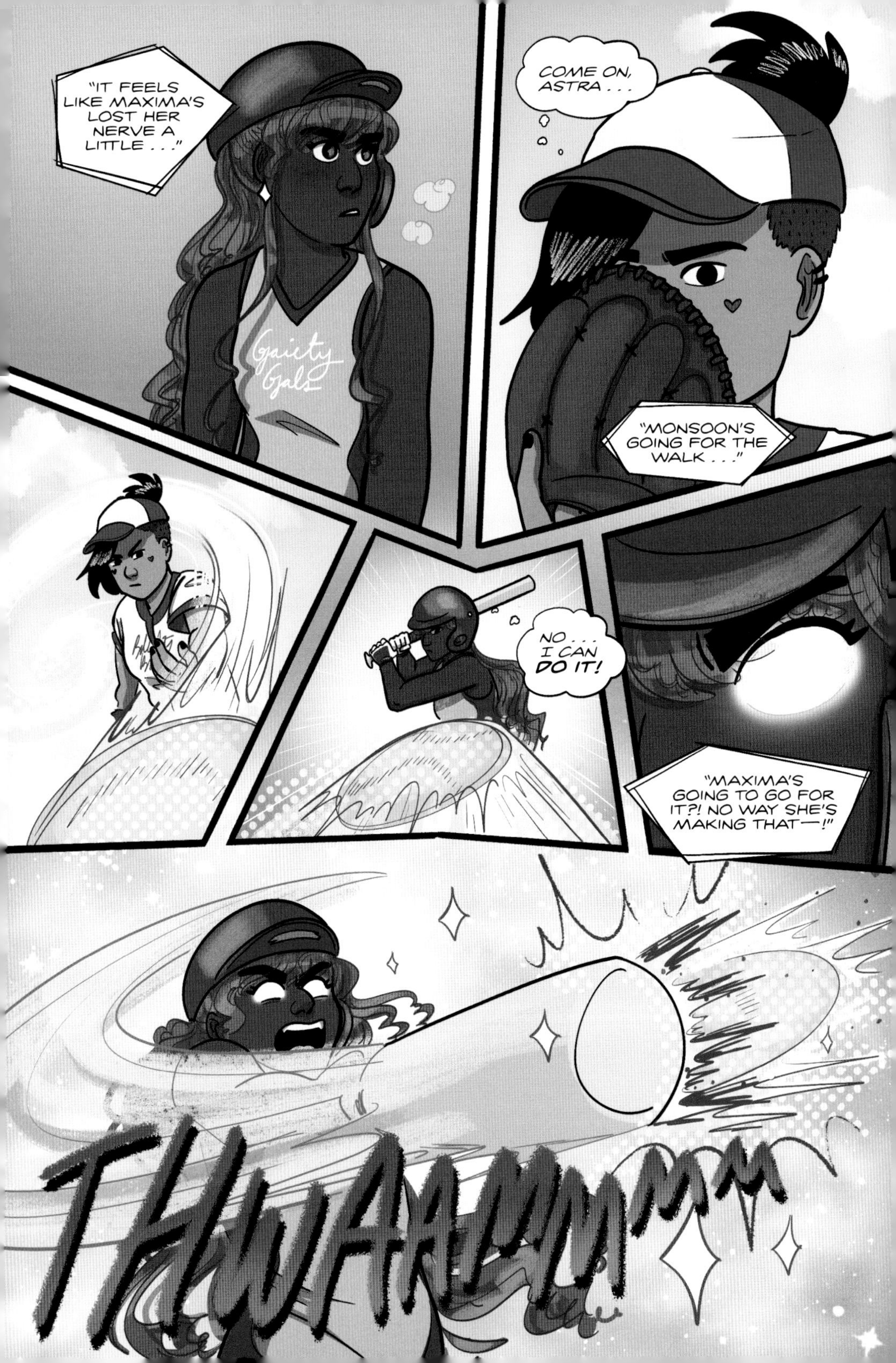
"IT FEELS LIKE MAXIMA'S LOST HER NERVE A LITTLE . . ."
Gaiety Gals
COME ON, ASTRA . . .
"MONSOON'S GOING FOR THE WALK . . ."
NO . . . I CAN **DO IT!**
"MAXIMA'S GOING TO GO FOR IT?! NO WAY SHE'S MAKING THAT—!"
THWAAMM

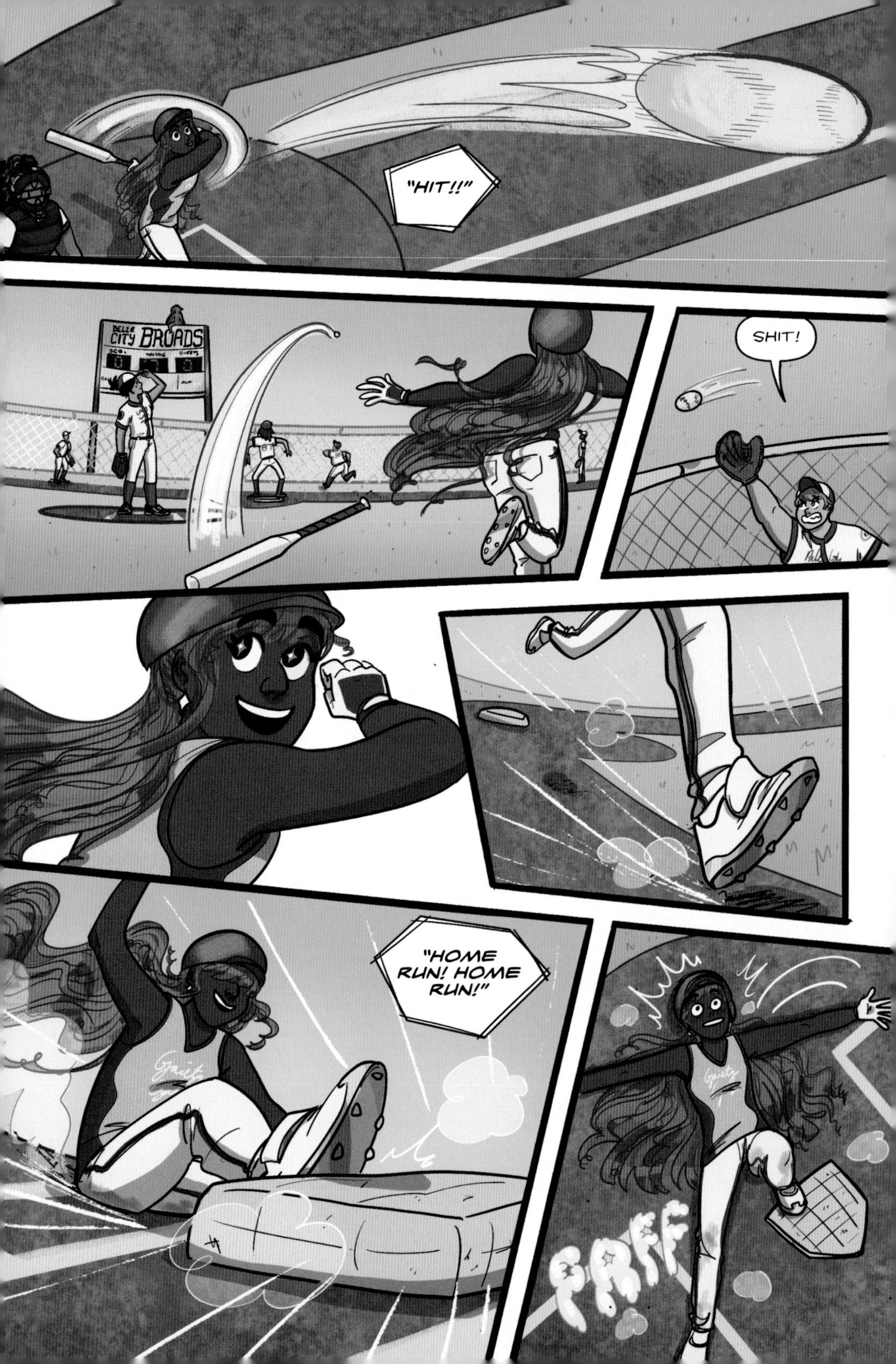
"HIT!!"
BELLE CITY BROADS
SHIT!
"HOME RUN! HOME RUN!"
PAFF

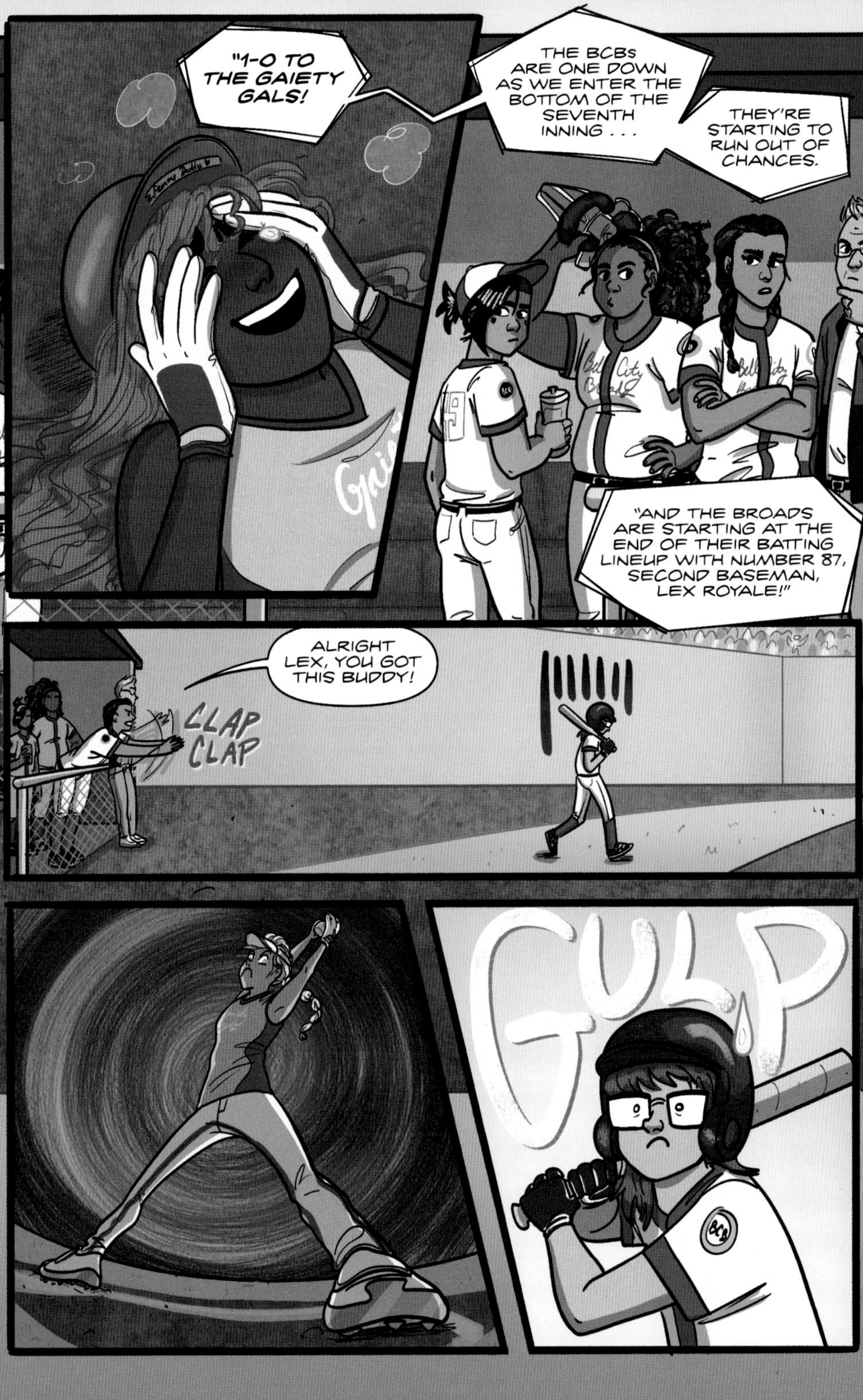
"1-0 TO THE GAIETY GALS!
THE BCBs ARE ONE DOWN AS WE ENTER THE BOTTOM OF THE SEVENTH INNING . . .
THEY'RE STARTING TO RUN OUT OF CHANCES.
"AND THE BROADS ARE STARTING AT THE END OF THEIR BATTING LINEUP WITH NUMBER 87, SECOND BASEMAN, LEX ROYALE!"
ALRIGHT LEX, YOU GOT THIS BUDDY!
CLAP CLAP
GULP

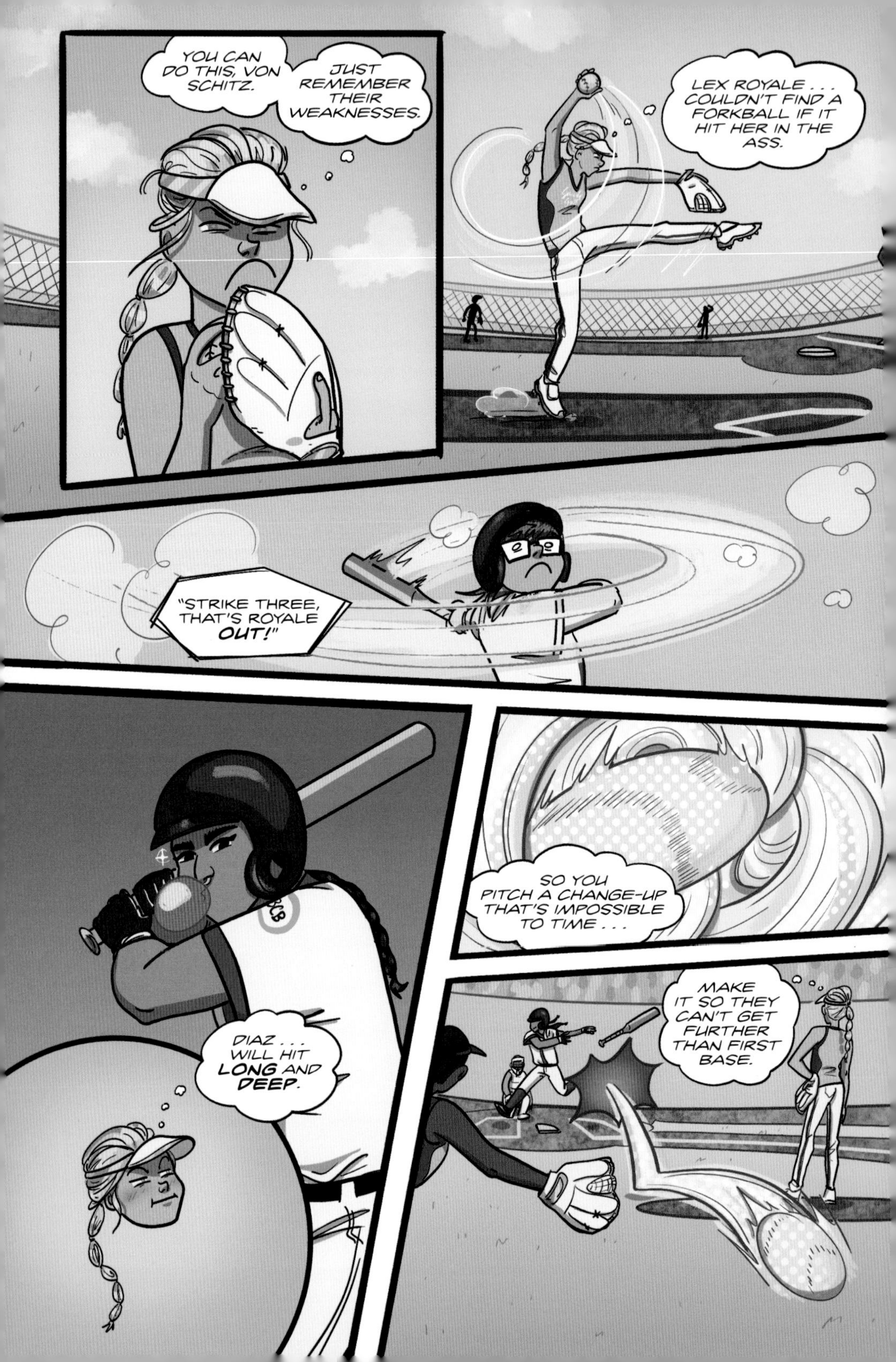

YOU CAN DO THIS, VON SCHITZ.
JUST REMEMBER THEIR WEAKNESSES.
LEX ROYALE . . . COULDN'T FIND A FORKBALL IF IT HIT HER IN THE ASS.
"STRIKE THREE, THAT'S ROYALE OUT!"
DIAZ . . . WILL HIT LONG AND DEEP.
SO YOU PITCH A CHANGE-UP THAT'S IMPOSSIBLE TO TIME . . .
MAKE IT SO THEY CAN'T GET FURTHER THAN FIRST BASE.

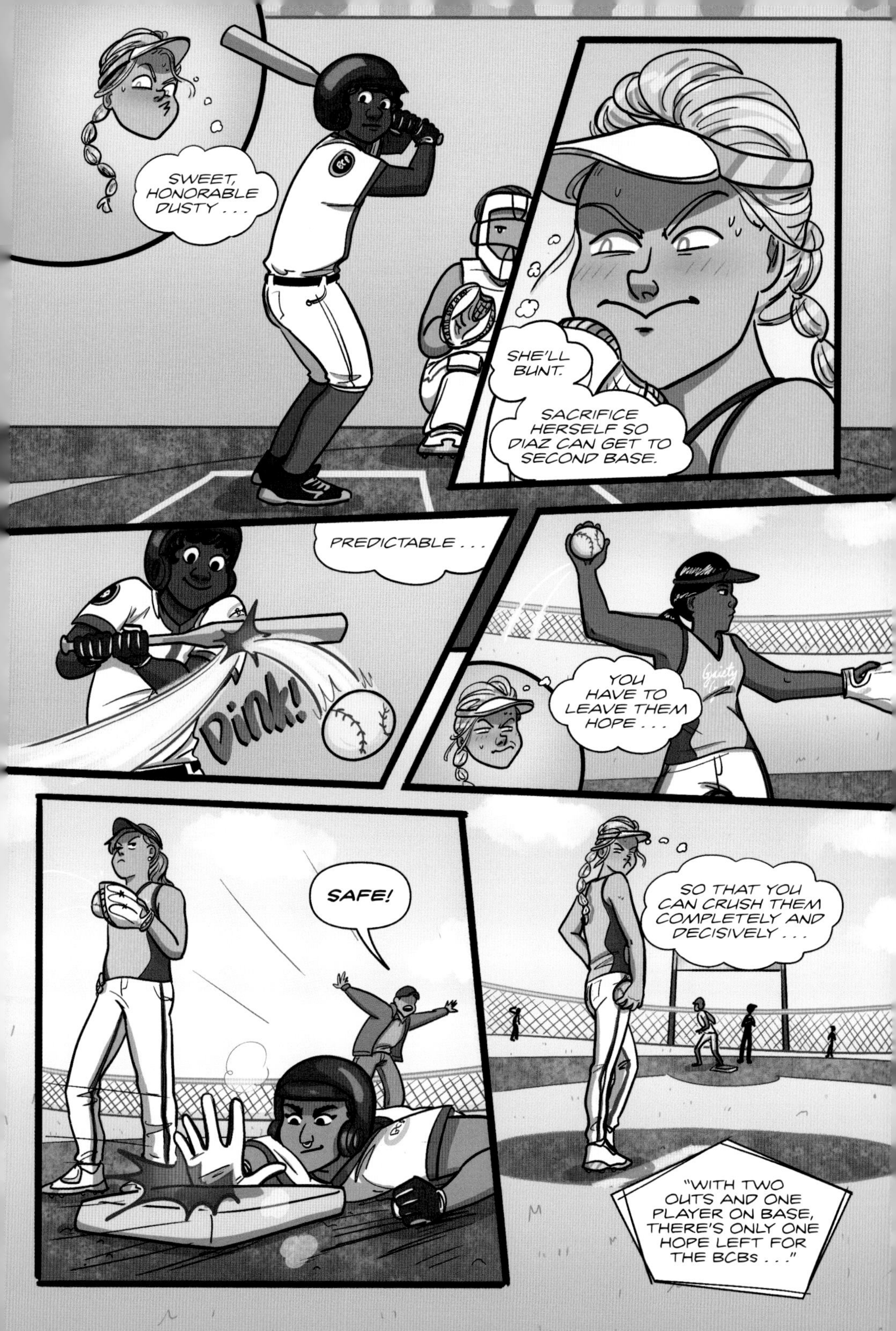
SWEET, HONORABLE DUSTY . . .
SHE'LL BUNT.
SACRIFICE HERSELF SO DIAZ CAN GET TO SECOND BASE.
PREDICTABLE . . .
DINK!
YOU HAVE TO LEAVE THEM HOPE . . .
SAFE!
SO THAT YOU CAN CRUSH THEM COMPLETELY AND DECISIVELY . . .
"WITH TWO OUTS AND ONE PLAYER ON BASE, THERE'S ONLY ONE HOPE LEFT FOR THE BCBs . . ."

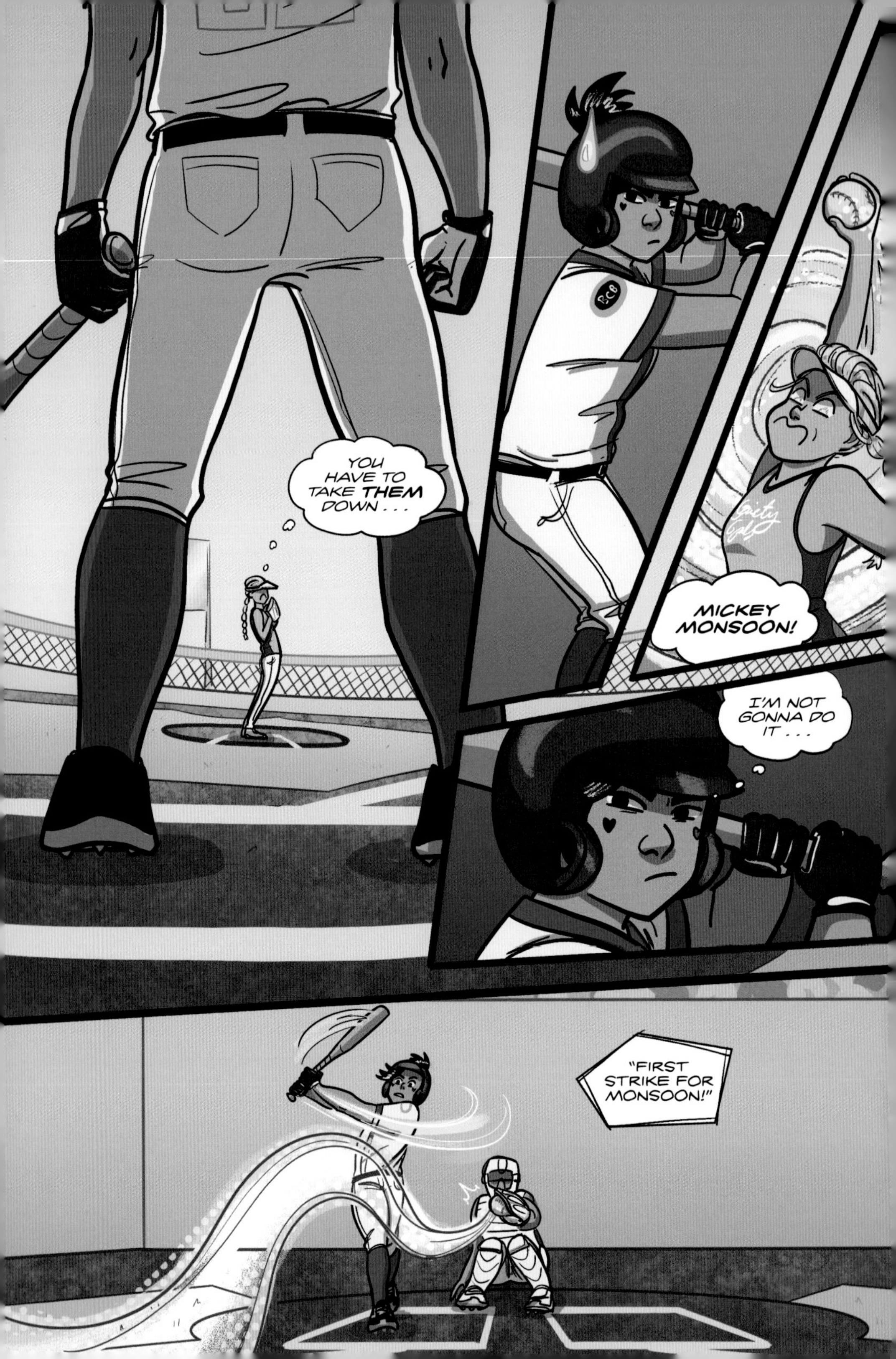
YOU HAVE TO TAKE THEM DOWN . . .
MICKEY MONSOON!
I'M NOT GONNA DO IT . . .
"FIRST STRIKE FOR MONSOON!"

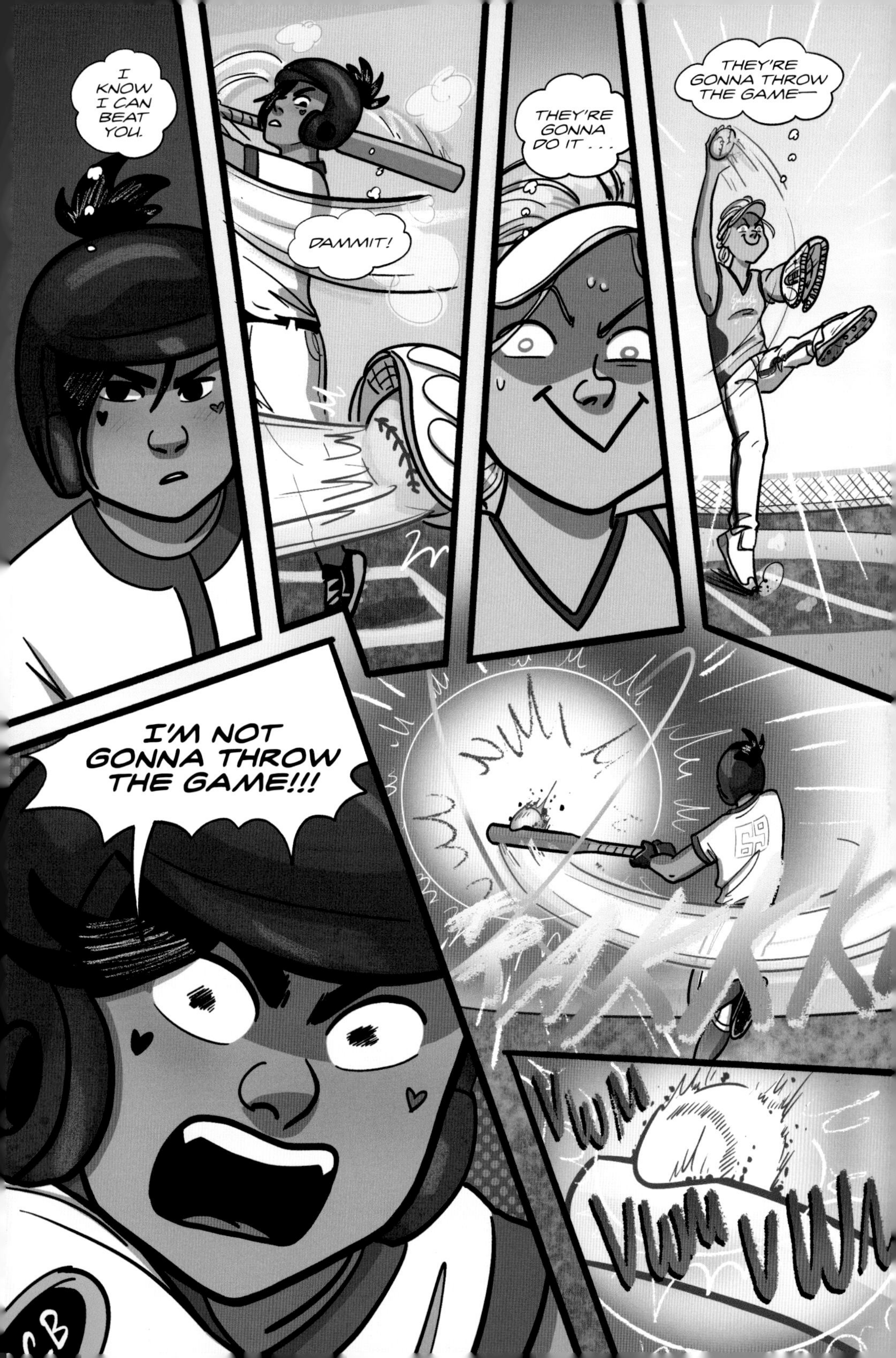
I KNOW I CAN BEAT YOU.
DAMMIT!
THEY'RE GONNA DO IT . . .
THEY'RE GONNA THROW THE GAME—
I'M NOT GONNA THROW THE GAME!!!
VWM
VWM VWM

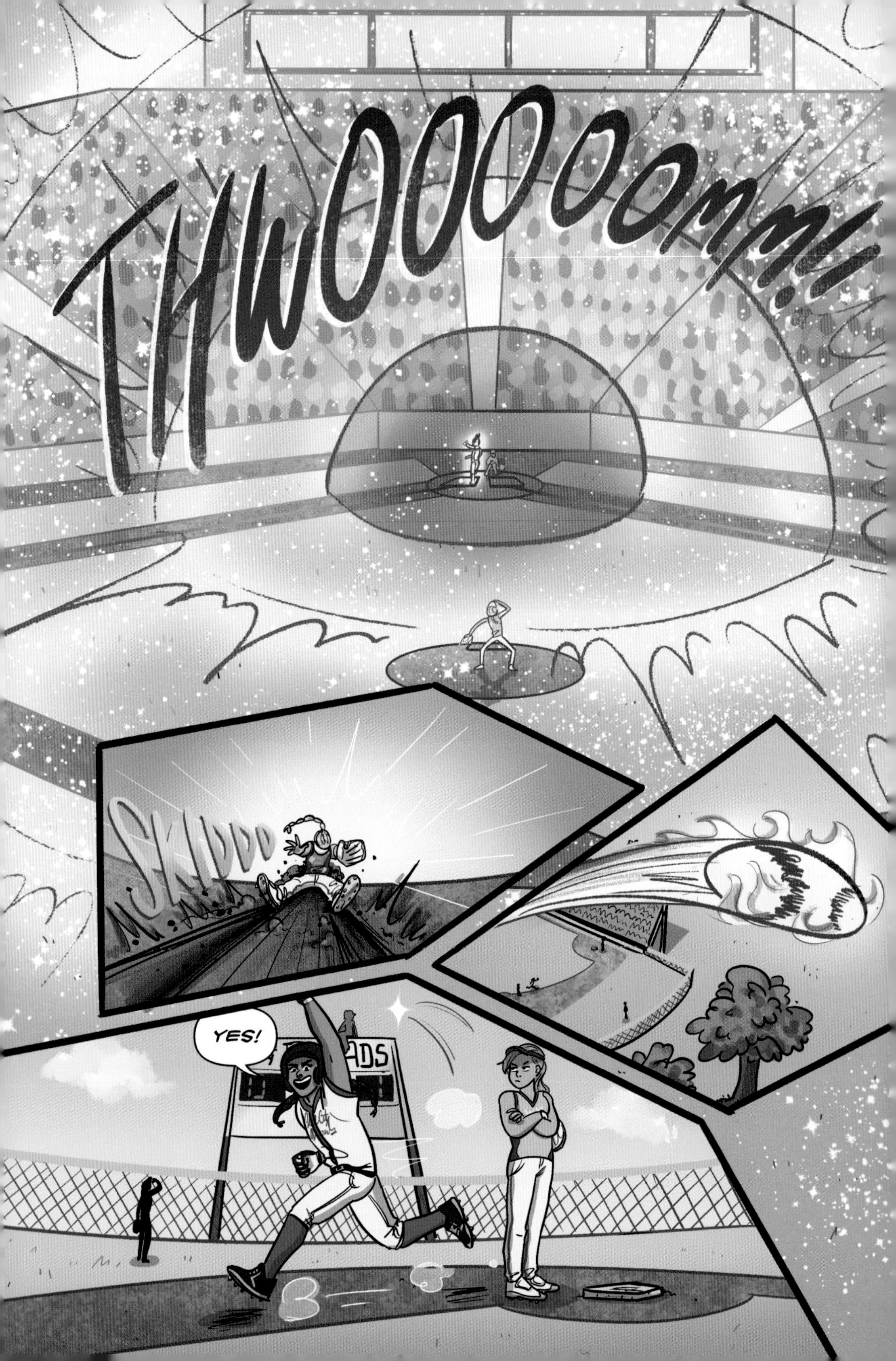
THWOOOOOM!!
SKIDDD
YES!

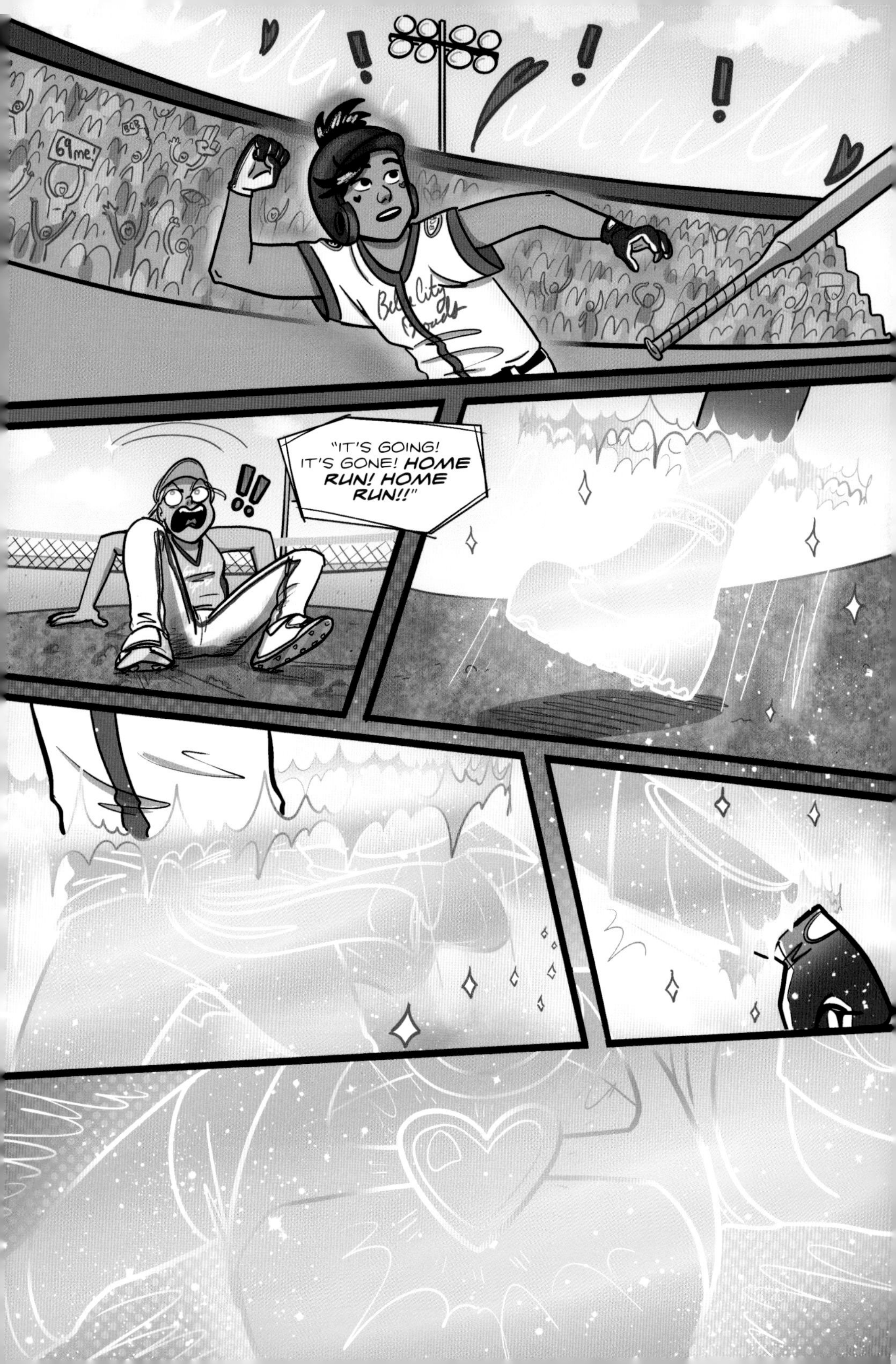
69me!
"IT'S GOING! IT'S GONE! **HOME RUN! HOME RUN!!**"

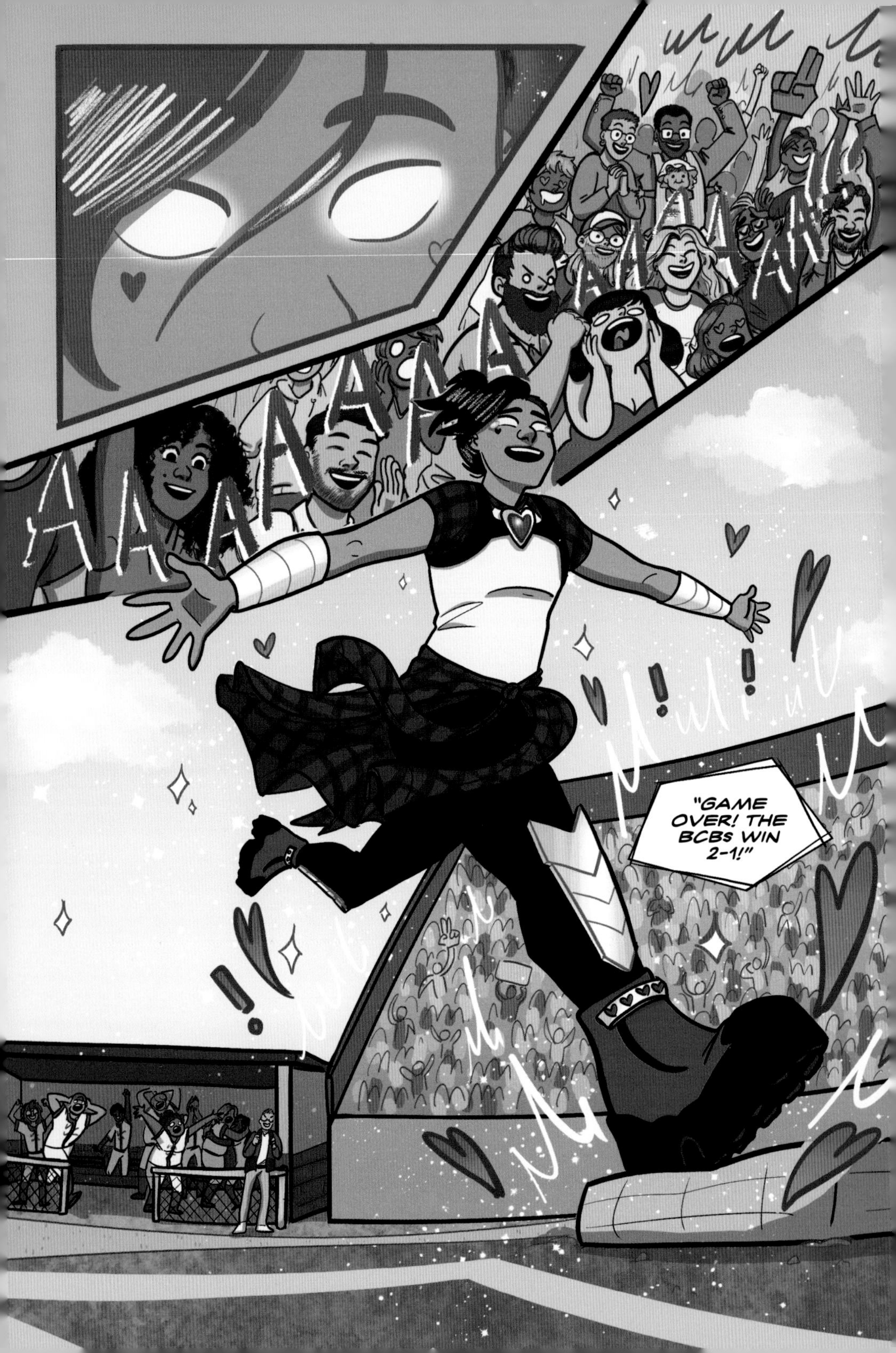
AAAAAAAAAAAAAA
"GAME OVER! THE BCBs WIN 2-1!"

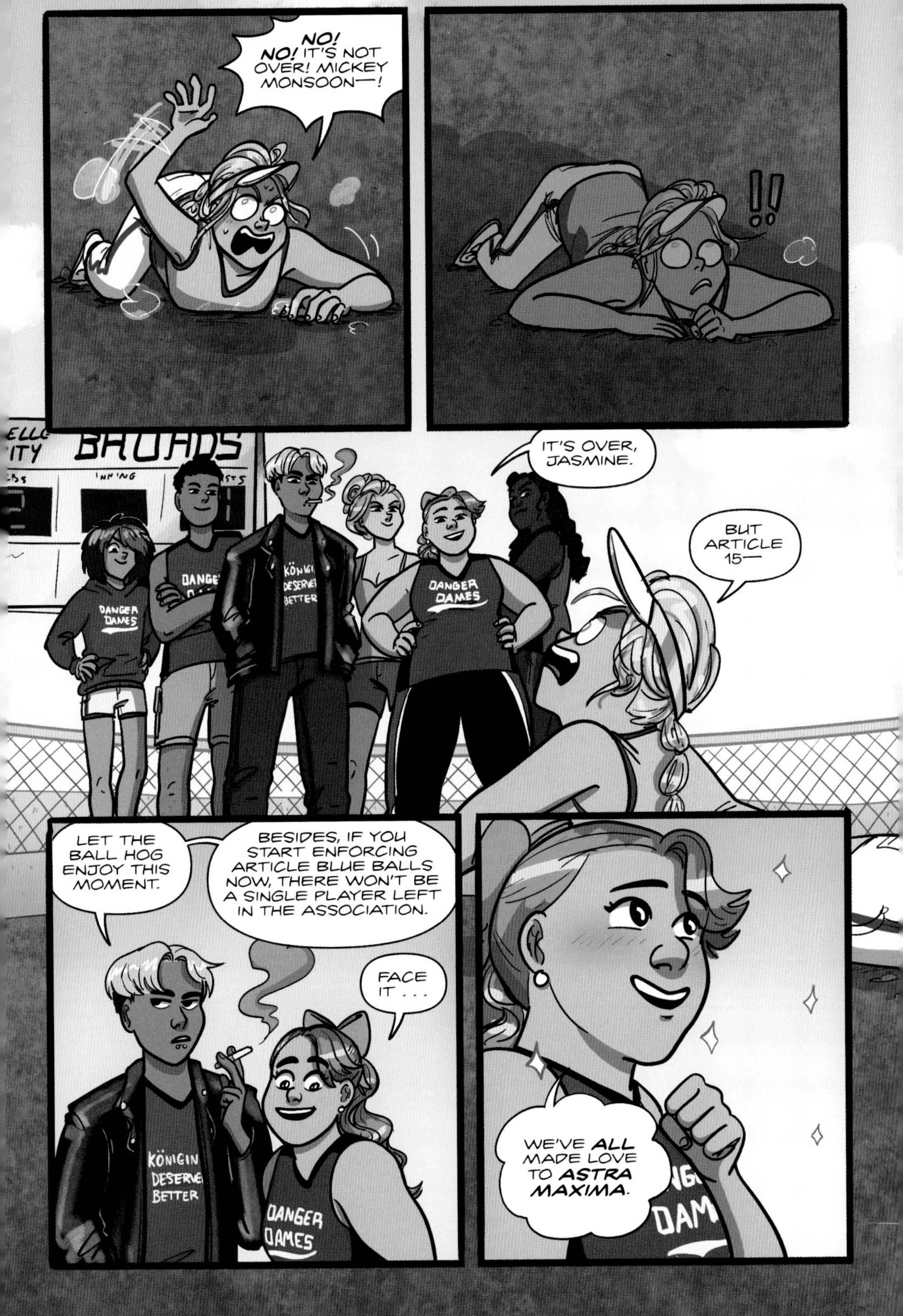
NO! NO! IT'S NOT OVER! MICKEY MONSOON—!
!!
BROADS
INNING
IT'S OVER, JASMINE.
KÖNIGIN DESERVES BETTER
DANGER DAMES
BUT ARTICLE 15—
LET THE BALL HOG ENJOY THIS MOMENT.
BESIDES, IF YOU START ENFORCING ARTICLE BLUE BALLS NOW, THERE WON'T BE A SINGLE PLAYER LEFT IN THE ASSOCIATION.
FACE IT . . .
WE'VE ALL MADE LOVE TO ASTRA MAXIMA.

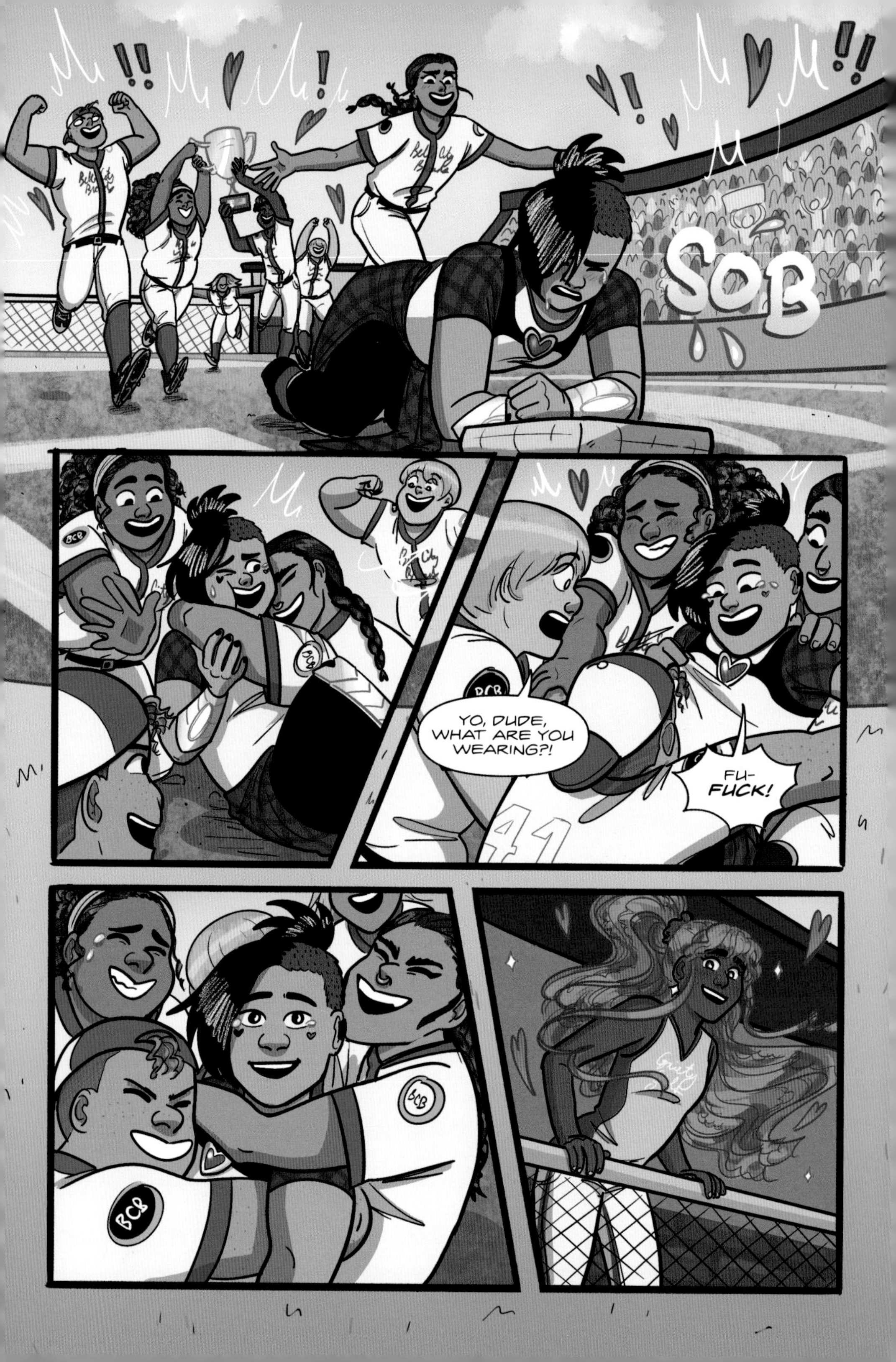
SOB
YO, DUDE, WHAT ARE YOU WEARING?!
FU- FUCK!

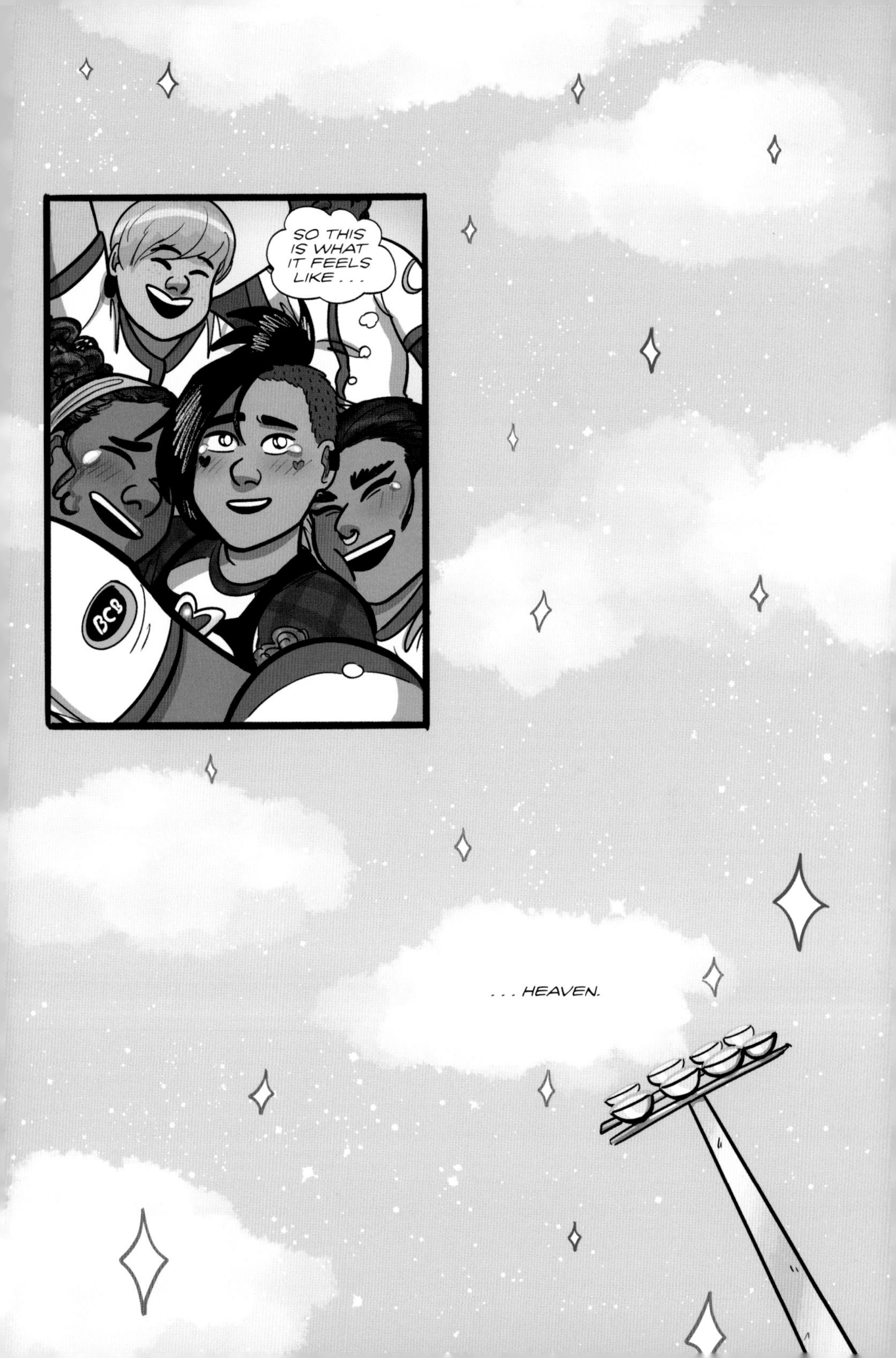
SO THIS IS WHAT IT FEELS LIKE . . .
BCB
. . . HEAVEN.

ACKNOWLEDGMENTS

This book came out of so many random coincidences that it's overwhelming. First thanks are for Joan Edam, who had to drop out of Thought Bubble 2019 because of impending parenthood, and David Robertson, who invited me to take his place as tablemate. And Mariko Tamaki, for noticing *Grand Slam* #1 on the table I wasn't even supposed to be at. I can never thank you all enough. You changed the course of my life.

At every stage people have generously pitched in to make this book happen: thank you to Yvonne Knop and Kim Acheson for checking my wonky high school Deutsch and to Carli Sauer and Cletus Jacobs for checking my even wonkier softball knowledge. Thank you to Georgia Battle and Jessica Burton who read early drafts of the GN pitch and thank you to Sid Galloway, Grace Hulme, Rachel Davis, Rebecca Horner, and Nyasha Hicks who read various early versions of the book and kept me going with their thirsty feedback, I write for the thirsty people!!!

Thank you to my friends not yet mentioned: Michael, Will, Norrie, Kerry, James, Cat, and Ricky, who have cheered for this book for a very long time, including going so far as to rearrange bookshop displays so our *Grand Slam* #1 zine was at the front or to dissect the locker room make out in book club. Everyone who stocked, reviewed, or championed the original GSR zine – thank you so, so much, and I hope you love what it's become.

Thank you to the incredible Grand Slamily who got this book to home base: Charlotte Greenbaum, my fellow Marzipan enthusiast; Lauren White-Jackson, our cheer squad; Andy Miller, our smashing designer; Wren Rios, who literally saved my wife's life by joining as our flatter; and Britt Siess, our agent and early Wolfgang stan.

My gratitude to my family: my mum and dad, Nathan, Nyasha (check you with your double mentions), Rosie, Jack, little Luana, Nanny, and my extended family. Thank you all for supporting me through this very long journey. Thank you to Peter, Val, and Sid: my grandparents who did not see this day but would have flipped out to see my name in the funny pages—thank you for indulging and loving my ridiculousness. Alli, Dan, Anna, and Drew, thank you for welcoming me into your home and putting up with my opinions so sweetly.

And finally, FINALLY!!! Thank you, Emma. You're so damn talented! Thank you for putting this whole thing into motion by one fateful day suggesting "well why don't we do a comic together?" Who knew that that nineteen-page story would become the thing that led us back to each other.

—OLLIE

I get sweaty thinking about how easily this book could have not happened. But through a long string of unbelievable coincidences, and with the un-wavering support of people who were invested in my future even when I didn't particularly care about myself, here we are and here it is.

Mom and Dad, thank you for always making me feel like my art is worth the world. Anna and Drew, you're the coolest siblings I could ask for, and I'm so proud of you both. Many thanks also to Mia and the rest of my wonderful extended family for their lifelong encouragement, and to my extremely sweet in-laws, for making me feel at home in a new country.

We were guided through this thrilling and terrifying journey by our agent Britt Siess, without whom I would have been completely lost. Mariko Tamaki has my eternal gratitude for plucking us out of the garbage and giving Grand Slam a home. Charlotte Greenbaum, Lauren White-Jackson, and Andy Miller have kept us well-fed with delicious compliments; you get the world's biggest thank you for loving our story and turning it into this beautiful beast! And Wren Rios, my flatter extraordinaire, you helped me churn this thing out faster than I ever could have hoped.

Jim, Deb, and Joan from CU Boulder, I owe you my life—or at least a fruit basket or something—not just for opening so many doors for me, but also for pushing me through them. Speaking of which, thank you to the Marshall Scholarship, for leading me to some of my favorite people in the world.

And now my friends! My infinite devotion and love to Devi for over ten years of bestfriendship, innumerable cups of tea, and being my intellectual artistic soulmate. I only started drawing comics because I wanted to impress you in high school. Jessica, dude, I cherish you. Words can't describe how your earnest queer joy has sustained me these last few years. Alex and Violet, I love y'all, please give Cecil a beef treat and a little kiss for me. Sid, Rachel, Emma, Andrew, Grace, Tony, and the rest of my MDes class, the things I learned from you are worth more than any degree.

It doesn't feel right not to say something about Mitch, who made me feel Teen Angst, Gay Pining, and a lot of other messy emotions which found their way into *Grand Slam*; Mitch, who broke my heart at sixteen and then again at twenty-four. Everything still comes back to you, even now. You were magnetic.

And finally, Ollie, not to be dramatic buuut how do I thank you for being the air I breathe? Our love is the grandest slam of any romance ever (I tried, okay, this is why you're the writer). GSR saved me, but only because I made it with you.

—EMMA

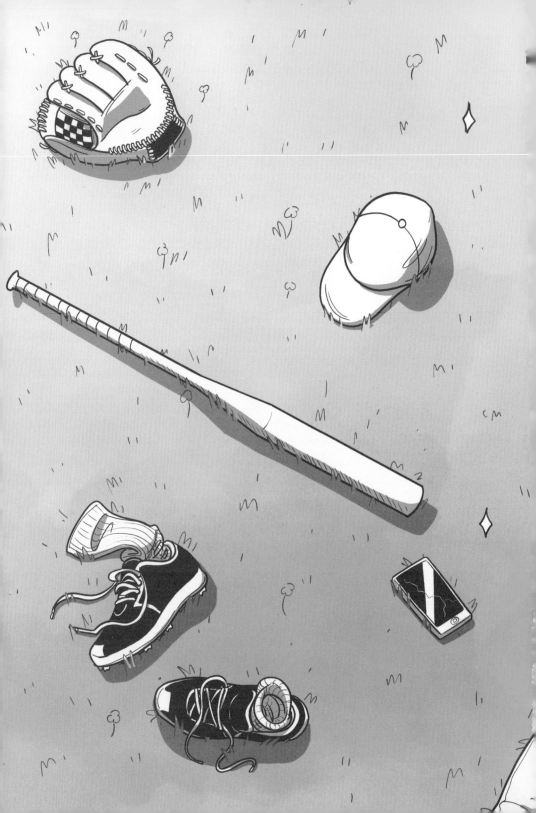